I0612778

Blood Eyes

By

Konrad Quincy Lewis

Edited by Terry Ivester
Cover Art by Yonatan Araya
Back Cover Graphic by Jamien Sills

2024

Published By

Truganini Productions, LLC
Kindle Direct Publishing

Blood Eyes

Volume One

Copyright 2024 by Konrad Q. Lewis

ISBN 9 - 798218 - 354442
ISBN 9 - 798218 - 338534
ISBN 9 – 798218 – 339579

Library of Congress Catalog Card Number: TXu 2-322-186
Effective Date of Registration: June 05, 2022

Published by Truganini Productions, LLC
Printed in the United States of America

To all those who imagine a world of peace and equality for all....

Thank You

Acknowledgements

I first of all would like to thank my ancestors for fighting and suffering for me and my family so that we may have a chance to honor their legacy. Huge thanks to my parents Jerry and Lucille Lewis who always championed education and showed me examples of the success you can have when you put your mind to something and never waver from your goals. Thanks to my wife Natasha and my daughters Simone and Olivia for putting up with my quirkiness and providing me with the motivation to complete this work of art. Big shoutout to Danai Gurira, one of this generations most beautiful and talented actresses, who saw the winner in me and gifted me the iPad that I used to write this book. My sincerest gratitude goes to my editor Terri Ivester and to Yonatan Araya for creating the cover art for this book. A tremendous thank you goes to my brother Jamien Sills whose graphic novel The Order of Heru's is an inspiration for me and my projects. Jamien also blessed me with the graphic that graces the back cover of the new editions of this book. And finally, thank you to anyone reading these words for giving a dreamer from South Nashville a chance.

Table of Contents

CHAPTER 1

Earth

Nothing on this planet is as it seems. The very matter that constitutes the people, places and things experienced by our senses has been proven to be nothing more than energy vibrating at various intervals to create the illusion of tangible material. The advent of powerful microscopes has revealed entire universes that exist within a single drop of water. In the same vein, cutting edge telescopes have revealed galaxies and quasars light years beyond our solar system that contain any millions of worlds similar to our own. Hidden beneath the façade of the governmental structures of every country there is a group of secret leaders who determine the policies and laws that affect the quality of life of all who inhabit this plane of existence. This ultra private consortium dictates mandatory guidelines to the top corporations, sovereign republics, nation states, and royal families of the world. Their misguided leadership has served only to foster their selfish interests to create a planet where the average person suffers a life of unfulfilled labor and relative unhappiness while an elite few are able to horde all the vital resources and live apart from the rest of humanity.

Over the centuries, the inequality created by these hidden leaders has contributed to opposition from those who pose a threat to their plans for planetary domination. These opposition leaders are given a special designation by the secret leaders and placed on a list of criminals who are to be neutralized at all costs and by any means necessary. A tiny fraction of the population is privy to the existence of this specially classified international criminal "most wanted" list which is not maintained by INTERPOL, the U.N. World Security Forces, N.A.T.O., United States Department of Homeland Security or any globally sanctioned organization. Past members of this unfortunate list consisted mainly of legendary drug kingpins who grew too big for their britches and turned against their handlers, tremendously talented hackers whose heist numbers sit somewhere in the billions of dollars, and certain revolutionaries that impeded the ambitions of top-level transnational capitalist elite.

It just so happens that I have held the number one position on this list for the past two hundred and twenty years. As such, all branches of the United States military have an "engage with extreme prejudice" mandate if they are to encounter me. I am listed in the Guinness Book of World Records for being the only "criminal" wanted in 193 sovereign nations in the world excluding Taiwan, El Salvador, The Cook Islands, and The Central African Republic. During the early Cold War years, right after World War II, U.S. President Harry Truman was forced to create the National Security Agency specifically to gather, track, and verify information of my whereabouts in order to keep me from falling into the hands of the Soviets and being used as a weapon against the Axis powers. Many of the advances in modern camera and video imaging technology in commercial use today were first developed by collaborations between the French and U.S. militaries in programs designed for my surveillance and containment. Hilliard Heintze, G4S, and other omega level international security firms and mercenary groups circulate one of the very rare pictures taken of me in 1913. It is rumored that if one was to be lucky enough to survive an encounter with me in the field and return to headquarters with at least one drop of my blood, they would be rewarded with 100 million U.S. dollars cash upon verification. My file remains the number one unsolved case for Foglight, the Pinkerton agency, and various other private detective and critical infrastructure security firms throughout the world.

History will reflect on mankind's affinity for stories of triumph, freedom and justice. From Jesus all the way to Neo in the 'Matrix' movies, stories and fables speak of heroes who fight for righteousness and always overcome evil in the end. Truthfully, the world is made up of various factions who prefer control and domination of the larger population and usually benefit from implementing the exact opposite of freedom and justice. And why must it be this way one may ask? To ensure the survival of a relatively small group of bloodline-connected oligarchs who feel it is their right to control the earth and all its resources for their own profit.

Recently, there was an all-out war between myself and these pugnacious forces that was so shocking and bloody that it resulted in a dynamic upheaval of the financial markets for the temporary benefit of the proletariat. The conflict began as an attempt to disrupt an unholy ceremony held by the global elite every year during the World Economic Forum meeting in Davos, Switzerland. This annual event is disguised as a business planning meeting for world leaders but is actually a ritual that uses earth energies to conjure demons and spirits from other realms while simultaneously causing dimensional shifts in the earth's biosphere that are meant to maintain a low vibrational frequency upon the citizenry of the planet. A disruptive and adversarial emotion is the result of this heinous ceremony that successfully increases its broadcast every year since it began fifty years ago and has gone conspicuously undocumented by the of the world's population. Some of the more sensitive souls upon the planet have been experiencing this unnatural vibrational shift and affliction to the timeline in the broader media as the Mandela Effect, time dilation, more frequent bouts of déjà vu or similar bizarre metaphysical phenomenon. I strongly believe that an attempt was made to reset the timeline using the Large Hadron Collider and other similar classified devices to benefit the ruling elite as recently as the year 2024 in order to mitigate the exposure of their diabolical plans caused by my infiltration of one of their most precious strongholds. No news agency in the world will ever be able to report anything about what took place that night and everyone involved in the battle was either vaporized or had their mind wiped by the controllers and handlers working for this secret control organization known only as the Incalculaba.

The Incalculaba...are better known as 'They,' the ephemeral group of individuals who control literally everything. They are the unknown cause and motivation for the feeling of hopelessness in the world, the ones called the Beast, the Archons, the Invisible Hand, the Illuminati, Majesty Twelve, the Syndicate, the Deep State, etc. They give themselves benign sounding monikers like the Trilateral Commission, the Council on Foreign Relations, The Bildebergs, The City of London, The Club of Rome, the Merovingian, the

G 30 and such. The web is rife with conjecture about worldwide conspiracies and every Tom, Dick, and Jane with a YouTube account will debate each other mindlessly every day of the week over exactly what extent of control these so called "clandestine" organizations have over the everyday ebb and flow of human life on earth. Most would agree that the direction humankind has been moving toward has been far from positive and that as it stands today, regulation of major global institutions seem to be concentrating into the hands of fewer and fewer people. The one percent of the one percent.

The average person recognizes these people as the untouchable elite who use offshore shell companies to hide their billions of dollars while everyone else pays thirty percent or more in taxes. They destabilize your country with unnecessary and impossible-to-repay loans for fake or inadequate infrastructure projects that wind up leaving the country in debt and its government a puppet. The ensuing poverty destroys once strong family units and communities and forces the people to battle amongst themselves for the little resources that are available. This sparks gang violence and creates sex trafficking havens amongst the women and children who are left with nothing but their bodies as collateral for food. They make billions on the processed meat industry that knowingly includes ingredients that are carcinogenic while simultaneously profiting trillions from the pharmaceutical, medical, and insurance industries when people's bodies degrade from the poor quality of food available. Ironically, they are the true blood suckers of the world. They rape the earth by pushing overconsumption and exploitation of fossil fuels and then sell you the climate change solution and place the blame on the consumer. They buy politicians by funding campaigns to guarantee their elections to government office and then turn around and assassinate them either physically or in character when he or she doesn't fall in lock step with their draconian policies.

On the surface, human cruelty and suffering seems to be married to life on earth, and the greed and avarice of mankind appears to be just the price of doing business in the third dimension. Much of this negative behavior is written off as by-products of human character— envy, arrogance, hatred, lust...it is supposedly all baked in from the start. Countless scholars have postulated that mankind's progression to recent technological heights would only be possible as a direct result of its inherently self-centered need to subdue nature in order to procreate efficiently. However, it is 'They' who create the atmosphere that forces the worst traits of humanity to bubble to the surface and wreak havoc on the planet and each other instead of focusing on the deep well of goodness on the earth. It is 'They' who are deliberately blocking our spiritual awakening and causing existence itself to feel at odds with human nature. Everyday suffering should not be conscripted as a permanent, inescapable phenomenon.

Is it necessary for 90% of the global population to work five or six days out of seven in the prime years of their life only to die in debt and leave a perpetual burden for subsequent generations? Why is it that you can count on one hand the number of people who control over half the world's wealth? Why should a few hundred hedge fund managers generate trillions of dollars through trading highly specialized currency derivatives, while most of the world makes less than ten dollars a day? We have more than enough resources to extend the basics of food and shelter to everyone on the planet and create a balance in the world but somehow refuse to do so. Darwinism has become the true planetary religion over and above basic human decency. Things do not have to be this way. I made up my mind that someone has to do something about this and since have experienced these heinous circumstances for over 300 years and near immortal, that someone has to be me.

•   •   •

The range of human capacity to feel things beyond touch, taste, sight, smell, and hearing is expansive but at times extremely subtle. These feelings are usually reasoned away with terms like instinct, intuition, a sixth sense etc. We express these abstracts in words through phrases such as: the feel of it all, it felt bad, weird, nasty, amazing, incredible. Feeling is paramount to all senses. How we feel when we meet someone. That special someone. The vibe, impressions... Their aura. The feeling of guilt, depression, bliss, pain. How it feels to fall in love. How you felt when you saw him/her going astray. The way the wind felt. The atmosphere at the party or the job.

11

The feeling of anxiety. The first day of…. How it felt when they said those horrible things. The touch of loneliness. The heights of happiness. The feeling once you knew. The spark of two lips touching each other. How we felt when they died. How we felt when they lived. First love/lust. The feeling a man and woman experiences in the nanosecond just before and after penetration. The morning after feeling. Hunger, anger, fear, joy, kinship. To feel is all. The heat, the cold, the shock, the embrace. All feel. Insect, mammal, reptile feel. It is conscious and unconscious, physical and ethereal. Inescapable. All must feel.

Famous last words: "I don't feel like ….."

You must feel, for feeling drives purpose. It cradles the anticipation of future, past, and present as feelings manifest. There are those who would burn or maim one's own person just to feel something, anything. Feelings are not in an arena unique only to humans, for all creatures use them to interpret their environment. Instinct is to manifest from within despite what reason would dictate otherwise. One merely feels the righteousness or erroneousness of his or her actions. As for now there is no definitive origination for the urge, the drive, the need. But we can feel it. A small word to encompass such a powerful sentiment, I feel, felt, am feeling. To express certain emotions of feeling, a universal language of wordless facial expression that all humans understand has been invoked. For the natural feelings of contentment, anger, sorrow, etc. can be witnessed in all species accessible to man's scientific inquest. The web is fraught with videos of slaughterhouse employees busily engaged in the task of chasing down their hapless victims who are not exactly enthusiastic about their fate of becoming sustenance for other mammals. Feeling is tantamount to any experience. How did they make you feel?

I feel that something does not feel right.

Chapter 2

I have never grown accustomed to cold weather. I laugh to myself at Jessie's shenanigans and how she used to make cheeky comments in earshot of the overseer whenever there was a rare cold morning in the bayou, and I was coming back from the fields. Frost covered everything and everybody and she would remark to me in her French Creole accent, "Madichon move tan fret sa a. Nou se yon pep twopikal" [To hell with this cold weather. We are a tropical people].

I have been driving for at least an hour on I-90 eastbound out of Chicago, and the less than reliable heater which has been running the entire time but has barely increased the temperature in the car above freezing. The passenger window is stuck about an inch and a half down so all the rain and snow leaks in, and the sound of the wind overpowers the weak clock radio speakers, drowning out the one decent station I was able to pick up in this area. You get what you pay for as usual in the Chi-town. It was providence that I found and procured this car from a fellow I contacted using the Backpages application. Sites like these are on their way to being obsolete but still have some services available that are coveted by the underground consumer who was not able to access mainstream services that require digital payment or proof of identity for purchase.

A few years from now social media will revolutionize person-to-person sales markets and when applications such as Only Fans, Tinder, Plenty of Fish, and Bumble are released, the sex-selling business will go super high tech, putting the old paradigm to shame. I pull a cigarette from the box in the cup holder and light up. Only eight remaining in the pack, I need to stop for more next time I get fuel. My cash reserves are getting low, so no carton this time, just a couple of single packs until I can get back to my stash in my hideout in Chicago. Dystopian surveillance laws are making it impossible to travel with large amounts of money and newer reserve notes contain tracking chips that law enforcement can scan from a considerable distance. I refocus my attention back onto the road ahead of me as I pass a caravan of trucks carrying military equipment. I light another cigarette and try to find some interesting talk radio like Coast to Coast AM with George Noory but I am unsuccessful and I am forced to choose between listening to evangelical propaganda or country music. I switch off the radio in disgust and kill the heater which is now blowing only cold air anyway.

Almost out of Illinois and a steady light snow begins to fall as the biting cold of the American Midwest winter decides to make its presence known through the crack in my window. It's a busy fall Friday night at ten o'clock, as I cross the state line into Wisconsin. As long as I maintain the speed limit, I should have smooth sailing as far as police are concerned. The inside of this pickup truck reeks of urine. A gift left behind from its last owner, I presume. This truck with its rusted fenders, sagging headliner and drab grayish green color certainly looks the part of a run-of-the -mill, Mid-western American vehicle, and my tags are legit under the name Alvin House. The same name that's written on my fake passport and driver's license, which should be good for me to use for at least the next 28 days. An American flag sticker on the window behind the passenger seat sits adjacent to a sticker bearing the image of two horses facing opposite directions, the logo of the International Teamsters Union. I am just your regular 'Johnny Apple Pie' with a leather jacket and dark sunglasses on while driving at night. I can count on two fingers the times I have risked driving since the world became a surveillance state, and I try to convince myself that every car that merges in behind me or has a ski rack on top is not law enforcement. The story I have ready for the police is always to first apologize for the sunglasses and explain my acute sensitivity to light and the need to cut down headlight glare when driving.

I have been extremely careful over the last seventeen years. Always moving in shadow. Watchfully remaining underground in every aspect of life. Building my case against *them* while keeping my actions to a minimum and making deadly sure that there were never any witnesses to any moves I made.

14

Not five minutes after entering the state, I pass a stationary state trooper vehicle sitting in the median of the highway holding a radar gun at oncoming traffic. A lump builds in my throat as I watch the rearview mirror for his headlights, but he does not move. I allow myself to breathe again. I cannot afford to let paranoia get the best of me now. Hopefully, I am right about it being a busy night for these middle America towns. Kids doing doughnuts inside the local Walmart parking lot on Friday night, high school football games, and methamphetamine infused domestic violence should be enough action to keep the law enforcement busy and off my ass. The next major city before I reach Madison is Janesville. I will stop for gas and cigs there, and if I maintain the speed limit, that should put me in Madison at around eleven o'clock pm. I need this meeting to go down with no snags.

Tonight will determine my next move, and if all goes well, it will provide me with a concrete connection to the mass communication and inflammatory aspect of my plan. I will finally be able to credibly expose everything the global elite and corporatocracy have been up to for the last one hundred fifty years and the dystopian future that they are planning for the so-called "unwashed masses" of the planet.

Just my luck, the Chevron at the exit had a Rock County Sheriff patrol car parked out in front of the gas pumps. There was a blond woman leaning on his passenger window who looked like she was ready to do him a service in exchange for money to buy whatever drugs she was using. I keep it moving and immediately reenter the highway for the next exit. A few miles down the road at the next exit I spy a Kwik Trip convenience station. No cops in sight so I make a beeline for the first empty pump. There is an older model camera on the corner of the roof of the gas station, and I am positive they have several inside the store. Within the last fifty years, they have been installing cameras everywhere, so I am always careful to maintain an extremely low profile whenever I am above ground. I put on my Chicago Cubs ball cap and pull it down to the top of my shades for further blending before walking into the store. By the looks of it, this service station has seen its fair share of hard winters. The main building is small and the fuel dispenser area is set up in a throwback design when this was once a thriving full-service gas station. A shed full of old tires sits adjacent to the main building. The damaged roof looks as if it is ready to slide off the front of the building and into the rusted, empty propane cages. Scars that serve as living testimonies to this building's resilience.

The acrid fuel smell attacks my nostrils, and I instinctively reach for my right jacket pocket for a pack of cigarettes that no longer exists. I involuntarily let out a small sigh before turning and walking briskly towards the store. As I approach the main building, two feet above the front door, I clock a three-pronged floodlight with a small camera hanging loosely by a few wires. As I enter the store, a young, olive-skinned Persian man stares at me as he stands behind the counter next to a seated older Persian gentleman on the telephone speaking Farsi about needing a new transmission for his wife's car. I try to make as little eye contact as possible with him and everyone else in the gas station as I walk toward the cooler. I find that the majority of people usually keep to their own mental bubbles anyway. The inside of the store smells of frankincense and mop water.

The urine concentration of thousands of weary travelers relieving themselves in this relic of a gas station created a miasma that emanated from the bathroom so strongly that my sensitive nose unwittingly caused my face to draw up into a deep scowl. An expression that I try to suppress but unconsciously wore most of the time when I was not smoking a cigarette. I hold my breath as I pass a large man wearing a cowboy hat leaving the bathroom rubbing his stomach with a look of relief. As I reached the coolers to grab a bottle of water, the smell hit me hard. It was comparable to the Chicago sewers after a hard rain. I sorely need to get outside and smoke a cigarette. I hurry my way up to the register and plop down my water and three 20 dollar bills. Without looking up I ask for two packs of Marlboro Reds, and request that whatever change is leftover to be credited to pump three. I grab the cigs as he places them onto the counter and I slide the 60 dollars towards the man all without making eye contact. I vaguely hear something about a receipt over the door chime as I am exiting, but I continue walking briskly back to the truck to pump my gas. Not many people here tonight except for an older couple in an RV taking their three dogs behind the station for a bathroom break and a couple of solo acts also refueling. One man is dressed as a lumberjack in a Toyota Tercel pumping gas and scrolling on his cellular phone, and the other vehicle at the pumps is a newer model F-150 truck, probably driven by the cowboy I saw leaving the bathroom. I open one of the packs and place an unlit cigarette in my mouth as I pump the gas. The aroma of gasoline carries a piercing quality that has always been unsettling for me. My anxiety is starting to get the best of me now as I notice two more cars of people pull up to the front of the gas station.

Being topside and under this much light makes me feel uneasy. Of course, the pump is slow as hell. The gas pumps are first generation digital, and the numbers climb slowly to the whirring sound of the dispenser. A three-minute eternity later, I have only managed to pump 29 dollars worth of gas with 15 left to go. As soon as I get to less than a dollar left to pump, I hang up the nozzle and close the tank. I jump back in the truck and light the cigarette that has been hanging from my lip absorbing saliva for the last eight minutes. I pull out of the parking lot and back onto I-90. Before long I am merging onto Wisconsin State Highway 30 East to Marquette and the Dane County Regional Airport. The light of the moon and the stars are finding it difficult to penetrate the thick layer of clouds, casting a rich darkness over the road and the surrounding landscape. Hearteningly, I cannot smell any rain or hear any thunder on the horizon. Bad weather is the last thing I need at this point in my mission. Mainly due to the fact that all attempts to re-raise the passenger side window only made it slide down further, and I now have to deal with the rushing wind and cold causing my cigarettes to burn faster and freezing me into a fucking popsicle. The windshield wipers are corroded and need changing. The last thing I need tonight is more rain or sleet or any other surprise from mother nature that could further impair this already unsound vehicle. There is a faint animal musk carried on the wind, and my senses are on full alert for the frequent occurrences of rutting deer that have a tendency to come crashing out of the tree line looking for a mate just in time for me to knock the shit out of it with my truck.

Slightly more than 45 minutes later I am in an area of Madison, Wisconsin, called Maple Bluff. It is a lily-white suburb north of the city near Warner Park, full of keenly manicured lawns and unspoiled natural enclosures. This area reeks of opulence and wealth, but I should expect nothing less from a blood relation to one of the most recognized names in the world. Someone from that family should be able to afford homesteads equivalent to this and a whole lot more. I toss my cig through the crack in the window and exhale a large cloud of smoke. I inhale deeply and the crispness of the midwestern night air fills my nostrils sharply as the breeze dances and rolls sharply off Lake Michigan. This neighborhood reeks of the 'monthly trips to Europe and chauffeur driven black SUVs for your children that attend elementary school that costs fifty thousand dollars a semester' type of wealth. That 'summer trips to the lake in your own yacht to your waiting lakefront property' life. The more I think of it, the more my anxiety flares out of control and my heart starts racing irrepressibly. I need to make contact, get back to the main highway and get the fuck out of Wisconsin and back to the Windy City A-S-A-P. I stick out like a sore thumb in this shabby vehicle and my grim appearance.

I check the time on my phone which happens to be a new type of Iridium smartphone Keith procured for me that uses encrypted end-to-end P2P communication. Developed for military use, but as with everything else in this world, for enough cash, all things are for sale. Especially over the internet. The phone operates over a pirated Starlink connection that includes web and voice calls and everything is unequivocally private. The GPS application provided with the phone works entirely on a mask network that codifies my location into information that scrambles the beacon signal every so often so no one will be able to ping my device and track me accurately. It estimates my arrival time at 37 minutes. The multi-story single family houses I pass give way to mansions and soon the mansions become estates. My next right turn puts me on a dark road that seems to run parallel to a humongous lake for miles. Lake Mendota according to the GPS. I am tempted to cut my lights but it would be my luck to pass a cop wondering what the hell I was doing and stop to question me about how I am able to drive in this darkness.

I try to go over in my mind what I will say to her but my anxiety bubbles to the surface, only filling me with more doubt. How do I even begin that conversation? What if she does not remember me or freaks out when she sees me and immediately alerts the police? What if she does not believe my story? What if she will not help me? Fuck it, I must try, and this is as good of a chance of unmasking this worldwide puppet show as I am going to get. It has literally been an eternity, and I have been extremely exhausted as of late.

The corner of my eye catches something white and reflective behind a large hedge on the passenger side of the car. Fuck! My stomach tightens and sweat immediately begins to bead on my forehead. My hands instinctively shoot up to grab the wheel at ten and two and reduce my speed like a 16-year-old who just received their driver's license. I tap out my cigarette into the ashtray, sit up straight, and turn down the radio. I hope it was an optical illusion due to fatigue causing me to see things out of my paranoia, but I am positive I caught a glint of metal in my peripheral vision as I passed that last clump of bushes. My mind was so preoccupied with my meeting and how I was going to break the ice that I was not paying proper attention to the road. Nothing in my rear view yet. Maybe it was just a vehicle broken down on the shoulder that was shaped like a police cruiser. Still no movement behind me but I absolutely saw a sedan shaped something posted back there behind those trees waiting in ambush position. Who else could it have been at this time of night in this neighborhood. He definitely got a good look at me.

Shit!...

Think!....

I cannot blow this, not when I am this close to connecting the pieces of the puzzle I need to exact my retribution. One chance at this and... Fuck me.

Looking in my rear view at the empty road I see the car's headlights pop on behind me and aggressively pull in the road, kicking up dust behind him as it drags its heavy framed sedan chassis up onto the concrete and rapidly begins to close the distance between us. My first instinct is to cut the lights and smash down the gas pedal but then I remember what type of vehicle I am driving and I realize that I do not stand a snowball's chance in hell at outrunning the 4.6 liter V8 of that Crown Victoria police interceptor. He probably waited a minute on purpose to make me sweat a little or to see if I would panic and try to take off and lose him just so he could have fun walking me down with his clearly superior vehicle. As the cruiser begins to accelerate and the wide toothlike grill grows in my rearview, the car flashes its berries without the siren to let me know I am the target. I turn on my emergency flashers and begin to slow down to a snail's pace, instead of stopping completely, hoping that I can stall him for a few more seconds until I can figure out what my next move should be while simultaneously looking for a more dark and secluded area to lure him into before I pull over. Holding the wheel with my left hand, I reach into the middle console for my fake driver's

19

license and car registration with my right hand and place them in the cupholder. I am not sure what the diversity mixture of this area is, but I think it is safe to assume that they do not get a lot of guys of my particular background driving through affluent neighborhoods in Madison, Wisconsin, in 15-year-old Toyota Tacoma pickup trucks after ten o'clock at night. I am doubtful that I would be able to sell him on the old 'visiting a sick mother' story. The tags and car are clean, but once he runs my ID or, even worse, if they have a dash cam and can run a follow up facial ID, it could be terrible for me in the short term and catastrophic to the plan in the long term. We are all certainly fucked if my mug makes it up the pipeline and gets tagged by *them*. Goddamn cameras!

In the cars, on the cars, on the buildings, in the phones, in the computers, in the sky. Everywhere you turn, we are being watched. The increasing pervasiveness of social media outlets promoting the 'video everything at all times' culture, is turning what used to be considered an invasion of privacy into a normal, acceptable way of life. They have schemed for centuries to develop the technology for full scale world domination and one of the key requirements to that level of control is establishing some reliable method to surveil the entire populace and make the general public accept this state of affairs without question. There are very few places left on planet earth that cannot be accessed by satellites with high powered cameras that can zoom in on a mosquito's pecker from outer space. This tends to create a monumental challenge if one is inclined to move in secrecy. I must think hard now and weigh the consequences of my next move. How to get out of this situation without killing this cop and thereby alerting the whole goddamn state of Wisconsin to my presence.

Shit, not to mention that any tarnishing of my reputation by local authorities could subsequently degrade my chances of having a civil meeting tonight with my liaison who will now have an actual reason to mistrust me or see me as a criminal. On top of the fact that I would be forced to return underground and wait for, at a minimum, another decade until the heat dies down enough for me to resurface. Meanwhile these bastards get richer and more powerful and make it increasingly more of an impossibility of ever toppling their empire. Just to arrange this meeting took damn near thirty years of scrupulous preparation and planning. If it does not happen tonight, I doubt if I will be able to track down and somehow gain the trust of another contact directly connected to one of the most powerful group of people in the world again without waiting at least another century or without some sort of modern-day miracle taking place.

I make the first right turn I can make onto Farwell Road and go down about a quarter of a mile before I pull over as far off the shoulder of the road as I possibly could without going into the drainage ditch. By now he is no doubt pissed that I failed to pull over on the main highway and is going to radio in for reinforcements before approaching me. Standard procedure for most traffic stops is to report in to dispatch once they have made contact with the driver so I may be in the clear for one or two more minutes. There are no homes I can see from the road which means I may have a chance of doing this without anyone witnessing the scene from their bedroom window or catching the traffic stop on their home security cameras. I cut the lights on my truck and remove my sunglasses. There is a cigarette already being raised to my mouth to calm my nerves. Funny, I can still get that twisting feeling in the pit of my stomach no matter how many times I go through a potentially perilous situation. My options are slim to none. I need this cop to be cool. I turn on my front dome light and hold up my fake credentials in my right hand so he can see them. Both hands extended up now to show my willingness to surrender. I wonder what he saw that made him decide to pull me over in the first place. I definitely was not speeding. My Illinois tags maybe…? Did he see my glasses? He should not have been able to determine whether they were tinted or not at the angle I was sitting when I passed him. Maybe the dilapidated pickup was too much for this part of town, at this hour.

"Driver, remove your foot from the brake, put the car in park, and turn off your engine," a booming male voice commands over the patrol car's loudspeaker. I can already hear the anger inflected in his cadence. Dammit! I bet dollars to doughnuts that he is already making a call to run the tags for stolen or unregistered vehicles. I am too far down the rabbit hole for any mistakes to happen. I close my eyes and take a deep breath to clear my mind and think. At the moment there is only one officer and one squad car. I can handle this. I look in my rearview and kill the engine. My driver's license and insurance card would fool the C.I.A. on their best day, so I felt safe in that

21

regard, but if this ends up being anything more than a traffic violation ticket, I am royally screwed. I took the chance of making the trip thinking that the short distance between Madison and Chicago would be a piece of cake. Forty-eight days was the time allotted for my credentials to remain valid so it was in my best interest to get the ball rolling on this operation tonight in order to give myself enough latitude to finalize the plan. I regret not waiting another week or two to get an additional phony Wisconsin tag and registration before I left Chicago. Anxiety flaring....Now more than ever I was feeling exposed and vulnerable. Once you are outside the big city, it always gets increasingly more troublesome to hide. A set of headlights crest the hill as another car approaches from behind the officer. If this is another cop, I am seriously fucked. I can take out one cop, maybe, and get away smooth enough to make it back to Chicago tonight, but two cops and disposal of two cars plus cameras and deal with any witnesses that may happen by without blipping their radar — Im-fucking-possible. Even for me. The car slows but keeps going. Just an ordinary nosy civilian. An older gentleman driving a late model diesel engine Mercedes, rubbernecking as he passes. I am calm and collected because I have been on the business end of many weapons before, and no matter what caliber bullet strikes you, they all hurt. Even the ones that manage to not lodge into your bone and pass right through really sting like a motherfucker.

The emotional fragility of humankind is responsible for the misuse of these weapons from the beginning of their inception in wars. Gone are the days when the nobility led the charge to battle and earned the right to their titles. On the contrary, the integrity of warfare has all but disappeared from the battlefield. To stare someone down for the prize of one's own life as the only plausible result and feel that same desperation thrusted at you in return...*THAT* is true warfare. Fucking airstrikes and drone kills reduces war to video games like Call of Duty. There is nothing that smacks of honor in a gun battle. Empires focusing all their resources on military defense and developing overwhelming firepower to remain relevant at any cost. Aggression mistaken for bravado. It baffles me how amongst a species so fragile you would foster this environment of gunplay being the solution to every problem. Bullets start flying, piercing flesh and vital organs so quickly the recipient does not even have a chance to mount a response or plead his case to this impossibly fast and final method of judgment. Some calibers are so powerful that bullets just whizzing by closely can be enough to remove limbs and incinerate flesh of the innocent and guilty alike. No, mon ami…give me a good sword or knife, a spear or similar melee weapons and then you will see the true measure of a man. Pulling a trigger from any range is a safe and disconnected way to kill. There is no connection to the life or lives you are attempting to alter when you point a pistol at someone. When two combatants meet on the battlefield carrying their rage and animus for each other with nothing more than sword or spear or even just your fists, only then do you see and begin to understand the fathoms of human will, determination and decisive thought.

What am I saying? Fuck it. I know the game, and I definitely do not hate the players. I have used guns to kill. I have never been proud of it. It just gets damn fucking hard to keep going through the same shit over and over with people. Most so-called gangsters these days are nothing more than cowards. Guns are always their only way out. That is until they meet someone that guns have no effect upon. Then comes the "shit the pants" moment. Today will unfortunately be a bad day for this police officer. Regrettably, I am all out of time, and I must remove myself from this situation immediately if I am to make my deadline. Katherine Reichstall is scheduled to leave on a flight to San Francisco tomorrow afternoon, and if I wait any later, I am going to miss my opportunity and have to start over again from scratch. That is not happening under any circumstance.

"Driver, using your left hand, slowly open the car door from the outside and get out of the car with both hands up where I can see them," shouts the officer.

I am racking my brain trying to figure out why I was pulled over in the first place. And now, how did things progress to me having to get out of the car? Does my vehicle fit a description? Whatever the circumstances, I cannot be detained or arrested under any circumstance. I was prepared for a ticket but this was too much. If they attempt to search my car, there may be a problem. If there is a dash cam installed in the police cruiser, as soon as I get out, they would simply have to run facial recognition on the footage, and I would be toast. I must make my move. My eyes are keenly focused on the driver's side mirror. The bed of the truck helps to block the blinding headlights of the Crown Victoria, and by squinting I can just make out the large silhouette of the officer putting on his hat and preparing to exit the car. I open the door slowly and I have to look at the rear view now which, because of the lights against the back of the truck, makes it harder to see exactly what the officer is doing. I focus on his door and as I lean forward and move to place my left foot on the ground, every muscle fiber in my body begins to harden in anticipation.

As soon as I see his car door crack open a millimeter, I pivot on my left foot and in one motion I am up and out of the car. My feet only make contact with the ground twice, once on the initial step out and the other step 15 feet afterward. I close the gap between cars in less than a second and grab the driver door of the patrol car with my left hand and yank it open for my right hand to grab him and lift him out of the car. He must weigh a good 270 pounds if he is an ounce, but my blood is hot and pumping now so I easily snatch him up by his collar like a bag of apples. The officer's eyes grow wide as saucers and his skin goes pale as a ghost as he is lifted high into the air, fighting the urge to faint from the sudden rush of paralyzing fear. The wild look of absolute terror on his face as our eyes meet for a solitary second betrays the poise and demeanor I expected from this man, considering his salt and pepper hair and the numerous stripes on his uniform. His mouth was gaping like a fish, not knowing how to react to the last one and a half seconds of his life. His training or his sense of fear finally motivates his hand to instinctively move toward his revolver.

I grab his hand so swiftly that I accidentally snap a few bones in his fingers, rendering his right hand useless. It has been many years since I had to do any hand-to-hand combat, and it is hard to regulate my strength when I get nervous like this. He lets out a weak 'Yelp' and his face winces in pain. I let go of his hand and wrench him around so I can wrap my left arm around his throat and keep my hip against his service revolver while freeing my right arm. The officer's heart is beating like a bass drum. I can feel his carotid artery against my bicep straining to pump precious blood up through to the brain and back down to the heart. I squeeze my left arm tighter around his neck. I must be careful not to snap it. I only want him to take a little snooze.

"S-s-s-s-t-t-t-ooop....p-p-p-p-l-eeasssse!"

Comes a raspy voice as the officer struggles in vain to free himself. His arms and legs flail and kick in mid-air trying to gain a hold of something to use as leverage, but he cannot budge my chokehold. He begins smacking my arm with his broken fingered hand out of desperation. The small-town life has left this man ill-prepared for anything like this to be happening. I have to be careful for fear of him going into shock from the overflow of adrenalin in his bloodstream before I can make him pass out.

"Ffffff-f-fuck-k-k-ing,.....Bassss-ss-s-s-sta -a-rd!" he manages to spit out as he tries to hook his le around mine and wrench his body around as much as physically possible.

"I am not going to kill you," I whisper to him softly.

His struggles begin to subside, doubtfully from my reassuring words, but from the lack of blood flowing to his brain. The excitement and physical strain of the struggle causes him to begin to lose consciousness and in a matter of seconds he is out. I ease off my grip accordingly. I have not heard any squawking from dispatch over the radio in response to him calling in the traffic stop which could only mean that I was correct to move on him when I did. His breathing slows to a raspy snore, and I lower him to the ground, being sure to cradle his head as I lay him down on the ice-cold concrete. I need to wrap this up quickly and get back on the road with all speed. If this predicament becomes any worse, I may have not only lost my window for tonight's meeting. I may have blown the entire plan. There are way too many lives riding on my back for me to fuck it up now. The drive from Chicago to Madison was only a couple of hours, and there was only the one cop at the gas station for the entire journey here. It blows my mind that I was able to make it all these years and get this close to my destination without having any major run-ins with law enforcement, and now here I am hunched over an unconscious deputy sheriff who is going to be far beyond pissed when he wakes up. If another car were to approach this scene and report what was happening, it would most certainly be a wrap.

Hell, no, not fucking happening! I yank out the body camera he is wearing in his shirt pocket which inadvertently rips a hole in his shirt up to his name badge, further exposing the thick hair on his chest which was also frothing out from the top of his neckline. Not wearing body armor. Probably

25

not crucial for police in this area like it is in the Windy City. I slide the body camera into my right pants pocket and continue the cleanup. The officer is fast asleep now and snoring away lying flat on his back half on the concrete and half on grass in the shoulder of the road. I bend down into the squad car to grab the rearview which has a dash camera attached below it. I yank the entire apparatus from the front windshield mount and drop it on the driver's side floor for the time being. I turn off the headlights and the flashing berries with my knuckle, making sure not to get any fingerprints anywhere. It is now pitch dark again on both sides of the street. I see only trees with no signs of residential lights behind them. The homes in this area are more like ranches with the main dwellings always located very far back from the road and entrance to the property. This part of the street sits in a valley where the road crests upward about a mile ahead of and behind where we are currently positioned. However, it is only a matter of time before someone comes up the road in either direction. I need this to be over as soon as fucking humanly possible.

Deputy Todd as his name tag proclaims him to be, is sleeping soundly but once he wakes up, I'm sure he will have the whole goddamn state of Wisconsin will be looking for me. I am facing no less than aggravated assault charges all the way to attempted murder on a constable of the law stemming from the chokehold and whatever damage I may have done to his right hand when I stopped him from grabbing his pistol. Destruction of state or county property for the body camera, the shirt, and the dash camera. Plus, when he wakes up he is going to need a ton of Aspirin for the giant headache he is going to have. While he is still lying on the ground, I tuck his shirt back into his pants and twist his buckle around to the front and try to smooth out some of the wrinkles caused by the struggle. If someone does happen to drive by before he wakes up, I want them to think that it is just a cop catching a much needed forty winks by the side of the road. Radio is still quiet. My luck just may hold out.

Once I am satisfied with Deputy Todd's appearance, I lift him off the ground and stand him up outside the open driver's side door. I dust off his uniform as if he was a store mannequin getting ready to go on display, holding his head upright by the back of his neck with my right hand. I unclip his radio with my left hand and slide it into the kangaroo pouch on my

26

hoodie. I then scoop his legs with my left arm and pick him up in a cradle slowly, like a mother lifting her limp child, and lower the pudgy, snoring man gently into the driver's chair. I recline him back into a comfortable position using the controls at the side of the seat. I am purposely being as mild as possible as to not jar him out of his stupor prematurely. With his head leaning slightly back on the headrest, Officer Todd's mouth gapes open and a buzzing sound emits from his throat on every exhale from what sounds to be a textbook case of sleep apnea. I take out a handkerchief from my back pocket and wipe down the outer door handle and then reach across the officer to wipe down the instrument panel for any fingerprints. I grab the dash camera from the floorboard next to the officer's feet, remove the SD card, and slide it into my pocket. I grab the officer's cell phone from the cup holder and, using the handkerchief, I throw it high into the air, sending it soaring deep into the woods across the street.

As Deputy Todd sleeps, the expression on his face is peaceful which should make it easier to fool any passersby into thinking he is just getting some much needed rest. I grab the keys out of the ignition switch and place them in my pants pocket. On a hunch, I reach across the sleeping officer to the closed laptop in the center console, and with the backside of my hand, I check to feel that it is ice cold like it has not been used in a while. This leads me to believe that he had no interest in running my tags. I was being profiled and whatever he said I did wrong was going to be the final word. Hardly surprising that he gave me the step out of the car treatment right after I stuck my hands up. Regrettably for him, I was the last person on earth you would want on the other end of that request. Tucking the dash camera and mirror combo under my arm, I close the door to the squad car. I wipe off the handle and around the door frame with my handkerchief for any residue left by my hands as a precaution. Having such a unique fingerprint is a major problem, and I have always had to be extremely careful about keeping them out of government databases.

Since the advent of the internet and legislation like the Patriot Act, law enforcement has been granted sweeping surveillance powers. Different police municipalities that in the past were hardly able or willing to share information across jurisdictions now do so readily and are provided with unlimited access to huge data stores which they use to spy on the

27

unsuspecting public whether they be criminally inclined or not. People like Cynthia McKinney, Chris Darden, Aaron Swartz, Snowden, and Assange all tried to warn us of the coming surveillance state, but distractions like reality TV and football triumph over common sense every time.

I look at my watch, I am completely out of time now. Now it is up to the ancestors to keep everything quiet long enough for the meeting to happen tonight. If I make it back to Chicago, it will probably be a good idea to switch out vehicles as soon as possible. I do a visual scan while sniffing the air for any signs of humans in the immediate area but all is eerily desolate. I walk quickly back to my truck and throw the mirror and camera combo into the passenger seat before cranking it up and slowly pull off without turning my lights on. I make a quick three point U-turn and take one last glance over at the sleeping Deputy Todd as I pass by before making a left back onto Farwell Drive. I gun the engine through the darkness as I push my little getaway vehicle to 65 miles per hour down the dark empty streets. I make another right onto Highway 113 and continue in the direction I was headed before the interruption.

The entire encounter with Deputy Todd took less than three minutes but every second I was standing there felt like an eternity. I see the glow of headlights cresting over the hill through the darkness ahead of me approaching southbound. It has been about a minute and a half since I left the scene with Deputy Todd, and this is the first car I have encountered. I slow down to match the speed limit and fumble for a second reaching for the switch to pop on my lights a split second after the oncoming car's high beams hit me like a photon blast. From here on out I cannot afford to make any more careless mistakes. I certainly do not need to solicit any more attention from the police or anyone looking to alert the police. I quickly turn my head as the car passes to determine if it may be another cop. It happens to be a royal blue 7-series BMW carrying an older couple. Hopefully they are not turning down the street I left Deputy Todd on and if so, I hope they fail to notice Cop Van Winkle sitting on the side of the road sleeping on duty and be concerned enough to decide to report it to someone. I dig around in the bag next to me on the passenger seat and fish out my cigarettes. I am so nervous I crack open a fresh pack instead of the one I already started and start chain smoking. I need to remain calm and trust that I bought myself some time as I

28

glance down at the dash camera. It has been ages since my nerves have had this much action. A weird feeling of fear mixed with anxiety that I had once considered myself immune to, began to pulse through me. I gingerly grab a cigarette and stick it in my mouth. I pluck my lighter from the ashtray and take my left hand from the wheel momentarily to block the wind and spark the cigarette. I take a deep five second drag before I allow the flaming tip to stop glowing. I exhale the smoke through my nose in an attempt to wash away the smells of sweat and funk lightly accented by Old Spice cologne, cholesterol medicine and the overall stench of fear coming from Deputy Todd. The cigarettes help immensely but the fucking odors get implanted in your brain sometimes and never really quite go away. This is why I need a break from continuous interaction with multiple humans because it can really start to confuse me as I try to interpret the information of certain pheromones that are emitted involuntarily from people. The cigarettes also help in easing my nerves somewhat but after my run in with the deputy, my sense of urgency is screaming that If I am to win the night, I need to hurry the fuck up. After another mile, I see more headlights approaching headed south. A dark colored F-150 this time passes by too fast for me to make out the occupants.

As soon as he passes, I grab the dash camera with the handkerchief and slow down to a steady 25 miles per hour. Holding the car steady with my knee, I wrap the dash camera rear view mirror up inside the handkerchief and crush it between my palms, destroying it thoroughly so whoever finds it will have one hell of a puzzle to piece back together. Once I am certain that the vehicles behind me are out of sight and that there are no cars coming towards me, I quickly swerve into the empty oncoming lane. I slow down to around 15 miles an hour to dump the contents of the handkerchief onto the opposite side of the road, scattering the pieces. I give the handkerchief one last shake before quickly retaking my proper lane and return to driving the speed limit. I grab my phone from the center console and enter the code on the lock screen to re-enter the GPS app. After the initial welcome screen loads the application asks me if I would like to resume my previous drive for the last address entered. I click 'ok' and the display reads that I have less than five miles until I reach my destination. After a short while of passing nothing but mansions hidden within the trees, a voice I can barely hear over the wind coming through the cracked window into the GPS announces:

(Electronic Voice): "In one mile, turn left."

ETA is 12:05am. Hell of a time for a first date. From our correspondence through email, Katherine Reichstall and I have had an excellent rapport. I have always tried to make her as comfortable as possible with my eccentric research requests, and she has always portrayed herself as genuine and trustworthy throughout the entire process. I need to focus now in case there may be a double-cross afoot. It's hard to believe in coincidences anymore, but the police just being randomly posted in this area waiting for me this close to my objective seems a tad suspicious. I put out my cigarette about two and a half miles from the house because I want the old sniffer to be working at full capacity. My hearing and eyesight are not too shabby either, but smells linger and can tell a story about a space. When I can smell you, I can damn near read your mind. That is why I chain smoke when I am not working. Otherwise I would be smelling every cock, cunt, and ball sweat from here to Timbuktu, and it would give me headaches and frankly piss me off in general. Making me a real pill to be around. However, this keen sense of smell has saved my life many times in the past for it can readily discern intention and deception in most mammals. Humans are probably one of the least aware species when it comes to hiding their presence and intentions through the pheromones and aromas they emit when they are confronted with different circumstances. Their underdeveloped noses seems to be the main reason why humans have routinely taken this aspect of the senses for granted which explains why their actions can become callous and arrogant towards nature simply because of their unawareness of what is literally right under their noses. Pun intended. Every living creature produces a scent and that scent translates into a language that can be interpreted through the nostrils of certain 'analytical' creatures.

I continue further down the seemingly never-ending River Road. All the properties in the area are covered with tall trees that smother both sides of the street. As the tree line gives way to the night sky, I can see the clouds racing across the face of the moon for a moment before it's completely covered by what looks like an incoming storm system, plunging the night deeper into darkness.

The electronic voice of the GPS speaks again.

..."In one mile, turn left...

...In half a mile, turn left...

...In a quarter of a mile, turn left"

I make the left turn onto a street lined on both sides with a white wooden fence, something like a large cattle farm or a golf course would erect.

(Electronic Voice): "In one mile, your destination is on the left."

Research indicates that as of 2002 the Reichstall family purchased most of the land in this area. Katherine moved here the following year with her then-husband and six-year-old daughter. It is incredible to imagine that ninety percent of all these thousands of acres of trees and farmland I have been driving past for miles belong to her and her family. I can smell multiple cows, horses, pigs, and other livestock nearby. My guess is they are also heavily invested into the dairy market, being this deep into Wisconsin. With the time crunch created by my run-in with the deputy, I decide to trust the earnestly straightforward and altruistic persona I glean from Katherine's email correspondence. I have researched, tracked, and monitored her and her family's lives for decades. I have poured over hundreds of books and spent countless hours combing through historical documents and internet articles for my research into the Reichstall family and their role as intermediaries for the clandestine rulers of this planet. Some of my most valuable research has been facilitated by the vast network of people that survive just below the surface of accepted society. People who for mostly horrible reasons are somehow connected to the power structure through their secret crimes and oftentimes uncontrollable yearnings and vices. I sought to gain her trust by indirectly providing her with insight for her various journalistic endeavors which garnered her a fair amount of professional recognition in recent years. I also planted a seed of curiosity for such lofty pursuits many years earlier when we met briefly in the early nineties when she was but a girl of twenty-five years old attending New York University.

Chapter 3

Katherine Reichstall grew up in a wealthy hamlet in upstate New York called Salisbury Mills. She was raised in a very conservative home, her main caretaker being her live-in-Nanny Sophia. Her father was away most of the time traveling for business while her mother busied herself shopping or traveling for pleasure nine months out of the year. After high school, she attended Stanford despite her parents' wishes for her to attend a more 'prestigious' institution somewhere on the continent of Europe. Katherine's resentment of her parents and eventually her entire family was the driving force behind her passion to expose the secrets that haunted the unwholesome narrative that followed her surname. While serving in a graduate program at the Rubin Museum of Art connected to her archaeological studies doctorate at N.Y.U., Katherine was able to convince the gallery curators to conduct a one-night exclusive display of her relatives' private art collection which had been kept behind closed doors in the vaults of her descendants for centuries.

This was an opportunity which the museum curators jumped at. This was around the year 1991 or '92. Our chance meeting was due to my acquaintance with an old homeless gentleman whom I had befriended while living in the sewers and subway tunnels some years ago. He was one of the few 'mole people,' as they are called, who was not afraid of me from the moment he met me. I happened upon him one night as I patrolled the streets and viaducts of New York at night looking for crooked souls that could use an attitude adjustment. Most of the time, I kept to myself and ignored the nasty things that went on in the city to avoid being detected by the Incalculaba. There were those rare occasions when I would be out patrolling and someone's cries for help were just impossible to ignore. One such person was a man being attacked by a group of punk kids wielding baseball bats and brass knuckles. After making short work of the leader of their little gang the rest of the kids turned tail and ran. The grateful gentleman that I rescued introduced himself to me as Kerwin Terrio. He was a former Wall Street executive and current smack junkie with a heart of gold who lost his shirt in the crash of '87 from too many over leveraged investments and an unshakeable cocaine habit. Kerwin is dead now. Stabbed to death in a homeless shelter around 2011 by a female junkie he had been living with under Grand Central Station for four years prior. Once upon a time, Kerwin was a brilliant hedge fund manager who lived in a beautiful Manhattan penthouse, drove a cherry red custom Porsche 911, and could have anything he wanted delivered with the snap of a finger. Kerwin managed portfolios for the likes of Mick Jagger, Clint Eastwood, and The Sultan of Brunei during those boom years of the early eighties in the U.S. stock market. He and his firm made tens of millions of dollars before it all went bust on Bloody Monday in the third week of October 1987, and in the blink of an eye, the market crashed and Kerwin and lots of other traders and fund managers hit rock bottom right along with it.

One night, Kerwin and I were smoking Camel reds in Washington Square on the corner of Sixth Avenue and West Fourth Street. Kerwin was trying to listen to the Yankees game on his Walkman which was by far his prized possession. He would always tell me how he used to own box seats directly behind the home team dugout at Yankee stadium. Whenever they lost, he would roll out a string of barely audible Italian curses and drink himself to sleep without sharing any cigarettes for the rest of the night. If the Yankees were playing the Red Sox absolutely no one could speak to him at all, not even me, because of the hissy fit he would throw over every bad play. Anytime I was in the park at night, I would stop and check on Kerwin in his tent and leave a few bills in his hand. He would in return provide me with cigarettes because he knew I had no desire to go into the stores. Reliably, he always had something he needed to tell me that required I give him back one or two of the cigarettes he had just purchased for me.

Kerwin had all the latest gossip about the goings-on in the sewers. He would always begin talking to me with a positive word about how no one bleeds to death or O.D. 's anymore because I was always carrying these

33

'sickos' to the surface for help. Every now and again, he would want to fill me in on some injustice that could use my version of redress. Usually, the culprit would be an asshole cop who may have gotten a little overzealous in his duties while kicking Kerwin and his drinking buddies off of some park bench. More than anything Kerwin hated the gangs who would shake down winos and hookers for 'scratch and dope'. One night over a couple of Marlboro Reds, Kerwin could not talk fast enough to tell me something he had found out that he thought would be of great interest to me.

"Remember I was telling you about how my brokerage firm functioned as a consultation hub, and I ran the commodities branch that made crazy money for all types of super rich assholes," Kerwin began. "My win percentage was so fuckin' good wit' such few drawdowns that I began gettin' referrals to manage a small percentage the portfolios of some of the richest of the rich. I mean fat humpback whale motherfuckers. One percent of their portfolios were worth over two billion dollars. These guys were so rich, they didn't fart in the same pair of underwear twice. One of the richest amongst rich cocksuckers, hell pretty much the biggest and baddest of them all was an heir to the Reichstall fortune".I flinched at the sound of that name and Kerwin noticed my change in demeanor.

"See, I knew you would know about 'em. Nobody can stand those assholes," he said before continuing. So you know these fucks own half of the world's wealth, no bullshit, and it's been that way for more than a hundred years." Kerwin paused to take a drag from his cigarette before continuing without exhaling. "They were rich fucks before Guinness and Ripley started keeping track of who the world's rich fucks were," he quipped before blowing the smoke in his lungs out of the side of his mouth. "Anyway, one of the egghead CPA's we had workin' for us came to my office one day with a statistic about these fuckers that said if you were to try and quantify all their money through all their limitless business holdings, it would take a team full of accountants and attorneys working around the clock for seven years to crunch all the numbers. Mainly because the dough is tied up in so many different little tax havens, shell companies, and blind trusts. The news can never report the twisted shit that goes on because they're complicit. These crooked bastards control every media outlet on the planet. Any hoo, you know not to get me fuckin' started on that shit!" Kerwin said as he took another long pull of his cigarette. "Back to what I was sayin', rememba' we were talkin' last year about this time afta that kid set that fire to that club in the Bronx, killing like eighty somethin' people." Before I could nod my acknowledgement, he continued. "Long story short, that kid's dad worked at a rival brokerage called Garner and Beck before it went belly up. Turns out the kid's dad ended up killin' himself after the market crashed. The head of Garner and Beck was part owner of that club, and the kid set the fire to get revenge on the jerk because he felt that the guy had left his dad out to dry after the shit hit the fan at the firm."

Kerwin threw his cigarette butt down on the concrete and stomped on it. Looking me square in the eye he said to me, "I don't know where I was going with that story but I thought you were gonna shit just now by the look on your face when I mentioned that Reichstall guy. I swear it was one of the only times I seen you give a damn about any story I ever told you." Kerwin said, pointing knowingly at me.

"*Reichstall* — Yeah...when I look back at what happened to me, If I could blame anybody as the ultimate cause of all the money manipulation that put mine and all those other firms in the toilet bowl, it was those Cornutos!" His Italian accent would get thicker whenever he got really angry. "They even got every family in the mob in their fuckin' pocket,"

Kerwin stood and paced back and forth a few steps rubbing his thinning hair and shaking his head as he cursed out loud toward no one in particular.

"*Cazzo!*" .....

"*Leccare il culo!*"

And a few other colorful Italian phrases I recognized like spilled from his mouth as he plopped down onto a milk crate and produced a small flask of what smelled to be Gin and offered me a sip before having one for himself. I lit another cigarette and offered him one, which he took and placed behind his ear while still holding about a quarter of the previous cigarette. He began again looking up at me and pointing his two fingers which held the remainder of the cigarette to emphasize the end of every other syllable.

"Half the goddamn misery on this god forsaken rock wouldn't exist if it weren't for those greedy bastards sucking all the blood from every fucking body and every fucking thing." He looked at me over his glasses and smiled and said, "No offense".

"None taken," I gravelly replied.

"I would be happier than a sissy with a bag of dicks if I could somehow get my money back and shit on those bastards' whole operation in the process," Kerwin continued, "but for now, it's just the dream of a homeless bastard living in the gutters of the Big Apple." He took the cigarette from behind his ear and placed it in his mouth, lighting it with the dying cherry of the previous cigarette. He took a deep drag and exhaled a large puff of smoke that engulfed me in the darkness and pirouettes away in the shards of streetlight coming down the block.

"I don't think even you"—he pointed his cigarette hand at me for emphasis— "with all the amazing shit you can do...you wouldn't stand a snowball's chance in hell against the fire power behind those bastards." He looked down at the broken glass littering the concrete.

"I wasn't sure if I should say anything. Shit, it would take at least a hundred of you to even.... fuck it. If anybody had half a shot of taking down a cat as fat as Reichstall then you could. I'd give both my nuts to see those bastards get taken down a peg, so I figured I'd show you this anyway."

He held out a folded newspaper to me. As I took the paper and turned to the article he had circled, Kerwin continued talking, mostly to himself.

"Made those cocksuckers boat loads of fucking money, and what do I get for all my fucking trouble?... I get to eat dog food out of a can every fucking night." Kerwin lamented. "Fucking Reichstall bastards are so rich God owes 'em twenty bucks," complained Kerwin to himself as he unscrews the cap on his flask and takes another sip.

I quickly flipped the paper over to read the rest of the circled article and to see how it could be of use to me. Usually I would dismiss Kerwin's drunken ramblings as nonsense, but the gravitas in the tone of his voice seemed to be more than just the alcoholic babbling that he usually lectured me with. The mere mention of the name Reichstall causes a knot in my stomach to tighten.

The headline of the living section of the paper read, *Reichstall Heir to Assist in Opening Night. One of the many members of the reclusive Reichstall family, Miss Katherine Penelope Reichstall, will be acknowledged as an honorary curator of an art exhibit featuring rarely seen pieces on loan from her family's private art collection. This unique show will be open to the general public for one night only at the Rubin Museum of Art on West Seventeenth Street in the Soho district one week from today.*

My mind begins to race and I immediately begin to formulate a plan. I never dreamed an opportunity like this would present itself in such an improbable place. I may have an opportunity to win the trust of someone in that family that can get me inside so I can expose their unmitigated evil to the world and destroy their empire from within. This will demand pulling off something terribly brilliant. Especially because I was sure a young debutante and socialite of her high status will have top level surveillance and bodyguards. Not to mention high security surrounding the exhibit itself. Whatever I do, I must do it publicly. I would have to get in her head and make sure our time together was brief but memorable.

New York at that particular time was the center of the universe. The golden era of the Big Apple: the late seventies all the way until the mid to late nineties. In 1985, I had just relocated back to New York because my basement apartment on Osage Avenue in Philadelphia burned to the ground along with the rest of the block when the police dropped a bomb on the MOVE headquarters. They shuffled the politics and used the media again to hide their complicity and scapegoat themselves with the very people they firebombed. They murdered men, women, and children under the guise of removing terrorists to suppress a grassroots uprising with the added bonus of an attempt to try to assassinate me. They resorted to the same heavy-handed tactics to destroy me and the truth as they did back in 1921 when they callously dropped firebombs from planes and destroyed thirty-five square blocks of Tulsa, Oklahoma. At that time, I had been living and assisting the Negro and Indian population in the Tulsa area for about a year when I received classified information from a reliable source that named all the

American corporations complicit in funding and profiting from both sides of World War One. I was bolder and extremely adamant about playing an active role in dismantling their empire in those days, and my idea was to use the independent black printing presses in Tulsa to distribute the damning information to the mainstream press. First through the state media, then nationwide and eventually broaden our reach internationally. But before I could follow through, the Incalculaba with their network of spies caused my plan to unravel like a spool of yarn. Many innocent people lost their lives and their lands in the subsequent massacre. I was forced to flee the country to keep myself and my accomplices safe. It seemed as if no matter what I tried, *they* were always five steps ahead of me.

Nevertheless, the vibration in New York City between the years of 1967 and 2001 was sublime. Even with the rats and the crime and corruption it was a place where any and every type of person could come and just blend into the jungle. There was always someone doing something more bodacious than what was done previously. New York was active, electricity itself. The entire world could feel it. A time where MTV actually played music videos, and the world boiled down to Michael Jackson and Ronald Reagan. Everyone dressed in the wildest most outrageous fashions. Leather and fishnets were everywhere, people wore gloves for no reason at all, and cut all manner of parts and lines in their hair and eyebrows. Men and women alike. Punk rock existed with hip hop, and New York was ground zero for everything that mattered on earth. The darkness of the night breathed on the party-goers, and blow glistened from the nostrils of smiling faces enjoying the Big Apple life and all it had to offer. A creature such as I could move freely at night and blend perfectly into the complexity of the metropolis without impediment. Wearing midnight black sunglasses at all times of the day and night would seem odd for most people not named Ray Charles or Stevie Wonder but not in New York City. I must admit to myself that I cut a striking figure in those days. My attire mainly consisted of black or dark colored slacks and shirt and boots. No matter the weather I could always be seen wearing a black or brown trench coat and a hat which was very useful to protect me from the UV rays on the rare occasion I would move during the overcast day. It was the eighties when I first began to wear black t-shirts instead of button down collared shirts. Since the turn of the century I learned that keeping up with rapidly changing fashion trends kept the questions from civilians to a minimum, and helped me to move amongst the greater population without detection. My many travels over the ages have allowed me to alleviate much of my ignorance to broader cultural changes and has instructed me very well on how to blend in with the night dwellers in whatever country or region I find myself.

About a mile before my destination, the police radio I forgot was in the kangaroo pouch of my sweatshirt makes a squawking noise just as an approaching car crests the hill and pulls me out of my daydream about New York. I am forced to squint because of the bright HID lights approaching me which appear to be rather high off the ground, signifying that this could be an approaching pickup truck or an SUV. Not the typical police cruiser lights but nowadays the police drive many different makes and models of vehicles. My paranoia kicks in, and my mind immediately begins running escape scenarios if it does turn out to be the police. The vehicle passes, and I cannot quite determine the physical characteristics of the driver besides the winter hat that he or she is wearing, but in my rearview, I can see the Illinois plates on the vehicle confirming this SUV was not affiliated with the local police.

My sources inform me that Katherine will be leaving for San Francisco tomorrow and then out of the country. She will be serving as an associate producer of a documentary based on one of her books about Jordanian folklore as it relates to the Old Testament of the Bible. In the last few weeks, I attempted several times to contact her by email and at her office mailing address anonymously but to no avail. I am sure she either just ignored the personal requests I messaged her or, more than likely, they probably ended up as spam in her inbox. Our correspondence began through anonymous emails where I sold myself by posing as an independent researcher and won her trust by offering my knowledge of the Dogon of West Africa and their archaeological connection to the Egyptian mystery schools. At her level of journalism, I imagine that she receives tons of research tips from fans and colleagues so mine were probably not significant enough to warrant her giving my correspondence any type of favor over the others. It was only when I included a drawing of the symbol that is branded on my neck that she began to take notice of my emails and reply on a regular basis. A face-to-face meeting is the only way to speak with her and ensure confidentiality. I will remind her of that night thirty years ago at the art gallery in New York then I

39

may be able to convince her that she has nothing to fear and that she has always been a part of my plan as the final component to exposing and dismantling the Incalculaba. My heart drops into the pit of my stomach at the thought of it. You would think being able to take multiple shotgun blasts head on and jump from helicopters without a parachute would make me immune to anxiety, but I am so used to taking what I need rather than asking for help from people that to do otherwise puts me at a loss for words and makes me more than a little uncomfortable. As I pull into the long driveway, I am met by a wrought iron gate and a call box equipped with the latest in camera doorbells. I am too far away from the main house to smell the occupants, but I can smell the strong aroma of a horse stable a few hundred yards to my left. There is a high probability that she will not understand a male stranger showing up at midnight on a Tuesday spouting nonsense about the end of civilization as we know it. I will need to talk fast before she alerts the authorities herself and they connect me with old Deputy Todd back there.

The wind begins to pick up intensity, a light rain begins, making it more difficult to discern how many people are inside from the lingering aromas in the air. If she has a husband or children that failed to make the report, there is no way I am waltzing in there at this time of night spouting some corny shit like "Hello. If you wouldn't mind, I need your help saving the world." I may as well drive myself to the nearest precinct and save myself the trouble because this is starting to feel like an exercise in futility. I listen intently to the call box as I press the button on the digital doorbell. Its digital chime makes a horrible attempt at mimicking the analog relic of its past. I wait and count to sixty in my head and reach out to ring the bell again. This time I count to one hundred and twenty, and I sit as still as possible while still checking my mirrors and peripheral for any approaching vehicles.

Shit! Maybe my intel was wrong, and she left already. My senses are unable to help me with any clues and now I find myself staring directly into the lens of the doorbell camera that could quite possibly be sending my image to the Incalculaba at this very moment. I push the button again and start a new count when about 23 seconds into my mental timer, over the device comes a groggy voice that's either an Australian woman who smokes five packs a day or a British man with a lilt of sweetness behind every last syllable.

In a surprisingly 'matter of fact' manner, the voice said, "I have not ordered any Uber Eats or Door Dash, and in case you did not know, whoever the fuck you are, it is fucking midnight and way past time to be ringing people's doorbell. The sheriff just so happens to be a close personal friend of mine and I assure you that whatever you are selling can wait until normal business hours."

She clears her throat, and her voice comes through the device sharper and crisper.

"If you're not putting your car in reverse and leaving within the next three seconds so I can get back to sleep, there is going to be hell to pay,". There is a calmness in the timbre of the speech that lets me know that this person is all business, and I need to start flapping my gums quickly if I am to convince them to allow me to enter.

"P-Please!" I yell, suddenly at a loss for words. "I apologize for my timing but I have an important message that can only be delivered in per—."

"3-2-1," she cuts me off, "Times up pal. I tried being cordial. Now leave before I have the whole bloody Dane County Sheriff's Department come down hard on your ass," boomed the voice, now sounding angrier and domineering. A sure sign that she is terrified that I may be calling her bluff. She more than likely has been studying the image on the doorbell video, trying to figure out why a black version of Inspector Gadget with dark shades on is trying to enter her property in the middle of the night. I do not blame her for being scared. I must do something drastic now before I lose the opportunity and my decades of waiting and planning would be for nothing. I quickly turn on the overhead dome light inside the car and remove my Fedora and sunglasses. I turn my back to the doorbell camera and quickly pull my coat down from my shoulders. I grab the nape of my sweatshirt in the back so that the back of my neck is directly in front of the camera. There, in full view of the camera, was something I wanted to forget, something no one knew was there.

"Oh my God!"

41

I hear the voice exclaim before going silent.

If I am mistaken about her character and disdain for her heritage, I could be exposing myself to their surveillance and putting my plan at risk. Even allowing myself to be recorded on this doorbell camera is a huge gamble. Many of these videos are saved in cloud accounts which are monitored heavily by private agencies that no doubt surveils family members and their day-to-day dealings. They could realistically be running a facial recognition scan and sending someone here this very second. I regret having to do this at night but if I am cornered by law enforcement, I will need all my strength to get away in a pinch. I wish I could have called or sent a letter, but I knew that providing a warning of my visit would be out of the question. I sit at the gate waiting for at least another two minutes. No cars have passed and the police radio I pilfered is quiet again. If she is calling the cops, I am going to have to ditch this truck and get back to Chicago on foot. That would throw a terribly unfortunate monkey wrench into my plans, but I must always be prepared for the absolute worst possible scenario. That is the only way I have survived this long. After another minute of silence passes I begin to lose hope. If the cops have been called and they are on their way, I need to leave now before I am boxed in. If this is a different jurisdiction than the one Deputy Todd works for, then they could presumably use a different radio frequency that would not register on the walkie talkie I stole.

My paranoia is raging now and I am beginning to feel like a Class One, Grade A idiot for even attempting something this risky. Defeated, I reluctantly throw the car in reverse and begin to back out of the driveway when the gate buzzes and slowly begins to open. The first part of my gamble worked. I put the car in drive and proceed forward down the path before me. The driveway is about half a mile of tree-lined road made up of immaculate cobblestone which ended at the mouth of a large roundabout surrounding a dazzlingly green patch of grass in front of the main house. The exterior mansion is an exact mimic of a French chateau made completely out of limestone and Italian marble slabs sitting atop a four-car garage. About sixty yards away and adjacent to the main house to the right is another smaller, two-story all brick bungalow which I deduced must be a guest house or servant quarters. As I marvel at the decadence, I think to myself that even the black sheep of the family still enjoyed the comfort provided by the tremendous wealth of the Reichstall empire. As I pull up into the roundabout, I pass the only other vehicle visible which is a dark blue late model Ford F-150 pickup truck in immaculate condition. I park on the left side of the hulking behemoth of a truck to block my comparably tiny truck from being seen from anyone approaching from the main driveway. I put my Fedora and shades back on as I get out of my vehicle. I tilt my head back and inhale deeply trying to gain awareness of my surroundings and assure myself I was not walking into an ambush. There are no signs of hostiles in the vicinity and the dark house looked empty through the large bay window, but I approach with caution nonetheless. As I draw closer to the front door I can smell the residual musk of canines and felines nearby. The blinding porch lights spring to life revealing more of the contours of this majestic home. Victorian style columns flank the front porch with its elaborate crown molding and sandstone tiles leading up to the huge and beautifully designed wrought iron double doors. I walk up the stone slab steps and try to remind myself to smile as much as possible to diffuse the tension this woman must certainly be feeling due to the suddenness of this encounter. As I approach the door, I see another video doorbell camera attached to the wall parallel to the more traditional doorbell embedded in the marble next to it.

From this doorbell camera comes the voice again. "Remove your hat and glasses and lean toward the light so I can see your face." I oblige and flash the biggest smile I have been able to produce in the last 30 years. I squint into the lens in an attempt to make my eyes soften and my face more palatable. I need this woman to be able to listen to me and be at ease with my presence because what I have to tell her is anything but pleasant. There is another camera above me on the opposite side of the porch which must have a better resolution for the person inside to be able to get a more detailed look at my face.

"That brand on the back of your neck is one of a kind and very specific to a certain time period per its use as a family crest. There should be no one alive under the age of 150 with those markings. And there are only a handful of researchers on this planet that would even recognize that insignia. So how the fuck did you end up with that symbol on your neck?" booms the voice, resuming the matter-of-fact but intentionally intimidating tone from before.

43

I look directly into the higher camera, still smiling and say,

"I received this mark from one of your ancestors who was once in control of my life a great deal of time ago."

A very long silence and then she states plainly, "There is no possible way that can be true…. because that would mean that you are over 100 years old. I'm sorry, it was a mistake to let you in here. Leave immediately or I'm calling the cops," she says sternly.

"I was property!" I blurt out, looking directly into the lens of the camera. "Ikh geven farmog, Ikh Bin a shklaf Ikh bin amok gevena hunt fun Reikstal" I say in perfect Yiddish which basically translates to, *I was once owned by her family.*

"My Yiddish is a little rusty,.." she paused for a moment "…but I think you just told me that you were once a slave for my family?"

After another pause.

"Listen you bastard, I don't know what kind of BLM publicity stunt you're trying to pull, but if you wanted money this is the exact opposite route you should have taken".

I begin pleading again trying to appeal to her academic sensibilities.

"I follow your work closely, and I have read all your essays published in the Journal of Anthropological Archaeology and subsequent articles in the Journal of Egyptian Archaeology that delves into the different categories and characteristics of people in the Atlantean races. I was particularly interested in the part that revealed startling evidence of the sunken remains of the Atlantean continent still in existence and details about their connection to the biblical histories of the Garden of Eden, Noah and the Great Flood and other related subjects. I damn near memorized your dissertation in the New England Medical Journal on your research into the suspected manipulation of the human genome by ancient scientists which artificially truncated human lifespans. That piece proved to the scholarly community beyond a shadow of a doubt that man was once able to live for hundreds of years and that the tales of the longevity of Methuselah and Abraham were more than likely true."

I rattle off all this quickly before she can talk over me again. I am careful to leave out the parts of our anonymous email correspondence lest she thinks I am just some fanboy/stalker coming to do a surprise face-to-face. There is another awkwardly long silence between myself and the doorbell camera. I continue, "I sought you out specifically because of that research, because I knew you were one of the few people on the face of this blue rock who could understand exactly who or what I am and can shed some light on my otherwise uncommon ancestry which requires me to travel when the night is darkest."

Silence for an eternity, the rain begins to slow to a halt, leaving as quickly as it came.

Wait —are you that guy that has been sending me emails about the Mali/Egypt connection? Your email address is ancient...Zulu something?

I nod my affirmation.

"And did you live in New York City, specifically during the late 80's, early 90's?" the voice asks over the video doorbell.

This question was the one I had been waiting to hear. The gamble I made all those years ago was finally paying off. It has been ages since I have had to genuinely resist the urge to smile. She remembered me. That night at the Rubin Museum of Art back in 1989. I was dressed to the nines in a blue Armani suit and a white mesh tank top with blue suede Bally shoes and no socks. Rocking my midnight black shades and a funky afro I pretended to be some 'Warhol/Basquiat' type who was really into the Bohemian art scene. I sauntered right up to Katherine with two glasses of Merlot in my hands and stuck one in her hand while introducing myself. I took her by the arm and whisked her away from a group of pompous, stereotypical, Soho art critics who could not help but look down their noses at everyone else in the room. I made quite the scene by interrupting her conversation with the exhibit curator, drawing the ire of Katherine's security detail as we walked through the gallery with my hand on the small of her back. I proceeded to impress her with my knowledge on everything from early Ethiopian Coptic Christian symbolism and its influence on Western societies to my thoughts on Gorbachev and the end of the Cold War.

We laughed and talked for the remainder of the evening. She was totally enraptured by my devilish charm and extensive knowledge of historical and archaeological benchmarks. I left her that night as abruptly as I had arrived, but I was sure that I had implanted the seeds that would cause her to question reality and to explore beyond the agreed upon historical accounts of the racist and sexist scholarship of the past. This impetus to expose the truth behind accepted historical dogma became the core subject matter for her doctoral thesis which she later expounded into a career in anthropological research that would clear up significant discrepancies in the historical concepts held by academics for years. Since then she has written four noteworthy books and given countless lectures and appearances as an expert in her field with multiple TedTalks on the subject of biblical archaeology that garnered her worldwide respect and recognition amongst the international intelligentsia community.

Back on the front porch, another eternity of moments passes when I hear footsteps inside sliding toward the door. I knew when she buzzed me in the gate, a total stranger wearing sunglasses and a Fedora at 12a.m.., that she must have recognized my face from back then. I probably would have been invited in even without me exposing my neck bearing the slavery brand that was her secret family crest. Maybe she just had to be sure. Just then the door cracks open and a small alabaster face sticks out above the door chain. The sad blue eyes on the face just stare directly into the colorless iris of mine. Neither of us are able to blink for what seems like a full minute. She then looks me up and down, cocks her head to the side, and the next words Kate utters let me know that my plan was a success.

"How do you look exactly the same as that night 30 years ago?"

She opens the door wider and my eyes cannot help but travel down her figure to the 12 gauge shotgun she is holding. She flicks the safety on and still looking directly at me she says, "It's mandatory to have one of these babies when you live this far into the boonies. And under the circumstances, until I hear more of your story, I will be hanging onto it while we chat," she says to me, looking directly into my eyes. I nod my silent approval and place my hat back on. As she opens the door wider for me to enter, I am accosted by a mixture of smells including but not limited to multiple cats and cat litter,

46

aromatherapy candles, and menthol cigarettes. I pause and take a moment to absorb the grandeur of the place despite its messy condition.

"You'll have to excuse the clutter. I wasn't expecting company this time of night, and I was packing for a flight out of town tomorrow." She uses the barrel of the shotgun to pick up a bra lying by her foot in front of the coffee table which she quickly stuffs in her robe pocket.

Katherine is a tall woman, at least five foot eight inches or more, and her body mass leans a little toward the thin side. Her strawberry blond hair, which was up in a protective bun, bears only a few traces of gray and her alabaster, makeup-less skin has not lost much of its elasticity over the last thirty years either. There are a few forehead wrinkles and a couple of lines around her thin mouth which unfortunately serve to betray her otherwise youthful face. There are visible freckles from sun damage on the bridge of her nose and her upper chest that I can see through the opening in her robe.

She stares at me again for a long moment with both hands on the shotgun and says flatly, "No wonder you wear those glasses. The lack of pupils and iris make your eyes look seriously disturbing. I figured the sunglasses at night were just part of your look back then. You know everybody being coked out and high in the New York art scene in those days, sunglasses were par for the course." Her unmistakable straightforward way of speaking is still the same as it was thirty years ago with an added edge instilled by the bitterness of life.

I put my glasses back on.

"I'm sorry, I do have manners," she says. "Would you like something to drink? I have some Johnnie Walker Black bourbon I keep around in case I have company which is rare, but tonight I think I may need a stiff drink myself."

"Yes, please, thank you Mrs.Reichstall!" I say politely, then gesturing as if I needed to wash my hands, I ask, "May I use your restroom?"

"Kate, and it's the first door to your right over there, just a bit down the hall. You can hang your jacket on the coat rack by the door there and please remove your shoes," she orders. Still cradling the shotgun under her right arm, she pulls a cigarette and lighter from her robe and lights it. As I bend down to unlace my boots, I see the source of the cat smells, one tubby black and grey British Shorthair and a sly sand colored Japanese Bobtail appear from behind the sofa. Both staring at me with their hair on end and their backs arched in a threatening manner. I walk to the bathroom and enter without flicking on the light and close the door behind me. The bathroom is large and covered in immaculate white porcelain, marble, and chrome with a bidet situated next to a regular toilet. I shoot for the regular toilet and flush by pushing the Roman numeral one on top of the tank. I wash my hands in the floating vanity, dry my hands on a towel, and walk out of the bathroom to find Kate pacing back and forth in front of the fireplace, cigarette in her left hand and holding the shotgun under her right arm.

The glass of bourbon is on an end table between a pair of 1950's style, fog colored, Italian leather swivel chairs. Kate gestures by raising her chin in a motion for me to take a seat. Her living room and dining room looks copied and pasted from an Mondini Arredamenti catalog. Italian white Carrara marble floors and tabletops. A large painting of a rustic lighthouse near the sea is flanked by two large bookshelves embedded on either side of the main wall. The huge modular, fog colored sofa is bound by two beautifully maintained palm plants and serves as a neutral ground between myself and Kate as we address each other across the living room. Her entire home screams of comfortable opulence. I do not detect any other recent human scents, and being privy to all her professional accolades and the sacrifices made over the years to develop important archaeological theories and procedures, I realize maintaining a family would be damn near impossible with her professional career demanding such a huge chunk of her life. In true Reichstall fashion, Kate lays right into me with the hard stuff.

"First of all, how did you find me? This address isn't listed anywhere, and my mail and packages all come through a private postal service."

"Well, I—"

She cuts me off. "I'm sorry, never mind that. First of all, something more pressing is troubling me. You never answered my question. How in the bloody hell have you not aged a single minute in thirty years?" she asks me as she takes a drag of her cigarette and stares directly in my face.

I clear my throat and sit forward, interlocking my fingers, and looking down at the floor searching for the right words before I begin to speak. "I came here to secure your trust and to recruit you in assisting me in my mission. I will tell you everything, but please bear with me. The full story may take a while, and you may find the truth to be much stranger than fiction."

"Try me," she says sassily, exhaling her cigarette smoke.

"In the interest of time, I will be as blunt as possible. Because of all the negative connotations attached to it, I try to refrain from using the word vampire, but for the sake of argument, I guess that is what you would call my condition. I move at night mostly. My diet consists mainly of water, meat and blood. My body is incredibly durable and from what I have learned about my physiology over the years from poring over hundreds of books in dozens of libraries around the world, I have discovered that my hyper cellular reproduction happens at such an energetic level that injuries that would kill a normal human become minor to me. As far as I can tell, once I reached adulthood, for approximately every forty human years, my body ages one year. Kind of like a reverse dog." I wait for a smile or laugh or even a raised eyebrow that does not come. I continue. "The movies have created so many myths about beings such as myself that I usually refrain from using the 'V' word unless I need to make a point. I have a reflection, and I can survive sunlight and garlic although they both irritate the hell out of me. Sunlight is especially toxic for me. Holy water and crucifixes are mainly pop culture bullshit but I have found evidence, mostly in Eastern Europe near Estonia and Romania, of some fringe underground sects that still dabble in the occult and invoke certain spirits that can be counteracted through the use of 'blessed or 'sacred' talismans."

As I am speaking, Kate takes a sip of bourbon from her glass on the mantle, swishes the liquid around in her mouth before swallowing, and puts the glass down hard before pulling another cigarette out of the pack. "Let me stop you right there and let you know that if it's virgin blood you're looking for, pal, then keep moving because that ship sailed a long time ago" she quips.

Not smiling, I continue. "I understand that for a woman of science like yourself, this all sounds far-fetched, but I assure you that joking about things is not a habit of mine,".

"I'm sorry. I'm half cynic and half Scottish on my mother's side, so you'll have to forgive me. Please, continue," she says as she flashes what I can only call a fake smile.

I sit there for a long pause just looking at her light and smoke her next cigarette. I spring to my feet and pull my pocketknife from my right pocket and flick the gleaming three inch blade out. Without dropping her cigarette and with military regimentation, Kate swings the barrel of the shotgun up and clicks the safety off all in one swift motion, leveling the weapon directly at my face less than fifteen feet in front of me. With the knife in a tight fist in my right hand, I hold my left hand up and draw a deep gash in the middle of my left palm. Kate's eyes go as wide as saucers watching me cut myself without flinching. I hold out my left hand towards her so she can clearly see. The separated skin merges with itself again starting at the top of the wound almost as if it was being zipped up from the inside. Only a small trickle of blood which was released in the initial stab slides down my hand and onto my wrist. I pull my handkerchief from my back pocket and wipe the blood before it falls on the floor.

Kate, still holding the gun at my face, says, "Immortal or not, I would have shot you right in the fucking face if you'd have gotten blood on my carpets. I get your point. I retract my call of bullshit and you now have my undivided attention." She grabs an ashtray from the mantle and takes a seat opposite me on the chaise part of the sectional sofa.

Now she was ready to get down to brass tacks.

"Would you mind if I record this? I want my report to be as accurate as possible, and I don't want to miss anything. Not that anyone will believe me..."she says under her breath. She pulls out her smartphone from her robe pocket before I can give my approval and swipes the screen to find the voice memo application.

"Before I listen to anything, I want to know what my role is in all this, and why you decided to show up on my doorstep tonight. Let's begin with that brand on your neck. What happened between you and my family that makes you think we have a connection and that I give a damn about that symbol? And why didn't the scarification heal like your hand just did?" Kate asks.

"The mark on my neck was created using a branding iron made from pure Sterling silver heated to an ungodly temperature and then left to cook my resistant flesh while I was unconscious. And to your first question, this marking was used to designate ownership by the upper echelon of your family's bloodline during the eighteenth and nineteenth centuries. It represented the top branch of the family tree to ensure that certain goods or property were deemed ceremonious or for use by only a select few top family members. I was a servant to your family and their subsidiaries for most of my life. The amount of suffering I endured during those centuries could fill an ocean with tears. It was during that period that your family went from being one of the wealthiest most connected families in Great Britain to being the top dog wealthiest family on the planet. And ever since the late 17th century, driven by profit and power, they have directly or indirectly gained carte blanche control over every institution on this planet. From the looks of it, I am pretty sure they are actively endeavoring towards making the galaxy their next conquest." I finish speaking, and she stares at me for a moment, rolls her eyes, and then vigorously smashes the cigarette butt into the ashtray to extinguish it.

"And now you want me to do something to help you stop or curtail that power because you feel somehow responsible for unleashing the great capitalist machine on the innocent world?" she begins. "Although I don't normally find myself defending my family's actions, I have news for you, buddy. With or without you, somebody, somewhere would have risen to the top and done what my family has done. It's human nature, survival of the fittest. Frankly, it's just good business and unfortunately, if you want to make an omelet, especially a good one...you have got to break some eggs. Today it's Europe, tomorrow it may be China or India. I should have my head examined for saying this, but if you've really been around for as long as you say you have, then you should know as well as anybody that mankind is just filled with avarice and selfishness. Can you please explain to me how the fuck you specifically are involved? I have a PhD in archeology and historical research with an emphasis on European dynastic legacy, and I am sorry but I have certainly never heard of a Negro who never ages and can't be killed being a part of the rise of any major elite families. Especially not the Reichstalls." Kate exclaims in an increasingly exasperating tone.

I see that I have my work cut out for me if I am going to convince her to use her resources and reputation to help our mission. I am going to have to pull out all the stops. I take a sip of the Johnnie Walker Black and take a deep breath to gather my thoughts. I shoot her a cold look and then stare down at my shabby, faded black socks against the expensive rug for a moment.

I clear my throat and begin. "I beg to disagree with you on the assumption of human nature. Granted, all living creatures are born with a survival mechanism that drives us to claw back at Mother Nature and grasp at the means to sustain ourselves and our loved ones, but most of us just want enough to survive the day. Then there's the infamous influence of the *they* who tell us we need to outdo the next-door neighbors by having the newest car or a bigger house. Heaven forbid you do not buy the latest sneakers or miss the President's Day Sale at the mall. *They* dangle their version of life, liberty, and the pursuit of happiness in front of an unknowing, population but what *they* tease is not reality or the truth. Wires get crossed, emotions get involved, and BOOM! War, violence, poverty, rape, you name it all begins to foment due to those lies. Basically, without certain influences of this relatively small group of ultra-rich, ultra-powerful people, most of mankind would live in relative peace surviving the day with enough shelter and food for the foreseeable future. The reason most of us cannot see the solution is because we are constantly being told that we are being denied something that someone else has. Conflict is artificially created between the masses, and the real controllers of all this continue on their merry way unobstructed."

"I'm sorry, but exactly what the fuck are you talking about?" Kate asks dryly.

"This! I say, pointing my index finger towards the ceiling. "Everything. Just fucking everything. The world rests neatly in the palms of a few dirty little hands, and I was the dog on a leash that helped them achieve it, both through my direct actions and through my years of complacency in the face of the truth. Of course, your books and scrolls do not reveal my existence. They have had control of all forms of the media damn near a hundred years before the fucking printing press was invented. Knowledge is power, and if they do not have anything else, they definitely have power. Do you actually believe that the notion of a Negro being somehow involved in creating the greatest banking and financial empire on the planet would be included in the accepted canon of history? The shit I was involved in is buried deep within the vault. In the catacombs under the Vatican type of arcane information. The secrets about my history and those like me are highly confidential and profoundly well-guarded."

"I get it! you're a big deal!" Kate says sarcastically, waving one hand over her head and rolling her eyes. Her phone chimes, and she picks it up and swipes away a message quickly before looking up at me and saying, "But if I'm going to be able to help you I need to be able to trust you."

I try to convey as much sincerity as I can in my facial expressions and tone, but I am met by a feeling of deep skepticism on Kate's part. I guess I should be happy that I was able to make it this far. She was at least willing to listen to what I had to say. She moves the phone that was recording our conversation to the ottoman between us, probably to get a clearer sound on the audio. Then she lights a cigarette, and I begin my story.

Chapter 4

For the first ninety years of my life I was a slave on multiple sugar and coffee plantations in San Domingue. My mother and I were put on a ship with about a hundred other slaves and transported to the Caribbean. I only knew my father through the stories my mother would tell. While my mother was alive she served as a buffer between myself and the rest of the world, and other than the demeaning treatment and the non-stop labor, we lived a relatively peaceful life. That peace ended abruptly around 1792 when the Revolution began and San Domingue was plunged into war. When the war ended, I was a prisoner of the French government. After serving time in solitary confinement in a French dungeon for five plus years, I was sold back into slavery to a rice and indigo plantation in Louisiana. I was in an extremely low place in my life. I was a mess mentally. Fit only to serve with no will of my own, functioning barely above the level of a vegetable. I was suited only for performing great feats of physical labor that did not require much complex thought. I was constantly chopping down large trees, pulling heavy plows and ox carts, chasing down vermin that plagued my master's harvest, digging irrigation canals and countless other tasks. Most of my work was done during the mosquito-filled nights. I seldomly slept more than four hours a day and I was forced to wear coarse burlap that covered my body from head to toe in order to protect me from sun exposure.

It was a miserable existence. I was treated with less consideration than the dirt at the bottom of the latrine by pretty much everyone on the plantation, white and black. There were only two people since my mother's passing who acknowledged the fact that I was a human during those American plantation years. One was a boisterous French Creole woman who worked her way up to being the plantation's main house cook named Jessie, and the other was her beautiful but painfully introverted daughter Colette. The three of us met as slaves under relatively peaceful circumstances in Thibodeaux Parish, Louisiana on the plantation of Doctor Jean Michel Carbonneaux.

Dr. Carbonneaux was very passionate about biological sciences and I was frequently the subject of his experimental research into the limits of human longevity. He would weekly require blood, urine, tissue, and stool samples from me and afterwards he would force me to perform all manner of testing to determine the limits of my physical capabilities. Dr. Carbonneaux conducted testing on many other of his enslaved workforce and much of his research required him to travel to Europe on a regular basis to divulge his latest findings amongst his colleagues. Because of Dr. Carbonneaux's busy schedule the day-to-day oversight of the plantation was left up to a goblin of a man named Bledsoe Les Bouton— a tall, effeminate but ill-tempered waste of a man who was notorious in Louisiana for being an extremely shrewd businessman and an even more merciless overseer. These particular traits made him the prime candidate to be Carbonneaux's liaison. Les Bouton found many lucrative ways to exploit my abilities, and under his greedy tutelage I became somewhat of a celebrity in the small Louisiana Parish where I found myself. On nights when there was little work for me to do, Les Bouton would force me to perform feats of strength and speed in front of paying audiences. I was billed as *Crocodile Man*—a *blindfold-wearing nigger who ate raw meat with the strength of a ten-mule team and who could run faster than a race horse*. And best of all, I came complete with a meek and mild temper that could easily be controlled. That was my best selling point. Every slave owner knew that an enslaved man is only as good as he is obedient. I was treated worse than a dog, and I conducted myself like a beast in return by sleeping only on the bare ground and eating insects and vermin as my primary forms of sustenance.

In the year 1815, After receiving the news of my astounding physical capabilities, the Reichstalls personally sent an envoy to secure me, and I was sold to an up-and-coming young ancestor of yours by the name of Nathan Reichstall. At the time, Nathan was an investment banker in the City of London working diligently at the family trade which consisted mainly of doing their level best to fill their pockets with as much wealth from the rest of the world as they possibly could. Their willingness to dabble in the occult to gain an edge, their shrewdness in mandating that they only conduct business transactions amongst the family using coded messages in an obscure Yiddish dialect and their willingness to intermarry between family members to further concentrate their wealth was uncanny. They would go to any extreme to remain above their competition.

Adventure seeking also seemed to be a trait that ran in your family's blood because your forefathers, especially Nathan, loved traveling and also loved to 'collect' unique and exotic human specimens and 'recruit' them as employees at his estates in England. He learned of my existence when one of his many agents was traveling through Thibodeaux Parish, Louisiana, on a report that there existed a negro who was faster than a greyhound, could fight grizzly bears toe-to-toe and wrestled alligators into submission in local death matches set up to entertain the white people and simultaneously punish disobedient black people. Apparently, this gentleman was present at one of the exhibition matches and was struck dumb after witnessing a night race between myself and several animals including two young Appaloosa horses and two British wolfhounds in which I proved the fastest by a landslide.

Nathan Reichstall paid an impossible sum to have Jessie, Collette and myself shipped from the Louisiana plantation we had been condemned to toil away on and removed us to Sussex County, England. An entire merchant vessel was chartered and a sailing crew hired to carry myself and my two closest companions under the proclamation of being special cargo of the Reichstall family. Les Bouton brokered the deal and was compensated so much that the sale was heralded all over Louisiana as one of the highest payments for human chattels in the history of the state. The news had the whole city in an uproar for months. When the rest of the Parish found out that the tight-fisted Les Bouton was selling not only me but two robust healthy negresses in their prime work years, one of them being the plantation's head cook at that, absolutely no one could believe it. For three years in a row I had been the biggest money-making sideshow attraction in LaFourche, Louisiana overtaking the previous record holders — the *'white nigger twins'* of neighboring Dubois Parish, who were actually just poor fraternal twins suffering from extreme albinism. Reichstall was rumored to have paid a sum equivalent to $250,000.00 in today's currency to secure my two companions and I.

As a cover story, we were told that the Reichstalls believed their enslaved responded better to kindness than cruelty and as such they did not want me to suffer loneliness by being transplanted so far away from home alone. My companions and I were left dumbfounded by this unique development. We had been so conditioned to associate heartbreak and separation with being sold as a slave, and this development was so surprisingly benevolent for members of our class that our departure was bittersweet. After we left, from that day forward whenever slave traders with English accents would come 'shopping,' all the hands and the house girls would wash their faces, slick down their hair with whatever grease they could find and rub their teeth shiny with a rag while chewing peppermint herbs all day in hopes to get sold into the British *lap of luxury*.

The British had already received a favorable reputation for being markedly more sympathetic to their slaves and free blacks who defected to their side during what history would later call the War of 1812. The story of a nightcrawler like me being sold to a *'good master'* only added to the myth of British benevolence. Back then, none of the enslaved were allowed to read or write so news came only by word of mouth delivered by eavesdropping Negroes situated closest to the white social conversations. We all foolishly believed that over in England and pretty much anywhere else on planet Earth besides Louisiana, "niggers" got treated better. A white man showing concern for any slave or group of slave's mental well-being was doubly extremely rare on the bayou. If a slave died or was sick or hobbled, they would have a new soul on a boat or a wagon headed that way before his predecessor's body was cold. Even the so-called 'decent' slave masters behaved this way because the work was so abundant and the money was too good to worry about improving the standard of living of the workers when there was an inexhaustible supply. By and by, we would taste the bitter lesson of being taken advantage of by something that seems too good to be true.

The morning we were to board the ship, Jessie and Colette were giving their bittersweet goodbyes to the cooks, servants and field hands already preparing for work that day at five thirty in the morning. Originally,

57

the pair came to Louisiana ten years earlier after being sold as a package deal from a West Tennessee slave merchant. Jessie stood about five feet seven inches, a hefty woman of about forty years old who always wore a scarf known as a tignon over her thick black hair. She was very spry and moved around better than the women half her age. Her powerful body and huge personality melted the hearts of all who had the pleasure of meeting her. She had a pair of large dark brown eyes. They would light up by the moonlight. They would shine when she smiled. That day she looked back at the big house, the house she cooked, cleaned, and warmed the master's bed for during the previous decade since she and her daughter arrived, but her eyes were not shining. They were filled with tears. Jessie wore a self-sewn shawl made out of a coarse navy blue material over her plain brown dress that went well past her knees. The shawl could be unfolded to make a blanket she could use. A small leather pouch with various medicinal herbs like dandelion root and stinging nettle herbs for emergencies, a piece of cheesecloth containing a chunk of cornbread, a slab of cooked bacon and the clothes on her back were the only possessions she carried. The remainder of her belongings were tucked away neatly in a knapsack that Colette carried on her shoulder.

Colette was the product of Jessie's first and only marriage. She had recently just turned twenty-two, the curves of her body seductively testing the limits of her ragged dress and petticoat. She covered her upper half with a large shawl sewn by her own hands from leftover materials from her mistresses' wardrobe. Jessie had gifted Colette the leather shoes she wore complete with a fresh piece of newspaper covering a small hole in the sole of the right shoe. Colette was a beautiful young woman, the spitting image of her mother in her youth. She kept her hair and face covered by a bonnet and scarf combination unless she was sleeping. She had a rich, even, chocolate complexion, darker than Jessie's and her features slightly more aquiline. High cheekbones with full pouty lips and a dimple on her left cheek would appear on the rare occasion she would smile. Her bright eyes were almond shaped with a deep dark brown pupa. It is said that her father was Senegalese or Kushite in origin. I am told he was working on multiple plantations by hiring himself out as a blacksmith, and he promised to come back with enough money to buy Jesse and Colette's freedom. The last information they received about his whereabouts was that he had been able to purchase his freedom and had successfully made the journey out of Tennessee. As he was traveling down to Louisiana in order to find his wife and daughter, he lost his manumission papers and was falsely accused of being a runaway and reenslaved. He was subsequently forced to work in a prison camp during the dead of winter where he eventually died in a holding cell in Opelousas Parish from hound dog bite wounds he suffered to both arms and his groin during his arrest.

As the story goes, Colette was a very bright and somewhat talkative child before she and Jessie were sold further south. During a few of the overnight layovers required for the travel from West Tennessee to Louisiana Colette was mercilessly raped and molested multiple times by multiple overseers, both black and white. The trauma resulting from these savage assaults rendered Colette totally mute for about five years. She withdrew into herself and became incredibly timid and shy. Colette rarely left Jessie's side, and I can count on one hand the words I have heard her speak louder than a whisper. Beneath the rags and dust and sweat, both these women were spectacular beauties whose radiance was muted by the horrors of that "peculiar institution."

I was never allowed to go anywhere or do anything without some sort of heavy gauge chains attached to my body. Les Bouton had an overseer named Marcel who was equally as cruel and twice as shrewd as his employer. Marcel was instructed to commission a well-known local blacksmith to create shackles and chains that were loose enough to allow me to complete my daily duties but thick and heavy enough to subdue any rapid offensive action from me toward my captors. I wore eighty grade three quarter inch iron chains on both feet and both hands. The rust-covered shackles cut into my flesh day and night with the simplest of movements. The lacerations and abrasions would bleed onto the increasingly rusty chains as I worked and before the callous could form over the wound my movements would cause the flesh to rip open again causing the hot blood to run onto the shackles and it would heal and the process would start over anew. Sometimes dozens of times a day. On rare occasions when the cane crops were bountiful and the rest of the field hands could not keep up with the work no matter how hard they were whipped, Les Bouton would grant permission for me to work without arm shackles so I could chop the cane, stack and haul it all off to the store houses. And in turn he would add heavier or multiple cannonballs to my leg irons and hire additional men on horseback with shotguns and some on foot carrying large barrel hunting rifles to keep me in check.

The most powerful thing holding me back was fear. Marcel the overseer made sure that he reminded me at least once a day that if I ever did work up the nerve to do anything as foolhardy as to escape or fight back, he would take it out on the other slaves. His preferred method of torture included skinning them alive and letting the dogs eat the freshly removed skin off their bodies before their very eyes. I became a trained elephant. The fear that my curse would cause another soul pain was enough that the chains I wore were no longer necessary to keep me in line.

The journey upon which Jessie, Colette and I were about to embark upon would be only the second time I had been able to travel beyond the boundaries of the plantation. As such I was made to wear a small cannon ball attached to each ankle with a chain about 6 feet in length. Instead of dragging the cannon balls behind me I carried them in my hands for ease of movement. My attire consisted of the usual burlap pant and long sleeve burlap shirt. My face was covered with a thick piece of cloth in anticipation of the sunlight that was fast approaching. Even when obstructed, my field of vision is extraordinary and combined with my enhanced senses I can interpret the world around me by changes in odor and responding to vibrational patterns in the air.

After Jessie was done hugging people and saying her goodbyes, we all walked solemnly toward a large and very ornate waiting carriage. I carried my chains and walked unhurriedly towards the coach and could not help but wonder where the hay trailer was. Enslaved persons such as ourselves were usually either made to walk behind carriages when traveling or they would ride in a separate supply trailer pulled by a team of mules. We had witnessed rich creoles from the Parish riding inside of carriages. Jessie used to tell us stories of the free negroes in New Orleans who rode horses every day, but not even she had ever seen servants riding *inside* a carriage. That was a dreamed-of fantasy for the Negroes in Thibodeaux Parish. When it was revealed that we all would be allowed to be seated inside the carriage alongside our new beneficiary, Jessie and Colette were as visibly taken aback as I was. The looks on their faces said it all.

60

"What the hell is going on here?" was the expression on Colette's normally stoic face, her eyes wide as saucers as she stood just gawking open mouthed at the coach. Jessie, who has never been at a loss for words a single day in her life, could only muster her signature three-word phrase.

"Lawd ham mussy."

A tall, broad-shouldered square-jawed, Negro coachman came from around the opposite side of the carriage in front of the horses, and after quickly checking all the harnesses, he greeted our small group, tipping his hat to the faceless croaker sac on my head, and smiling and bowing deeply to the ladies next to me.

"Please, madame," the attendant said in a deep baritone voice as he gestured for Jessie to take his arm. They walked toward the side of the coach to another dapper, black footman who graciously assisted her up the step and into the coach. The coachmen were equally as dainty and careful with Colette as she entered the carriage behind Jessie.

The two men looked me up and down taking in my poor condition while maintaining their cordial smiles. Both men looked to be pondering how the hell a six-foot-two blindfolded man wearing the equivalent of a ship's anchor was going to mount the stairs and step over into the carriage, without being carried. The taller coachman who seemed to be the senior of the two extended both hands in an attempt to reach for my upper arm in order to guide me towards the steps of the coach. Before he could assist, I briskly stride up the stairs past him while carrying my 50 pound cannonballs in each hand. The rusty chains clanking and dragging against the step as I climb inside. The lurching motion made by my entry into the carriage startled the team of horses and the young man sitting in the driver's box. My near 300 pounds rocked the entire wagon back and forth as I plopped down in the seat opposite Jessie and Colette. Because I spent most of my time alone and outdoors, I became used to sleeping outside under a dense brush or under the floorboards in the crawl spaces under the slave quarters. As such, I had become oblivious to how I appeared and how I smelled. Since my mother passed, I rarely gave hygiene a second thought. But inside this cramped carriage, I suddenly became very self-conscious of how I looked and smelled being enclosed in such a small area with other people. I had been instructed to bathe in the nearby stream the night before and given new rags to wear, yet I still smelled like a wild animal. In my embarrassment, I tried to physically make myself as small as possible so as not to offend anyone.

At the sound of a set of footsteps I did not recognize, I quickly hopped from the opposite bench in front of the ladies to their bench next to the soft fleshy thighs of Jessie. I attempted to nestle up against the side of the coach, and I crunched my body against the carriage walls as much as I could to give the women as much space as possible on the bench we shared. The man approaching was probably our new patron and should have the bench opposite us to himself. It was not considered polite company for Negroes to sit with gentlemen, especially if they were white.

After a few moments, I smelled the fragrance of a woman's perfume and I thought I must have been mistaken when I heard the approaching footsteps. But then I heard the elegant British accent skillfully giving instructions to the driver to stop in at the general store in town. Jessie informed me the day prior when I was given my new clothing that we would be taking a boat.

At the door of the carriage appeared an immaculately dressed white man in a navy-blue double-breasted coat over a dark colored waist coat and a crisp white linen shirt underneath. Black Hessian boots with buckskin breeches, a black top hat and a cane crowned with a solid gold lion's head bearing its fangs. He was tall and gaunt with salt and pepper hair and eyebrows. His eyes were close set, and his eyelids were heavy as if in a state of perpetual fatigue. He spoke with a strong British accent and ended some words with a humming sound. His lips were non-existent, and his nose pointed permanently southward. He introduced himself as J. Phineas Gellner without extending his hand and sat down and began checking the time on his golden pocket-watch. After the introduction, no one said a word for the first leg of our journey other than the exchange of names. I never spoke. There was no need. I was a beast. A tool. I existed only to serve others. I had no will of my own. Jessie and Colette were my mouthpieces. At least Jessie was. But now she, like the two of us, was literally struck dumb by the never before seen fineries inside the carriage.

After about five awkward self-conscious minutes, the magic of the fanciful carriage and the jolt of VIP treatment wore off on Jessie. She began to loosen up a bit and returned to her usual jovial talkative demeanor.

"Marse Gelna," began Jessie, "I do pologize bout my havia. But Lawd we aint neva seent the inside of no carr'age be fo'. Ev'n dat'n ova dere was s'prised," gesturing towards me. She must have seen my body shift briefly as we approached the vehicle. "Dat boy, what nothing don't stir em, not e'en two hunnit' lash cross de bare back. Looked like he done seent a ghos' and almos' trip ova his own foots when he seed us walkin up towars dis here buggy. I cain't see his eyes, but I know'd dey was buggin' out 'is head," Jessie stated as she belted out one of her punctuating chuckles.

Mr. Gellner smiled at the ladies with as little condescension as he could summon. Addressing us all he began, "there is no need to call me master for I am under the employ of the man who you will come to know as your master. For the purposes of this journey, you are legally bound to me per the laws of this country. But please, for my benefit, call me *Mister* Gellner." He turned to face me and looks where he thinks my eyes should be and said slowly as if to add emphasis, " *Do-you-under-stand?*"

Again, Jessie chimed in. " Marse,…I mean Mi-ser Gener suh. You may as well be talkin' to dat tree stump out dere cause dat boy don' talk nun at all. Onliest time I eva hear him say sumthin s' like a wud is when dis chile here," pointing to Colette, "liked to got runt ova by a wild hoss. Alls we herd was soun' like ef a damn wolf was to say sumfin. So low and scratched up like a storm was a rumblin'. Next thang we know, dis boy dun got tangled up wit' de hoss where bofe um was rolling in de dut. I swea' fo' God de boy was dead but he got up fo' de hoss did. Colette, her head bowed offers an audible

"Um hmm" for emphasis and corroboration.

Gellner nodded his head as he feigned interest in Jessie's tale. The exhaustion from the negotiations and all-night preparation before the prior day's journey as well as an eagerness to return home to England seemed to create a growing sense of disgust in Mr. Gellner. Both for the task he was commissioned with and for his fellow passengers. He appeared to be growing quite perturbed, maybe even questioning what he may have done to incur such a wretched assignment in having to babysit what he felt were three morons. The combined stress of the long return ride began to wear thin on his demure and no-nonsense attitude. He flashed an almost imperceptible smile as Jessie finished her tale and responded with a series of nods and a counterfeit "Oh my".

Jessie, perceptively taking the hint finishes, with a "I says all dat to say dat he don' talk wit wuds, but he un'stans mo dan ya thank. And he kin nod yes and no when ya ask im." Colette concurred with her usual appropriately inflective

"um hmm" to punctuate Jessie's statements.

Mr. Gellner looked as if he was fighting the urge to roll his eyes and smiled patronizingly at Jesse and Claudette saying thinly, "Noted, Madame," before once more looking at his pocket watch and staring quietly out of the window. The next few hours were spent in relative silence as our merry band of passengers bumped along the relatively smooth road which was little more than a horse trail less than five years ago. In about one hundred and fifty years, it would become the path for development of Interstate 10 and the Pontchartrain Expressway through Downtown New Orleans.

After a few hours, our party was forced to stop in Destrahan, a small little burg on the way to the main body of the river, to refresh the horses and switch out a few of the older mares because they were being worn out from the extra weight of my chains. There was a small slop house located on the outskirts of town where Mr. Gellner and the ladies were able to eat and relieve themselves in the woods behind the adjacent stables. I remained in the carriage during these stops to avoid causing any commotion amongst the gentry. Les Bouton had been instructed to feed me well for the long journey, and I was given an old and dying milking cow to drain of blood and devour last night just before we were to begin preparing for our journey. The ladies were not used to sitting in one place and being still for this long so both found themselves dozing off in spells as we resumed our long arduous ride. I rarely slept. Especially not in plain view of someone I did not know.

Although I must remark that the sharply dismissive manner of our host did not smack of the usual dark intention I felt from most white men. He

64

seemed to be a man of profound indifference. His dress and southern dandy-like manner was that of the planter class but I sensed no trace of the seething contempt that sloughed off of most slave owners when they first laid eyes on me.

I could sense the change in the barometric pressure of the air and heard the faint rushing of the water as we got closer to the mighty Mississippi River. In those days, there was something called packet boats which were steam powered vessels that were used to carry humans and cargo such as bales of cotton and other goods from plantations to markets up and down the Mississippi river and its tributaries throughout the South. I suspected Jessie and Colette had also realized that we were getting closer and closer to the river, a development none of us foresaw. We could potentially be traveling to another part of Louisiana or maybe even as far as Mobile on one of these boats. Slaves were always being hired out and moved around on the whims and necessities of their masters so none of us had any idea that not only were we leaving the state, but we were about to leave the country.

It would have been nice if we were able to just *ask* where we were going but questioning white men was a tricky task that Negroes had to approach with caution. Enslaved persons were constantly trying to gauge the moods and personalities of their employers so as to not incur the wrath doled out to Negroes who were deemed too 'nosy' or 'uppity.' Fortunately for us, Jessie was of a special class herself — 'The overbearing black mammy.' This black woman trope could be found throughout the South and although she was technically classified as a slave, her pivotal role as cook, nurse, teacher, disciplinarian, and psychiatrist for both the black and white members of the plantation thrust her into an important position within the jumbled hierarchies on the plantation. Many planters even allowed their 'mammies' to serve in unofficial managerial roles and found that allowing these women to supervise the mundane duties of the other slaves was crucial to the desired level of harmony needed to maintain a successful plantation. Jessie was certainly this type of woman, physically capable of working as hard or harder than most men her age. She was the archetypal black woman who, through her sheer force of will, placed herself on equal ground with those

65

she was constrained to refer to as master but who, in actuality, were dependent on her.

Jessie blurted out in her usual way. "Marse Gellna, now I been quiet on count of I din' wanna go an sour you 'gains us since you aint never met us befo', and we was thown togedda in dis here coach. But I aint never seed dis part of de bayou befo' and we shoulda long ben at de river. Jus where on God's ert' is a we goin' xactly. Marse, I means Meustuh Gellna." She began again before he could answer. "Such as it's one thang to be on a steamboat headed roun' sout but we ain't got no clothes nuff to be goin nowhere up Norf to Phi'defia an such where it git cole, as de devil."

Gellner, amused at Jessie's worries, smiled wryly before addressing her. "My dear Jessica, do not fret. I have been provided with more than adequate accommodations to make your transition into Lord Reichstall's conglomerate as comfortable as possible. My employer has such a great interest in this young man and his abilities," gesturing in my direction, "that he has instructed me to make certain that he and his companions are treated with the very best of care. In hopes that you will find happiness in your new home, and thusly work your hardest in the employ of my and, soon to be, your benefactor," Gellner replied.

Sitting forward with one hand on her hip and the other resting on her knee, still not satisfied with Gellner's vague responses, Jessie retorts, "Das all well and good suh' but wit' all 'spect due, you still aint tell us where we is a-goin. If it's Flo'da den say dat, I knows dem British folk got ran down dere wit da injuns since the wah bin on. I got folks in Jawjah too whet jes' might be a suvis to you an yo 'ployer like we is',suh," Jessie finishes with a hint of nervousness.

Gellner looked robotically down at his pocket watch again even though it was too dark to see without a torch or candlelight. Looking up at the patiently waiting Jessie who is politely staring at him quizzically, Gellner complied in such a nonchalant tone that I was not sure if he was serious or not.

"I'm sorry I failed to mention it before in my preoccupation, but we are going to neither Georgia nor Florida, madam. We will be boarding a

66

chartered passenger vessel and traveling to the country of England, also known as Great Britain. The Fatherland of these so-called United States in which you reside, my dear. Your services have been requested by the Baron Nathan von Reichstall. Lord Reichstall resides in an area called Sussex to which we will be conveyed by chartering a privateer vessel to navigate us safely through hostile waters. If all goes to plan, we are scheduled to arrive in the city of Felixstowe in ten days, barring any unforeseen weather anomalies."

The carriage was silent for the next few minutes as both women sat stupefied at the news of our final destination. I had absolutely no clue of where or how far this place named Britain was, but judging from the amount of time we will be at sea and the reactions of my companions, it must be much farther than San Domingue.

Out of nowhere, Jessie went into panic mode. Flailing her arms dramatically and screaming "O my Lawd Jesus we is goin ova da oshin!" She exclaimed, grabbing her tignon with both hands and shaking her head. "Lettie gul, I tol' you to get that wool dress from Dana cause I know you ain't got nutin dat a stan' up 'gainst no win, Lawd ham mussy. Suh," Jessie says, turning her attention to Mr. Gellner, "we women folk ain't got no b'iness on no sailboat. Aint no place to use da pot, ah to cook a good meal a nuthin. And dat boy ova deah," she says, pointing to me, "he gone need to hunt and eat raw meat, and I'se sorry, suh, but fishes aint got nuff hot blood in em for dat boy to go no ten days on de oshin. He cain't get too much 'rectly in de sun on de boat neither on de count a his faintin' spaills an weak cons'tution in de sunlight... If is not too much trouble, suh, I know I'm gonna need some croaker sacks to sew together fo' a cover if we is gon' be on a wide open ship," protests Jessie.

"Lawd ha mussy Jesus son a Mairy. Bein nanm nou Seye Jesus! We gone need to stop fuh provisions fuh us women folk fo we gets on de boat. Dis beaucoup fou sho nuff suh. I still cain't b'lieve I'm ridin' inside a hoss coach wif a bainch tuh set on 'stead of a pile of hay for a cha'." Jessie talked on and on about her excitement and expectations for the majority of the final leg of the trip. It was hard to contain her once she got worked up about something. It was how she dealt with nervousness and pressure. I stared silently out of the window soaking up the world through the burlap sack on my head pretending not to understand what was being said as I was accustomed to doing.

Gellner quietly humors Jessie's frantic tirade, although distantly. His head tilted back, looking down his nose with eyes half open, both hands steadfastly holding the top of the cane which is perched on the floor between his legs. Nodding at intervals, trying desperately to decode Jessies's Creole-French-English dialect into something intelligible. Jessie would refer to me as 'dat boy' in third person as if I was not sitting next to her. She knew I could understand every word people spoke to me, but she also knew that if I exhibited any cognition higher than that of a sheepdog, then I would be too terrifying for people to allow me to live. Much less allow me to walk around freely. Jessie's heart was too big for that world.

Gellner, having heard quite enough, cut Jessie off mid-sentence. "Madam, I assure you that my Lordship has spared no expense on guaranteeing your pleasant journey and all the required amenities have been provided. His Lordship has also made special arrangements to provide for any dietary peculiarities that may require singular attention."

After that last explanation by Mr. Gellner, Jessie dropped the subject and became relatively quiet for the remainder of our time in the coach. Her mind was occupied with anticipation over the new possibilities that lie ahead of us and the sudden expansion of her world that for most of her life had known only heartache.

As we reached the city limits, we were all too busy gawking at all the unbelievable sights, sounds and scents of New Orleans with its impressive Spanish architecture, and its zestful French nightlife rolled together with the gumption and flavor of Africa. As we wound through the streets trying to process all that we were seeing for the first time, Gellner would repeatedly check his pocket watch at more frequent intervals with an exasperated look on his face like he was hopelessly worried about something.

As we approached the wharf, the air was filled with the smell of humidity, water-logged wood and the tar that was used to seal the hulls of the ships. The salty sea stench was soaked into everything— the structures, cargo, and people in the harbor. An aroma that carried a strange yet familiar

68

association for me personally. I could hear goats and pigs calling from their crates at the end of the pier near the point where we ended the land portion of our journey and parked the coach. On the pier, I could see many Negro men loading heavy barrels alongside white men who seemed to be laboring right alongside the Negroes. Jessie would later relate to me that the black men I saw were probably former slaves who bought their freedom and worked as sailors to remain free.

It was not until the scent of the livestock hit me that I remembered that I had not used the restroom since 3:00 a.m. this morning and a sharp pang of needed release stabbed me in my midsection. I had grown accustomed to holding my bladder and bowels but the jostling of the carriage over the cobblestone streets of the city and the strange yet enticing smells began to get the better of me.

Our carriage began to slow to a halt as we approached a large stack of wooden crates and as soon as our vehicle came to a complete stop, Mr. Gellner was quickly up and exiting the carriage. As soon as his feet touched the earth, we watched him march directly to the foot of the gangplank to speak with a tall, broad-shouldered, red-haired fellow directing the men from the bottom of the gangplank into the ship. Colette was first of our trio to disembark from the carriage, followed by Jessie with the help of the sturdy footmen. Myself and my extra hundred pounds of chain made up the rear. The men working on the dock stopped momentarily and glanced in my direction at the loud 'CLANK' of the chains as I hop out of the carriage and land on the solid wooden pier.

The carriage driver dismounted to tether the horses, and the two footmen were moving at top speed to carry Mr. Gellner and the ladies' bags over to the bottom of the gangplank to be loaded by the crew, tipping their hats at Colette and Jessie before returning to the carriage. The ship sat imposingly large before our small bodies as we walked along the length of it. There were four large cannons visible from small rooms on the side of the ship. I was illiterate at the time so I was unable to read the letters that loomed large before me. Men and a few young boys moved to and fro, busying themselves with the final preparations for departure. There was a team of black men readying row boats to tow the ship away from the dock to open waters where it would be safe to unfurl and hoist the sails.

Rory Sullivan, I would later find out, was the name given to the tall, red-haired man that Gellner was speaking to who was now looking over his shoulder in our direction as he and Gellner spoke to each other out of earshot. Abruptly, Sullivan turned and walked toward our group and introduced himself by kissing the ladies' hands. He then turned to me and waved his hand in front of my face to test whether I could see through the shroud covering my face.

"Dat boy can see" stated Jessie addressing Sullivan. "He gots to wear dat rag on his head on de count of his eyes cain't stan' no sunlight."

"At's right, the geezer did say sumthin' bout 'I'm needin' cover from the sun" Sullivan retorts. With that, Sullivan reached out and grabbed my hand in both of his hands shaking vigorously causing my chains to rattle comically.

"Welcome aboard" Sullivan said with a yellow toothed smile. He then extended his arm to Jessie who graciously stepped forward and accepted the gentlemanly gesture and they walked side by side up the gangplank with Colette behind them and myself bringing up the rear. As we walked Jessie repeatedly made a crucifix over her chest and recited her Catholic prayers under her breath. I thought that Colette would be catatonic with fear and anxiety but to my surprise, her head was up and looking forward, heedful but nonetheless undaunted.

•   •   •

The decommissioned privateer ship that Gellner chartered was a huge three masted barquentine model, known at the time as a Baltimore Clipper. The crew was composed of mainly British, West Indian, and American sailors but there were a few Polish, Italian, and Portuguese aboard also. All the deckhands were moving to and fro frenetically, industriously working at whatever tasks they had been assigned by the deck foreman. I was careful to avoid the paths of the laboring men. Normally, whenever I am amongst strangers I receive unkind looks and catch people staring at me

70

whispering about my appearance. Strangely, no one seemed particularly concerned with my presence. I think we were all surprised that most of the men did little more than cast a quick glance or merely nudge each other and nod in our direction as we walked along the main deck. Some of the men threw lustful gazes at Colette but none of the men's behavior felt like intimidation. It was more of a brief acknowledgement of a beautiful woman then quickly forgotten as they went back to their work. The sun began to drop below the horizon while Sullivan escorted us around the main deck while filling us in on the do's and don'ts of ship living. He told us he was the first mate and had been sailing on that ship since he was a lad of nine years old which explained his rank among others twice his age. All around us men were pulling mast lines and hoisting the sails, securing the anchor while yelling instructions peppered with obscenities to each other as they prepared for departure.

I could feel the ship now, gently being tugged away from the pier and slowly into the open harbor by the rowboat crew. We followed Sullivan down the length of the vessel to the rear of the ship where the captain and officers' quarters were. The mildew smell of sea-soaked wood hit my nose as we passed through a doorway and into a narrow corridor with rooms on either side. Sullivan removed an oil lamp from the wall and lit it before we continued.

Mr. Gellner stopped in front of the first large door we came to. Turning to us, he said directly to Sullivan, "The ladies will reside in one of the midshipman's quarters, and this young man will sleep in the cargo hold in the bow of the ship. There are no portholes there, so he will have the darkness and privacy he requires." Turning back to the ladies, he continued. "Sullivan here has been instructed to give you ladies a parcel of food every three days which will consist of salt beef, pork, dried fish, rice, flour, oatmeal, sugar, molasses, tea, a portion of lard, a jug of fresh water and a chicken to split between you. Since you are our guests of honor, you have free use of the kitchen. Simply ring for the cabin boy, and he will clear out the mess deck on your behalf for your unabashed convenience." Pointing at me but not looking in my direction, Gellner said, "Have an adult goat brought to this man's quarters before dawn and tell whomever completes the delivery to be sure not to linger or attempt to engage this young man once the goat is in his grasp. It may prove fatal," warned Gellner.

"I'll send that cabin boy, Warren. 'E's a fast one an slicker than axle grease. He'll get the chap fed soon as we reach open water and don't need him on the clewlines. 'E looks as if e'll hold til then," Sullivan remarked, sizing me up. He is probably wondering if the goat is for me to eat or have sex with by the look on his face. He turned his head and launched tobacco juice into a spittoon in front of the living quarter door before continuing. Looking at the women, Sullivan remarked, "Ye lasses should stay in 'eir room 'til second bell. That way, the men 'ill be cleared out to the focsle by then. Ye shunna have any problems from the crew fer I told them that if one of the scoundrels lays a hand on ye, 'e'll get the lash and a salt packin` by strict orders of the Captain."

And with that, he opened the door to a relatively compact room with two small beds and a dresser with a small vanity mirror attached, a chair with a chamber pot, a beeswax candle, and a hand carved tinderbox on the seat. Jessie said alluringly, "Merci beaucoup, suh," as both she and Claudette curtsied their thanks to Gellner and Sullivan, and then Jessie shot me a "behave" look before they both entered the room with their meager belongings and closed the door behind them. A meaningful "*Hallelujah!*" could be heard from beyond the ladies' door as we continued down the narrow hallway to Mr. Gellner's room who instructs Mr. Sullivan saying, "After showing this man to his living quarters, please reiterate to your men not to bother him if they encounter him after nightfall. He suffers from severe allergies when directly exposed to sunlight, and as such he is essentially a nocturnal creature. You and the crew should have been briefed by the captain on his unique nature."

Sullivan looked over at me and said, "I could hardly b'lieve the Cap'n when he was tellin' us. I 'spect he could hardly b'lieve it 'imself, way it sounds. But jest watching the lad move in them thar' irons tells me 'e must be as strong as bleedin' Samson. Those be the very same gauge irons we use to haul our anchors."

"Indeed," retorted Gellner. "He is a guest of Lord Reichstall so he will be treated as such, but the chains are to remain in place at all times. They were crafted with a special lock that can only be opened by an impossibly difficult-to-come-by key that rests solely in the possession of Lord Reichstall's chief of security. In addition to the fact that the chains are made of molybdenite alloyed with steel so they cannot be cut away with iron or steel tools, nothing less than a diamond bladed saw could undermine their integrity."

Sullivan looked at me with sincere sympathy in his eyes. "Poor devil," he said as he turned to spit another glob of saliva and tobacco into the spittoon opposite Gellner's door. The entire time these men were speaking, I held my head down and remained completely silent.

"Again…" Mr. Gellner starts as he reached into his bag and handed Sullivan a folded sheet of paper, "…use your discretion when dealing with this man. I know you lot can be a bit *rowdy* but I sincerely warn you, no matter how timid and harmless this man may seem, there is a reason he is adorned in those chains." And with that, he turned and opened the door to his elegantly furnished room. "Goodnight gentlemen," he says as he disappeared into the darkness of the room, closing and locking the door.

"Right this way, boy-o, follow me to yer suite," Sullivan flashed his signature yellow-toothed smile and I followed him to a door that opened up back onto the top deck of the ship. He blew out the lantern and placed it on a hook just outside the door. Sullivan turned to face me and said "You'll meet the Cap'n in the 'morrow. He's at the helm and doesn't like to be bothered til we get out of the gulf. 'specially during a night launch. Seein' that the sun 'as fell beyond the horizon, how about ye tekin' off that mask so I can see yer mug.

After an awkward pause, I slowly reached up and pulled my shroud away from my face. I kept my eyes down as was customary when talking to a white man. Sullivan stared at me for a moment, his expression remained deadpan. With a hint of exasperation on his voice he said "Lemme see yer eyes mate." Slowly, reluctantly, I raised my eyes to meet his.

"Bloody hell! What are you?" asked Sullivan rhetorically. His lip snarled with disgust at the sight of my colorless eyes. He turned wordlessly and gestured for me to follow him.

73

As we walked I could not help but look up and envy the men of all backgrounds high up in the topsails, nimbly climbing across the rigging, manning the ropes, and fulfilling their individual tasks on the ship with expert precision. Able to earn a wage and live as free as they wanted. Another group of sailors behind us screamed commands to each other as they began luffing the boat around ninety degrees to point the nose of the ship toward open water. As we reached the center of the ship, Sullivan and I went down a set of stairs which took us 'tween deck' as they call it. This level of the ship consisted of a small kitchen adjacent to the crew bunk quarters. At the top of the next set of stairs Sullivan removed an oil lamp from the wall and lit it with a piece of kindling from the kitchen oven. The next level we descended into was the gun deck. To my left sat two of the cannons that were visible from the gangplank when we were approaching this behemoth of a ship. We descended another set of steps into the belly of the ship which was crammed with wooden boxes and large burlap bags filled with everything from rice to cotton. We walked in silence towards the dark corridor of wooden bins filled with coal briquettes until we reached a wall of crates marked with a red and blue Union Jack stamp. On the other side of this artificial wall was a small pallet of hay covered with a yellow sheet and a thin burlap blanket folded at the foot of the pallet. There was also a chamber pot and a wooden apple crate turned upside down to serve as a chair.

Sullivan pulled a canteen of grog from his hip and handed it to me. "Ye can fill it back up again in the galley. Ere's a bucket in the corner next to yer pallet for shittin' and pissin'or yer welcome to visit the head at the front of the ship. I'll send one of the cabin boy's to fetch ye that goat fer yer supper soon's we catch a break in the headwinds and the Cap'ns happy with setting the tack." Sullivan cautioned me, "Best ye stay 'ere out of the way mate, least for another couple of hours. Til the work's done. I can't leave ye a candle down here fer risk of fire. Captain says it won't be necessary because you can see even if it's black as the Earl of Hell's waistcoat about." I stood there holding my shroud in my hand, too nervous to speak the few English words I knew. I froze in place as Sullivan raised the oil lamp toward my face. He leaned in and turned his head sideways in order to try and get a better look at my eyes and face to gauge whether any of what he was saying was sinking in.

Still looking down at my feet, I croaked out hoarsely, "I wait".

Sullivan flinched slightly at the sound of my dry voice. He cracked a toothless smile and without extending his hand to shake mine he said, "That'll do then. Welcome aboard, mate." As he straightened up and gave a half salute, he turned and walked back around the wall of wooden crates and back up the stairs. Alone in the dark, the first thing I did was empty the overflowing contents of my bladder into the chamber pot. Once relieved, I anxiously perched myself on my apple crate chair and tested the limits of my excellent hearing in order to listen out for any distress calls coming from the quarters where Jessie and Colette were sleeping.

A couple of hours or so after Sullivan left, I heard what sounded like the door to the stairs being opened, and I could smell the animal musk and hear the hooves of a goat clip-clopping its way down the stairs. Behind the goat walked the naked feet of a person with a very light and sneaky footfall pattern. I stood to receive my guests just as the approaching sound and the bouncing lantern glow of my approaching visitors stopped abruptly behind the wall of crates. A small pale white face and arm holding an oil lamp poked around the edge of the boxes trying to cast light into the darkness seemingly to pinpoint my exact location. I had moved the box into the opposite corner of the partition opening where it was darkest so when I opened my eyes only the red glow of the sclera in my eyes could be seen flashing in the dark. The boy let out a shriek and dropped the rope around the goat's neck and ran as fast as his 12 year old feet would carry him up and out of the cargo hold. In the next moment, I heard the hatch to the cargo deck open and close, and just like that, he was gone.

The goat stood there in shock for a moment at the abrupt disappearance of her host. She bleated a couple of times into the seemingly empty room, sniffing at the air in complete darkness. She then began to innocently chew on the guide end of the rope still around her neck. Two seconds later, my teeth were at the jugular of the small beast. The goat let out a bleat in protest and tried in vain to free herself from my clutches but, I was too powerful. Her cries died down to whimpers as I began draining every last drop of her savory, warm blood. Using my claws I separated her head from her body to dig into some of the soft flesh of her internal organs. It had been a very long time since I had this abundance of meat within the span of three days. And it was rarely anything fresher or larger than a fat possum or raccoon. Before I knew it, I had devoured the top half of the body and picked the meat from the skull clean including the spongy brain matter.

That night, I remained downstairs in the cargo hold for fear of being persecuted if I were to walk around on the upper deck unescorted with people that had never been around someone such as myself. I cleaned up my mess as best I could, and I sat and watched the walls of the ship until I let myself relax enough to drift off to sleep for an hour or so. As I sat in the dark throughout the next day, I tried to keep my mind from harboring negative thoughts and being anxious about Jesse and Colette and what this journey had in store for us. I found myself nervously pacing around my small nook, unsuccessfully trying to work up the nerve to venture upstairs and check on my friends.

I suddenly heard the hatch being opened and the voices of men approaching. Rounding the corner of my nook came the first mate Sullivan carrying an oil lamp and being followed by another man, a short balding Negro also carrying an oil lamp and a bucket of sea water. They had both come to retrieve me and to clean up whatever remained of the goat carcass. In my gluttony, I had used my claws to tear away the skin of the goat which lay neatly in a pile next to its skull and lower torso. I was filthy from the blood and viscera that splattered onto my shirt and had now dried into a smelly brown mess.

"Follow me so as ye can meet the Cap'n and see yer lasses again," says Rory Sullivan who is now standing in my living area holding an oil lamp high in order to survey the mess I had made. "Bruno here will clean up yer mess." He pointed to the nervous black man who was just rounding the corner of crates. "Take that rag of a shirt off and leave it with Bruno. "Sullivan said to me. We'll find ya some'n to cover you on our way through the galley," and with that he began walking towards the stairs to the upper decks. I grabbed my shroud from the floor and followed him.

I placed the burlap sack back over my head and passed Bruno who scowled at me in disdain for having to clean up behind a freak show like me. As Sullivan and I ascended the stairs, men were buzzing about the middle deck floors. The rhythmic 'clank' of my chains as I walked silences the

76

boisterous commotion coming from the living quarters and drew many curious stares from the men. Sullivan walked over to a cupboard near the kitchen area and retrieved an old, tattered piece of a sail. He tossed the fabric at my chest and said "Put this over your shoulders til we can get ye some proper slops soon as we can.

And what are ye lot gawkin' at?"

Sullivan asked the men standing around silent and slack jawed. I must have looked ridiculous wearing the dirty cloth over my shoulders while carrying the shackle weights with a burlap shroud over my face. The seamen all watched me walk past them as we approached the next set of stairs. As soon as we were on the landing leading up to the main deck, the men began clamoring amongst themselves again. Many began to debate as to why a slave would be forced to wear such heavy chains even in the middle of the ocean. Some seriously doubted the prudence of having me on the ship, concocting rumors that I was a convict wanted for murder or a demon controlled by the two witches. They all knew this vessel was not commissioned as a slave trading ship and some thought of me as a seriously bad omen for sailors due to the warning given by the captain to keep their distance from me. I kept my head down while still following Sullivan like an obedient puppy. As we stepped up onto the main deck a few of the braver men stopped what they were doing and moved closer towards me to get a better look at the slave with the huge iron shackles and the sack over his head.

The lack of sleep I received due to me having trouble getting accustomed to the smells and sounds of the constantly moving ship was now catching up to me. As I slogged behind Sullivan across the deck, my body all at once felt tired. It was uncommon for me to sleep for more than four hours a day, but the last few days of upheaval and travel had left me unexpectedly exhausted. The Caribbean slave system, especially in Saint Domingue, was thought to be to some degree much more brutal than what I experienced in the United States these last few years. Mainly because the Caribbean model was to maximize profit by working slaves literally to death because of the continuous supply of fresh labor coming from the west coast of Africa. At the height of French sugar production, in the West Indies, the average lifespan for a person once they landed and began the grueling labor was about six to

77

seven years. My mother was able to withstand that hell for over 60 years because of the blood we shared. There were countless times where I was forced to work all night, but since it was still seen as unheard of for a slave to be asleep while the sun was up, I would be forced to catch mice in the cellar or trudge and clean the dark disgusting latrines. Les Bouton ran his operation in a similar way. Around the clock there was always work that needed to be done, always some godforsaken tasks that would be placed on my shoulders so it became extremely rare for me to sleep more than a few hours while the sun was still up.

Sullivan and I emerged up onto the main deck and to my surprise, the sky was overcast and dark grey clouds could be seen blocking the late day sun. As we approached the bow of the ship, I heard the signature "Lawd have mussy," and both Sullivan and I turned to see Jessie and Colette emerge from the officers' quarters in the rear of the ship and approach us followed closely by a very large man who was dressed noticeably better than any of the rest of crew. Besides Sullivan, this was the only other man wearing boots. As the large man approached, he extended his right hand to mine that was still unwashed from my goat meal. I dropped my head out of embarrassment and my trusty mouthpiece Jessie immediately stepped up to interpret my actions to this man so as to not upset our gracious hosts. She quickly snatched the burlap sack from my head and began to explain my behavior—

"Suh, dis man aint got da sense God gave a road lizard. He don' know nuffin' bout no gentmen or nuffin like dat. He is a wukin nigga and das all, but when I tells u he da bes' wukin nigga, thas God's truf!" said Jessie.

The captain had not taken his eyes off of me, and instead he quickly bent down and grabbed my right hand with his and began pumping it gingerly and proceeded to tell me: "My name is Captain Thaddeus Ridley of His Royal Majesty's Reserve Corps for Special Conveyances."

Captain Ridley was only slightly taller than Sullivan but quite a bit broader in the chest and shoulders. He was a very robust and sturdy man with a shock of grey in his otherwise jet-black hair pulled back into a rugged ponytail that rested just under his tricorne hat. His face was worn and showed every bit of his fifty-some-odd years, but his eyes were shining with youthful power that burned with intent of action. His bearded face parted

78

with a tobacco speckled smile as he looked me up and down. His strength was very apparent by the ease with which he manipulated my shackled hand. I bowed my greeting as he released my mitt.

"Welcome aboard mate! Mr. Gellner has briefed the entire crew on the importance of you and your companions reaching the shores of England swiftly and securely. Please feel free to avail us of any needs you may have," Captain Ridley said confidently.

I looked first to Colette whose face is incredulous as her arm is now intertwined with this Captain's, and then to her mother Jessie who is grinning wide enough to wet both her ears. I nodded my head and bowed deeper than I have in many years, an atonement for not being able to respond vocally. Captain Ridley, seemingly satisfied with my response, turned and began walking the ladies back towards the bow of the ship, strolling and chatting as if on the boardwalk in downtown Charleston. The overcast sky and the sea were the only witnesses to this strange phenomenon of white men treating negroes as equals.

Both Jessie and Colette have had their fill of pain and suffering under the current institutions in the world that dictated that the darker peoples must build nations for the lighter. Intra-racial conflict also occurs amongst our own people as the same stratification paradigm prevails. When I was brought to the plantation where I met Jessie and Colette, I was little more than a beast and the clothes I had worn as a prisoner of the French military were literally falling off of my body they were so threadbare. Because of the inability to unlock the shackles, it was nearly impossible for me to remove or put on clothing. Jessie and Colette were assigned to literally sew the trousers and shirt onto my emaciated body the first day of my arrival in Thibodeaux Parish. They were the first humans to touch me out of kindness since the death of my mother. I have loved and cherished them both deeply since that day. I always worried that my curse had now entangled our fates inextricably and that they would one day be swallowed by the abyss that always seems to rob me of everything I hold dear. I pray that this time will be different.

That night, Captain Ridley asked me to remain on the top deck instead of being locked away inside the cargo hold. Jessie went to fetch a needle and thread from her belongings and took to sewing the old piece of sail I was wearing into a makeshift shirt. Once she finished, I returned to the main deck, and I was allowed to hang out and sit in the darkness and watch the waves and the clouds pass in front of the moon. The sailors not needed for work detail that night had retired to their living quarters and only a few of the men remained on the deck to make the rounds. First Mate Sullivan was manning the helm and barking to the men present about adjusting the sails to the tack. The novelty of my occupancy had worn off for the sailors, and as such most of them would simply ignore me as I sat maskless mutely watching the waves in my shadowy corner.

There were a couple of sailors nearby who spoke to each other in English and another language I did not recognize that were drinking copious amounts of rum which persuaded them into disobeying the captain's orders about approaching me. They staggered over and began chatting me up in English and asking about my chains while offering me a swig of their extremely pungent rum and a greasy plug of tobacco. Both of which I declined with a shake of my head in polite protest. As I sat taking in the smells and watching the dorsal fins of dolphins crisscross each other a few hundred meters in the distance, a large rat darts out of a shadow scurrying a few feet in front of me. A second later, before it can react to my presence, I am crunching its skull between my molars as quietly as I possibly can as its still moving body struggles to free itself from my hand. Catching vermin is an old habit of mine and, my self-proclaimed contribution to keeping the ship tidy. I toss the rat's carcass into the sea, wipe my mouth on my sleeve, and retire to the cargo hold just as the sun is cresting the eastern horizon.

The following morning, I awoke with a start, thinking I was late to report to the fields. After a second or two, I began to remember that I was still safely sprawled along the pallet of hay near the rear of the cargo hold in the belly of the ship I had forgotten I was aboard. Sleeping unfettered was a new sensation and proved to be very disorienting for me. This entire experience has been counter to anything I had ever experienced over the last one hundred years.

Jessie and Colette were drinking tea with actual sugar cubes for the first time in their lives with Captain Ridley and Mr. Gellner, and they all sat at the same dinner table. I could not help but feel responsible for their being torn away from what little connection to friends and family they had made in

Louisiana in order to chaperone an idiot like me. I would never forgive myself if anything foul ever befell either of them because of me. That first night and every night following, I would move to the rear of the cargo hold and listen intently with my ear to the ceiling under the officers' quarters where Jessie and Colette slept. I had to be sure they were safe during the night and at sunrise when I heard them stirring, I would retreat into my corner of the cargo hold. Throughout the day, I was forced to stay below deck on account of the high level of sun that shone down hotly during our fortnight sea journey. Those first few days aboard the ship, I would crack the door leading up between decks and scan the air for Jessie and Colette's scents to make sure they were still on board. I would then close the hatch and sit at the bottom of the stairs in the darkness and listen to the voices above me until I heard Jessie's signature laugh which, once confirmed, would temporarily put my mind at ease and I would slink back down the corridor and around the wall of crates to get a little rest before nightfall.

Colette was the only one of us aboard who had never been aboard a ship, and after trying her best to fight off seasickness during her first day at sea, she ended up regurgitating the complete contents of her belly into a wooden bucket and off the starboard bow for the majority of the second day. By the third day she was able to eat some bananas and dwarf apples and sip grog provided by the only other female aboard besides herself and Jessie. This black-haired woman was a half a head taller than most of the men on the ship and wore men's dungarees and an overcoat. Her pale, whisker-less face was the only factor that distinguished her from her male counterparts. She offered me the same meal that same night as I sat quietly near Colette and Jessie.

"You eatin'?" The woman queried of me in her British Cockney accent.

Jessie immediately piped up for me as I raised my head. "He don' talk an' he don't eat, lest you got some raw coon or possum meat. Tha's the onliest thangs that boy don't do is eat much, udder dan dat, dat boy can work any other nigga into his grave," she proudly proclaimed.

The woman cut her eyes at Jessie as if to say 'butt out', then turned back to look at me, quietly nodding her head. Life at sea must have prepared this woman for all manner of strange and different creatures this world had to offer for she showed no fear of me whatsoever. The woman just stared down at our little group for a moment with a look of pity. "More for me, I guess." The woman said as she shrugged her shoulders and turned to walk back to the galley with the leftover food.

When the woman was out of sight, Jessie scolded me in her stern teaching way. "Boy, dem Son Dominga niggas dun mess u up so bad, u don' nose wen white folks is treatin' you lak tresha. Nex time, mek like you gwine et it and den let me and Lettie have yo` pohsun. Even tho' she a bull dagger, I still woulda' took it from her on de coun' of I wanna be puhlite tuh dese here Bridish. I ain't spect tuh thank no womans tuh be on da boat I'll tell yuh dat much." Jessie reflects for a moment then back to me. "Lawd I aint neva seent a nigga as touched as you is." Jessie complains, shaking her head from side to side in disbelief and unwrapping a cheesecloth filled with cornbread that she brought with her to snack on.

•   •   •

The two weeks aboard the ship passed rather uneventfully except for a small storm that blew in from the northwest. I overheard some of the crew members remark that the storm had pushed us slightly ahead of schedule. I learned more details about our hosts while listening to a talkative West Indian sailor named James.

James had lots of grey in his hair and beard and looked to be one of the more senior members of the crew. He had been enslaved in British Jamaica and was fond of telling the story of his escape to the sea and how he lost the three fingers on his left hand to a tiger shark when he was working on a whaling ship. He also relayed to me the fact that Captain Ridley was a former pirate-turned-privateer who now worked for the British monarchy. According to James, Captain Ridley had earned himself a Letter of Marque which gave him official use of the Union Jack whenever he was in British waters. I had absolutely no clue what that meant and it would be years before I understood the significance of what James was telling me. That very flag was hoisted as we approached a group of islands just outside the mouth of the English Channel. I was told that this land mass constituted an area known as the Isles of Scilly and was a sign that we would be landing in Great

82

Britain soon. At the sight of land, Jessie expressed her excitement with one of her signature *'hallelujahs'* and a couple of *'Lawd ha mussy's'* for good measure.

Old Man Wind was kind enough to glide our ship right smack into the Strait of Dover, and we put in for disembarkation at the port city named Felixstowe just southeast of Ipswich, located just about seventy miles northeast of London.

When we arrived in the harbor, it was so busy that our ship was forced to wait to be approved for disembarkation until a suitable pier was made available. Captain Ridley, realizing the situation beforehand, was kind enough to arrange an alternative method for getting us ashore. He bid us farewell with hearty hugs and handshakes before he had Sullivan, Bruno, and two other crew members I had not seen much of during our journey load our meager belongings into a couple of the tender boats attached to the side of the ship. Captain Ridley gave instructions to ferry us to the pier in order for us to "grab some land" while the ship was waiting to be anchored in the harbor. Jessie, Claudette, and Mr. Gellner rode in one tender with one of the Portuguese sailors paddling them several hundred yards to shore.

Myself, Bruno, and one of the Polish sailors named Lukashz used the other tender to ferry to shore. Lukashz was an unbelievably large man, even taller and broader than Captain Ridley. Despite his size this man moved with great agility. I watched him leap up into the tender boat and using the pulley attachment he lowered himself down into the sea with no assistance. Still up on the deck, Bruno then proceeds to attach a rope around my waist and using the pulley and assistance from a few of the deckhands they lower me over the side of the ship into the waiting tender below. The added weight of my body and my chains cause the small vessel to sink low into the water and the churning seas splash over the side of the boat onto our feet as Lukashz and I attempt to steady ourselves. Bruno stared down at us with trepidation as we tried to steady the tender and balance the combined weight of myself and my oversized chauffeur. Seeing that the small boat was already having issues staying afloat, Bruno yells down to us that he will remain on the ship for fear that the weight of my chains would capsize the boat if we were to attempt to make the junket with any more people. Bruno reminded Lukashz that my safe delivery was top priority for the captain who had promised to

83

reward them all with a grand feast and a day off to visit the famed brothels of London after the transaction was complete.

We exited the ferries carefully and swiftly as the sea was churning with a sentient animation that felt overwrought with the excitement of our arrival. Once on land with our few belongings, we sauntered a short distance down the pier to a waiting coach. The town of Ipswich, we were told by Captain Ridley during one of his long dinner rants, was fabled to be one of the oldest established cities in mainland England and has always served as the home of some of the wealthiest Anglo-Saxon families in all the Empire.

As I walked with my chains and weights in each hand toward our waiting conveyances, I could feel something of a sinister energy pulsating through and underlining the opulence and niceties of the ships in the harbor and magnificent architecture of the buildings near the dock area. A dark history that traces its roots back to the times when the Roman empire used this port as a major trading hub. The coach that awaited us was of a very grand design. It came equipped with a six-horse team and two drivers, and another man with a dark mustache, dressed in a military uniform seated in the top rear of the coach holding a musket rifle with a pistol and a cutlass in his waistband. This man did not acknowledge our party of four in the slightest as we approached the carriage but instead looked around in all directions in a watchful manner.

Colette and Jessie slowed down their approach and stared at the sight of the heavily armed man. Pushing down her fear in an attempt to ease the tension, Jessie turned to Gellner and asks, "Zat ahmy fella up dere looking to shoot sum rabbits on de way?" gesturing to the man holding the rifle atop the carriage.

Gellner dismissed Jessie with a wave of his hand and a cruel scowl on his face to punctuate his disdain at the absurdity of the question. He then adjusted his lapel and explained to us in the calmest voice he could muster "Do not worry yourself my dear Jessica. Your security is a top priority to us and out of an overabundance of caution the baron thought it wise to have a bit of extra protection to ensure that his investments are kept well out of harm's way which, at times, warrants the use of heavy artillery by our staff."

Satisfied with Gellner's answer, Jessie nodded her approval and stepped up into the carriage with Colette and I right behind her.

As we entered the vehicle, the weight of my chains barely registered any movement as I climbed into this extremely spacious and sturdily built buggy. I eagerly took my seat against the wall of the coach with Jessie in the center again. As Gellner entered the carriage he took the seat opposite Colette instead of his usual center position. More than likely to avoid having to answer another hundred questions from Jessie this time. Gellner again checked his pocket watch and released a small sigh and rubbed his eyes as if the journey with us was beginning to take a toll on his patience. Jessie took the hint and remained relatively quiet, only making small talk with Colette about the fineries of the interior of the carriage as we waited for the final preparations to be completed for our departure.

After a few tense minutes we heard the crack of a riding whip and the coach lurched forward as the eight sizable Yorkshire Trotters effortlessly pulled the noticeably heavy carriage. The infamously rough and uneven English roads were no match for the large wheels and metal springs of this coach which must have cost a small fortune to possess such modern engineering.

Nightfall approached, and as the sun tumbled below the horizon, I inhaled deeply under my burlap shroud as the cool English air brought the smell of freshwater and the sound of the bullfrogs along the river calling to their lovers in the cool late summer night. As we continued down the roughly hewn lane, there were a few ruts and potholes created from recent rainstorms that would jostle the stagecoach from time to time causing the three of us to bump together. Colette was thoroughly amused at the prospect of a new life in another country and would quietly giggle at the sensation of the bouncing vehicle. The mood inside the carriage was very light, and Jessie was now quietly commenting to herself about what she wished she would have brought on her journey as she looked out of either window for most of the trip. Jessie not speaking for more than ten minutes was a feat unto itself and the strange feeling of giddiness and whimsy crept into all our hearts taking in all the new and breathtaking sights and sounds of this regal country. Our buoyant mood was a symptom no less of something akin to being hopeful, the root emotion behind every enslaved person's smile.

The faint but distinct smell of roasted meat crashed into my nostrils just as the lane we were traversing became wider and the incline of the road caused the horses to strain for a few miles before it began to level off again. The sun was far below the horizon now, but through the darkness, I could see the outline of a massive structure less than half a mile ahead. As we drew closer, I could also now smell the beeswax and whale oil of the torches lighting the windows of this incredible estate. There were also torches placed at the main entrances and on the ornate entry gates that gave a rather gothic dimension to the Palladian architecture. The building completely engulfed the entire skyline, the moon giving it shape and breadth unlike any of the castles or plantation estates homes I was privy to in Saint Domingue or Thibodeaux Parish. Even the massive French forts paled in comparison to this palatial structure. We were now close enough for everyone to be able to smell the meat roasting and see the details cast by the torches burning and illuminating the building and we were all taken aback by what we saw.

Jesse turned and leaned across Claudette to get a better view from her window and said with a huge smile on her face, "Lawd ham mussy, we dun came cross de oshun ta wuk fa de Kang of Angland. Sol'mon an de Quain a Shiba aint seen quotas dis big. Dey mus got beaucoup niggas wekkin fa dem, jes to clean all dem winders. Hell, Geoj Wash hisself aint sittin' dis high on de hog."

The last statement was directed at Mr. Gellner who was in the middle of checking his watch again in the partial moonlight coming through his window. He glanced up at her and smiled, more with his eyes than his lips as he replaced the watch in his left breast pocket and pulled a small logbook out of his other pocket and opened it toward the moonlight streaming into the window to check one of his many personal calculations.

As we drew nearer to the complex, our coach began to slow as we approached the main entry gate. There were two white men armed with rifles and swords at their hips dressed like the military gentleman seated above our coach. From seemingly nowhere appeared a short, thin faced Negro with jet black hair that laid down neatly across his forehead. He was dressed in an immaculate green suit complete with coattails and patent leather Souvaroff boots. The man bounded ahead of our carriage to open the Byzantine wrought iron gate wide enough for our coach to enter the enormous estate. An ominous feeling began to overwhelm me again, but I suppressed the overwhelming urge to run and hide again in hopes that my hesitancy was merely caused by my nervousness about being in unfamiliar territory and fear of what was to happen next in this unbelievable maelstrom of events.

Once inside the gates, I saw that the main building was fronted with four enormous columns. In the center of the courtyard stood a gigantic spire jutting majestically into the night sky. It would be over one hundred years from that moment before I would visit a place called the Place de la Concorde where I would learn that what I was looking at was a replica of spires built all over the world. In ancient Egypt, the symbol was an Obelisk shape that represented the sun and the power of the male energy. One of the largest representations sits in the United States Capitol today. There were two additional structures that were an order of magnitude down in grandeur from the main building connected on either side of the center structure by curved colonnades. The building to my left was spewing smoke from its chimney, and I reckoned this was the source of the fabulous smelling meat. Specifically lamb and pork with some absolutely succulent smelling fowl I did not recognize that certainly was not mere roasted chicken or turkey.

The carriage entered the roundabout drive and as we pulled closer I could see the massive oak-hewn double doors, each with a grand brass lion's head holding a formidable circular door knocker in its teeth in the center. In front of the doors stood two identical twin mulattoes adorned in green wool and silk velvet tailcoats with metallic buttons. Both had their hair shorn close to their heads revealing their very odd-shaped skulls.

As the carriage came to a halt, one of the twins approached the side of the coach gracefully and placed a large block that he was holding under the door of the carriage as a step. As the door opened, Mr. Gellner sprang from his seat and bounded wordlessly out of the carriage. His demeanor signified both his delight at being successful with the delivery of his bounty, mixed with happiness he felt to be freed from the revulsion of having to accommodate such a motley crew.

The twin attendant, now holding the carriage door open, addressed Gellner with a deep bow in a nasally very proper English accent, "Sir Gellner, on behalf of His Greatness Lord Reichstall, it is a pleasure to have you back in the land of the Saxons during such tumultuous times."

The other twin, now helping Colette out of the coach and down the step, flashed a handsome smile at her causing her to blush, chimed in saying, "The Baron has been eagerly anticipating your arrival and hopes your trip has been comfortable and expedient."

Jessie extended her hands next as the man effortlessly pulls her full weight up from her seat and gently guided her out and down the steps of the coach as if she were arriving for the Governor's ball.

As the valet turned back towards me, his smile dropped momentarily as he looked me up and down, probably wondering how I would be able to walk with a sack over my face while carrying such an amount of weight and why anyone would need such huge restraints. As I slid forward to get up the man offered both of his hands in assistance. I paused to think about how absurd everything felt in that moment for me after being accustomed to such harsh treatment. I slowly and timidly extended my right hand while holding the shackle weights with my left.

Jessie's eyes grew to the size of dinner plates as she snorted. "Lawd Jesus you can tek muh soul ret nah, cuz I dun' seen evathang dere is tuh see in dis life!" as she flailed her hands in the air mockingly. "Dis boy thank he on de cakewalk down in de paddy," she screamed and emitted one of her boisterous laughs.

As I stepped down to ground level Jessie reached up and removed my shroud from my head and stuffed it in my pants pocket.

"Ac' like you got some damn sense now please, hear?" Jessie said to me pleadingly, looking directly into my colorless eyes to make sure her message was coming through loud and clear.

The massive front doors of the castle slowly began to open and out steps a humongous black man. The man was so tall he was forced to duck under the top of the door as he exited. This man was impeccably dressed in a wool and silk navy blue tailcoat, white trousers, gloves, and black leather knee high Brunswick boots. He wore a gold ring in each ear and was completely bald. He stood half a meter over any man present. Looking down at the three of us, his deep voice boomed in heavily accented English,

"Welcome to Woolverstone Manor. I am called Albert and I am the Chief of Staff here. You will be shown to the servant's hall where you each have your own room to freshen up and change to prepare for dinner at which His Greatness Lord Reichstall, your new master, will be in attendance in order to personally welcome you into his employment. My Lord enjoys greeting his new charges in person and making them feel as comfortable as possible as they acclimate to their new environs." And with that, the giant Albert bowed deeply and gestured with his arm for our party to enter.

Jessie and Colette looked at each other and clasped hands. Jessie let out a heartfelt Lawd ham mussy" As Colette let out another involuntary little squeal as if she was a seven-year-old girl.

"We is gonna has a room all tuh ah'selfs?" questioned Jessie, mostly to herself. "I 'spect Saint Peta mus' be in dis here place, cuz I sho nuff dun died and went tu hebin," she cackled.

Colette piped up uncharacteristically, tears welling in her eyes. and said just above a whisper, "I caint 'member las' time I has a hot baf indose befo'." Now breaking into a full toothy smile, "An maybe fetch us a new dress fo nes' Crismuss." Quietly to herself in French, she said, "Ca doit etre le paradis pour de vrai." (This must truly be heaven).

They both marched boldly into the front door without looking back and disappeared to the left of the main entrance and into the main hall.

I looked at Albert again before I hesitantly began my clunky approach. I cannot help but notice his powerful arms bulging beneath the material of the suit and the scarification around his ears resembles the warrior markings of the Wolof tribesmen, a group of proud warriors who were amongst the many different peoples who were enslaved with me in Saint Domingue. They were known for their cunning and fierceness in battle and for their stubbornness in captivity.

I shuffled past him and entered the mansion that was brimming with the smell of torches burning, roasted meat, and the French eau de toilette that all the servants were donning. In the main hall facing the door, there was a large mural on the wall depicting a serpent with the head of a lion. And directly under the carving was a large portrait of a man and a woman naked in a garden with a serpent standing between them. Jessie would later explain to me that this was a scene from the Bible story of the Creation, and the two people were Adam and Eve and the serpent was Lucifer. The high ceilings were gilded with ornamental crown molding painted to resemble gold. Instead of torches on the wall, there were dozens of candelabras placed strategically throughout the house that were held by neatly sculpted Promethean hands that appeared at regular intervals throughout the rooms and along the corridors. Plush red carpet runners covered the hallway marble floors, and the center floor carpet was a dark, reddish color with floral decorations that had an Oriental flair. There were statues of cherubim juxtaposed next to grotesque gargoyle faces along with other symbols that resembled crosses, arrows, and stars all along the corridors. As we passed an impressively large room on my right, I could see the disembodied heads of animals such as deer, crocodiles, and large cats including a tiger displayed on the wall like paintings.

The ladies were walking and gawking at the decor about twenty feet ahead of me and were at the point of hysterics while thrilling at the luxury of their new accommodations.

"We is bein' blest sho nuff chile." Jessie said, addressing Colette who just nodded her head emphatically and smiled.

As Albert reentered the foyer, he clapped his huge hands twice, and three demurely dressed young women appeared from a door under a painting of a black woman and her child and each led us respectively to our individual quarters for us to wash and change before dinner. These women were unlike any I had ever seen before. They were not Negroes but they were not white women either. Their hair was long and jet black and their skin was pale but their eyes were very dark and almond shaped instead of rounded. They wore long, decorative robes, red dresses adorned with intricate beads, and metallic sashes that tinkled with every step. These women did not smell of eau de toilette but had the aroma of jasmine spice and saffron that was very pleasing and alluring.

My quarters were altogether separate and on the complete opposite side of the main hall from Jessie and Colette's rooms. The sweet-smelling woman guided me down a long corridor lined with ceiling to floor stained glass windows depicting scenes from some medieval battle. As I continued to follow the exotic looking woman down the never-ending corridor, we made a right turn onto another slightly narrower corridor lined with statues and paintings of historical figures from around the world. As we approached a door that led into the adjacent wing of the main hall I immediately caught a whiff of gunpowder and as we entered I could see ahead of us a bearded white man dressed in the attire of a military officer donning a helmet with a large red plume. The man turned to us as we approached the door to the room that the woman seemed to be leading me. He was a tall, very broad-shouldered man with a barrel chest that gave him ample surface for displaying the many medals he wore. The man appeared to be middle-aged but his movements were very supple and deliberate as if he could still handle himself in combat very well. His hand rested on a pistol tucked into his waistband and the look on his face was more akin to the expressions that I was used to being greeted with. I looked down at the floor instinctively and turtled my head down between my shoulders in deference to this intimidating brute. As we stopped in front of him, he reached down and grabbed my shackles causing me to drop the cannon ball weights. They crashed to the floor with a heavy 'thud' but did not crack the marble tile. He straightened his back and placed one hand on my shoulder as if to further establish his dominance before he began to address me.

"I am Colonel Berners of His Royal Majesty's Fifth Regiment and personal bodyguard to the Baron when he is in Sussex. I welcome you and offer you freedom from your shackles in exchange for your cooperation. I must admit I personally think it is a mistake to have a Negro such as yourself traipsing around the castle unfettered and without proper safety precautions. To be honest the very notion of it is absolutely ludicrous to me." He sighed heavily, looked over at the female attendant then continued. "But as a soldier, I must follow orders, and I must acquiesce to the Baron and his wishes on this matter."

Colonel Berners reached into the top of his shirt and pulled out a very strange looking key hanging from a silver chain around his neck. He pulled the necklace with the key over his head and proceeded to use the back end of the key to turn a keyhole located on the side of my wrist shackles. He gave the key another rough twist and a quarter inch panel is released to reveal another uniquely shaped keyhole underneath the newly opened panel. The Colonel then uses the head of the key on that lock to open my wrist shackles. After a furtive attempt to turn the corroded lock, a loud click was heard and the shackles on my hands fell to the ground with a reverberating clang. Colonel Berners then handed the key to the woman with the almond eyes and stepped to the side, all the while watching me like a hawk with his hand on his sidearm. The woman dropped to her knees and proceeded to repeat the same procedure to unlock the shackles around my ankles. The raw and rotten flesh of my forearms and legs emitted a sickening smell after being exposed to air for the first time in six years. In utter disbelief I rub my fingertips across the mutilated patch of skin that had grown thick with a calloused ring of pale flesh from being damaged and healing hundreds of times a day over all that time.

I stood there dumbfounded, in a state of shock, staring down at the shackles and chains that I was certain would never be taken off again.

"Megumi here will get you cleaned up and presentable for your dinner with the Baron this evening." Berners says pointing to my beautiful escort who gracefully bows her greeting. Now be a good boy and don't even think of doing anything that would make myself or the Baron cross." With his index finger to his temple, Berners leaned in and said, "Know that we are always watching you." In an instant and as if on cue, four soldiers, three of which I had already smelled, appeared from doors hidden in the wall panels opposite the entrance to my room. They were all carrying pistols and swords at their sides with their lower faces covered by scarves, leaving only their piercing eyes visible. "These are some of my best men, recruited from militaries all over the world and trained to deal with the most dangerous and extraordinary of threats." I nodded my head in compliance but my eyes continued to stare down at the floor at the heavy cannon balls and chains that I could still feel the phantom weight of.

Colonel Berners continued his briefing. "And as an added incentive to curtail your behavior, your companions in the other hall will be held accountable for any mischief or disobedience on your part and will be punished according to your transgression including but not limited to death by hanging."

At these words, I raised my eyes from the floor towards Colonel Berners, but I am careful not to make direct eye contact. I nodded my comprehension as the colonel cast one final look of disgust at me before slowly turning and walking back toward the main foyer. His soldiers silently disappeared behind the wall panels again. I turned to follow Megumi just as she advanced into the room ahead of me. She walked over to the hearth located in the center of the room and removed a large pot hanging over a blazing fire and poured its contents into a waiting tub of water next to the bed. Another beautiful woman entered the room holding a long white garment over her arm and closed the door behind her. This woman was coffee brown and she greeted me in Creole with a seductive,

"Bonjou, ou Ka rele m Claire" [Hello my name is Claire].

Claire looked like she could be from San Domingue, but her eyes were as blue as the summer sky. She placed the garment on the bed and then approached me smiling and motioned for me to remove my shoes and clothing.

The pleasant smell of this woman standing before me combined with the overwhelmingly tantalizing smell of the food coming from the other building swirled together and enveloped my senses fully. Suddenly I was aware of another aroma intermixing with the others. This scent I immediately recognized as one of the most horrible and disgusting fragrances that I have ever had the displeasure of experiencing. The smell could only be described as that of a perspiring animal wrapped in moldering rags, soaked in swamp water. The source of the offending odor I soon realized was myself and blushing with embarrassment from my offending odor much more so than my nakedness in front of these two women, I removed my rags quickly and hastily sank into the warm water waiting in the tub. Both women exited the room with my pile of dirty rags and for a few minutes, I was left alone to soak and take in my surroundings.

After a few minutes of sitting in the tub, the clear water grew gradually more opaque with the dirt and grime coming from my body. There were many fine pieces of art and furniture in the room but for some reason I could not take my eyes off the soft blankets and alabaster sheets of the bed. Never had I been in the same room as such opulence. I was hypnotized by its allure, and I wished with all my soul that my mother could be here to see it. I have called many places my bed over the years. Whether it be a pile of straw, a bundle of dirty rags, a patch of grass, a hole dug into the side of an embankment, or usually just a bare wooden floor. However, in all my nearly century of life I never imagined lying my body down upon something so magnificent. The mattress was the size of a hay trailer, with large wooden posts carved with intricate floral designs and draped by canopy curtains that hung lavishly from the molded oak with brass trimming for accent. The high goose feather mattress was a cloud with linens made of the finest silk and a large duvet quilted in a pattern that resembled tiny fleur-de-lis amidst red and gold accents.

Claire reentered the room with another kettle of hot water which she hung over the flame in the fireplace. She then walked over and kneeled next to the tub. I froze as she unabashedly plunged her bare arms into the bath water and reached between my legs. After searching for a second, she found her target and pulled out a small brush and began to scrub the dirt from my shoulders and back. A few rich black curls bounced from beneath the bonnet she wore as her hands deftly moved the tallow soap against the horsehair brush and then against my skin. A sensation of joy returned me to my childhood when my mother or one of the nurses in the slave quarters would wash us three at a time in the metal tub behind the huts. As she lifted each arm to attack some of the more offending areas, her smile never left her face but I on the other hand, now conscious of my proximity to this very comely woman, grew more and more bashful by the second. As her firm but gentle caress moved down my chest to my abdomen, she rose to her feet and gestured for me to do the same. I reluctantly obeyed, the cold of the damp room embracing me as my body reached full height. Claire, still smiling, then proceeded to wash my legs and buttocks. My manhood involuntarily began to lengthen in approval as she moved toward the front of my torso. She paused almost imperceptibly and emitted a cheeky giggle and then continued to scrub my body even lifting my penis and testicles with her left hand in one deft movement without ever making eye contact and without a word passing between us.

Just as Claire was finishing my scrub down, there was a rap at the door and promptly Megumi reentered the room holding a garment that resembled a military uniform in one hand and in the other hand she held another pot of water. Claire took the pot of water from Megumi and exchanged it with the water already warming over the flame. My eyes moved down to the sway of her hips as she approached the bathtub. Being alone with these women made me extremely nervous. Although I was over 100 years old I was clueless when it came to sexual matters and I sheepishly stood waiting with both hands covering my penis, mortified by my involuntary arousal in the presence of strangers. She pretended not to notice as she poured the warm liquid onto my shoulders and down the front and back of my body.

"Baisse la tête s'il te plait," [please lower you head] she asked me, and as I obliged she poured the remainder of the kettle onto my head and face.

The smell of sandalwood and cedar filled my nostrils and as I wiped the water from my eyes I noticed that the calluses on my wrists had begun to heal rapidly and reverse the damage caused by years of wearing iron against my flesh. Claire then placed her hand under my elbow and gently led me out of the tub towards the bed. She then picked up a linen robe and wrapped it around my shoulders. The material felt like soft chicken feathers against my skin. In my ignorance, I begin to dry off with the robe. I pull it from my shoulders and wrap it around my waist. This time instead of a chuckle, Claire smiles and shakes her head and she and Megumi shared an amused look as she approached me holding the uniform.

In perfect French Megumi said "[Lord Reichstall sincerely apologizes for the lack of proper dinner attire for you. The tailor will take your measurements first thing in the morning to begin crafting your new clothes. Please accept this as your dinner wardrobe for tonight, and we will be able to accommodate you more graciously in the morning.]"

She then bowed her dismissal, and both women scurry out of the room. As the door opened, I saw the armed men stationed directly outside my domicile. I stood there partially covered by the robe, still reeling from the day's events. The house was quiet, and the fragrances of the women lingered softly in the air. The peace and tranquility of the moment was betrayed by the sound of someone moving inside the wall behind the bed and the faint smell of gunpowder sat under every other scent and seemed to be all around me. With all the kind treatment I am being afforded, my hosts were still very much on their guard. Still, for the first time in my life, I felt like more than a tool. My thoughts wandered to Jessie and Colette, and I prayed that this would truly be an upgrade from the rotten plantation at Thibodeaux Parish with all its indigo planting, bed warming, and general uncertainty that permeated enslaved life under the thumb of Les Bouton and his lascivious behavior.

The suit I was given was that of a military officer which fit snugly around the chest and shoulder area. The pant legs were a little short but overall, the fit was proper. I was having trouble with the buckles and buttons, partly because I usually fastened my pants with a rope, and I had only known buttons in my youth when I attempted to help my mother with fastening her petticoats. It also didn't help that my nails were so long they hindered me from successfully threading the buttons through the buttonholes.

I smelled the sweet saffron moments before Claire reentered with another mulatto woman who looked to be nearly two meters tall with high cheekbones, bulging brown almost black eyes, and full lips pressed in an appealing tight smile. Her long black hair hung down in two long braids past the back of her knees. She was clearly much older than Claire but every bit her equal in beauty. She was dressed very chastely and the only bit of skin showing was from her hands and face. She held a large tool which I first mistook to be a fire tong for removing hot coals, but as she moved closer, I recognized it to be a tool used by the stable boys to trim the hooves of horses. Claire's soft hands gently glide over my left hand to present it to the tall woman who, still smiling, began to chop my thickly overgrown claws down to a more manageable size. Each nail resisted a bit and then gave way with a loud "KRITCH."

As the woman finished clipping both hands, she then gestured for me to have a seat on the bed and while kneeling in front of me, she proceeded to deftly chop the nails on either foot just as neatly as she did my fingers. As I am prompted to stand up again, both women helped to finish dressing me; buttoning, pants, shirt, vest, and waistcoat, even sliding stockings over my now civilized feet. A pair of thin black leather shoes with a golden silk bow on the tongue are brought through the door by the spicy smelling Megumi.

In her perfect French she remarked, "[I hope these suit you until we can fetch the cobbler in the morning to outfit you with a more comfortable pair. Dinner is served, and the Baron would like to see you now.]"

I nodded my comprehension and as she turned to walk out of the door, I looked at the tall long-haired woman and Claire who were both bowing their goodnights and extending their hands as a gesture for me to follow Megumi which I most certainly oblige. As I exited the room, the two guards now flanking the door just glared at me briefly before returning to their statue-like poses. I am enthralled by the decor of this magnificent dwelling. Large, eccentric portraits lined the hallway, many of them depicting women in various levels of undress and striking animal-like poses. One portrait that still stood out in my mind was of a woman wearing only a flimsy skirt made of palm leaves, suckling what appeared to be a goat with the face of a man. Along the walls and amongst the floor coverings, there were many triangles inside triangles that formed star shapes alongside depictions of the lion, the bull, the eagle, and other animals that I later learned were representations of the zodiac.

The smell of the meat was now overwhelming throughout the castle, and I assumed most of the servants and valets were assisting with dinner preparation because there was not another soul on the corridor until we reached the doors leading into the main dining hall. My escort then turned to me and bowed and gestured for me to continue on my own through the doors. The two white gloved men standing on either side of the double door each proceed to open his respective portal, and I am smashed in the face with the aroma of tantalizing meats, fruits, and sweetbreads, the quality of which my impoverished palate was certainly not accustomed. All was laid out on a large dark oak table to my left. In the center of the room was another smaller table that sat four. Two stunning negro women were seated across from each other with a blonde-haired white man who looked to be in his late forties seated at the head of the table wistfully engaging both women in what must have been an enthralling conversation because neither of the group had acknowledged my entrance into the room as of yet. As I approached the table the man finally looked up at me and said from his seated position,

" Ah, our guest of honor has arrived," now placing his napkin on the table in front of him and standing. "Welcome, my good man. Now we may begin the dinner."

And with that a parade of a dozen servants appeared through the doorway and began to service our four-person party. I was led by the arm to my seat by Claire, now dressed in a black and white valet type uniform. Every one of the servants were perfectly manicured and dressed in the finest quality clothing and many of them seemed to have some unique physical characteristic that set them apart from the Negroes that I was accustomed to seeing. I was nonplussed at the two new but familiar colored women sitting on either side of this middle-aged, white man who wore a black shirt like a clergyman and a large pendant bearing double triangles around his neck. The same symbol was depicted in a portrait which hung over the bed in my room.

My mind was reeling at the sensory overload I was experiencing but as I began to focus, I could not take my eyes off my two companions. Jessie and Colette could very easily have been mistaken for Parisian mademoiselles with their elegant silk gowns dripping with ornate lace and tassels. Their scarves no longer adorned their heads, but in their place was beautiful black hair, black and gray in Jessie's instance, expertly coiffured to enhance their natural beauty. Colette's slender face with its full lips, high cheekbones, and enchanting eyes was framed by two bouncy curls that hung down on either side of her temples making her even more bewitching in the radiance of the candlelight. They both wore elegant ball gowns with white gloves that stretched completely to their elbows. Colette was a vision of beauty in yellow with white lace and gold inlay with a tight bodice that perfectly accented her dark brown skin. My eyes unwillingly drawn to the plunging neckline that displayed her ample bosom. Jessie was a completely different woman entirely in her sky-blue dress and pearl necklace with pearl earrings.

Both women were beaming like the uppity wives of the plantation owners or the proud, free creole women of Port De Paix as they paraded the boulevard after Easter mass. Their faces were expertly caked with powder, blush, and lipstick, and the smell of perfume emanating from both women held a power over me that was so strong I did not notice the two male attendants coming up behind me who gently touched my back on either side to guide me to my chair. Both men bore distinctly Negro facial features but were pale white with blond hair wearing thick spectacles that clung to their noses.

"Allow us, sir," they both say in unison, and I sat down eye to eye across from this white man, and the first thing I noticed about him that was remarkably peculiar was that I could not detect his scent.

"My name is Baron Nathaniel Devereaux Von Reichstall," he began, "and I want to be the first to thank you for joining me. Before you arrived, I was apologizing to the ladies for the secretiveness of my identity and my reasoning for summoning you so abruptly to such a distance from your home. I hope your accommodations and the service provided by my staff was a blissful boon to your mood, the Baron said, smiling graciously and staring directly into my eyes while addressing our party. "Madame Talbot *(Talbot being Jessies given last name) here tells me that you are uncommonly prone to privacy so I hope my servants did not offend you in any way." A stunning dark brown skin woman wearing a silver turban and piercing green eyes poured water from a pitcher into a glass in front of me.

"Bon jou zanmi mwen," the woman said in a sultry voice. Her creole impeccably articulate. Her smile trapped me for a moment as she moved to refill the water glasses of the other parties at the table.

While the Baron spoke, all manner of men and women with foreign features and accents the likes of which I had never encountered dashed to and fro nimbly placing dishes and pouring wine and water while setting the different courses on a service table with all sorts of meats, cakes, pies, and various trays of fruit.

"When my agents first told me of a man who could outrun a coach horse, I must say my insatiable curiosity got the best of me. What might I call you old boy?" Baron Reichstall inquired.

Jessie took that opportunity to speak as the ambassador of our trinity, finally broken from the spell created by her whirlwind of an experience up until now. "Bike home in de bayou, de creole folk call 'im 'Je Blan'. Wat mean white eyes on de coun' a his eyes lightin' up like a hoot owl at night. Sum a de color' folks call dat boy 'Dyab' or 'move Lespri', what mean devil man in Creole. Marse Beauchamp, one a de ovaseahs, give de name a La Terreur' when he fus get tu da plantashun, prolly as a joke knowin him an his damn foolery," she adds. "Mos' folks ain't too keen on talkin' to da boy on count a his bein up all night wukin and catchin' crittas. Marse Reichstall, I feel like I speaks fuh' all bofe me an' Lettie an dis boy heah an' says that we shole preciate evy'than' you is doin' fuh' us. I says dat cause this gal so bashful she don' har'ly knows how to speak tuh white foke. An' dat man deh," Jessie said pointing to me, "ain't says two words cross a month. So I haf tuh thank ya on dey behaf…"

A short man with long jet-black hair, gently placed a bowl of soup in front of Jessie which momentarily distracted her. "Lawd and de food smell so gud! I knowed fo' a fac dat I never spected in all my yeahs dat dis boy was gon' tract dis kinda fine life. I knew sumthin' was gon' happen but I be damn' if I cain't hones'ly say t'was gon be sumthin mo n' beaucoup det an 'struction." Her voice filled the dining hall with her infectious joy.

"You're quite welcome, Jessica,"replied Reichstall, "and quite the opposite of bedlam awaits you and your compatriots, madam. This young man is destined to be the crown jewel in my assemblage of the finest humans and superhuman beings walking the planet. I have been thoroughly briefed of his unique constitution and, believe it or not, I have met men and women of his kind on my travels." "Through the rural areas of eastern Europe where the climate painted the sky a dreary overcast grey for the majority of the year and the endless nights accompanied by a dense fog that seemed alive." His eyes flashed as he winked at Jessie and continued. "Ah, yes, my fine fellow, in my exhaustive research of the occult and the mysteries of the ancient orders of Atlantis, I encountered them, the rulers of the night. Using my family's great wealth, I was able to parlay a meeting with their leadership. I learned of all their amazing and unique qualities and I was also privy to their many weaknesses. Which is why I have ordered all curtains drawn during the daylight hours and for all the staff to operate under the light of oil lamps and candles for the first few days of your stay to accommodate your nocturnal nature."

And with a dramatic swish of his hand, two large, dark haired white women approached my end of the table and place an immense, covered silver platter in front of me. The woman on my left then removed the heavy silver cover from the platter revealing a large pile of bloody lamb parts, mostly consisting of the hindquarters and tongue, liver and various other premium cuts of the meat. A leather canteen skin is presented by the woman on my right and she began to pour a substance I was all too familiar with, but with a cut of purity unlike any I had encountered up until today. The crimson of the liquid was hypnotizing and even with the keenness of my sense of smell that up until now has never betrayed me, I could not place the source animal from whence this blood could have come from.

Baron Reichstall spoke up. "I learned from those ancient noble men and women of Eastern Europe the secrets to procuring the purest of blood to satiate the most demanding of connoisseurs. Their faces were the palest of whites and their bodies were pure works of art. The strength and speed that they exhibited was like that of the gods. Many of them secretly ruled many areas of Eastern and Western Europe, and some even had influence as far as India and Persia. My fascination with their abilities has occupied scores of hours within my imagination. The sheer will and ability to survive the great cataclysm speaks to your kind's temerity of spirit which metaphorically spit in the face of God's will. A handful of your original kinsmen remain walking the earth after countless ages. Their only flaw was that they could not surmount any prolonged exposure to pure sunlight due to their severe lack of pigment which caused their skin to spoil and burn relentlessly beyond the regeneration capabilities of their nigh immortal constitutions. But, as with the case in many affairs concerning the Reichstall family, eternal providence has befallen us once again and brought to my attention an ancient of African descent blessed with all of their great strengths and a nominal fraction of their weaknesses. Forgive me, where are my manners? I am truly sorry for rambling on while our meal sits in front of us growing colder by the second."

Baron Reichstall clapped his hands and the servants and attendants all descended on the table to bring over the many dishes of the multi course feast that we were to choose from. "We will have plenty of time to discuss this topic and more at length in the days and weeks to come," the Baron remarked as he took a lusty gulp from his wine goblet without tearing his eyes away from mine.

"Please eat and drink your fill. Also, do not be embarrassed at the differences in dining manners. We understand the necessity of these differences. After all, as my new employees, all of you will be treated with fairness and compensated justly over the course of your tenure with me.

I could hardly believe our good fortune. After all the suffering and heartache we have had to endure in our lives. I looked at Jessie who was whimsically giving her best impression of a lady eating soup and sipping her red wine. I glanced over to Colette whose gaze darted down to her soup coyly just as our eyes meet.

Baron Reichstall then clapped his hands again, "Please fetch the curtain," he said to one of the swarthy attendants wearing a turban standing nearby. The man disappeared into the rear door and very soon reappeared with another gentleman with red curly hair that resembled the whites who operated the mill during harvest and sold produce and Souse meat to the Negroes in the slave quarter of Thibodeaux Parish. The attendants then proceeded to stretch a black satin sheet between myself and the rest of the table with the two men positioned facing away from me and my pile of food.

"Please dispatch this dinner in your customary fashion. I want your experience under my employ to be as unencumbered as can be so please, eat and drink until you are content, and we shall talk more history and business in the hours and days to come," the Baron said to me through the curtain.

I looked down at the rich, savory meat and the metallic smell of the fresh warm blood accosted my senses again. I could no longer contain my hunger. The sound of crunching bone and slurping blood was all that was heard between short breaths of air from behind the partition. The soft bloody meat was like nothing I had ever experienced before. I was eating like a prisoner on his first day of pardon. My fangs extended involuntarily reacting

102

to my hunger. I gorged myself, my bloody face and hands well hidden behind my veil of privacy provided by our new master. I dropped all pretenses, and I made short work of the stack of raw meat. My lack of table etiquette caused my attendants to become squeamish as the black satin cloth they held began trembling. I force myself to breathe between huge bites. My gut stretches to its limits to meet the demands of my self-indulgent behavior, and a sensation that has eluded me for my entire life fell over me: gratitude.

I heard Jessie speaking apologetically to Baron Reichstall about my behavior saying, "Dat boy ain't et lak dat since marse Bouton had to shot dat young mare on a count it had cum dine wit de loc jaw. He cided to let dat fool there have 'er fo' his suppa' 'stead of da possum and coon meat he was use ta etin. He dragged dat mare behin' de shed and you aint even hea no holling from dat hoss. All use heard wuz teef nashin', bones brekin' an' beaucoup skin a tearin."

As she trailed off, "L'homme Crocodile" followed the sweet voice of Colette to punctuate Jessie's outburst.

"Das is name child, I plumb fu'got! Das what us really call de boy. Heh heh, Lawd Jesus das 'is name!" Jessie cackled.

"With all due respect, madam," Reichstall interjected, "this man sits as far above humans as we sit above sheep and cattle. A species so magnificently rare that it was thought to exist only in mythology but somehow has permeated throughout all cultures and regions of the earth. In my many years spent doing anthropological research, I kept coming across the same legends and accounts of tribes dedicated to the bat spirit. Noble and revered rulers of the night that kept the balance of power within the earth realm before the great deluge."

An elderly but spry black man wearing white gloves and long grey ponytail appeared from the doors at the rear of the room and walked directly towards me carrying a basin of water which he placed in front of me and gestured for me to rinse the blood from my face and hands. I do as instructed, clouding the water in the bowl and staining the bowl bright red. The elderly black man yanked a large white linen handkerchief from the inside of his coat and thrust it in my face to wipe the remaining blood from

103

my visage. The two men holding the black cloth between myself and the rest of the dinner party were visibly shaken by my uncouth dining habits. I snuck a look up at their once stoic faces, now aghast with revulsion at what they just witnessed.

"BL-E-E-E-R-R-G"!…. I reflexively let out a huge belch that echoed in the room and immediately, I tried to shrink into my chair and disappear from embarrassment.

"Pawdon yo'self, boy!" Jessie scolds. "You know I tawt you mo' manuz' dan dat," chuckling to herself she then turned to address Baron Reichstall. "You haf' to 'scuse dat chile on da coun' a he aint the shahpess knife in da draw'. But he got a heart a' peo' gol'! An' he suhtin'ly mean well," Jessie explained.

Baron Reichstall takes a sip of his red wine and wipes his lips with his napkin before he addresses Jessie with a straight face. "That sound comes as gentle music to my ears, Jessica. A physical manifestation of a man's satisfaction with his meal. A badge of honor, and nothing to be reprimanded about."

After satiating myself with raw meat and two goblets full of that enchanting blood, the two curtain attendants removed my barrier and disappeared as quickly as they had appeared behind one of the many doors to the dining room. I sat quietly listening to the other guests at the table and rubbing the newly healed skin on my unshackled wrists. The conversations involved mainly Baron Reichstall and Jessie, bantering between each other about various topics.

Although a slave and not 'officially' allowed to read, Jessie would pick up things from being privy to the bed chambers and sitting rooms of the slave owners. White people had the tendency to speak frankly about their affairs in front of Negroes without a second thought that their servants who seemed dull and uninterested would really be listening keenly and intently and memorizing every word and detail so they can relate whatever important information or news there might be regarding their futures and the future of the plantation to the rest of the servant class. Jessie was a master of this deception because of her loud, seemingly uncontrollable, unfiltered

104

opinionated way. Everyday white people saw her as the 'quintessential mammy' and did not give her antics or anything she said or did a second thought. As a matter of fact, if she did not act that way, they would more than likely question her health and mental state. If anything, the white people felt comfortable airing out their business in front of her. At times, they would even confide in her their secrets, and solicit her advice in matters of the heart or even matters concerning the business of the plantation.

I sat absorbing the sights, sounds, and smells of our new unbelievable circumstances as the rest of the dinner party were finishing their dessert course when Jessie said, "Lawd I shole hope my po mammie is lookin' don on me an' her gran'chile an' is a-smilin sho nuff, he he," she chuckled as she wiped her mouth on her napkin before placing it in the bowl in front of her and leaning satisfactorily back in her chair and rubbing her corset restricted belly.

Colette uncharacteristically even squeaked out her own approving, "hallelujah" as she beamed across the table at her mother and then looked toward me with a beautiful grin of contentment. Baron Reichstall clapped his hands again and the servants swarmed the table, removing plates and silverware while depositing steaming hot cups of tea in front of each guest. Another large goblet filled with the delicious blood from earlier was placed in front of me in kind. The red liquid was still pulsing and warm. It had to be from a freshly slaughtered young animal due to its purity and crispness. It was basically potable life enshrouding my entire body with a blissful sensation after every gulp. I felt intoxicated as I guzzled it down.

Baron Reichstall spoke up. "As you can see, I prefer to surround myself with a variety of servants who are unique in their own way. From Circassia to the Fiji Islands, whatever exotic setting I found myself in, my philanthropic efforts would always be rewarded with my pick of the local gentry as a show of fealty and good will between myself and the many chieftains and spiritual leaders of the various places I visit. When I am traveling out of the country or indisposed on business in London or Manchester, most of my employees here are able to earn money for themselves in the town or on the wharf. As you can see, it is a far cry from the indigo and rice plantations that you lot were recently accustomed to," finished Reichstall.

"Praise de Lawd tuh dat," shouted Jessie, laughing and slamming her heavy mitt on the table in front of her for emphasis, causing the teacups and spoons on the table to 'PLINK' together loudly. "We cain't thank yuh 'nough fa tekkin us 'way from det hellish plantation. I hope I'se neva haf tu wuk thew 'nother roulaison in my life! You aint neva gonna 'gret wut you dun did fuh us, sho as you is bone!" promised Jessie, looking directly into the eyes of Reichstall, something I had yet to do. She was sure to hold her gaze with his as if to say that *on this point I am being sincere*. Colette began nodding emphatically to co-sign the sincerity behind Jessie's words.

Reichstall raised his glass and said, "To new beginnings!"

 To which we each raised our glasses and drank. Shortly after our toast, the Baron bids us adieu and exited through a door on the east wall of the huge room. Gradually we all retired to our respective quarters. The ladies were escorted back to their rooms by one of the tall curly haired white women. I was escorted back to my room by the exotic looking Megumi who Reichstall referred to as being something called Japanese.

The next few days, Jessie and Colette were shown the entire campus and given tasks in the kitchen and housekeeping service respectively. I remained in my room during the days and I was assigned to manual labor work that could be done at night. The groundskeepers would show me my duties using a lantern which included chopping firewood and removing large stones from one area of the grounds and transporting them down to the riverbank to serve as a homemade levee against the occasional swelling of the River Orwell. Since there was an ongoing war with France there were armed guards everywhere. I was always accompanied by a small regiment of Colonel Berners' men whenever I was working on the grounds around the main estate.

It was the first night of the full moon and Jessie, Colette and I had already been a month in England. The climate was very different from Louisiana. Even though it was almost June when we arrived, the weather consisted of mild heat during the day and cool to moderate nights. The fog rolled off the river creating a very thick veil that added to the already ominous mood of the evening. Earlier that same night while I was replenishing the firewood at the back door of the kitchen, I was briefly able to talk to Jessie and listen to some of the latest gossip about what she had seen and heard during her tenure in the cookhouse and guest dining hall. Jessie narrated a tale of working with strange foreigners and cooking for and serving a captivating array of lavishly dressed men and women of all ages, wearing flamboyant wigs and heavy face paint and perfumes. Jessie would go on and on about the endless amounts of food they were required to serve at these sumptuous dinners and how she was learning to prepare all manner of delicacies that we never heard of in Louisiana, such as roast pheasant, venison pie, and deviled kidneys.

"I wouldn't reckon a wah's goin' on out dere way dey be carryin' on, drankin' wine an' spirits de whole night gettin' full a' *Dyab." [Devil] Jessie says in a whisper so as not to be heard. "Wukin' ova heah so fah way from de guest kwatus, I harley eva' sees Lettie anymo'."

It was becoming increasingly rare for me to see Colette also. During that first week in Reichstall's castle, our paths would cross often as she was bringing linens or toiletries to or from the guest cottages and the main building. I would stare at her until she noticed my presence, our eyes would meet, and she would wave at me and smile, and I would raise and lower my hand quickly in response. She would then bounce away happily and continue with whatever her housekeeping duties entailed. I had yet to lay eyes on Baron Reichstall since that unforgettable first night and that amazing dinner. Jessie also mentioned that she had not spotted him at any of the dinners herself since that night even though he must have been present to have been hosting the parties he held almost weekly.

Just then Jessie jumped with a start as a bell rang from inside the kitchen. "I'se bin sot out heah, runnin my mouf, and plum forgot we was s'posed tuh be learnin' bite cookin' dem li'l chickens lak we et on dat fust night." Jessie touched my shoulder as she turned to go.

I grunted my goodbye to Jessie and headed out to complete my nocturnal chores. Once the sun had dropped below the horizon, I was able to remove my burlap hood as I walked toward the front of the main house to my usual spot where I check in with the overseer/ groundsman. He was a medium height, pale, thin man with a cockney accent named Richard Mathew. My work at Reichstall's estate began a full three days after our arrival. It was the only time Mathew spoke to me directly about what was required of me in the service of the baron. Each subsequent night, Mathew would have one of the other servants train me on whatever task was required of me that evening. Typically, Mathew used one or two of the teenage male servants to carry torches or oil lamps for him as he supervised my work. Due to the unrest associated with the conflict with France and Colonel Berners' mandate to maintain a security detail near me at all times, our work party was usually accompanied by a regiment of anywhere between three and four soldiers as escorts. This night for some reason, we were accompanied by an additional garrison of twelve or so men in addition to the normal handful of soldiers that accompanied me at my night work of wood chopping and boulder moving. Over the previous few weeks, I had been welcomed and accepted by seemingly everyone I encountered. As long as the work got done, we were given Sundays off, and there was always more than enough food for all the hands to eat their fill without stealing from each other or stealing from the kitchen when the dinner slop provided was not quite enough.

That night, I was carrying a particularly heavy boulder towards the shoreline of the river when the thought crossed my mind that the extra reinforcements were retained in response to some specific threats made against the Baron and his estate, and that the additional security measures were being taken to protect myself and others that the Baron held dear. The smell of gunpowder coming from the soldiers' rifles sat heavy in the foggy air and that is when I noticed that the men who were positioned around the levee where I do most of my work had formed a semicircle around me with only the rushing river to my back. The other half of the men seemed to have established a sort of human wall just before the shore path was swallowed by the forest between Woolverstone Estate and the river. I placed my boulder down amongst a growing pile of rocks that was being installed as a new enlargement of the previous levee. As I walked slowly back toward the area of the woods where we had been quarrying the rocks, I observed that all the soldiers were holding their rifles out in front of them tonight instead of shouldering them casually or using them as a prop to lean on. The restless demeanor of the group was creating anxiousness and tension that triggered the nerves in my stomach to begin churning involuntarily. This was the first time since I had been living and working at the manor that I had felt any obvious animosity towards my person.

I committed myself to being as docile and timid as I could possibly be from the moment we landed in England. I was determined to please my new master to ensure that Jesse and Colette would be kept safe and cheerful in their new home thousands of miles from their country of origin. I was racking my brain trying to recall if I had said or done anything too bold or offensive that might be misconstrued as me being ungrateful or unhappy. I mentally tried to retrace my steps and actions over the last few days and weeks, but nothing in particular stood out in my mind as being the reason for the heightened scrutiny I seemed to be receiving. Tonight, every soldier seemed to be monitoring my every move. Odd, since for the last two weeks it seemed as if everyone had gotten used to my presence. The guards acted as if being my 'security' detail was an extremely boring and low rank assignment. Watching a slave carry stones and chop and stack lumber for hours on end in the cool summer night air was not what most of these men who were either current or former British Special Forces had in mind as being fulfilling employment.

My status as a slave was never in question but overall, my experience here at Woolverstone Manor has been nothing but paradise in comparison to the misery I endured as a slave everywhere else in the world. Tonight, something of that oppressive, depressing feeling was slowly creeping its way back into my world. The gradually building fog seemed indicative of the ominous mood that was bubbling just beneath the surface.

I noticed that Mr. Mathew, who tended to be very jovial and talkative while everyone else worked, was very quiet and pensive tonight. Normally he droned on and on about British politics and how the price of tobacco and tea have gone through the roof since the war began. He would either talk to the servants holding the lanterns or some of the soldiers that were our nightly escorts, and his loud, cockney voice would be the background noise to my nightly duties. Mathew was standing near a large elm tree still holding his own lantern in one hand and checking his pocket watch with his other hand. Normally Mathew would make a small campfire, and he and a couple of the more regular soldiers would roast rabbit or fish for a meal overnight. Mathew would always use those lunch breaks to go into

109

full-fledged storyteller mode and would divulge stories about his life as a younger man in the service of some notorious privateers in the Mediterranean Sea. But this night, Mathew was solemn and pensive, pacing back and forth in the dark under a leafy elm tree with a worried look on his face, periodically glancing back down the path toward Woolverstone Manor but never looking over at me as I worked.

It must have been near midnight when I heard a brief guttural scream coming from the direction of the manor. A noise too low and too far away for human ears, but my ears caught the unmistakable sound of anguish. Something in the tone of the voice shook me to my core. I stopped walking with my boulder and glanced around, surveying the soldiers and Mr. Mathew, who looked down to check his pocket watch just as our eyes met. He knew something and the reason for this large entourage of soldiers had something to do with what was going on back at the house.

They were purposely stalling me…. but for what. I placed another large boulder which caused me to have to kneel to lower the heavy stone from my shoulders without making a clatter. The behavior of Mr. Mathew and the soldiers coupled with the mysterious scream I know I just heard sent my mind racing. What should I do? Leaving in the middle of the night's work to travel back to the manor to check on things was an impossibility for sure. Even forming the words and having the gumption to ask Mathew's permission to check on things at the manor was inconceivable. I tried to calm my mind and dismiss the sound and the evidence before me, but instinctively I could feel that there was something very strange about tonight. Time was running out for whomever it was that was feeling pain enough to cry out like that at this hour.

My breathing started to quicken and I felt as if I was being forced to make a decision. Colette's face wearing a frown flashed in my mind and before I could consciously register my actions, I exploded from my position and the ground below me shreds as my boots searched for traction and dug into the soil. As I pivoted away from the riverbank towards the path back to Woolverstone, time stood still for a moment. My sudden movements caught the soldiers nearest me off guard and by the time their first fusillade came, I had reached the edge of the forest. I was well past their line of defense and near the mouth of the path where the remaining regiment of soldiers and mercenaries were gathered and were now drawing down on and firing at me. I dropped to all fours and galloped from side to side to avoid their bullets.

Any musket fire other than a direct hit to the face would have been ineffective anyway because my adrenalin was pumping hard, and I was absolutely determined to make it back to that house to check on my friends. I prayed that I was not overreacting but my gut told me something was seriously wrong. I needed to be sure that my friends were not in danger. I will deal with whatever consequences may result from my actions, but I made a solemn vow to myself on the journey over to this country that I would tear down heaven and hell to protect those two women.

I plowed into the first soldier blocking the path and threw him into another man frantically reloading his weapon. I grabbed a third man and swung him by his shoulders around and into a group of soldiers approaching from my rear who toppled backwards from the impact of my human projectile. I am at too close a range for them to fire effectively and most had not had the chance to reload their muskets, so I blasted through the rest of the half dozen or so men on the road, knocking them about and sending them flying out of my path. Once through the blockade, I resumed bipedal running as the crack of muskets followed the sensation of bullets whizzing past me as I sprang headlong down the lane… past the garden… through the rear courtyard… past the guest quarters. In my agitated state, I mindlessly ran straight towards the kitchen even though it was well past midnight, and it was highly unlikely that Jessie would still be there because she would normally have long been finished with the cleaning by now.

As I flung open the side door to the cookhouse, slamming it into the wall, the startled kitchen help all jumped with a start and stared at me wide eyed and frozen as if they were all in on this cruel gag and now the jig was up. I looked around the room wildly and then stopped to snort the air.

Blood.

Human blood.

The smell was below us. I dashed out of the room and back into the courtyard towards the root cellar, tore open the locked doors and rushed down the stairs but the smell of the blood seemed to be getting more faint. I sped back to the kitchen and grabbed the night cook, a short man with slits for eyes and a long black ponytail which I use to lift him into the air.

"WHERE?!" I growled at the terrified man who shakily pointed to the door leading to the main dining hall and the adjacent chapel.

I dropped the man in a heap on the floor and crashed through the locked door to the main dining hall. To my surprise it was unguarded and empty, but all the torches and candles were burning as if in anticipation of a dinner service. The aroma of blood came from behind a large ornate door in the back of the room. I was told by Jessie that it led to a chapel where in her words "folks use ta be conjuring haints". From where she got this information I did not know. This place had long ago been a site Druidic priests used for rituals to their gods. Once the Reichstall family purchased the land and property and built the monolithic estate around it, there were rumors that the rituals were resurrected and were undoubtedly terrifyingly sinister.

I smash my shoulder into the locked heavy oak door, but the iron hinges and multiple deadbolts hold fast against my initial onslaught. I took a few steps back and began to slam my shoulder against the door repeatedly. Each time, the iron hinges sing within the stone frame and loosen ever so slightly with each barrage. I ran away from the door to the middle of the room and slid to a stop, dropping to all fours to create friction. I turned and ran full speed toward the door. I leapt into the air with both feet extended out in front of me, slamming into the door with my full force, which splintered the thick wood around the hinges and bent the deadbolts. The door landed flat on the ground with a very loud 'Whoomp' that echoed through the castle. My boots ruptured and were torn apart when they impacted the door, so I scrambled to my bare feet, ready for whatever might come next.

To my astonishment, Baron Reichstall was there, wearing a robe and blood-covered apron, holding a bloody knife. He was standing next to a wooden platform, and on it was a horribly mutilated, decapitated body of a large woman with various symbols carved into her flesh. The recognizable smell of the woman's skin caused me to go into panic mode, and my body was frozen from the shock. It cannot be her, there are plenty of other Negro women here that this man could have murdered, but not her. Not this again.

Reichstall's mouth was moving. He was staring directly at me saying something, but I was too traumatized to hear what it was. After a few moments, I perceived him speaking some foreign language in which he kept repeating the same phrase repeatedly. I snapped to reality and regained my focus. I must kill this man if it be my final act upon this earth. A fury inside me began to build in the pit of my core, and the heat of my blood gave rise to cold beads of sweat on my skin. Just as I was about to pounce and eviscerate every molecule of this person, something like an invisible chain clamped around my entire body holding me stock-still in my spot. My muscles strained mightily to make even the slightest movement against this unseen foe.

"Eureka!!! shouted Reichstall, I have conquered the abyss, and now the devil himself is mine to control!"

As I flexed and struggled against my invisible bonds, my eyes began to fill with moisture. I did not want to believe that I would never hear another one of Jessie's "Lawd ham mussy's" again and large heavy tears reluctantly begin to fall from my eyes.

"WHHHYYYYYYY"!!!!

I screamed, my voice speaking not to Reichstall, but to address the heavens directly.

Baron Reichstall's steel blue eyes glared down his cruel nose and his mouth formed a sickening sneer.

"Why? Why, you ask? Why does anyone do anything? The very reason you are not able to move despite all your incredible strength and speed and supposed immortality. All that might is nothing compared to the demonic power that rests between dimensions in the spirit realm. An overwhelming power that can be manifested through the unique vibrations in the substance that runs through the veins and arteries of all creatures on this godforsaken rock.

You see, I have researched and studied alchemy and sought out the elusive philosopher's stone. I have traveled around the globe searching for answers to the mysteries of the universe interpreted through archaeology,

113

magic, and astrology. Acquiring from the celestial intelligences of the cosmos all the secrets from the most brilliant shamans and mystics my wealth could afford an audience with. I learned that the most powerful of ceremonial magic on this plane involved the utilization of blood.

The rites needed to summon and exorcize demons became my main focus, and I was compelled by my ancestry to apply my knowledge practically for the sake and welfare of my family's prosperity for a thousand generations in the future. While conducting my experiments on all manner of creatures, I discovered that the most compelling incantations occurred when necromancy was performed with the blood of the African woman. The potency of the ritual is increased exponentially if the cause of death is a traumatic or violent one. The woman's heart races, her body produces adrenal enzymes that flood into the subject's organs and endocrine system due to the severe emotional distress..."

The Baron looked down at the mutilated body with a depraved smile and continued, "She was made to watch her own feet be devoured by hogs, and I must say, the screams that woman emitted were some of the most shrill and pitiful noises I have ever heard. My, how they like to call Jesus' name. All that cheeky talk she was known for vanished in an instant once she surmised that the pleasant treatment and fineries that she had been experiencing under my employ were nothing more than a charade that had all been constructed for this very night. The night of the blood moon." Reichstall touches his brow as if recalling a lovely Sunday morning. "The look on her face was priceless when I told her that her torture and eventual death was a necessary sacrifice in order to gain absolute control over a living weapon like you. This particular incantation would not have worked without the fresh blood of someone emotionally linked to the target. The energy infused within that hot primordial native blood, flowing out of those black veins instantly amplifies the magic into such a compelling force that one could easily use it to topple mountains."

My breathing was ragged, my nails and teeth began to extend and grow respectively as the hair on my entire body bristled like a porcupine. My muscles began to tense and bulge, stretching the fabric and breaking the inner seams of the fine cotton shirt and trousers I was wearing. Not wanting to believe what this man was saying to me, I closed my eyes and grinded my teeth in vexation. The rage in the core of my being was a dagger in my soul and agony began to build so rapidly I felt as if my heart would explode from my chest. A transformation was taking place inside my body. It felt like another layer of my souls had been peeled away... something familiar but alien and foreign at the same time awoke in my conscious existence. Something that lay dormant until this moment. This betrayal by Baron Reichstall was the deepest hurt I have felt since my mother was taken from me.

This betrayal involved people that had grown personally dear to me, who trusted me to protect them, and I was fooled into letting my guard down. I was the very reason that they were brought here, and to have them be destroyed and dissected like vermin after being teased with hope for a truly better life was unforgivable.

It was at this moment that the giant doorman Albert appeared, needing to bend down slightly as he walked through the doorway behind the altar next to Reichstall. Albert took a position next to the altar, and it was then that I could see that he was carrying the decapitated head of Jessie in his massive right hand like it was an apple. His face was expressionless as he stretched his long arm toward me so I could see the full horror of Jessie's once smiling vibrant face now twisted and contorted, tongue lolling disgustingly from her mouth. Her once beautiful black and silver hair was matted and caked with blood and viscera. Her once caring eyes now bulging and straining with a look of sheer terror forever frozen on her countenance, lamenting the despicable fate she met at the hands of these demons.

My body moved before my brain knew what was happening, and I broke free from the invisible grip around me through blind force of will. I was instantly airborne, leaping across 40 feet of the banquet hall at Reichstall and the giant Albert. Just before I reached the altar, Baron Reichstall's hand went up, and I was somehow suspended in mid-air less than a meter from the altar where the pair and Jessie's body lay. I strained and twisted with all my might to free myself, but it felt as if the air itself had again formed into a gigantic

115

hand or living chains to bind me in place. I was suspended at least two meters off the ground, hanging in midair, under the complete control of Reichstall.

"Binding magic was a craft I excelled at from the beginning of my tutelage." the Baron says as he visibly struggles through his words. His raised fists shake as I strain against his magical bonds. "I-I-It involves a summoning of invisible creatures that are composed of dead souls that can manifest as hands to hold or push things. A form of magic originally perfected by the ancient order of Saturnalia and has been used by the illumined class throughout the ages. As I told you that first night you arrived... the only thing in this world more valuable than silver and gold is information. And the only substance comparable in value to information is time."

He swung his wrist and tightened his fist which caused my arms and hands to be forced to my side and my legs straighten involuntarily. I was seething with anger, and I flexed every sinew in my body against my invisible foe. With each passing second, I could feel that my efforts were causing whatever was binding me to strain desperately in an attempt to match my force.

The Baron's fist began shaking reflexively while trying to maintain his ghoulish restraints. "Please calm down before the same fate befalls the other wench you're traveling with," Reichstall threatened in as calm a tone as he could achieve under the stress he was experiencing.

At the thought of Colette being subjected to the same fate, I tried to calm down, but the monster borne of pure hatred and hidden within my heart had already escaped and began to seep into my very atoms. It was becoming extremely difficult to maintain my senses. I tried to preserve my sanity by taking shallow breaths as Reichstall began to speak again.

"The man before you," Reichstall nodded to the black giant, "whom you've come to know affectionately as 'Albert' was once a proud Ashanti warrior of unsurpassed skill and military prowess. On the battlefield, he was undefeated and nigh unstoppable when fighting at full capacity. I lost many good men invading his village and nearly lost my own life to this tower of a man when I faced off against him. For you see, my knowledge of alchemical magic was still fresh, and I had not the competency and mastery that I wield today. But now, Albert has learned to respect me as a most powerful witch doctor, and it is his custom to obey the will of the powerful."

Still visibly straining, Reichstall motioned to Albert with his other hand. Albert placed Jessie's severed head onto a small stone table next to the Baron Reichstall who took a seat in a large chair behind the altar. Albert then walked over and opened a chest near the wall behind the chair and pulled out the heavy iron anchor chains that I wore upon my arrival at the castle. As Albert approached me, I could see that his eyes were dull and glassy. He seemed to be completely unconscious of his movement.

As Albert began to robotically clamp the irons onto my legs, Baron Reichstall began again. "You see my friend I would like for us to preserve our working relationship with each other. The terms of which being that I trade the life of that wench you love so dearly for your services. It is dreadfully important that you understand the absolute severity of the situation. My family's fortune was built upon banking and finance, and the glue needed to be successful at those businesses hinges on information, and more importantly, time. Meaning speed of information. That is why we also established and maintain one of the fastest coachmen courier services in the world, rivaled only by the Royal Postal Service. In our present situation, British and Prussian forces are trying to quell a resurgence of the French, and that blasted Napoleon is running roughshod through Belgium. The outcome of this war will determine who will emerge as the leading power in Europe. Whether Britain and the allied forces win or lose is of no consequence to us. The value here lies in knowing the outcome first so we can control the flow of information for the benefit of the family and our vision for this world."

Albert returned to the chest and produced a pair of wrist shackles and slowly turned to approach again to complete my binding. Reichstall's hand was straining terribly now. The shaking of his arm was causing a vibrato in his voice as he tried to speak to me while still holding me under his spell. The more time that passed required the Baron to exert more concentration on his part to maintain his hold over me now that my rage was in full bloom at the sight and smell of poor sweet Jessie's severed head. My arms began to break their invisible captors and slowly rise from my side as Baron Reichstall continued speaking.

"T-t-t-hat is where your speed comes into my plan." He stuttered uncontrollably now, attempting unsuccessfully to maintain his composure. "Over t-t-the next few d-d-days, the news from the battlefront will be delivered, and reliable s-s-sources point to the fighting reaching a c-c-c-climax soon. Whatever the outcome, the markets w-w-w-will b-b-b-be thrown into turmoil. Vast fortunes stand to ch-ch ch-change hands depending on the results. I want you to w-w-w-wait at a storehouse near the harbor that I own, and when the n-n-n-news from the Belgian front is delivered at the usual sh-sh-sh-shipping post, I want you to run the eighty miles as fast as you can to deliver a personal message from the warfront to the stock exchange in London before dawn. If y-y-you are successful a-a-a-and are able to return here swiftly and stealthily enough so no connection is m-m-m-made with my courier service and your movements, then I will release you and the wench unfettered and unharmed. I will also provide a ship for s-s-s- safe passage back to the c-c-c-c-colonies with fu fu-fu-full manumission pap-p-p-pers and a substantial stipend as a t-t-t-t-token payment for the blood of this vulgar wench."

At the mention of Jessie, I flexed hard against the invisible bindings, pushing against them with all my might and causing Baron Reichstall's invisible hold on me to break completely. Reichstall tumbled backwards and lowered his hands, grabbing the armrests of the chair to maintain his balance. This in turn dissolved his hold over me and dropped me to the marble slab floor. I scrambled to my feet and took a step towards Reichstall now leaning forward in his chair, holding his head between his hands, massaging his temples with his palms, when Albert's fist which was the size of my skull crashes into the side of my face sending me flying head over heels into the wall behind me. The strength of that punch being imbued with some otherworldly power in addition to his own natural brawn stunned me for a few seconds, just long enough for Baron Reichstall to begin chanting again to try and reestablish his magic and grab me with his invisible tentacles again.

"I will only warn you one more time that any unnecessary outbursts by you will spell the end for the wench for whom you pine so openly for, so I suggest you calm down," cautioned Reichstall. "Albert, bring me your handkerchief."

Albert turned and walked towards the Baron, reaching into his breast pocket with his massive left hand, his right arm hung limp from being shattered by the blow to my face. So deep in the trance, the pain of his broken fist does not register for him. I was beyond angry and had crossed into furious mode. I was incapable of stopping now. The weak hold that Reichstall had over me allowed me to move as if in slow motion towards him and Albert. The leg irons now attached added another level of difficulty as I gradually made my approach. With every step, his spell became weaker and weaker.

Reichstall stood there in disbelief and held the handkerchief to his bleeding nose with his left hand and clutched his magic right hand into an impossibly tight fist. His eyes blazed with fear as he desperately tried to invoke the binding spell again by chanting the main phrases over and over. He had shed all his pretentious and pseudo-regal manner now as his eyes bulged, sweat poured down his face and spit flew from his mouth as frustration mounts at his inability to control my approach.

"Albert!!!" yelled Reichstall. Albert spun deftly on his heels, and just as I reached the altar, he pulled back his huge left hand to slam a colossal haymaker into my battered face. The massive force of Albert's left hook cleaves the air, and just before it connects, it is met with the equal and overwhelming force of the palm of my hand. The impact of the blow gusts the air of the chamber, and a 'crack' sounding like splintering wood is heard. My index finger and thumb were broken, but Albert? My rage combined with my dense bone structure withstood his death blow, however it caused his entire wrist bone and forearm to shatter from the impact. His arm hung comically limp as he mindlessly attempted to kick me or move in close enough to deliver a head butt or bite me. The deep trance not only rendered Albert completely obedient It made his body impervious to pain as well, although it greatly diminished his ability to fight. I dodged his attacks easily.

119

Reichstall finally recognized that he overestimated his knowledge of spell casting and that he would soon lose what little control he still had. He used the fight between Albert and I as an opportunity to run to the back of the room and escape through one of the side doors, slamming and locking it behind him.

I dodged a kick from Albert and with the back of my right fist, I viciously slammed into his jaw breaking it and sending him down hard to the stone slab floor knocking him out cold. I leapt over the huge unconscious body and took one more look at Jessie's severed head as I ran towards the large oak door Reichstall fled through. With three consecutive heavy kicks, the hinges broke loose from the stone, and the door fell with a *'THOOM'* of dust and splintering stone and wood.

BLAM!

BLAM!

BLAM!

I was met by three gunshots, all of which I dodged with incredible speed. I lunged at one of the mercenaries hired personally by Reichstall as his last resort bodyguards. This was a wall of a man with scruffy facial hair and a scar across his right eye which was as pale as mine. I attacked in the brief second between the man firing his first weapon and trying to cock a second pistol, chomping down hard on the carotid artery in his neck. The blood spurting from his arteries sprayed my face and eyes. I could taste the foul swill this bastard drank to give him the courage to beat defenseless women and fight monsters like me. I tossed his lifeless body against the wall which it hit with a 'thud' and fell in a clump onto the floor.

It had been a long time since I tasted warm human blood. My God.... even blood from an alcoholic goon produces a powerful sensation. A life contained in that red substance, transferable and intoxicating, the human equivalent of drinking a vintage wine.

120

"YOU BLOODY BLACK MONSTER!!!"

I spun around to face two other members of Reichstall's personal bodyguard unit.

BLAM!!

BLAM!!

They both fired their guns at me and a bullet hit my left shoulder and bounced off the bone while another whizzed by inches from my face. I charged at the man on my right before he could reach for another pistol tucked in his waistband and snatched him up by the left ankle and slammed his body to the ground like a wet rag. Blood and brain matter sprayed out as his skull yielded its contents onto the stone floor. I scurried on all fours dragging the weight of the cannon balls shackled to my feet around to the man now leveling a pistol style crossbow.

"DIE NIGGER!"

The arrow fired but missed me by inches. I could smell the poison it was laced with. Without hesitation the man pulled his pistol from its holster and fired a shot. My speed put me in his face as the gun flash was still clearing the muzzle of the gun. The ball glanced off my right cheekbone, splattering blood in my eye. My left hand slammed his weapon-wielding hand against the wall, shattering the bones in his forearm.

"AAAAGH"

The man screamed just as I grabbed him with my right and lifted him by the neck. Sweat poured down his bald head as he flailed his arms and legs in the death throes of his final moments.

I had not felt this sensation in a decade. The bloodlust was off the charts. I looked up at the man who still wore a defiant scowl even as I squeezed the very life out of him. As his eyes bulged out of their sockets and his nose and ears began to bleed from the pressure I was hit with the faint smell of Colette.

"STOP THIS!!!"

Baron Reichstall boomed over the pulse of adrenaline and blood in my ears just as I am about to rip this scumbag's throat out. I looked behind me to see Baron Reichstall emerging from another door holding a pistol to Colette's head. Behind him was another tall fat ogre of a man with red hair hanging to his shoulders and a long red beard, wearing a suit of armor complete with helmet. His aura smacked of something ominous. A vibration that I had not experienced since the days of living in San Domingue when the conjuring Elders were called to banish an evil spirit that had inhabited some poor unsuspecting soul. It was difficult to see the man's face beyond the helmet he wore but his eyes bore no emotion whatsoever, much like Albert's.

"Please let Jonathan go or I will blow this wench's head off right here and bloody now" said Baron Reichstall, grinning malignantly.

I released the mercenary's throat. He dropped to the floor, flopping like a fish and writhing in pain while holding his crushed right hand with his good hand and gasping for air.

"I understand your anger over Jessica's death", Still holding the pistol to Colette's temple, Reichstall takes a few steps into the room followed by his fearsome bodyguard.

"Our ties to the weak will always stand as stumbling blocks to our path to enlightenment. In another world we could have been partners. If I had my druthers, I would have liked for you and I to come to a mutually beneficial agreement concerning your employment, preferably one without coercion. But as a businessman, I have found time and again that allowing

122

circumstances to unfold without direction is unwise and ultimately bad for trade. I was really hoping the blood ritual with that talkative wench would be enough to make you my mindless servant like Albert and the others. You proved to be more powerful than you yourself even realize. I knew it was unwise to allow you to exist without some type of guarantee to restrain your behavior."

Nodding to Colette, "this girl was always to be my insurance in case of a miscalculation on my part. I do hate to stoop to such vulgar tactics but the window for me to implement my plans successfully will be closing soon. I require you to perform one simple task. Upon completion of which I will render you and your friend here clear of your obligations toward us, and you will be able to count yourselves among the ranks of the free Negroes of the United States."

I could hear Colette's frightened heartbeat thumping loudly over Baron Reichstall's speech. He repositioned the gun to the small of her back holding tight to her arm with his left hand and stepped back to stand next to the man in the suit of armor who had not moved a muscle since he walked through the door. I was less than twelve feet from the group, and my rage for Jessie's murder was fueling my desire for blood. The pain of involving the only people on this planet that meant anything to me was tearing me apart.

"I don't know if you've had time to really reflect on why you are here and how I know who and what you are, began Reichstall, "but think of yourselves as being specially commissioned for service in my family's most esteemed employ. And I will be the first to say that it is an honor to have a being such as yourself in my charge."

The sound of his smug voice was grating my ears. Every syllable I allowed from his filthy mouth felt like a knife in my heart. My fury and frustration grew to be irrepressible over the knowledge that a sweet, beautiful woman died at the hands of this barbaric bastard in a misguided attempt to control me.

"Let...her...go!..."

I snarled out slowly and gruffly as if a grizzly bear were taught parts of the English language and decided to test out some of the words it knew. I was seething with indignation. My chest was heaving with shaky breath as I stared directly into Colette's eyes. The once hopeful eyes that I promised to protect now terror- stricken and reliving all the pain she had been forced to endure since childhood. With all my being, I wanted to convey to her that everything was going to be fine, and that whatever happened, I was going to avenge Jessie and kill every last one of these fucking bastards, doing to them tenfold times worse than what they did to her.

"Unfortunately, old chum, I cannot let her go. As I said I am a businessman, and I need this wench as leverage." At this, Baron Reichstall tucked his gun into a side holster while still holding on to Colette's right arm, twisting it behind her in a restraint maneuver.

Again, he flashed an evil smile.

"You see, I was privy to the research of my dear family friend and colleague Count Constantine De Volney and was instrumental in pressing him into the service of General Bonaparte and the First French Empire. His essays and writings first whet my appetite for the occult with his stories regaling the Heptamaron, The Lemegeton , Peter of Abano, and ancient magicians and sorcerers of the days of Isis and Osiris, and the connection between our world and the spiritual ether of the netherworld. Many of the royal and aristocratic families across the planet share the common thread of being high level initiates of supreme wisdom and knowledge that afforded them certain insights or influence over mortal men. I decided to travel to Egypt and the Sudan on my own to study and research the rituals and incantations I needed to invoke that would bring myself and my family to the pinnacle of wealth and influence. It was during this time that I spent inside the forbidden tombs of forgotten queens and pharaohs that I came across information regarding, fairies, pygmies, gnomes, dryads, nymphs, dragons and all manner of vile and wondrous creatures. I also came across information about vampires."

At that word, I leapt towards the trio, my first thought being to grab Colette away from Baron Reichstall even if I had to rip his arm off in the process. In the nanosecond it took me to reach them, the man who I previously thought was a breathing statue reacted supernaturally fast. He moved between myself and Colette, not only blocking my attack with his knee with an incredibly swift move, but also following with an immediate right jab that stopped my forward motion, knocking me backwards onto my butt. The man's punch had the impact of gun fire like Albert, but with something otherworldly behind it. My eye socket felt broken, and I was having difficulty closing my mouth. I stumbled over my leg irons and as I scrambled to my feet, I was hit again and knocked down with a right hook that felt and sounded like it broke my lower jawbone.

"Enough! Enough! My God, enough!" Reichstall shouted. "I must say, old boy, you are most certainly a monster. You were just hit by a man who has been known to cripple his opponents with his combat skills when he's in his normal state. At this moment, he's been imbued with superhuman strength by a technique known as shadow possession. It is a way of invoking demons to inhabit a body to magnify their physical and mental capacities in exchange for their soul. This is the culmination of my time spent in ancient catacombs of Egypt and gothic castles in Romania." Reichstall paused for a moment as if he was remembering a distant memory. Back then, "I wasn't satisfied with the promises of immortality. I wanted the power that great men like von Wöllner, Merlin, and Faust were able to wield by allowing powerful spirits into their being in order to achieve absolute wisdom and authority."

Reichstall pointed to the man standing next to him. "Lieutenant Reginald here is actually an entity named Marzriel. He was known in prehistoric times for his great physical speed and bodily strength. The stories tell of his ability to topple entire nations with a wave of his sword. I knew that if we could not control you with your sympathetic feelings for this wench, then I would need someone who could deliver extra persuasion to keep you under control. Still… the fact you were able to withstand not one but two of his blows that would normally explode a rhinoceros' skull speaks directly to the fact that my decision to bring you here was correct. I dare say

125

that if I were to allow you to continue battling, you brutes may well bring down London Bridge," he scoffed.

"Guards," yelled Baron Reichstall. He stamped his foot and twelve of the family's mercenaries entered and made a half circle around me and Lieutenant Reginald with bayonets pointed at me. Two of the guards carried large chains attached to thick wrist and neck shackles. "Ahh, my dear boy, your replacement bracelets have arrived."

Tears began to stream down Colette's face. I knew she blamed herself for being too weak to do anything for her mother. I wanted to tell her not to worry, but her whole life had been worry. I guess I should be happy that she was not dead along with Jessie, but maybe death would be a welcome respite for a slave in this miserable world. The mercenaries approached slowly from either side. I resigned myself to my fate for the sake of Colette, lower my head, and extend my hands to be clapped once again in heavy irons. There were various arcane symbols and insignias etched into the metal which felt much heavier than any of my previous restraints.

"These manacles have been specially designed by Swiss mechanical engineers, engraved with holy symbols, and chanted over by the high priest of this district who was ordained by the Pope himself. You will find it very difficult to remove them without the key which requires two people engaging the locks simultaneously to permit the release mechanism to function," said Reichstall

"Tomorrow evening you will be briefed on your duties and after your mission is complete, yourself and your companion will be returned to the city New York with manumission papers and a stipend for you to rebuild your lives as free Negroes as previously promised."

Colette was sobbing openly now, her hands covering her face, her heart atomized to dust. She was led out by Reichstall through the same door they entered. I am prodded by the business end of twelve bayonets in the opposite direction through the main, now broken, door at the opposite end of the chamber. The demonically possessed man just stood like a statue in

126

the middle of the parlor watching me as I walked out of the room. His malevolent face was added to my memory banks and place at the top of my list of bastards I vow to kill. I was led away down the corridor and out into the courtyard toward the brig. I was too distraught to even react to the pain caused by my broken jaw. The physical irritation of my flesh was a small but fitting penance for not being able to save one woman's life.

Meanwhile inside the east corridor of Woolverstone Manor, Reichstall shoved Colette forward while giving orders to his servants.

"Have Renfort and Lenfort ready my bath, and alert Colonel Berners that I want to have that boy placed in the stockade below the castle. Remind him to be sure to keep a round-the-clock watch by at least ten of his best men armed to the teeth on that scoundrel. Tomorrow, he will be instructed on the details of the errand that he is to perform in return for the life of this wench." Reichstall squeezed Colette's arm and looked at her up and down hungrily.

Claire and Megumi floated into the corridor from a side chamber and approached Reichstall and Colette. Megumi produced another white handkerchief from her kimono and handed it to the Baron. He shoved Colette towards the women as he snatched the handkerchief and used it to blot a fresh trickle of blood escaping from his nose.

The Baron addressed them saying, "Take this wench and bathe her then bring her to the red room and make sure she is secured fast to the bed."

Both women nod in affirmation to Reichstall and each took Colette by an arm and whisked her near limp body away.

127

Chapter 5

I was roused from my intermittent dozing by the sound of a key turning in a door far above me on the main level of this foul dungeon I was thrown into the previous night. My body had healed but my mind was laden with worry and regret since Baron Reichstall and his demon-possessed crony were able to lock me up in thick chains made to anchor naval ships. After a few hours that felt like an eternity I felt a sharp jerk then a tug on the rope that was affixed to my leg shackles, then I am suddenly upside down as I am being pulled up by the rope out of this shithole.

Once I was dragged to the surface level, I was forced to shuffle my way through the castle by a group of soldiers and mercenaries up to the main dining hall. There I saw Baron Reichstall standing with a stoic Colette between him and another man who was shirtless and completely hairless. The man stared at me with piercing blue eyes, his chest heaving as if he was out of breath and smiling like a lunatic. The sudden shock of snake urine filled my nostrils. I could not tell if Colette was injured, but the shocking heartbreak of her sad face gave me pause. Her eyes. Those once hopeful, simple, beautiful eyes, in less than a day's time, now bore all the weight of the world and seemed distant and dead. Reichstall had dressed her very elegantly in an alabaster gown that draped completely over her ankles and feet. She wore two polished pearl earrings that accented her flawless chocolate skin. I wanted to apologize for not being able to save her. I wanted to ask forgiveness for not being able to save Jessie. All this so-called devil in me, and I could not even save my only friends. The emotion of the moment was so overwhelming that the first half of whatever Baron Reichstall was saying failed to register with my ears.

As my senses gradually began to return, another blast of snake urine hit my nose as the man with no shirt began hastily untying a burlap sack which contained at least two vipers. I quickly snapped alert watching the man closely as Reichstall was saying,

"...inhabited by a familiar who is immune to all forms of the venom and holds a supernatural command of all things of reptilian blood."

The shirtless man was now holding two venomous snakes that in later years I will learn were called cobras wrapped around his right forearm. Colette seemed indifferent at the sight of the deadly creatures, gone were her natural reactions to scream. Her will was so broken, she just stood and waited for whatever heartbreak and anguish that was to come. Snake man was now staring directly into the eyes of the two serpents. As I watched him, he seemed to be communicating with the animals as his eyelids flutter rapidly and the snakes begin to writhe in unison. Suddenly he snapped out of the trance, our eyes met, and a madman's grin spread across his obnoxious face. One of the snakes leapt from his arm, slithered lightning fast across the carpeted floor, under Colette's dress, and bites her just above the left ankle. She did not scream or flinch but only let out a gasp of air as if she had been holding her breath the entire time. She pulled up the ruffles on her dress to reveal her injury as she dropped to one knee grabbing the freshly bitten leg and trying to stem the bleeding from the two puncture wounds.

As I stood there barely able to move because of the restrictive chains, I could only watch in horror at the display of madness by Colette who seemed to be more concerned with keeping the blood from her wound from dripping onto the expensive pearl-colored shoes she was wearing than her own well-being. Was she so broken that she had lost all sense of what her priorities should be? Could she be so far gone now that the first pair of white shoes she had ever owned held more value than her very life? Chains be damned. I swore, as God as my witness that I was going to kill everyone in that nightmare castle.

"Before you go jumping to any conclusions and do something rash, please be assured that this girl will be fine. The venom is nonlethal if the proper antidote elixir is administered within a few hours," Reichstall said mockingly.

"Now to business. As I see it, my poor brute, the only thing in this godforsaken world worth more than silver and gold is information. And the speed with which that information is acquired is extremely crucial because as with most things of value... information expires. And the spoils go only to the swift of foot. That is where you come in, my boy. When I give the signal to have my men release your chains, you are to use that incredible raw speed of yours to run to the London Stock Exchange in the heart of the city deliver this parcel to the office of Lord Thomas Cochrane. I have already arranged to have one of my agents meet with you at the rendezvous point."

I looked from Reichstall to Colette who was now seated with her dress over her knees, her arms holding her legs, all traces of modesty and chastity were gone as she silently and slowly rocked from side to side with tears streaming down her face. Her eyes did not come up to meet mine. She just stared blankly at some invisible object in front of her. Seemingly resigned to whatever fate befell her. Death would be a gift to her now in comparison to the horrors of living at the whim of these devils.

"I sorry!" I croaked in her direction, tears filling my colorless eyes, but she did not acknowledge my words at all.

Two soldiers approached, each holding long skeleton keys to undo my wrist and neck shackles. The task required two other soldiers to assist in carrying away the heavy shackles and neck brace combo. Four different men approach and unlock my leg irons. Each pair dragging their respective weights into the corner.

Reichstall continued with his direction. "Upon your return of the verification flag that my agent will give you, you are to be shackled once more before I administer the antidote to that woman. If you fail to return the verification flag or are tardy returning or should you fancy a notion of deserting her, rest assured this woman will be tortured mercilessly before we destroy her. I will also most assuredly bring the full weight of my family's fortune to hunt you down anywhere you may try to hide upon the four corners of this earth and make you my slave once again. "

A soldier approached me and handed me the parcel with Baron Reichstall's official seal and a scroll which was actually a small map with a very fragrant cologne soaked into the paper.

"Since you haven't the faculty of literacy, the map has drawings of how to proceed from the River Orwell to the River Thames to mark the boundary of your journey. The rendezvous point will be adjacent to the tallest church spire in the heart of the city. You know to follow Ursa Minor to bear seventy miles southwest from here. The fragrance on the map is a secret family formula that is not used by anyone else in the world so there should be no confusion. Memorize that smell, it is unique to only my most trusted operatives. Find him as expeditiously as possible and get back here with the confirmation flag without delay. I understand even though you are nigh immortal you still require an issue of blood to perform at your peak. At the western gate that leads to the riverbank, my stable hands have staked a fat calf to provide stamina for your journey," instructed Reichstall.

I looked at Colette to try to assess what she thought about the things she was hearing, but she was gone. Indifferent to her fate, she curled her arms even tighter around her legs rocking almost imperceptibly from side to side staring at nothing with tears silently streaming down her face.

I was led to the courtyard exit and as the doors are opened, I looked behind me to see a regiment of the Baron Reichstall's soldiers pointing rifles and swords at me, pushing me towards the exit. All I could think of was Colette and how there was absolutely no way I would fail to protect her again. I tore out of the gate and five seconds later, the bellows and bays of the calf were heard cutting the night air as I devoured its throat, savoring the blood aroma and its warm life-giving essence. While locked in the Reichstall's dungeon overnight, to keep my strength up, my menu consisted of mostly the cockroaches and earthworms that I could get my hands on. To now be drinking blood of this quality and purity, my body was being fully revitalized. I quickly drained the calf of its blood and cleaned my hands and face in the river, drying my hands on my trousers before I pull out my map and examine the relative direction I should follow one more time. After examining the crude road drawings, I look up at the stars to get my bearings on which way was west. I cleared my mind and tried to calm myself down as I called upon all my senses to help me find the quickest, straightest direction to the city and back before it was too late.

The Peregrine Falcon which can be found in many different regions of the earth is recorded by National Geographic as the fastest mammal in the world. When diving for its prey, the falcon slices through the air at nearly 250 miles an hour. The most remarkable thing about these creatures is their ability to process information from their senses while moving at such velocities. The next closest land-bound animal to reach peak speeds is, of course, the cheetah which can reach up to a whopping 75 miles an hour. The American quarter horse is a magnificently built creature that can effortlessly blaze along at nearly 60 miles an hour and can generally sustain that speed for longer intervals than most mammalian speedsters. As far as bipedal animals go, there are very few creatures with enough leg strength to be able to move on land at speeds that could rival their four-legged counterparts with the exception of the mighty ostrich. An ostrich's legs are said to be strong enough for them to sprint at 60 miles an hour and sustain speeds of up to 40 miles an hour. A great deal of the ostrich's success in running belongs to their stable center of gravity and their specialized toe structure that keeps them aloft at high speeds. The humanoid frame with its upright vertebrae, lighter bone structure, relatively small feet, and lack of long claws or paw pads specialized for creating grip and traction when running is not the ideal body type for reaching maximum speeds for land travel. My body compensates for this shortcoming by the extreme density of my bones and muscles that generate incredible strength when compared to normal humans. In my more agitated moments, the natural strength is exponentially increased in accordance with my emotional state.

The forests, the meadows, the roads all became a blur as I shrank the world and time slowed to a standstill. My bare feet, already calloused and ossified from being shredded and healed over and over throughout my century of life, barely register the contact made from each step. The word 'run' is inadequate when trying to describe such swift movements. What I was doing was more like free falling horizontally.

Immortality, if I were to paraphrase it scientifically, would be the constant replacement or regeneration of cellular matter to retard injury and decay that occurs naturally through physical exertion and organic age progression. My body multiplies natural human regeneration and healing such that my leg muscles do not experience the same fatigue and lactic acid build up as a normal human does, so I am able to sustain a speed of near 50 miles an hour when running at no consequence to my body. Walk in any modern L.A. Fitness, and the first thing any gym rat will tell you is that to build muscle, you first have to tear it down. Thus, the need to rest between sets or take off days between workouts. For me, the muscle is rebuilt in seconds and minutes rather than hours and days, causing my body's strength potential to be off the charts when exerting long term physical activity. I am pure acceleration. To be able to process at this speed, my sense of smell and hearing are dulled to levels on par with most humans. I depend solely on my keen eyes that see at night as well as the most gifted sighted man can see at high noon. I will deliver this fucking letter and get back to Colette if it was the last act I performed on this earth. No one else that I love would die because I could not protect them.

At this period, the Royal Mail Service was the gold standard in reliable delivery. They consisted of many networks of loyal postmen who had to traverse roads that were in very poor condition, many not being able to travel more than five miles an hour, a journey which was hard on the horses and the riders. There was also the added danger of robbery by the many bandits and highwaymen that dotted the English countryside. The Royal Mail Service used only the swiftest of horses to meet their critical deadlines. When I was a child, before the widespread expansion of roads for vehicle travel, Negro men and boys were used to run between plantations to deliver breaking news or deliver messages. I was spared this task as a child because most people thought of me to be blind or nearly blind, and likely mute, so they left all the running to the more "normal" boys. Tonight, I would put all forms of delivery to shame. Despite the distance and the steep, narrow, rocky precipices that kept pounding my feet across this shitty English terrain, I was laser focused on my mission. The English countryside still possessed many trees in those times and at intervals, I would take to the trees and glide between branches, sending showers of leaves down to the forest floor and startling many a creature not accustomed to being troubled by branch swinging humanoids at this hour. The entire time, my mind was drifting to the memory of Colette's dead eyes and the paralyzed way she was sitting and rocking as if she had already seen hell and welcomed death as a relief.

At times, I was forced to slow down and look up at the night sky to recalibrate my bearings. At this hour, I would follow "Mintaka, premye zetwal la," the first star in the tristar belt of Orion to head due west. Buukman taught me how to read the stars during the Revolution.

I was pure adrenaline now, the time it took to traverse the nearly 65-mile distance to London was shortened drastically. By the sky's reading, there were still more than four hours until sunrise. I tore through farms and villages avoiding human detection as much as possible. As I converged on this massive city, the downwind currents accosted my nose with a horrible stench. That was the hidden cost of having so many humans living in such a densely packed urban environment. This city was large enough to swallow New Orleans whole.

As the landscape around me changed from rural to urban in a flash, I am cautious to move quickly amongst the shadows of the buildings. There was light everywhere in this huge city. It was customary for people to leave candles and oil lamps burning in their windows at night and even more light was being created with the recent advent of gas street lighting and state sponsored lighting for business and government buildings. The light pollution emanating from the city was making it nigh impossible to use the stars as an accurate way to order my steps.

I took a quick break in the bell tower of a large church to stare down at my crude map and try to narrow down the direction I should be traveling. The rancid stench of the open sewers made it difficult to distinguish which way the river lies but my instincts told me to continue on the same course, and I moved in a northwestern direction from the church and further into the center of the city.

As the number of structures began to multiply and the ground below me changed from dirt and grass to cobblestone streets and row houses and shops, I did my very best to avoid anyone because there were tons of people, including children, out and about even at this late hour. London proved to truly be a marvel for it was not very common in Thibodeaux Parish for there to be this much bustle after midnight. The specter presented by the sheer multitude of life activity in the city forced me to slow my rush down a bit as I moved from shadow to shadow and hid behind trash bins and under horse troughs as people passed me by mere inches. There were so many societal castaways of all ages lying in the alleys and gutters of this unforgiving city that, inevitably, I was spotted by a few people who reacted either being indifferent to my presence or being too frightened to speak as if confronted by the devil himself. I elected to take to the rooftops to further avoid people and to seek out the streets and alleys that had the least number of streetlamps. The reddish moonlit night further mocked me, reminding me of the bloody face of a mutilated Jessie. I began to panic as my mind turned to thoughts of what those devils would do to Colette if I was not able to find the financier's office and return to Woolverstone before time ran out.

I climbed a tall building in a part of the city now known as Stratford. Hanging on to the roof with one hand, I pulled the map from my pocket with the other hand and sniffed the distinctive smell again. It was rose oil mixed with peppermint and accented with lemon peels, saffron and cinnamon. An extremely distinct cocktail of spices that only the wealthiest of people had access to. The map drawing showed a smaller river near my current location that led into a much larger river that served as the boundary for my rendezvous point.

I deduced by the horrid odor that seemed to be growing stronger and stronger that ahead of me must be the larger body of water I was warned about by Reichstall to not cross, else I would have gone too far. Amongst the many smells throughout the city, incredibly I began to pick up a very faint hint of my target. Someone expecting my arrival must have left markings of

135

that specific smell and currently must be wafting the fragrance in the air from some unseen window for now it came even stronger on the wind.

I flew through the night streets, darting past barking dogs and scaling walls of crowded flats, past candlelit windows and idle chimneys. The matching aroma emanated from a well-built Baroque four story structure. There was a candle situated under a metal pan filled with pungent liquid in a third story window. As I drew closer, I could see the smoke created by the heated oil was being fanned out of the window by a Negro manservant. I vaulted up onto the side of the building and scaled the wall by digging my claws into the grout lines between the stones and climbed acrobatically into the window. To my surprise, Mr. Gellner was there wearing a crisp grey suit and looking down at his watch, as usual, which he held to the light of an oil lamp for a better gander. He was seated next to another robust middle aged gentleman wearing spectacles and holding what looked and smelled like brandy in a crystal glass in his hand.

"You are late!" Gellner said flatly. "You have something for myself and Mr. Cochrane I presume?" he asked in an exasperated tone as if annoyed at the interruption caused by my sudden appearance at the window.

I reached into my inner coat pocket and retrieved the letter from Baron Reichstall. He snatched the letter and read it quickly. His eyes went wide.

"Oh my word," he said to himself as he handed the paper to Mr. Cochrane who also seemed to go into shock after reading whatever message the note held.

He snapped around to look at me as if he couldn't believe I was standing before him and then pulled a small green flag with a symbol of a snake with a lion's head on it from his coat pocket and handed it to me.

"You may go now boy," Gellner ordered as he put on his hat and ran out of the room, leaving the door open behind him. He ran down the stairs to the back of the building where a carriage and a horseman were waiting. The driver took off like a flash as soon as Gellner sprang into the carriage.

I stood there stunned for a moment watching Gellner's carriage speed away, and then the vision of Jessie's disfigured body snapped me back to reality. I vaulted from the window onto the adjacent roof top and began the long trek back to Woolverstone Manor and Colette. My feet were shredded, and my body's regeneration and immortal stamina were working overtime to keep up with the limits I was pushing it to. I stopped just outside the city to check the sky for the Drinking Gourd and adjust my bearings to the northeast toward Ipswich. The stars told me it should be just after two o'clock in the morning, which puts me arriving well before dawn to rescue Colette. God help anyone who gets in my way.

I was exhausted, my muscles burned, what was left of my clothes were soaked through with sweat. My feet were numb from the pounding of the dirt, rocks, sticks, briars, streams, and brooks that were my runway. The claws on my hands and feet were broken and bleeding from running on all fours to give increase to my speed. My chest heaved mightily from the non-stop movement. Despite the physical strain my body was under my mind was laser focused on rescuing Colette and I managed to make it back across the treacherous English countryside in no time. My heart lifted somewhat as soon as I could smell the perpetually roasting meat and hear those damned bullfrogs that inhabited the River Orwell signifying the fact that I was drawing near to Woolverstone Manor.

The thought of Jessie being dead was still surreal to me, and I was sure...

No! I won't let my mind go there now. It was already too much with Jessie but if he touches....

I need to pull myself together. I was now close enough to see the torches lit in the main tower of the manor. I began to cross the massive lawn when I saw one of the castle guards walking in the darkness and holding a musket but without a torch or lantern. This being the night of the blood moon, he may have surmised that he would be able to see well enough without light. I am at least thirty meters ahead of him, making a beeline directly past his patrol. I was determined not to stop until I saw Colette again, and by the time the soldier was able to make out my silhouette and hear my feet slicing through the grass, I was already upon him. I lower my shoulder into him which he tries to buffer with his rifle, knocking him one way and sending his rifle flying in the opposite direction. I was expecting the alarm whistle to come in the next moment but when I heard no shouts or bell alarms, I guessed that Colonel Berners must have informed his men that I would be returning tonight and that I would be approaching at a frightening pace.

The air was rank and very cool here for a summer night, which proved beneficial to my sense of smell. I was picking up scents of all the servants and guards coming from the first floor of the manor, and I slowed my approach velocity as I passed the newly built fountainhead that sat in the middle of the impeccably landscaped front lawn. I could not smell Colette or Reichstall, but there was a faint hint of the incredibly strong bearded man and a faint tang of blood.

I grabbed the knocker on the oversized front double doors, and I pulled the ring completely out of the jaws of the brass lion serving as its holder. I tossed the ring and smashed the door repeatedly with my right fist making a thunderous racket that I was sure the entire estate could hear. I had returned well before dawn and now it was time for Reichstall to keep his end of the bargain and set Colette and I free. I impatiently banged my closed fist on the door again, this time rattling the hinges with each blow. Still no response. I decided to knock a third and final time before I destroyed the whole fucking place. I raised my hand to knock or more like punch the door. It swings open, and a tall, sharply dressed, dark complected man with a turban wrapped around his head stood before me. The man bowed deeply, held out his right palm and spoke.

"Le drapery s'il vous plaît monsieur" (The flag please sir)

Initially I was too angry to understand what the man was asking me and I just stood there panting and staring until after a few seconds I had calmed down enough to comprehend. The sound of this man's heartbeat was very gentle. He did not seem to be the least bit startled by my actions or appearance. I pulled the flag from my inner coat pocket and gruffly slapped it

138

in the man's hand. He places the flag in his pocket and as he bid me to enter, my panting began to subside. As we walked my body began healing all the cuts and bruises received during my marathon, but mentally I was becoming severely more and more fractured. I walked wordlessly three paces behind this man as we traversed a long corridor which led to an area just behind the kitchen hearth that I never realized existed until now. The man pushed against loose stone and the wall slid left revealing a hidden door that opened onto a small stone lined corridor that sloped at a 30-degree angle downward.

I continued to follow the odd man until the end of that corridor opened into a grand study lined with volumes of books of all shapes, sizes and ages. At each corner of the room stood a suit of armor bearing a variety of different family crests. Another impressive space built on the toil of others. The more of this overindulgence I was forced to stomach, the more furious I became. My guide turned to me and bowed his dismissal to me saying six words in French but with another underlying accent.

"Veuillez attendre ici pour le maitre." (Please wait for the master)

My patience was wearing thin, but I nodded my compliance as the man walked toward the wall, pressed against another stone, and disappeared into the wall that swings closed behind him with a scraping thud. Oddly, I could no longer smell any of the servants, only the smoky chicory tea smell of my foreign guide still lingering in the air.

From the looks of the stone used to build this room it appeared I was in a very old part of the manor. There was some sort of geometric pattern on the floor with lettering similar to what I saw drawn on the walls in my bedroom and throughout the main gallery of the manor.

Just then, torches sprang to life all around the room, and disembodied voices began to come from each of the empty suits of armor. I did not understand the words, but the cadence was very driving and mimicked holy chanting mixed with guttural animal calls. The chorus of sounds was joined and overshadowed by the sinister voice of Baron Reichstall reciting the same idiosyncratic witchery that he was spouting when he murdered Jessie. The smell of blood became stronger and seemed to be wafting in from every direction. After thirty seconds of this noise, I began to feel very strange as if someone was slowly pulling my mind out of my body. My once throbbing leg muscles now felt as if they were no longer affected by gravity. I felt as if someone else was carrying me or should I say standing for me. As the chanting got louder and stronger, my body spontaneously began to move toward the wall opposite from where the turban donning fellow entered moments ago. I was still somewhat tired and recovering from the frantic run to London and back which was making it impossible to physically resist these forces that seemed to have taken control of my motor functions while leaving my mind conscious. This must be something akin to what was invoked on the giant Albert when he appeared holding Jessie's head.

Precious anger began to build again as I watched as my left hand reach out involuntarily toward the wall in front of me and press a strange symbol shaped like an eye engraved into the stones of the wall. I could hear the gears of some mechanical device on the other side of the wall begin to turn revealing a narrow door, half the size of the one the turbaned man exited through. This smaller door opened to a corridor inside the wall. The same symbols and letters that were inside the circle and triangle on the floor in the main room line this hallway and the chanting seemed to be getting louder and more rhythmic as my feet and legs compel me forward against my will.

As my body healed, I could feel some of my strength returning and I tried, with little success, to stop my body from moving forward towards whatever designs these evil bastards had in mind for me next.

I had only walked a few meters when I smelled a fetid mixture of blood, sex, and human feces. My mind went insane at what I knew was the smell of Colette's skin and hair. I tried to focus my hearing past the chanting to catch the sound of her breathing, but the chorus of voices was too loud. I also smelled the bearded man I fought earlier, and my fangs began to grow instinctively. I could feel adrenalin coursing through my veins and my blood vessels dilating in response to my increasing anger. Halfway down this corridor, the solid walls were interspersed with what looked like prison doors, some of which contained what smelled like squalid animals but were more than likely humans degraded and tortured beyond identification. The hellions controlling my body brought me to the threshold of one of the last doors on the left side of the hallway. I watched as if in a dream as my hand reached out and pushed down the latch of the door, and I was hit with the sight of revulsion.

Colette's face and mouth are covered in blood from having her teeth knocked out, lying naked on the stone floor in a pool of her own blood, urine and excrement. The large, bearded man stood naked next to her with his penis and face dripping with blood and saliva. I looked back down at Colette, the white dress clung to her sweat drenched body, her once radiant brown skin was ashen and pale. Anger overflowed as my worst nightmare became a stark reality. My body began shaking uncontrollably, gradually chipping away at the unseen controllers of my movements.

I wanted to run to her with all my being but the spell I was under held me firmly in place. I was prevented from going to her and making sure she was gone because if there was even the slightest hint of breath, I could give her some of my blood and she may be able to heal and continue with so-called life. The chanting voices and the now glowing symbols on the wall were still preventing me from moving and as I stood there helpless and sobbing the symbols began to pulse a sinister red color and the chanting grew considerably louder.

I was in shock as I stared at Colette's motionless body and with every nanosecond that passed, my blood began to heat up like lava inside a long dormant mountain. I fought to move my legs, but the pulsing of the walls and the chanting began to increase according to the amount of effort I exerted to keep me at bay. I was incensed and every molecule in my body was fighting hard to regain control of my movements. I was able to slowly, gravelly spit out the most complete sentence I have ever spoken aloud.

"GOD...DAMMIT! YOU PROMISED.... YOU WOULD NOT KILL HER!!!!!!"

The bearded man took a step toward me and leaned down with his bloody, slimy face and said to me, "We kept our end of the bargain, we didn't kill her. We just raped her all night after you ran off. When Emir came to check on her, she had already chewed through her own damn wrists and bled out before we could stop her. She must have shit herself when she died and her bowels released. It was still warm up until a little while ago. And I must admit...." the vile man was now inches from my face and shooting putrid

141

spittle with every syllable, "...she was even better after she had croaked." As he spoke, he broke into a wide, rotten, bloody smile.

At that moment I blacked out.

All rational thought was gone.

Pure rage flooded my mind, rage and hatred and vengeance.

My right hand shot out and grabbed the bearded man's throat and began to lift his huge bulk up and off the floor slowly while I burned through him with my eyes. He began clawing at my forearm and hands, tearing at my flesh with his massive strength to get me to release my grip. Then he began trying to pummel my face and chest with his large strong hands, but his demon powered brute strength and iron skin could not compete with the furor that was inside me. I was so enthralled with anger that I had not noticed that the chanting had stopped and the glow from the symbols on the wall ceased its pulsations and began to fade.

"Gelpppp...Meeeeehhhhh,"

the bearded man coughs out as he flails and slaps against my arm and hand just before I hear his windpipe collapse and blood began to trail down his neck as my claws sank into his flesh. My plan was to continue squeezing until his spinal cord is ground to dust. A different chant began emanating from the four corners of the room which appeared to reinvigorate the now frantic bearded man giving the frantic blows from his powerful arms somewhat more impact. This new spell was more than likely an incantation to increase this man's strength instead of the spell to restrict my movements, I deduced.

But it was too little too late.

I was too far gone now.

 I slammed the bearded man into the stone floor sending dust and debris flying into the air. I could hear several bones breaking upon impact but in his demonic puppet form, he continued to struggle. His mouth opened wide as he futilely attempted to scream in pain. I grabbed the top row of his teeth with my left hand and the bottom of his jaw with my right hand and

142

began to pull for all I was worth. Animal-like screams and moans emit from the still intact vocal cords as the man shudders in agony while the skin and sinews in his cheek begin to tear. I can feel his hot breath and cold flailing tongue against my hand as the popping sound of his jaw being ripped apart is dwarfed by one last blood curdling scream as my anger rips the top his head apart, sending blood splattering against the walls which are now no longer pulsing with red light. The huge body of the bearded man fell to the floor with a 'thud' and I watched as his large frame gradually began to shrink. After a moment, this once bulging hulk of a man was now shriveled down into his original pale average sized humanoid form.

The room was quiet, and there was only the light from a torch on the wall in the far corner and the waning Gibbous blood moon coming through the window at an angle that perfectly illuminated Colette's beautiful, bloodstained face. I walked over to her to stroke her hair and gently lifted her and cradled her body in my arms, much as I had done my mother after her murder. The tears flowed freely for what seemed like hours, but my grieving was interrupted by the sound of someone applauding.

"It seems that Mr. Reginald got a little cocky, aye, old boy?" comes the voice of Baron Reichstall through openings at the top of the walls. "I never dreamed that the combination of my alchemy and his summoning combined were able to be overcome, but I guess I never calculated, or should I say rather never fathomed the unbelievable strength that a real devil would possess. Your usefulness has served me extraordinarily well, and I am no longer in need of your unique services. Thus, after this most recent display of disdain for me and my subordinates I hereby find your presence in England to be too dangerous. Especially considering your proximity to the crown and seat of power for the empire. As such, I am shipping you back west as promised to that godforsaken country of rabble rousers where there are plenty of slave wenches that you can find as a replacement for this one."

I just sat rocking back and forth and sobbing profusely while holding Colette's lifeless body in my arms. Not hearing anything and seeing only tears, I did not notice when the turban wearing servant inserted a tube into an opening in the door and began filling the room with a heavy foul smelling gas. I was still too distraught to move. I was ready to die now anyway.

I had nothing to live for any longer.

After a few minutes, all the oxygen in the room was completely replaced by this mysterious gas. The voice of Baron Reichstall came piping through the room again. "Oh, how the mighty have fallen. That wench was always slated to die just like her fat obnoxious mother. You may be a marvel of physiognomy, but your mind is still that of a mere child," Reichstall scoffed.

"My family were financiers of most of the French Colonial expansion over the last century, and the island of San Domingue was the crown jewel of the Empire because of the vast riches being made from the sugar exports there. If things would have continued as planned, the Reichstall family stood to corner the market and expand our empire throughout the Western Hemisphere and stop the upstart British colonies from dividing European interests. All the while raking in tons of revenue from the expanded slave markets. But you and that bastard L'Overture decided to rebel and somehow thwart the three most powerful militaries in the world with only your jungle education, a few slings, and garden spades. When I first received the report of the losses we were taking in San Domingue, I could hardly believe it. Then a report came into our offices from the war front of an unstoppable creature who would only appear at nightfall or on overcast days armed with only swords and axes who could single handedly murder entire battalions of men. It was reported that this man could not be killed even after receiving mortal gunshot and cannon fire wounds at point blank range. Not only did we lose billions in revenue from your little 'declaration of freedom,' we were forced to sell some of our vast land holdings to the American colonists as a means to recoup a fraction of our losses. You black devils and your *revolution* nearly finished us by giving hope to other so-called freedom movements that nearly upended the control mechanisms we had so diligently worked to place throughout the world. Many of the royal and wealthy elite that were vested for centuries in that business model were forced to change their approach to how they wielded authority, and our plans for world domination were set back indefinitely by your bloody black rebellion."

As he spoke, more and more of the poisonous gas replaced the oxygen in the room, but the efficacy of the gas was being neutralized by my body's regenerative abilities and my pure vexation. An absolute refusal to

144

bend to the will of this maniac before I spilled his blood and exacted my revenge.

Reichstall began again. "This very battle that rages in Belgium is an indirect result of the tumultuous times caused by you and your rebels."

I sat on the floor clutched by grief, still cradling Colette's lifeless body. Ultimately, I began losing the campaign for my lungs, and I could feel myself slipping into unconsciousness from the effects of the deadly gases continually being pumped into the room. The cloud of gas was so thick I could no longer see anything past Colette's body. The room had become so thoroughly filled with gas and despite the best efforts of my virtually immortal biology, I began to be outpaced by the toxin.

Before I completely succumbed to the gas, I heard Reichstall add, "Just so you are aware of who you are dealing with, I always planned on killing those women because of their importance to you. And I want you to always carry the burden of their lives on your soul. Unfortunately for you, you won't be able to join them in the afterlife as of yet. Your life belongs to us now and you will be a servant of the Incalculaba until all the useless eaters have been wiped away from this miserable planet. And once mankind conquers the galaxies and colonize the heavens, you will still remain a servant until the flesh falls from your immortal bones."

I looked down into Colette's inert face once more before whatever this malodorous substance I was breathing caused me to succumb to its effects. My eyes and body grew extremely heavy. It took every ounce of muscle I had to fight passing out. I made a solemn promise in those last few moments of consciousness. I promised to take down the Reichstalls and the demonic Incalculaba if it was my last act on earth. With my last bit of strength, I leaned down to kiss Colette's bloody forehead and before I knew it, I was unconscious.

Chapter 6

"My God...that is quite the tall tale," Kate interrupts. Cynicism dripped heavily from every word.

"Is that when you received that secret family crest burned into your neck?" Kate asks, reaching into her pocket for another round of cigarettes? "I don't understand how it's still visible after two hundred years. Wouldn't you have healed after all this time?"

"From that day forward, I would forever bear the mark of Reichstall and the reason it has not been able to heal is because the brand that left this mark was made of a very pure form of silver, a minting technology that only wealthy families like yours was able to procure at the time." I tell her.

"I'm truly sorry to hear such a sad and tragic story," Kate begins, trying to suppress the sarcasm in her tone and attempting to display a genuine look of concern on her face. "But what I guess I fail to understand is how someone as powerful as yourself ended up a slave in the first place? If you're truly immortal and that powerful, how did you become a slave and remain one for ninety freaking years?" She lights another cigarette then leans back and uncrosses her legs. Out of habit, she carefully perches her lighter on the arm of the loveseat, the smoke from her lungs wafting up into the air. I must admit that I have never had anyone ask me such an obvious question before. And when put so bluntly, I was somewhat given pause on how to answer her truthfully. I stared up at the ceiling to thoroughly search my memory banks for the best way to answer her question honestly. I smash out my cigarette in the crystal ashtray and lean forward in my chair and tell her,

"To answer that question, I truly need to take you back to the beginning of things."

• • •

"During the ancient times when the last of the great lizards still roamed the earth...
...the connection with the outworlders that traveled within the Wheel still visited this plane regularly...
...the galaxy surrounding Tiamat knew peace...
...the era of Thoth and the great gods within the Halls of Amenti...
...the times prior to the creation of the Moon and the Great Sleep of Leviathan...
...before the Great Flood that destroyed the spectacular civilizations of Atlantis and Lemuria...
...our people existed."

"The elders taught my mother that my kind were always connected to her people by a representative Queen Goddess due to the feminine nature of the Moon which is as central to our mythos as the Sun is to Western mythos. That may explain why vampires, especially the females, can be exceptionally stronger during a full moon. I always thought the blood and menstrual cycle thing was kind of ironic and may be where legends of our origins began because of the woman's loss of blood, she would need to feed on the blood of others to replenish her strength. Modern scientific research even points to the fact that men are chromosomal duplicates of women save for the minutest of differences in amino acid content. Thusly men have inactive nipples that do not produce milk, and a penis is just an oversized clitoris."

147

"Ha! Some of them aren't oversized at all. Ask my ex-husband," Kate quips, mainly to herself. Not being able to resist the opportunity to make light of what probably sounds like hogwash to her. I roll my eyes and pull another cigarette from the pack and continue.

"As I was saying, the Elders also relayed to my mother that this connection to the Lunar Goddess placed us in a very ostentatious ranking amongst the many peoples, tribes, and nations of the world known to inhabit the planet before the flood. A world which possessed spiritual and physical advancements of civilization far superior to the disease-ridden, fossil fuel driven, wasteful world we live in now. Unfortunately, that very same amazing knowledge and technology was used for exploitation by a few wayward souls and led to foolish pride and arrogance amongst the rulers and the elite of the ancient world. Over time, the lower vibrational entities won the battle for human souls and even with all their vast knowledge and power the great alchemists and thought leaders of that era could not prevent the wars that led to their own self-annihilation. After the cataclysm, most of the ancient civilizations either died out, went inside the earth, or left the planet completely. An innumerable amount of knowledge was lost to the barbarians that now ruled the earth realm.

To preserve the knowledge for future generations, sites like Stonehenge, The Gavrinis Passage Tomb and the Great Pyramid of Giza were created to remind mankind of the greatness they were once capable of. Regrettably the ignorance of man prevailed and once again, they allowed fear of the unknown to rule the day. The cycle to rekindle knowledge and wisdom upon the earth by way of the Akashic record that happens every few millennia was set in motion again. Just as the skin of a serpent sheds and is renewed within its better image, so must the earth reform itself.

When civilization emerged again, my kind's numbers had greatly diminished, but many of our clansmen survived the Wuurmian Ice Age in lands far to the North which would now be considered Eastern Europe and Russia. Braving the cold climates for access to longer nights, our people survived and served mainly as teachers and protectors. But as it was still our custom to be affiliated with the lunar gods and goddesses of the night, our observances were misinterpreted by the masses and became associated with negative practices like sacrificing the hearts of children for occult rituals and manipulation of women for sexually deviant purposes. When men are blinded by superstitious faiths, they become very irrational, and when these beliefs are organized into religions, they tend to ignite conflict in the world. Eventually pushing aside the knowledge of the ancients and in their ignorance they began to conflate *'darkness'* and everything having to do with the ancient occult with negativity instead of balance to the light."

"In the Mediterranean, it was Artemis or Diana. In Asia, she was known as Chandra or Heng'e. In the Americas, her moniker was Coyolxāuhqui or Maya. On my native continent, she had countless names and iterations and was called Abuk or Inyanga. In Egypt, Thoth himself was represented by the moon. As mankind began to rebuild civilization, it found that scattered throughout the planet there was enough of the knowledge of the ancient times and sufficient contact with the inhabitants of the Wheel to replenish the earth with vital information that birthed great cultural achievements near areas like Gobekli Tepe, Macchu Picchu, and the Borobudur. Only to have everything dissolve back into ignorance and crumble once again into oblivion. In the case of the African continent, a scientific breakthrough amongst the Nubians of the North led them to dabble in the splitting of atoms to harness energy for war and accidentally unleashed an explosion which destroyed much of the land permanently and created what we know today as the Sahara Desert. The Ancient Brits and Europeans perverted and exploited the leftovers of the ancient wisdom into control mechanisms like the Holy Roman Empire and the Catholic Church. The rest of the world fell into ignorance and darkness by subscribing to superstition and sacrificial offerings to various gods and goddesses that suited their mortal needs and desires."

"As a result of all this misuse of information and perversion of the truth, my kind were persecuted and misunderstood in a sort of global genocide. Due to our supernatural abilities, people feared us. They could not understand our gifts and they feared us because they could not control our power for themselves. Across the world, my kind was forced into the fringes of society, and we became synonymous with demonic legend and folktales. Many of my kind began to embrace this defamation and were sure to murder humans, gruesomely at times, as a source of pleasure and sustenance. As a result of this conflict the night, and the things that go *bump* in it, were forever relegated to all the evil and horrible things that mankind fears.

Woefully, myself and others like me who thrive in the darkness have been branded as malevolent and have all been permanently stained with this nightmarish reputation."

"Fortunately, there were a few cultures who correctly realized that their ultimate survival and the success of their clan could be improved through a symbiotic relationship with my kind. In return for loyalty and worship, we provided protection, and we received a sense of belonging again as night creatures that could wield the powers of immortality, incredible strength, unbounded speed, and in some cases even flight. Imana, Kuguruka Imbeda or Mbweha Anayeruka, the god who lived in the caves, we were called. My mother's tribe resided in the foothills of the Ruwenzori mountains near what is now called Lake Edward. Because of its proximity to the ancient ones' underground dwellings, my mother's village became the custodians of the knowledge of the ancient ones and each generation of elders were required to oversee and maintain the peace between the human and vampire worlds. My mother told me that her bloodline ruled over a vast territory that covered much of the land just below the equator in what is now known as the Eastern Congo, North Rwanda, the majority of Uganda and western Kenya. This was an area that covered thousands of miles and would be comparable to the size of Texas, and Western Europe put together. The legend of my ancestors warned that anyone within this jurisdiction who was guilty of injustice to his fellow man would be punished in the night by the Kuguruka Imbeda :

'The Great Bat Spirit who would swoop down on silent wings and slaughter your livestock, drink the blood of your wife or daughter and chop off the head of your firstborn son all before you could grab your spear in defense.'

These myths and legends kept people in line for hundreds of years in that kingdom. To this day there are multiple tribes and nations in Africa who drink the blood of animals for ritual divination, perceived invigoration, or as tributes by imitation to the ancient protectors in our present absence."

The griots of the villages in my native land retold some of the oldest tales recorded in this section of the galaxy. Tales of when the earth was frequented by giants and the dragon seed from beyond the firmament and accounts of the settlements they created for themselves by carving out the rivers and the lakes of the Rwenzori Valley. Myths are told that our village came into existence shortly after these mysterious beings introduced the bee, the ant and all the other insects and animals that still inhabit the land and serve the planet as custodians of natural order. The legends state that the mountains surrounding our village were once hollow and served to house these beings and their offspring, of whom I am directly descended. The caverns and tunnels that remain underground there are said to be ruins from a once great transportation system that the ancients used to travel to every corner of the globe. By the era in which I was to be born, these legends were now stories told to children before bedtime. As the Ouroboros depicts the cycle of life as a snake eating its own tail, everything that has a beginning must also see its end. Our once great society met its end at the hands of ignorant, greedy men. As the slave trade ramped up around the world, the hearts of men became clouded by greed and the indigenous people across the world were made to heel under the boot of imperialism. I was to be born into that era of extreme degradation.

My mother was the last queen of the Kuguruka Imbeda tribe before our kingdom was infiltrated and destroyed by imperialists seeking their fortune through the enslavement and exploitation of their fellow man. She was eight months pregnant with me when the village was invaded and plundered. We were taken thousands of miles from our homes and forced to work under the yoke of slavery in the French colonies. My mother was treated very poorly. Starved beaten and raped many times in order to break her defiant nature. Burdened with a child that everyone believed to be a blind imbecile and because of my extremely introverted nature and my need to remain covered from head to toe when the sun was out. During those many years of enslavement in San Domingue my mother held on to the pride she had for her tribe, and she made sure that I knew all about our regal ancestry. No matter what horrible circumstances we found ourselves in she was always sure to remind me that I carried the power of the Ancients within my blood and that one day when the time was right, I would manifest those powers and become the hero of all those who are suffering under the current regime of negativity. The one foretold to reestablish order in the chaos.

151

"And that was supposed to be you?" Kate asks incredulously.

"I've been wondering that very thing all my life," I reply.

"If so, we're in deep doo doo." Kate winks at me as she lights another cigarette and non-verbally offers to refresh my drink.

I lean back into the sofa as she tosses me the lighter which I catch without looking and light my cigarette. After a few puffs, I lean forward and place the lighter next to Kate's still recording phone. She still seems a little skeptical of all this information I have been dropping on her. Even the most open minded of people would find it hard to believe that the subject matter for Hollywood teenage horror movies may genuinely be rooted in reality.

"Atlantis, huh?" Kate half-heartedly asks as if she almost did not want to.

I drop my eyes. "I am truly sorry. I was debating on whether I would be saying too much but I wanted to convey how far back this grudge originates. I-I-I guess I thought I could appeal to the historian and archaeologist in y–"

She cuts me off abruptly. "--I dated a guy when I was an undergrad at Stanford," she says, looking directly at me. "He was a history major named Ethan who was tall and skinny but had the most beautiful strawberry blonde hair and hazy blue eyes. We would smoke a joint in his car and afterwards walk to Wilbur Hall to get some food and talk about the most interesting things. I remember our conversation turned to Egypt one day because of some funky earrings I was wearing at the time… Anyway, as we talked, the subject changed to personality traits and we divulged our zodiac signs to each other, I think he was a Leo if I remember correctly." She takes another drag on her cigarette. "He loved telling me all about these ancient cultures – Akkadians, Nubians… I forget the exact fucking civilization we were discussing at the time, but he ended up doing his graduation thesis on the subject. The entire essay turned out to be a scathing condemnation of the accepted chronological canon of history in which he discovered huge discrepancies with the accepted timeline which appeared to be purposefully tainted to entertain biased ideologies that printed misinformation due to government and corporate influence over modern day historical academia.

152

I should have married that guy instead of the beta male that I'm paying alimony too," Kate scoffs, "but back to my story...Ethan would love to explain to me how these ancient, primitive people had been able to learn and record libraries of knowledge and were also somehow able to create a detailed map of the procession of the zodiac across the Milky Way which is roughly about a twenty-five thousand year cycle. He would ramble on and be totally bugged out about the true length of time these ancient people had to have been actively studying the stars. He theorized that the real human timeline would need to the extended by tens of thousands of years longer than accepted history says that these civilizations actually existed. For the uncomplicated fact that they would have had to at least been around long enough to have noticed the first procession of constellations to have had the wherewithal and technology to have been able to record the second procession which would mean that the numbers we have for the accepted timeline of mankind is way off, and human beings are way older and have been hanging around creating and destroying civilizations a lot fucking longer than we've been led to believe." She exhales the remainder of the smoke from her lungs.

Kate stands now and folds her arms, looking up at the ceiling nostalgically while still holding her cigarette in her right hand just inches from her mouth. Smiling to herself now she says, "Ethan had a habit of repeating scholarly sayings from old farts like Churchill and Hemingway and random shit his professors would tell him whenever he got high. He would pick me up from my apartment and hand me a bag of pot and Zig Zag rolling papers as soon as I got in the car, and we would ride to Menlo Park in his money green Mercury Cougar. Sometimes we would drive to a lookout point in Palo Alto or just find a quiet spot near campus and smoke and have sex in the backseat. Ethan would get stoned and want to talk again, and I would just sit and stare into his beautiful blue eyes as he rambled on about the problems with the world at large. One of the little quotes he would always recite that I used to just chuckle at was an old saying that went... Shit how'd it go? ... something like– 'Mother Earth has shaken many civilizations from her back, and it is not beyond reason that the principles of astrology and astronomy had evolved millions of years before the first white man appeared.'"

Sitting forward in my chair, I take a long drag from my cigarette and without lifting my eyes from the floor I say, "Stanford huh? Makes sense."

"I'm going to assume you mean that in a complimentary manner," Kate says, cutting her eyes at me.

"Now... now, go back to the part about your mother," Kate says, waving her hand at me as if to shoo away the last five minutes of conversation. "If she was a human, then what was your father? You have yet to explain how your mother came to conceive a vampire baby in Haiti or San Domingue whatever you were calling it," she asks, taking her seat again and ashing her cigarette in the tray. Turning towards me she checks the phone to make sure that it was still recording our conversation then sits back and crosses her legs with a serious look on her face as if to signify that I have her undivided attention.

I put my half-smoked cigarette in the ashtray and began my story again.

Chapter 7

My mother must have told me this story a thousand times in my youth. I begin it just as she would.

It was late spring and at this time of the year, there was a pungent yet delightful smell unlike any in the world, wafting everywhere, permeating all creatures across the savannah. A plethora of flowering plants dance and woo their future lovers with the mist of love pollen that flies and surges throughout the atmosphere like an invisible tsunami signifying a crashing vibration of pure molecular energy. A tangible spirit that can burn as well as it can freeze. The time when all that is natural executes her yearly menstruation that facilitates the growth of the innumerable plants and animals that flourish across the various terrains that comprise this continent. The quintessence of nature, an invisible force which if bottled could power today's dynamos at maximum output infinitely. To wield such power falls only to those with absolute intelligence, cunning, and shrewdness. To be able to bring forth life continually and abundantly while also understanding the necessity for all of it to wither away. Repeating the cycle again and again. Across cultures mankind always marks that unfathomable power with the pronoun "she." Nature is always "she."

Africa throughout ancient times was renowned for the magnificent creatures it produced, and my mother Zoya was no exception. At seventeen, she was two years past the marrying age for this part of what is now called Tanzania. Her lithe, tall body with ample hips and thighs, a signature feature of the women in this sphere of Terra, moves silently across the dirt floor. Her bare feet step with the muscle memory of her morning meal routine. As she

155

begins fire preparation, she is accosted by the storm of fragrance coming from spring plants mingled with the heat that rises from the loins of all animals and insects who are also entranced by the time that their bodies require them to seek the future no matter the cost. This beautiful brown girl who wears her family's traditional colors of red and white on this day knows that her yearnings and desires, however natural, must be curtailed. For her future is one that has been decided since the first moon of her existence. She is to be life-bringer and teacher to the one who is destined to maintain the crown and become the symbol that is most important to her family's way of life and stability for her kingdom. *'The Great Protector,'* as sometimes it was called, has dwelled in the mountains and caves surrounding those of Zoya's lineage since before the ancients built the Sphinx. Antecedent to the Alcheringa or the "Dream Time" referenced by the indigenous Australians as the period that shaped their clans. Prior to the time when man and beast understood each other as kin and there was no conflict between the two. Her people are said to have "indizela phansi njengokhokho" ("flown down like the falcon") and "kuthathwe konke okhule" ("seized all that was good") to create the abundance that they and their neighboring tribes enjoyed during those days.

"Sawubona," a voice from below calls to greet another villager. Recognizing the voice, Zoya stands up from her work and walks over to the window and looks down just as a group of young warriors going out for the day's hunt are passing. All were laden with bows and arrows in their quivers and sharp knives at their hips. They were on their merry way to capture hares, okapi, and waterfowl that will serve as dinner for the royal compound. Her usually serious face softens and she almost begins to smile as she watches the young handsome men proudly marching toward the bush

Behind them, a group of farmers and cattle herders approach with various domestic animals being shepherded into the village. In addition to the cows, they also managed a handful of large, stout goats, chickens kept in boxes made from reeds, and pigs on leashes being dragged unceremoniously between the strong men who approached the village in pairs in preparation for the feast. All the livestock have traveled here from their various farms to have their throats cut and their blood extracted for consumption along with their flesh. Some of the animals were already hanging over bowls with their throats slit in order to drain their blood. The women will then skin the slaughtered animals to prepare the meat for roasting. Each animal being carefully selected from surrounding villages for their size and quality to be the absolute best choice amongst the herd.

One of the stragglers from the hunting expedition slows his gait when he sees Zoya peering from the window down onto the parade of men. Emboldened by the impetuosity of youth, the young man cries out to Zoya. "Sawubona, beautiful one."

Zoya darts her eyes in both directions to be sure that she was the one being addressed with such temerity before she speaks. Her brow wrinkles and her delicate, expressionless face now fills with hot anger as she focuses on the speaker.

"How dare you open your foul mouth to address me in such a way," she spits at the young man.

"I carry the blood of the Ancient Ones, the founders of this world, the protectors of this land.

The ones feared by the lion and served by the falcon.

The very night is my precious sibling!

And you!

A common archer, dare to address me directly before the sacred home of my forebearers!"

Her brown eyes dance with blue flame at each inflection. Without raising her voice, "You will have to answer to my father for this insult." She hisses at the young man whose face is now in utter shock.

He meets her eyes for a brief moment to confirm the real anger he is sensing and quickly darts his eyes to the ground as he stammers..."I...I...apolog-"

"Too late!" she blurts out, cutting the young man off.

157

Zoya marches back into her empty hut with all the fake outrage she could muster. There was no one there that could voice her complaint to her father even if she were really inclined to do so. This was Zoya's way of causing drama to redirect her thoughts from the fear and frustration she was experiencing due to her apprehension about being betrothed to a complete stranger. She had been isolated in a hut on the edge of the family compound for the past 39 days, as required for the mental and physical preparation needed to enter the sacred caves and be judged worthy by the Spirits to carry the seed of the Ancient One. She must be able to overcome the overwhelming fear of descending into the caverns alone and weaponless and facing the perils of the Ancient One's domain alone.

She left the window and retreated down to the ground level where she began preparation for her morning meal by starting a fire in the hearth and grinding cassava into a powder to make bread. Her heart which longed to experience normal teenage 'puppy love' was again placed into a tiny hole and hidden away. Tears streamed down her face as she walked to the center of the room and collapsed to the floor sobbing quietly over the disappointment and unfulfilled ambition she felt in her life.

That year's spring rebirth festival marked the 720th solar cycle, a unique event that was to bring forth the next defender of the new age. According to the Elders the earth was approaching a new paradigm shift in the galaxy as we knew it. At the dawn of the next full moon, Zoya was to be crowned the next Queen Mother of the village to usher in this coming time of forecasted tumult. Her fate was marriage to the son of the moon. No matter what her heart may have yearned for. An arranged marriage was always met with antipathy, but the weight of these nuptials came with the added responsibility of her acting as a gateway between two very different worlds. A living wormhole to another dimension that will birth a child who is prophesied to be the next savior of this realm.

For over one thousand years, relative peace had reigned over this vast area in East Africa which consisted of parts of countries known today as the Democratic Republic of Congo, Uganda, Burundi, and Kenya respectively. All those territories were allowed to bask in decades of serenity due to our tiny village hidden halfway between Lake Mwitanzige (Albert) and Lake Rutanzige (Edward) in the southwestern part of the Ugandan Valley.

Before the Berlin Conference of 1884 and the carving up of Africa by the European powers at the time, there was only a minuscule fraction of the war, corruption, and famine that the continent of Africa is experiencing today. Most of the major issues stemmed from greedy foreign and domestic slavery exploitation. The chief priest of our village was very proficient in the ancient ways of summoning and conjuring and thus had exclusive access to the great and powerful Kuguruka Imbeba spirit who was immortal and could single-handedly destroy entire armies with his great strength and speed. The legend tells of the great Imana that soars in the shadow of the moon to drink the blood of his enemies.

Beware all who dare to leave their home under the watchful eyes of the moon goddess to seek bloodshed amongst their brothers.

This edict kept many a skirmish or land dispute from becoming a war because all parties desired a diplomatic approach to ending disputes instead of risking one's village and people to the wrath of the Kuguruka Imbeba.

As far back as even the eldest of the clan could remember a blood sacrifice was required to be delivered every fourth moon as the toll for the protection of this great Spirit. The sacrifice consisted of either the best female goats or cows which would be left staked to the ground in a circle drawn with limestone in the center of the ceremonial grounds. No one was allowed to venture outside or even have a window that was not covered in their home during the night of the sacrifice. The animals would be heard bleating and mooing one second and the in the next, the sound of the wind being sliced open would be heard right before dead silence and all traces of the animal sacrifice completely vanished along with the sound of every other creature in the area including the crickets and the cicadas. All of whom were said to be too frightened to speak in the presence of such a powerful aura.

Our village basked in the abundance and prestige showered upon them by the other nations and tribes in the surrounding region that coveted the protection afforded them by the Ancient Blooded One. Everyone lived with an outstanding sense of pride and achievement, especially the direct members of the chief's family. Zoya, being the eldest daughter of the chief's brother, had been groomed by her mother and kin to be the bearing vessel of the next savior which she, at first, understood to mean she would marry someone from her extended family and give birth to the next chief as was the usual custom. Love versus duty is an age-old dilemma for women ever since they were used as the first forms of currency. Sold by their fathers for a dowry to benefit the wealth of the family. Unbeknownst to her, she was to become the gateway to a being foretold to appear once in a star cycle who would prove to be far more exceptional than an ordinary chief, or shaman. Her belly was destined to house the lion disguised as a lamb who would bring ultimate salvation to the wickedness that was slowly creeping across the face of the earth.

As a child, Zoya always thought she would be very happy and excited at the opportunity to be queen, but deep inside her heart of hearts, the fear of what being betrothed to an unknown person known as *Kera Maraso* (The One with Ancient Blood) was not something that sounded pleasant for a young woman. Zoya sighed heavily as she poured a mixture of ugali and wali (rice and maize porridge) into a bowl for her breakfast. She sat on the floor and ate alone as the women of her tribe before her have done for eons to prepare for the moon cycle feasts of the past. Their belief was that a wife must have solitude to attain a clear mind and heart to prepare for her impending nuptials.

Zoya's mind was anything but clear as she sat on the floor lost in thoughts of all the scintillating and horrifying things she had been experiencing during her solitary confinement for the last month and ten days. The recurring dream or, better yet, nightmare that haunted her sleep night after night is one that found her naked in her hut lying on her back atop a firm bed of palm fronds arranged on the ground. Her virgin body is covered by a thin piece of an incredibly soft material, a texture unlike any she has ever felt before. Her back arches unconsciously and she feels the pressure of someone pressing their lips against her mouth and neck and the squeezing of each breast while simultaneously the bulb of a river reed is torturously being slowly dragged across the length of her body beginning at her feet and continuing up her ankles and shins, knees, and thighs. Her heart races as the moisture between her legs causes her to release her clinched lower regions and be nudged ever so gently by some still invisible but increasingly massive being. Zoya's eyes remain open during the seduction, never able to fully focus on what or who is creating this incredible sensation that begets such a throbbing of her soul. It is as if her body were hummingbird wings, vibrating between fiction and reality.

Zoya was now caressing her own form. Her left hand glided along the left side of her hips and ribcage up until it finds the full brown breast and taut round jet-black nipple slicing through the night air. Her right hand cautiously slides down across her stomach, past her navel, inching through the pungent bush of hair just above her sex. As her middle finger ever so slightly reaches the crest of her flower and her head falls to the side in total abandonment, she sees two yellow glowing horrible eyes looking at her from outside in the darkness. In the next instant the eyes are within the skull of a giant scaly brute of a man who is now climbing into the window of the hut and running at her with the fangs of a jackal and the claws and skin of a crocodile.

Zoya always awakened screaming, drenched in sweat. She had to force herself to go back to sleep and not to cry all night until morning like she used to do when the nightmares first began. Seeing those terrifying eyes piercing her through the dark in such a vulnerable moment felt so real to her.

Alone again in her hut to deal with the terror the best way she knew how. No one was permitted to come to her aid for this part of the tradition was to simulate the *solitude of the caves* in which every woman who was chosen to bear the next Chief or descendent seed of the 'mtu aliyekuja kabla ya wakati' (Man who preceded time) must endure. This passing of the seed had not happened for over 700 years. It was held to be an esteemed honor so great that Zoya's father has been elevated to Imana umwami w'abantu a wapanda bawa or Chieftain of the Winged Bat Clan as per the tradition. Thusly his brother was forced to honorably abdicate the throne. Being connected to the vessel of the *Great One* was such a high honor for the entire clan that there was not a hint of bad blood between family members during the transfer of the crown.

As the day of the fated event grew nearer, the celebration attendees came by the thousands from every corner of the territory wearing beautiful garments and adorned in the finest of jewels as testimony to the fabulous wealth that the area had been experiencing. My mother's family was said to be on par with the most revered royal courts of history and were world famous for their extravagance well before the great monarchies of the Queen of Sheba and Mansa Musa. Despite the accolades that she and her family were experiencing, Zoya still questioned why she was not happy to be taking part in something that would bestow such a high honor to herself and to her family? Why was she absolutely terrified of this marriage when she had never feared anything or anyone before?

The Elders consulted with Zoya's parents when she was but an infant and warned them that the new iteration of our ancient protector would not reveal himself until our darkest days were before us and that the future is indeed going to require one that is exceedingly strong to raise *this* savior to be a powerful warrior for when he is called to bring order to the chaos. These same Elders were present at the ceremonial feast to inform Imfume, Zoya's mother, to

"fear not because the seed that Zoya will carry was the one true champion that can finally defeat Ekwensu,(Evil or the devil) and bring balance and peace to the world once again. But first he must be born through the fire and must suffer the worst miseries this life has to offer one thousand times over. A cruel fate worse than any human could possibly endure."

The elders also spoke of a coming time of unimaginable tribulation that would topple every kingdom, including our own, which would last for hundreds of years. It will be during our darkest hour that Zoya's seed must shoulder unmentionable hardships before peace may be delivered and our kingdom will be restored."

Imfume was even more conflicted after hearing these words because as a mother she would have liked for her daughter's life to be free from hurt, harm, and danger, but she also knows that what was happening to their family was a preeminent honor and a deeply established and necessary tradition of their clan. How unlucky she was, Imfume thought to herself. To invest so much time and effort in raising such a beautiful and regal daughter only for her to suffer supreme heartache in order to fulfill a 700-year-old prophecy that to her was now feeling more like a curse. Imfume forced her emotions deep down inside her heart and wore a mask of composure for herself and her family throughout the ordeal so as to not be rude to the celebration guests despite her worries and misgivings. For in the end, she knew that whatever lay ahead must be shouldered by Zoya alone.

The sacred site of the Ancient Blooded One lay deep within a mountain range east of the impenetrable forest of the Bwindi and north of Lake Rwenshama amongst the Rwenzori peaks. It was a half day's journey for the swift of foot. The entrance of this sanctuary lies beneath the great waterfalls past the eucalyptus groves and the valley of the Nyamuragira. When Zoya would accompany her parents on the yearly pilgrimage to this site as a child, she would play here with the other children and they would all swim and play in the cool waters beneath the waterfalls, completely naked without a care in the world, utterly unaware that she was splashing and frolicking right next to the ancestral lair of the sentinel of her homeland.

The day prior to the night of the betrothal ceremony in the lake near the mouth of the sacred waterfall, Zoya was bathed and dressed by four royal attendants in addition to Mama Kassa and Zoya's mother, Imfume. Once she was made ready, she must enter the mysterious mountain alone, successfully traverse the precarious cave structure, and survive a trial by fire to be worthy of her future husband. The attendants carefully washed and adorned Zoya with pleasant fragrances. Her young adult body was covered from head to toe in a long yellow dress that struck a beautiful contrast with her unblemished dark brown skin. The dress draped down over her sandals so she had to hold it up with one hand while she walked to avoid stumbling. She also wore a belt made of cloth dyed a deep purple that perfectly bifurcated her hourglass figure. On her head, she wore a dazzlingly colored scarf made by her mother, who created it using the same deep purple material as the belt which acknowledged her family's royal standing during the feast ceremony. After a brief prayer by her father the chief, and four other elders, Zoya is carried on a bed of reeds and leopard skins by six of the strongest warriors trailed by two of the priestesses from the village into a dense patch of trees surrounding the sacred entrance to the forbidden forest and the vast cavern in which lie her goal. Zoya dismounted the bed of reeds, is given a final blessing by the priestesses, and then left alone in the forest as her traveling party returned to the village.

As she walked through the bush, Zoya's demeanor betrayed no thoughts of fear or worry though her heart was pounding inside of her chest. She had been groomed for this moment from infancy, and she knew she must face this ordeal head on. Not only for the honor of her family and tribe but also for the safety of the nation. Zoya had always been athletically inclined and throughout the village, she carried a reputation of being a fearless and capable warrior, but tonight this exterior façade was merely a mask for her true feelings that harbor a distinct wariness of becoming not just a mate but also a meal for this *man* who was simultaneously a *beast*. Alongside the fear she tried desperately to suppress, Zoya's spirit harbored a feeling of loss for her heart that would never truly be able to explore falling in love with someone of her choice and having that love reciprocated.

"What is one woman's heart compared to the hearts of nations?"

Zoya asked herself as her sense of duty returned to fortify her resolve against the doubt and fear that would cause her to turn and run for dear life. Minutes became hours as she walked amongst the dark silent trees. Every shadow reminded Zoya of some creeping thing. It was as if the silent trees of the impenetrable forest were watching her every move. Zoya came to a clearing in the forest and managed to suppress her fear enough to look to the heavens and adjust her trajectory towards the sacred entrance to the caverns hidden within the trees. After three hours of anxious walking through the perilous forest, Zoya could finally see the grove of tall, one-meter-thick brown mahogany trees in a tight formation around a humongous Ceiba tree with massive, twisted roots that were well over seven feet above ground. Inside one of these gigantic roots lies the pathway into the underground caverns of the ancients.

Zoya climbed up onto the lower part of the root system where a small entrance caused her to have to pull her dress above her knees and walk in a crouched position down a short corridor and into a small, ornately carved chamber. The clan that Zoya was born into has always worshiped the night and the moon as their primary deities and evolved to have pupils and iris' that gave them very good vision in low light. However, the tunnel leading to the interior of the mountain was extremely dark and the builders of this pathway were wise enough to install a handrail that jutted out from the wall to guide clan members through the darkness.

After a relatively short walk, Zoya reached a familiar landing that marked the top of a spiral staircase. This part of the journey was familiar from her childhood. Zoya groped on the wall to her left until she found a cut out where sat a small bowl of palm oil mixed with animal fat. Next to the bowl of the flammable mixture in a hole chiseled into the rock face was a flint rock and striking stone. Zoya remembered the way the elder would strike the stone and send sparks into the dish that would ignite and bring an amazing yellow glow to everything in the tunnel. It was so dark within the tunnel that even that small amount of light made a huge difference.

As she walked deeper into the tunnel Zoya physically began to tremble with fear. The solitude training she took part in during the last forty days was not helping her cope with the realization that she was all alone, hundreds of feet below the earth's surface. Soon Zoya could hear the roaring waters of the sacred waterfall ahead of her. As she reached the opening to this mighty naturally occurring phenomenon, there was another cut out in the rock face for Zoya to place the bowl of still burning palm oil mixture. The mist from the crashing water of the waterfall was so heavy that it almost extinguished the flame. As Zoya approached, the mist began to be absorbed by her dress causing the shape of her voluptuous 19-year-old body to be revealed even more so as the delicate material of the garment clung to her flesh. Her body began to shiver as the temperature of the cavity behind the waterfall was much lower than the upper parts of the cave.

At times Zoya had trouble keeping her balance as she traversed the stones leading down into the inner cavern while the sound of the water bellowed from the rush of the falls. She stepped onto a surface with three roughly hewn steps on the side of the stone that led to a flat shoal area just beneath and behind the main waterfall. The sound of the crashing water is heard above all else, and Zoya must keep one hand against the wall while the other hand has a fist full of dress being held up to allow Zoya's legs to move more freely. Once fully behind the crashing water of the falls she began to carefully traverse the narrow walkway path which led deeper into the pitch-black cave at the bottom of the waterfall where her frightening journey into earth will begin.

Although fearful, she began the arduous journey full of energy and stamina but after hours of trekking, Zoya was exhausted. She stopped to rub her sore feet again after what seemed like miles of walking in the twists and turns of the voluminous cave system. She was lost as to which direction the mountain lay, confused by the many crisscrossing paths throughout the endless tunnel. The only saving grace was the fact that the pathways were surprisingly well lit due to the presence of peculiar flocks of fireflies that clustered around a sticky paste-like substance that oozed from the cracks in the rock-face. At a few intervals along the path, the strange substance appeared to be smeared and unnaturally caked in certain pockets as if done recently by human hands. Zoya hesitantly continues along the path, jumping at every noise she hears. Her heart beating out of her chest with fear as she journeyed all alone, deeper and deeper into the bowels of the earth.

A grueling 48 hours had passed since Zoya entered the cave system labyrinth. The insects that flitted about and provided the only light were once cute and unique to Zoya, but now they only served to confuse and annoy her. She was now hopelessly lost, miles beneath the surface of the earth. Despite her rigorous training in the bush, Zoya was not mentally prepared for the frustration and despair she would encounter being lost in a maze of dark tunnels full of jagged crystal growth. Zoya's stomach burned with hunger and her feet bled from wounds caused by the rough terrain. After another few hours of walking in the dimmed tunnels, Zoya reached an area with no connecting pathways, what she deduced was the 'end of the line'. The walls and ceiling of the small cove where the trail ended were covered in crystal formations and twinkled brightly as the night sky lit by many clusters of the glowing insects covering the room, crawling busily along the surfaces of the room, flying around the gaping chamber and gently landing on Zoya's exhausted shoulders and head scarf like little bits of starlight.

On the wall directly in front of her, the glowing insect bodies illuminated an area with no crystals jutting from it. Carved into the flat space was a winged eye shaped symbol that closely resembled the talisman that the Elders wore on the night of the ceremonial feast. She ran her fingers across the etching in the stone admiring the skill with which it was carved, perfectly with no signs of chiseling or digging. She looked all around but cannot find a way up or out of the progressively darker cavern now that the fireflies have for some reason decided to begin to disperse, having consumed their fill of the sticky material. Zoya tells herself not to panic and that she is of royal blood and as such she should be brave and level headed in times of adversity, but after about an hour of sitting in the dark on the ever colder stone floor without a solid plan, she began to hallucinate that the air was

166

getting thinner and that at any moment an earthquake would occur and she would be crushed under the weight of the millions of tons of rock above her. Or worse, she may simply starve to death on this damp floor as a pitiful offering to a nonexistent deity to appease some archaic tradition of her people. Dying alone...never knowing true love.

Lightheaded from thirst and exhaustion, Zoya's vision began to deteriorate along with her mental state which was spiraling downward rapidly from depression and self-pity. Her once intrepid and fearless attitude had now turned into anguish and heartbreak after hours of sitting in the pitch dark on the bare floor in a thin dress with no possible way out and no expectation of anyone coming to rescue her. Cold, hunger, and thirst were now ripping through her body in waves.

The utter torment of coming to the realization that her fate was always to die alone in order for her village to accommodate some unseen deity who only cherishes blood began to enrage her. In her desperation, Zoya released an earsplitting scream. She stood up and violently began to smack and claw at the walls of the cavern. Her emotional state grew quite erratic. Gnashing her teeth and cursing the Elders and the wisdom of the Ancients one minute and in the next she was sobbing and begging the gods desperately to provide her a way out of the damp dark cave. As she clashed against the shadows, she cut her hand on the jagged crystals jutting from the wall and blood began to pour from the wound uncontrollably, causing her to become dizzy and stumble around blindly in the darkness. Her fury returned as the faces of people like her parents and the Elders appeared before her, all of whom she felt masqueraded as wise counsel, but were just selfish tyrants who could callously decide the fate of a young girl to be sacrificed to appease some myth. A fairy tale betrothal to an imaginary creature that somehow was supposed to protect the kingdom. She remembered the symbol of her pain etched masterfully into the stone and gropes in the darkness along the floor and up the wall until she finds the shape of the eye with her fingers. Tears streamed down her face as Zoya bashed the symbol with her bloody fists all the while cursing and spitting virulent profanities until she collapsed from dehydration and exhaustion. Her hand smeared the warm red liquid gushing from her wound down the wall as she tried to stop herself from falling face first onto the ground. She slumped to the bare floor, unconscious and taking very shallow breaths, sadly approaching her very lonely, ignoble death.

Chapter 8

Zoya awakened with a start, as out of breath as she was before she blacked out. Was it all just another nightmare? After a few more moments, she realized that she was still inside the underground tunnel complex, which was completely dark except for a small gathering of glowing insects high upon the ceiling above her. The small amount of light against the darkness was enough for her eyes to begin to adjust, and she realized that she had somehow been moved to a different space than the one she collapsed in. This area of the tunnels had flat, smooth walls, undoubtedly hewn by human hands. There was a cushion of infinite softness between her and the ground which she could not help but glide her fingers back and forth over. In disbelief that there existed an animal with fur that soft. She reached for the wound on her hand and felt the armored bodies of a neat line of siafu (ant) heads used as a suture to hold the skin of the cut together of the once wicked gash which was now healing rapidly. She ran her hand across her face and over her head and down the back of her neck where she felt two small bumps from a puncture wound that she somehow received while unconscious. Zoya attempted to stand clumsily, still woozy from the blood loss and as she reaches her feet, she called out hoarsely

"S-S-Sawubona (Hello), i-i-i-is anyone there?"

168

She was grateful that her life had been saved but was somewhat fearful as to what manner of mysterious people could be living this far under the mountain. Zoya willed herself to continue to stand as she listened for a response, but the dizziness returned and forced her to lie back down onto the soft cushion. She closed her eyes as a sharp headache began to form behind her left eyeball. It was then that she noticed that she was no longer cold, and it occurred to her that she could feel a jet-stream of warm air from some unseen vent in the roof of the cavern, creating a very pleasant temperature for a pit several miles below the earth.

A trickle of lights floated into the room from unseen crevices and began to congregate on the moisture on the walls as if they were released on cue by someone who knew she was awake. The fireflies gradually began to congregate in mass giving Zoya enough light to see her dungeon which, when exposed to the light, revealed itself to be a rather beautiful nest. The massive rock walls were indeed polished flat. Smooth as sheets of ice and again with no chisel marks. One of the walls of the room was riddled from top to bottom with intricate carvings, illustrating things she recognized such as lions, elephants, men carrying spears, yams, people dancing, and depictions of bodies in the solar system like the moon, sun, and stars. There were also many shapes, symbols, letters, and numbers that she did not recognize. Boats and canoes with no sail or oars and men and women with the faces of animals such as reptiles, birds, hyenas, and leopards.

It was then that she noticed her soiled mavazi ya harusi (wedding dress) was gone and instead, she wore a garment of a material many times more luxurious than anything she had ever felt against her skin. The frock hung lightly from her shoulders and was smooth and cool to the touch. It was nearly the same yellow but more vibrant, almost gold in color which further complemented her radiant dark brown skin perfectly in the glow of the insect lamps.

She inspected her wound again in the light and could barely believe her eyes at what looked like three days of healing on such a deep cut taking place in what seemed to have only been a few hours. The smell inside the cave was noticeably pleasant. Not the stench of mildew or bat guano and sulfurous gasses that she imagined would be emanating from such a foreboding dwelling, but a wafting of burnt materials like lemongrass oil or patchouli, the same as what she and her family used in the spring rituals in the village new year celebration. Zoya could also swear that she heard the faint sound of running water nearby.

The next thing she noticed with her nose were five small stone pedestals with polished granite trays each with a different selection of fruits, nuts, vegetables steamed and non-steamed, dried fish, fruit juices, and various roasted meats. Some of which she had seen before but most of which proved to be exotic delicacies from lands and cultures far distant from the Kikorongo Valley of her upbringing. Directly in front of her on a separate pedestal rested a large gourd with a carving of what appeared to be her image wearing a crown of flowers carved into the side of it. Upon closer inspection, Zoya found the gourd to be filled with the purest, most refreshing water she had ever passed over her lips. The water crashing down into her empty belly coupled with the smell of the food produced a pain in her gut which jarred Zoya further out of her fear of dying miserably in a dark mountain cave. She fell upon the delicious food, her dehydrated body not caring from where it came or who prepared it. She made sure to taste a small portion of each dish, filling her belly gluttonously. Zoya capped the meal off with a beetroot wine that was in a shallow challis positioned behind the fruit trays.

After eating and drinking her fill, Zoya fell languidly back onto her cloud pillow. Her headache now subsided, before she knew it she had fallen back into a deep sleep again. During the nap she dreamt of seeing the bush from above as if she were a bird flying at night. In the dream, she could still see all the nocturnal creatures and the people very clearly even though the stars were ahead of her and there was no sun to speak of. In the dream, she lands near a large stream babbling peacefully near an area that resembled her father's birth village. The sound of the water pulls her gently out of her dream and back to the reality of the dark cavern. As she dreamily blinked back to the present dimension, she realized that she had to urinate. The embarrassing thought that she must have involuntarily relieved herself during her unconsciousness washed through her mind because she did not remember using it since before she passed out. She stands up on still slightly unsteady legs and looks around the now dimly lit cave. She noticed that the trays of food had been removed and only the water and wine remained.

170

Uncertainty and fear began to return, gripping Zoya in a fit of paranoia.

"What if the food was laced with some type of sedative that is causing her to let her guard down." Zoya thinks to herself "Maybe this person or these people are fattening her up to be a human sacrifice to the Ancient Blooded One."

"S-S-Sawubona......" she calls hoarsely, her voice still weak since falling unconscious. "Sawubona...." she said again in a more normal tone with an added hint of sweetness.

As if she flipped a switch, a path on the floor began to take shape, illuminated by the peculiar fireflies again. Zoya reluctantly follows the trail of insects for about three hundred feet to an opening in the rock face that leads to another chamber riddled with a dazzling variety of quartz crystal formations jutting out from the walls and ceilings. To her surprise, between a row of the stalagmites ran a small stream of crisp, clear water flowing freely through the maze-like cave system. Zoya was slowly led by the firefly path to an area behind a rock formation that, to her surprise, revealed a polished granite squat bowl over a discreet hole in the cavern floor, complete with tembo majani ya sikio (elephant ear) leaves for hygiene.

After relieving herself and freshening up in the stream, Zoya walked back down the path to her bed chamber and began to inspect the murals and hieroglyphs on the walls again more closely. Her curiosity led her to follow the carvings around the main enclosure and into another part of the antechamber where the subject matter of the wall carvings changed into depictions of the Ancients in the lands beyond the valley before the sea swallowed them. Zoya discovered detailed drawings of the creation epic, including a mural representing the truth behind who the original teachers of her ancestors were and the tales of their glorious empire that delighted in the thousand years of relative peace over earth realm. As she wandered further, she speculated on what advanced tools the people who inhabited these caves used to be able to excavate the tons of dirt and stone out of the cavern while creating the walls and the narrow paths that she walked on which had been smoothed and leveled so expertly with only the dim light provided by these insects.

Zoya forced herself to overcome the irrepressible sense of dread she felt from being miles beneath the earth alone with some yet unseen person or group of people who are clearly watching her every move. After silently wandering and exploring her surroundings for the better part of an hour, Zoya could find no signs whatsoever that anyone other than herself had been in the cave recently. There was no trace of other animals or insects other than the strange fireflies which Zoya began to find very odd. Especially since the food she ate was freshly harvested. Emboldened by her familiarity with her surroundings, Zoya began to venture deeper into the tunnels. She noticed that there were certain corridors that had noticeably fewer fireflies. Her eyes adjusted accordingly as she felt her way around in the darkest areas of the cavern. Determined to find her hidden hosts, Zoya ventured further into segments of the cave with the lowest visibility. She eventually stumbled upon a corridor with rough-hewn walls and floors. Much more jagged and rocky than the surfaces in the main chamber. Zoya's thick-skinned feet were unfazed by the rough terrain as she cautiously followed the obscure corridor about one hundred yards until the tight hallway opened into a large curved open space within the substrata of the cave.

"Ayiiyyyee!!"

Zoya shrieked.

Startled by the unexpected change in the texture of the ground.

Someone had placed a large amount of grass straw here presumably to not only soak up the moisture but also to provide a resting area for livestock. Zoya took a series of deep breaths in a struggle to control her fear. She reminds herself that she is the descendent of the great Ikiyoka priestesses and that she must show strength as representative of her nation.

Zoya's eyes had adjusted enough to the darkness to discern more of the details of this inner chamber which also seemed to have been crafted by human hands, only the walls were not polished smoothly as the walls within the main chambers. She thought to herself that for a cave hidden miles beneath the earth, her surroundings had been surprisingly elegant and sophisticated. Her eyes had adjusted enough to the darkness that she could make out shapes of objects and move around somewhat easier without the risk of stumbling. As she scanned around the large chamber, she could see that there was a structure in the room. It looked to be a heap of straw, about ten feet in length and five feet in width, shaped like a bed, and covered with various zebra and okapi pelts.

"Who sleeps there?" she thought to herself absently.

As she looked around squinting in the dark, there were other shapes nearby that looked to be merely smaller tufts of straw randomly scattered around the room. One massive lump of darkness that she had not noticed before now sat directly opposite her. The smell of dried perspiration hits her nose. The same aroma she would smell when someone who was recently outside came inside the house. Other than the bed, she swore that there was nothing else this large in the room moments ago. Her eyes locked on it now, and a sick feeling began to grow in the pit of her stomach. Zoya knew that this huge lump could not have been there when she was making her way into the room or else she would have surely bumped into an object so broad. That was when two burning yellow-orange flames appeared near the top center of the dark lump. Zoya froze with panic and her throat went desert dry. The dark lump rose and seemed to rise forever as the huge frame of a man stood and filled Zoya's field of vision. As he stood, not only did he get impossibly taller but something from his back extended both ways horizontally making the creature before her seem to completely fill what she once believed to be a huge space.

For all her fearlessness, her courage, her preparation...nothing readied her for this.

She could not move.

She could not scream.

She was frozen in place with terror.

The creature approached her slowly, feeling her dread, smelling her need to run. As he reached her, Zoya tried to open her mouth and say something, anything to protest being killed and eaten by this huge creature but no words would form. She wanted to scream in protest, but no sound

173

would come out. A huge hand darted out, grabbed her forearm, and pulled her effortlessly from the ground and into his huge heaving naked chest.

Zoya's faculties began to return as she gazed into the now, sharp, silver eyes at first thinking she should use her nails to claw at them and try to escape from this beast, but the firm yet gentleness of his embrace did not feel like malice or ill intent. His dark brown stoic face reflected the reverence and care that he had for the frightened Zoya as he caressed her back and shoulders as if attempting to comfort a crying child.

Zoya felt her muscles relax as the hypnotic gaze of the creature activated the venom that was injected into her bloodstream from the bite she received while she was unconscious. The effects of the creature's saliva influenced Zoya specifically by flooding her mind with the memories of the ancestor spirit of Nzambici (Goddess of Essence, Moon and Sky.) Her thoughts of fear and hesitation vanished and she transformed spiritually into the embodiment of the great Goddess. Zoya's body began to respond in kind as she relaxed to receive the caress of the giant scaly hands of the creature moving eagerly across her solid frame. Their passionate petting progressed rapidly. As Zoya descended deeper into the trance, her mind was opened to the wisdom of the Ancients and serenity swept over her in waves as she absorbed years of maturity in mere minutes. Soon Zoya would become a vessel of transition to a supernatural being powerful enough to topple nations.

The massive wings of the creature slowly enclosed around itself and her, its lips pressed against Zoya's waiting mouth, and her body responded by softening totally. Her dress is pulled up and over her head in one fluid motion and tossed onto the straw covered floor. All her muscles began to unclench and allow the two to begin to become one flesh. Her body was assaulted by a flurry of gentle kisses and large powerful hands caressed every inch of her supple skin. Her eyes fluttered with ecstasy as fluid within her system surges to the area between her thighs. The tender strength of this brute's touch seemed to play her body like a banjo, sending shivers up and down her spine that vibrated with a feeling of connection to the universe that was embodied in all the sensual parts of her recurring dream.

After an eternity on the edge of mortal rapture in the arms of her hypnotic lover, Zoya felt a large pressure against her leg, moving up her thighs, between her ample hips, and then suddenly the pain and pleasure she felt from the penetration of this man-creature touches a place inside her that she herself did not know she possessed. Thrust after thrust, the creature released a powerful electricity into her soft, quivering flesh. It held her body tightly like a loving boa constrictor as her heart raced in her now exposed breasts. She wrapped her legs around the creature's waist as her body was suspended by its powerful arms. It unwrapped its wings from around them, and with one mighty flap, they were airborne. Its arms held her securely against its chest as they ascended above all light, gliding on the currents flowing through the cave. Naked before the gods, united in the carnal dance of the deified rite to create an Immortal being that will upend the evil machinations of modern man. Her moans and heavy breathing echoed through the miles of tunnels call forth the ancestral spirits from the nether realms to bear witness to this union of mortal and immortal flesh to produce a unique and blessed being. As their bodies writhed together rhythmically like a dragon undulating through the clouds of the night sky, Zoya's eyes rolled up into her skull.

"Aaaaaaaaaayyyyyyyyyyiiiiiiiiiiiiiiiieeeeeeeeeeeeeeeeee!"

A flap of the creature's mighty wings kept them airborne as Zoya liberated a reverberant scream from the pits of her diaphragm, unleashing a shockwave of emotion as she climaxed with a tremendous force. Wrenching her head back, her eyes shut and soaking with tears of ecstasy her body reverberated and trembled like a tuning fork. Inflamed neurons sent the muscles in her body into spasmodic fits that gripped around the substantial member within the walls of her vagina clenching and releasing constantly and rhythmically causing the Ancient Blooded One to also explode with a tremulous growl, bathing her uterus with his special seed that would flow throughout her nubile young body and forever change her molecular structure to become something more akin to a god than a human being. As Zoya's mind left the trance, her body became heavy and she could barely keep her eyes open. She fainted into the arms of the creature, falling again into a deep satisfying sleep.

The following morning, Zoya awoke in the main hut of the compound next to her mother, not unlike what she would have done in her recent youth. Her mother sat quietly humming while she busied herself weaving a basket from discarded Millet stalks and dyed raffia. Zoya sat up with a start and began touching herself to see if she was still in one piece and had not been devoured.

"Was it all a dream?" she wondered.

The last thing she remembered was being airborne in the arms of her winged lover. The only blemish she could find on her body was a small scratch on her hand where she nearly bled out only a few hours prior and two small marks on her neckline where the scabs had already fallen off and were already close to being completely healed. She looked down at the blue kanga dress covering her body, relieved that she was not still naked but perplexed on how she came to be home so quickly after traveling for days and so many miles beneath the surface of the earth.

Zoya began recalling everything she could remember to her mother and, as she spoke, it all seemed too surreal to be factual. As she told her story, Zoya noticed how her mother's face beamed as she listened intently while her swift fingers expertly threaded the Millet and colorful raffia into beautiful patterns on the outside of the basket. She did not utter a word other than sounds of acknowledgement as her daughter recanted every detail she could remember.

Chapter 9

There was a monumental nine months of feasts and celebrations following Zoya's impregnation and initiation into the Imana Ubwami Royal bloodline. In seven hundred years, there had not been a commemoration of such magnitude. From the West, East, North, and South all the tribes of the land sent representatives, some from over one hundred miles away who brought gifts of food, fine cloth, exotic animals, trinkets, and gadgets from their respective nations to honor the tremendous occasion. Everyone was keen to pay tribute to the 'Warrior of the Night' for providing for their safety and prosperity with ceremonial tribute dances and songs, wearing luxurious garments as well as fine jewelry, and presenting traditional dishes and ambrosial delicacies from all over the territory.

Singing and merrymaking went on around many fires all night long, and everyone rested in the large comfortable compound during the day. Partygoers were encouraged to stay for at least a week before returning to their respective homelands, and all were accommodated in the spacious royal estate. As each new group of guests would arrive, they would sleep until sunset the next day and then arise to sing and dance all night once again to pay homage to Nzambici the moon Goddess and the spirits of Imana.

Each day, new celebrants would come in from another country or village bringing food and drinks to replenish the feast from the previous night's festivities. It was all to congratulate my family, as an offering to Imana for blessings and protection over them and their kin, and for prosperity for the future. There were tribesmen at the celebration that had traveled from the far outskirts of the kingdom and would regale the royal court with tales of the world and the changes happening in the surrounding nations.

One subject that seemed to be a reoccurring topic of conversation were the tales of men with white skin who had made alliances with the old slavers amongst the Arabian nations and those from the Northern provinces to kidnap and trade for the men, women, and children. Blind ambition and jealousy had fueled some of the neighboring tribes' people into aiding the flesh trade in order to acquire the foreigners' weapons, rum, textiles, and trinkets which they will resort to all manner of underhanded tactics to acquire. The invaders were said to be learning our ways and customs and then instigating petty disputes between tribes into full-on wars with the purpose of dividing the people and making them weak for plundering. There were those who spoke privately with the elders about whole villages disappearing for the sake of profits for these slave traders. They say that the scale and cruelty inflicted upon the people is magnitudes worse than the operation maintained by the Islamic slave holocaust that began many moons ago and continues to ravage some of our countrymen on the northeastern border of the kingdom. There is fear amongst the allied nations that even the great Ikiyoka (Dragon) will find it difficult to defeat these foreigners who use greed to make enemies of brothers and sisters who, under normal circumstances, would never resort to violence and subversion.

Despite every effort by the clan chiefs and elders to dissuade the people against losing faith in the power of the Ancient Blooded One, it was clear that this year's feast was seriously marred by an atmosphere of worry and trepidation. Zoya was now the equivalent of Empress over every mountain, river, lake, and blade of grass she beheld. She was assigned twelve female attendants, one from each of the main surrounding tribes. She was moved into her own separate compound which was guarded by twelve elite bodyguards, each from the primary surrounding tribes. As the months went on, Zoya's belly grew with the seed of the Ancient Blooded One and at the full moon of each month, there would be a mini feast attended by one of the heads of each tribe to mark the nine cycles which corresponded to the eight planets and the moon. Zoya always tried to remain modest and gracious despite all the attention and adornment she was receiving. She was still a young woman at heart who had yet to experience life outside of her village, and now she was stuck in a pampered lifestyle serving as a vessel for the coming savior. A role that with all her grooming, she still felt unworthy to fulfill. Now that she was head of state, at times she would be expected to make decisions that could impact the kingdom, a task in which she also felt entirely unworthy. All because of this strange little being she carried in her womb, a being who would remain perfectly still until nightfall and then would begin to move around restlessly until dawn.

Strangely, Zoya did not experience any sickness or nausea related to the pregnancy. As a matter of fact, she noticed a strength and litheness of movement that she never had before. In her fifth month of pregnancy at the new moon feast, she was cutting a large piece of roasted goat, against the wishes of her attendants, to share with her nieces and nephews. The blade she was cutting with was very sharp and she accidentally cut herself, making a very deep gash along the ridge of her thumb on her left hand. After washing the blood away with water from a gourd, she wrapped the finger tightly with a piece of palm leaf to stem the bleeding. The next morning when her attendant came to change the leaf and clean the wound, the cut was already closed as if it had been healing for a few days. By the end of the week there was only a keloid from where the scar had been. The Ancient Blooded One was already blessing her with his strength.

During the feast of the moon for Zoya's seventh month of pregnancy, there came a warning from the East by Chief Araya who lived on the coast in the country that is now called Eritrea that the legends of The Ancient Blooded One had reached the ears of foreigners that resided in northern Alkebulan, just south of Kemet. The invaders were being told rumors that our villages were selfishly hoarding untold riches that are coveted by the white man. They said that many who would normally have made the journey to commemorate the Moon Goddess are now unwilling because of the fear of ambush by slavers who work for the pale-faced man. Brother Araya spoke of the fact that when the men with white skin first came, they were welcomed as guests and everyone humored their attempts to convert the people to their strange gods and superstitions which they openly believed to be more powerful than our ancestors. We saw them as no more than a curiosity until they returned with some of our brethren and began to make very hostile demands. They boasted of great weapons and traveled with a wagon full of chains built of iron for all who defied their authority. When our brethren informed them that this was the land of the Ancients and that they should beware the wrath of the Son of the Moon, our people were mocked. They laughed at them outright, stating that their savior was the true Ancient One who would vanquish our nonsense and make them his footstool. The Elders gasped at such blasphemous speech.

To Zoya's surprise, her father, who was usually very passive, stood up and stamped his staff into the ground to call for silence. With a grave look on his face he spoke to the crowd in Kinyarwandan saying, "We should be reminded of the prophecy of the coming end times. The prophecy states that before the Ancient Blooded One can triumph, there must come a time of wickedness. A time when the elephant and the lion spirits will be under the jurisdiction of a man, and the people will be strangers within their own lands."

Every night during the ceremonial feasts the young men and women danced about the fires to the pulsating drum beat in wild abandon. They were blissfully unaware that just a few hundred feet away their fate was being decided by the Elders who brooded over this new foreboding information. The married women and the children sang their traditional songs in their trill contralto voices, singing praises to the Ancients and the ancestors amongst other sounds of joy and abundance. The festivities continued well into the night as the roast meat and Makayabu (salt fish) along with the Urwagwa (banana beer) was still bountiful. However, as Zoya's belly grew and the time for each month's moon festival came around, the surplus of food began to dwindle due to the drop in attendance. This noticeable absence was attributable to the people's fear of making the long journey to the Kikorongo Valley under the threat of slave trading foreigners. Zoya tried to greet everyone with the same joy and exuberance she usually showed during the moon festivals, but the news of the kidnappings of the people never to be heard from or seen again concerned her more than anything ever had before.

The next full moon would mark Zoya's eighth month of pregnancy. Her day began as normal with her being bathed and dressed by her attendants before being served ugali with Ntaba (roasted goat) and groundnut stew. The next moon festival was less than two weeks away and tensions were mounting because of a strange message that was delivered the night prior. The message said that slavers attacked a Kasenyi village just east of the Kikorongo Valley and a battle ensued in which there were men with their modern weapons mixed in among those traitors who led them to the populated areas of the bush. The brave men and women of the village were said to have put up a valiant defense effort but were overwhelmed by the long-range weapons of the white-faced man. A third of the men were killed by having their heads removed in front of the rest of the villagers to serve as an example of the cruelty their new captors were capable of. It was said that women were raped and the children were beaten in front of the remaining men to further humiliate and degrade the citizens.

The survivors were chained together in a long line and made to walk to the river where they were forced to board large rafts that would take them to the sea, never to return. The message also said that the entire village was burned to the ground and since they were careful to begin the attack at dawn, they believe that someone working with their group was coaching them on how to avoid the wrath of the Mwana w'ukwezi (Son of the Moon). The messenger added that by noon, the entire town was scattered to bits and the people crushed and corralled. They would then march their procession of the defeated immediately back to their well-disguised camps in the forest with the aim of avoiding the Ancient Blooded Ones air patrols over this area of the bush at night which further suggested that someone with deep knowledge of our culture was assisting those slave traders and mercenaries. Whomever it was, they were very well versed in the legends of the people of the region, and they were being careful to use the Ancient Blooded Ones's rival, the sunlight, as their shield when they planned their attacks.

Zoya was visibly shaken after hearing such a horrible account. She touched her cool hand to her warm belly as its little inhabitant shifted restlessly in accord with mommy's preoccupation. Her father had already issued an order that all warriors were to prepare as if for battle and to station a handful of swift footed men just outside the main valley that led to the village to warn us of any enemy approach. There was also an additional ceremony given by the chief priest Ometwetwe who fervently prayed to the Ancestors for protection and guidance by the Ancient Blooded One, the great

Kera Maraso. During the ceremony, tears of blood ran down the silent face of the elder shaman who spoke in the ancient tongue of the primitive times. His visions revealed the coming decline of our peace in the hope of ushering in a new age and allow us to learn from our mistakes and petty quarrels that have plagued our past.

A few weeks before Zoya's delivery time, there was an immense fire in the forest to the north of the village. The fire threatened to destroy a very lucrative Okapi hunting ground near Lake Mutanda which supplied the surrounding area with meat from the large game that visited the lake and various streams as their watering hole. Some of the men who were standing guard around the village were forced to leave their post and use their weapons and tools to create a fire break between the main village and the approaching fire. Another group of the men chopped down palm leaf branches to smash out the flames while others shoveled dirt from the fire break onto the fire to smother it. The alarm went up in the village a few hours before daybreak. It was after dawn when most of the flames had been extinguished when,

BRRRRTCH! BRRRRRTCH! BRRRRTCH! BRRRROW!

 a sound echoed from the direction of the fire. It sounded like a series of large trees snapping or a rock falling from a high distance.

KATHOOM! KATHOOM! KATHOOM! KATHOOM! KATHOOM!

Another series of sounds like that of thunder and shockwaves felt for miles came from the sacred mountain. Plumes of smoke were seen in the distance coming from the entrance to the underground cave system where the Kera Maraso's home lay deep beneath the earth. Whoever was attacking Zoya's village knew enough about their defense systems to ignite large amounts of gunpowder throughout the sacred mountain geared toward hindering their protector. Reports from the men stationed as lookouts high in the trees sent word of clouds of dust and smoke coming from a gaping hole in the side of the mountain due to the collapse of the caves and tunnel systems within. In spite of efforts by the Chief and the Elders to calm the people, the fires and the unsettling explosion sounds had the villagers in a full-on panic. Zoya ran to the window of her bedroom to see the plumes of smoke rising in the distance as her attendants hurriedly made preparations for her to escape into the bush in case the fires threatening the village could not be contained.

The next noises Zoya heard was the sound of men yelling and the hooves of animals outside the walls of the village.

KAPOW! KRRRRTCH! KAPOW!

Gunshots!

The screams of women and children ripped through the compound as the invaders broke through the defense perimeter of the main gate into the village and indiscriminately began whipping and beating the fleeing villagers. Children were snatched from their mother's bosom, tied up with coarse rope and dragged away spitting and screaming for their parents. The invaders went about killing the lame and the elderly by bashing their heads with rocks or the butts of their rifles to save ammunition. The men and women who could fight took up spears and swords and tried valiantly to protect the village from the murderous slave catchers, but their superior weapons and savage combat tactics quickly overwhelmed the defenders.

"Your highness we must leave NOW!!"

Lieutenant Zawadi Sabo, Zoya's second cousin and the head of her personal security detail, ran full speed into the room and grabbed Zoya by her arm.

"Your Highness we must leave now before we are surrounded by these barbarians!

Running down the corridor to the rear entrance, Zawadi, Zoya and her twelve attendants were met by a vanguard of the remainder of her security detail who encircled them within a wall of shields, swords and longbows as they exited the backdoor into the lower courtyard.

Zoya's heart broke as she ran past walls splattered with fresh blood and bodies of friends and extended family lying strewn about like bits of rubbish in the road.

KRAPOW!!!

Blood splattered Zoya's dress as one of the royal guards protecting her is killed by a headshot. In an instant —

THWIP, THWIP, THWIP, THWIP, THWIP, THWIP THWIP!

Arrows flew almost in unison as the elite royal guard at Zoya's rear returned fire with deadly accuracy. But for every mercenary that the archers killed more seemed to appear, cutting off their escape routes.

KRAPOW! KRAPOW!

"AAAAAAAAIIIIIIIIIIII!!"

"KIMBOTI! NKENGE!" Zoya screams not wanting to believe what she is witnessing.

Another hail of bullets directed at the royal party took down two of Zoya's closest personal attendants. Zoya tried to pull away from Zawadi to check on her friends, but he held her tight as they ran through the melee. She looked back with tear filled eyes at her fallen comrades, but she was helpless to do anything now except run for her life. Arab men on horseback crash through the broken outer walls of the settlement, trampling villagers and setting fires to the homes. Everywhere Zoya looked was bedlam. A village that had never even witnessed a shouting match and has known peace for a thousand years was now thrust into utter pandemonium. Mercenaries carrying rifles and swords rushed in from all sides, massacring the brave men and women desperately trying to defend the village with only their spears and hunting knives. Black men dressed like foreigners used clubs and whips to disarm the villagers then tied their hands and feet together with ropes made from vines to prevent them from running. The unscrupulous mercenaries took children as hostages and held knives to their necks threatening to kill them on the spot if the adults refused to surrender. One of the pale men carried two adolescent girls bound by their hands and feet and draped them trophy-like over the back of his horse. Most likely to be taken back to their base camp to indulge their sick pleasures.

KRAPOW! KRAPOW! KRAPOW!

Bullets and shrapnel barely missed Zoya and what was left of the escaping royal entourage.

Of the twelve royal guards only four remained. Zawadi, their leader, held tightly to Zoya's hand as he and his men slashed their way through the hordes of menacing invaders. Visibility was poor due to the smoke from the fires and Zoya had lost sight of her remaining attendants as she struggled to keep up with the pace of the security detail. As they reached the edge of the village Zawadi stopped abruptly and turned to Zoya. He pulled a long knife from a sheath hanging on his hip and Zoya could see blood gushing from a gunshot wound to his stomach.

Completely exhausted and out of breath he tells Zoya "You must escape into the bush and wait for nightfall. You are too important to die here. I apologize for not being able to do more to protect you. Surely Imana will appear and avenge us, but you must stay hidden in the forest until then." Zawadi hands her the knife and wraps his leopard skin cloak around her shoulders.

KRAPOW!

Zawadi is struck in the back by an enemy bullet but remains standing.

GO!!!!

He yells at Zoya, pushing her away as he charges back toward the fighting in the village, his body running on nothing more than pure adrenaline and courageous determination. Zoya could not believe the nightmare she was living. However, the emotion that had been growing inside her was not one of fear but of anger.

No sooner than Zoya turned to run into the forest her escape was cut off by a white man on horseback emerging from a thicket of trees holding a burning torch. The thought that this man was here to commit arson and destroy everything she and her family held dear caused something inside Zoya to snap. Before she knew it, she was charging the man on the horse, running at an unnatural speed. She leaped at least six feet off the ground and with one slashing movement she chopped off the man's left arm at the elbow. Her strength and speed augmented by the blood of the Ancients coursing through her and the child growing inside her.

"AAAAARGH!" *WHUMPH!,*

the man screams falling backwards off the horse with a thud knocking the wind out of him.

Zoya knew these forests like she knew her mother's house. She could have easily escaped into the bush and remained hidden until nightfall when the great Kera Maraso spirit would come and devour these barbarians. Zoya looked over her shoulder at the burning village

The crumbling walls...

The trampled gardens and burning crops...

The scores of dead and imprisoned men women and children...

There was nothing left...

Nothing left but....

RAGE!!!!

She turned away from the forest and ran back toward the man writhing in pain on the ground. Her heart pounded in her chest as she raised the heavy knife high above her head and plunged it down into the man's eye socket and through the back of his skull, killing him instantly.

Zoya charged back into the fray, she reached down and grabbed a spear from one of her dead compatriots and with a weapon in each hand she fearlessly unleashed a whirlwind of deadly attacks. Moving like a lioness, her strength, speed and stamina all enhanced, Zoya sliced the throats of several mercenaries closest to her and impaled two others on her spear before any of them knew what was happening. She moved swiftly, using the smoke and chaos as cover. If she was to die, she would die fighting. It took five of the slavers to overpower her, finally stopping her rampage by knocking her unconscious with a blow to the back of the head with the butt of a rifle. They quickly clapped her in irons and forced her to sit on the ground with the rest of the captives.

The entire scene was heartbreaking. It took less than six hours for the attackers to destroy the centuries old royal compound at Ruwenzori Village. The people who were not killed or maimed had their hands and feet bound and were made to lie on the ground in rows of ten separated by gender and age. The shame and disbelief on the men's faces and the sorrowful wails of the women and children spoke volumes about the unprecedented nature of the holocaust that had befallen them. A little less than an hour after losing their entire way of life, the survivors were made to stand up and everyone was forced to drink a ladle full of water before beginning the arduous 180-mile journey to the mouth of the Upper Nile.

KRAPOW!

One of the men on horseback fired his weapon into the air and said something to a black man dressed like a foreigner who translated to the captives in Swahili, ["If you try to run you will be beaten and the toes on your left foot will be removed"]

In groups of ten they walked two-by-two through the horrific scene. Zoya did not see the charred bodies of her father and mother, but she did see the dozens of scorched and mangled bodies of the people she knew and had broken bread with mere days ago. The now smoldering forest was deathly quiet. All the animals were forced to flee and very few birds could be heard in the canopy of the trees which only hours before were teeming with life.

Every last one of the poor prisoners were exhausted from the first day of walking but as the sun began to dip below the horizon, they still had strength enough to pray under their breaths for the Ancient Blooded One to appear in the night and free them from this hell on earth. To Zoya and all the other captives from Ruwenzori village's surprise the Ancient One did not make an appearance that first night. Instead, they were visited by some of the slave drivers came that in the night and took some of the women and young girls into the bush and raped them while the rest of the villagers sat helplessly, forced to listen to the cries of their wives, mothers and daughters as they were violated by these despicable excuses for human beings.

The next day the sun shone down relentlessly on Zoya and the other prisoners as they walked for a full fourteen hours. Several of the villagers collapsed and died from fatigue and had to be cut out of their bindings to allow the rest of the group to continue walking. Along the way Zoya and the other captives pass the charred remains of other villages that had previously been decimated by the slave traders. The smell of death was heavy in the air and Zoya vomited multiple times as she passed predator-gnawed carcasses of both slavers and other villagers. It was almost too much to bear.

After the third night passed without any sign of the Great Imana many of the people grew bitter and instead of offering prayers to the great one, they cursed his name and vowed to never worship the bat spirit again. Even the children were beginning to believe that the mighty protector of the Rwenzori village was a phony who in their darkest hour left them to suffer at the hands of barbarians. Zoya rubbed her belly to quiet the restless little being inside her. She was heartbroken. The same question rolled around in her mind again and again—why had the Ancient One abandoned her and her people? Her mind took her back to the huge explosion she heard just before reports of the sacred mountain partially collapsing. Could that mean that the ancient one might be buried under the mountain and not able to come and rescue them? she pondered.

The prisoner caravan from Rwenzori village started with roughly 240 captives but after six days walking through the bush only 117 weary souls remained. At close to nine months pregnant, forced to walk many harsh miles, Zoya made it to the mouth of the Upper Nile with the rest of the survivors. She was sold to French slave traders for a very high price considering she was a two-for-one deal. The mixing of our blood made my mother's body strong enough to withstand the fatigue of the long walk, the physical abuse by her captors, and the disease-ridden ships that carried her and the other destitute souls to their doom.

Through sheer stubbornness she willed herself not to deliver me on the long arduous journey to this unknown land and was able to wait an entire day after arriving at Port de Paix, San Domingue before she could wait no longer. Her water broke early on a Monday morning while she was perched on a pile of straw that rested on the floor of a shabbily made cabin while surrounded by strange speaking women including a caring midwife who assisted in her labor. That was somewhere in the ballpark of the year 1713, the year I was born.

Chapter 10

I grew up in San Domingue now known as Haiti on a French plantation just South of Port De Paix between Le Gros Morne and the city of Plaisance. I was always very sheltered by my mother who told everyone that I was born with a severe eye and skin condition that required me to remain inside or be covered from the sun or else my skin would burn and blister horribly. Living in the Caribbean required me to wear long sleeves and oversized trousers and otherwise be completely covered from head to toe. Because my eyes were extraordinarily sensitive to sunlight, most times I wore a blindfold or a burlap sack over my head. It was also to lessen the pointing and staring by people who were disgusted by my pigment-less pupils. I naturally gravitated to being nocturnal and once I turned eighteen months old, my mother would allow me to make myself useful by catching vermin around the main plantation house at night. At three I was tasked with keeping watch over the chicken coop for brown racer snakes which my mother knew I loved chasing through the surrounding forest and back into their burrows. When I was seven years old, the older male slaves would sometimes take me along at night to hunt hutia, a large guinea pig-like rodent which was a good source of protein for the people. At ten years, I still appeared as a five-year-old, but I was old enough and already more than strong enough to do small tasks at night that were more related to the work of the plantation. Jobs like dragging and loading heavy logs that were too cumbersome for some of the men to carry.

My master during those years, whose name I cannot recall, hailed from an aristocratic French family. Since they traveled often, most of the day-to-day management of the plantation was left to the cruel overseers who would oftentimes be another slave promoted over his fellow captives or a mulatto freedman who worked on the plantation for wages. Many of the darker skinned blacks grew to resent this middle class of Negroes who felt that they were better than their brethren even though they were only one generation removed from chattel themselves.

I was raised to be very meek and mild because my mother did not want anyone to associate me with evil spirits or demons because of the appearance of my eyes, my great physical prowess, or the need for me to eat raw flesh. When I would walk places with my mother, many of the other slaves who were otherwise friendly to her would see us together and cross themselves and spit as if to ward off a curse. None of the other children were ever allowed to play with me, which made for a very lonely childhood.

On the days and nights that the enslaved were given to rest, usually a Sunday, my mother would talk for hours about her childhood in the Ruwenzori Valley and what it was like growing up as a member of the royal court. Her stories would usually include details of the pristine lakes that supplied the surrounding villages with food and recreation. Sometimes her stories would be about the majestic snow-capped mountains that surrounded her village and the cave systems within them that housed the millions of our kuguruka ibeba (bat) brothers and sisters. My mother told me of the first time she visited the great forest and how she was taught to read the stars and live in the Bush. She taught me everything about how to interpret the language of plants and animals to attain a better understanding of my surroundings. She recalled stories of her beautiful village and the wonderful peace they enjoyed. Her memories of the royal court conjured images of elegance and grace that were difficult for my limited imagination to fathom. She spoke of how she missed the amazing food that was always plentiful, the sweet honey that was harvested from bees living on the side of the mountain and the amazing fruits that grew wild in abundance. She never spoke directly about who my father was but would always remind me that I was descended from greatness and should be prideful of my heritage. At

190

least once a week she would reiterate to me that would be a time when I would reach my full potential and when that day arrived, I would use my gifts to help cure this world of its ills and reclaim the throne of the great Kera Maraso (Ancient Blooded Ones).

Because the French plantation owners were inundated with such a large supply of labor, they conducted a very cruel form of chattel slavery that would work human beings so hard and for such long periods of time that their bodies would break down. Muscles would literally detach from bone due to repetition of movement and oftentimes enslaved men and women would collapse and die right where they stood, literally worked to death. There would be another soul to replace the battered bodies the next day, and the plantations continued to make inconceivable profits for the French empire. My mother and I were forced to bury many of our colleagues during our years of enslavement in San Domingue. The blood we shared kept my mother more youthful than normal women, but her heart and mind took a heavy toll over the years as she watched her friends and acquaintances all die sad, cruel deaths under the yoke of servitude.

My mother and I worked our fingers to the bone but still managed to outlive two of our previous owners, being passed from the father down to the son who then went into debt and was forced to liquidate some of his assets. Subsequently, we were sold to our new owners after sixty years living and working on the same plantation. Our former master was able to fully recover financially once we were sold because we fetched such a high value for being so durable. The only caveat was that we be sold together which surprisingly, my mother negotiated. She would make it a point to inform the potential buyers that if separated, there would be no one to rein me in if I ever lost control. Knowing how strong and fast I had become, no one, black or white, wanted to see that happen.

We were now the property of the stately Laferriere family who hailed from the Forez now Loire province of France. They traded in mostly coffee and sugar and were very wealthy with close ties to the Belgian crown. Due to my unique physiognomy, at the age of thirteen human years I noticed an exceedingly sluggish progression in my growth. Imagine going through puberty for fifty years. Once I finally reached adulthood physically, my aging slowed to a crawl. My mother? She was reaching her century, but she looked like someone less than half that age. One balmy night in august of 1791, during the European conflict known now as the French Revolution, there was a huge *Bwa Kaye Imam* ceremony being planned that evening in the Le Cap Francais region of the island. Which lie north of the plantation we now lived on at the time. I was oblivious to the careful stratagems and rigorous planning that had been going on for months and probably even years by Buukman, the fiery revolutionary leader strategist, and Mama Fatiman, another important revolutionary organizer along with countless other valiant and cunning men and women enslaved by the French.

After decades of reflecting on the way it all transpired. I now suspect that my mother was also one of these brilliant co-conspirators. I worked during the night with only the overseers to keep me company so I was never privy to the machinations going on behind the scenes with the other field hands. Very few people on the plantation were brave or courteous enough to speak to me so I was shut out from any information that did not come from my mother or eavesdropping with my extra sharp hearing. I was too introverted and awkward to notice anything out of the ordinary. My mother's kindness, her incredible cooking and her knowledge of mushrooms and herbs that could be foraged for health benefits made her an invaluable asset to both races on the plantation. They also feared her for being the mother of a monster. She was the only person who could effectively communicate with me. The only person who could stop me if I ever went out of control. Amongst the black population my mother was highly respected, and people went out of their way to help her. The people believed that she was covered by the benevolent spirit of Iwa Ezili Freda due to her agelessness and wisdom. They also pitied her for having to be burdened with a son who was so odd.

The night following the beginning of Bois Caiman (Bwa Kaye Imam), I returned to the slave quarters to find something dreadfully wrong. My mother, who was always faithfully involved in the food distribution for the workers after they returned from the cane fields, was nowhere to be found. As a slave, there were no sick days or time off or breaks unless you were on your deathbed or there was some type of recognized religious holiday. Something had to be terribly wrong for her to miss mealtime because she was always so concerned with making the meals enjoyable and hearty for the downtrodden souls she was nourishing. For the last seventeen years of being on this plantation, my mother has only not been there to oversee the evening meal only once. I immediately knew something was wrong.

Pascale, one of the elderly slaves assigned to help my mother prepare supper for the field hands, was one of the rare few who would greet me when I came to sit on the floor behind my mother as she worked. Today, he would not look up from his pot of porridge as he served it to everyone in the cabin who also seemed unusually quiet as they ate. There were unfamiliar smells of talc and French cologne lingering in the air around the quarters which gave me a very uneasy feeling. I had grown accustomed to people leaving me to my own devices because of my strange behavior and the fact that I wore a burlap sack over my head.

I was used to being ignored and to be honest, I enjoyed it. But today I noticed that even the small children who were too young to do field work and would usually be making noise and playing games outside the 'slop house' while they waited for their parents, were all just staring at me as I walked around the building to the serving area again to try and pick up mother's scent. Armand, the stable man and lead coach driver who sometimes would thank me for keeping the mouse population low in the stables, was silently staring at me with a melancholy look on his face. I stole glances back at him through my mask, wondering what had everyone in such a strange mood today and how was this behavior connected to my mother?

Just then Estee, Armand's wife, walked around the side of the 'slop house' cabin humming a gospel hymn. She was a tall thin woman with very average features who was almost twenty years younger than Armand. As soon as she saw me, the smile disappeared from her face and she hurried over next to her husband who was still staring right at me. Everyone who came to the quarters for their meal that night walked noticeably more sluggish. They all seemed to look toward the corner of the yard my mother and I usually occupied as they came in and out of the slop house. There was a solid tension present that I assumed had something to do with the unrest my

193

mother had spoken about between the French crown and the French people that was undermining France's power at home and in her colonies. After the meal service I usually sat at my mother's feet and waited for her to finish eating before I took my meals. I was starving from the day's work because of a mishap involving one of the draft mules on the plow stepping into a deep hole and breaking a leg. I was awakened by Gaspar, one of the messenger boys, and told to get up and head to the fields even though it was many hours before sundown to help drag the huge animal out of the mud hole. Since the mule was now out of commission, the yoke was then placed on my shoulders and I was forced to finish the job in its place.

My dinner that evening consisted not only of three fat mice I had captured in the field earlier, but Mother had left me some cow skin and rabbit bones with a lot of flesh still on them in an old rusty tin bucket covered with a piece of burlap to keep insects off of it until I arrived. Since no one usually gave me a second thought, I was never conscious of what my eating sounded like to others. I would simply slip the food under my hood and into my mouth and wolf it down. The others were always too preoccupied with unloading their burdens of the day, their own meals and interaction with their fellow slaves and children to worry about me anyway. But for some reason, today everyone was stealing glances toward me, and it was much quieter than usual inside the slop house cabin, making it hard for me to crunch bones and slurp blood which was my usual modus operandi during meals. Mother, being the only person who spoke with me, would smile and dote on me as all parents equate their children having a regular appetite as a sign of normalcy. That is when it hit me. I could not smell her. Not that my nose was sensitive enough to smell all the way to the master's house where I suspected she was whenever she was not able to be there to greet the other slaves from the field, but her scent was so faint that she must have been gone for many hours prior.

As stated previously, I was attached to my mother by the hip and could count on one hand the times when she was outside the range of my senses. Once in my recollection when I was very young, around eight human years old, Mother was sent on an emergency errand to help assist in a difficult pregnancy of an unmarried white relation to our mistress on another

194

plantation owned by the mistress's father three miles east of Plaisance. She was forced to leave abruptly in the middle of the night while I was out in the forest hunting raccoons so that when I returned at dawn and she was not in our cabin, I immediately began to panic and ran into the woods following her scent. The fastest horses and dogs had to be recruited to retrieve me because I tore through every fence, vine, bramble, and briar directly through two plantations and a forest to reach my target leaving a wake of trampled vegetation and broken wood and branches behind me. When the trackers finally caught up to us, I was with my mother, serenely strolling back from the direction of the neighboring farm while being cooed and petted by her as she removed thorns and twigs from my skin, clothing, and hair.

The next day, Le maitre forced me to start wearing leg irons to slow me down. That was over seventy years earlier. Nowadays as a man of more maturity, my initial reaction is not one of panic, but I am still very worried. Combined with the way everyone was being so solemn at a time when slaves are usually able to relax and speak their minds, it was causing the fear that something bad had happened to grow inside me.

I stood and untied the rope attached to the bucket containing my meal and walked outside. As I moved, I could feel the eyes of everyone present upon me. Fear and paranoia began to build up inside me like steam inside a boiling kettle. I tried desperately to suppress the negative thoughts flooding into my mind as much as possible and keep my wits about me, but my stoic facade was beginning to crack. I knew I was in trouble when I became so nervous that I couldn't bring myself to eat the food my mother had left for me. I left the slave quarters and walked toward the main house to check if she was there. As I came down the dirt path between the cabins, I was stopped by Norris who happened to be one of the former coach drivers and considered one of the wisest of the elder slaves on the plantation. Norris usually worked as a shoeshine in the big house since it did not require him to stand as much anymore. As he limped closer towards me, I could see that his face was wet and huge tears were hanging in his eyes and his gray lower chin was quivering like mad.

195

"Bondye gen pitye (God have mercy)," he began in Creole. "I-I…. I saw them t-t-ake her," Norris said, as he began his tale.

He related to me that he was sitting on the porch scooping out some boot black when he heard arguing and scuffling inside the main house. A minute later he said he looked up and saw a white man he had never seen before bursted out of the front door of the main house dragging my mother by her collar and shouting rude things at her and the other slaves in their path. Evidently the man was a guest of the master visiting from a nearby newly purchased plantation. Norris said that he was told that one of the children mistakenly spilled a cup of tea on the man and he flew into a rage and started viciously beating and spitting on the boy. Mother stepped in and tried to apologize for the child and offered herself up to be punished instead of the boy.

"Mwen regrèt pitit mwen men yo se kèk move lespri pou sèten" [I'm sorry my boy, but they are some devils for certain"] Norris proclaimed.

"Kote li ye? (Where is she)" Were the only words I could croak out. This was the first time I had spoken directly to anyone other than my mother in at least five years.

Norris replied, Blan yo pè kounye a e sa fè yo danjere. Poutèt sa modi lagè an Ewòp gen yo tout pè. Se sa yo te di m anvan mesye a trennen l. Mwen sispèk fè yon egzanp soti nan li. Yo te kite alantou midi nan cha yo se konsa sa te gen yon ti tan de sa. Mwen vrèman regrèt pitit [The whites are afraid now and that makes them dangerous. Because of that damn war in Europe has them all spooked. That is what they told me before the man dragged her off. I suspect to make an example out of her. They left around noon time in their carriage so that has been a while ago. I am truly sorry son.]

At these words, I began to unravel. My skin became a flame and sweat began to pour from my forehead and hands. My mouth dried up and my breathing became increasingly more rapid. Even though Norris could not see the distress on my face under the burlap sack, he could see my body shaking from the emotion welling up inside me.

196

He said again, looking down at the ground and shaking his head, "Mwen regrèt."

There had been skirmishes and fighting in Le Cap Francais early in the year 1791 between the free blacks and the white planters or "grand blancs." Because of the Declaration of the Rights of Man and of the Citizens being widely available for consumption by the literate blacks in the area, there began to be grumbling of the necessity for the free blacks to have an equal footing with whites, at least the poor ones who were known as "petit blancs." The free blacks fought courageously to undergird their plight for equal treatment under the law with little to no regard for their fellow Negroes who were still under the yoke of slavery. It was quickly made plain by both classes of colonizers that no one of color, slave or free, would ever be considered the equivalent of the white man. The very idea was believed to undermine the European power structure. Nonetheless, the genie was out of the bottle.

It is funny reading in modern times about something that you were directly involved in. The official and accepted story is usually way off the mark. And although there was not much formal communication between the main slave force and the free blacks known as the gens de couleur, we all had connections through our various leaders. The Northern province where my mother and I lived and worked was known as The Plaine-du-Nord and was renowned for its fertile soil so the land was riddled with plantations all swarming with enslaved men and women. The white man's greed and arrogance created this huge conflagration of people and that proved to be the very catalyst for their undoing. Once the tales of these free black heroes daring to defy the seemingly insurmountable French empire reached the ears of slaves throughout the world, a psychological threshold was crossed with no hope of turning back.

The first attempts at revolt led by the free blacks of San Domingue were utterly crushed after a few months of fighting, but the revolutionary hymen had been busted, and there was no stopping the wave of freedom that was to come. The response from the French planter class, their

197

supporters, and the royalists was cruel retribution. They employed the most inconceivably heinous torture techniques known to man on the leaders of the revolt to make examples and try to foment fear amongst the black slaves and anyone else who had the gall to defy the colonial class structure. But the blacks had also been secretly laying plans. The effort to crush their spirit backfired, and the cruelty dealt by the French upon the slaves and free men and women up until that point was replayed upon them and the rest of the European powers twentyfold. This impending war would be the first domino to fall that would serve to dismantle chattel slavery all throughout the western world.

The man who tied my mother to the back of his carriage earlier that day was totally incapable of fathoming the faux pas he was committing. He undoubtedly thought he was meting out the proper punishment befitting a slave who, during these tumultuous times, needed to learn that French patriarchy was still ultimately in charge. This small unassuming woman had led a harrowing and difficult existence and absolutely did not deserve the display of anger and assault she was subjected to in her last hours of life. She was burdened with being the only gatekeeper to a black devil harboring an untapped bloodlust capable of destroying nations.

From what I was told, she was dragged behind the unknown white man's carriage to master Laferriere's brother's home in the plantation adjacent because his property still maintained a whipping post next to his barn. My mother was then stripped naked in front of everyone and whipped and beaten brutally by the Frenchman and his overseer who took turns between hitting her repeatedly with a wooden plank and flogging her with a rawhide whip. I was told a few weeks later by people who were at the beating of my mother that "bleeding seemed to come from all over her body and yet she still never cried out in pain." They would also tell me later how everyone witnessing it wondered how it was possible that she was still able to draw breath after that sadistic flogging. A detail I chalked up to the fact that we once shared blood, and she was more resilient and healed better than other humans.

She endured the pain and did not cry out because I might have heard her and would have run top speed through any obstacle to get to her. I am told that when they cut her down from the whipping post, she was very weak and unable to walk or talk. Some of the women ran over and put a sheet around her and used it to carry her bloody body back to the quarters to a waiting tub to wash the blood off her and lay her on a straw bed. I was told that she was delirious with pain and lay sobbing and shivering and under a quilt one of the women provided. They say she only said my name over and over as if she refused to die until she saw me one last time.

· · ·

Back in the present-day tears spontaneously burst from my eyes and roll down my face and onto the expensive rug but my voice does not waver as I continue to spell out my pain.

Kate moves to hand me some of her Kleenex but I wave her off and continue my narrative. "This is my first time I have ever spilled my guts about my life so openly to anyone so you will have to excuse me."

She nods a sympathetic acknowledgement.

"Even after two hundred years of suffering enough death and disappointment to span a thousand lifetimes…. It still destroys me when I speak of her final day."

Kate's face softens a bit for the first time since I arrived. This woman may be willing to help me after all. I wipe the tears from my eyes with the sleeve of my shirt and continue with my story.

After receiving the news of what happened from Norris, my body moved on its own, and I tore out of the yard stretching the links on the iron chains on my legs as far as they could go with each stride and ripping the flesh away from my ankles until the metal of the shackles was almost grinding on bone. I tear down the path to the neighboring plantation, and the world becomes a teary blur as I bolted through the woods. As I came to the clearing, there was a gathering of men and weeping women outside of the cabin that I knew to belong to an older couple named Jean Luc and Celine. The loud rhythmic clanking of my chain alerted everyone of my approach and they all turned to look at me with mourning faces, opening a lane for me to enter the house. I dragged my torn bloody feet down the dirt path made by the parting bodies like a sad parade of one wretched man, up the stairs, and into the shabby cabin where my mother lay dying.

As I walked in, my mother was lying on a hay-stuffed mattress wrapped in bloody bandages and covered by a homemade quilt. As my eyes focused through the tears, I could see her face was swollen and misshapen. I dropped to my knees and began to sob uncontrollably with my face into the dirt floor. I let out a soul wrenching cry. Squeezing the tears from my eyes, pushing the air from my lungs, and moaning like a wounded animal. Water streamed from my face so hard I completely soaked the shroud I wore before I tore it from my head and tossed it aside. Snot and tears mixed with dirt from the floor covered my face, and now I was sobbing and rocking and shaking my head frantically next to her still body, not wanting to confront reality.

Her left arm weakly moved from beneath the blanket and planted itself gently onto my shoulder as I rocked back and forth weeping into the floor. I immediately began to calm down and I forced myself to stop crying and I tried wiping the mucus and tears from my face with my sleeve, but I only succeeded in smearing more dirt across my already filthy face. I did not want to see her like this. I did not want to feel the shame of not being there for her when she needed me the most. She was trying to say something, but I was sick with despair and convulsing with too much emotional pain to realize it. I wanted to die at that moment. I wanted to command my own heart to stop beating if it meant I could carry on by her side.

200

My mother used the last of her strength to whisper to me, ".....Sois forte... maman t'aime.[Be strong mama loves you]."

That was the last time I would hear her sweet voice say those words. That would also be one of the last times I would ever consider love. Hatred consumed every fiber of my being.

My recollection was not very clear as to what happened over those next few hours. I remember being on the floor of the cabin, curled up in the fetal position, crying for what seemed like days until I was dehydrated. I also remember wrapping her body tightly in the quilt she was under. The next thing I recalled was being hot and walking outside, not caring if the sun cooked my skin. I wanted to die along with my mother.

Night had already fallen and as if coordinated, enslaved men and women all over the territory had begun taking up the ax and the cane knife and demanding their freedom. The first smell that hit my nostrils was the gunpowder from the musket and cannon fire. And below the gunpowder, the pungent smell of fresh human blood. The fuse on the rebellion had been lit.

I was a different creature after my mother died. I was Le Diable, I was a monster. I reached down and pulled at the shackles on my ankle, my anger fueling a strength I never realized I was capable of and ripped them both completely in two. With my legs now freed after so many years of bondage, I bounded off the porch, past the women who were keeping their silent vigil outside the cabin containing my mother's body and ran like a gazelle towards the smells and sounds of the battlefield. I wanted to murder the entire population of France. I wanted to drink the blood of every colonizing bastard I could get my claws on.

Before that day the only human blood I had ever tasted was my mother's to sustain me as an infant until I was old enough to hunt. I had never been violent toward any human and my mother always forbade it. I had never seriously considered attacking a human because I understood the consequences of what would happen to my mother if I were to ever be seen

201

as unruly or unmanageable. However, tonight I wanted nothing more than to spill blood.

Tonight, I would have my vengeance.

Tonight, I would feast on the flesh of my human enemies.

I ran nonstop toward the scents and sounds of battle. Without my leg shackles I was able to move like the wind. My eyes gleamed in the darkness as one single thought ran through my mind —revenge.

No one was prepared for the killing spree that I unleashed that night. I began ripping throats with my bare hands spraying blood everywhere as it gushed from the arteries of my victims. I moved from one soldier to the next either ripping their throats out with my teeth and claws or body slamming them and breaking their skulls against the ground. I used no weapons; my fists were enough to cave in nasal cavities or crack the skulls of my enemies. One of the soldiers managed to stab me from behind with his sword and before he could remove it, I turned and grabbed him by the throat and slammed him viciously head first into a nearby tree.

KRAKOW!

I dodged another soldier's point-blank rifle fire. I run at him as he retreats to reload and catch him by the back of his shirt.

KRRAATCH!!

With both hands I twist his neck cracking his vertebrae and dropping his limp corpse on the ground. I used my hand to pierce straight through the ribcages of the French soldiers. I moved from victim to victim, too fast for any of them to target me with their rifles. I was a harbinger of death. In less than ten minutes I had murdered or maimed over fifty soldiers. The rebel forces were confused by what was happening. They at first believed a wild puma was attacking the French troops. The darkness and the smoke from the musket fire made visibility poor. They only heard the blood curdling screams of the French soldiers and saw the leftover carnage of my rampage. Men with their throats and intestines ripped out. The battlefield was covered in blood. When the rebellion force finally did get a glimpse of me running through the mayhem upright like a man, they swore I was Satan himself.

I was covered in blood.

I ripped and slashed my way through dozens of soldiers like they were paper dolls. I even managed to destroy three rolling heavy artillery apparatus that were pinning down the advancing rebels who fought back bravely with mostly machetes and billhooks.

I ran wild all night, spilling the blood of well over two hundred of the French infantry and local French militiamen sent to quell the rebellion in Plaisance. Victory went to the freedom fighters that evening. Most of my clothing had been shot up or ripped off during the battle, and I began to hurry back to the quarters to find shelter and clothing before sunrise. When I arrived at the Laferriere plantation it was in shambles and the main house was partially burned. The rebellion confiscated the property during the night and there I was approached by one of the main leaders of the revolution.

My mother called him Buukman and I knew of him to be one of the few people who spoke to me kindly whenever he would visit our plantation. That night, he officially recruited me into the rebellion and gave orders to the rest of the freedom fighters to spread the word to everyone that I was no longer to be seen as a pariah or a bad omen to the people, but as a weapon of liberation and a gift from Papa Legba. Buukman told me that many people were frightened of me. He said that when I appeared in the combat zone that evening, many of the other rebels were initially afraid because I ran on all fours like an animal. I appeared so abruptly from the forest, moving faster than a bird could fly. He relayed to me the pride he and others felt when I appeared during the battle. Just as the French militia began to advance on the rebels with reinforcements, before they knew what was happening, I was airborne above their heads, leaping eagerly into the crowd of heavily armed French soldiers with not even as much as a club as a weapon in my hands. The subsequent bloodbath that those French soldiers received in my wake was so swift and decisive, he said, that the entire French battalion had to retreat and leave their dead and or wounded soldiers to rot on the battlefield. The rebels that were present to witness the battle earlier that night had their breasts swelled with confidence. They were able to find the will to continue to fight valiantly even though they lacked serious leadership, food, water, and basic gear such as shoes and gunpowder with the knowledge that they had such a powerful ally in their corner.

The first few weeks of the uprising, most of the black revolutionaries were armed with only farming tools and the rifles and swords that they could steal from the colonists. Over time, they were able to secure more proper cutlasses, rifles, and pistols, to place themselves on a more level playing field with our enemies. There were times that the European forces would overwhelm the freedom fighters in multiple battles, and the plight of the revolution would look very bleak as the armies of the colonists began to advance. When there would seem to be no end to the losses on a particular battlefield and the morale amongst the rebels began to wane, stories of Le Diable being nearby or headed to the conflict zone would be circulated throughout the ranks of the African rebels. This news would serve to reinvigorate the bravery amongst the rebels and provide a morale boost to overcome the near impossible odds.

The news of my proximity would have the opposite effect on the colonial armies for when they would receive word that Le Diable was on his way to the combat arena, they would lose their will to fight at the thought of guaranteed death. I was not able to spend much time under the tutelage of Buukman, for he died a few months after the rebellion began. However, his martyrdom coupled with my mother's and the sacrifices of many other fellow freedom fighters were all just rocket fuel for my pent-up fury.

On another occasion I made it just in time as the revolutionary army was near giving the order to retreat and regroup. The rebels recalled hearing a sound like the howl of a mad dog above the noise of the gunfire followed by an explosion. Initially they thought a cannonball was misfired by the enemy because of the scattering of bodies that occurred as I slammed into the front line of the French troops. I was moving so fast and hit them so hard that my initial attack disabled two mobile artillery gun installations and plowed completely through the commanding officer's wagon. I had taken out most of the heavy machinery and half of the mounted cavalry before anyone realized it was a person that just rocketed past them.

Meting out death and destruction seemed second nature to me, and I began to attack anything—horses, soldiers, supply wagons, mobile artillery cannons— by just ripping them all apart like they were a bundle of dandelions. All the time charging forward covered in blood, "operating more like a demon than a man." I was an absolute terror. I annihilated entire battalions with little more than claws and teeth. I would run on all fours like a leopard into an oncoming regiment of infantry and light artillery and all advancement would stop. As the bodies began to pile up in my wake, the rebels would then signal the 'all clear' and attack the soldiers who were now collapsing their reinforcements on my position, leaving their flank wide open for an ambush. Unfortunately for the French Military and its subsequent relief regiments, it was the rainy season so every morning would start overcast and I would still be on my rampage well into the first hours of sunrise.

The insurrection in Le Gros Morne and Pilate eventually spilled over to Port Margot, and many of the insurgents were able to secure weapons, strategic logistical information and locations that would prove invaluable to the success of the revolution. The string of triumphs that the rebellion experienced also created a rumor of the power that the Haitian deities held was able to defeat the European gods. The Haitians possessed the ability to summon an unstoppable demon who was immortal and powerful enough to snap a horse's neck with his bare hands. Outwardly I was a coldblooded butcher and supreme thorn in the side of the French colonist regime. But inwardly I was a mess. I was a coward. I did not want to believe that my mother was dead. During most of those bloody battles my eyes shone in the darkness because of all the tears that flowed from them. Killing the people responsible for her pain was the only way I could mourn her.

Three and a half weeks had passed since I began my rampage when something inside my brain clicked and I realized that I had not given my

205

mother a proper burial. I left the battlefield abruptly and ran like a madman back to Plaisance where my mother was killed. The people must have been expecting me because when I arrived I was told by some of the women there that her body had been taken back to the Laferriere plantation and buried behind our old cabin by the wives of the rebel soldiers who knew her during her long life. The order to have her body carried back to our home and honorably interred was given by another one of the leaders of the revolution named Jeannot Bullet. When I made it back to our cabin on the Laferriere home ground to pay my respects to my mother, I was greeted by an older man named Biassou who explained to me that the paths to retribution for my mother lie in the destruction of the French colonial power structure and their allies. I prayed on my mother's soul and openly wept before my comrades who prayed with me and helped me give her a spirit filled eulogy. I walked into the woods and returned a few minutes later with a boulder larger than any human could think of lifting without hiring a dozen men and a wagon team. I gently placed the boulder down next to the pile of stones already marking my mother's grave. Zoya Mbabazi Anyango, my amazing mother, was dead. I had now been officially recruited into the rebellion, and my strength was used strategically by Jeannot and the others. I returned to the battlefield the next night near the city of L'Attalaye ready for anything.

My mind and spirit grew exponentially during that grieving period, and the guidance and training I received from those early revolutionary leaders would prove invaluable over the course of the next ten years. I was entirely unaware but mother was preparing me for this day little by little. She knew I would someday prove useful to the revolution when the time came. I would now be a weapon of the people even though most of them feared me for they misunderstood what I was. Many still believed I was a tool of Beelzebub who would turn on my comrades viciously one day and require their blood as repayment for my assistance in defeating the French. Buukman and others tried to convince our troops that I was truly a tool of Vodou, a flesh and blood manifestation of Ogou Feray and friendly to the struggle of the slave. But unfortunately, he was captured and killed early on in the first few months of the war, so I was forced to go it alone and gain acceptance through my actions.

206

Battle after battle, the memory of my mother and the bravery exemplified by so many men and women who were just recently obedient chattel fueled my blood thirst for colonist souls. For every wound I received, I would snap the neck, decapitate with my sword, or bite the throat open of at least three of the enemy soldiers. My presence on the battlefield affected French military strategy to the point that the French and their various European allied troops would fight their hardest up until sunset which proved very difficult for them because of the heat, humidity, and insect bites. At nightfall, the colonists developed the tactic of retreating and regrouping their battle lines. They utilized a strategy of placing several of their cannons toward the rear and flanks of their position, with the aim of defending the more vulnerable lines of their perimeter. Each battalion was given orders to reallocate their artillery fire this way because if there was not at least some form of heavy arms available for my initial charge, it would almost certainly mean a guaranteed defeat for the squadron because of the high casualty rate delivered by my fists and sword. With one swing I was known to cut a man so nearly in two that the dull blades would lodge in his spine and I would be forced to appropriate another sword elsewhere on the battlefield.

Nonetheless, even with all my efforts, the fact that the Europeans had a clear advantage of superior wealth, access to the latest in military technology, and were educated in historical war strategy could not be ignored. The courageous men and women of the rebellion suffered many more casualties than the French, Spanish, and British combined. Tens of thousands of men, women and children were lost to the Cause. Many went to their graves lamenting the fact that Le Diable, Kwokodil La, Je San Moun (Haitian Creole for the Devil, the Beast and Blood Eyes respectively) or whatever sobriquet I was being called at the time, was not there in time to save them from the heartless colonists. Many survivors who were imprisoned and punished after losing on the battlefield met their fate cursing my name for not being present in their final moments of freedom. This was the burden of power. The hero bears the weight of every life he could not save. Every ten people you rescue in one city, fifty lives are lost in another.

For the next decade, I walked past the corpses of all ages and genders. Lives that never tasted their freedom but willingly exchanged their own existence to save the lives of unknown generations to come. A dream deferred in the fight to remove the yoke of slavery from the future progeny.

As the years went by and the enemy's military technology improved, I would occasionally have a limb blown off from cannon fire or be riddled with musket balls so thoroughly that my clothes would fall away from my body, and I would have to rest for days or weeks depending on the severity of the wounds. Many times, I would have to leave my comrades fighting desperately on the battlefield just before dawn and find some hollow tree or cave to sleep and recuperate in while the bright sun of the day blazed over its domain. In some instances, I would retreat into the bush, dig a hole until it was deep enough for me to lie in and cover my body. I would enter the hole feet first and collapse the dirt on my face leaving a small opening for air. My lungs needed only a fraction of the oxygen a human requires. Occasionally, large insects or small critters would happen by and provide a sorely needed replenishment of nutrients.

When I would emerge from my hole at nightfall, my first action would be to drink either the blood of the first enemy I came across or some other large mammal I encountered to accelerate my regenerative healing factor. The blood from humans is exponentially more potent for my metabolic system than that of the capybara or iguanas I usually consumed. Although I had existed on earth for more than eighty years, I was only now beginning to live. Freedom came to me in several ways during those years. I happily followed the orders of Buukman and Biassou who, along with Toussaint L'Overture, Francois Mackandal, and Jean Jacques Dessalines, led the black people of San Domingue, now known as Haiti, out of bondage.

•   •   •

"Wait, wait wait," …Kate interrupts, "you mean to tell me that Blacula is the reason the Haitians beat the French, Spanish, and British armies? How come there is nothing about this in any of the historical records? Why has no one ever heard of you?" she asks.

"One would barely believe that Haiti had won its independence all those years ago by looking at the condition it is in now," I calmly explain to her. "The embarrassment of losing to uneducated, unsophisticated, underfunded, mere slaves sent ripple effects around the world that eventually toppled chattel slavery throughout all the European colonies. The effects are still being felt by colonial powers this far into the twenty-first century. That is why Haiti has always been disenfranchised, forced to pay reparations to France. Its leaders and people have been exploited beyond recognition and continue to be suppressed to this very minute. San Domingue went from being one of the richest countries to being the poorest in the world despite the industrious and proud nature of its people. Do you really think they are going to report the history properly after suffering the biggest financial loss of the millennia? And then as a cherry on top, those same superpowers allow the official historical report to state that the main cause of their loss was due to the Haitian's control of certain supernatural forces?" I ask her rhetorically.

"Touché," Kate says, rolling her eyes. She stands up to top of her wine, and then returns to her ottoman perch sitting on one leg.

"The rabbit hole is a mother fucker," I tell her as I sip my drink.

"So, wait… how do you go from being this bad ass devil incarnated secret weapon from 1791 to 1804 to being re-enslaved by my family just few years later?" After all that fighting, did you become a capitalist all of a sudden?" Kate smirks at me wryly through a sip of wine.

I continue my tale reluctantly, thrown for a loop by her continued skepticism.

Touissant L'Overture was a brilliant leader and hero of the revolution whose war strategy and fierceness were unparalleled during the twelve years of the revolution. After his invasion of the Spanish slave colonies of Santo

Domingo, we were essentially dismantling the myth of the all-powerful white man and destroying his financial base in the process. A crime that we were soon to learn was seen as an unforgivable offense. Touissant, as intelligent as he was, allowed his noble designs to naively be projected on his enemies, and this mistake would lead to his ultimate downfall.

The revolution was not just black versus white, there were some Negroes and mulattoes who remained loyal to the French and assisted in the attempted re-enslavement of the black population. L'Overture's naïveté of European cruelty and deception led to his capture and ultimate death in an obscure prison in France. With Touissant gone and Dessalines and other leaders pacified by French promises of political power, myself and others still continued to wage war against what we knew to be inevitable if we did not continue the struggle: the return of slavery. When word reached the mainland countries of the "Diable" that was controlled by African magic who could destroy a warship single handedly and was defeating European forces faster than yellow fever, a cry went up to have me put down by all means at the petition of the French Crown. The age-old trope of 'divide and conquer' was ever present among the colonists' tactics and was rule number one amongst the slave holders. Slaves are given different ranks and vie for the praise of their masters. If they were faster, stronger, more obedient, better at cane chopping – basically anything they could do to be favored by their masters so they could put on airs in front of their peers. It became a kind of contest with some of the enslaved who chided their own people for not pleasing the masters.

The internal hierarchy classifications amongst the enslaved was just as diabolical and centered around frivolities such as who was lighter or whose hair was straighter or whose nose was smaller or any number of insults to their natural appearance to positively associate themselves with their oppressors. The main offenders being the free mulatto class who, through their yearning to be on level footing with the white man, were also impassioned by the Revolution on the mainland as a rejection of the ruling class amongst the colonists who treated them little better than when they were chattel. However fiercely the mulattoes fought the white man for their individual rights and recognition, they also fiercely opposed being equated and lumped in with the majority black population. For a period after Touissant's capture, the leaders of the revolution were given land and political appointments to appease them and get them to reveal my location and the secret to my magic. The French crown had always dabbled in the occult and alchemy and equated my existence as proof that a demonic spirit could be controlled for military applications. Nevertheless, the credit for my exploits in facilitating an extreme number of deaths of European soldiers had been given to yellow fever.

As our rebel forces began to win key battles it served to bolster the efforts of the guerrilla movement and there was a palpable sense of hope amongst the people. Our actions brought to pass a new fear campaign by the French colonists to re-enslave all the rebels by inflicting some of the cruelest torture and murder tactics they could imagine. Captured young men would have their penis and testicles removed violently by tying one end of a rope around their genitals and tying the opposite end to the yoke of a horse or bull. When whipped the animal would take off ripping the poor souls nearly in half. The women would be systematically raped and the discarded ones would have their breasts removed and afterwards be tied to a stake in a standing position while they cooked under the hot sun or where eaten alive by insects.

All this was perpetrated to give nightmares to the current and formerly enslaved. The French colonists wanted to create the impression that even with my assistance, the European forces were still ultimately in control. Many captured rebels would be held in dog pens and starved to the brink and then tricked into eating their dead comrades that were burnt alive and served to them in a trough with cornmeal. Many men would be castrated in front of their wives and children while soldiers raped the latter. One of their favorite tactics was to take a woman heavy with child and tie her arms together and suspend her by her wrists above the ground to the point that only the tips of her toes would touch the ground. As she struggled against her own weight and the awkward position, a soldier would then slice her stomach open causing the baby and all the woman's entrails to fall upon the ground where the woman would watch and scream in horror as the booted soldier would crush the head of the baby and grind it into the ground, splattering blood and tissue. It was during one of these tortures that a man named Jacque had the unfortunate fate of watching his wife about to be split open in one of these horrible displays of human cruelty.

Jacque was the eldest son of Armand, the coach driver from the Laferriere plantation. He had been one of the main lieutenants who was responsible for arming the resistance, and I knew him to be effective in many of the battles we fought during the early years of the uprising. Jacque was a high-ranking lieutenant amongst the rebels and was recently living in a maroon village where he met and married his wife after the fighting was believed to have subsided in that area. Jacque was also one of the few people that knew my secret strategy of burying myself somewhere near the battlefield with the intention to rest and regenerate my wounds. That was why, to the enemy, I would seem to vanish during the daylight hours. Fortunately for me, no one from the enemy camp had ever stumbled across my regenerative hiding places, but occasionally when one of the enslaved would witness my burrowing into or emerging from the earth at dawn or dusk, the sight would solidify my connection with the underworld. This made many of the people I was fighting for just as suspicious and afraid of me as they were the white men trying to kill and re-enslave them.

Jacque and his pregnant wife Marie were recently captured in an ambush on a maroon encampment in Maguimbo. Jacque was singled out from the rest of the captives for being a top-ranking member of the rebel army. Two French soldiers half dragged him out of the holding pen and forced him to his knees with his hands tied behind his back, helpless to rescue Marie as she was shoved toward a breadfruit tree by two disgusting soldiers. The soldier on her left sported a long black beard stained with tobacco. He shouldered his musket and began to tie one end of another rope between the bindings on Marie's wrists and tossed the other end of that rope over a thick branch of the breadfruit tree and yanked at the rope as he catches it on the other side of the branch causing Marie's arms to stretch up high over her head. She let out a heart wrenching yelp that shattered Jacque to the core. His body went cold and he yelled at the top of his lungs as the other soldier's right hand moved to the saber hanging on his left hip.

"AAARRETEZ, S'IIL VOUS PLAIT!!!!!" yelled Jacque at the cusp of total despair.

(In French):
"Please pardon my wife and child! Please allow my life to be taken in their place!
I am a lieutenant in the rebel army. I have a cache of gold I will give you. It's hidden nearby! I stole it from the High Command in Port-Au Prince. It's worth a sum of over 100,000 francs!"

The non-bearded soldier looked at him and held a solemn countenance as if briefly considering Jacque's plea. In the next moment, he wordlessly cracked a rotten toothed grin, drew his saber high into the air...the blade reflecting the glint of the afternoon sun as he made ready to deliver the fatal blow...

Jacque screamed out in absolute anguish as loudly yet intelligibly as he could through his tears. "Je peux te donner Le Diable!! [I can give you The Devil"!!!!!]

"QUOI?!", asked the bearded soldier before he spits a huge wad of tobacco juice right on Marie's dark bronze feet.

With his chest heaving from sadness, Jacque took a series of breaths and tried to compose himself as much as he possibly could before speaking. The soldier behind him clapped a hand on his shoulder gruffly and pulled him up to meet the eyes of the bearded soldier for a response. After a moment, Jacque was able to speak a little more clearly.

(FRENCH): ["I-I-I c-c-an give you L-L-Le Diable, I can t-t-tell you his secret."]

(FRENCH:) ["And how would you know? How do I know you aren't just saying anything I want to hear just to keep us from splattering this wench and her pup all over the dirt?"] the bearded soldier asks.

Jacque's eyes left the ground and traveled up his wife's tobacco-stained feet, up across her distended belly plump with his seed and in danger of never knowing the free life that they fought so hard to achieve. His eyes traveled up further to meet the eyes of his wife which reflected the memories of happiness in their brief few months of relative freedom together. Her eyes also reflected the unmitigated terror of the situation they now found themselves in. All this emotion transpired within a millisecond, and the look of dismay in her eyes surprisingly shifted into a different sentiment.

Anger.

Her eyebrows bowed toward each other and her expression turned hard as she shook her head and mouthed the words. "Non ne parle pas" (Don't tell them!)

At this Jacque's eyes drop back to the ground.

(FRENCH): ["Well, what's it going to be? Answer me or I will kill this wench and make you clean up the guts with your teeth if you don't start talking fast,"] the bearded soldier commanded.

After another eternal moment, Jacque broke the silence (French): ["I am from the same plantation as the demon known as 'Yeux de Sang'. He is known to be immortal save for his weakness to bright sunlight."]

"Jacque! Non!!!" yelled Marie in protest. But the bearded soldier took one filthy hand off the rope holding Marie up and grabbed her face, covering her mouth, preventing her from screaming, and severely restricting her breathing.

Jacque continued. (French): ["If you spare her, I will tell you the secret to his immortality and where to look for him….and…." his voice trailing off, "a-a-and…how to capture him."]

The bearded soldier who held Marie looked at the younger soldier who was holding his sword near Marie's belly. A knowing nod passed

214

between the two, and the younger soldier lowered his sword and placed it back into his scabbard. The bearded soldier then released Marie's rope allowing her arms to drop and causing her to collapse into a heap on the ground weary and sore. Her eyes were unable to meet Jacque's for the shame she felt for causing him to break his pact with the Revolution.

(FRENCH): ["We're going to have to go and talk with General Rochambeau himself considering this level of intel," says the bearded soldier, leaning down into the tear-stained face of Jacques. "And boy, you mark my words, God help you if what you have to say is not useful. Not only will we kill this wench and her pup, but we will make sure the whole platoon rapes her before we split her open."]

Jacques was silent, as was Marie. Both spirits were impossibly crushed.

Chapter 11

Jacque Duplantier was only sixteen years old when the 'Armee Indigene' spread to his plantation in 1794. He was tall with a powerful build and his skill with a musket kept him alive through countless skirmishes. He was one of the few surviving lieutenants from the Plaisance area of the island who survived the start of the Revolution, so he was very familiar with our war protocols.

For example, whenever there was a prolonged battle, our support team of women and other auxiliary non-combatants would breakaway and set up an encampment hidden in the forest area as a base camp to treat the wounded and feed the troops. To ensure that our outposts remained very well hidden, we would always build our camps in the mountains and hills obscured behind a thick wall of brush. At least four lookouts with rifles were posted high amongst the treetops facing each cardinal direction 24 hours a day on rotating shifts. The barracks inside of the brush wall consisted of three main temporary structures to serve the needs of the soldiers and support staff but most everyone else slept outside. Our hideout would usually also have an animal pen about six hundred feet from the rearmost hut of the main encampment. Standard procedure for setting up this vitally important part of the base consisted of collecting the different types of wood needed for the building materials from the forest and constructing the pen with sturdy branches for fencing and tying it all together with vines and sweet grass reeds. After the completion of the fence the animals are loaded into the pen. The support team would immediately begin chopping down young saplings and leafier twigs and vines until they had enough to completely obscure the enclosure. Not only did this addition add protection from crocodiles it also kept nosy humans at bay.

Many times, these structures would be built at night, and whenever I was present, I would help gather what was needed. Given my abilities, there was no shortage of material for building. The duality of my presence being a boon and at the same time a source of fear and awe was ever present, even more so amongst the volunteers than the soldiers. They called me 'Dyab', which meant 'devil' or 'Je Blan' which was Creole for 'white eyes.' Many people would force a smile and look towards the ground to avoid making eye contact when I approached the camp carrying a huge bundle of sticks for firewood and building shelters. Their heartbeats thumping against their rib cage echoed loudly in my ears. "Dyab la kom yon sove (The devil as a savior)," they would shake their heads in disapproval and whisper.

Whenever there was a fierce skirmish that lasted into the morning hours, I would retreat from the battlefield in anticipation of the sunrise, running like a mad man looking for a safe place to dig into the earth for my day slumber and recuperation. In my hunger from physical exertion and fighting, I would look for something or someone to prey on to replenish my strength while I retired from the sunlight. Whenever I was fortunate enough to be near a Maroon encampment, I would help myself to a chicken or a goat from the pen, take it into the forest and feast on it. When I was able to eat at my leisure, I was usually careful to peel back the skin and fur layer with my claws. The remaining hide I would leave for my comrades to tan and turn into leather. But at times when I was racing the sun, there was precious little time for table manners, and I would quickly and gruesomely dismember my meals covering myself with blood before digging into the earth for shelter.

It was revealed to me years later that the very same Jacque who confessed to knowing me and to knowing my secret, was also betrayed by the French military. He lamentably wound up dying in a stockade a few months after I was captured. After witnessing our revolutionary army overcome so many impossible obstacles, Jacque went to his grave believing that I was invincible. He had convinced himself that I would somehow still

217

overcome the white man and his god because our cause was just and we had the great power of the Gran Met on our side. The night of my capture, myself and a group of rebels from a plantation near Duplessis were retreating from a rout by a relatively small French regiment. Their superior firepower led to many casualties on our side. Defeating us handily, the French soldiers suspiciously seemed to be wise to our latest tactic of using decoy retreats and guerrilla tactics to break up the ranks of attacking enemies. Using our knowledge of the terrain, we would feign surrender and then quickly double-back and re-engage our pursuers from the rear. Unfortunately, that strategy got most of our squadron killed that night, and I received a coconut sized piece of shrapnel in my left side from a palm tree that splintered right next to me due to a cannonball strike. At the approach of daybreak, we all scattered back into the bush and retreated to the maroon camp just east of our position near Le Grande Rivière du Nord. I broke off and ran ahead of my compatriots as was our usual strategy and after fleeing into what I thought was deep enough into the bush to secure my escape, I doubled around to a small maroon encampment that was not far from the previous night's battle near a commune known as Milot.

That is when I saw the pig.

I should have known better. No one would be careless enough to leave a fat sow tethered to the trunk of thin breadfruit sapling. The protocol would be to hang it from a tree branch first because of the noise they keep up when rooting in the brush. I made for the little sow in a flash and as I grabbed the animal and snatched it up and away, the rope around its neck stretched taut to reveal a chain connected to one end of the rope that held fast, jerking me back and halting my forward motion. Out of blind hunger, panic, and equal amounts of stupidity, I continued to pull against the chain as the flesh on the neck of the pig began to rip. Instead of cutting the rope in those first seconds, I opted to pull harder against it, the muscles pop and bones crack as the animals neck stretches into thinner pieces of tissue, and the pig releases an ungodly scream as it struggles in vain to free itself from my clutches.

Extreme hunger and greed clouded my judgment, and I failed to register why this pig was tethered to a chain in such a strange way in the first

218

place. The few extra seconds of trying to rip the animal from its leash slowed my movements and distracted me enough that I failed to smell the gunpowder. Enemies in the shape of four French Imperial Forces Speciales hidden in the thick underbrush behind me with large shotgun muskets. As if on cue they each fired simultaneously from about fifteen meters away into my back sending me flying forwards onto my face into the ground. I was somehow still holding the now headless blood spurting pig. The close range and the large caliber of the gunshots felt like they had broken one or two of my ribs. I spring up and leap in the opposite direction to hide behind a large palm tree as the soldiers reload their rifles. A shift in the wind direction sent me an odor that caused the hair to stand up on the back of my neck.

Something dangerous was coming.

Under the ringing in my ears from the gunfire, I could hear the yelping and howling of dogs. These dogs were of various breeds, but all were highly trained to be vicious man-eaters. Tracking and subsequent torture using dogs was a favorite pastime amongst the planter class. This infamous group of canines were imported from Cuba and became world renowned for their savagery and uncanny success rate in hunting down and retrieving runaway slaves. I had encountered them and dispatched them quickly on the battlefields near Port Du Paix, but at the time, there was only a handful of them accompanying the Spanish regiments. Many stories had been circulating recently of their reputation for maiming and devouring disobedient slaves who dared to support the effort for rebellion. These dogs consisted mostly of Great Danes, bulldogs, and mastiffs who were fed a special mixture of gunpowder and raw meat that most of the slaves suspected of being pieces of missing comrades and family members. The torture these canines endured as puppies made them mindless killers, devoid of any compassion, sometimes devouring members of their own litter from hunger.

I dropped the pig to free my hands to defend myself from the incoming monsoon of sharp teeth and claws. As the first of the barking dogs entered the clearing, I struck them down with overhand blows, breaking the spines of the first three leaping attackers. My back was turned when I felt the

219

teeth of one of the canines sinking his incisors into my left arm. I tried to fling it away but the strength and voraciousness of the jaws of these creatures rivaled the bite pressure of the crocodile. As fast as I could grab one of them and toss them into the bush, break their necks or slam them into the ground to break their skulls, another three would try to bite at my groin or latch their teeth into my ankles. All the while, the sun was cresting the horizon and the soldiers continued to fire off pot shots at me and the dogs to keep me off balance, even at the risk of killing their own animals.

The fatigue from the night's previous battle coupled with the sustained injuries, the loss of blood, and lack of quality blood for me to drink were beginning to take their toll and my movements were becoming sluggish. Two dogs hung from both elbows, shaking and snarling and trying to drag me down. I successfully kicked and slashed down all frontal attacks, but they circled around and snipped at my Achilles' tendons and the backs of my calves with their sharp teeth. I spotted the dog trainer out of the corner of my eye leveling his rifle. Before I could react,

BLAM!!!

A bullet struck the side of my skull. The force of the buckshot caused me to spin off balance and tumble to my knees. As I fell, I dragged all my canine attackers to the ground with me. A large Great Dane beelined for my throat as I managed to place one foot on the ground and tried to stand from my kneeling position. I watched as all four of the Great Dane's' feet left the ground as it lunges at me from seven feet away. At the last second before its sharp teeth reached my face, my right hand jetted out and grabbed the Great Dane by the neck.

KKRRRTCH!

I squeezed with all my forearm strength and crushed its throat until I could feel its spinal column. The pressure caused the animal's eyeballs to explode from their sockets. Blood spurted from its nose in a jet stream. I tossed the lifeless body of the Great Dane aside and sank my teeth into the neck of another canine attacker and quickly sucked out as much blood as I

220

could to assist my body which was gradually becoming weaker from exertion, the wounds inflicted by these vicious mongrels and the encroaching light now cresting the horizon. If I had to fight in the raw light of the sun, it would mean a drastic reduction in my strength and healing abilities. Leaving me helpless to defend myself against this horde.

From the corner of my eye, I noticed a small brigade of soldiers coming from the same direction as the dogs running shoulder to shoulder in groups of four and carrying what looked to be miniature cannon barrels. I rose to my feet and began twisting my body back and forth and flailing my arms to shake loose my two new appendages. I managed to shake off the larger of the two mastiffs who took a chunk of my right arm as it went flying into another hound. I bent the other dog's bottom mandible back with my right hand until I heard it crack like a walnut. The pain in its jaw made it come to its senses and retreat, shaking its head and causing its loosely hanging mandible to flail back and forth, spewing blood and saliva. I turned on my heels to run in the opposite direction of the approaching soldiers with the aim of escaping deeper into the shadows of the forest. The artillerymen holding the mini cannons between them stopped abruptly as the remaining soldiers continued forward in a V-formation.

KRAAKOW! KRAAKOW! KRAAKOW!

Another round of buckshot riddled my body pushing me toward a patch of Chenn trees. Distracted by the searing pain of the gunshots and the dogs, I ran right into their trap. The instant I caught a glimpse of something in the trees above me, a group of soldiers holding a huge net about forty feet across made of iron links dropped down on top of my head. The soldiers all had mud heavily caked over their faces and uniforms to hide their scent from me as they waited amongst the branches. A grayish brown pit bull, now trapped under the net alongside me, bit my left hand with its full force, striking a tender nerve, sending a huge jolt of pain up my arm. I reflexively brought my right hand crashing down upon its skull, caving it in with a muffled 'scrunch' sound. The jaws of the dog now reflexively locked and would not release even though the animal was no longer conscious. The weight of the net, the tugging and biting of the dogs, and the force of the

221

now more than twenty soldiers pulling down and trying to stake the trap to the ground with ropes attached to the ends of the net causes me to drop down to my hands and knees.

My muscles screamed with pain and fatigue, but I fathomed that if I did not somehow free myself, and soon, I would certainly number amongst the enslaved once again. In the next few eternal seconds, I think of the years with my mother, all my fallen comrades, and all the blood and tears shed in the conflict during the last eleven years against three different slaveholding empires, only to allow myself to be snared like a wild, unthinking animal. Caught in the trap of men who thrived on a business model that required the enslavement of their fellow humans. In that next frantic moment at the literal bottom of the dog pile, I called upon every ounce of strength that I could muster.

"RRRAAAAAAAAAAHHHHHHHH!!!!!!!"

I let out a primal scream of desperation, what I can only describe as the roar of a delirious animal, straining with all the strength I could muster, I managed to stand on my feet. Suddenly a throng of French soldiers and British mercenaries who were waiting in ambush swarmed the area. I grabbed a fistful of the chain material in each hand and began pulling against the soldiers who were doing their level best to hold onto the ropes tied at intervals around the chain net. There must have been thirty men now trying to hold down the heavy iron net. I dug my toes into the dirt to square myself and gain some leverage with my feet. A lethal game of tug of war began between myself and the squadron of soldiers. Luckily for me, the dogs had gotten tangled in the net also and were no longer an immediate nuisance.

'KERCHINK'!....

'KERCHINK'!...

'KERCHINK'!...

The chain rattled loudly as I labored with all my remaining strength and slowly took three steps forward. The net buckled as it strained my efforts to free myself. The voices of the soldiers went up and began screaming at each other to dig in and resist in response to the fact I was beginning to drag them with each defiant movement. I poured my strength into each leg. With each small step the fear of the soldiers intensified. None of them could believe that I was still able to stand and defend myself under the weight of the net while bleeding so profusely.

In all the commotion and the low visibility caused by the net and the blood and sweat that was pouring into my eyes during the brawl, I failed to notice the twelve pound Gribeauval cannon being uncovered from its hiding place and rolled through a preestablished path in the woods into a position just five meters in front of me. I smelled the phosphorus and magnesium of the flint just before the wick was lit on the cannon.

KKKAAAAAATHOOOOOOMMMMMM!!!!!!!

One of the last things I remembered from that morning was the sound of that cannon being fired point blank into my chest, sending me flying back into the trunk of a large Chenn tree and feeling it crack in half from the impact of my body and the thrust of the shot. The dogs remaining under the net were killed by the force of the blast, however, I was still entangled by the now mangled iron chain net.

"AAAAARRRRRHHHHH"!!!

I willed myself to remain conscious.

Through the smoke and dust of the cannon blast I looked down to see my right arm was missing.
Torn flesh and shattered bone hung in its place. The blast had the positive side effect of tearing a hole in the iron chain-mail net and the shockwave forced the soldiers surrounding me to release their grip on the net. I was beyond weak and unable to feel the entire right half of my body. I quickly reached out to try and stretch the hole made by the cannonball, grabbing

one side of the hole with my left hand and placing my left foot against the other side.

"RRRRRGGGGUUUUHHHHH"!!!

I growl. Straining to break free as the soldiers began preparing for another point-blank range cannon blast. Visibility was poor but I could hear the soldiers giving the order to reload and reposition the barrel of the cannon to aim as low as they possibly could without allowing the ball to roll out. While I squirmed to extract myself from the net, I managed to rip the links in the iron webbing enough to crawl through the hole made by the cannonball. With the feeling returning to my right side, I was able to move at near full capacity. In a flash I made a beeline for the five men now making the final preparations to blow me to smithereens again.

I smashed my left shoulder into the soldier standing beside the cannon, knocking him into two other soldiers.

"WHOOEE-UUEET"

I hear a loud whistle behind me. Was the dog trainer calling for the remaining dogs to regroup and attack? I backhand another soldier who attempted to stab me with his bayonet, sending him to the ground. Before I could take a step in the direction of the dog trainer, I was hit with a volley of musket balls from the heavy-duty rifles. The force of the blasts spun me around and sent me crashing face first into the dirt knocking the wind out of me. Day was breaking fully now. I fought hard against blacking out to push myself up from the ground with one hand and will my legs to keep moving forward. I desperately needed to escape into the thick tree cover of the bush where I could maybe make it to the river and disappear until nightfall. Before I could move…

'BLAKOW!

I was struck with another volley of rifle fire by four soldiers standing within five meters of me, riddling my body with buckshot. The sound from the explosion of the gun powder and the flash of fire from the muzzles were the last things I saw before losing consciousness. When I came to a few minutes later my ears rang, my body ached and I was blindfolded lying on my stomach with my left hand and feet tied behind me like a pig on a platter. A disgusting brass horse bridle held my mouth open, bearing my fangs and causing me to drool uncontrollably. Humiliated beyond comprehension.

I could smell the sickening aroma of Eau de Toilette popular with the French aristocracy approaching. I heard a man's nasal voice speak who I surmised was their commanding officer.
"Donc le diable est noir. [So the devil is black?]," he remarked bemusingly. "Bonjour, mon ami. Êtes-vous réveillé? Pouvez-vous me comprendre? Vous êtes par la présente mis en état d'arrestation sur ordre de l'Armée Royale Coloniale Française" [Are you awake? Can you understand me? You are hereby placed under arrest by order of the Royal French Colonial Army.]

"Emmenez le au loin [Take him away]." I heard the man say, and I felt myself being lifted and carried off like a captured beast by two rows of soldiers.

Years later, I would discover that the rebels had negotiated a surrender by the Allied forces. In what was supposed to be a unilateral iron clad deal with the French, British, and Spanish military leaders, the leaders of the Revolution wrote up specific terms that were to go into effect upon my successful capture and delivery to the enemy. Their agreement came with the promise of the immediate retreat and removal of all allied forces from the territory of Hispaniola known as San Domingue. The terms of my capture also gave the men, women and children of San Domingue, now known as Haiti, full recognition as an independent country, the second country to duplicate a successful transfer from a dictatorship into a republic in the western hemisphere behind the United States. And the first and only independent nation to be created from a successful slave revolt. Our resistance and subsequent victory had bankrupted France and sent the fear of God through the European powers that still resonates to this day. I would like to feel that the decision my comrades made to sell me out to the French as a term of peace was the only way to save the lives of the people and end the war, but deep inside, I could not help but feel used and discarded. Their misunderstanding of what I was and the fear of the power I would be capable of wielding if I was allowed to remain amongst the people fueled their need to be rid of me.

Our *Lame Endijen* (Indigenous Army) had either decimated or ousted the main colonial forces and their reinforcements, sending them running into the sea. Thusly, the French and other colonists never forgave little San Domingue for having the effrontery to demand their independence. A spiteful plot to forever disenfranchise her was hatched by the ancestors of the capitalists who still hate her and treat her like dog shit today. My capture and the settlement on the terms of surrender took place mere months before the betrayal by Napoleon against Touissant L'Overture and his subsequent imprisonment and death.

•   •   •

I was a state secret of the French government from that day forward. I was transported in complete darkness inside a coffin-sized steel box with walls six inches thick and three holes drilled into one side for oxygen. Inside the box, I was restrained with chains and thick ropes tied so tightly that I could scarcely move enough to scratch my nose, much less generate enough force to push or punch my way out of my new prison. I could smell the sea, and I could hear the crash of the waves so I knew I was being transported by sea somewhere. Compared to my first experience at sea, this was loathsome. My fate was now once again left up to my enemy. It was inside this box that depression crept its ugly little head into my psyche, and despair began to take a permanent seat in my heart. I was in a pitiful downward spiral into indifference and apathy about my tragic life. Devoid of all hope.

I lost track of how much time I spent at sea until one day I felt the movement of the ship slow to a gentle bobbing. A few hours after the ship had halted its forward movement, I heard men approaching and feel the box being lifted and unloaded from the ship and then loaded into what I deduced from the smell was a horse drawn carriage. I suspected there must have been a large regiment assembled to transport me to my prison because I smelled what seemed like a dozen horses, and I could hear many heavy footsteps of booted men walking behind them. After a relatively short ride, I heard the locks being released on the latches surrounding my coffin. I was extremely stiff from being cramped inside this stifling uncomfortable box for so long. Despite my predicament, I was not going to allow myself to go peacefully back under the yoke of slavery. I was angry. I wanted to fight. I knew that the instant the lid of the coffin was raised, they would be vulnerable to my speed and if I needed to rip through a thousand throats until I was free again, then so be it.

As the last lock was removed from the latches, I readied myself for whatever abuse I would need to endure before I could free myself and begin a counteroffensive. To my surprise, I felt the box being hoisted into the air. I anticipated being thrown into the sea so I inhaled deeply to give myself enough oxygen to survive underwater until I could free myself from these ropes. For a few seconds I felt the weightless sensation of falling then...

KRRRADUUSHHH!

I am ejected from the box as it smashes apart into the rocky ground. I tumble hard into the dusty hole, the impact being enough to snap the ropes binding my arms. I laid on the ground stunned for a few seconds before rolling onto my stomach to take inventory of the dismal hole that was my new home. Before I knew what was happening the soldiers at the top of the hole yanked the two pieces of the broken iron box up swiftly by two ropes still attached to each half. I scrambled to my feet and tried to jump and grab onto it before it was gone, but I was too late. This was the trap of someone who had watched me on the battlefield and knew the exact limits of my strengths and my weaknesses.

I was thrown into what amounted to be part of a large well or the abandoned beginnings of a mine shaft about forty feet deep straight down into the earth with about fifteen feet in diameter of floor space. The soil at the bottom was hard and rocky but the walls were made of clay that crumbled so easily that it was impossible to climb out. I hesitate to imagine

227

the backbreaking work it must have been for the people forced to dig such a crater. I chewed the rope away from my left wrist but in addition to the ropes on my ankles those bastards had chained my feet together at the ankles with an additional shackle linked to a small iron ball shaped weight. The top of the hole was well beyond the range of what I could jump vertically, especially with the chains severely restricting my limbs. Someone had done their homework on the extent of my abilities.

Imprisonment in this dungeon was my first true test on the limits of what it meant to be immortal. The first three months in that hole, I ate nothing save for a few earthworms and other insects that had the calamitous fate of crossing my path. I drank only water from the small amount of rain runoff that made it to the bottom of the hole. I wanted to run from my failure. Suicide consumed my thoughts, however I had to face my uniquely cruel reality—no matter how much I wished death for myself every second of the day. It would never come. My body rebuffed decay as if drawing sustenance from the very air. The soldiers sent to check on my supposed demise were shocked, to say the least, when at the end of the first month with no food or water I was still alive and well. There were soldiers that seemed to be military medical personnel who would appear at the top of the hole and lower a special oil lantern about halfway down the shaft so they could see the condition my body was in and take notes on their findings. My right arm had grown back completely after the first two weeks in that pit and I could hear the guards remarking in astonishment about this and the fact that there seemed to be very little to no solid waste present in my enclosure. This was due to my immortal constitution rapidly adjusting my food requirement levels and minimizing the waste my body produced in proportion to consumption.

After the second month of my imprisonment, there appeared to be more frequent instances of medical and military brass at the top of the hole. I could hear them openly discussing the need for further research into the phenomenon of my physical durability and their desire to weaponize those traits. There was also talk of burying me in hopes that I would suffocate under the weight of the dirt and rocks. Afterwards they could safely dig me up and do an autopsy on my corpse to discover my secrets. Presumably, I was too expensive and too dangerous to be restrained for long and the word from the high command was that I would serve their purposes more when I was dead. Inevitably the lure of profit and the argument for potentially unlimited military strength led the discussion and my execution was postponed.

After the third month of lying in that prison hole, the French military research scientists were giddy with curiosity. So much so that they were willing to attempt to retrieve a specimen of my hair and blood for their soldier enhancement experiments. I sat leaning against the side of the chasm one morning as the sun shone halfway down into my prison. The hole, I deduced, had to be located on the side of a hill or elevated area for the sun never shone directly down into my dwelling even when at its apex. A flaw in its design that would one day serve in their undoing. I watched quietly as a beeswax torch was dropped from above and rolled, still flaming, against the wall opposite to where I was seated. In the next moment, two thick ropes covered in a thin wax were tossed from above along the opposite wall where I sat and close to where the torch lay burning. I raised my head to see two armored men wearing helmets, thick leather gloves and cuirass', repelling swiftly down into the shaft. At the top of the hole beyond them, I saw a ring of soldiers peering down into the chasm. Some of the soldiers stood in firing positions and were aiming high powered muzzle loaded muskets at me. I heard a familiar nasally voice above me say
[In FRENCH]:
    "You are hereby ordered to cooperate with our scientific research in the name of His Imperial Majesty, Emperor of France, Napoleon Bonaparte. Any resistance to our efforts will be construed as treason and a direct affront to the authority of the French military."

Just as the lieutenant had finished speaking, the armored men landed in the increasingly cramped space with a thud sending up a cloud of dust up into my face as I sat motionless but looking innocently up at the top of the hole at the party addressing me.

    "After securing your pledge to cooperate we will—"

I was on my feet before either of the soldiers could react.

229

I slammed the soldier on my right into the wall, lifting him up off his feet with my left hand and tearing off his helmet with my right. With the soldiers' face and neck now exposed, I bit down hard into the milky white flesh of his throat so hard that I nearly crushed his vertebrae. I could feel the hot bullets from the musket fire above me on the top of my head and shoulders, but I was unfazed. The roar of the booming guns echoing in the hole amongst the smoke and confusion was something to behold. No one present would soon forget the raucous scene. The other soldier, being an uneager witness to my gruesome display of hunger, remembered his training enough to swing his rifle from his shoulder and fire a shot into my back and then proceeded to ram the business end of his bayonet into my lower lumbar region as I gorged on the blood and flesh of his fellow comrade. Seeing that I was wholly unbothered by his attack, the soldier abandoned his weapon, removed his helmet and began frantically scrambling up the rope and screaming for the soldiers at the top of the hole to pull him out, which they did with some effort because of all the man's floundering and panic.

For weeks following that incident I was subjected to all manner of abuse consisting mainly of unprovoked shootings by the soldiers at all times of the day or night. I received hundreds of bullet wounds, many to the top of my head while simultaneously dodging rocks and boulders thrown from above to crush me and make my already dismal living conditions even more unmanageable. Men were urinating and defecating into the hole for weeks until they grew bored of it. When the soldiers suspected a servant of stealing or if one of the workers showed disrespect in some way that required reprimand, they would hang the poor soul upside down by their ankles over my dungeon hole. The offender would inevitably scream bloody murder until tears and mucus streamed down their faces begging to be forgiven and swearing to cooperate provided that they were not thrown into the devil's pit.

The scratches I had been making on the walls and floor marked the fact that over four months had passed since the debacle with the armored soldier being murdered. The guards and infantrymen had stopped their revenge attacks on me weeks ago and now only the research soldiers who

230

would peer down at me then jot something down on their notebooks before leaving were my only regular visitors. After nine months, when it seemed that no one would be able to study my physiognomy more closely without meeting a horrible death, even the scientists seemed to have given up on their research. No one visited my dungeon for long intervals at a time.

Not that I cared. I was ready to die a long time ago, the only person I ever loved in the entire world had been taken away from me in the most tragic of ways. With all my so- called power, I was unable to do anything to protect her. And to add insult to injury, the very people I shared my abilities with and risked my exposure to liberate were the same people who betrayed me to the enemy. The feeling of grief was too overwhelming for me to bear. Lamentably, I was still seen as a valuable curiosity for the State and the French military played up the rumors of my existence to use as a hedge against their enemies. Napoleon's government would frequently threaten my return to the battlefield under their control as a trump card during diplomatic discussions with the British and the Prussians.

The French bullied both foe and ally, threatening more than a few times that they had only to give the word and I would be unleashed to go on a bloody rampage through Europe. The resulting political situation was a kind of Cold War standoff with me playing the part of the nuclear warhead at the beck and call of Napoleon and the French military machine which had its eyes on expanding its empire throughout the rest of the known world.

It had been almost a year since I had any blood or meat. Even the earthworms started getting wise and avoided my dungeon like the plague. As the years passed, on very rare occasions, the French troops would toss one or two of a captured enemy into my pit while their fellow captives would be forced to watch the gruesome scene. I would be impossibly hungry, but I would try my best to fight the urge to extinguish these men's lives for the benefit and entertainment of those depraved French bastards. Inevitably, the captured soldiers would be so frightened by my presence that most attacked me unprovoked. I began not to pity them at all. A warrior should be prepared to die was how I began to see it. I began to savor ripping their bodies apart and scarfing down their blood. The hoots, jeers, and screams from above only fueled my savagery.

The prisoners who were forced to watch their comrades be torn apart would be released to report back to their respective homelands that an actual demon was under control of the French military, held captive through their mastery of esoteric magic and alchemical science. The stories of my existence were oftentimes enough of a deterrent to procure surrender from France's enemies which in turn increased their strategic power and their financial coffers. This led to even more boldness from the leadership under Napoleon. France was able to expand her empire and grow their military exponentially which only added to Napoleon's temerity. It would be this arrogance and greed that would eventually cause him to feel that I was too expensive to keep in lieu of mounting debts in Paris. Napoleon also began to feel that I was no longer needed as a preventative measure in view of the fact the imperial military had become so formidable. I would later find out that because of all the hyperbole surrounding my abilities, I had thrown off the delicate power balance amongst the nations and I was becoming a threat to the real power brokers who had come to the consensus that France and her leadership was becoming too haughty and needed to be taken down a peg or two.

These invisible power brokers had plenty of capital and were willing to pay a fortune to possess me with the objective of harnessing my abilities for themselves. The numbers that they were offering France were utterly irresistible, and the government felt the infusion of capital was necessary to continue their aggressive military campaign across Europe. But Napoleon was also smart enough to know that if I were to fall into the wrong hands, it could cause an imbalance in power in the years to come. A sinister scheme was hatched to accept payment for my transfer and then kill me and report that I was assassinated shortly after the transfer by a rival third party in a staged attack that would release France from all liability with the power brokers and neatly dispose of the nuisance I had become.

By my reckoning, I had been rotting in that miserable hole for a little over six years when one fateful morning, I was awakened by the sounds and smells of a horse drawn wagon, freshly chopped wood, and what must have been a large amount of pine tar and gunpowder. A tall, bearded man with an eye patch over his left eye and no mustache wearing the uniform of a highly decorated officer began to address me from the top of the hole explaining (In French).

"This day, by order of His Imperial Majesty, Emperor of France, Napoleon Bonaparte, you are to be executed by fire until dead."

When the man had completed the reading of the edict, as he looked down into the hole for a moment, our eyes met, and we just stared at each other in contempt. Abruptly, the officer saluted and turned on his heels. The soldiers encircled the top of my dungeon's hole and all at once, they began to dump wood, pine tar, and some other substance that I assumed to be another form of accelerant that smelled like gunpowder but had the viscosity of slime. The combination of the fuel odors threw my senses into a tailspin. I frantically began to stack the firewood up as quickly as possible in order to create a platform high and sturdy enough to be able to leap out of this hole and eviscerate these bastards. I knew what was happening and I was not going to sit idly by and let them kill me.

BLAM! BLAKOW! BLAKOW!

The sounds of musket fire reverberated loudly in the hole.

My back was sprayed with buck shot.

BLAKOW! BLAKOW!BLAKOW!

Another deafening series of shots.

Bullets were striking me square in my shoulder and one even nipped my right ear, taking part of it with it. The soldiers were trying to prevent me from stacking the wood. Before I knew it, three lit torches tumbled down into the hole. Time slowed to a halt as I scrambled with my chained feet up the little pile of wood I was able to create in those few seconds. I thought I could

233

time my jump to use the force of the blast as lift to push me out of the hole and avoid being blown apart and burnt to a crisp. There was a spot on the wall that was just out of reach of the sun that I had been chipping and scratching away at for the last two years to create a small foothold that would give me enough thrust to be able to leap to the top of the hole. Just as I was about to make my leap the chain around my ankle that had the cannonball gets lodged between two large rocks that had been tossed down in a previous barrage. I watched the first torch being flung down and skid off the wall. It flips and lands innocuously on top of a pile of bones. In the following milliseconds, I reached for the leg chain to yank out the cannonball so my legs were free to make the jump. That was when I saw the second torch fall and land directly onto the gunpowder-laden substance.

KATHOOOOOOOM!!!!!!

Instantly, the entire bottom of the hole was on fire, and the flames surged upwards. I held my breath, squat down into the flames and spring skywards toward the ledge. My hair, beard, eyebrows and every other piece of hair was burned away from my body. The rags I wore were soaked through with perspiration, but they were barely surviving the roasting blaze. The exposed flesh on my body was raw and surging with pain from the initial explosion but began to heal as soon as the pain reached the epidermis. This burn was merely a tickle compared to what the sun was going to do to my exposed legs and arms. In the following moment, I sprang up onto the makeshift ledge and from there, I jumped with all the strength I could muster. In a heartbeat I was, at long last, near the top of the hole. I clawed frantically to pull myself up over the edge, the dirt giving way with each handful I grabbed but eventually I succeeded and immediately went into action.

For years as I languished in that hole I dreamt of the first skull I would sink my claws into once I was free from my underground prison. No sooner had my feet touched the surface, I grabbed the first two soldiers I saw and ripped out their throats. None of the guards imagined me to be able to jump out of the pit so they had all backed away at the initial surge of the explosion giving me plenty of room to run. The sight of me on the surface put everyone in a panic. There were black male slaves present that were being used to transport the barrels of tar and gunpowder who discarded their work immediately and struck out running for their lives at the sight of my smoldering body. Suspiciously, only the two soldiers I killed were on duty to guard the hole. In the next instant I caught another very strong smell of gunpowder mixed with the faint scent of something that conjured up bad memories for me.

It was the stink of that bastard dog trainer from the ambush years ago that landed me in that shitty dungeon six years ago. I caught sight of him and noticed that he was the man who read my execution pronouncement wearing the eye patch over the wound I inflicted on him as I was going berserk to escape the iron net in San Domingue years ago. He had been given a promotion as a reward for taking the lead in subduing me the first time and now I guess they figured that he was going to be able to do it again. Unfortunately for him, I had other plans. I saw him drop his hand as if giving a signal and I spun around to—.

KKKRRRRRAAAAATTTHHHHHOOOOOOOMMMMM!!!!!

Flash and smoke of the muzzles of ten Gribeauval guns, firing consecutively from left to right. They were seriously trying to kill me. Instantly I dropped and began to run on all fours. I dodged the first shots by adroitly twisting my body in the air like a cat. My still chained feet were barely touching the ground as I ran zig zag toward the line of artillery and soldiers to escape the cannon fire. The explosion I absorbed and exposure to sunlight were making my movements a bit sluggish, but I was determined to escape from this hell on earth and live free. In my anger I misjudged the toll my weakened condition would have on my reflexes.

I am grazed by an oncoming cannonball and my wrist and hand shatter upon impact. I slam against the ground on my left side hard into the dirt. My right shoulder was significantly dislocated, and my body would not stop vibrating like a human tuning fork. Both wrists were broken, and my

235

right forearm arm was totally shattered with part of my radius bone piercing through my skin at the wrist like a jagged knife. I coughed out a breath and forced myself to inhale. A second later, I was on my feet. The dog trainer anticipated my determination on getting out of that hole and had prepared a contingency course of action to prevent me from escaping. I grossly overestimated my ability to handle the updated technology of the French artillery. All around me there were strategically placed gun nests full of heavily armed soldiers to be able to contain any threat that was foolish enough to try and escape that pit. Considering my surroundings, I could see that the area that I had been imprisoned within for all those miserable years was nothing more than a small military installation near the coast. Probably set up for housing top level prisoners and exiles far away from the seat of power.

KRAKOW! KRAKOW! KRAKOW!—

   Slugs from the rifles hit me in my side that felt like little pops of pressure through the numbness in my still trembling body.
 Their concentration of fire seemed to be pushing me towards an opening in the fort. A panel built into the east wall dropped to reveal another row of other cannons…

KKKKAAATTTHHHOOOM!!!!!!

   I would have been able to dodge their fire with my speed at this distance but instead of the guns firing cannonballs, two giant steel harpoons attached to an improved version of the iron net wrapped around my body like a bolo entangling my arms and legs causing me to fall face first into the dirt. My uninjured arm was tangled helplessly and rendered useless and I flopped on the ground like a fish out of water trying my damndest to free myself from the heavy net but only serving to drain what little strength I had left.

   I kept asking myself: How could I fall for the same trick twice?

I let my anger get the best of me. The dust and smoke choked my lungs. I could barely see anything, especially with the sun being so bright. I squinted hard but I can only make out the shapes and smells of several men approaching with a new and improved steel box much like the one that I arrived at this prison in over half a decade ago. Behind that group of men, I smelled the one-eyed dog trainer and as he drew closer I could now make out his silhouette approaching with his saber drawn as a precaution. He said something inaudible in French to the men surrounding me and in the next moment, an iron muzzle was placed over my mouth and I was secured with heavy rope and chains while the iron net was removed. I was hoisted up and slammed into another steel box. As the lid closed, I was thrust back into darkness. I could hear the dog trainer telling someone that he wished he could just drop me into the ocean and be done with it. Instead, I was to be auctioned off for the purpose of funding the increasing ambitions of the French imperialist machine. Allegedly, Tallyrand, one of Napoleon's ministers, felt it unwise to go against the Incalculaba and kill me as Napoleon had instructed. As an alternative he decided it would be more prudent to make sure I was secretly delivered to my new owners alive so as not to incur the wrath of those who would not be too receptive to Napoleon's defiance. Tallyrand wisely understood that to go against the Incalculaba would surely spell the downfall of the French Empire at the hands of the true rulers of this world.

Chapter 12

.... BZZZZ...BZZZZ

Kate's phone goes off, interrupting my story. She looks towards it and frowns at it as if this was the first time she had heard the noise before. "Let me guess, now Frankenstein is at the gate and wants revenge" she says sarcastically as she stands to grab the phone from the sofa table. She swipes up to end the voice recording and opens the video doorbell application.

"That's odd," her eyebrows contract as she stares at the screen.
"Is everything okay" I ask her, turning in my chair to face her.
"It's the police, the police are at the gate. But..." she trails off. Giving me a suspicious glance as she walked into the foyer.

"Have the police of this area ever been to your home before today?" I ask her as the phone chimes out a digital recreation of the classic doorbell sound.

What? ... you think I called them?" She asks incredulously, "This is the last thing I needed tonight. I should be asking you why the hell the police are at my door at two a.m. the very same night Count Chocula decides to pay me a visit. If you are going to have me help you, it's time to tell the fucking truth, and all of it. Is there something you did that I need to know about because I can't stand liars!" She walks over and picks up the shotgun from beside the fireplace.

"I already could be charged for simply harboring a fugitive if everything you've been telling me isn't a crock of shit."

Her phone rings out with the doorbell chime again.

"You should answer it. I promise everything I have been telling you is the truth and I will come clean and tell you what happened but first try to get rid of them. Please!" I stare at her pleading with my eyes.

"Hello?" she said into the phone. "Is there a problem officer? Did something happen? It's almost two in the morning."

"Good evening, ma'am," the officer says with his southern via the Midwest twang. My name is Deputy Milford of the Dane County Sheriff's Department. We sincerely apologize for disturbing you at this time of the morning, ma'am, but we had a serious incident take place tonight. One of our deputies was injured, and we believe the suspect to be armed and extremely dangerous. We are advising all residents in the Three Foot Bay, Governor's Island area to remain indoors and be on alert for the next couple of days. We are also urging residents to report any suspicious people or vehicles to local law enforcement immediately. One of your neighbors told us that he saw a suspicious looking gentleman wearing sunglasses and driving a dark colored pickup truck turning onto this street shortly after the incident"

"Was the officer injured badly?" Kate asks the police officer, taking a drag of her cigarette and squinting her eyes accusingly at me.
"He's expected to make a full recovery, but our main concern is this perp out here on the loose with absolutely no respect for the law. We believe it to be related to the rise in gang activity surrounding the meth epidemic this county has had to deal with for the last few years," replies Deputy Milford.

"My word, I hope to God you find whoever it may be. I have a flight out in the morning, but I will be sure to keep my doors locked and stay close to my phone in case I see or hear anything out of the ordinary," Kate says convincingly.

239

"Thank you, ma'am, and again, we apologize for bothering you so late and scaring you with all this business. We've set up roadblocks and active patrols in the area so if you must leave your home for any reason within the next twenty-four to forty-eight hours, please be sure to bring your identification or you may be delayed or detained by the roadblocks our deputies are putting in place. Presently, we are checking the identifications of everyone traveling in the vicinity and for now, no one is allowed to turn on this street without proof of residence," Deputy Milford finishes.

"I don't anticipate needing to drive anywhere. I am having a driver come pick me up and take me to the airport at eleven but they should have car service credentials to prove themselves so it shouldn't be an issue. I had become sort of a recluse even before this COVID stuff and everyone started working from home. But I will keep your advice in mind if I do get a wild hair and decide to travel anywhere," Kate says.

"Thank you, ma'am. Again, we truly apologize for disturbing you at this hour. We also very much appreciate your cooperation in this matter," Tipping his hat to the video camera, "As a routine procedure for cases like this, another officer will most likely do a follow up with residents in the area tomorrow morning after the sun comes up."

Of course, thank you, officer, I will keep my eyes peeled for anything out of the ordinary. Kate gives me a pointed glare that lingers too long and makes me look away nervously. "And I will absolutely call you if I see or hear of anything out of the ordinary. Thank you, and goodnight." Kate ends the connection. With the shotgun now tucked in the crook of her right armpit again, she takes a long drag of her cigarette, stamps it out in the ashtray and exhales. She stares at me for a prolonged moment before speaking.

"Did you attack a police officer tonight?" she asks me, placing the phone on the back of the couch and pacing back and forth in front of me.

"Let me explain, I had t— "

"Listen, let me stop you right there." She cuts me off abruptly, and there is a long dramatic pause before she speaks as she glares at me holding one finger in the air like a mother scolding her child. "The only reason I didn't scream bloody murder into that phone just now is because for some stupid reason, I was beginning to believe your sob story when you were speaking about your mother and Claudette..."

"Colette" I interject. "Kate, everything I have said is truth, I— "

"Goddammit, let me finish!", she cuts me off mid-sentence.

Kate stands with one hand on her hip looking down at me and says sternly, "First of all, *'IF'* I am going to help you, then you need to know that you cannot be wantonly attacking police officers or anyone else for that matter. Because once I am involved, you need to make absolutely, positively sure that you understand that in my eyes once you cross the line and start assaulting and killing people, no matter how justified, you become a terrorist. At that point I will consider you as having gone rogue from any agreement I may make to help you. I certainly can't justify murder, no matter how big of a schmuck these people are. If you can somehow manage to bring them in alive, I will help you with litigation and we can lock their asses up and throw away the key. And I promise I will do everything I can to roast them in the court of public opinion and make the world understand the implications behind their schemes for total domination. But, before I lift one fucking finger, I need to be able to trust you," she says angrily.

I look at her and exhale my cigarette smoke through my nose like a dragon. Our eyes lock at the end of her last sentence. My look says it all. We both know that this conspiracy is so enormous, we would be lucky to get just one person arrested, and like Oswald, Epstein, and countless other exposed assets, they would never live to rat on their conspirators. Moreover, at any point in the operation, if I am captured or our connection is discovered, they would disown and exile her, if not worse, and wipe out our entire existence from the public record. And once they get bored with torturing me they would probably, put my immortal ass in a one way rocket to the moon.

"The matter with the deputy tonight was unavoidable and unfortunate, but I assure you other than a few broken fingers and a terrible headache, he should be fine," I explain to Kate.

" I was careful that no one saw me intercept the deputy, and I was sure to destroy his onboard surveillance systems so no one would be able to track or identify me. I have confessed my truth to you tonight, and I feel that if I am allowed to divulge the rest of my history, you will come to understand why we are out of time and desperate measures like the ones I took to be here tonight are indeed necessary. But, before I continue, I must ask, is there a garage or shed on your property large enough for a vehicle. If the police are using helicopters or when they come back with a warrant during the day, they may ask to enter the gate to speak with you in person and they will surely spot my truck," I tell her.

She looks at me for another long moment with one hand holding a freshly lit cigarette aloft and the other hand folded across her chest. The shotgun now rests across the arms of the chair in front of her. Her mind is at a crossroads. Kate must be honest with herself that the idea of what I was proposing excited her more than it scared her. She rolls her eyes with a sigh and says, "There is an empty horse stable about a quarter of a mile past the guest house. You can put your truck in there, and it should be fine, but over the past two years since we sold the horses, I have been using it as a storage area so you may have to move some things around to make space for your car to be able to fit through the door. The breaker panel for the stable area is just left of the door of the main barn out there so unfortunately, there are no lights out there to guide your path, and it gets pitch dark out here. But if you are telling the truth that shouldn't be a problem for you," Kate says.

"Thank you," I tell her as I stand to walk towards the front door and my boots.

"Turn the porch lights off as you exit in case they have someone watching the house already. You don't get to be an award-winning journalist without being able to shift into full paranoia mode," Kate says through a cloud of cigarette smoke.

She follows me to the door as I run out into the darkness. I open the door to my truck and lean into the cab. I insert the key but only turn it to the first position to engage the power steering without cranking it up. Putting the truck in neutral, I hold onto the steering wheel and the door frame as I push it around Kate's truck toward the back of the house and down the access road to where the barn was. The sound of a distant helicopter moving slowly closer to my position confirms what I feared. It will be next to impossible to get out of the state for the next few days but if this episode with the local police hits the wire and raises any red flags with the upper echelon, all my decades of careful planning may go to waste. I pick up the pace, pushing the truck at a light jog when I arrive at the stable door. I jump into the cab and apply the brake to stop the truck's forward momentum. I hopped out and hurried over to the barn entrance. As I undo the latch and open the door, I see the piles of boxes and bins along with various covered items of furniture including several eight-foot stacks of horse saddles. I hastily begin to stack the boxes and bins to either side of the door and clear a space large enough for me to wheel the truck inside. As I am working, I can hear the chop of the helicopter hovering in the near distance so in the interest of time, I hurriedly lift as many saddles as I can get through the door with and place them in stacks outside the front of the stable.

I see the spotlight of the police helicopter as it makes a sweeping approach over the neighbor's property and edges ever closer to my position. I hurriedly pushed the truck in the barn deep into a corner stall and covered it completely with some canvas tarp and rotting bales of hay. I ran back to the front of the stable to swiftly re-stack all the bins, boxes and saddles inside before closing the front door of the barn. Through the gaps in the wood, I could see the spotlights from the helicopter orbiting the main house and then sweeping over the guest house before eventually hovering over the building I was hiding in for a long moment. After an infinity, the helicopter finally seemed to be moving on. As soon as the buzz from the helicopter had faded sufficiently, I finished hiding the truck, crept out of the barn and glided my way back into the darkness to rejoin Kate at the house who was standing at the door smoking as I approached the front porch.

"Jesus, you really do have night vision. I didn't see you coming until you were at the edge of the carport," she says as she turns to re-enter the house. "They are serious about finding you. This is probably the first big case they've ever had in this podunk town. I'm sure the local sheriff is going to use this as an excuse to acquire more of the many toys they've already been buying second hand from the government at dirt cheap prices. I wouldn't be surprised if they rolled down the street in a tank tomorrow. Your provocation has given them the green light to go full fascist," she chuckles as we enter the living room. Kate pours a glass of wine for herself before we resume our respective seated positions. She resets the voice memo recorder on her phone and gestures for me to continue my story.

"I believe we were interrupted just about the time I was recaptured and sold to the highest bidder for a sum nearing one hundred million francs. That was around the year 1810, Indeed I had reached a low point in my life. Not only was I physically bound by the chains of the French military, but my mind had begun to accept that I was an abomination. Destined to serve my enemies and condemned to loneliness..."

Chapter 13

      I was sealed inside that steel box for at least a week during the transport to the vessel that was to take me overseas. This box was specially engineered to prevent me from escaping. This coffin was made of Wootz steel, a very strong and durable form of crucible steel that originated during the ancient times in Southern India. My right arm had healed almost completely, but I was very weak and stiff. There were at least two dozen soldiers, mercenaries, and corresponding attendants securing my arrival, and they were sure to open the coffin in the middle of the day under the blazing hot sun causing me to be even more defenseless than I already was. During my unconsciousness, the iron net was removed and it was replaced with wrist and neck shackles connected by thick naval yard chains, complete with a muzzle over my mouth forged of the same type of reinforced iron material. At first, I lost the will to fight. Making my transition back into a mindless servant was welcome if it meant never having to feel again. I was utterly distraught mentally, and my body had become weak and emaciated from spending the last six years eating very infrequently at the bottom of that prison pit.

      Unbeknownst to me, I was now being shipped to the United States as the property of a very wealthy and scholarly French family who also happened to hold the exclusive status as being one of the main thirteen bloodline by the name of Carbonneau. The patriarch of the family, Dr. Regnault Gillet Carbonneau, made a fortune in pharmaceuticals and wrote multiple academic papers that delved into the studies of blood diseases such as hemophilia, ogbanjes (known today as Sickle Cell Disease") and porphyria (also known as the 'Vampires Disease'). Through his wealth and high-level connections in the French military, Dr. Carbonneau knew well of my condition. His timing was also impeccable in choosing to inquire about me through a personal letter to Tallyrand himself around the deadline for the decision as to what exactly should be done about me. The good doctor was able to outbid many of the other families of the Incalculaba who all were vying to be in control of my *gifts*. My sale to Carbonneau was a win-win for Tallyrand and the French government who were able to secure more funds for the war effort and to make me someone else's problem all in one transaction. Carbonneau was a very intelligent man and his dubious connections with the Reichstalls placed him head and shoulders above the rest of the bidders.

From the small island colony of Guadeloupe on which I was being held captive for the last six years to what is still known today as Thibodeaux Parish, Louisiana I traveled for over a fortnight, more than four thousand kilometers inside that godforsaken box. During that time, I experienced hallucinations about my mother who reminded me that I still had a long way to go before the evil ones were vanquished. She reminded me of my royal ancestors and the fact they no matter what happened I should never give up. The bloodlust I tried to bury under self-pity and depression slowly returned and I again vowed to myself that I would escape my bonds and have my revenge on these evil doers and once and for all purge their wickedness from this earth.

I could feel the warmth of the noonday sun through the box as I was unloaded from the ship and onto a waiting caravan of wagons at the port in New Orleans. I was unable to see anything through the tiny air holes cut into the box, but I could smell and hear my captors as I was hoisted onto an ox cart led by armed men on horseback. After a few more hours of traversing uneven, bumpy roads inside the oven-like steel container, I began to feel the temperature subside and heard the insect sounds change from the high-pitched whine of cicadas to the monotonous chirp of crickets. My old friend darkness was returning.

Another handful of hours trudging through muddy bayou passed when the wagon finally came to a stop. I could hear voices surrounding me and speaking a foreign language in excited tones in anticipation of my arrival. I tried to interpret my surroundings from the myriad of scents of the mules, the horses, gunpowder and of the men who unloaded me in the thick humid night air. If I was going to fight, the first thing I would need is blood to replenish my stamina. Whilst the locks were being removed and the heavy lid was slowly withdrawn from the box, I prepared myself to leap from the casket and grab a hostage. As the locks sealing the coffin shut were released, the hair on my body stood on end and I braced my muscles in preparation for action. To my astonishment I was hit by an aroma strikingly reminiscent of the spices the women who used to cook with in the kitchen with my mother back in San Domingue.

At once I lost my nerve and allowed my body to relax. I heard a woman's voice from directly above me saying the words, "Lawwwwd ha mursy!" These were the first words of English ever spoken directly to me. I lie there staring up at a group of Negroes, men and women gawking at me under the light of a torch. There was a large woman who seemed to be in charge of the group who greeted me with "Bon-joe!" Pa Le Vu Francie?" in a sort of lazy French mixed with Creole that she had to repeat a few times for me to finally understand her. She asked me to nod my head if I could hear her, which I reluctantly obeyed. After every few words in French, she would punctuate with her signature

"Lawd Ha Mussy"in English.

I was removed from the box by the men present and placed in a seated position on the ground where a pair of teenage boys began to unlock and remove my muzzle. A tall and beautiful young woman then walked nervously towards me with a mid-sized female goat on a tether strolling sleepily behind her. I could now see that there were many people present, including white men who also held torches and rifles a short distance from the circle of Negroes and myself. One of the men on horseback spoke to the Negroes in English and a man wearing a hat and shoes came over and held a torch to my face so those gathered could get a better look at me. Everyone stared at my dirty emaciated body and the look on most of the faces present

247

was that of disgust. The man wearing the hat and shoes made a gesture which prompted the woman leading the goat to walk over and hand off the animal into his custody. Her eyes showed pity instead of disgust though she was cautious not to come too close to me. One of the men on horseback said something else in English and I was led along with the goat about twenty feet away from the crowd. The man stopped abruptly and placed the rope holding the goat in my hands and walked away. I looked down at the unsuspecting animal and imagined its warm blood pulsing through its body. As the saliva built in my mouth, a bit of drool began to form on my lips. I glanced at the men on horseback who were sneering in revulsion yet eager to see what such an expensive slave was capable of.

It had been literal years since I had a meal so large, and I was terribly hungry. I was unable to control the urge to tear into the creature. I ripped the poor animal apart and splattered its hot blood onto the dusty ground. I made a pure glutton of myself in front of these total strangers. In a matter of minutes, I completely drained the poor creature of all its blood and devoured all of its internal organs except for its intestines. After ten or so minutes of uninterrupted feasting, I was splashed from behind with a bucket of water thrown by the man wearing the hat. I stood up from the remains of the goat and turned to see the large black woman fearlessly approaching me with her own bucket and scrub brush in hand. Presently, I was nearly naked save for my loincloth shirt hanging loosely about my waist which was now stained with fresh goat's blood.

I must have smelled like shit for my new compatriots, led by the large black woman still punctuating every action with her signature "Lawd Ha Mussy," poured buckets of water mixed with copious amounts of lye soap on me. Brushes at the ends of broomsticks were used by three of the Negro servants to scrub off any lice and disease perceived to be on my body. My loincloth was snatched away from around my waist, and I just stood there like a naked dumb animal as the men finished scrubbing and the two women poured buckets of cold water over my head and shoulders, baptizing me under the stars and torchlight as the white overseers looked on from their mounts. I was given a thin shredded burlap blanket to cover myself and made to walk with my legs and hands still chained led by the two boys that removed the muzzle from my mouth. For the rest of the night, I was closely

248

guarded by over a dozen armed men while I waited inside a barn just about 100 yards from a huge structure which must have been the master's main dwelling. My senses told me that there were at least another ten men on patrol outside of the barn, and the same four white men with rifles that were present for my unboxing were standing guard inside the barn, watching my every move until dawn.

Doc. Carbonneau, as everyone on the plantation called him, was a very shrewd thinker and had rightly deduced that I would not attack a group of enslaved black people, even in my feral state. Employing a matronly figure like this woman was an even greater stroke of genius because her fearlessness and familiarity with Creole disarmed me completely and I was made to feel somewhat at ease upon my arrival.

The next morning, I was brought into the main house to meet my new master, the esteemed Dr. Carbonneau. He was a tall pale man with silver white hair who was very curt and dry in his manner of speech. His first instruction was for me to discard the horsehair blanket I had wrapped around me. He proceeded to perform a physical inspection of me as the four armed guards, two lab assistants and the large black woman that greeted me upon my arrival watched unashamedly. Dr. Carbonneau drew blood, took hair and fingernail samples and thoroughly examined every inch of my body with his stethoscope and various other medical measuring devices that were state of the art in 1810. This madman was my new master, and my heart sank even further into my chest as the depression of my hopeless situation took hold. I would be forced to be a beast of burden to enrich another coven of villains. As Dr Carbonneau finished his humiliating exam on me, I was dismissed into the care of two of the larger of the armed white men and the boisterous woman who I now presumed to be one of the main housekeepers for Carbonneau.

"Lawd ha mussy! We gon has teh gitchu' sum propa' britches boy. Cain't have no men's workin' wit' dey pecker out. He He! One a' dese here mutts be dun' came and bit it right oft," the woman says to me as she hands me an oversized long-sleeved shirt made of coarse material. She blushes somewhat as she peeks down at my jungle covered manhood. "Say gal!" the woman yells back towards the taller younger woman. "Fetch me dem needle an dat croacker sack an' sizzus. Lawd, ha mussy! We gon' haf' tuh mek' yuh sum darn breeches!"

Over time, this woman and her daughter not only taught me English and Creole, but they also protected, nurtured, and instructed me on how to be a proper servant over the next five years until I slowly transformed from a monster back into a man. I came to rely on them and love them as dearly as I loved my mother, and I swore with all solemnity that I would protect them from this world. Their names were Jessie and Colette, the women I spoke of before in my earlier tale of woe. Back then, I was totally ignorant of the fact that everything that had happened in my life from the moment I was betrayed by my compatriots in San Domingue and used as a bargaining chip to end the revolution, my fate had always been in the hands of the Reichstalls. They saw my life as a trinket for their amusement. As the new head of the Incalculaba, Reichstall funded and directed Carbonneau to purchase me. They had always planned to use Jessie and Colette to lower my guard and exploit my vulnerabilities by teasing me with hope and acceptance, only to return me to the deepest pits of despair by taking them from me violently and using our emotional connection in a blood ritual against me. This they perpetrated on top of the fact that they used me as an accomplice in a crime that manipulated the financial markets in a way that only served to enrich and solidify their wicked monopoly over the world economy. Every day the first thing I would do was repeat my vow that no matter if it took me a thousand years, I would have my revenge on the Reichstalls and the Incalculaba.

That saga concluded during the summer of 1815. As you will recall, it was the end of the Battle of Waterloo, and I was beyond anguish at the brutal murder of Colette, but before I could exact my revenge, I was knocked unconscious by Reichstall's tranquilizer gas. I next found myself chained stiffly in the lower level of a slave ship chartered by the Baron and furnished with an entire crew with only myself as its cargo. I was on a return voyage from England to the American mainland to suffer even more baneful tribulations under the servitude of another one of Reichstall's landed and moneyed plantation owner colleagues within his vast web of influence. As I lay in the dark, the back of my neck burned with an excruciating pain. The discomfort consisted of a nagging and throbbing pulse the likes of which I had

250

never felt before. Every injury I have ever received would eventually heal no matter how severe, but this burning on the back of my neck was like nothing I had ever experienced before because the wound seemed to be getting progressively worse instead of healing. Considering that I was bolted to the floor with thick steel chains, I was helpless to do anything about the sensation besides tilting my head back and forth and moving it from side to side in a futile attempt to soothe my searing flesh. For the life of me, I could not dissipate the pain. The flesh on the back of my neck felt as if it was being bored through with a hot, dull knife. I must have inhaled the gas so thoroughly that I was comatose and completely oblivious to whatever manner of tampering they had done with my body.

At the time, I did not understand why this mark was so painful and why my body took so long to heal it, but in later years, once I was able to learn to read, I began more in-depth research into old books and manuscripts about the legends of my species. I grew to understand how certain pure grades of silver can retard our healing process when introduced into our bloodstream. The less impurities in the silver, the more lethal it becomes for us and the more vulnerable we are to its effects. The branding iron used to create this mark was made of such high-quality silver that the insignia would probably endure for another five hundred years. The searing pain of this marking would last for nine full days before it began to scab over and heal into a keloid that resembled the head of a lion with the body of a serpent. An eternal mark of shame that forever identified me as the property of the Reichstall conglomerate.

After ensuring my perpetual bondage, I was shipped away from the shores of Great Britain as the sole parcel on a merchant ship owned and operated by one of the Baron's subsidiary companies. Express cargo designation was given to the vessel I was ferried on. The trip lasted just over thirteen days before we touched down at the Isle aux Maraguans, an area in the Gulf of Mexico just south of what is today known as Mobile, Alabama. Mobile, in those days, was a remarkably bustling French port city with a Spanish influence that was annexed by the American government in 1813. The specific plantation I was shipped to was a two day journey northeast of Mobile. A huge cotton plantation that spanned the Alabama River which is now marked by a city called Grove Hill or closer still—Gosport, Alabama.

Chapter 14

     Gosport, Alabama, present day, is a microscopic, one stop sign town in the southwestern foot of the state between Mobile and Montgomery, and it is still recognized to this day as being the heart of Choctaw country. There are large tracts of forest still separating the few farms that still exist there now. Most of the properties there belong to the descendants of the wealthy landowners of the old cotton plantation abundance that this area was notorious for. Mobile originally was the jewel of the French empire in the Americas and still to this day hosts a Mardi Gras and Fat Tuesday that boasts of its decadent French culture. I arrived here in the year 1815, locked into servitude. My life was never to be my own again. My gifts were to be used to further enrich the Reichstall empire via their associates and business partners. The whole lot were sick, depraved individuals who would go to any length to ensure their power and influence for generations to come. Crashing the London Stock Exchange that year and repurchasing everything for pennies on the dollar and getting away with it was the crime of the millennia. The Reichstall family now controlled the crown jewel in the world of finance and banking. I will forever bear the shame of being an unwitting accessory to that crime and receiving absolutely nothing for it except for more misery and regret.

     My heart had become a void from the despondency I suffered every day for not being able to save Jessie and Colette. The memories of their blood-stained faces and eyes that pleaded *"where were you?"* haunted my every waking moment, so much so that I was too depressed to fight anymore. All this so-called power and I still amounted to being nothing more than a helpless sycophant.

The merchant ship I came over on was staffed mostly with rejects from the Napoleonic regime, exiled after their defeat. Under strict instructions I was to be delivered during daylight hours to my new master, a wealthy cotton tycoon named Rufus Walker who owned an enormous plantation right alongside the Alabama River. Walker had European business connections through his associates in the Incalculaba that were the catalyst for the rise of his family's small empire. Rufus Walker was a short, stocky man who wore a beard and a straw hat but never wore a blazer or overcoat like the other landowners no matter how formal the occasion. Only plain white linen shirts with the sleeves rolled up and always black or brown trousers with red suspenders were his everyday attire. Walker always gave the impression of an overseer rather than the plantation owner mainly because he was so hands-on with all his business affairs. Including the lives of his chattel. He was said to be distant bloodline to King Charles II and wore a permanent scowl on his countenance as if his mind always dwelled on the most diabolical of subjects. Reichstall chose him above all others because of his reputation for breaking the most difficult and stubborn Negroes. It seemed that after every ten words, Walker would spit a wad of tobacco, and he did not seem to give a damn where it landed most times. In our first encounter, I could hear his distinctive baritone voice through the hull of the ship as he was speaking very loudly barking orders to the workers there.

"Fetch that devil from de' galley and be sure to fasten that sack o'er his head and keep clear of his hands and feet dammit," Walker screeched.

Instead of being transported in an expensive box this time, I was forced to wear heavy freighter chains around my wrists and ankles that attached directly to the ship, making my movements extremely limited. Sleep came sporadically, and I was delirious with hunger. I just lay there, naked, neck throbbing with pain, waiting quietly for the next level of hell I was to experience. As I heard the latch being removed and the door opening, I could smell the sweat of my new compatriots coming down the steps to carry me into my next term of servitude. Eight of the largest men money could buy, all over six feet and bearing powerful arms and legs from being forced to work in the shipping district from the time they were boys, began the process of

253

unbolting me from the floor. All the while a kind cabin boy of no more than ten or eleven years held an oil lamp with his arm stretched high above his head to light the men's work. The only people wearing shoes in the room were the armed white men with rifles in their hands and pistols on their hips who stood guard wordlessly as the laborers worked to ready me for transport.

I had been locked in a position with my arms stretched above my head and my legs stretched down in the opposite direction by chains that were bolted to the hull of the ship. There was about eighteen inches of ship anchor chain that held my arms together around the wrist and the same apparatus held my legs together around my ankles. Attached to those chains was a slightly smaller chain that held my body in place by attaching to a huge shackle that was built into the bow of the ship specifically to prevent me from being able to escape without ripping apart the main bulkhead. I listened as the men used their tools to turn the huge bolt that unscrewed the latches to my chains top and bottom. They spoke in a form of Creole French Pigeon that Jessie would sometimes use but I did not understand very well. From what I could interpret, the men seemed to find it peculiar that there was a need to go to such great lengths to secure one man but still went about their duties as instructed. A long wooden plank was inserted between my arms and legs and the men lifted me like an animal hanging on a spit with four of them shouldering the weight of my body and the chains on each end. A man standing to my left produced a small croaker sack from his pocket and proceeded to unfold it and place it over my face and neck before they began to march toward the stairs leading up to the main deck.

While unconscious, I had been stripped of all my clothing. My entire body was totally exposed and when we emerged up onto the deck into the sunlight of southern Alabama, my skin began to burn and itch almost as bad as the cattle brand on the back of my neck. In my depression I no longer allowed myself to register pain. I wanted to die. I was numb to the world now and I could not feel anything inside or out. I had also become so weak from the lack of blood and meat consumption that the exposure to direct sunlight began to be too much for my system to handle, and I started having trouble staying conscious. I heard the heavy footsteps of a large man walking rapidly in my direction as I was lowered to the ground and made to stand up straight, the smell of hair pomade smacked me in the nose, and I presumed that this was my new boss approaching. Shuffling with my chained feet I was marched away from the dock until I was under a thicket of trees just out of reach of the hot late summer sun. My exposed skin immediately began to heal and rehydrate once we were out of the direct sunlight. The sack covering my head was snatched away, and I was blinded by the unexpected rush of light causing me to turn my head to one side as a reflex to shield my eyes. The heavy-footed figure leans over me to examine his new merchandise and gets very close to my face where his putrid tobacco breath fills my nostrils.

"Humph" a nigger what cain't stan' the sun." I 'spect I can die now 'cause I done seent eveh thang," he grunts out a laugh and spit tobacco over my shoulder and onto the ground, the overspray splashing on my face and body. He then stepped back to regard me up and down before replacing the croaker sack hood gruffly.

Walker then spoke to his men saying, "Get this nigger tuh de stables and delouse 'im agin 'fore you bring 'im to da quarters."

The men then lie me down on my back again and insert the plank between my hands and feet to hoist me like an animal once again as we walk towards a waiting wagon. I am placed in the back of an empty wagon cart and secured to the frame of the vehicle with thick jute rope tied across my chest and thighs. I am forced to ride like this to my new work assignment under a cloudless sky in the full sun roasting in agony as my entire body was cooked repeatedly the entire trip which took well over forty-eight hours. I was in and out of consciousness for most of the daylight hours of the hellish journey. As we left the coastal areas, the salty smell of the air grew more faint, and another strange but not unpleasant smell accosted my nose for miles during the journey. I was later to find out that the source of this odor was the product that solidified the economic superiority held by the southern states and which America still benefits from today: cotton.

Mercifully for me, the sky was cloudy and it rained sporadically for the majority of that second day. The roads became muddy which caused the horses to slow their pace, impeding our progress somewhat, causing our small caravan to arrive at Walker's farm in late afternoon. That first night at the plantation, I was locked in a circular stone structure that looked to be a former corn crib or some other storage facility. My legs each sported new looking iron shackles and cannonball weights that were misshapen into ovals, making it slightly more difficult to maneuver than the rounded weights I had grown accustomed to. My waist was fitted with a heavy chain that attached through a hole in the wall, on the other side of which was an iron anchor that gave me just enough slack in the chain to be able to reach the opposite side of the hut. The small building was filthy and the floor was covered with moldy hay. There were two other inmates already occupying my cell when I arrived, one brown goat and another black goat with white spots around its eyes. I presumed these animals to be my first meal. From Walker's cautious behavior, I was sure that Baron Reichstall and Carbonneau had included some instruction on how to keep a pet such as myself satiated.

Despite my deep depression, I was starving. It had been over a week since I tasted any flesh. One sick and tumor ridden hen, graciously left next to me by the kindhearted galley boy on the ship, was my only meal during the voyage here. I tear into one of the goats, draining its blood as it kicks and bleats wildly against me. After eating the meaty areas around the face and neck of the animal I begin removing the skin from the top half of its body with my claws while the other goat is silently in the corner gnawing on tuft of hay extruding from a pillow made from a burlap sack unperturbed after witnessing the demise of her compatriot. The blood and the night fully restored my body, but my mind was damaged beyond all repair. Constant tears flowed from my eyes when I thought of all my loved ones that I had lost over the years. My only wish was to perish tonight in this cell to prevent ever being used as a tool again. All creatures who suffer find peace in the afterlife.

I made up my mind that I absolutely was not going to be forced to work as a slave to enrich another undeserving capitalist asshole. I was ready to test the definition of immortality. I was ready for peace. I had resolved myself not to budge no matter how much torture I was subjected to. I would rather be dead than to lift another finger to advance another diabolical regime. There was no one left to protect. Everyone I ever cared for was dead and so was my reason for carrying on. However, Baron Reichstall in his infinite shrewdness had calculated for this eventuality and Rufus Lafontaine

Walker saw it as a personal challenge and a once in a lifetime opportunity to break a "special nigger" such as myself.

There were small, holes drilled into the structure I was imprisoned in that allowed air to circulate and gave me a few different windows to peer out onto my new world. During the day, the bright sun made it difficult to see much unless there was prolonged cloud cover, but at night I could see that my prison was just one of many structures on the vast Walker estate. From the constant sounds of work being done I could tell that everyone on this plantation was engaged in some industrious activity from daybreak until it was too dark for humans to see without candles and torches. The aroma of cotton mixed with human perspiration overpowered all other scents which spoke volumes on the vile nature of this factory of horrors. None of the other Negroes present seemed to pay me a bit of mind. They were all kept so busy with their myriad of tasks that they barely had enough time to eat and close their eyes before they had to be up working again. People and wagons passed by no less than fifty feet from my enclosure. Most without giving a glance in my direction.

I had been there about four and a half days when one late afternoon as the sun was falling below the tree line, I was awakened by a commotion outside my cell of a child sobbing loudly. I was leaning on one shoulder on the hay pile I had made into a makeshift bed. I shifted my weight to my left elbow so I could turn around and peer out of one of the holes behind me. A white overseer was cracking a whip on the backs of a naked man and woman who were tied at the wrist. They were some distance off but appeared to be walking toward the prison I was being held in. At the end of a leash being pulled behind the couple by the neck was an equally naked sobbing little boy of about six or seven years old. I could not help but stare at the poor little child whose dirty face was streaked with highways of tears. Bringing up the very rear of this sad procession was Walker mounted on his horse slowly following behind the poor creatures but staring past them in my direction. He stopped his horse just before it almost trampled the still wildly sobbing child and dismounted very nimbly for a man of his girth. One of the servants came and collected the reins of the bridle from Walker as he began to walk briskly toward the building I was housed in. He stopped about ten feet from the building and began to address me from the outside.

"Hey, boy! I know you kin hear me. I need ya teh git up." Walker commands. "You been 'vouring goats and living high on de hog without doing no work. Least you kin do is set up heah an' look at what I got to show yeh. You hear me boy? I know you sleeps during the day, but I needs ya up to see sumthin'."

I hear him come around the front of the structure where the iron door is and a pair of hard blue eyes appear in the door slot.

"Good evenin', boy, I 'pologize iffen I'm disturbing ya. Now I don' know what they do in London or Paris with all that dam tea drankin but here in South Alabama, ever' man gotta work fuh his vittles. Hell, I own ever'thang you can lay your devil eyes on for at leas' thuty miles in any direction on this here place. But I works jus' as hard as any one of my niggers. An' sometimes hard'uh cause of the fact I gotta makes 'em mind." Walker spits a huge glob of tobacco onto an ant hill just outside my cell then continued speaking. "Now most of my niggers know me to be a hard master but dey also know I am a fair master. They know that if we mek our numbuhs, they gets every other Sat'day and Sundays off. Hell, fuh Chris'mas, I gives all my niggers two whole weeks off. Sumuvum even 'llowed to get married and visit they wenches and chillun on sum nights and weekends, and any nigger worth a nickel will tell ya I'm one of the few white men in this area what 'llow his niggers to do such. You should consider yo'self lucky," he said before I heard him liberate another massive glob of spit and tobacco.

"Now I ain't got much patience for much of anythin', and I most suh'tainly do not have the benefit of sufferin' niggers what don't or won't work fo' dere meals. Cab'aneaux said you would need some type of motivation, and he give me a damn book of notes on his so-call obs'vations an' studies he done took on you while you was his boy. I aint so keen on that scientific hoss shit so I reckon to m'self," he puts his hand to his chin and rubs it, looking up as if pretending to be thinking, "what can motivate a monster nigger crocodile man? You wouldn't b'lieve the brilliant plan I came up wit'."

Walker smiled wide at me through his tobacco-stained teeth. "I figure I would just show you what yo refusal to wuk' would mean fuh the other niggers 'round you. Fust time in my life I was paid a bonus fuh housin' a slave. Hell, I got so much money to take you off that limey bastard

258

Reichstall's hands that I can 'ford to kill a pack a niggers and it still won't hurt my bottom line." Walker paused again to release tobacco spit. This time his spit lands on the outer wall of my cell. "You jes' sit tight, cause the show is about to begin soon. Just holla when you thank i's enough," he said wryly. And the peep hole in the iron door slid shut.

I refused to watch this gruesome display and I turned around so that I was facing away from whatever Walker had planned for that poor family. A couple of minutes later, I heard a lash cutting the air, and I heard the all too familiar *Thwack* of the cow hide leather moving at the speed of sound against human flesh. I hear a male voice scream out hoarsely,

"My Gawd!"

as he frantically struggled to break free from the ground-stake he was tied to. After countless rapid consecutive strikes, the pain racked the man's body so much that he dropped to his knees writhing and convulsing in excruciating pain. I smelled the fresh blood that was now streaming down the muscles of the man's naked back. There was an intermission, and then I heard the whip *whoosh* back...the *thwack* of the whip was followed by a blood-curdling shriek from the female. Each *whoosh* of the whip was followed by repeated *thwacks* that split apart her brown skin. The crack of the whip sang between desperate wails for mercy. The old me would have broken by now and put a stop to this by just doing what I was told to prevent trouble. That was what mama would have had me do because she knew that I was weak. She knew I could not handle the emotional pressure, and it would just drive me mad with anger if it were any other way. The woman was whipped so brutally that she sank to her knees onto the ground next to her husband. Curling into a ball, I could still hear her moaning weakly. Out of her mind with pain. Her naked body was covered with blood and red clay.

It was then I began to hear the loud protests of a child saying "I be gud, I'se sorry!!! P'ease massa don' hit me, I be gud!! Mama! Maaaama! I be gud I'se sorry tell 'im mama, I be gud boy" I'se sorry mama an' , please massa, don' whup me. I......!" The boy's protests are met with the whistle of the whip cutting the air, and the next sound I heard made me question whether it was even coming from a human being and not some nightmarish creature or some hellish machine. The shriek the boy released, this being his

259

first time at the end of a bullwhip, was so shrill and ear splitting that you could audibly discern his heart breaking in that very moment. This pain was confirmation to him that this world was broken and there was nothing in it for him or anyone like him. I was beginning to get uncomfortable. After what sounded like the second whip strike against the boy's back, the sound abruptly ended. The boy was either dead or unconscious for there was no other sound heard from him thereafter.

"Cut em loose, and tek 'em back to de quarters." And get that pickaninny to Doc Iverster, I hear Walker say, he then yells out, seemingly addressing me.

"Nigger, you is responsible for them folks getting whupped. And tomorra' dis same time, I'm gonna whup some mo' niggas til I can count on you to wuk, an do what I tell ya,.. wit'out causin' no trouble. " At this I hear the whole sad affair pack up and move back down the hill towards the main house.

The next afternoon around the same time, I am subjected to déjà vu with a fresh trio of torture victims, but in place of the young boy they flogged yesterday, there was what sounded to be an adolescent girl whose unanswered pleas for mercy and deafening shrieks shook me to my core. Why must I continue to live this nightmare? Everyone around me gets sucked into my curse.

"You can stop dis, boy! Just say the word, and this will be the end of dey suffrin," yells Walker through the walls of my prison. That night, I finished off what was left of my other goat friend. While I ate, I tried in vain to take my mind off the events of the last few days. I tried to block out the screams of those people… those children from my thoughts. A cruel world indeed.

I did not doze when the sun came up. I busied myself stacking the bones of my departed meals and placing handfuls of hay over the blood that spilled onto the floor to keep the fly population down. The bug infestation in my cell was already getting out of control since I was forced to defecate in the corner just a few feet from my bed. The sky that next day was overcast, and it smelled as if it would rain soon. The afternoon was drawing near and there was no sign of Walker and his torture committee. Maybe they decided to be merciful and would spare the beatings for today. The sky became dark and threatening but only light rain fell. I pulled at my chain in a futile attempt to try and bend or break the heavy bar at the other end, but all my effort only managed to work up a sweat. The room was too small to get any momentum and the iron too thick to break. The clouds burned off in the early afternoon sending lasers of sunlight into the small building. I covered my skin where I could but there were many holes that still allowed the sun plenty of chances to sting me. The usual time of the beatings came and went, and Walker seemed to be a no-show.

The sun was retreating west once again as night approached. That was when I caught a whiff of human blood. I next heard Walker's voice barking orders and heard a whip snap followed by what sounds to be a young girl scream out in pain. Another sad group of slaves are being led to the horse post outside my prison, and I prepare myself to block out the cries of these poor souls as I did their unfortunate predecessors. From the sound of the footsteps, there were at least two adult men with their feet bound making them walk in short quick steps but there is also either a woman or a boy stumbling along carrying the strong smell of blood mixed with sea water. As they come closer, the scent becomes vaguely familiar. I know this person.

"Shit!" I thought to myself. The sun was still lingering on the horizon but I stood up to look through the hole where the whipping post was set up. I recognized his smell more than his face but unmistakably it was the young galley boy who brought me the chicken while I was locked in the belly of the merchant marine ship.

"I got one of yer buddies here, boy, "Walker shouts in the direction of the shack. "This nigger came cheap on the count of him being skinny, specially 'sidering what I was paid to tek' yer' lazy, good for nothing ass in. So cheap in fact I think we'll make sport of this nigger and see how long he can stan' dat cowhide." And with that, I see Walker glance at the overseer, a tall and thin cruel vulture of a man who raised his whip and cracked it across the young boy's back, sending him to his knees. The boy's face was wet with sweat and tears but he did not cry out.

"We got ourselves a tough lil' pickaninny, huh?" coughed Walker who nodded again at the overseer who immediately fires off another crack of the whip which sent the boy face down into the dirt hard, but still no cries.

"You can die quiet as a titmouse, don' make no diffuns tuh me. I cain't do nothing with yo scrawny ass 'cept to stan' ya in da fiel's and make ya a scarecrow." Again, Walker nodded to the overseer who brought down the whip hard with a loud *thwack*, and I could see the boy grimace, his young face looked as if it has never known a smile. Silent tears began to stream down the boy's dust-stained face. A dark blob moved across what's left of the back of his shirt as the blood oozed from his wounds.

"Don't cry now, nigger, we jes gittin' started." Again Walker nodded and the overseer began to go into his wind up. Just as the man's elbow flew up to strike what could well be the final blow, his attack was halted abruptly by something like a Dragon bellowing hoarsely, "Stooooooop, Stop, Stop Goddammit.... Stop!!!!!!"

It had been so long since I heard my own voice, I scarcely recognized it. Everyone but the sobbing boy turned to look at what or who made the noise coming from the stone structure.

"I work, I no run!," I sputtered out loudly in my broken English.

"I work!" I shouted to Walker, pleading with my voice.

Walker's face broke into a huge grin as he spit a chunk of tobacco that landed right at the back of the boy's neck. "Well, Jasper, even a croc'dile niggers got a haut sum weah. I figured right, all we had to do was fine' us a nigger you was sweet on, and dat was da trick. We jes might hol' on to dis boy fa sum insu'ance 'gainst ya iffen ya eva 'sides to act up," Walker threatened. "And don't you damn fu'get it," he emphasized pointing his fat finger at the hole my eyes were behind. "Jasper!" Walker shouted to his overseer, still looking in my direction. "Pick dis boy up and let that nigger conjure woman patch him up. I aint paying that damn quack a full two dollars jest to come check out some little pickaninny what got one foot in de grave already no how. And get the rest of dese niggers bike down to the quartuhs. Den, once you done that get Luke Samuels and his boys and tell em to brang them hunting dogs wif' 'em and meet me up here tonight round ten."

"You want all dem Luke Saumels boys down here, you thank we gon' need dat many folks fu dis one niggah?" asked Jasper, the overseer.

"Hell, yes, we will, all seven of 'em, and tell 'em to brang dey rifles too. Mek' sure dey come wit' the guns already loaded and with extra dry powder and ammo," Walker instructs. "And on yo way back up here, brang one of dem Guinea niggas what speak Franch case we need ta translate fa dis boy how ta wuk da cotton," Walker punctuated his instructions with another huge wad of tobacco spit.

"Ruf', with all due respect, you and I both know Luke Samuels and dem damn boys is gone be dranking and cutting up dis time of day. How I'm gonna 'splain det we need 'em to watch one nigga pick some damn cotton in da pitch-black night?" questioned Jasper. "Luke an' 'nem gon' look at me like I'se one egg shawt of a dozen."

"Jes' do lak' I tells ya. And if anybody gets fresh, jes' tell 'im I said they living on land that my pappy loaned to 'dey family and if they 'spects to keep it, they need to come ouchea and hep us wit 'dis crocodile nigger," said Walker, pointing in my direction, sounding as if his fuse was getting shorter and shorter and now approaching the overseer menacingly as if to assault him.

"OK Ruf', you aint gotta be like dat." Jasper the overseer turned to walk back down the hill towards the quarters and the main house. Two male servants were instructed to carry the now unconscious boy back down the hill and the two adult male slaves who narrowly dodged receiving a beating shuffled along behind them with their feet still bound together. I watched as Walker mounted his horse and trotted off toward the area where the cotton smell seemed to be the most potent. I punched the wall in anger which left an impression of my fist in the stone and began to sob quietly as I took inventory of all the people whose lives have been destroyed by my curse.

About three hours after the sun had fully set, I could smell Walker's horse approaching. As he began his dismount. I also heard and smelled another gathering of people and what smelled to be multiple dogs coming up the hill behind them. Walker may be thinking that I may run so he can use the dogs to hunt me down out here in the dark. I wanted to tell him that he would not need them, because at this point, I was one of them now. Just another obedient dog.

I heard the men struggling with something heavy and metallic outside that hit the ground with a solid *thud*. The iron door is then swung open allowing the fresh night air to replace the moldy, fly-filled, rancid air of my prison. I am greeted by multiple musket barrels and Walker in the center of them holding a torch. Walker held his hand to his nose as the sickening smell of the inside of my prison escaped past him.

"Jasper unlatch dem leg chains from the wall anchor dere and 'ttach dat chain round dis boy's neck. Be careful and do not unlock his hands or leg irons. Dis nigga is a hundred times stronger than he look."

The overseer reluctantly did as he was told and clamped the neck iron with a lead chain around my throat which rested heavily on my collarbone. Walker pulled me up into a standing position by the chain. Forced to waddle and hop with the leg irons still attached, I am led between Walker and his night ensemble of seven or eight white men, all carrying rifles and passing around a jug of rum as we all walked down to the cotton fields. There was also a bald well-built negro of about forty years of age in our party who carried two large empty croaker sacks on his shoulder and lead the horse Walker was riding. The dogs they commanded ranged from pure bloodhounds to common mutts, and they all ran to and fro around us, staying close to the group and sniffing and investigating every shadow on our path. After about ten minutes of walking, we came to a vast field of cotton that stretched for miles, well into the darkness.

"Rooster, hand off that hoss' tuh Jasper and brang them croaker sacks over here." Walker barked at the black man and he immediately ambled his way forward towards Walker and myself past the disdainful looks of Walker's goon squad. "Rooster here been wit' me since he was fi'teen yea's old an' he one of my hardes' wuking, and mos' loyal niggers I ever raised," Walker gloated as he released another glob of tobacco and mucus onto the ground. "He also my stah' cotton picka! Damn nea' wort' fi'teen hunnid dollars, e'en at the ripe ol' age a' forty. Show em how it's done Rooster," commanded Walker.

"Yassuh Massa Walk," Rooster said. Almost too enthusiastically, as if he had been waiting his whole life for this moment, basking in the praise that Walker was raining down upon him. The next thing I knew, under the light of a few torches held by Jasper and the Luke Samuels crew, this man called "Rooster" began to grab and twist the small balls of cotton from their shells with such deft motion his hands seemed to fly across the plants. After twenty or so minutes, the once empty croaker sac bag now appeared pregnant with a substantial lump of freshly picked fluff despite his having to work by lantern light.

After about fifteen minutes of watching this man pick cotton at breakneck speeds, Luke Samuels had had enough. The corn liquor was providing the courage he needed to let Walker know that he was no one's flunky. Samuels blurts out in the direction of his crew. "I don' car whet my deddy owed 'im, it ain't wuth the torture of havin' tuh watch niggers pick cotton while muh wife layin' in de bed all by 'er lonesome wit nuthin tuh quanch the fi'e t'ween 'er legs." All the men laughed at Luke Samuel's statement except for Walker who merely shot him a death stare and grunted disapprovingly which seemed to be enough to end this line of questioning and discontinue the laughter.

"Now boy, you see what you gotta do now, don't ya? Le's see ya stuff," Walker said to me as he shoved the empty croaker sack in my chained hands. "Now I don't s'pect you to be good as Rooster here but I s'pect you can fill up dat small bag fo' de nights ova wit. Jasper, git ova heah and hol' dis damn torch fo dis boy. I'll hol' da chain."

The chain connected to my neck shackle was around fifty feet long and gave Walker enough leeway to step over toward his horse and the group of men talking and drinking just on the edge of one of the shorter rows of cotton. I began to grab the soft white blooms and twist them away from their sharp housing to release the valuable part and drop it into my bag. I tried to mimic Mr. Rooster's exact hand movements but ended up cutting myself quite a bit on the sharp edges of the cotton bolls. Jasper looked over at me with his lip curled into a snarl while holding the lantern less than four feet from my face and suggested that I "get on a hoss" if I wanted to have my bag filled by the time the sun came up. The glare of the lantern being annoyingly close to my face was preventing me from being able to see well enough to complete my task.

"Un possu piu vedi," I murmured.

Jasper spit a wad of tobacco down at my feet and cooly said, "You gone haf tuh learn anglish, nigger. I don' spik no Franch."

"No see suh" I repeated in English in a slightly louder but not forceful tone.

Rooster, my teacher, must have understood my poor French because he spoke up for me saying, "I thank he say he cain't see nuffin, suh. On de coun' a' de toach, suh." Rooster coyly suggested.

"Caint see, huh? asks Jasper, looking from Rooster to myself. Well, open dem blind nigger eyes a yorn' den maybe you kin see sumthin."

Just then, Walker, who had been watching the whole exchange, marched over and snatched the lantern out of the overseer Jasper's hand and walked away back to the crowd of men squatting and standing in the dust a short distance away.

"What the hell you do that fer, Ruf? Now me nor dis nigger gonna evah git out of heah tonight on count of neither one us cain't see."

As he was speaking, I began to make that cotton disappear into the bag. Almost as fast as my teacher Mr. Rooster. The thick skin on my hands would occasionally be cut by the sharp bolls on the flowering cotton but would heal immediately. Walker and his men could only hear the constant clank of the wrist and ankle chains and even Rooster had to pause and look on in awe once his eyes adjusted to the dark. After about six back breaking hours bent over hundreds of cotton plants, I had filled up both bags until they were stretching and overflowing with the white commodity

"Sweet Jesus alive, look at that nigger go"! I heard one of Luke Samuel's posse blurt out as I easily lifted both bags and approached the men shuffling as usual per my leg irons.

Jasper then chimed in immediately saying, "An' in de pitch dark night wit'out ever pickin' no cotton befo'."

"Jes' what type of steam powered nigger is you done got ya self, Ruf Walker?" asked Luke Samuels.

Walker grinned slyly as he rocked on his heels with his thumbs in each pocket, gloating over the praise he was receiving. He spat tobacco and chuckled to himself contemplatively.

Chapter 15

    Every night for the next five years, I worked on that plantation like a faithful dog. The only time I was not toiling away at some back-breaking task to make Rufus Walker and his empire richer were the breaks given for the Easter and Christmas holidays. Despite all the work, I lived in relative peace under the unspoken but iron clad agreement that none of the other slaves would be harmed *unjustly* as long as I did not try to run away, did not disobey an order from my superiors, and that I kept working for Walker and his family enterprises forever. I was strictly prohibited from fraternizing with my fellow slaves too often because Walker always feared one of them could convince me to go on a rampage to free them all. Evidently, that thought consumed much of Walker's leisure time during those first years of my re-enslavement because I was constantly accompanied by armed men whenever I was not in my enclosure.

    My tasks included but were not limited to cutting and hauling trees, chopping wood, assisting the mule team in removing stumps, picking the cotton, and hoeing the weeds when it was in season, turning the soil, and threshing the stalks during the planting season. Sometimes I would chop wood and drag the small saplings back to the quarters for the other slaves to use for their warmth and cooking needs. During the day if it was overcast or raining, I would be dragged outside with a burlap hood over my head to do all manner of work needed to fulfill the hectic demands of a successful plantation. My clothes were little more than oversized rags. My shirt was full of holes and tattered at the end of the sleeves causing the material to flop over and cover my hands and wrist shackles. The oversized pants I was given were shredded at the bottom to provide cover for my feet and allow room for my ankle chains. I was never given shoes, but I would receive new burlap pants and a shirt at the end of every other year.

The other one hundred forty or so slaves on the Walker plantation were expressly instructed to avoid me. They all knew implicitly from Walker's all too visceral demonstration that their survival and well-being hinged on their strict adhesion to the rules. I would constantly feel the eyes of the other slaves watching me closely whenever I was working near one or a group of them. On the rare occasions that I was left alone in the company of other servants, a few brave souls spoke to me, but most were sure to avoid even making eye contact with me. To save their families from incurring the wrath of Walker and his sadistic staff, mothers were forced to tell their children lies about me being cursed by the devil and that if they got anywhere near me, I would snatch them and take them into the woods to be eaten alive.

The main source of my loneliness was caused by the fact that I hardly saw anyone I could relate to because all the other enslaved people toiled during the daytime. I worked mostly at night and was forced to remain in my stone prison during the sunlight hours. The speculations on my affliction and the fact that I never let anyone see me eat or drink were the fuel for wild stories and superstitions about me and my lifestyle amongst the servants, cooks, and field hands. I would hear people say I was a half demon or I would become a wolf or a fox at night so the white folks could use me to hunt runaway slaves. There were rumors that I wore a mask because if anyone was to make eye contact with me directly, they would fall dead on the spot. The majority of the despicable rumors about my actions were concocted by Walker himself and to test my loyalty and obedience I would receive savage beatings at all hours of the day and night for the most minor offenses.

The first pitiful three years on Walker's plantation everyone avoided me so much that I rarely spoke to anyone. I had forgotten what my voice sounded like. Over time most people became accustomed to my quiet presence and considered me as being harmless. I was a machine when it came to hauling timber, clearing brush and digging irrigation canals and due to my ability to work proficiently at night, Walker was able to maximize his harvest output and broker a string of financial successes which positioned his plantation to supply forty percent of all the cotton exported to Europe the through the port of Mobile. Walker's financial success began to translate into more leniency in his work mandates. He went as far as implementing a new policy of rewarding his slaves with every other weekend off instead of just Sundays and allowing married couples to have two days off as a honeymoon. Because of the trickle-down effect of Walker's better treatment, some of the black people on the plantation even began to smile or nod as I passed at night or early in the morning while headed to my work.

After toiling in the fields during the day, many of the men would hunt possum and raccoon at night to supplement their diets that lacked sources of protein. Coon hunting was a very difficult and time-consuming endeavor due to the high intelligence and the cunning of the prey. Many times, the men would be just finishing their hunting before dawn and would have to turn around and be back in the fields for work without sleeping. Subsequently, they would receive severe whippings from Walker and his overseer for being lethargic and drowsy while performing their daily tasks. I was unmatched in chopping wood and picking cotton, and not even the strongest mule could tear through the sod with a plow like I was able to do. As such, I would complete my assignments with time to spare and oftentimes be left alone in the fields because the driver or the overseer assigned to my night watch would usually be asleep if it was a black man or be drunk and asleep if it was a white man. It was at these times that I would strike out into the woods and use my keen senses and my speed to catch the coveted critters my brethren preferred to dine on. I would break the necks of the animals and using a vine I would hang them on the porches of the cabins I knew to contain field hands, allowing them to sleep without worrying about having a source of protein for their families.

Every blue moon, Walker would choose a Saturday night that he would allow the servants and field hands along with their respective families to gather and barbecue a hog, drink and dance and sing away their sorrows. I would listen to the sounds of merriment and marvel at how a people subjected to such misery and disrespect could laugh and frolic with such genuine fervor despite it all. The only person that would speak more words to me than 'hello' or 'goodbye' and who would occasionally leave a slice of delicious smelling, roasted piece of fat meat for me, donated by one of the kindly cooks in charge of the Saturday night barbecues, was Quimbo.

Quimbo was the young galley slave from Senegambia who showed me mercy while imprisoned on the ship. The same skinny kid who displayed so much bravery while being beaten by Walker and his overseer when I first arrived. Quimbo had been taken from his mother at Bordeaux when he was very young and made to work as a pageboy to the captain's first mate on the merchant cargo ship that brought me over from Great Britain. He was tall for a boy of only twelve with long thin arms and legs, a strong jawline and very bright dark brown eyes. His smile was riddled with rotted teeth because of a penchant for dipping snuff and chewing tobacco that he developed when he was six years old. Quimbo relayed to me that growing up on a ship, he had seen men killed for the simplest of offenses so to ensure his safety he learned to speak and read English, French Creole, and some Spanish. His intelligence made him valuable as a message boy for Walker. As Quimbo grew older, his tobacco habit only got worse. Subsequently he began to use his time off on Sundays to pick up extra work on neighboring plantations to make money. Hiring themselves out was a custom that most slave owners benefited from and did not care what slaves did on their own time, but we all had to be careful because we knew that Walker was very particular when it came to loan out work. Walker felt that every bit of energy in his slaves' bodies belonged to him and him alone.

Quimbo would translate my French and help me with my English as he would pass me returning to my shelter for the day while he and the rest of the slaves trudged sleepily out to the fields before the sunrise for another day's work. On overcast or rainy days when no one was around, Quimbo would draw the letters of the alphabet in the mud with his finger. The lessons would be in triplicate so I would learn "chat," "gato," and "cat" all at once, an education that would serve me well in the years to come.

When he first arrived on the plantation Quimbo's main job was to deliver messages, supply the slaves in the cotton field with water, tend livestock, and sometimes look after younger children while their parents worked. But because of his height and sturdiness from surviving life at sea, he was soon made to pick cotton and chop wood like all the other men even though he was barely twelve years old. One Thursday morning about six

271

months after Quimbo had begun picking cotton and living in the adult quarters with the other single young men, he was heading towards the field as I was just finishing my work and the sun had not yet broken through the overcast, late August sky. Quimbo stopped to speak to me in French when Jasper the overseer came rushing up to us on his horse. From thirty paces away, I could smell the moonshine emanating from his pores. He approached so fast that it seemed he was trying to run us both down with this beast, his whip was in his right hand as he held the reins of the saddle with his left. We both pivot to face the charging animal ready for whatever nonsense this crazy man has planned. He stopped short right in front of us, sending a cloud of dust and rocks flying at our faces. Quimbo backed away slightly, tripping over a tree root.

"Get to wuk, you black bean pole!" Jasper yelled at the boy. In the next moment,

"*WHOOOSH*" the sound of the whip slicing air is heard and the "*CRAACK*" of the rawhide leather finding its target is heard.

Quimbo fell to the ground. His forearm was bleeding from trying to protect his eyes from the slash of the whip. He scuttled backwards to escape the next blow Jasper is already winding up for. Quimbo's legs become jelly in anticipation of the pain of the next blow. Instinctively he balled himself up into the fetal position to protect himself from Jasper's drunken tirade. The supple leather of the whip moved faster than the speed of sound as it descended towards its young prey when just before it struck Quimbo, I grabbed the fall hitch of the whip, stopping it in midair just before the '*CRACK*' sound catches up with the motion. Jasper tried to free the whip from my grasp but was unsuccessful. He turned to me slowly, his eyes glassy, his facial expression that of bewilderment, as if in a dream. His whole head turned instantly beet red with a deep hatred in his bloodshot blue eyes.

"YOU STAY OUTTA DIS, YOU CROCODILE NIGGER, ELSE I'LL BEAT YOU TIL YOU ROPE LIKE OKRA!"

Jasper screamed at me through his tobacco filled jaw. Staring down at me with all the vinegar-laced hatred he could muster, I stared right back at him unyieldingly. The look in my eyes must have conveyed that today was not the day to try me, and he decided to back down without reporting the incident to Walker. He was probably so smashed that he did not remember it happening anyway. By this time, Quimbo had scrambled to his feet and was trailing the other slaves into the field, wrapping a piece of torn shirt around his wound so as not to get blood on the cotton.

By virtue of his intelligence and amicable nature, Quimbo became a sort of ambassador between the black help and the white help. If necessary, he would oftentimes use his relationship with me as leverage to intimidate others. Which would have been fine if he were only intimidating fellow enslaved people. His mistake was trying to prop me up as a symbol of resistance for the slaves. A black man that the white men feared was what he tried to sell me as. Unfortunately for him, none of the other slaves would believe that someone as meek and mild as myself would ever be anyone's savior. I could not even save myself. Walker was very shrewd and employed spies amongst the enslaved to report any suspicious activity.

Quimbo was always very careful to conceal his comings and goings but eventually Walker's spies caught wind of what he was up to. When Walker found out about the divisive talk that Quimbo had been spreading and the fact that he was teaching letters and working on other plantations to make his own money, Walker went ballistic. Quimbo had ceased to be a boy long ago, and Walker knew this. Walker suspected that Quimbo also knew how valuable he was to plantation logistics and was becoming too independent and harboring too many dangerous ideas that could spoil the minds of the other slaves. Especially at risk was persuading someone as powerful as myself to realize my own potential. On that one plantation alone Walker had over of a little over three hundred slaves now, considered one of the largest and most prestigious plantations in the region. That season, the climate was perfect for growing, and Walker was able to reap a bumper crop, and the demand for American cotton on the global market was at an unprecedented level. Walker was too busy making money hand over fist to properly handle his disobedient slave issues and that was the only thing saving Quimbo from being beaten within an inch of his life or sold off to some low-class farmer in the Deep South that would only work him to death.

Sure enough, once the harvest season was over that year, Walker sold Quimbo without breathing a word to anyone else. He sold him far away

273

to some sleazy Texas slave merchant who arrived while I was busy digging a new well on another one of Walker's land purchases. My only friend gone without a trace, never to be seen or heard from again. I was again plunged back into relative solitude, determined never to attach myself to anyone again.

Walker's plantation was in an area of Alabama that was seen as a waypoint between Montgomery and Mobile. Because of the success stories of many of the plantation owners in the area, citizens with expansion on the brain began to flock into the territory. Andrew Jackson was stirring up the local Native American community with his campaign to exterminate as many of them as he possibly could to make room for the white citizenry that was growing exponentially. Many people in the Alabama gulf area still spoke French even though the Spanish and British both once laid claim to the area. As the American expansion continued, the ability to speak English became more and more desirable. If I remember correctly, it must have been after the harvest of 1820, almost a year since Quimbo was sold. I was still very awkward and very much alone, but as time went on, I was no longer such an oddity to my fellow slaves and others who frequented the Walker plantation. Still, I was never fully accepted by anyone black and certainly no one white.

One night in December of that year, I was hot after a raccoon, running on all fours with my chains clanking loudly as I bounded through the forest like a leopard zeroing in on my prey. I was within four feet of my victim as I leaped through a thicket of bushes when, out of nowhere, I was confronted by human forms. I was genuinely surprised to have come upon them so close without detecting their presence. A small group of nearly naked, dark-skinned men. I knew from what Quimbo had taught me that these men were what they called Indians. The Choctaw whom the other slaves say once owned this land before the colonists came and took it away from them. They were moving downwind and very silently through the brush. I was so focused on my quarry that I did not hear or smell them before we were less than ten feet away from each other. I stood up immediately and there was a tense moment between us as I watched and waited for them to reach for the knives hanging at their waist. We all just stood there in the pitch darkness staring at each other. In the next moment, the tallest and darkest of the men slowly removed the belt he was wearing across his shoulders which I saw now was a pouch carrying a freshly killed animal. He walked toward me and with his right hand reached into the pouch slowly and pulled out a large possum and gestured for me to take it. I reached out cautiously to grab the gift and as I did, the other three men bowed their heads and touched the center of their chests. The man before me, whose face was harrowed with deep wrinkles around his mouth and crow's feet around his dark eyes, nodded his approval and flashes a decayed and missing tooth smile. He then also placed his right hand over his heart.

That night marked the end of my fourth year as a slave on the Walker plantation. and with all the torture, betrayal and loneliness that had happened to me from the time my mother drew her last breath. Through all the war, through all the death and pain, watching my compatriots die or be sold away and my time as a slave in San Domingue, Louisiana, England and now here in the cotton fields of Alabama I can count on one hand the times I was able to trust anyone blindly. This very night was the first time I had the pleasure of smiling at a total stranger. I bowed my gratitude to the men, and we parted ways from each other. Before returning to my quarters that night, I came across a large tortoise and another medium sized possum. A bounty that should make a good soup and stew respectively for the coming days of the Christmas season.

There were rare instances when Walker acquiesced to hire out the male slaves on the plantation. One was if the men had pretty wives or daughters he fancied. Another was if it was government sanctioned dock work in Mobile. When the field hands or house servants chosen for employment on the docks in Mobile were all rounded up, Walker and his men would mount up on their horses and march the caravan of men along the road which entailed a three-day journey. After being paraded down to the coast, the men and boys would be hired out as deckhands for military ships, cargo frigates, and fishing boats that frequented the port. In some cases, they would be contracted to work for multiple months and years at a time. It was fairly common to have Negro sailors on all manner of sea vessels until the creation of the Negro Seaman Act in 1822 which was a direct result of our involvement with the Denmark Vessey uprising.

Many slaveholders frowned upon allowing their slaves to work on merchant ships because they were exposed to free blacks with independent livelihoods. Plantation owners were worried that ideas of liberation and equality might foment in the minds of the slaves as a result of this exposure. Let the record reflect that despite the tremendous threat that ideas of freedom and equanimity posed to the bottom line of Walker and all other business savvy plantation owners like himself, the notion of passing up a guaranteed 27 cents a day per head hired was seen as a greater evil. Plus if they were able to secure a federal contract to hire out to a Naval operation, Walker could pull in damn near 80 cents a day per man. An astronomical sum for day labor at that time.

My first exposure to this type of work happened in my fifth year at the Walker plantation. I was a very loyal slave and as such considered a very low risk of running away. Walker could not ignore the prospect of making nearly a dollar a day per man so he organized a group of about twenty working age men and boys to travel to the docks in Mobile. After the three days journey to Mobile, I was exhausted from having to trudge in the caravan with the rest of the enslaved men under the unforgiving sun while during the night I was forced to keep watch for coyotes, bandits and Indians. The rest of the men and boys slept soundly on the grass or the dirt with a stone beneath their heads to prevent bugs from going into their ears and noses. The six overseers, including Jasper, took shifts in pairs to watch me and the horses at night. By the third day, I was so fatigued that I would try to steal moments of sleep standing straight up while our caravan would be stopped during the day to relieve themselves and water the horses. Given that I never spoke and my face was always covered during the day, no one noticed me sleeping. I awoke only when my chain was pulled along with the caravan as it continued.

When we arrived at the pier in Mobile, it was nearing nightfall. The workers and people on the dock were all busy trying to finish their business before the sun went down. I was put right to work which consisted mainly of unloading and loading cargo that was too heavy or too difficult or bulky to manage for the regular deck hands. Due to my extraordinary abilities Walker was able to land a government contract and once a month we made the grueling journey from the Walker plantation in Gosport to the docks of Mobile. Walker was making a fortune and I was learning my way around merchant sailing ships. Oftentimes I would be given dangerous tasks on board these vessels, such as loading barrels of gunpowder or climbing high

276

up onto the main mast to reattach the principal topgallant stay ropes that had become frayed or damaged.

One Saturday night in late September 1820, I was hauling huge bales of cotton on a hire out job for a trader out of New Orleans, by the name of Phineas Alabaster Dufon, a local businessman and former colleague of Walker's when they both dabbled in the slave cargo industry. Because of my incredible display of strength and speed when loading the cargo, Mr. Dufon asked Walker if it would be possible for me to accompany his ship overnight back to New Orleans to pick up a large shipment of rice and other commodities that were to be delivered back to Mobile in three days' time. Dufon offered a whopping twenty dollars for each day that I was gone. The frequency of business they conducted with each other and Walker's correct presumption that I would not have the audacity to try and run away, especially by boat, made the deal plausible for Walker. But for good measure I was accompanied by four of Walker's hired hands that all came equipped outfitted with rifles, pistols, and cutlasses. I was also made to wear my customary 50ft chain attached to my waist while working anywhere outside of the ship. The end of my leash was held by two of Walker's men, and the key to release the apparatus was deposited with Mr. Dufon who I mistakenly thought was the captain of the ship.

Dufon was physically the opposite of Walker. Tall, thin, clean shaven, a chiseled face with a soft expression, and impeccably dressed for a businessman who sometimes had to oversee large shipments of goods amongst crass filthy sailors. He seemed unperturbed by the heat and appeared not to sweat or give credence to the gnats and mosquitoes that constantly hovered about. As the ship pulled out of Mobile Bay headed southwest, Dufon was eager to disappear into his quarters in the fore deck but before he did, he instructed the captain via the boatswain to put me to work immediately helping to hoist the sails and assist moving the rest of the cargo below deck which included two bulls, twenty bales of hay, forty fully loaded burlap sacks of grain, twenty six barrels of Dominican rum, five heavy wooden trunks of animal pelts, and seventeen pigs, one of which was allotted to me as my meal for the three day trip. We loaded all the goods remaining on the upper deck into the cargo hold and prepared our ship for the short errand. The sea was serene and the wind favored West so we should arrive in New Orleans just after dawn.

We arrived on a Monday morning, sailing around the Rigolets into Lake Pontchartrain and the main interior of the city. The bright sun forced me to wear my shroud while unloading the heavy boxes of animal pelts and loading the rest of the indigo and building materials which were stacked in a large pile some distance from the pier where the captain chose to dock. There were people pointing and whispering about my appearance as I passed them, bent over, carrying impossibly heavy loads to and from the ship all while wearing heavy chains and a mask. We finished our work just after four o'clock, and all the Irish and Italian ship mates decided to venture into the city for various forms of fun including gambling, drinking and chasing women. The Negroes and darker Indian hands and ship mates were forced to stay near the ship for any mischief that could be found in the immediate vicinity. They all feared going too far away from the dock into the city due to the tendency of white men and law enforcement types to lock up any free black and Indian sailors they could get their hands on in exchange for hefty fines levied against their ship captains. Many times, these marauders would try to turn a profit by selling the men into slavery or forcing them to work for the local parish as free prison labor. *[FOOTNOTE 1]

We waited until just after dawn when the tide was perfect for us to travel out of the bay. The captain was a bald man with a gray beard and a huge scar across his forehead who barked incoherent orders at the men through a megaphone as they all scrambled to ready the ship for departure. Once the sails were raised and secured, I would usually spend my time in the darkness of the cargo deck, either sleeping or staring blankly into space. In my loneliness I would try my best not to think of the past or the future.

The weather was clear and more than suitable for sailing but a couple of hours past noon, just as we were exiting the mouth of the bay and passing Cat Island, I heard stomping and raised voices of the crew above me which shook me from my daytime slumber. The sun was still high in the late afternoon, so I elected to remain below deck and just listen as intently as I could to all the commotion above me while I awaited orders. The partition of the cargo hold I resided in was a dark corner at the bottom level of the ship. On the other side of my partition was a larger area which served as the dwelling for the other contract workers. Above us was the middle deck which served as the living quarters for the rest of the ship mates and galley hands. When there was no immediate work to be done, protocol dictated that the contract crew was to remain below deck. There, we would await word from the overseers or the first mate as to what our next instructions were. At that moment, we were waiting and listening for whatever the source of the trouble on the main deck could be.

Not two minutes after the disturbance began, the first mate's sunburnt Scottish head appeared in the hatch above us screeching,

"Bleedin' pirates off de' port bow! Get tuh da guns fer da cannon crew, and the rest of ya get yer scobberlotching asses up here and help trim these sails so we can try to outrun em."

At the time, I did not understand what pirates were, but I understood the panic and agitation they were causing, and I presumed that they must be dangerous. Since it was still bright and sunny outside, the captain thought it would be best to send me to the gun deck to help in the ship's defense. I was led to my post by one of my fellow contract hires. It must have been a real emergency because I was allowed to travel between decks unaccompanied by any of the men Walker hired to babysit me. The person sent to guide me to the gun deck was a young man named King. King was merely sixteen and he had the official title of 'powder monkey.' His mother was from Martinique and she taught him to speak French fluently by the time he was six years old. This put him in a prime position to train as a merchant sailor for Dufon and his various enterprises at sea. King, myself and a slew of other men ran like hell to the gun deck and began prepping the cannons to fire at the pirate ship. The plan was to keep them at bay long enough to buy us the time we needed to turn around and outrun them back to the mouth of the Black Bay where we would be able to enlist help from the naval vessels that were harbored near New Orleans. The pirate frigate was moving much faster than we were, at speeds upwards of 25 knots, approaching westwardly from the direction of Horn Island just as we were passing Chandeleur Sound. This area had apparently been plagued with pirates, and now the ship's Jolly Roger was reportedly clearly identified from the crow's nest. When the captain heard the report, a grim look fell across his stern face. The worst of his fears seem to have been confirmed.

"Get those goddamned guns ready double time!" The captain shouted through his thick Welsh accent. "Give no quarter to the bloody heathens! Tis the rag of some of the worse freebooters 'pon these waters as of late," the captain shouts to the crew as he realizes the rapidly approaching pirate vessel must be decidedly bold for them to attack merchant vessels this close to a naval patrol route.

The captain took a swig of a flask pulled from a hidden pocket in his petticoat trousers, replaced it, then drew his sword for emphasis and began giving more orders to the men with his megaphone again, sending them scrambling around the upper deck like a herd of squirrels as they manned their various battle stations. Our ship was unfortunately too slow and too far out in the open sea to successfully turn around and outrun these pirates. We were being attacked less than thirty miles from a safe area where we could be rescued by the United States Navy who, since the War of 1812, regularly patrolled the southern border to protect and solidify its coastal economic interests.

The Spanish galleon we piloted had the unfortunate task of sailing between a peninsula on our starboard and an island on our port side which meant we ran the risk of running aground onto either of those land masses if we pivoted too hard to either side to evade the pirates. Most of us contract hires were used to running supplies back and forth to the gunners. Those of us with the most experience were recruited to load powder and stuff cannons as fast they could move without crashing into each other.

'KATHOOM!'

'KATHOOM!'

'KATHOOM!'

The deafening cannons of our ship went off, as we desperately tried to shake off our attackers. Despite the herculean efforts of all our gunmen and support staff, we were no match for the swift moving pirate frigate whose guns were newer and could reload and fire faster and more accurately than our older model cannons. Before long, the pirates were bearing down on us in the open sea, blocking our path back into the relative safety of Chandeleur Sound. The swift moving pirate vessel was able to maneuver past every volley of cannon fire we sent at it. They closed within a thousand yards of us and in on us, the next thing we heard was a rapid succession of cannon fire

'KAAATTHHHOOOM!'
'KAAATTHHHOOOM!'
'KAAATTHHHOOOM!'
 'KAAATTHHHOOOM!'

that sounded like thunder rolling through the sky. The bow took a direct hit, rocking the ship and sending shockwaves throughout the hull of the vessel strong enough to send a few of the deckhands flying across the gun room. I was running through the shadowy corridor of the ship wheeling a 1,500 lb. cannon barrel that I was ordered to reposition from the starboard side to the port side of the ship for return fire. Gabe, one of Walker's field hands who was regularly hired as out as a shipmate was injured severely when he was thrown by the shockwave of the cannon blast. He was slammed into a wall about four feet in front of me as I had dropped to one knee and struggled to steady myself with the load I was pushing. The knock Gabe took into the wall was absorbed mostly by his right shoulder and the side of his head which was gashed open on impact and hot blood began drizzling from the fresh wound down his face and into his eyes and mouth. He looked up at me, as I was struggling with the heavy cannon to keep it from crushing me against the hull of the ship.

"BASTARD!"

"Dis yo dam fault!" Gabe hisses as he weakly crosses himself with his left hand and points two fingers at me. A menacing scowl on his face as he sputters out the words "I knew you was a janx on de watuh" Grimacing with pain and dripping blood profusely Gabe somehow manages to stand to his feet run down the corridor leading upstairs to the main deck.

'KAAATTHHHOOOM!'
'KAAATTHHHOOOM!'
'KAAATTHHHOOOM!'
'KAAATTHHHOOOM!'

Another round of cannon fire from the pirate ship that sounded like the sky had cracked open.
Above us, I could hear the chaos and the stomping from the men upstairs trying to pull down the sails to avoid them being destroyed by the constant cannon fire.

'KAAATTHHHOOOM!'
'KAAATTHHHOOOM!'
'KAAATTHHHOOOM!'
'KAAATTHHHOOOM!'

Another fusillade of hell.

The pirate guns managed to land hits on the side and rear of the starboard decks just as we were turning. This pirate crew was smart. Their *modus operandi* was using three-pound cannon balls and chain shot to destroy the masts and the rigging so they could disable ships in order to loot them without burning valuables or sinking them. Despite the damage we were taking on the main deck we continued to load the cannons and return fire as ordered by the gun captain. With our old-fashioned artillery each shot and reload required the efforts of at least eight men. Once the cannons were positioned and loaded the heavers positioned the cannons into their gun ports and tied off the cannons with thick rope attached to a block and tackle fitted around hooks in the wall to absorb the recoil of the blast.

'KAAATTHHHOOOM!'
'KAAATTHHHOOOM!'
'KAAATTHHHOOOM!'
 'KAAATTHHHOOOM!'

Shockwaves from another round of enemy fire rattled the ship so violently it felt as if it would crack in two at any moment. Over the ringing in our ears, we could hear the voice of the captain bellowing something unintelligible to the men on the main deck. Presently, the ship began to slow down considerably. Still no order came to cease fire and after a brief pause we continued with our preparations. Out of the eight guns our galleon had, five were still operational. We were finally locked and loaded for the third volley and the gun captain lowered his hand as the signal to fire just as the port side of our ship became perpendicular to the approaching bandits. The touch hole in the breech was primed with gunpowder and the fuses were lit. Three seconds later,

KAAATHHOOOOOOMMM!!!!

KAAATHHOOOOOOMMM!!!!

KAAATHHOOOOOOMMM!!!!

exploded the cannons, vibrating the entire ship like a huge bell and filling the gun room with smoke and dust. We feverishly pulled the nose of the cannons back in and began reloading to fire a fourth volley when the second mate appeared at the hatch and came flying down the stairs. He was a balding white man with a slight French accent screaming at the top of his lungs,

 "STOP! STOP! CEASE FIRE DAMMIT!!
BY ORDER OF THE CAPTAIN! CEASE Fi….

'KAAATTHHHOOOM!'
'KAAATTHHHOOOM!'
'KAAATTHHHOOOM!'
 'KAAATTHHHOOOM!'

The cannons of the pirate ship returned fire in a murderous hail of chain shot which shook the entire ship violently and injured a few of the men on deck who were hit by flying wood and metal shrapnel. The explosions managed to tear up the foremast and the adjoining ropes and tackle. The watch leader Diego, a stout fellow of Portuguese descent who was filling in for the injured gun boatswain, was running down the corridor behind the second mate, and went down on his knees hard as we all lost our balance under the shockwaves from the cannon fire. Standing again Diego yelled:

"Cap'n's orders! Abandon zee gons n' git up top to 'elp drag down de' rest of de' sails and rigging' else we all en' up at de bottom of de sea!" Every man present dropped what they were doing and began running toward the stairs to the upper deck. As I passed Diego, he grabbed my arm and pulled me aside. Pointing towards the hatch leading to the lower cargo deck, he yelled, "Cap'n want fer you to 'ide in da bilge 'til de trouble blows over."

We stared at each other for a moment, and then he snapped his finger in front of my face to get my attention.

"Voce entende! Can't you heah me, boy?" Spit flew from his rotten-toothed mouth. Again, he hollered at me. "Git yur' black ass down tuh dat bilge room and find da deepest, darkest cowener tuh hide in, and stay in it til I tells ya tuh come out. Now! Corra, gottdammit!"
He then shoved me in the direction of the access ladder. I glared at him for a beat before turning and following orders. Putting aside my pridefulness, I was relieved to not have to report to the upper deck. In the mayhem, I had lost my shroud and would have been weak and uncoordinated under the full brunt of the afternoon sun. Mr. Dufon seemed like the shrewd type of thinker who would reckon on this fact and considered the best ploy was trying to hide me away until after sunset when I would be most useful. The bilge room, being on the lowest deck of the ship, made it impossible to eavesdrop on what was going on above me. All I could tell was that the ship had stopped all noticeable forward motion.

284

After about half an hour of sitting in the darkness of the bilge, I heard heavy footsteps on the floor directly above me and approaching the rear door that led to the ladder hatch down to the bilge room. I follow the sound of the footsteps over to the ladder area and listen as the hatch is unlocked and opened. Two agile men slid down the ladder without touching a rung. One with a thick black afro coming out of his monmouth cap and a scarf around his neck with a deep scar across his right eyebrow, wearing an animal pelt coat with white linen trousers. Behind him was a short but very muscularly built man whose bare arms each held a pistol that he never let go of as he descended the ladder. The room is pitch dark to human eyes and until their eyes adjusted, neither man could see their hand in front of their faces.

I was crouched in the corner behind a large part of the bilge pump in the back of the room, as still as a statue only moving my eyes as I watched a hand jut down from the top of the hatch holding an oil lantern to illuminate the hold. The man that handed down the lantern stuck his greasy face into the hole, and I could see he was a half caste Negro with a patch over one eye and two gold teeth shining in contrast to the filthy smile on his face as he belches,

"Dis where dey shore tuh hide de madmoisselles and les enfants." The one-eyed man says as he descended the stairs.

These men emitted an ominous aura. I felt like a possum waiting to be flushed out of a bush by a hunting party. My heart was pounding, and my breathing began to be shallower and more pronounced. Hot blood started pulsing, my body started to grow, my canine teeth began to protrude in response to my building angst. Dammit, I needed to calm down. If I killed someone out here and messed things up for Walker, he would surely torture King, Gabe, and the other slaves mercilessly in order to teach me a lesson.

Meanwhile, up on the main deck, Mr. Dufon was seated on the floor of the ship. He had been reduced to tears and was wiping blood from his nose with his handkerchief while the captain and the rest of the crew were all on their knees in a circle around the main mast of the ship. They were all being held at gunpoint by a band of twenty-five of the most hard-boiled men to have walked the earth. Next to the defeated crew was a pile of begrudgingly surrendered swords and muskets. The pirates used rowboats to reach our ship, and then they used hooks and ropes to climb aboard. Moving with uncanny speed and precision, they swarmed the ship and overtook the crew before anyone could form a worthwhile defense. Now they sat surrounded by mostly Negro pirates of all shades who spoke to each other in a French creole patois dialect sprinkled with English. Evidently, they were known throughout the Caribbean for their fierceness and for being a compilation of some of the most skilled sailors in the Western Hemisphere.

A few of the pirate stragglers were still climbing up the side of the ship and up onto the deck when at the middle rope a very tall, Negro with a muscular physique, wearing leather boots and tricorn hat with a sleeveless trench coat pulled himself over the side of the ship. Just as this bodacious man landed on the main deck, one of the pirate crew members loudly proclaimed in English,

"This ship and all her goods are henceforth the property of Black Cesar— the Emperor of the Caribbean Sea."

'AAAAWWWWWOOOOOOOOO!!!!!"

The pirate crew begin to howl like wolves and make barking sounds in unison to emphasize their introduction. Some of the pirates who were first to infiltrate the ship were already ransacking the officer's quarters, bringing out wooden trunks filled with the fine suits and other clothing items such as Hessian boots and silk scarfs that were signature to the style during that period.

Dufon, the captain, and the crew never imagined that their short, and by all accounts, lucrative journey would take such a turn for the worse. Dufon went pale at the thought of the barbaric pirates finding his cache of gold and silver coins he kept hidden under the floorboards in the officer's quarters. Tears begin to stream down his face even harder.

The pirates brought out all the heavy bags of rice and sorghum, forty chickens, twenty goats, 10 fifty-pound bags of sugar, 25 crates of Indigo and 13 barrels of molasses, most of which were traded for or purchased fresh in New Orleans. As the provisions were being loaded over the side of the galleon into the waiting boats of the pirates Black Caesar approached the contract hires sitting quietly around the mast and bellowed in his deep voice,

"Who amongst you would like to throw off the shackles of bondage and be a free man on the sea as a part of my crew?"

Not one of the contract hires looked up from the floor as Caesar paced in front of them.

"Take heart men, and fear not your masters, for the sea is a victim of the lies told by mamas who don't want to see their boys to grow up and for buckra's who don't believe Negroes should be free."

He glared at the black ship mates with a big easy smile on his face that was more gold and silver than ivory. Dufon made it a point to frown in the direction of the hired hands as if to discourage anyone thinking about running away. Caesar understood the kinds of pressures and connections Negroes made in slavery. Connections that bound them to the land and the people, so he did not press them. He tried to hide his disappointment, but you could tell by the defeated expression on his face that he felt a small pang of pity for the degradation heaped on the people trapped within this loathsome institution.

KRAKOW!

KRAKOW!

The sound of two consecutive gunshots rang out from the lower deck. Some of the pirates drew their weapons and moved toward the rear hatch to investigate when without warning the hatch at the bow of the ship flew open and slammed against the deck with a loud *'KNOCK'*. The short muscular man that was part of the scout team came scrambling out of the

287

hatch with a smoking pistol in each hand as fast as his arms and legs would carry him with a look of horror on his face. His pants clearly stained with urine, the man crawled away from the hatch screaming bloody murder and pointing his already discharged guns towards the hole as he scooted on his butt backwards and into the legs of Caesar.

"Sur quoi Diable tirez-vous? (What the devil are you shooting at)?" Caesar asked the man with a stern look on his face, grabbing his shoulders and trying to quiet his tirade. "Qu'as-tu trouve? (What did you find?) and Ou est Karim et Two Feathers? (where is Karim and Two Feathers?)

The frightened man, Clovis, was in his early thirties and in excellent physical shape. He had been with Caesar almost from the time he left Haiti at the beginning of the Revolution to become a free man. Clovis had seen bloodshed and had faced down many an enemy with ice in his veins and was known to be one of Caesar's most fearless lieutenants. For him to be shaking like a leaf due to some routine encounter on a merchant vessel was a bad omen.

"What the fuck you got down there connard" shouted Caesar in English, wheeling around to face the captain and Dufon and addressing them directly.

"Speak up you dirty bastards or I'll have my men cut your peckers off and stuff 'em down yer throats!" Caesar gave a nod and one of his crew members bounded over with a long sword and pressed it against Dufon's groin area.

With his teeth clenched Dufon reluctantly muttered,

"C-c-c-crocodile...m-m-m-man.

The man holding the sword to Dufon looked back at Caesar and began to chuckle at the seemingly ridiculous answer from Dufon. Other members of Caesar's crew also began to laugh at the response from the obviously scared shitless merchant.

The only person not smiling was Caesar. He was now staring at the dark pathway leading to the belly of the ship. The men he sent to retrieve the hidden goods were some of his most hardened, battle tested men. For them not to have returned by now and for Clovis to be this distressed by whomever or whatever he saw down there did not bode well. Caesar walked over to Dufon, grabbed him and lifted him to his feet by his lapel, shaking him and screaming in his face,

"His eyes, what color are his eyes?!"

The shock from fear and the embarrassment of being treated like a nickel rag doll by a Negro seemed to have paralyzed Dufon's tongue, but eventually he managed to say but one intelligible word through his tears...

"Blanc".

Caesar released his grip, and Dufon crumpled to the floor. Slowly he walked over to the open hatch leading down to the middle deck and cargo hold. He looked up at his first mate, the skinny black man who spoke English to Dufon, and boomed,

"Do not follow me!"

In a flash, he removed his belt, dropping his sword and pistol, and before his men could protest, sprang like a cat down the ladder and into the darkness alone. As Caesar's eyes adjust to the darkness, he could see the second ladder that led to the lower decks and into the bilge room where his men were sent to patrol. As he climbed down the ladder, he began to speak softly in French.

"I was born a slave in San Domingue and given the name Henri Caesar by my mother and father who were also both born slaves. We all worked for a greedy and cruel family named Arnaut. While still just a boy of eleven years, I was forced to work in a lumber yard because I was big like a man for my age. My boss beat me for stealing something that was rightfully mine, so I killed him with my bare hands that very day." Caesar laughed to himself and continued, "My very first thought afterwards was that I had killed a man before I had ever known a woman. I ran far away from my home because I knew when they found me out, they would kill my mother and father and all my siblings." He continued speaking in an even tone as he entered the dark room where I sat lurking, listening intently to his story.

"I ran away to try and protect them even though I was still only a boy. I was forced to live in a runaway slave encampment where I met a great and wise man named Buukman who told me of the prophecy of the Revolution that would soon set myself and my family free. He told me that there would be beaucoup bloodshed and innumerable deaths on our side, but our victory was all but guaranteed because Legba had shown us favor and sent one of his strongest sons to be a secret weapon that would fight on our side. Yon nonm nwa, [a black man] who could run faster than a sparrow, was stronger than a team of oxen, and was enchanted by Mami Wata with a body no white man's weapons can kill." Caesar told me that he held this man in high esteem because this man was willing to protect the people and struggle for their freedom despite being feared, hated and misunderstood by the very people he was fighting to save."

Caesar slowly made his way down the narrow corridor and began speaking again as his eyes adjusted to the darkness of the room. "I was eager to join the revolutionary army if it meant that one day I wouldn't have to worry about the safety and well-being of my family. I saw too many comrades fall on the battlefield against the colonists and one day I told myself that I had seen enough. I decided I wanted to see the world before I drew my last breath. My plan was to go to Port-de-Paix and smuggle myself to Cuba. I was fortunate to be taken in by other black privateers like Jose Gaspar who taught me the sea. After a year I raised a crew, returned to Port-de-Paix and liberated a Spanish galleon and a gunboat from the Corps des Marines Imperiaux. From there we began a campaign to undermine the French and British by confounding their warships, looting their merchant vessels, and freeing their ill-gotten gains." Caesar continued talking as he walked toward the back of the bilge into the total darkness.

I could fully see the man connected to the voice now for the first time. Very little facial hair for a pirate but a swagger of maturity tinged with fearlessness. A man among men. At only 25 years of age, this man smelled thoroughly of the sea, and I could sense no hostility. I remained quiet as he continued to talk.

"I was always told that the only reason we were able to defeat all the superpowers of Europe was through the unity of our people, the invocation of our deities, the righteousness of our cause, and through the Herculean efforts of the one who was called many names by the people: Mons La, La Monstre, Le Diable, and Crocodile to name a few. But known to Buukman, Touissant, and the inner circle of generals as 'Yeux Blancs,' the one with the white eyes."

I listened as Caesar continued.

"I have dedicated my life to freedom, and I owe my life and the safety of my family's lives to Yeux Blancs. Early on during the war when the French were rounding up Negroes to torment and use as examples to strike fear in the hearts of the revolting masses, my parents were to be beaten and executed and my siblings were to be sold to separate plantations. However, the firing squad never arrived that overcast day because all the soldiers in the area had been summoned away to serve as reinforcements in Chansolme. The main legion there were having such a hard time with the revolutionaries led by a man who was said to be half beast. A man who in mere minutes could take out whole battalions single handedly. As a result of the distraction that man created, my family was able to escape execution and being split up. I regretted never being able to thank that person for such a gift. Today, providence has shone upon us once again, and Legba has reunited brothers in arms." Caesar was now standing about six feet in front of me. He dropped to one knee next to the two unconscious bodies of his men and extended his right hand as if to greet me. Staring into the darkness, he said,

"Please allow me to return the favor and release you from your bondage. Sail the sea with me as my brother."

It was about midday and the sky was overcast due to a distant storm rolling eastward of our current position. It had been a quarter of an hour since Caesar had entered the hatch and Cesar's first mate Rene was at his wits end on what to do next. The longer they waited, the more they risked a navy vessel passing by and intervening in the heist. With one of the top lieutenants incapacitated and the captain nowhere in sight, Rene feared that some of the miscreants on the crew may be getting ambitious ideas of taking off prematurely and high tailing it with the loot. Rene was a stocky, bald man with a grayish goatee. Not a big man by any measure, but he was certainly fearless. His boxing skills were unsurpassed, and legend has it that his hands and knuckles were made inordinately tough from being forced to work as a mechanic since boyhood. So much so that it was rumored that his punches felt like being kicked by a horse. Rene looked up at the setting sun and back down at the hatch next to where Caesar's gun and scabbard still lay. He decided to make a general announcement in order to stem any chaos.

"You bastuds put yer willies back in ya pants cuz we ain't budgin' til I hea from de cap'n. An I' aims to shoot any one of you rum gaggers that makes lak 'e's got a pro'lem." Rene yelled out to reiterate the seriousness of everyone understanding that the captain's orders were final.

Just then, the motionless body of the mulatto with the eye patch is pushed up out of the hole and the voice of the captain is heard.

"Little help here!"

A few of the pirates rush over and pull the limp man up out of the opening and drag him off to one side. Captain Caesar then emerged from the hatch smiling,
"Hope you girls didn't miss me too much."

As he put his belt, sword and pistol back on his waist, the unconscious body of the man with the afro named Karim emerged from the hatch opening, tossed up from below by some still unseen force.

A few of the pirates began to revive and administer first aid to their crew mates, Caesar looked at them and laughed.

"Ou sont tes manieres [where are your manners?] You should thank your brother for not killing these men who were so rude as to interrupt his day sleep." Caesar dropped his smile and addressed the crew directly. "Gentlemen, I want you to put everything we took from this poor buckra's vessel," pointing to the weeping Dufon, "and put it all back on this ship just like you found it."

Caesar's crew stared blankly at him as if they had not heard him correctly. Even the first mate Rene was dumbfounded at the request. After a few awkward moments Rene speaks up,

"But, Cap'n Caesar, we —"

Rene was cut off by Caesar.

"No excuses, ye bastards! They were hidin' the real treasure in the bilge. A man fully worth a thousand gold pieces fer each of ye bastard's heads alone. I plan to bargain with this here wretch of a slave trader and make him an offer that will beaucoup work out in his favor."

Caesar walked over to Dufon and carefully stood him up, giving him a handkerchief from his coat pocket to wipe his tear-streaked face. Caesar, now looking eye to eye with Dufon, said

"I will give you back every bit of your cargo and return your money and jewels...hell, I'll even return your weapons. Plus, you get to keep your miserable wretched lives. All in exchange for that so-called 'Crocodile Nigger' you were keeping below deck."

The pirates looked at each other in disbelief, as if what Caesar was suggesting must certainly be a joke. Even the crew of the merchant galleon and Dufon were not too sure if Caesar was just having a little fun at their expense before locking them in the cargo hold and burning them all alive within the belly of the ship. Caesar continued calmly,

"I'm dead serious."

Caesar glared at Rene who got the message and gave the order to return the loot, whistling loudly to the rowboats to turn around despite their being nearly back to the pirate frigate with their stolen goods. Caesar walked back over to Dufon and cut his wrist bindings with a large knife and stuck out his right hand gesturing for Dufon to shake it.

"Une affaire d'homme! Do we have a deal that upon return of your lives and all your goods and money, you will, in exchange, allow that man to sail with my crew. I am sparing your lives and your wares because I want you to make sure that he is not personally held accountable for his absence and none of those people on your land catch hell for his being stolen from that plantation you and your business partner run."

Still shaking hands, Caesar pulled the terrified Dufon close so only he could hear what Caesar had to say.

"This is my sea, and my people talk to the shadows. If I ever catch wind of any mistreatment of those people because of our agreement today, I will consider that a breach of contract." Caesar flashed his brilliant smile, and said solemnly to a cowering Dufon, *Je reviendrai et te tuerai a mains nues.* (I will come back and kill you with my bare hands.)"

•   •   •

That was my last day as a chattel slave. For the next several years, I sailed the Caribbean under the yoke of no man. I was free to become who and what I wanted to become. In my travels throughout the Caribbean, the Gulf of Mexico, and South America, I advanced to being one of the top lieutenants of the Black Caesar pirate crew. My first few days aboard Caesar's ship, I was greeted with jeers and hostile looks. Lots of the men would either spit or cross themselves whenever I came near them. During the day, I remained in the cargo hold with a small pile of hay as my bed. The chore boy would bring me freshly slaughtered chickens with the feathers soaked in piss as my dinner. A subtle reminder from the crew about how welcome I was aboard the ship. At night, I would climb high up onto the main mast and serve as lookout because of my excellent night vision. As hardened as these men were and as much as they hated me, no one came within twenty feet of me for they knew it to be folly after seeing me climb the mast in seconds and heave full barrels of rum with one hand onto my shoulder.

It had been a week since I ate anything not soaked in piss, other than an unsuspecting rat or two, when I heard the alarm go up at the top deck. The man that was posted in the crow's nest had fallen asleep in the warmth of the afternoon sun and failed to see two American warships bearing down on us from either side in a pincer move to trap us between themselves and the Florida Keys. This area had recently been officially annexed by the U.S. from the Spanish. As a show of power, the U.S. navy began patrolling the area heavily at the behest of Andrew Jackson who had taken it upon himself to rid not only Alabama but also Florida of all Native Americans he felt were posing a threat to the newly founded United States. It was too late to run, and Caesar was not one hundred percent he had the firepower to shoot his way out of a duel with two navy battleships. The entire crew began to prepare to burn the ship and transfer any portable loot to the rowboats for an escape attempt into the confusing islands of the Keys. Unfortunately, there was still a lot of open sea between themselves and the nearest island. Chances of even a quarter of the crew escaping were looking very bleak.

I remained below deck in refuge from the sun and cupped my ear against the ceiling. It was difficult to discern what was happening as I could hear nothing but jumbled shouting and confusion while the men argued over what was the best course of action. The sun was just beginning to set as the American naval battle cruisers began to come into cannon range. Caesar had not given any official instructions to the crew on whether to run or try and fight their way through and the men were becoming frantic. They all knew that capture meant that they would all be tried and hanged or at best imprisoned in some godforsaken work camp for life. Caesar was nowhere to be found and Clovis and some of the crew became worried, even going as far as barging into his cabin to get orders, but the captain could not be located anywhere.

Amid the tumult, a familiar voice boomed,

"Pipe down, ye Mary's! You call yourselves pirates and you let a couple of Navy whelps get your britches in a bind," Caesar shouts, climbing out of the gun deck hatch.

"Quit yer blubbering and trim them sails so we can put out away from the coastline and get them two bastards to approach us from the starboard side. Some of you lot get busy taking down the Jolly Roger and run up the white flag. They must respect the law of the sea and take us into custody without firin' on us. After that, all of ye get down to the cargo and bilge deck and wait there with all yer guns and cutlasses and keep yer fucking mouths shut until I give the all clear. Cyrus, get my rifle and then run down and get Yeux Blancs from the hold."

Cyrus' brown skin went pale from the last order and the man looked at Caesar with terror in his eyes. "B-b-b-eg pardon suh, b-b-but I'se fraid of that, well uhhh…. Y-y-yoyo wolf nigga down dere. I-I-I-I ain't riskin' my hide tryin' to go down dere wit' dat dyab," squeaked Cyrus.

Caesar looked down at the floor and took a deep breath before looking back up at the quivering Cyrus. Speaking in his even baritone voice Caesar says, "Goddammit, I said go get 'im right now or I'll teach yer ass who's the real wolf nigga. The rest of ye dogs get those sails down and get downstairs as soon as ye can."

Cyrus half-heartedly shuffled his way to the back of the ship and reluctantly lowered himself down the rear hatch to the middle and subsequently, the lower deck. I heard him enter the pitch darkness of the rear cargo hold. The metal of the lantern rattling in his shaky hands.

"H-h…e, h-h-h-h-hey b-boy. C-c-c-c-ap'n need yuh own top dack ret noo," Cyrus blurted out quickly to the darkness before him, looking around nervously, not able to tell where I was standing in the dark room.

I stood up to face this man sent to fetch me from my solitude and only the light of my pale eyes was reflected in the glow of the lantern.

"Christ alive!" yelled Cyrus who hurriedly skittered back up the ladder and out up onto the top deck again.

I placed a burlap sack over my head and ascended the ladder and then the stairs, up onto the deck just as the sun was beginning to drop below the horizon. As I climbed the ladder to the main deck, I hear a deep voice say,

"It's time to show these devils the power of Sango and Oya, my friend," Caesar says, as he walked over to the ladder I was ascending and held his right hand out to me. I grabbed his large, powerful hand as I stepped off the ladder and onto the deck.

Looking to the crew remaining on deck Caesar shouted, "ye lot hurry up and secure those ropes and get yer asses down to the galley."

Caesar pulls me to the side to address me personally — "Try not to kill them all mon ami." and he gave me a knowing wink.

The last of the men remaining above deck scrambled to tie down the main sail and accompanying rigging. Two Feathers and another crewman I did not know were busy clipping a dingy white sheet to the flagpole when in the next moment we hear the proper voice of an Englishman amplified through a megaphone from the closest warship.

"By decree, these waters fall under the jurisdiction of the United States of America and you are hereby deemed as trespassers in restricted waters. You are hereby under arrest for plundering and piracy under British maritime law. Surrender immediately and your ship will be boarded, and your vessel confiscated as contraband."

297

"Hide behind those empty rum barrels for now my friend until I give you the word to begin," Caesar commanded, pointing to three empty casks on the starboard side of the ship. I ran and hurriedly crouched down as instructed.

Caesar nimbly climbed onto the bow of his ship wearing a huge smile with his hands in the air. While the crew was securing the sails Caesar had equipped himself with a leather gun holster with pistols on either side and a musket rifle which he wore strapped around his back.

"Don't shoot, I surrender!" he yelled to the U.S. navy battle frigate holding up his empty hands.

The warships closed on our free-floating frigate in no time. The closest of the two aligned their starboard side guns on us at what amounted to be point blank range as it dropped anchor a mere fifty meters from our ship. I removed the burlap sack from my head and from my hiding spot I could see the naval soldiers aiming pistols and rifles at Captain Caesar. Some of the soldiers began lowering hooks attached to ropes in what looked to be preparation to tow our ship back to the mainland. The other warship made a wide circle around us at a distance of about a quarter of a mile cutting off any chance of our being able to escape. My heart began to pound and the familiar bloodlust that accompanied conflict began to course through my veins.

"You navy dogs will rue the day you dared come against the Black Caesar Pirates!

DEBUT!"

Caesar yelled as he pulled his pistols and fired at the naval soldiers nearest to the bow of the ship. Still holding the pistols, Caesar acrobatically ran along the lower jib arm, leapt onto the deck of the ship and rolled safely behind a row of wooden crates as the U.S. naval soldiers returned fire.

Simultaneously I spring from behind the rum barrels and ran straight up the main mast and leapt high into the air and onto the closest Navy vessel, eyes, claws, and teeth glimmering from the light of the lamps. I wasted no time in blitzing the crowd. They were scarcely able to draw their swords before my claws slashed out eyeballs and ripped throats apart. I indulgently gorged on the blood of the first unfortunate victims of my attack in order to replenish my strength. This served to strike fear in hearts of all who bore witness to my savagery. Prior to our assault Caesar asked me to kill as few people as possible and I tried my best to oblige him. Caesar understood that, although we were pirates, it would not bode well for our future endeavors on the sea to massacre an entire naval regiment. The smell and taste of human blood was like revisiting an old friend and before I knew it I was feasting on those poor bastards. Becoming a monster was what I excelled at and I had to fight hard against my inner nature to not go on a killing spree. Instead, I snatched sailors up by their ankles and sent them flying overboard where their only fight was with the sea. For those I did not kill or toss overboard I would mercilessly body slam against the floor or bash their skulls against the masts of the ship, knocking them unconscious. I moved with such blinding speed the naval defenses never stood a chance. I snapped the lower jib arm of the middle mast with a vicious leaping knee. I ripped their sails apart and slashed the ropes until they were useless. I even tore out the steering wheel and threw it overboard. I was a fox in a hen house. While I distracted the main forces Caesar was able to get a few shots off during the melee, even taking out the signal captain with a well-placed shot to the shoulder. Within minutes we had disabled the ship and left most of the crew swimming for their lives. Their cutlasses and small arms fire were not prepared for my rampage that evening.

The trailing marine vessel, responding to the commotion on their sister ship, was approaching at top speed. They seemed to be attempting to maneuver across the bow of their comrade's ship and line their cannons up to fire upon Caesar's ship while suppressing the threat terrorizing the lead ship with rifle fire from their starboard deck. Unfortunately for them, I had already cleared the deck of sailors, and those too afraid to fight had barricaded themselves below deck during the onslaught. By the time the trailing vessel had sailed close enough to fire the first volley of shots, I was already moving towards the bow of the ship.

"Six O'clock!!"

Caesar yelled to me from his ship but before I could react!

'BLAM!BLAM! BLAM!BLAM!'

BLAKOW! BLAKOW!BLAKOW!

The thunder of rifle fire. I was struck by multiple balls of shot that spun me to my left side.
The pain of hot bullets is something one never quite grows accustomed to. I had forgotten what it was like to run freely without the weight of leg shackles and as the muscle memory returned, I caught myself from falling and tore across the deck. Dodging enemy fire, I ran like a cat up the main mast and out onto the top mast arm. With every movement I could feel hot bullet shrapnel that found its way into the meat of one of my lungs and I am reminded of the revolution and the rivers of blood we spilled only to realize the futility of war. Below I saw the sailors robotically reloading their rifles and taking aim. I tried to remember that my enemies were also men. Men who were only following orders to fulfill a contract for compensation. I cannot be certain that they hate me. I do not hate them. But today, we are enemies.

I dashed down the arm of the mizzenmast and somersaulted high into the air. Bullets whizz past me as my forward momentum carried me over and down onto the main deck of the second warship.

'WAHTHOOMP!'

I land hard, cracking the wooden deck beneath me.

My attack was swift and brutal.

After having my fill of blood from the victims of the first warship I was more mindful of using deadly force against this group. I darted from man to man yanking their rifles from their hands and effortlessly tossing their bodies into the sea. I would grab men by the throat and slam them viciously against the floor of the ship. Instead of slashing with my claws I closed my fists and ran top speed at my assailants, knocking them out with single blows to the gut or the jaw. I overwhelmed their defenses so quickly that they were unable to drop anchor, leaving the ship at the mercy of the ocean currents. Men cursed my soul and cried out for their God as I ran amuck aboard the huge naval vessel. Once I cleared the deck of combatants, I disabled the ship by tearing apart their sails and rigging. As reinforcements emerged from the lower decks, I darted between destroying the ship and attacks on groups of desperate sailors trying futilely to get me to stop. With most of the commanding officers unconscious or swimming for their lives the ship fell into anarchy. Regiment and training had all but disappeared and many of the sailors began abandoning their duties and loading the lifeboat tenders to escape being maimed or drowned. This day would set in stone the infamous name of Black Caesar and would cement his pirate crew in the annals of time as being one of the fiercest crews to sail the Caribbean.

'Phooooweeeeet'

Caesar pierces through the sound of men yelling and torn fabric flapping in the wind with a loud whistle, the signal to wrap things up and return to the ship. With all the damage I caused it would be impossible for the navy ships to follow us. I escaped as quickly as I had arrived, diving head-first over the side of the vessel I swam to Caesar's ship which had drifted about one hundred meters away, leaving both United States naval vessels stranded and in states of respective emergency. I clawed my way up the side of the ship and I was leaping back onto the deck when Caesar was yelling the "all clear" to the men below. Caesar's crew timidly began filing back out onto the main deck to hoist the sails again and make our retreat. After seeing the two naval ships on fire and in total disarray, they all just stared at me in awe.

The blood flow from my heightened state caused my eyes to reflect the blood onto the vitreous humor in a deep red due to the lack of pigment in my iris. From that day forward, I was called 'Je San', which in the creole of San Domingue translated to 'Blood Eyes', by Caesar and the crew. The atmosphere surrounding my occupancy on the ship changed drastically after that. The attitude of the men went from near mutiny over my presence to everyone on the entire crew displaying the utmost respect for myself and the decisions Caesar made no matter how outrageous. I was treated like royalty from that day forward. Each man would take his turn spinning yarns of their recollection of how I single handedly defeated the United States naval phalanx. Some of the more colorful tales about that evening included one which swore that I *'picked the warships up and slammed them upside down onto the sea.'* Another storyteller stated that I *'flew overhead and breathed fire on the sails of those navy scoundrels.'* As the night progressed, the tales would get taller, and the men would get more drunk and begin to fight each other as to who was my closest companion on the ship. The destruction and mayhem caused by just myself and Caesar that day felt liberating in many ways. We once again overcame what seemed like impossible circumstances setting a precedent in the seas surrounding the Caribbean for the next several years that our krewe of privateers was not to be trifled with.

Caesar and his fraternity of rascals taught me many things, but most of all they taught me to live free and to see my curse as a gift to use against tyranny. They reminded me of the inequalities of this world and made me promise to always be a thorn in the side of the establishment. We sailed together for the next eight years. In our travels, we despoiled many slave traders and imperialist dogs trying to exploit the weak and vulnerable. We confounded authorities in every jurisdiction we found ourselves while enriching our personal treasuries at the same time. With our many successful adventures myself and each of the lieutenants of the Black Caesar crew were able to amass a small fortune in loot that many of us had the wherewithal to hide in various places like some of the more obscure islands of the Keys and in the Sea Islands off the coast of what is now the state of Georgia.

In 1822, the first year I sailed with Caesar, we were commissioned by Peter Poyas to secure weapons and another ship off the coast of South Carolina to allow a large group of soon to be freed men and women from South Carolina to return to the west coast of Africa. The massive revolt plot, led by a man named Vessey, unfortunately was betrayed by an informant. All the conspirators involved in organizing the revolt were tried and publicly hanged. To prevent another large-scale rebellion by enslaved blacks in the future, the state of South Carolina drew up a charter to establish the Citadel, America's first private military training academy. Although most times driven purely by profit, Caesar and his pirates continued to clash against the system until his untimely death from tuberculosis in 1832.

Those were my truly formative years, and there are three things I learned that will kill a pirate the fastest: yellow fever, a bottle of rum, and a woman. Caesar's crew had become public enemy number one in the eyes of the British and Spanish navies, but they knew to give us a wide berth out of respect for our fierceness in battle. The U.S. on the other hand was bolder and less cautionary. As a fledgling nation, they had something to prove. The United States had begun expanding her mission of Manifest Destiny and at the time was waging an all-out war on the indigenous population. Under the questionable leadership of Andrew Jackson, the United States military had issued a warrant and was actively trying to arrest our pirate crew for aiding the Seminoles in and around the southeast. My last years with the Caesar crew were spent gallivanting around the Gulf Coast of the United States and the Caribbean as far south as Isla de Providencia near Nicaragua. Most of that time was spent skulking the waters of what is now called Fort Lauderdale, Miami, and the southern Florida coast. We would frequently visit Key Biscayne which served as a trading post during those years where the crew would be able to trade bullion for leather goods, beer, salted beef, hardtack, and weapons.

It was out at one of these trading posts that I met and fell in love with a Afro-Seminole woman named Bella who worked at a brothel that the men would all frequent. Bella was the first woman I had sex with, and I admittedly had to hide the fact that I was deeply in love with her from my pirate mates. They all respected me enough to not treat her like a pariah for being willing to have sex with me when the other women rejected me and refused to take my money. Bella was a stout woman with large breasts who wore a black horsehair wig whenever she left her room. Otherwise, she wore a multicolored tignon over her neat cornrows. She was stunning. Tall for a woman, with a caramel brown complexion, full lips and nose and piercing brown eyes. Her dress danced in the back as she walked by, a testament to her African heritage. She spoke French, English and local dialect of Creole and could read and write more than just her name. When we made love, she would wrap her legs around me, take me into her, and scream obscenities into my ear in her Seminole Creole as I plunged deeper and deeper inside her. She never treated me like a monster and I think that is what I was most grateful for. I was making Bella very wealthy every time I went to see her because I wanted to make sure she knew how happy she made me. Bella consumed my thoughts to the point that I never spent money on anything other than her and over the years, I had stashed enough loot away to rival Cornelius Vanderbilt. I wanted nothing more than to marry her and sail away to our own island where we could live in peace. Far away from this wicked world.

Whenever our ship was to be harbored near the Keys, I would rent the best room and buy her out for weeks on end. I would have been happy with a minute if it meant we could be together undisturbed. Since birth I was always unable to express myself verbally very well and it was Bella who taught me to speak like a normal human being. She also taught me to read and write in English. If I had a weakness, she was it. I longed for her whenever we were apart. It was much more than just sex for me, Bella restored my will to live and gave me hope that even a devil like myself could find a place to belong in the world.

Florida was becoming an integral part of the southern border of the fledgling United States and the land was highly coveted by the Monroe White House. Around 1817 the United States military under the direction of then General Andrew Jackson accused a group of Florida Seminole of harboring runaway slaves which was against federal law at the time. Subsequently the U.S. military invaded the Seminoles' land leading to a string of battles that began what was recorded by historians as the First Seminole War. The result of this War conducted under mostly false pretenses was the transfer of the remainder of Spanish territories to the United States. After the annexation, the tension between the natives of Florida and the U.S. military lasted for years, sometimes flaring up into shootouts that would last for days and weeks. It was during one of these skirmishes that took place near Key

Biscayne where the brothel we frequented was raided under suspicion of harboring renegade Indians and runaway slaves. In the ensuing scuffle, Bella was injured by shrapnel from stray gunfire between U.S. troops and suspected fugitives. By the time I and the Black Caesar crew received the news of the raid and were able to return to Florida, Bella had succumbed to her injuries and her body was taken into the swamp and she was sent on her journey into Paradise in a mass Seminole funeral rite.

When Caesar broke the news to me, I was livid with anger. I wanted to rip this entire world apart. For a month after I found out about Bella's death I did not eat or sleep. Racked with depression, I simply sat in the darkness of the cargo hold of Caesar's ship wishing I could join her in the afterlife. Again, someone I loved was taken from me in a violent manner. That was my last sea voyage with the Black Caesar pirates. I took the remainder of my share of loot and left permanently for life on the mainland. I reminded myself of the vow I made over Colette's lifeless body to take down the Reichstall family and their imperialist plans to control the world. The same imperialist forces that had now taken Bella away from me.

I would soon learn that the Reichstalls along with other global elites already had me on their radar. During my outlaw years with the Black Caesar pirates, I unknowingly became the focus of an international criminal ranking roster that was being compiled by the earth's wealthiest oligarchs. This roster listed names of people from all over the world who, in some way, impeded or stood to impede their plans for global domination. The Guy Fawkes', Joans of Arc or Huey P. Newtons of this world who were targeted and systematically killed or driven into obscurity. Any so-called *"Messiahs"* that sprang up as leaders amongst the people were either bribed into compliance or categorically crushed. I had cost them untold amounts of riches through my efforts to dismantle their capitalist institutions in San Domingue.

Caesar was also on this list because he frequently made it his mission to raid the merchant ships that flew the flags that represented these corrupt corporations and individuals whose business models seemed to be unable to function without the employ of slavery, exploitation, and genocide.

Andrew Jackson had killed and displaced so many native Americans in order to expand the United States that he was awarded the job of President where he continued his persecution of Native Americans by ushering the Indian Removal Act through Congress. Battles between Native Americans and colonists raged on leading to a second Seminole War over the theft of more Florida territory by the deceitful U.S. government around the year 1835. I deeply regret not getting my fangs into Jackson and apparently I was not the only person out for his hide. An assassination attempt was made on Jackson's life that year by a gunman who failed in his endeavor and was captured. The newspapers reported that this man wore a ring with the symbol of a snake with the head of a lion. The secret symbol used to identify the tools of the Incalculaba. This was the first time anyone would attempt to assassinate a sitting president.

Years later my research would reveal that the global elites were not happy with Jackson's blockage of their attempts to create a Central Bank in the U.S. and needed him taken out. I and many other brave men and women fought valiantly against insurmountable odds in defense of those native lands. However, the policy of the United States government was that of deceit and betrayal when it came to making treaties with Natives concerning ownership of the land. One of these policies culminated in the biggest breach of trust to the Native Americans, their forcible removal from their ancestral homes to unknown territory west of the Mississippi commonly referred to as the Trail of Tears.

Over the next thirty years I took up the crusade for the poor and downtrodden wherever I found myself. I lived and fought with the Seminoles, Creek, Blackfoot, Yamasee and Choctaw to name a few against the imperial designs of the United States. It was during these years that I developed my strategy of operating from the shadows and never declaring a particular affiliation when it came to helping the weak defend themselves or creating a distraction to facilitate their escape to freedom. Nonetheless despite my best efforts, the machinations of the empire proved to be too mighty to curtail. Many times, we would have our liberation efforts thwarted by other Negroes and Indians who saw no merit in being free from the yoke of slavery and thought to curry favor from the very devils that kept them oppressed by becoming traitors to their own kith and kin.

By the time the American Civil War broke out, I had fought in countless battles in an effort to slow the spread of imperialism in the west. For years leading up to the war I believed that if I could inspire the enslaved of the United States to take up arms against their oppressors then we could curtail the spread of injustice. However, after witnessing the poverty and wage slavery of the North being just as bad or worse than the chattel slavery we were fighting in the South, the line between whose ideals we were fighting for began to blur. On one occasion around 1864, during the War Between the States, Confederate troop advancement had been overwhelming the Union forces as of late. I could cover great distances by running at night and whenever the opportunity presented itself, I would raid Confederate encampments. I would set fire to their tents and weapons caches and scare off their horses and soldiers, most of whom were just drunks and young men looking for a reason to raise hell. General John Brevard Kershaw commissioned a special mercenary unit of skilled marksmen and foragers to track down and dispatch me with extreme prejudice. Unfortunately for them, communications technology at the time was still too primitive so by the time the information was relayed about an ambush I had made on Confederate forces, it was already days too late and I had moved on to my next mission. One night during a raid on a Confederate encampment I ransacked an officer's tent and by chance found invoices from a British company to the United States. On some of the paperwork there was an insignia of a snake with the head of a lion. The documents revealed that not only did the Reichstall empire and the Incalculaba own insurance policies on thousands of enslaved people, but they also profited handsomely from supplying both sides of the war with weapons and equipment. All these people knew was constant war and suffering in the name of expansion. Colonization became a term used to replace the word tyranny. I could feel it. The shift had been taking place for a long time, but now it was beginning to become palpable. Brother killing brother over imaginary ideals fomented through a propaganda machine of falsehoods controlled by an oligarchy with a very powerful and a very singular point of failure. The power of the

Incalculaba was only increasing and despite my best efforts, I only ended up losing the people I cared about the most.

[1][FOOTNOTE:*According to the statute, county sheriffs henceforth were obliged to arrest all "colored" sailors, regardless of nationality, until their ship was ready to leave harbor. The captain of the vessel was monetarily responsible for a bond to cover the expenses of their incarceration. If the captain refused to pay, he was "liable to be indicted, and, on conviction…be fined in a sum not less than one thousand dollars and imprisoned not less than two months." If this penance seemed a touch harsh, it paled in comparison to the one doled out to the sailors of the recalcitrant captain, as "such negroes or persons of color shall be deemed and taken as absolute slaves and sold." Essentially free black men could be sold as slaves. (Navigating The Dangerous Atlantic: Racial Quarantines, Black Sailors And United States Constitutionalism, pg. 36 Michael Alan Schoeppner)]

Chapter 16

The assassination of Lincoln had the stink of the Reichstall conglomerate and the Incalculaba all over it. The very same day he signed into law a bill that would create the Secret Service to combat counterfeiting of the U.S. currency, was the same day he was murdered. John Wilkes Booth, his alleged assassin, was a card-carrying member of the Knights of the Golden Circle, a secret society dedicated to creating a country where slavery was permanently legal. When Booth was finally cornered and killed he was said to have nothing in his possession except a small folded piece of paper with three lines of indecipherable code stamped with the symbol of a snake with a lion's head on it.

In the years that followed my vigilante style exploits became something of legend. My main focus was assisting in defense and resettlement of newly freed blacks and displaced Indians. Time and time again I would come up against property magnates denying township to natives or racist sheriffs harassing the formerly enslaved who thought they were just doing their respective jobs but were unknowingly on the payroll of a gigantic network run by the secret government. Their ultimate plan being to centralize world power into one dystopian nightmare for all.

I quickly became one of the biggest thorns in the sides of the invisible rulers since the Protestant Reformation. Operating exclusively at night I was always sure to maintain a low profile as I roamed the countryside as a vigilante nomad. Constantly moving in the darkness, drifting from city to city, and avoiding human contact as much as possible. Unable to bond with the very people I had sworn to advocate for. For as much as I tried to use my abilities to help people, it became nigh impossible to remain hidden in an area for too long before talk of my exploits reached the ears of those connected to the blue bloods. In consequence I would be forced to flee the area before mercenary groups loosely employed by the Incalculaba would appear in the town harassing the people and inquiring of my whereabouts. These international mercenary sweepers were the predecessors to the assassination friendly organizations such as the CIA, MI6, and the KGB.

It would not be until after World War One when two-way voice transmission radio frequency technology became widely available and advanced enough to track my whereabouts in real time. It was also around this time, after the first war, that the League of Nations and the ICPO(Interpol) was being formed. This was a few years after the formation of the Federal Reserve System, a major step by the wealthy elite that signified one of the first overt attempts at globalization.

I had been freelance fighting for the disenfranchised and downtrodden for almost one hundred years, and after many close calls I was always able to evade the Incalculaba led by the diabolical Reichstall family and their unrelenting need to possess my power again. Critical advancements in technology brought about an exponential increase in the surveillance powers of the Incalculaba. Their tracking devices and radar were now developed enough to pinpoint my location with some accuracy, and I found myself at the center of a major disaster on American soil. During this incident it became clear to me that, going forward, it would be considerably more difficult for me to stay off of the Reichstall syndicate radar.

From my time living with the natives of America I learned that this leap in intelligence gathering technology was no coincidence. Numerous tribes spoke of the *Lizard Men* who had been influencing the earth from another dimension using restless humans like the Reichstalls to do their dirty work. Supposedly the goal of the Lizard Men is to create misery and strife on the planet so that they can feed off the emotions of sorrow and hatred which is like food to them. In exchange for creating a low vibrational frequency for the entire world, the Reichstalls and the Incalculaba are rewarded with earthly riches and alien tech which they reverse engineer to develop advanced machinery that will further their monopolistic ambitions.

After the riots of 1919 and witnessing all the hatred and greed mankind was capable of, I grew weary of constant fighting and death so I decided to head west of the Mississippi for a less chaotic lifestyle. I was living in an abandoned J.J. McAlester coal mine on the outskirts of what is known today as Tulsa, Oklahoma. This was mainly Creek Nation and the stories of my sympathy for Indian causes won me a lot of favor with the locals so this seemed like the perfect sanctuary for laying low for a while. The discovery of a massive oil reserve south of the city sparked a huge rush of entrepreneurs and speculators to the city and Tulsa was growing by leaps and bounds as a booming commercial center for migrants seeking their fortune in oil. The influx of settlers from the east began to conflict with the current inhabitants of the city and the Indian nations who were already basically prisoners on their own land. With the limited amount of resources to go around the entire situation was a powder keg waiting to explode.

The influence of the Ku Klux Klan had been growing rapidly in the area since the turn of the century and causing trouble for the citizens of blacks and the Indians in the area alike. The Klan in the Tulsa area were colloquially known as Night Riders, and they would make it their business to attack unwary citizens of color to prevent them from creating any meaningful roots in the area. One early summer night as I was collecting bullfrogs for meat, I looked up to see a thin plume of smoke. I was being summoned. I went to a prearranged rendezvous point at the northern border of Tulsa at midnight where I was met by a Muskogee woman named Dancing Cloud. She was a friend, one of the few I trusted with the whereabouts of my lair. The message was concerning trouble brewing in the majority black owned Greenwood District. Two black men were accused of raping a white woman and the settlers from the surrounding areas were using this incident as an excuse to call for blood. There were many whispers in the air warning of the coming backlash from the Klan and other disgruntled whites in the Tulsa area who were jealous of the success of the businesses and the high quality of life in the Greenwood community. Dancing Cloud also told me that carloads of white men with weapons were seen as recently as this morning gathering on the outskirts of Muskogee land. This rape accusation would give them all the reason they needed to go in and burn the place down and displace all the residents. I thanked Dancing Cloud and hurriedly made my way south to the city.

The men of the Greenwood District had gotten all the rifles and shotguns they could find and organized themselves into a militia of sorts to protect their friends and families from the coming violence. As I recollect, it was just after eleven p.m. on a Wednesday night when the shooting started. The volunteers of the militia were holding their own against the mob for the first couple of hours of rioting when I arrived on the outskirts of the town square near Pershing Street. I was hauling ass, making my way south when the mobs began arriving from the surrounding counties and all hell began breaking loose. The way the droves of armed white men descended upon the city, allegedly organized in a matter of hours, was absolutely astonishing. I fought like hell to protect the people and stamp out the fires being started at homes and businesses everywhere, but the scene was pure chaos. People were being shot in the back as they ran holding their children. Elderly people were dragged into the street and trampled by the mobs. Looters were pilfering money and jewelry from the homes of the affluent blacks that had already fled for their lives amidst the chaos. Brand new Model T Fords were overturned and on fire and the smell of blood and gunfire dominated the air. I fought tooth and nail, literally, against the hordes of plunderers, some of whom toted dreadful military grade weapons that they mastered as veterans of World War I.

As I made my way south of the city, I saw a large group of marauders heading towards the courthouse where many of the families had barricaded themselves. I was ambushed by a group of attackers carrying an incredibly lethal weapon and forced to retreat towards the town square, unable to stop the destruction of dozens of lives. I would later find out this handheld machine powered rifle that could fire thirty rounds without reloading was called a Tommy gun. Years after the massacre, through my research into the global syndicate I deduced that these men were actually high-level mercenaries trained and deployed using Reichstall's unlimited resources to keep me at bay until dawn when the majority of the plundering whites were scheduled to arrive.

That next morning when the bright summer sun came up over the gruesome scene, there were dismembered arms and legs, severed by the barrage of rapid gun fire, littering the streets. I was forced to take refuge in one of the hulls of the burned-out buildings and listen to the cries and screams of the dispossessed until late in the afternoon. By the time I was able to rejoin the battle, the entire Negro section of town had been abandoned by the residents, and military planes flew overhead dropping incendiary devices on my position wherever I tried to flee. The pilots kept tabs on my location by corresponding over the radio with the ground forces who transmitted my location to the bombers to accurately drop their payloads and blow me into pieces. I was hiding just South of Greenwood and Haskell streets when the bombing runs began again which pushed me to duck behind the remains of a demolished schoolhouse. No sooner had I caught my breath when a loud *THUD* of a metal object struck what remained of the roof followed by a thunderous *KABOOM*!!!!!The remainder of the building came crashing down on top of my head. I braced my muscles as wood beams and plaster were piled on top of me. I coughed and sputtered, trying to breathe enough oxygen to be able to dig my way out and regroup before they circled back around. Through the dust and smoke of the crumbling building, I could hear what sounded like liquid being poured onto the ground. The stink of gasoline came strongly into my nostrils, and seconds later, smoke began to obscure my vision.

They were burning me alive!

WHOOOOOOOSH!!!!

Flames rose up all around me causing the rubble to shift. I rolled onto my left hip to avoid the avalanche but some of the debris caught me, pinning and crushing my left leg with a massive slab of bricks and plaster up to the knee. The bones in my leg were completely crushed. As the heat from the flame grew closer, I could hear the plane circling overhead, coming around again for another bombardment. I shoved as much of the wood and plaster wreckage off of my leg as possible, but I was unable to completely free myself due to the impossible weight of the bricks still pinning my left foot. Frantically, I began to tear away at the skin and muscle tissue just below my left knee, ignoring the agonizing pain, clawing through the bone to tear off my lower leg. I ran like a three-legged dog as fast as I possibly could, clearing the area seconds before the decommissioned World War I plane released another firebomb, this one crashing down and obliterating the building I had been pinned under moments before.

To my chagrin, I underestimated the lengths these sadistic fucks would be willing to go to accomplish their goals of world conquest. The newspaper reports and official historic records were altered to fit the narrative that the Negroes caused a disturbance, and the white militias and National Guard had to be called in to quell the insurrection. To this day, the entire incident is mischaracterized as a riot amongst indignant Negroes instead of being portrayed as a massacre by jealous, greedy white men who did not believe in the American dream for black people.

Chapter 17

I ran, if you could call it that, nonstop to the Arkansas River and disappeared downstream before the mob could find me. That first night, I traveled as far downstream as I could go before daybreak. I remained in the forest near the riverbank the next day by hiding in the canopy of a thick patch of oak trees. As soon as the sun had fallen behind the horizon I made my way to the ground and broke a young sapling to make an improvised crutch. I decided it was time to head South into less inhibited areas and figure out what my next move should be. I was forced to abandon the few possessions I had including a small fortune in gold bullion and a book of newspaper clippings with articles pertaining to the Reichstall family and their business dealings over the last decade. It took over a week for my leg to heal, making it very difficult to hunt. I hobbled across the dark, empty plains at night and during the day I would either climb into a thicket of trees or find a cave to wait out the sun. I seriously underestimated the sophistication of the Incalculaba's intelligence network.

The stakes had been raised and I decided that because of its burgeoning military industrial complex, the United States was no longer safe. The Incalculaba, led by the Reichstalls were organized, willing and powerful enough to order bombs to be dropped on American soil and annihilate an entire community, murdering hundreds of people and displacing thousands of residents under the false flag of a racial dispute. All to eradicate one man. The military industrial complex in America, particularly the espionage community, was growing much too influential to remain within its borders. After the brief Reconstruction period and the Southern Loyalists regained power in Congress, the moneyed elite resumed shaping America into the vanguard country of its agenda, doing the dirty work in policing and dominating the rest of the world. After I healed completely, I left Oklahoma and headed further South to Texas where I spent a few weeks moving at night and avoiding human contact as much as possible. While passing through what is now Round Rock, Texas just north of modern-day Austin. I was able to meet and visit with the chief of a group of Tonkawa Indians that were sympathetic to my plight and provided me with clothing, a hunting knife and a deerskin satchel for my journey. With two functioning legs I could move much faster and reached the Mexico/Texas border a few days shy of July. I continued my journey further into the interior of Mexico until when, in early October, I reached the Sierra Madre del Sur mountain range. The sparsely inhabited hills and mountains of this part of the world were riddled with connecting cave systems that spread throughout the surrounding landscape and, upon further evaluation, I realized that I could find peaceful refuge from the Incalculaba and bountiful wildlife for food in the area. I decided to make this land my new home and live free in the caves on the outskirts of Oaxaca, in the southern regions of Mexico. I disappeared from the world of man.

I lived as a hermit in the hills outside the tiny city of Santa Maria Huazolotitlan for the next four decades. The chaotic life I led up until now became a distant memory for me. I hunted, fished, and foraged for my food, running with the jaguar and puma at night. Rumors of my presence began to circulate amongst the natives. The indigenous Zapotec and Mixtec people in the surrounding area believed me to be a descendent of the Camazotz, guardian of the darkness and emissary of death. For fear of reprisal, many a farmer or villager would look the other way when one of their goats or domestic fowl came up missing from time to time. I would always leave something like Ocelot or Cacomistle pelts, turtle shells, anything useful that I felt would compensate the individual or family that I had pilfered from in return for my meals.

Some of the men who worked various jobs outside the village would bring home bundles of discarded newspapers and use them for lining shoes, starting fires, wrapping fruit to preserve freshness, as cleaning rags and numerous other ingenious uses. I learned to read and speak Spanish during my time with Black Caesar and on the nights where there was no moon to speak of, I would sneak into the village and steal these editorials to keep abreast of what was happening in the surrounding area and beyond. Most times, the papers would be filled with news of internal strife within the government of Mexico, occasionally, there would be international editorials concerning political rhetoric around events in Cuba, Jamaica, and even as far away as Venezuela. It was rare to get anything from as distant as the United States or Europe, but what little I did receive piqued my interest to the point that I seriously began contemplating leaving the peace of the mountains to rejoin the struggle against imperialism. I became particularly intrigued with the various people's movements that I was able to read about regarding Africa and its recent endeavors for liberation. I decided one night as I watched a commercial airliner fly high above me as I sat atop my mountain throne that I had stayed hidden long enough. I still had to keep the vow I made to repay the Reichstalls for the personal pain they have caused me. 39 years should have been enough time for me to have fallen off their radar and for them to have given up on the hunt for me. I was sure that if Reichstall had even an inkling of the fact that I was still alive and hiding out in a place such as this, the entire peninsula would have been obliterated by now.

When I escaped from Tulsa like a bat out of hell, no pun intended, I carried a small bag of gold coins in a satchel I kept strapped around my thigh next to my groin. An old habit I held onto from my days as a pirate. I never needed any money because the forest and the hills provided plenty of bounty, but as I stated before, occasionally I would donate anonymously to various members of the community that believed me to be a benevolent force in the area. In particular, I would donate to a small Catholic Church on the outskirts of a tiny town called Santa Maria Yavesia. The priest would subsequently use the coins to buy medical supplies and food in order maintain a small orphanage. By the time I made the decision to return to civilization, I had dwindled my treasury down to only five gold coins. More than enough to get me back to the States, but I certainly could not just waltz into the port and purchase a ferry ticket. Using a piece of charcoal, I wrote a note to the old priest on one of the *pagina deportes* of one of my stolen newspapers. The note simply read:

"Ropa de hombres, zapatos talla doce, una maquinilla de afeitar, quinientos dolares y la mapa de La Veracruz, por favor." [Men's clothes, shoes size twelve, a razor, 500 dollars, and a map of Veracruz please.] Three weeks later as the August rain fell in large drops, I perched upon the mouth of my cavern which overlooked the town when a small plume of smoke, uncharacteristic for summertime, began to rise from the tiny church steeple just after midnight. I rushed down into the sleeping hamlet and when I arrived at the portico behind the narrow church building, there sat a small duffel bag covered by a parasol on a stone bench. The only scent present was that of the priest who must have been somewhere inside watching from a safe distance. I grab the loot and briefly inspect the contents for completion before leaving my last five gold coins on the bench in a neat stack and disappearing back into the hills as quickly as I came.

Safely back inside my mountain lair, I took inventory of the bag which contained two pairs of slacks — one navy blue and the other colored black — and one pair of Levi's jeans, a clergyman's white button down shirt, a black and red lumberjack shirt, a plain white t-shirt, a green t-shirt, a lightweight jacket, a grey fedora, two pairs of thin black socks, a brown pair of penny loafers, and two pairs of brand new brief style underwear. Only one pair of the pants fit me but everything else suited me fine. I repacked all the contents of the bag except for the two smaller pairs of pants and the map which I studied in the darkness until the morning light appeared at the mouth of my cave. The priest had drawn arrows to the city of Heroica, Veracruz, which was the major port city, and circled a pit stop on the map near the municipality of Yanga with the word 'amigos' written next to it. Most likely to signify his connection with the area and that I had allies there if I should need them.

The following evening, I hunted, killed, and devoured a female white-tailed goat entirely before setting out through the miles of forests and over wide arid mountain ranges. Periodically, I would stop to dine on a fat bullfrog or a sleeping iguana to regain my strength before finding a resting place at dawn. To rebuild my stamina, I ran most of the way heading North toward Veracruz wearing one of the pair of the too small pants, modified into shorts that stopped just above my knees and nothing else except the duffel bag full of clothes and supplies strapped across my back. On the third night of my

318

journey, I ran without stopping for food and just half an hour before dawn, I reached the outskirts of the Yanga province. There, I found a dense patch of trees to rest and wait out the sun amongst the thick canopy before continuing my journey. As the sun set on another day, I descended from the trees onto the forest floor to hunt some of the reptiles and birds that make up this unique ecosystem for my breakfast. After feasting on the flesh of a large boa, I removed the skin and hung the remains on a branch for the natives to use for clothing and crafting bags. I left the Yanga province shortly after my meal and began my approach to the main city of Veracruz from the south. I passed through forests and over large tracts of farmland marked by thriving towns with such names as Mundo Nuevo, Los Bajos, and Santa Rita. My trajectory led me smack into a mid-size river known as the Jamapa, just below the sleepy city of La Pepehua.

I laid down my bag and tore off my filthy shorts and bathed the sweat and grime layers from my body. I put on the underwear, blue jeans, the faded green t-shirt with a Mexican flag on the front, the tan windbreaker, the first pair of socks I can remember wearing in my life, and the shiny pair of dark brown loafers from the duffel bag. I was trying on the narrow-brimmed fedora when an item fell out of the bag that I had overlooked in my first inspection — a small pair of browline dark glasses usually worn to hide the eyes of blind orphans in the monastery infirmary.

I look up at the clear night sky for the drinking gourd in order to recalibrate my bearings and start walking northeast from the Jamapa which ran me directly into La Carraterra Federal 150, the highway that terminated into the heart of Veracruz at its eastern end. According to the map, from my current position if I follow this road, it was eleven miles until I would dead end into the harbor. The sun would be rising soon and if I did not make it to the ship or find a place to hide soon, I may be in serious trouble. I do not dare run for fear of attracting attention, but I doubted if I could walk fast enough to beat the sunrise. Hitchhiking was still seen as a safe form of travel during those years, but for me, it was out of the question. The less people that knew I still existed the better. I did not want to risk being identified by the Incalculaba as being alive before I had the chance to take my revenge.

319

Moving only at night and staying as far away from human interaction as I possibly could, I followed the riverbank north, walking as normally as any man past houses and streets, towards the lights of the metropolis in the distance. This city was known simply as Veracruz and boasted a rich and distinguished history as one of the major port cities in the Western Hemisphere. One of the newspapers I happened to read earlier this year stated that the U.S. President named Kennedy had visited Mexico and made a stop in Veracruz in an effort to extend a diplomatic hand and mend relations between the neighboring countries.

The city of Heroica Veracruz was magnificent in the early morning darkness. The moon and stars illuminated the fog that rolled in from the ocean to obscure the picturesque landscape. The architecture of the churches, homes and buildings, and the relatively smooth and pristine roads reflect the economic success this city has enjoyed since the sixteenth century. The smell of the food and the sound of the people reverberate throughout this town with its rich mixture of Spanish, Caribbean, and African culture.

As I got closer to the center of the city, I saw the five-lane highways I read about in the newspaper jam packed with thousands of motorized vehicles of all shapes and sizes whizzing past each other by mere inches. I was sure there would be an accident at any moment. I could remember when people were afraid of electricity and preferred to pipe gas through their homes because they thought it was less likely to set their house on fire. Now the electric light has made it possible for humans to conquer the night. So much has changed in the last forty years.

I was close enough to the coast now that I could smell the ocean. I ducked down a dark alley and leaned against a pickup truck with its passenger side wheels on cinder blocks and read my map. The padre was kind enough to mark on the map the exact direction of the main shipping harbor where I would be more than likely to find a cargo vessel headed for the States.

Near the shipping district, I passed a huge stone head monument with the visage of a Negro man wearing a helmet labeled Cabeza Olmeca. A fitting guardian for such a majestic municipality. As I continued walking,

320

Carraterra Federal 150 becomes Avenida De Miguel Aleman, a massive street that served as the main thoroughfare through this tremendous metropolis. The contrast of the hills and bush of Oaxaca that I had grown accustomed to living in for the past four decades in comparison to the modernity of Veracruz was shocking. The technological level of the world had grown by leaps and bounds. Streetlamps illuminated every nook and cranny of the city and huge billboards advertising items like Coca-Cola and Goya littered the scenery. Motorcycles, semi-trucks, and cars choked the streets and avenues everywhere I walked.

I made a left on Avenue Ignacio Allende, and I think I was less than half an hour from the Zona de Ferrocarilles and the main port labeled Portuaria de Veracruz on the map. I made a right onto Calle Jose Montesinos and spotted two police cars parked next to each other partially blocking the street. There was no visible way for me to get around them and reach the dock without passing directly by them. I pulled my hat down, stuck my hands into my jacket pockets and walked purposefully toward the docks, trying to blend in with the other men headed to the pier to start their workday. I was taller than most of these men and the way I was dressed did not exactly imply dock worker or sailor. I was positive I was the only person here wearing loafers and dark glasses to work at 5 A.M. I walked right past the police on the opposite side of the street and neither of them paid me one iota of attention. I exhaled and continued walking until I was out of their range of vision.

I dipped into the shadows of a shipping warehouse and scaled the barbed-wire fence serving as the barrier to anyone not authorized to be in the area. I crept out of the shadows and tried as best as possible to blend in with the other workers milling around and slowly making their way to their respective jobs. I could read and understand Spanish perfectly well, but if I was required to speak it, I may respond slowly and stumble over words, mainly because I was alone in the jungle with no one except the animals to talk to for four decades.

As I reached the east end of the pier, the distinct aroma of coffee wafted my way, and I see a group of large crates labeled *Granos de Cafe"*, *Para Exportacion: Estados Unidos, Florida*. I watched in awe as the large gas-powered hook and tackle machines lifted the sizable metal and wooden crates onto the ship at the end of the pier. As the machine lowered to lift another bundle of crates onto the ship. I zipped over into the shadows between a large empty wooden spool and an eight-foot stack of railroad ties that I ducked behind to remove my shoes and socks and placed them in my bag. I ran east down the pier and hid amongst the crates being loaded one by one onto the ship. I spotted a metal container with a latched top filled with the aromatic beans and opened the latches on either side and climbed in before I was spotted by anyone.

After about an hour of sitting quietly amongst a sea of raw coffee, I heard the men outside my container close the latches and attach span sets at each corner and then to the hook. I felt myself being lifted and lowered into the dark cargo hold inside the belly of the ship, and if not for the overpowering odor of the coffee beans, I might have remained within that container for the entire journey. After a few unpleasant hours of waiting for the load to be completed and the sound of the crane motor to subside, I felt it was safe enough to exit my hiding place and find a new one that did not involve being submerged in coffee beans. As I climbed out of the sea of beans, I had to turn out all my pockets and shake the beans out of the cuffs of my pants and the creases of my jacket. The acrid smell of coffee seemed to be permanently etched into my clothes and body, making it difficult for me to discern how many humans were aboard this vessel and the nature as to what else they might be transporting. Upon further inspection the cargo hold was empty of all life bigger than a rat. The huge room was pitch dark and filled with neatly aligned rows of crates and boxes, all seemingly filled with coffee. I chose a corner towards the bow of the ship and maneuvered some of the crates around to form a high wall around me that would give me time to escape if anyone were to venture down here in search of stowaways.

After three sleepless, hunger filled days I arrived in Tampa, Florida. The ship was not unloaded immediately because we arrived in the late afternoon on a Wednesday, and the port authority administration was backed up already with international shipments. The dock workers were in no mood to check and receive a huge shipment like this when it could wait until tomorrow morning when more personnel would be on duty. The shipment was not technically due to arrive until the morning, but with the favorable weather, we were able to arrive ahead of schedule.

Once night had fallen, I waited a few more hours to allow for the darkness and the crew to settle in before I carefully left my hiding place and climbed the ribs of the walls of the cargo hold up to the open hatch and onto the forward deck. Most of the crew were either in their rooms or out in the city so there was hardly anyone on duty when I emerged from the bowels of the ship. Keeping to the shadows, I stealthily leaped over the side of the vessel and down onto the pier. Sitting about twenty yards to my right was a row of large metallic shipping containers stacked in a way that created a secluded nook to duck behind and put my socks and shoes back on. I tried to be as unassuming as I possibly could, blending in with the crowd of longshoremen leaving the pier and into the industrial area surrounding the docks. I followed the Hillsborough River north and made my way up and out of the city as quickly as possible. Tampa had not yet grown to the busy cruise ship port and tourist destination that it is today, so it did not take me very long to reach the outskirts. Walking through the small town, I was fully aware of a concealed tension around racial relations that lingered in this part of the south.

I constantly worried that walking around at this time of night, I was a target for bigots and if things were still as bad as they were when I left the United States, then I could be questioned and detained on the whim by any white man who had the notion to inquire. Until I reached the forest and Indian country, I felt like I could be ambushed and attacked at any moment and all my senses remained on full alert. I consciously willed myself to walk with purpose without looking suspicious, going over in my mind how I should respond if stopped and detained by anyone. I absolutely could not wait to get back into the bush and the swamps that I had grown familiar with a century ago during my time with the Blackfoot and Seminoles.

As I continued trekking northeast, I ran into the huge tract of manicured lawns and large institutional buildings that I later learned was the main campus for the University of Florida. This was the last obstacle of civilization I had to endure before I reached the Cypress Creek marshlands and relative sanctuary. There were a surprising amount of people still moving about in the wee hours of the morning throughout the campus, forcing me to be extra cautious as I maneuvered my way through the countless buildings littering the property. I found a shadowy spot beneath a large oak tree on the edge of the swamp and stopped a moment to remove my clothes and shoes and deposited them into my duffel bag before plunging myself into the backcountry and setting out walking across the panhandle and down the east coast of the state. I took my time with my movements, reintroducing myself with the flora and fauna of the southern United States. For food, I hunted deer, capybara, and raccoons at night and rested in the thick green canopies of the forest and swamps during the day. Although remote, the region was still inhabited by a few people who still valued traditional living, so the families survived in small communities away from mainstream society here on the swamp. Given the number of tourists in the area I always made sure to conceal myself well during my day's rest and covered my tracks thoroughly after a hunt to avoid being detected by anyone.

In a little over sixteen days, I made my way South to the Everglades and Key Largo area where I kept a stash of loot in the form of gold and various other precious metals and gemstones hidden away from my days as a privateer. The plan was to find some black-market gold brokers outside of Fort Lauderdale and convert at least 25,000 dollar's worth of gold into cash. Going underground was the only way to fence the bullion because most of the currency exchange brokers would either try to swindle you and not pay you the full value of the coins or get nosy and start asking too many questions about where a Negro got so much money and what I planned on doing with it. Racism created a vacuum in the mainstream market. Many goods and services that we were either excluded or prohibited from accessing, made it necessary for many black people to resort to off the grid measures to achieve even the most basic of tasks that white people had unencumbered access to services such as securing loans for cars, homes, and paying for higher education were kept well out of the reach of the average Negro. Looking back, there was a silver lining about financial transactions in the black community in 1962 and the years prior to majority digital commerce, and that was that if you had enough cash, you could get anything done even if it had to be done in the middle of the night. And it was all untraceable.

My stash was buried in a heavily wooded area of southern Florida known as Dog Beach that sported a hidden cave system just under the rocky shoreline at the northeast tip of the Manatee Bay. We chose this hiding spot because the terrain was so incredibly uneven and difficult to walk upon that it would be impossible to build or develop any human settlements there. I grabbed what I thought would be enough loot to last me the next few years in case I had trouble getting back down here. I reburied the remaining loot and left Manatee Bay that same night. I followed the eastern coastline up into the city of Miami. I was moving cautiously, so it took me two nights to travel the forty miles to a small lake south of Hollywood, Florida, that was dubbed Leaping Cat Lake by the Blackfoot Indians. Once there, I was able to bathe in the cool lake water. I cleaned the filth from my body and put on the slacks, the flannel shirt and loafers before traveling toward the downtown area of the city to try and secure a newspaper. I wanted to find out the where the Negro section of town was because it was getting late and I was worried that the streets would empty out before I could find a bar to duck into.

I yanked open a newspaper box and grabbed a Miami Herald and quickly flipped to the classifieds to find which area of town rented mainly to Negroes. It took me a while, but I finally figured out that Dania Beach was to be the closest city with a majority a Negro settlement that I could reach on foot before dawn. I tucked my paper under my arm and flagged down a brother riding past me on a bike with a shoeshine box attached to the rear of the seat to ask for directions. After thanking the man profusely, I began walking north a few blocks to my destination. I crossed a set of railroad tracks into a small section of town that fit the description of what the man on the bike said it would look like. A few office buildings, a couple of churches, a school and a few blocks of houses made up this quaint little Florida town where the Negroes of the area had created a relatively comfortable environment inside the ever-expanding Miami metro vicinity. The only places still open were either gambling houses or brothels, but after frequenting a few bars and pool halls in northwest Hallandale and the 'Black Bottom' of Dania Beach, I was able to grease the palms of a few brothers who 'pulled my coat' to where I could get everything I needed.

There was a Madam named Lady T in a large Victorian home at the corner of Seventh Avenue and Northwest 8th Street that bade me come back the next night to exchange $15,000 worth of gold for $12,000 American dollars. I returned the next night and collected my cash. I purchased a used dark green 1955 Studebaker Commander from a black stud named Eddie (Edwina) who was one of the madam's frequent customers. Eddie was a brown skinned Cuban who made money trading cars to black people who could not get them through traditional methods. The car she sold me had been run into the ground but still had a decent engine for the amount of mileage it had. I ended up paying 1200 dollars, twice what it was worth, in order to bribe Eddie to keep her question asking to a minimum. For an extra 75 fins, I was able to get a Florida driver's license and a fake registration thrown into the deal. The name on the license read Karl Torres Jr and other than the race designation and the black face on the card, none of the other information on the document matched my appearance.

The last time I drove a car was around 1920 so it took me about half an hour to figure out the gear shift and clutch. This was a big leap from the Model T's that were all the rage when I last operated a vehicle. In retrospect, I came to the conclusion that not much had changed other than the dirt roads being replaced by asphalt and concrete. It took another half hour to figure out the grid of the city streets. Once I got my bearings and felt comfortable, I cruised into a Pure filling station on the outskirts of South Broward county where, according to Lady T, there was a large Haitian and Trinidadian community. I paid the attendant and asked him to fill it up. I forgot about the convenience and anonymity that the city provided. Everyone was too preoccupied with their own lives to pay me any attention. I went inside the tiny convenience store attached to the garage and purchased a Miami tribune newspaper, a map of south and central Florida, a couple books of matches, and four packs of Benson & Hedges cigarettes.

From what I read in the newspaper, Alabama seemed to be a hotbed for many of the people's struggles in the South, so I decided to head toward ground zero: Birmingham. The Klan was said to have permeated all levels of government in the state and were doing everything in their power to deny the human and civil rights of the Negroes there. If the bastards only knew that the Reichstalls and bloodline families like them, used these hate organizations to perform acts of terrorism and widen the chasm between the races of humans. Causing them to remain poor and fight each other over the same table scraps while the ruling elite just sit back and reap the rewards.

Chapter 18

Kate gets up and walks over to the marble credenza behind the sofa to refill her wine glass.

"You know, "she takes a sip of merlot before beginning again.

"I have to admit that I have been highly skeptical of you the whole night, but something you just said a minute ago made me remember a story my dad once told me. As the family tells it, Nathan Reichstall was rumored to have been stricken with severe dementia in his later years due to lead poisoning from the paint in his mansion. The symptoms he was said to experience were manifested as massive delusions where he would say and do things that were contrary to his otherwise sound and even keeled manner.

The story my dad would tell us is that Nathan Reichstall was so obsessed with a particular rare slave that he spent half the family fortune scouring the world for this one man and nearly bankrupted the famliy's financial services business. A man that he, for some reason, felt was extremely valuable. Nathan Reichstall was also known to be very heavily into the occult and nearly banished from England for some of his more heretical dialogue against the Protestant church. But if you are that man that my great-great-great grandfather was obsessing over, what I don't understand is why you would seek help from someone like me who hails from the same family that has ruined your life and hunted you like a dog for two centuries? You're taking a huge chance right now, so please explain to me a little better how you came to the conclusion that someone like me would even give a damn and help a stranger like you exact their *'undying'* retribution on my, albeit estranged, but nonetheless family?" Kate sits with her new drink and checks the phone to ensure the voice recorder is still running.

I take a drag from my cigarette and exhale the smoke before I look at her solemnly for a moment and say plainly,

"The Art of War, my dear. Keep your enemies close. I assure you all will be revealed shortly. May I continue?" I ask her over-politely while tapping out the flame end of my cigarette in the ashtray next to me.

Kate crosses her legs and waves her hand in a circle as if to say *'get on with it,'* giving her approval exasperatingly.

I sit forward in my chair and begin my tale once again.

"As I said, I was headed to Birmingham to confront the beast that I vowed to defeat. My only thoughts were of staying underground and off radar while I gathered intel on how best to proceed. There is an ancient African proverb that states 'God looks after fools and babies. Given that I am as big a fool as they come. Providence shone down upon me once again. It was during these next few years in Alabama that I would meet the person that would suggest that I try and contact someone close to the Reichstall family who may not be happy with how things were being run and ask them for help in infiltrating their inner cabal. From the day I received my freedom, I had been hell bent on finding an Achilles heel that would give me an advantage over them if I were to ever try and mount an attack on their empire. When I read about your activism toward wanting to expose some of your family's more closely held secrets in hope's of making your lineage's name more palpable to the world, I figured I may be on to something. I confirmed my suspicions about you when we met at the museum exhibit in New York all those years ago. From that day forward, the plan included you as the perfect Trojan Horse into the inner sanctum of the Reichstalls and eventually the top brass of the Incalculaba.

Kate shifts in her chair uncomfortably at the boldness of my statement, her lips involuntarily curling up into a scowl as my words suddenly

328

touch a chord of truth that she has been suppressing up until this very moment.

I point to Kate with a fresh cigarette between my index and middle finger, looking directly into her eyes and say, "Your open rejection of the imperialist system was the spark of hope for me that this world could be different if people only knew the truth."

For a moment it seemed as if the words landed a blow to Kate Reichstall's tough, cynical demeanor but it was only in passing because she shot right back at me,

"Spare me your psychoanalytical bullshit," she says, mockingly rolling her eyes. "I've come to terms with my family's shit a long time ago, and you know what I've come to realize?" she asks rhetorically. "I don't hold anything against them for rising to the top. Sure, they may have owned slaves but so did everyone during that era. Sure, there were some back-office deals made or some market manipulation to sway financials in our favor, but it's nothing worse than what Chase bank and Goldman Sachs do every day of the week. Let's get one thing straight here, buddy. I carry no shame for the history of my family and for you to imply such is rude and out of line. Now I suggest you hurry up and finish your story before I lose the little patience you've already managed to tread upon."

Kate finishes her scolding of me. Her chest heaving, she is visibly shaking after her mini tirade. She walks over to the fireplace and grabs the shotgun which is leaning against the mantle and places it on the floor next to her chair before taking her seat again. There is a long awkward pause between us and without looking up to meet her watery eyes, I continue my story.

"I think I left off when I was just arriving back stateside because of my deep curiosity about the American civil rights movement. I felt that the United States drove the overall global movement for liberation. Some of that was due to its robust national media infrastructure that loved the ratings jumps when it reported on racial conflicts. After leaving Fort Lauderdale and heading northwest through Georgia and into Alabama, I stopped in a city just outside of Birmingham called Fairfield that boasted a thriving Negro population centered around a historically black university called Miles College. I decided to remain in this area for a while to gather intel, gauge the atmosphere of the movement, and ascertain whether I could be of some assistance while maintaining a low profile. I managed to find lodging through ads for boarders in the local Negro gazette, and I wound up staying in the basement apartment of an elderly widow named Thelma Garner or, Ms. Thelma as everyone in the neighborhood referred to her as.

Ms.Thelma was skeptical at first but eventually she bought my story about working at night because of my sun sensitivity after I offered to pay her six months' rent in advance on top of the deposit. This God-fearing little community of hardworking people was exactly the cover I needed to find out information about the world at large and still blend in and keep a low profile. I knew if I resurfaced with any fervor, it would be no time before agents of the Incalculaba realized that I was still alive and all hell would break loose again so I was sure to keep a low profile whenever I had to move in public. I needed to feel the pulse of the people. I truly wanted to know if this movement was really a heartfelt cry from the Negro populous. A solid attempt to throw off the yoke of second-class citizenship or if the whole thing was some type of sick deception by the elite to use integration by Negroes into mainstream society as a tranquilizer to quell any future revolution. At night, I would visit the campus of Miles College and check the student organizing bulletin board for notices of civil rights organization meetings being held on campus or at local churches and homes of activists. I needed a connection with the people if I was to be able to assist them in any meaningful way, but finding someone I could trust and who would not be terrified of what I was seemed a bridge too far.

There had been violence against some of these black organizers by the local Ku Klux Klan who disguised themselves by wearing plain clothes. They weren't working alone either. Police officers, sheriffs, pretty much the rest of the Southeastern United States during the tumultuous years of the Fifties and Sixties were violently attacking Negroes. Oftentimes the church deacons and other men of the community would carry shotguns and pistols to serve as security for the meetings and rallies held around the city. This security was especially crucial during the night hours when the Klan was sure to be out cruising for trouble.

During many of these night meetings, I would lurk in the shadows on dark rooftops and under the crepuscular spaces of homes and other structures and listen to what was being said. One night, I was prowling above an old storefront on 16th Street and 6th Avenue North near downtown Birmingham where a voters registration signup was taking place for members of the church next door. As the people filed in, I leaped onto the roof of the church so that I could better hear the message. A patrol car turned left onto 16th and was suspiciously driving slowly past the front door of the church. The line of people was out the door as people packed into the sanctuary to hear the dynamic young speaker. I read in the newspaper that he was one of the leaders of the bus boycott movement and the main voice in leading the charge against segregation using nonviolent protest. The wind began to pick up slightly on that early October night and I settled into a stable position near a window as the last few stragglers filed into the church. I watched from my perch as another police patrol car pulled into the parking lot of the Jockey Boy restaurant next door and parked with its headlights facing the front door of the church. I put aside my immediate concerns and tried to listen to the rousing message being given inside the building.

Afterwards, as the people finished registering to vote and began to file out, it was coming on 9:00 p.m. The congregants who lived in walking distance were encouraged to leave in groups for safety against attacks by the Klan and their sympathizers. The irregular actions of the police patrols were beginning to unnerve me. One of the worst pitfalls about organizing and combating the system in the fight for justice is the betrayal risk by your so-called brothers and sisters that was ever present. I knew there were some informants at the meeting who were at this very moment reporting back to their superiors some of the inflammatory remarks that were being made tonight about local law enforcement and their ties to the Klan. I had only reentered the world of mankind a few short weeks ago and from what I had learned of the constantly increasing influence of the bloodline elites and their military industrial complex, corrupt financial systems, and rigged political structures, it seemed absurd to try to organize an offensive against them. I had yet to find any real connection to the movement, and I was beginning to think it was pointless to try and that I should just return to a remote cave in the jungle for the next thousand years and hope that maybe society will have changed for the better on its own. Unbeknownst to me that night, I was to meet the very person who would provide my reconnection with the grid and with humanity.

"Let go of me, Goddammit!!!!

AAAAAAUUGH"

I heard a short, muffled scream of a woman. Instinctively, I raced down the side of the building towards the sound which was about two blocks east of the front door of 16th Street Baptist. I had not noticed anyone walking this way because I figured everyone would avoid directly passing the Jockey Boy restaurant because of the known frequent police presence there and the fact that teenagers and other troublemakers were always waiting around to harass passers-by. I asked myself who would be stupid enough or maybe bold enough to go that direction to get back to the neighborhood at this time of night knowing the racial climate we were in.

I kept to the darkness as I approached the site where I heard the scream, and I could see two male figures scuffling with a smaller female figure between them. One of the men was restraining her arms and attempting to cover her mouth while the other man switched between fondling her breasts and punching her in the gut. I leapt from the rooftop and landed hard on the cold concrete of the alley. As I ran towards the trio, a third man, who I did not detect because of all the odors coming from the dumpsters filled with rotten food in the alley, sprang from his crouched position behind a pile of debris and swung at me with a blackjack. I caught his weapon wielding hand with my left and squeezed it hard, crushing his bones and causing the blackjack to fall to the ground. I lifted him up into the air by his neck and body slammed him to the pavement into unconsciousness. We would find out almost two decades later that the man who I left crippled on the ground that night was the nephew of a local grand wizard of the Ku Klux

332

Klan who, in retaliation to what happened to his nephew, would plant a bomb inside 16th Street Baptist church the following year that would kill four innocent young girls.

After their accomplice failed to be much of a deterrent, the man holding the woman makes a deft move with his right hand, spinning the woman around before she falls to the ground. He and his partner book it up the alley in retreat. As I started to give chase after the cowards, the rich smell of fresh blood struck me and I froze in my tracks and ran back towards the woman on the ground. A pool of blood was forming around her head like a halo, and now I could see that the man had slashed her throat open as he was pushing her to the ground.

I lifted her head off the cold concrete floor, and I saw the light from her beautiful, scared brown eyes begin to fade. For a second, she reminded me of Colette the night I held her lifeless body. Saving her life may prove to be far more of a punishment than allowing her to perish here. My curse would only guarantee her a life of misery. I was not completely sure if it would work. Before I knew what I was doing, I slit my wrist with my claw and squeezed out a few drops of blood into the open wound on her neck. It was quick but I was able to get a decent flow before my body began to heal. The blood seeping from the gash on her neck stopped immediately and the skin began to seal itself as if on a zipper. I pulled out my handkerchief and wiped the excess blood from her face and neck. I looked over at the guy I just K.O.'d and realized that this could turn into a real mess if I didn't leave soon. The woman's breathing was very weak but once I was satisfied that she would not go into shock I scooped up her limp body from the ground and carried her to my car. I quickly drove to my basement apartment in Fairfield.

After a tense two days passed of constantly placing cooling rags on her forehead, lowering her body in a bath of cool water to fight her dangerously high fever, and watching her unceasingly through fits of restless sleeping, the woman awoke from her stupor at 3:04 a.m. on a Sunday morning to two colorless eyes staring right at her from across the dark, unfamiliar room. To my surprise, her initial reaction was not to scream or run and cower away from me. Instead, she silently and slowly pulled the covers up over her head.

Still not believing that she was alive, she felt for the wound on her neck with her right hand. Her fingers caressed a small keloid in place of the hole that should have been across her caramel neck. "How am I alive?" she wondered as she vividly remembered the cold steel of the knife slashing across her collarbone.

I put on my shades to keep her from being any more frightened than she already was.

It was dark but she could tell that the sheets and blanket were clean. She can feel that she's wearing something like a long nightgown and not the dress she wore to the voter registration meeting. The last thing she remembered was being on the wet ground of the alley

Questions flooded her mind — "What happened? Where Am I? How did I get here? Where are my clothes and pocketbook? How long was I unconscious? What kind of human has eyes that glow white in the dark?"

She wondered why she didn't scream and run like hell out of there. She was always very empathic and despite the circumstances, none of the energy she was receiving at the time gave her any signals that she was in any danger.

"This must be the person she saw in the alley just before she was cut" she remembered. She owed this person her life. The least she can do is thank them. The woman took a series of deep breaths in an effort to regain her composure and arrange her thoughts. Politeness was a virtue that her mother and father always stressed to her. Gradually, she poked her head up from under the covers.

Her eyes searched the dark room for me. She noticed a bubbling sound coming from the area near the door. As her eyes adjusted she saw the silhouette of a broad shouldered man seated about fifteen feet away from her. She tried to speak but the muscles in her neck and throat were still raw from the attack, and she was only able to produce a hoarse, brittle whispering sound at first. "I-I-I'm sorry for my poor manners but, where am...?"

PHWWEEEEEEEEEEEEEEEEEEEEE!!!!!!!

She gasped and nearly jumped out of her skin at the shriek of the tea kettle whistling on the stove across the room. I moved over to the kitchen to stop the noise and poured the hot liquid into two cups. I flipped on the dull light in the kitchen. This was the first time I had used it. The woman attempted to sit up on her own but her body was still weak and shaking like a leaf from the shock of the attack. I helped her into a sitting position and placed a cup of tea on the nightstand. After a few sips she whispered to me again.

"Thank you for the tea." Pausing between sentences, "My name is Lynn... Lynn Chesimard.

Can you please tell me what happened?"

When I didn't answer immediately, Her eyes filled with tears as her mind recalled the terror and desperation she felt during the attack.

Whispering, she said, "Wh-Who are you? How long have I been here?" she mumbled, her voice trailing away. She wiped the tears from her eyes. "I'm sorry this is all a little much. I forgot to ask you what your name is?"

My mother had given me a name, but it had been over 150 years since I went by that moniker and I was a completely different person now. Rather, I thought of the name that Bella would call me in her playful French Creole accent. After a very long awkward pause, I say

"Dusange"

"I owe you my life Mr. Dusange but I must be leaving now my mother must be going crazy looking for me..." As Lynn spoke she swung her legs over the side of the bed and she tried to stand but she was still too weak and the world started spinning as she passed out and fell back down onto the bed.

Ten minutes passed before Lynn's eyelids began to flutter to life again and she slowly opened her eyes to the dimly lit room. As she remembered where she was Lynn just lay there as she stared at the cracks in the ceiling for a full minute and without turning her head.

Lynn's breathing was fast and shallow. Suddenly she turned to her side and vomited a mixture of tea and stomach acid onto the side of the bed and floor before passing out again. Over the next few minutes, I monitored her pulse and watched closely for any signs of seizure or any stoppage in breathing. As I knelt down next to the bed to clean up the mess I heard Lynn whisper,

"Where am I?" "How am I still alive?"

"You are safe here. Please try to rest so your body can become stronger. Your injuries were so severe that I had to take drastic measures in order to save your life. I was not sure it would work but I shared my life force with you and I was able to heal your wound and prevent you from bleeding to death on the floor of the alley that night. That was three nights ago"

"Lifeforce?" Lynn asks.

"You were losing blood at a rapid pace and there was no time to take you to a hospital that would accept Negroes. I thought that if I shared some of mine with you it would heal the hole in your neck. My hunch was correct but you had already lost so much blood that your body had turned pale and your pulse was extremely weak. Not knowing what else to do I brought you here to my apartment in Fairfield. I admittedly did not think you would survive through that first night."

Lynn slowly turned her head toward me and sat up onto her elbows, weakly, solemnly she said in a low whisper, "Thank you for saving my life. Overwhelmed by emotion, tears began welling up in her eyes.

"When those men grabbed me and I felt the cold metal of that knife across my throat, I remember thinking how my father always used to quote Isaiah 54 — *No weapon formed against me shall prosper.* I immediately began to ask the Lord for deliverance from those evil men. That's when you appeared. When the man cut me… and I felt the blood running down my chest. I thought, please God, don't let me die here in this filthy alley. He sent you to be my guardian angel." Lynn reached out to wrap her arms around my torso and began to sob uncontrollably. I gently placed my arm around her.

"God sent a miracle" she moaned through an ocean of tears.

We sat in that position for what felt like an hour or more until Lynn was completely out of tears.

"The sun will be up soon and I must take you home." I reminded her in a low tone.

I offered to carry Lynn to the car but she was adamant about walking. I had stolen the nightgown she was wearing from a neighboring clothesline, but the fit was perfect. I washed as much blood as I could from the clothes she was wearing during the attack and had placed them neatly in a paper bag along with her purse.

I put on my hat and jacket before wrapping a blanket around Lynn's shoulders and helping to put her shoes on. Once we were sure she could stand and move around without feeling dizzy, I gathered her things and we slowly and silently made our way to the car. Lynn gave me directions on how to get to her house which was a little less than a mile from 16th Street Baptist Church where she was attacked.

"I will walk you to the door and then I must take my leave" I said to Lynn not turning to face her as I spoke.

"Please?" Lynn said pretending to be insulted. "You have to at least meet my parents." Smiling at the thought she continued, "they gone shout hallelujah when they see me. They'll be so happy that I'm home. And when I tell 'em it's all on the count of you saving me from some crazy white men, I'm sure my father will give you a hero's welcome. And my mother is surely going to want to bake you one of her signature German chocolate cakes."

Lynn searched my expressionless face for some type of reaction. She could sense that what she was proposing made me uncomfortable and did not pursue the subject any further. We exited the car into the darkness of the early morning. I carried the paper bag with Lynn's belongings in my left hand as she used my right arm to steady herself. Her unstrapped shoes scraped the concrete of the driveway as we approached a door near the carport of the house. As we reached the door, Lynn quietly rapped on the screen. After about fifteen seconds muffled voices were heard and a light in the front room flipped on, feet were heard shuffling towards the front door.

"Is prolly is the police come to tell us sumpin bout CoraLynn, you ain't gon' need dat shotgun Jerry!" A voice was heard coming from inside the house.

"Seem mighty early fa da police." An you know they don' be tappin' light like dat." Replies another voice as it approaches the door.

"Who is it!?" A man's voice shouted threateningly.

The curtain covering a small rectangular window on the door is pushed aside and a serious looking wrinkly brown face with a gray beard and mustache peered out. The man's eyes went wide as If he had seen a ghost.

"JESUS!! LORD!!

LUCILLE!!!

CORALYNN OUT HERE!!!!"

338

The sound of fumbling with the door latch was heard over the thump of a stampede of horses barreling toward the door. The dingy white wooden door swung open,

"AAAAAAIIIIGGGHHH,

THANK YOU LAWD!!

JESUSSSSS!!

MY JESUSSSSS!!!"

Lynn's jubilant father, mother and two sisters exploded out into the cool early morning air with nothing but their robes and nightgowns jumping and shouting and praising God in wild abandonment. Some of the neighbors getting up for work turned on their porch lights to see what the commotion was about.

"MY GOD!!!!!"

"He answers prayers!!!!" proclaims Lynn's mother as she squeezes Lynn while rocking back and forth.

"Are you OK?"

"Did they hurt ya?"

"How did you get here?"

"What happened?"

"Where did you get this gran'mama nightgown?" Lynn's sisters fire off a barrage of questions while searching her body for scratches and bruises.

"I'm fine, I'm fine. Just fine thank the Lord Jesus Christ! He sent Mr. Dusan…"

Lynn looked around in every direction past her doting family, but I was nowhere in sight.

"Mister who child?" questions Lucille, Lynn's mother.

"He was—He wa—" Looking into her mother's eyes Lynn bursts into tears and hugs her tightly. Something inside her breaks loose and she begins sobbing uninhibitedly.

"It's alright baby, you wit mama now. You wit' yo' family now. You safe!". Promised Lucille.

All members of the family were crying now as they huddled around Lynn. The sun slowly crested the horizon of the new day.

Chapter 19

That winter was rough for Birmingham and the entire Civil Rights movement. All over the country the pushback against segregation and discrimination sparked racial tensions and violent clashes. I avoided as much human interaction as possible, only speaking to Ms. Thelma twice in a five-month period. Allowing myself to get close to Lynn was idiotic on my part. Any relationship I could not walk away from in a moment's notice was too dangerous to entertain. Her entire family could be at risk of being murdered simply for being seen with me. For weeks the image of her beautiful sleeping face haunted my every waking moment. No matter how much I tried to suppress it, I could not shake the thought of her. It was like an irrepressible flame on the tip of a match being battered by the blizzard within my heart.

I sat in the darkness of my apartment one afternoon smoking a cigarette and reading a copy of Frantz Fanon's Wretched of the Earth I acquired from a book bag I found near the college. I thought I was hallucinating when the scent of Lynn's hair and skin wafted through the room. I closed the book and sat up in disbelief as to what my nose was telling me. I thought I had gotten over my infatuation with her weeks ago. I hear footsteps on the stairs leading to my basement apartment and they do not sound like the slow careful steps of Ms. Thelma but of someone younger with better balance, moving on the balls of their feet.

I extinguished the cigarette, stood and put on my shirt and dark glasses. There was a gentle tapping on the door and — "Mr. DuSange It's me... Lynn Chesimard."

I opened the door and just stared down at her in disbelief. She was even more beautiful than I remembered.

"I wanted to return this blanket and the nightgown." She says while holding the neatly folded items out towards me.

I snapped back to reality and my paranoia kicked in. I looked up the stairs behind her.

"Are you alone? ... How did you find me?... You should not be here. Your life could be in danger if we are seen together." I told her as I pulled her into the apartment and closed and locked the door behind her.

Lynn was crushed. "I'm sorry, I just—I wanted to..." she stammered

Realizing my faux pas, I softened my tone and apologized. "It is I who should be sorry. Please forgive me. I am not used to visitors. Thank you for returning these. Please, sit and I will make you some tea." I offered her the only chair I had and moved to the kitchen to turn on the light.

"Thank you!" She said with a smile as she took her seat still holding the blanket and nightgown on her lap.

"You are a very difficult man to find Mr. DuSange. I grew up a couple blocks over on Court F and I thought I knew this neighborhood. Between me and my sisters we know every family over here but asking around, no one had ever heard of or seen anyone like you. If it hadn't been for Ms. Thelma's gossiping to my mom at church about the new hat and dress she was able to afford because of her new tenant, I wouldn't have had any clues to go on. My mom had to press her but she let slip that you were a tall man who kept to himself, so she rarely saw you.

342

My mother and father took me to the hospital that day you dropped me back home to make sure I wasn't raped or anything. The doctors said they could tell I had lost a lot of blood and received a concussion recently but there was no sign of my throat being cut open. They even suggested that it might not have happened and that maybe the trauma of the incident may have caused me to create the part about being cut in my mind. But I know what I felt. My bloody blouse and jacket are the only real proof I have of that night. My family says it was a miracle from God and I should just be happy that I am alive and well. But for some reason I can't let it go. And I also can't stop thinking of you."

Her words hung in the air between us.

"Please explain to me what you meant when you said you shared your... lifeforce with me."

Being the empath that she was Lynn could tell I did not feel totally comfortable spilling my guts to what amounted to a complete stranger so to make me more at ease she began by telling me her life story.

Cora Lynn Chesimard was born in 1937 to a loving family of three children, she being the youngest, near what is known as Dolomite, Alabama. A town rich in the mineral it was named for. Her parents were both literate and felt that it was important that Negroes get an education in order to be able to provide for themselves. A few years after Lynn was born the family moved to Fairfield for better work opportunities near the city. Both of her parents were Garveyites and raised their children to be proud of their race and the achievements of their people no matter what. In 1945, her father was one of the millions of black men who registered for the draft during World War II to prove their bravery and intelligence to the dehumanizing American society. He was injured on the battlefield serving with the 761st Tank Battalion in a French city called Morville-les-Vic. When he returned stateside his injuries severely limited his options for meaningful work. To supplement the income lost from her father's disability Lynn's mother and older sisters began working at the textile processing factory which afforded the family a near middle class lifestyle for Negroes at the time. Over the next few years, Lynn's family was able to scrape and save enough money to afford to send Cora to Hampton University in Virginia where she received her bachelor's degree in education. The night she was attacked, she had just been elected as one of the lead organizers for a *March on Washington*, planned by the Westfield and Ensley high school student committees and local Hopewell Missionary Baptist churches in which her father was a founding member.

Lynn said she felt so energized by the speaker at the voter registration meeting that night that she decided to take that shortcut because she believed Negroes should start acting fearlessly to invoke the protection of Jesus against their enemies. She also told me repeatedly me that *"the Lord sent me to rescue her so that she could continue the fight for Negro rights in the Jim Crow South."* She talked at length about her aspirations to make the world a better place than how she found it. She expressed to me that she felt I was sent by God to be her 'guardian angel' and watch over her during times of peril to allow her to truly fulfill her calling. During our subsequent years together, I would realize that it was *she* who was the true angel who would provide the catalyst for me to have the courage to change the world.

We talked for a few hours that first day although Lynn did most of the talking. I explained to her my need to avoid sunlight, but I was careful not to reveal anything about my life that might frighten her away. I also managed to avoid the subject of my blood and how she was healed that night. We were both smitten but I stressed to her my need to maintain a low profile for the sake of both of our lives. We decided to meet every second and fourth Wednesday of the month at 9 p.m. Our courtship was very non-traditional. Many of our dates were spent just sitting in my car for hours discussing politics and the social climate surrounding us. Lynn was a dreamer. She was also very passionate about civil and human rights for all marginalized people. I delighted in listening to her talk about her ideas and theories on how to create a more egalitarian world. As we discovered safer, more secluded areas to meet, our car discussions evolved into late night strolls and picnics in the dark where we drank wine and I watched her eat.

After eight months of regular meeting Lynn's mother and father confronted her about where she was going and who she was spending so much time with on a regular basis. She was forced to tell them about our relationship and to her surprise they gave her their blessing to be with me. They merely wanted to confirm their suspicions. They could tell that she was head over heels for me and that the joy for life that she had before the attack in the alley had returned since our dating began. Her family's only stipulation was that if we decided to elope and leave Alabama Lynn would come back to visit them from time to time.

Lynn and I were active lovers for the next five years living between Atlanta, New York, and D.C. She was my everything. I entrusted her with the knowledge of all my strengths and weaknesses. We were so inseparable that when she was unable to find a job teaching at night, I attempted to force myself to sleep during the night and function during the day just to be able to spend more time with her. I totally lost myself in her. She, in her wisdom, would always remind me of my purpose and mission and the need to stay focused on the larger struggle that our people were immersed in.

I provided for our lifestyle by supplying Lynn with income in the form of gold and jewelry from my years with Black Caesar. She would transfer it to cash and use the proceeds to buy whatever we needed which included multiple cars, our home in the Kirkwood neighborhood of Atlanta, Georgia and a two-bedroom apartment in Harlem. She would also send money home to her parents which allowed her mother to be able to stay home and care for her father. Since Lynn's family were the main trustees of the church, all our cars, clothes, and food and necessities were able to be expensed through the church to keep the I.R.S. off our trail. Much of the treasure was used to set up investment accounts and make real estate investments that provided funds, land, and housing to the poorest of the community.

Many stumbling blocks presented themselves in those first few tumultuous years Lynn and I spent together between 1963 and 1968. The enemy we had chosen to face was indeed a formidable one. As with any movement involving humans, the use of assassination against figures like Medgar Evers, Malcolm X, and countless others served to infuriate the masses which reinforced awareness but also put the fear of uncertainty about the efficacy of the movement into the minds of the masses. The Panthers tried, and we really had hope that there was finally an organization that could really create a grassroots foundation for nation building without a religious bent, but the *'behemoth'* under the guise of the United States government used its many influences to dismantle and sow discord within that organization and was able to unravel it completely and scatter its leadership. The bloodline elites coordinate with the major Anglo governments of the world to keep doing everything in their power to keep the masses disenfranchised and impoverished economically while politically and socially touting democracy and independence. It always seemed that despite our best efforts, there was no end to the war with the beast in sight. Some of the darkest times faced between me and Lynn was the day Martin Luther King was assassinated. The cohesion of the movement seriously began to deteriorate, and the unbiased anger of the multitude spilled into the streets again.

My own anger towards the founders of this globally oppressive system began to balloon out of control. I tried my best to keep myself grounded by spending my time worshiping Lynn and trying to reinforce any and every initiative she was involved with as far as human and civil rights were concerned. However, with the focus of our strategies leaning mainly toward nonviolent methods of retaliation, I started feeling like I was neglecting the larger mission and should be more active in the hunt for the main lieutenants of the Incalculaba starting with the current Reichstall heir.

Two nights after the assassination of King, Lynn and I were in the living room of our Harlem brownstone having a huge argument. I felt that blacks integrating with whites in America would destroy the networks and value systems that made us so formidable in the eyes of the powers that be, and that any black people pushing integration were knowingly signing the death certificate for Negroes in America. It was a sentiment that she totally disagreed with because there were many people who fought and died for Negro rights who were not Negroes themselves, all in the hopes for the world to be more accepting of all races. In my anger, I went too far, I broke Lynn's heart when I let slip that I had entertained the thought that she may have

346

been sent by the Incalculaba as a deep cover agent assigned to fuck me and keep me distracted from my mission to exact my revenge. She annihilated me in return by revealing that she had secretly undergone several abortions and had been faithfully taking birth control pills. She was afraid that if she was to become pregnant that she would have some type of aberration for a baby that she could only raise at night and feed with blood and raw meat until one day it would devour her.

After that night, we began to spend less time together. Eventually we broke off the relationship when she accepted a day job back in Alabama as a principal of a recently segregated Jim Crow school. Unbeknownst to me, Lynn had been growing disillusioned with the greater movement. She felt that she could do more for children and Negroes on a grass roots level as a part of the rural school administration. Lynn gave me most of the cash she had converted from gold and transferred all our business holdings and properties to her parents' church foundation and left our apartment in Harlem a month later. After receiving her forwarding address, I could no longer stand America, and I left for Angola, Cuba, Ghana, Kenya, the Soviet Union, and Vietnam amongst other controversial hotspots where I felt I could thwart the plans of the Incalculaba and the bloodline elites on the battlefield which is where I did my best work.

During our time together, Lynn had fake credentials created for me to be able to travel abroad and made me an authorized user on all her charge card accounts which remained active well after our split. I made sure to leave a substantial portion of the treasure in Lynn's possession that would maintain her and her family's lives for generations. That was the year 1970, and it would be another fifteen years before I would return to the States. While I was globetrotting on my one-man army crusade to bring freedom to the world, Lynn was starting the family she always wanted but was afraid to have with me. Two years after our separation, she married Dr. David Alexander White who was a Meharry Medical College graduate and was able to open a small general practitioners' clinic in Manila, Alabama, a few miles from the school that Lynn a headmaster position. They had three children and many more grandchildren, all of whom received great educations and were taught to be pillars of the community and staunch supporters of civil and human rights throughout the decades. After teaching for thirty years, she retired from the school system and bought a small self-sustained farm near Gosport, Alabama, to live out her days and enjoy her family in peace.

When I finally returned to the States in the summer of 1984, I decided to reside in Philadelphia as opposed to New York to give myself some new surroundings that would not remind me of my time with Lynn. I was able to rent a small studio apartment in West Philadelphia near Osage Avenue. During my time there, I befriended some activists that organized themselves under the moniker of MOVE which was originally the Christian Movement for Life. After listening to John Africa and his philosophies on the advocation of family values, I began assisting MOVE and some of the local community activist groups in persuading some of the dope pushers and pimps that continued to prey on the community to move on while keeping an eye on the corrupt police forces of the city that were actively engaged in a war on the people. The independence and civil rights movement of the sixties and seventies dealt a serious blow to the colonial holdings of the Incalculaba and they were forced to come up with alternate ways to divide and conquer the masses. The 1980's saw a tremendous influx of drug use and subsequently a disproportionate use of law enforcement and unfair prison sentencing to disrupt and neutralize many of the leaders and activists of the previous decades.

Ever since I resurfaced in Soweto in 1976, The current Reichstall heir and his agents had been busy building a worldwide network of task forces specifically assigned to identify and neutralize me and anyone aiding and abetting me. I was wholly unaware of the level of surveillance tech and portable computer technology the Incalculaba possessed. I believed that I still had the advantage of anonymity, but I would soon find out I was square in their bullseye. To send a message, the Incalculaba resorted to using a shocking amount of force to get rid of me again like their near successful attempt in Tulsa sixty years ago.

The Philadelphia police issued warrants for the leadership of MOVE and when the police arrived, tensions flared out of control and there was a gunshot heard which instantly broke down communications between the two sides and a gun battle ensued. During a firefight between police and some of the members of MOVE, the police dropped a bomb on the main building in broad daylight, causing a fire that would get so out of control that it would burn down the entire block of Osage and Pine Streets, destroying dozens of buildings, leaving hundreds of people stranded and homeless and killing much more than the eleven victims reported by the historical text. The police and national guard were given explicit orders by the top state and city officials to treat MOVE like a rogue terrorist group and were ordered to fire on anyone trying to flee the building to finish off the survivors and stamp out the flames of resistance in the black people of Philadelphia and the world for that matter. My apartment and everything in it burned to cinders, and I was left without anything except the clothes I was wearing and 78 dollars in my pocket. I lost all my books, my identification and over 63,000 dollars in cash to the fire. I was forced to hop Amtrak and flee to New York to get lost in the shuffle of the metropolis for a few months. Stalking the streets at night and eating whatever vermin I could get my hands on for sustenance, living in subway tunnels and sewers to escape detection by Reichstall's agents. It was December, six months since the fire in Philadelphia, when I finally had the gall to contact anyone. I had to find Lynn.

I called her collect at her home in Alabama from a phone booth on 125th Street and St. Nicholas Avenue in Harlem. As soon as we heard each other's voice, all the years of animosity melted away, and we both were moved to tears as we caught up on old times. She used her husband's business credentials to rent a one room apartment for me on Gun Hill Road in White Plains New York, just north of the Bronx. After a week in the apartment, I received a birthday card from her with 5,000 dollars in large bills inside. This would serve as operational money while I figured out what my next move should be. I felt that the plan to topple Reichstall was missing something. I needed someone that could prove to the world what I knew about the wickedness of the bloodline elites and their unnecessary negative influence on the world. Someone close to the matter with an ironclad reputation that could validate my accusations as the truth. That was when my attention was brought to you, and I took my chance that night in Soho at the Rubin Art Gallery.

Chapter 20

Kate rolls her eyes, and trying to sound as nonchalant as possible, she asks, "About that...in the movies, they always portray vampires that can control women and certain animals with their mystical powers of hypnosis. Oftentimes ravaging them sexually under a mesmerizing spell. Once eye contact is made, they can't resist the mojo." She stands and walks slowly toward me. "The women, of course. Not the animals." Then her voice changed from a playful one to a more serious one. "Did you use that power on me that night at the art gallery just to disappear and show up on my doorstep as a crazy person thirty years later?"

I look at the floor and after another of many awkward pauses, I begin quietly. "I hate to disappoint you," I tell her. "I wish there was some 'arcane telepathy' I could use to have my way with people, but that's just something that Hollywood came up with to sell movies. Now that being said, I do possess enhanced senses that allow me to feel when female creatures are pregnant or experiencing their menstrual cycles. There is also a certain confidence that comes with being immortal that translates as fearlessness and confidence to humans, especially women, who all seem to possess some degree of supernatural intuition. In addition, certain sensitive non-domesticated animals that are traditionally connected to the ancient mysteries such as wolves, ravens, dolphins, and snakes respond with a certain degree of agitation when in my presence — "

"I-I get it," she says, waving me off and lighting another cigarette.

My response does not seem to suffice for Kate, and there is another long uncomfortable silence between us as she paces back and forth in front of me, searching for the right words to express her feelings. She walks over to her chair and picks up her ashtray and taps the cherry of the cigarette violently into the glass, nearly extinguishing it. Her body tensed with frustration and irritation as if my answer was nowhere in the ballpark of what she wanted to hear.

"You made such an impression on me that night at the art gallery," Kate begins earnestly. "Being a Reichstall, I've always been in the spotlight and been treated as 'special' by everyone who thought that by befriending me, they could finagle an inroads to my family's wealth and influence for their own selfish purposes. And so, from a very young age, I had always been very wary of strangers and avoided trusting anyone who showed undue interest in me outside of our tight knit family circle. But that night, after our whirlwind conversation, I felt an incredible connection between us, and I etched your face into my memory banks."

Kate takes a long pull of the cigarette, reigniting it and then exhales cigarette smoke over my head looking directly into my eyes for the next few sentences.

"Being in New York and living with a family like mine...at times you meet a hundred people in a day and maybe one or two of them make enough of an impression on you that you might remember their names the next day, if you're lucky. Everything moved constantly, frenetically...It was those formative years when I networked my ass off, even using a misspelling of my last name to hide my connection to my family because I was determined to make it 'my way' and on 'my terms', the rest of the family be damned. I literally have flown all over the globe studying tons of fascinating people and I've documented several incredible cultures while researching ancient civilizations and their connections to the advancement of the sphere of human life in search of something that I was missing." Her staring eyes are wet now and her voice begins to crack. "I have had the privilege to meet some of the most interesting humans on the planet." She pauses and takes a breath, regaining her composure. "But for the last thirty years, I have never forgotten your face or your smile. And what you told me that night… it opened my eyes to what my calling should truly be. You were the catalyst that sent me on a burning quest for the truth." She puts down the ashtray, wipes her eyes with the sleeve of her robe and walks over to the kitchen counter to grab a Kleenex to wipe her nose. She crumples the tissue into her hand and stuffs it into one of the pockets of her robe before walking back into the living room to address me face to face again.

"That night we met was the early nineties," she says, exhaling smoke before wiping her runny nose. "If I was the final piece to your stratagem, then why did you wait all these years until they were able to achieve this draconian level of surveillance and control? What took you so long to try and contact me and why now, why tonight?" Her serious eyes frantically searching mine for some profound, heartfelt sentiment that regrettably, the frost on my heart won't allow.

"As the old saying goes, 'the best laid plans…' I wanted to move much sooner and fill you in on what the plan was and what would be required of us to dismantle this despicable system, but enhancements in surveillance tech over the last twenty years have made it extremely difficult for me to move. As computer and global positioning technology grew exponentially and the globalist indoctrination program began with everyone carrying pagers and then cellphones and now smart watches, before anyone knew it they had eyes and ears everywhere. With the advent of the World Wide Web and the interconnection of previously independent institutions, they made moving above ground anonymously increasingly more and more difficult. The 90's and the early 2000's ushered in an age where the use of cash for car rentals, hotels, and airplane tickets became synonymous with criminality."

"In my travels, I taught myself to take meticulous notes, and I had compiled an extensive handwritten database of damning information that connected the Reichstall's and other bloodline elite to the Incalculaba and everything wrong with this planet. From causing the Great Depression and the Pandemic to the assassination of Martin Luther King, Jr. and Abraham Lincoln. My original plan was to approach you during the Christmas holiday season of 2001. Back then, I was fortunate to have been connected with an inside informant who was an old civil rights acquaintance of Lynn—my ex. This informant's husband had been working in Building Seven of the World Trade Center eight years prior to 9/11. This woman was apparently willing to divulge your family's personal information as a repayment to Lynn for bailing her brother out of prison in 1979 during the Levittown Gas Riots. This woman explained to Lynn that the entire building her husband worked in was a facade which really housed a group of shell companies run for the Reichstalls and other bloodline families. One of their main vectors for moving funds was to create these companies that operated in tax haven zones, registered as consulting firms that managed shipping specifications and tariff allotments for the elites and their North American import/export investments. The informant's husband was afraid that he could be implicated in criminal wrongdoing if anyone ever found out what was really going on so he planned on smuggling out documents that could prove these allegations and expose Reichstall and his cronies to the court of public opinion for their wrongdoings. She and her husband were found dead of carbon monoxide poisoning in her home on September 10th. Any other evidence about Building Seven and its connection with the Incalculaba and the Reichstall family was disintegrated when a couple of hijacked airplanes changed the world as we know it. After that devastation, New York City became a police state and it would be years before I was able to gather enough credible information and risk resurfacing to find you and somehow recruit you in aiding me in taking down your own family and their wicked empire."

•   •   •

I return to my narrative

In the years following the MOVE incident, I continued to build my case against the Incalculaba, but with the advent of smartphones and other giant leaps in surveillance technology, there seemed to be no stopping those devious bastards who held no qualms about stooping to the lowest levels of barbarity to obtain the absolute power necessary to completely control and suppress the populace of earth. For safety's sake, I decided to live in the sewers and subway tunnels deep under the city of Chicago for the next eleven years. New York was already compromised and all my former contacts were either dead or in hiding. I was no longer able to get cash because my correspondence with Lynn had to be discontinued for fear of them ascertaining our connection. It was during those years that I made the shocking discovery that the militarization of law enforcement and the forced increase in the public's acceptance of constant surveillance being used by the global elite was to make certain that their totalitarian agenda to control the world by 2040 was on schedule. The Patriot Act which immediately followed 9/11 seemed to be the next genius play in the realm of draconian governance; enabling the the Incalculaba operating in the United States to create a vast cohesive network of law enforcement out of what was once a jumble of many different agencies and jurisdictions that were reluctant to share information with each other.

My movements became severely restricted, but I was able to stay up on current events by reading discarded newspapers and accessing the internet with an old PowerBook G4 laptop I found in the dumpster that I was able to make work again. I would frequent Internet cafes at night and surf the web anonymously until just before dawn. The internet in those early years was full of .ftp sites that just dumped declassified information onto low security servers which provided me with a veritable treasure trove of information about the secret government and their dirty dealings with multinational corporations and politicians. What became painfully apparent during my research was that globally, there was an outcry from everyday citizens who recognized that humanity was undeniably trapped within a losing race to defeat the forces of the Incalculaba before they obtained absolute and unrestricted domination.

Life below the city served me well. I drew maps of every tunnel and drainage junction I came across and after the first three years of traversing the Chicago underground, I was more than proficient in navigating all the subways and sewer pipes in the city. I could find almost everything I needed from the dumps and landfills throughout the city. All my shoes, clothes and furniture were found items. I even managed to salvage a small rowboat I found in a storm drain near Lake Michigan that had a baseball sized hole in its floor. I lived mostly on rats, pigeons, and other vermin I could find within the tunnels. For some reason I could not bring myself to kill and eat the tons of stray cats and dogs that I encountered in the streets and alleyways. Something about the emotions in their faces just before you snapped their neck was so accusatory.

I could count on one hand the times this happened but, occasionally, I would gorge myself on the blood of the rare human that happened to piss me off. Usually a mobster, gangbanger, crooked cop or belligerent hobo that was unfortunate enough to be committing some type of unforgivable offense in my presence. The people that lived or frequently visited below the pavement had an unspoken agreement to generally leave each other alone and for the most part to be helpful to one another if ever called upon by their fellow social outcasts. Thusly, in and around the immediate vicinity of my lair, I was rarely presented with the opportunity to bare my fangs at anyone so, as a result, it had been a very long time since I tasted human flesh.

Early March 2012, Chicago was still under the thumb of Old Man Winter and despite the talk of global warming, this city was experiencing the exact opposite. Recent upgrades to the sewer and railway systems were creating a negative ripple effect amongst the subterranean population, causing a lot of upheaval at the worst possible time. Whole tent and cardboard cities were being wiped out by Chicago public works crews. The jack hammering and drilling from construction workers around downtown and Magnificent Mile district was constant. Some work crews were taking out entire swaths of concrete from the streets above and replacing it with 8ft. steel plates in order to access and fix the aging pipes and worn-out drainage systems. My hideout was deep below the areas where most humans dared to tread, so I remained relatively safe from any construction projects planned by the city.

After a lifetime of research, crunching numbers and connecting all the pieces of the puzzle that I could gather on my own, I decided I had more than enough information needed to hang these bastards twice and generate an international peace movement to dismantle their stranglehold on the planet once and for all. I required lots of cash to make this thing work, so it was time for me to make my way south again and withdraw the remainder of the treasure I kept hidden. I decided that the best route to avoid detection by

355

the Incalculaba was to travel south by boat down the Mississippi River and reconnect with Lynn in Alabama. She should be able to help me secure the funds and items I need. Once I get the information I have been compiling to someone in the media who was credible and willing to expose these depraved bastards, I could awaken mankind to the notion of bringing the peace of true reality back to the earth.

I still had $1,227 in cash on me. I was carrying about $2500 on me the day I left New York over ten years ago. Living in the sewer doesn't require much capital investment. The only time I used money was to buy parts for my computers, new sunglasses if they were damaged or when I was helping my fellow sewer denizens with donations from time to time. In preparation for my journey, every night I would leave at dusk to travel topside, and I would always emerge from the sewers in an alley behind Walgreens on West 47th Street. In the days before my trip south, I purchased a few different maps of Chicago and the surrounding states at the Walgreens, and I walked over a few blocks to Pulaski Road to purchase some trousers, a hoodie, and another pair of socks from the Crossroads Trading Consignment and Discount Clothing store. I left the Consignment store and quickly headed east back down West 47th Street to Lembke and Sons True Value Hardware to purchase marine glue, duct tape, Bondo, a sheet of rubber, and two cans of matte black spray paint in order to patch up the rowboat. I packed my duffel bag with one complete change of clothes and personal effects including my research files and thumb drives in a large sealable bag that tucked inside my backpack. Using the supplies from the hardware store I patched the hole in my boat and spray painted the entire thing black inside and out.

My hideout sat far below Millennium Park just off Michigan Avenue and East Randolph Street. It was a one room affair built inside a distribution hub which consisted of three large hollowed out caverns that I deduced from the tools I found lying scattered throughout must have been a pre-Civil War era coal mine. The dense population created by the influx of tourists and locals made the area above me the ideal portal for me to pop in and out of the topside world unnoticed.

In order to get out of the city safely and travel nearly five hundred miles south to Alabama, my plan was to row my boat during the night using the current as much as possible and take the Chicago River until it connected to the Chicago Sanitary and Ship Canal which dumped into the Des Plaines River, then down toward Joliet where I would turn southwest into the Illinois river. From there, I would continue southwest down the river into Peoria and finally dump out into the waterways outside of St. Louis, Missouri. My preference for taking cover during the daylight hours would be to find lodging under a bridge or overpass that I could use as a temporary shelter and conceivably pass myself off as homeless and safely rest a few hours until the sun set again. St. Louis should be big enough for me to blend in and lay low long enough to locate a large vessel heading south down the Mississippi River to stow away in. It was ridiculous that a trip that would take only five hours of driving would take me almost three days because of the risk involved if I were to be stopped by police or had a facial scan run on me at a gas station.

As I set out the first night, I carried my boat through the sewers and up to the drainage tunnel that linked with a service canal that I could use to travel down a few miles until it connected into the murky, freezing depths of the Chicago River. Because of the recent rains, the water was moving with more force than usual and as soon as I placed the boat in the water and jumped inside, the vessel was grabbed by the current of the river which jetted the rickety dinghy up to a full 25 knots before I could gain control. I grabbed the oars and paddled like mad to control the tiny ship and keep it from smashing against the concrete walls of the tunnel. I had not tested the seaworthiness of the boat before setting off and I could see why whoever owned it before had discarded it. The thin aluminum seemed to flex with every movement of the oars and my patch job was already looking as if it would give way at any moment. I somehow managed to steer my way towards the proper canal junction that would spit me out into the river and take me further south. The water here reeked severely of feces from the millions of souls that inhabited this sprawling metropolis depositing their waste and sending it downstream to be a problem for someone else in the future.

357

After an hour on the river, the air quality became noticeably different. The water further downstream did not carry much of a stench at all. In fact, it had a very refreshing redolence this far out from Chicago. Unfortunately, it felt as if the legendary icy wind had followed me in order to reach a new clientele out here in the suburbs because it was just as brutally cold here as it was in the city. The wind blasted me through my jacket and clothes, bristling my skin against the unwanted intrusion. My muscles churned the homemade oars against the swirling currents to the point of breaking them, the wood rattling in the oarlocks. Even still, the bracing cold of the wind was trouncing my best efforts to generate body heat. I found my stroke at two second intervals and coupled with the river's flow, I was hurtling along downstream and had already reached the Illinois River, cruising at damn near fifteen knots. Mama Night concealed my getaway for it was very dark on the river, and there were few ships moving westward on this crescent moonlit evening. As the temperature approached freezing, the snow began falling and combined with the wind, it seemed I was paddling through a blizzard. My face and hands would have surely been suffering from frostbite if not for my body's healing factor. Snowflakes rushed by, reminding me of my first few months getting acclimated to living in Chicago. Although out on the open river proved to be very cold, it still paled in comparison to the slicing winds coming from Lake Michigan at night when I would walk between the silent Chicago buildings that would at times create the perfect wind tunnel for chopping a person's very soul apart.

My thoughts were interrupted by pangs of emptiness in my belly. I had hoped to be able to catch some fish or scare up a beaver or some other large river rodent for a meal soon because the physical activity of rowing was creating a cavity in my stomach region. Hell, I would take a good old possum or a fat raccoon at this point. Anything would be a welcome change to the rats and discarded meat of Chicago that made up the majority of my diet the last few years.

As the snow and wind began to subside, I decided to take a small break in rowing to inspect the sturdiness of one of my oars and make sure I had not cracked it. As I drifted along, I happened upon a couple of large freight liners carrying hundreds of shipping containers. They passed majestically, silently pushing my little dingy closer toward the shore in their wake. The sliver of moon revealed my presence to these ships who probably saw fishermen all the time. I was sure they would not particularly be alarmed if they saw me, but I still did not need any reports being filed on me as some random, crazy enough to risk navigating a huge river like this at night without a proper light. Suddenly I felt the cold river water rushing in over the top of my boots. Whatever miracle was holding this boat together for the last four hours had disappeared, and I was forced to paddle faster to avoid taking on too much water.

Fifty miles south of Peoria, I was letting the river current pull me along so I could bail water out of the bottom of the boat using a rusty thermos that I snagged back in the Republic Services landfill and kept conveniently under the seat for just such an eventuality. I was bailing water so much now that I was only paddling when I felt myself drifting too close to the shoreline, so I decided to make for land at the next underpass which happened to be U.S. Highway 72. I dragged my boat into the darkness and hid it the best I could in the shadows under the bridge. The walls of the bridge were scribbled with crude penis drawings and statements ranging from declarations of love like 'Marty loves Rebz' all the way to political notifications in pink spray paint 'Obama = Osama.'

I sneak my way up onto the highway and see a sign that reads 'Pike County Conservation Area.' I moved into the darkness of the nearby forest to find a raccoon or anything to eat and all at once, my nose is hit with the aroma of deer pheromones. The smell caused my fangs to extend involuntarily, I looked down to see a very large and deep set of fresh hoof prints in the mud near the tree line. She was nearby. Probably here with her family living a carefree life in the nearby nature preserve. I removed my wet boots and socks and rolled up my pants cuffs to my calves. I removed my jacket, sweatshirt, and t-shirt and folded them neatly and stashed them below a bush just below the 'Highway 72 South' sign near the bridge.

As I returned to the forest barefoot and shirtless in the cold night air, I got another hint of her…. she was within 100 yards. I shot through the thicket and up a large pine tree, clawing my way about thirty feet up to get a

359

better vantage point and to prevent my scent from being picked up by anything. Several minutes later, I could see her and two smaller deer cross below me, stopping periodically to nibble on newly sprouted foliage. The large female was still about twenty feet to my left and totally oblivious to any threats from hunters due to the peaceful life it had been living in the nature preserve. Before any of them could react, I leapt from the tree and landed four feet in front of her. In that instant, her instinct was to turn and kick before trying to escape, but I dodged the attack and grabbed her by her left flailing ankle and swung her into a nearby maple tree stunning her as her body slammed hard against the trunk of the tree. I was quickly on top of her and placed one hand behind her head and another around her mouth.

"KRRRTTTCH"

The sound of her neck breaking was that of a coarse crunch. Afterwards, all was silent except for the wind rattling through the empty branches above. I drained her of as much hot blood as I could before dining on her flesh. As I split open her torso, I watched the steam dance like fairies from her still warm body whisked away by the cold night air.

After gorging myself on venison, I searched the vicinity for strong, young saplings, and I found a immature sweetgum tree about three inches thick and about nine feet high. I bent the tree down and grabbed it with both hands about three feet up from the root, pulling it toward me and bending the trunk until it snapped away creating a pointed tip. I stripped the tree of its branches and I used my new spear to skewer the carcass of the doe right under the shoulder blades and below the spinal column. I hoisted her up, holding one end of the stick over my shoulder with the deer bouncing behind me to avoid carrying her in my arms and getting any remaining blood and viscera all over me before I reached St. Louis.

A half mile later, and I reach the bridge and shoreline to the river. It had been ages since I had eaten so heartily, and I was reluctant to toss the rest of her in the river yet. I sat on the shoreline deep in thought and just watched the water flow by in the cold night air for over an hour. I needed to dispose of this doe's body in case some 'Nosy Nancy' stumbled along and reported the mess as a Chupacabra attack complete with a half devoured body that had been drained of blood to prove it. That type of news on the police blotter might unintentionally blip *their* radar and draw the attention I absolutely do not need.

The forest was quiet and still. I forget about the cold. The air flowing into my nostrils was so pure and crisp that I even ignored my cigarette craving. My mind kept envisaging Lynn and wondering what type of hardships she has had to endure over the years. My hope was that she was still alive and my prayer was that she still gave a damn about me and the cause we fought for all these years.

"You won't get anywhere if you don't swing the bat." I tell myself out loud, trying to remain as positive about the situation as I possibly could.

A rustle of briars to my left awakened me from my stupor, and my body went rigid as I scanned the area intensely. I sniffed the air, but I was upwind of whatever it was so I was having difficulty determining whether it was something I should be worried about or not. Moments later, I saw a brown and black rabbit dart from under the brush and run deeper into the forest. Relieved, I sat back on my elbows and looked up at the stars for another few minutes. The only sounds betraying the tranquility of this natural oasis were the rush of the river and the steady hum of diesel engines from the tractor trailers crossing the nearby Highway 72 overpass in succession like a line of giant ants cruising into the distance. There was no telling how long it might be until I will have meat and blood this pure again so I opt to take a few more large bites of my deer dinner and fill my belly with as much of it as I could before I continued my journey.

I returned to the area where I hid my belongings and went to my bag and grabbed a t-shirt and a bundle of clothesline sash. I cut a 20ft. hunk and took it back to my meal. I found a large, jagged rock under the bridge and secure one end of the rope to the rock and the other end of the rope around the hind legs and uneaten portion of the deer. I dragged both to the shore and once there, I hurled the rock in an awkward shot-put throw which sent the pair out into the deep reaches of the Illinois River. I washed my face, feet, and hands in the river water and sacrificed my undershirt to use as a towel. I wrang out my waterlogged t-shirt thoroughly and stuffed it in my back pocket before returning to the rest of my clothes and belongings. I put my shirt and jacket back on and tied my boots together with another piece of clothesline and attached them to the outside of my bag. My nicotine craving started going nuts and I allowed myself to indulge in one cigarette from a pack that I kept with a lighter inside their own Ziplock baggie.

The cloudless sky began to turn its change to blue far in the east, and I am reminded of my need to secure protection from the sun and get some rest before I continued my journey. I walked back where I had the boat hidden and after inspecting the shitty condition of the hole that had reopened in the hull, I made preparations to take refuge under the bridge for the day until I could figure out my next move. I hid the boat amongst some dog fennel overgrowth under the bridge about halfway up the shoreline. I checked my shoes but they were still wet so I put them in a spot where they could get a little sun before I climbed under the bridge. I tucked my body in the shadow made by the support joists and the underside of the bridge and tried to make myself comfortable on the concrete slab. I lay there with my eyes open for a long while wondering how I was going to make the rest of the journey without a boat. Listening to the cars and trucks passing above me became white noise in my brain and along with my full belly, I was hit with the perfect combination to create enough drowsiness to overcome my paranoia and permit me to doze off in short intervals, waking every ten or fifteen minutes to smell or listen for anyone or anything that may be passing nearby. After a couple hours of that schizophrenic snoozing, I finally felt like I was hidden well enough to relax a little more.

I slept soundly for an hour and a half before being awakened by a truck 'jake-braking' loudly above me as it crossed the bridge. By the shadows on the bushes, I calculated that it must have been close to noon. I lay there with my eyes closed just listening to the rushing of the river and the rushing of the cars on the highway. I spent the next few hours of daylight meditating and going over what I would say to Lynn until it was dark enough to leave the safety of the overpass.

I took out a roll of duct tape from my bag before repacking and putting my boots back on. After thoroughly drying the breach in the hull of the boat with my sleeve I applied copious amounts of the tape. All I could do was pray that my crude patch job would be enough for me to be able to make it downstream at least another 25 miles. According to the map that would put me in Kampsville, Illinois, where I could maybe find more repair supplies or a replacement vessel. As soon as I put the boat back in the river it began leaking again. Slowly at first so I convinced myself that it was not so bad and continued to row vigorously, but before I could get a half mile downstream, my ass was completely wet, and the stern of the boat was hovering just above the waterline. I stood up in the boat and zipped up my jacket and cinched my bag tightly up onto my back. Reluctantly, I took one last look down at the water now rushing into the breach of my vessel before abandoning ship and diving into the icy waters of the Illinois river. Using my strength to fight the current, I swam toward the shore when I heard the horn and bell of a barge approaching. As I reached the shore and pulled myself up onto the muddy tree line, water poured from my bag and my clothes were heavy and sloshing with water. The cold wind across my wet body felt like little razors poking into my flesh.

My condition was for certain not ideal for moving on land and as I stomped a few feet onto the shore, I could tell I was already making too much noise against the soundless night. Walking anywhere would prove difficult right now, especially since the sun was only a few hours from returning, and I could not take the risk of running into law enforcement on foot without knowing the area. My plan B was always to stowaway aboard one of these mega barges headed South but that was easier said than done. With the freezing temperatures of the water I was certainly not eager to go for another swim tonight. About half an hour later I saw the lights of a barge approaching and I ran down to the shoreline to get a better view. It was a single tow boat pulling two large river barges that must have each been one hundred fifty to two hundred feet in length. Both loaded down with shipping containers of all different colors tightly packed together resembling a hunk of mismatched LEGOs. I figured that a ship of this size must certainly be making a stop in or at least passing the city of St. Louis, and I decided to make my move.

I removed my waterlogged boots and checked my bag to make sure all the important stuff was still dry inside the plastic. I closed the backpack and tied my shoes to the top handles before cinching the pack as tight as I could to my back without restricting my arm movement. As the tugboat passed in front of me, I walked slowly back into the water and once I was at chest height, I took a deep breath and crouched down into the water and rocketed off from the river floor, swimming with my full strength to be able to move cross current swiftly and intercept the barge. The drag created by my clothes and bag slowed me down significantly, but I managed to close the gap and get within ten feet of the back quarter of the second barge before it completely passed me. I glided up next to the hull of the barge which was so slippery that I had to use my claws to climb and puncture the side of the container skiff about an arm's length above the water line.

After about three minutes of being dragged by one arm half underwater and half out, I slowly clawed my way up the side of the barge and onto the side of one of the containers. There was only about half a meter of wiggle space around the edge of each of the neatly fitted containers and from a crouching position, I peered over the top to try and get a gauge on how many people may be aboard. The main personnel for these bulk transport river barges usually remain on the tugboat for the majority of the trip, but I imagined they would occasionally walk this lip in order to inspect the load periodically to check the shipment for any abnormalities or shifting of the cargo. The night swallowed all the light on the river so I doubt anyone would be able to see me, even if I was standing straight up on top of the containers. The lights on the tugboat were focused on piercing through that dark veil and not one could be spared to shine back upon me, so I felt relatively safe from detection for the moment.

Since this was a central time zone, by my calculation, I had six to seven hours of darkness before dawn. The cold night air was almost unbearable with my wet clothes on. I would surely have frostbite all over my body if it were not for my vampire stamina. Once I was sure that the coast was clear I removed my jacket and overshirt and wring them out over the side of the barge while sitting on my knees. The cold wind blasted my wet chest, bristling my ashen skin against its onslaught. I put all the damp clothing back on except for my wet shoes which still hung from my bag. I squeezed myself between two of the large containers and leaned back into the shadows with my head elevated on my backpack which gave me a greater vantage point to see anyone approaching from the direction of the tugboat.

As the night gave way to day, I could see frost forming around the still damp cuffs of my pants and jacket. From my vantage point, the surrounding scenery consisted mostly of barren trees with the occasional passing cargo or trash barge and their accompanying swarms of birds. Every now and again, we would pass a small city or town sporting a tiny marina with a few ships moored there, quietly bobbing up and down in the darkness. As we glide further down the river, I could make out signs with quaint town names like Beechville, Otter Creek, and Goat Cliff. After about four hours of this freezing cruise we reached a town called Grafton which sits on the intersection where the Missouri river merges into the Illinois river and those waters combine to become the Mississippi River. Going over the map in my mind and judging the distance traveled since I had to abandon my dinghy, St. Louis should not be much farther now. The stars confirmed that I was once again headed southwest, but the lack of clouds also told me that very soon there would be no protection from the sun. If I am caught out on the top of this barge in the morning, my goose would literally be cooked.

Checking my options for shelter, I most certainly would not be able to remain hidden topside until morning due to the spaces between each container being too narrow to provide a decent hiding spot. If anyone were to come within five feet of the shallow overhang, I would be spotted immediately. A few hours ago, I contemplated punching a hole in one of the containers to hide totally out of sight but decided against it because of the noise it would make, and the subsequent investigation of the hole ripped into a container of this thickness by some clawed animal would definitely reach the authorities. St. Louis should be very close now, but the barge did not give any indication that it would be stopping soon. By the frequency of the passing ships and the lights from the shore, it seemed highly plausible that I would reach the main city in the early morning hours, and my only wish was that the long winter night would conceal me until I was able to secure a better means of conveyance.

I noticed the channel ahead getting narrower at what now must be fifteen or twenty miles away from St. Louis. I made up my mind that I should bail when the opportunity presented itself instead of waiting until the barge stopped and risk sun exposure or being seen by any of the dock workers. I collected my bag and shoe combo and moved into a crouching position between the containers facing the tugboat to assess my options. I saw a shadow move across one of the tugboat windows which caused me to duck down lower. It was probably just one of the crew members checking on the navigation, but I did not want to take any chances and remained totally still. The river made it hard to pinpoint smells but there did not seem to be many people inside the vessel. Regardless, I was careful to stay low and in the darkness, moving cautiously but speedily toward the far end of the containers.

As we approached the city, I saw what looked like spotlights coming from an amphitheater just off the river near a large marina to the left side of the barge where I was lying prone in the darkness. Ahead of us, I could make out a large suspension bridge highway supported by huge concrete columns. As the barge glided beneath the overpass, I slyly moved closer to the edge of the containers and took a three step running start before leaping straight up from the top of the containers, soaring through the darkness like a rocket until I was able to grab one of the concrete columns. I dug my claws into the stone and climbed like an insect onto the blue steel girders which vibrated with a low whirring sound from all the cars and trucks speeding above. The pocket created by the steel support structure and the concrete columns below this bridge created the perfect barrier to conceal me from the approaching sun.

I sat on one of the large girders taking inventory of my belongings before returning my bag to my back. Looking down at the water I could see the sky changing more rapidly now from black to blue as the sun revealed itself in the reflection of the river. I pulled myself up onto another one of the huge girders under the bridge until I reached a relatively flat surface with a width of about two feet where I decided to hunker down and pass the day watching tugboats pushing and pulling their various barges as they ambled beneath me.

The day was long and uneventful and as night fell, I checked in all directions to verify that the coast was clear and that no other boats were approaching. Once I felt that the boat traffic had stopped, I crawled across the length of the bridge, alternating between clinging to the concrete ceiling with my claws or hanging on the beams below the bridge gripping along the edge of the girders with bare hands and feet. The brown grass and leafless trees below me did not offer much cover for ground movement, so I continued scampering along the underbelly of the highway until I reached a small dark patch of dense boxwood bushes just under the tail end of this massive trestle. I dropped fifteen or so feet to the ground and ducked behind a row of scraggly bushes. I sat on the ground and put on dry socks I kept inside one of the sealed bags. I slid my mostly dry shoes on and dusted off my clothes in the hope of looking as non-homeless as possible.

I needed to find a gas station. A truck stop would have been even better so I could take a shower and get a better map. The lights along the bridge were bright with two cherry red beams at the tips of each set of suspension cables. I put my shades on and walked as naturally as possible toward the off ramp leading from the bridge until I reached a chain linked fence topped with some nasty looking barbed wire and a sign pointing to the entrance of a nearby boatyard called Alton Marina. The place looked completely deserted except for a few random cars parked along the street and a stray dog sniffing around an overflowing trash bin. My nerves were tense and my senses were on full radar mode for any signs of lurking law enforcement. I followed the fence line around to a junction and made a left onto a brightly lit highway. The label on the street sign read 'Landmarks Boulevard,' a large, four lane highway, busy with the monotony of the rat race.

It was still early evening and judging by the threadbare neighborhood, the locals should not find it unusual for pedestrians to be in the area after business hours. The police in a city of this size more than likely had their hands full with real criminals and did not have the time or the resources to waste on vagrants and loiterers but, for safety's sake, I tried to walk as close to the tree line and as much in the shadows as I possibly could.

I smelled a familiar note that stopped me dead in my tracks. I tilted my head back and took a deep breath again to make sure I was not hallucinating. The bastion and sanctuary to all the weary travelers throughout the American countryside was just about two hundred yards away and once I saw those familiar golden arches in the distance, I knew my luck must still be holding on by a thread. I pulled the straps on my backpack tight and prepared to cross the street at the intersection as cool and calmly as possible. I walked in the front door and there were a couple of teenagers working the registers with an older gentleman in the back cooking and a middle-aged woman running between windows taking orders at the register, bagging up food, and completing orders at the drive thru. A pair of guys wearing green work vests were in front of me in line and after they ordered, I moved up. The teenager I was hoping would take my order got occupied on fry duty and I was kept waiting while they rushed to catch up the drive-through line which is beginning to wrap around the building.

Finally, the woman who was dressed in a management uniform complete with the sweater vest, steps up and says in a southern drawl, "I apologize for the wait. What can I get for ya hun?"

In my raspy voice, I managed to croak out, "Five Big Macs and a bottle of water, please."

She rang up my order and said, "That'll be $12.84."

I handed her a $20 bill.

"Out of $20 even? $7.16 is your change. Would you like to donate a dollar to the Ronald McDonald house?

"No, thank you," I replied.

I got my food and walked to the tables and sat in a small two-person booth away from as many people as possible. I removed the meat from each burger and ate it quickly, leaving the bread and other toppings inside the box. Contrary to popular belief, McDonald's meat contains higher concentrations of beef than any of the other major fast-food restaurants. This was the best I can do for now to hold me over until I could find rarer meat to consume. Before I opened the last Big Mac box, I left it and the bottle of water on the table and go to the bathroom to change clothes. The bathroom was empty when I entered, and I went straight into the handicap stall and latched the door behind me. I quickly changed into the blue jeans and flannel shirt I had still sealed in the same bag I had the socks. When I came out of the bathroom, my food was still on the table untouched but I saw one of the teenagers wiping down tables, hovering nearby. In all likelihood to determine if I was coming back or if he should just trash the stuff.

"Excuse me, sir," I choked out in a dry, baritone voice, trying to replicate as friendly a tone as I could muster after not speaking on a regular basis to people for weeks at a time. "Is there a gas station nearby?" I inquired.

The kid who could not have been more than seventeen, his pants sagging and the signature short dreadlocks in a mop fade that all the young guys were wearing. He looked at me for a second and then looked up as if he was thinking before he said,

"Yeah, uh, it's a Phillip's 66 down the street on the left," pointing to the street opposite the door I came in. "But there's a police station next door."

That last bit of information was a sign that this young kid was no slow leak, and he probably picked up on the vibe that I was trying to stay off the radar of law enforcement. The slight accent I still carried from all my years on French plantations also probably hipped him to the fact that I was not the average Midwestern brother. I thanked him and collected my food and took my leave walking briskly and holding the bag of leftover McDonald's and the unopened bottle of water.

Once I was outside again, I stashed the leftover food and water bottle in my backpack and continued walking east towards the gas station. After a little less than a mile, I came to the intersection of East Broadway and Washington Avenue. The City of Alton Police Department that the young man warned me about must be the large building looming ominously across the street. There was also a Dollar General store just on the other side of the police building that I trusted was still open and I could buy a new set of clothes and a pair of socks for the rest of my trip.

The Phillips 66 gas station was buzzing with people but there were no police in sight. I purchased a map of St. Louis and a map of the United States along with a cheap black baseball hat with a white Cardinals logo on the front, another lighter, and a pack of Marlboro Reds, all the while trying my best to avoid looking up into the cameras at the register. As soon as I exited the gas station, I slid the ball cap on my head. I took out the pack of cigarettes and lit one up as I walked back down the block towards the dollar store. As I came around the police building, I saw that it was actually a police records facility with a small precinct attached. I walked purposely around the parking lot towards the adjacent strip mall. I tossed my cigarette when I reached the door of the dollar store and saw a young woman in her early twenties approaching with a wad of keys in her hand. The woman wore her hair in long red braids pulled back into a ponytail, and her black pants and yellow shirt were filled to capacity with her ample body. She was approaching the door, keys in her hand... she was probably going to lock up for the night. She gives me an exasperated look and puts her hand on her hip as I was opening the door.

"Sir, we are closed. I am sorry but you will have to come back tomorrow," she tells me in an exhausted voice.

The clock on the wall read 8:53 so I had at least seven minutes before they officially close.

"I am very sorry, madam," I said, opening the door wider before she could grab it and flashing a seductive smile at her, emphasizing the French in my accent with every word, " but if you would allow me to grab just a few items, I promise that I will be quick. I only need pants and a shirt for an oil rig job I landed that starts tomorrow, and it will be impossible for me to make it to the Walmart because I am on foot currently. Please allow me just me two minutes." I clasped my hands together in a beggar's motion in front of me and raise my eyebrows above my sunglasses and smiled as friendly as I could.

The woman stared at me for a long second with one hand on her hip looking me up and down. With a deep eye roll, she swung the wad of jingling keys into her hand and steps to the side, gesturing for me to come in.

"Okay but make it quick." she says. "I'm gonna lock the door behind you because I don't want it to turn into a damn parade in here. I'm trying to go home. We got families too, you know?" She turns the top latch on the door to the locked position with the key. With her back still turned to me, she says, "And you gonna have to take that bag off and leave it at the register while you're in here.

"Yes, Ma'am," I answer and remove my bag and place it by the door. I can smell the presence of at least three other unseen people in the back of the store.

"Two minutes," I say back to her as I walk to the clothing section and pick out a long sleeved blue and black flannel shirt and black cargo pants.

I can now definitely smell two other male scents in the storeroom which explains why she felt safe enough to be in here with me alone. At the register, I picked up a waterproof, black Casio watch, a small 4-inch folding knife and purchased it along with the clothes. Walking from the store I heard the loud click of the lock behind me and saw the yellow sign out front darken.

I stuffed the plastic bag of clothes into my backpack, and I walked with a purpose back in the direction of the gas station. Once there, I slipped around to the back of the building, into the darkness, and out of sight of the cameras. I leaned down and used a pile of boxes on top of a grease trap to block the wind and light up a cigarette before I pulled out my map. The map confirmed that I landed in the city of Alton, Illinois, which sat just northeast of St. Louis. I calculated that I was about fifteen or sixteen miles from downtown St. Louis and the large wharf area where I should have no problem finding a ship to carry me south down the Mississippi River. Unfortunately, walking may take me all night and running would draw too much attention. I would prefer not to wait out the sunlight until tomorrow night, but I may have no choice. I would risk buying a prepaid card to call a cab but the odds of finding a pay phone that actually worked these days was like hitting the lottery. I thought about approaching a stranger and maybe paying them to use their phone but at this time of night, I would be hard pressed to find someone willing to lend their phone to someone they did not know. Shit, even if it were broad daylight, I doubt if I would have much success. I personally would be against trusting a stranger to use my phone if I had one. Dammit!... I truly did miss pay phones. An impossibly vast and convenient communications network that seemingly disappeared overnight. One day with the stroke of a pen, they made the entire country switch to digital and discard their analog devices without any real significant incidence of blowback. The next day, they stuck tracking devices in everyone's hands and called them smartphones which somehow triggered everyone to go apeshit and start videotaping every moment of their lives, providing even more intelligence for the already massively extensive database that the ruling elite uses to manipulate us.

"My kingdom for a fucking cab," I said out loud to no one in particular. I folded my map and surveyed my surroundings. It was pitch dark behind the Phillip 66 building from the shadow thrown from a huge billboard in the adjacent lot advertising the coming release of a motion picture version of the updated 'Three Stooges.' I remember when those guys were just a struggling vaudeville act. My, how things are different but the same. I needed to think back to what we did before cell phones, before pay phones. Hell, before phones period for that matter.

Then it hits me.

372

There must be a bar around here that takes cash. It should be nothing to persuade the barkeep to call me a cab. I can ask the clerk in the gas station if they can suggest a nearby bar. I resist the urge to light another cigarette and put my map away and walk out of the shadows around a dumpster to the front of the gas station to ask the clerk if he knew of a bar in the area. No cops in sight as I walked toward the front door passing a short, smelly man, with a grimy, bearded face and dressed just slightly shabbier than myself who was loitering near the ice cooler. He looked up at me and lifted one corner of his mouth like he was about to ask me something, but then he looked away towards the pumps searching for wealthier appearing patrons I suppose. Before I reached the door of the gas station, I turned around, walked back toward the man, reached into my coat and pulled out a small wad of bills. I snatched off a twenty out of the roll and held it out in a way the man could see the exact denomination.

"My apologies sir, no disrespect intended," I begin. "But I am new in town, about to start working over here at the shipyards, and I needed to ask somebody familiar with the local area if they could point me to a nearby bar that might be a cool spot to pass the time, shoot some pool, maybe find some women?" I inquired, being as amicable as I possibly could.

The man took the money, inspected it for a nano second to confirm its authenticity, and then folded it into his fist as he began to speak.

"I could tell you wasn't from around here, can't be too careful nowadays. Some folks I don't even asks for no money. Want to know the reason why?" he asks, pointing his finger up at me.

Now that we were facing each other I can see skin tags forming on his neck and behind his ears due to lack of proper hygiene.

"For fear of gettin' cussed out. Or worse, beat up, shot, stabbed, all types of crazy shit can happen to you on the street. You just never fuckin' know anymore. You wanna know why they doing it?" he asks again with the pointed finger. "Cause they ain't got no military draft no more. These young boys nowadays are crazier than cat shit!" He becomes extremely animated in his movements, pointing and making sweeping hand gestures as he spoke. "And you walking around with them damn shades on at night, I couldn't tell if you was gonna be cool or not so I didn't say shit to ya. Cause you never know these days."

He rubbed his arthritic hands together to warm them and looked around as if to make sure no one was in earshot of what he was about to say next.

"But I should know better than any of these fuckers not to judge a book by its cover. You wouldn't know it to look at me but I used to be one of the best fighters out of Southern Indiana. Eddie '*The Kid*' Whitfield. I went from doing amateur fights for not even enough money for bus fare home all the way up to going semi-pro and getting an agent and everything. I was the man— a local celebrity— a regular hometown hero. Back then and I could walk into any bar in this neighborhood and take home any woman in the joint. Eatin' at the finest restaurants in the city and I didn't even have to pay. This is how I can say without a doubt that around here the best women and the best pool games used to be down yonder at Schuster's which ain't but about seven or eight blocks up the street here."
The man said pointing a crooked finger west of the gas station.

"I would take you there if Skip, that's the fucker who owns the joint, hadn't banned me from coming in there. You think you would think a big-time boxing legend like me could get a second chance or somethin'. All I did was come out of the toilet with muh' britches around my ankles once." The man reflected as he stood and wiped the dust from the back of his trousers.

"Now on the other hand, the closest joint you can get a decent drink around here that I know of is this shitty little hole in the wall that's filled with nothing but hard legs from the shipping yards." He turned and pointed eastward. "It's about two blocks back down East Broadway. Hang your first right on Langdon Street and you'll come to a red and black door across the street from a fenced in parking lot. Right there, you'll be looking at a place called Hank's Hideaway which is what they call it now, but it used to be a skanky old Irish pub. I forget the old name it used to go by though."

His face turned serious as he leaned in and said, "But it's plenty of blacks and 'spanics folks in there too nowadays. The man broke into a huge rotten toothed grin after stating this fact. I used to go in there all the time but the price of whiskey is higher than giraffe pussy these days so I just stick to gettin' my kicks from this here Mad Dog 20/20 and Manischevitz... I can always find down here at old Phillips for the same price", the man said, as he nodded his thanks to me and proceeded to pass me to enter the gas station.

I reached out my hand to thank him with a shake for his help, but he doesn't notice the gesture and enters the store with the confidence of the King of France.

I left the gas station and walked up the street towards the bar. I stopped at the corner to light a cigarette then resumed walking purposefully but not too pointed so as to not draw the attention of any law enforcement types. One and a half cigarettes later, I reached a faded black door in the wall of a red brick building with a small, faded placard over the door that simply read 'Pub.'

As I entered, the place was small and dimly lit with a long bar along the back wall and about seven or eight tables between the front door and the bar. There was a couple seated at one of the tables sitting so closely to each other that the woman may as well be in the man's lap. At the bar, there were two men seated one stool apart and an older woman seated at the tail end of the bar. I walk to the bar and get the attention of the bartender. "An Uncle Nearest, double, straight. No. Sorry. Make it two of those and a Sam Adams draft, please."

The bartender looked to be in his late fifties or early sixties, average height, clean shaven with thin greasy hair and a body to match his flimsy grasp on life. In a strong Irish accent, he asked me,

"How about I give ye yer two doubles in one glass if it's all just fer you? Save me from having to wash another glass y' know?" The man glared at me as he wiped the inside of a glass with a rag before placing it down behind the bar.

"That will work," I said, and I laid two 20 dollar bills on the bar and told him to keep the change.

The two men sitting at the bar glanced over at the bills, then up at me, and continued talking about the basketball game on the television above the bar.

"Thanks," the bartender says and then asks me, "You on the job too? We get a lot of guys in here working river barge gigs. Hell, half my business is you fellers, and the other half is the local diehard drunks that still owe me money," the bartender says pointedly, nodding to the two men seated at the bar. One of them raised his half empty glass of beer in a mock toast. The bartender continued. "I can tell by your accent you ain't from around here, and if you don't mind me saying, them Terminator glasses you're wearing aint helpin', if you know what I mean." He slid me my glass of beer.

I began my usual explanation about my extreme light sensitivity which is why I needed the cataract glasses, and I confirmed that his suspicions were correct on me being a river barge hand. Seeming to be satisfied with my answer and why I was there, the bartender proceeded to pour my drinks and I took them and walked to a table as far away from the frisky couple as possible. I downed the whiskey first and then the beer and walked back to the bar and ordered another round of each, leaving a generous tip for the bartender again who this time had no questions for me. Because my body processes sugar radically different from a human's, it would take a barrel of whiskey to actually get me drunk but I feign a little intoxication as I walk to and from the bar. On my third trip back to my table, the woman who was seated at the end of the bar decides to come over and sits next to me. A move which merits a chuckle from the bartender and the two guys at the bar.

"Hope you don't mind me joining you, sugar," as she sat her martini glass down on the table and placed her jacket across the back of the chair

376

before taking her seat. "Oh, don't mind the hun, they just jealous I ain't sitting with them tonight." Her red lips parted to reveal a jagged and cigarette-stained set of choppers embedded in a pile of makeup and fake eyelashes.

"That's a lot of empty glasses," she said, gesturing to the table. "Is it a woman you're trying to forget, I bet that's why you wear these dark Terminator glasses at night. So no one can see you cry. Am I right?" she asked, sarcasm dancing on her tongue as she leaned forward and reached both her hands out to grab for my shades. I gently but firmly moved her hands away and she fell back into her chair laughing to herself as she continued. "You know what they say, hun? The best way to get over a woman is to get under one."

Her charming demeanor sharpened to a razor's edge from years of getting what she needed the best way she knew how. She leaned in closer with her pungent vodka and cigarette breath, speaking just above a whisper,

"I'm old but this twat is still in great shape and it will wrap around your big black cock like a velvet glove. My place is only a block over. Come on, what do you say? I'll give you the new customer discount."

Her eyes searched my face for a reaction and after an awkwardly long pause, I smile and say,

"Ma'am, I am flattered. Truly. I have the inclination, but unfortunately, I do not have the time. I only have enough time for a few drinks before I must report to my barge."

Undaunted, the woman breaks out into a huge smile that accentuated all the wrinkles and skin damage from whatever path brought her to this point in life. She then placed her pale, spotted hand on top of mine and in a very seductive fashion and looking directly at me, she says with all sincerity. "Well could you at least let me suck your dick in the bathroom for 25 dollars? It's been a super slow night and my boyfriend is gonna be pissed if I don't come home with somethin'."

I reached under the table and peeled off two 20's and slid them as discreetly as possible to her over the table. As she took the money, she held the two bills under the table to examine their denomination for a moment and then looked up at me and smiled while tucking her reward deep in between her freckled breasts.

"If you're ever in town again, sugar, I owe ya one." She winked and downed her martini, stood up, put on her coat, and blew me a kiss. Calling to the bartender, "I'll settle up later, kay Patty?"

The bartender did not look up from his filling of a mug of beer for one of the two guys at the bar. She turned with a flourish and walked out the door past me, pulling out a pink Nokia phone from her bag and dialing a number as she walked out of the door. I finished the rest of my drinks and walked to the bar and said, "I hate to ask you, sir, but I recently lost my cellphone between here and Chicago, damn thing being so small. Would you be so kind as to call me a cab to take me down to the shipyard? If I leave now, I can check in with the captain by eleven tonight?" I slid him another 10 dollar bill.

The bartender's eyebrows went up as he grabbed the ten from the bar and said,

"Sure thing pal. Give me a second." He wiped his hands on a cloth hung over his shoulder and walked to the end of the bar, pulling out a pair of reading glasses from his shirt pocket. He picked up the phone at the end of the bar and looking at a small list of names and numbers taped next to the phone, he began to dial the number to the taxi service.

"Which rig company you running with?" Asks one of the men sitting at the bar. He was a heavy-set man with a week-old beard and his St. Louis Cardinals cap turned to the back. He turned to me and the look on his face said something about my story was not sitting right with his spirit.

"I think the name was Tidewater, headed South to the Gulf," I lie, recalling one of the recurring names I saw written on the many barges that passed below me as I sat meditating and staring at the traffic under the bridge earlier that day.

The man put down his beer and then cuts a glance over at the bartender for a second. Then he turns on his stool to face me and for almost fifteen seconds the man just stared at me before releasing a snort and breaking into a smile.

"Hell, you gonna like working with them boys. Me and Mitch here was doing fourteen day runs with sixteen days off and getting paid damn near five dollars more than most companies was paying anybody back in those days. The few years I ran with Tidewater anyway. You must be green though because most people check in with one of the ship's gangbosses or the crew chief, hardly ever the captain nowadays. You look too young to know anything about that river life before all this climate change bullshit started." And with that, he took a large gulp of beer and put his glass down hard.

"I used to drive trucks. I have only just recently started to do this kind of work so I still have a lot to learn about this business," I replied to the man glancing in my peripheral at the bartender to see if he was making any progress with finding the cab number.

"Look here," the man seated at the bar began again. "I ain't gonna lie to ya, this fucking job will chew you up and spit you out if you're not careful. Ain't that right Mitch?" he slapped the man next to him lightly on the arm, prompting his equally wasted friend to raise his glass in agreement.

Just then, the bartender hangs up and in his Irish accent said, "Cabbie is on his way here now."

I thanked him and excused myself to the guys at the bar as I scurried off to the restroom at the back of the room. I pushed the door to the filthy stall open with my elbow and had a good long piss before taking out the rest of my cash and counting it. Just a little over 1,100 dollars left so I needed to be careful if this was going to last me long enough to get back down to Alabama. Depending on how long it took me to find Lynn, getting the rest of my loot may take months so I had to play it cool and not throw cash away on some wildcard shit like that pushy prostitute tonight. I put fifty dollars in each side of my zippered pouches inside my bag, a hundred in a money clip in my left pocket and the rest in my right. I ran the water like I was washing my hands in case anyone was listening. Before leaving the bathroom, I pulled out another 10 dollar bill. I exited the bathroom, glad I decided to bring my bag with me because there were two new patrons seated at the bar that seemed to know the other two gents that were chatting me up about barge life. I walked to the bar to give the bartender my thank you tip and overhear the man that was addressing me earlier lamenting about the river barge life saying, "Yeah, it's just like driving trucks except with five to ten other guys and you can't leave the truck for three weeks." This got a laugh from the rest of the peanut gallery just as the bartender was putting down their beers.

As the two newcomers took a huge swill from their ice cold beer mugs, I thanked the bartender and slid him the ten, another cherry on an already generous night of tips. I told him I was going to go outside to wait for the cab while I smoked and as I turned to walk out, I hear the same guy ask one of the newcomers,

"Hey, Tom, didn't you say you lost your gig with Tidewater 'cause they shut down most of their North American operations and closed the St. Louis hub forcing Ralph and Little Gary to move their whole family to Memphis?"

"Yeah, the damndest timing it was too because we had just bought a new car for my daughter Morgan," answered the large, balding Tom. "That's when I started doing construction work over in Chesterfield. Shit, Frank, you ought to know well as I do 'cause you got laid off the same time as I did."

I was sure they suspected my story to be bullshit now so instead of waiting around to have to answer any questions from these assholes, I hot footed it out of the door, lit up a cigarette, and walked about forty feet up the block trying to will that damn cab to get here before those guys got full of liquid courage and became more indignant about wanting to know what my actual reason for being here was. I was halfway through my second cigarette when I saw a sedan with a yellow glowing "Taxi" sign pull up and double park in front of the bar. I jogged a little to close the distance between myself and the cabbie before he drove off or before he called inside the bar looking for me. As I got within ten feet, the cab driver stood up out of the cab, with a vexed look on his face. He looked to be a very no-nonsense, middle-aged man with very black hair on his head and face, his dark eyes and bushy eyebrows furrowed and were almost touching from the scowl he wore.

I started to speak, raising my hand as if I was hailing him when he cut me off.

"I'm already waiting for a fare. Sorry buddy."

"I am the fare," I said to him. "I had the guy in the bar call you for me. Patty I think his name was."

At the sound of Patty's name, the man paused for a moment and then said, "Look, my friend, no offense, but I don't go to East St. Louis at night. I'm sorry."

"That is great," I replied, "because I do not want to go to East St. Louis. I would like to go to the Municipal River Terminal, I have a river barge gig and I need to get there as soon as possible please." I pulled out a 20 dollar bill and handed it to him over the roof of the car. "Consider this down payment."

He examined the money for authenticity and then I heard the click of the unlock button on the car doors, and the man slid back into the driver seat as I got in the back seat which was divided by a thick plastic sheet with a small square hole flap for driver/passenger access.

"Specifically, I would like to be dropped off opposite the Warren Street side and closer to North Market and North Wharf if I could please. I think it is just a couple miles down from The Arch." I told the man, using a location I chose arbitrarily from my earlier examination of the map. I had a feeling that it was an ideal spot to smuggle myself aboard a barge headed south.

"I know the building of which you speak for I have passed that area many times when I am first arriving here from Syria and driving first time for tourists, always wanting to see Arch. Let me know if it gets too hot, I will lower the heat setting."

Just then, his phone rang, and he answered by hitting the speaker button. The name 'Wali B.' is displayed on the screen. In Arabic, ["My friend, I will call you back. I have a shady abīd in the car, and I need to question him. Is everything OK?"]

The caller answers in Arabic as well. ["I wanted nothing only to tell you what Hassan spoke of in his trip to Pakistan last month. I will tell you. Call back when you are free."]

Then the driver hung up and said to me in English "Please forgive my manners. I have trouble sometimes with drunks and druggies wanting ride from bar. My name is Abdullah. What is yours sir and where from originally?"

It had been a while since I needed to speak it, but in my best Arabic, I answered his question with a question. "Hal yumkinuni 'an 'athaq bik mae alhaiqiqa [Can I trust you with the truth?"]

Abdullah flinched a little and swerved to the right slightly before correcting the vehicle at the sound of his native tongue coming from the backseat. Instantly, his demeanor changed, and he began to apologize for calling me abīd, and said that he was only trying to protect his business from gangsters and thieves.

"May I ask how you came to know Arabic? Are you Muslim?" Abdullah asked me, now in a much friendlier tone.

I told him I was an interpreter in the American military during Operation Iraqi Freedom and worked as a ship mechanic after the war. I throw in a line about not being Muslim, but I respected Islamic culture which prompted me to learn it for more meaningful conversations with the locals. Truthfully, I originally learned Arabic in 1973 when I traveled between Petra and Beirut and was involved in a little land dispute during my crusades to take down the Reichstall conglomerate.

" 'Ana huna lilitahqiq fi mumarasat alshahn ghyr aleadila [I'm here to investigate unfair shipping practices."]

"Ahhh," Abdullah acknowledged..

"I need to be discreet because of the agency I work for, so I would appreciate it greatly if you did not mention my business here to anyone."

"Bismillah, 'uweidak,"[I give you my word] he promises and continued in English. "I will not tell a soul." Making eye contact with me in the rear-view mirror to convey his earnestness.

The rest of the 20 minute trip to central St. Louis was spent in silence smattered with intermittent talk about politics and weather. Abdullah would often stare at me in the rearview and mumble things in Arabic to himself. I think my appearance juxtaposed with my ability to understand Arabic had somehow short circuited this man's perception of the world. The fare was $57, I gave him $60 bucks on top of the twenty he already had and he left me with a parting " 'as Salam Alaikum" and I fire back perfectly " 'wa-laikum as-Salam." I watched him drive away as I lit another cigarette and headed towards the shipyards.

Cranes and rusty metallic shells of storage containers littered the area amongst the warehouse buildings. Dust and smoke swirled together in the blustery wind that battered the shoreline carrying the stench of the rushing river. The high metal fence to the municipal docks was closed and locked from the inside so I walked north on Wharf Street down the fence line

383

past Grossman Iron and Steel to a shadowy area where there were fewer streetlights to search for a safe access point. I could see piles of debris waiting to be loaded onto barges and a large conveyor belt was actively transferring one of the large piles of what looked like gravel and a black substance that resembled coal into smaller piles inside the huge container of an open face barge floating near the dock. There were a few men milling around while supervising the load, but the crew seemed very sparse tonight.

I scaled the 12ft. fence effortlessly, being careful not to rip my clothing on the barbed wire at the top. I land catlike on the other side of the fence and run to one of the material piles located near the fence line. The men working around the rig moved with a similar lethargic gait. Every one of them seemed beaten down with the never-ending workload as they milled about between the containers saddled with various tasks such as monitoring the flow from the machine or loading and prepping the tugboat. Unfortunately, none of the markings on the cargo provide any intel on the destinations of the shipments. At this point my strategy may need to change from finding a barge that was headed to New Orleans or Mobile to just securing a ride as far south as possible and then transferring to another ship if the need arose. The sunrise was only six hours away, and I would like to secure something and be well hidden and on my way before the first cock crows.

As I moved closer, I realized that one of the materials being loaded onto the barge was grain, probably for supplying food to farm animals south of Tennessee. As I watched the giant conveyor belt finish loading the grain, the container it was transferred to was then covered and sealed for transport.

Jackpot.

I darted out towards the back of the shipping containers, being sure to stay in the shadows made by the piles of raw material. A large bulldozer with four high powered lights approached and I quickly ducked behind some unlabeled metallic drums strapped to a wooden pallet. I went unnoticed as he passed me and deposited a load of coal into a metal bin about 80ft. to the left of where I was hiding. When the bulldozer turned to go back for another load, I skulked towards the containers farthest from the tugboat and noticed a couple of cameras high on a power pole overlooking the operation. I was careful to move fast when I was forced into the lighted areas, and I was extremely careful to avoid the sections in the line of sight of the cameras. The moonless night did the most work in concealing my presence but with all the lights near the barge and around the port, it would be impossible for me to jump the gap onto the barge without being spotted. My only choice may be to slip quietly in from the water and board the barges from underneath. Which also meant I had to go down into the cold water. I began to dread the prospect of having to get fucking wet again. I could not be sure if I would be able to wait until the barges were finished loading to make my move for it may be too close to dawn and I would lose the darkness as my shield.

A huge stack of pallets and crates lay thirty meters from the dock to my left which gave me an idea. I dashed over and crouched down onto one knee and looked over the crates for any packing or destination material to try and get information on the load. They were all marked for arrival instead of departure. The longer I waited, the more of a chance someone would spot me, so it was now or never. I had to take the chance and climb aboard anyway and hopefully I would select the right one.

I removed my hat and stuffed it between the crates and ran over and grabbed one of the nearby pallets. I dipped into a dark area in the blind spot of the cameras facing the river where a huge pile of gravel kept me out of sight from anyone dockside while simultaneously also creating a natural barrier from the fence line and the pole cameras at the rear of the facility. I spun around twice holding the pallet in my hand discus style gaining a huge amount of momentum and launched the pallet high into the air towards the river over the conveyor belt loading machine and the tugboat.

'SPLAP!!!!'

The pallet hit the water flatly making a loud sound which grabbed the attention of all the ship mates and dock workers nearby. I could hear voices yelling instructions to one another and men running over to the vicinity of the sound. After a moment, I saw the large spotlight atop the tugboat turn to focus on where the sound came from. As soon as the lights were turned towards the water, I zipped out of my hiding spot, sprinting at top speed, and leapt from the edge of the marina in a straightforward trajectory, soaring about 40 feet into the air and landing on the second container out from the pier, a distance of about 30 meters. My knees absorbed most of the landing and my boots made a loud resounding thudding noise as I landed and rolled a few feet before catching myself and lying completely flat on my stomach in the darkness, not even breathing for a solid two minutes just to be sure no one heard me.

Once I felt it was safe enough to move, I rolled over into a crouching position and peered over the tops of the containers back toward the wharf. The workers on the dock had slowly begun to move back to their various tasks after the excitement over the pallet hitting the water had dissipated. I allowed myself to relax somewhat before taking inventory of my cruising accommodations and looked for a suitable hiding place to pass the coming days.

Each container was about 40 feet long and about 8 feet across and capable of holding about 61,000 lbs. of material. One river freight haul can consist of up to fifty of these monsters rigged together. The sheer magnitude of the whole operation was amazing considering that all those containers can be managed by one tugboat navigating this humongous, raging river.

There were a handful of people on the barge from what I could see and smell, making it easier to slide imperceptibly quick and quiet between shadows as I moved across the containers. I ran in a crouched position for nearly fifty feet before dropping down into the nearest open-air container on the back left side of the barge. The material I landed on was some type of pulverized gravel-like stones that released a puff of dust as my body weight plopped down hard. I quickly scrambled onto my knees and lay down prone on my stomach until I saw the spotlight return to its original position and the unsuspecting crew continued to load the ship. My landing created a small dust cloud that choked me up in the moment but did not appear to be caustic. I crawled to the far corner of the container and tried to regain my composure and get a sense of my surroundings. The load I landed in, upon closer inspection, was composed of a mixture of dirt, iron ore, and sand. The other encapsulated barges I saw probably contained food grade items like grain and what I thought, from the smell of it, was a huge amount of cow manure. With my back to the far wall of the container where I could face the tugboat from the darkness, I sat and waited. At nearly 3:00 a.m. I heard a loud whistle sound off from the tugboat twice before hearing the engines roar to life, and I felt the craft finally moving out into open waters and downstream towards my goal.

Apollo had hitched his chariot, and I could hear birds in the trees on the shoreline chirping loud enough to be heard over the dull roar of the tugboat engine on this cloudless March morning. Soon the sun would burn the clouds away and I would be in some serious trouble. More than likely the deck hands will do periodic checks on the containers to make sure there were no leaks or breaches so I could not risk cracking into one for a hiding place. I decided to hunker down in this partially covered container with the pulverized stone bits that were more than likely destined for some concrete factory or the like. I removed my boots and socks and put them in a plastic shopping bag which I attached to my backpack. I stripped off all the clothes I purchased at the dollar store along with my under shirt and stuffed them inside of my duffel bag and zipped it all shut. I moved down the side of the container which is covered by a waterproof canvas shell except for about a 15 x 5 inch opening in the center of the container. I moved under the far corner of the covered section and I dug a hole for my bag and buried it leaving only the top of the bag strap visible. Next, I carved out a body length sized hole deep enough for me to lay down on my back below the surface of the sandstone material. I lie down and pull the dirt and rocks over my legs and torso until just my right arm and my face was visible. Any prying eyes or sunlight would have a difficult time reaching my hiding place, so I allowed myself a few hours of sleep just as the sky began to transition to full day.

After only two hours I found it very difficult to remain asleep. I unburied myself and just sat against the side wall of the container and stared at the blue sky safely from the shadows through the opening. The tugboat pace was very slow and I really wished I could smoke to pass the time and try to placate my grumbling stomach. I dug my bag out and removed a couple of the burger buns I kept from my McDonald's dinner. I broke up the bread and tossed out a few pieces into the exposed area of the container hoping to attract a few pigeons, gulls, or any other opportunistic bird that may be passing overhead. After a couple of hours with no bird sightings, I began sniffing around the hold of the container, hoping there was a stowaway rat or two on board to hold me over until we got further south.

That night, I watched the captain use a bright spotlight to navigate the choppy waters which were apparently unseasonably high for this time of year. The light was so bright, it lit up the entire top portion of the rig, and I was hesitant to make any movements outside of the container lest I be spotted. Subsequently I was forced to pass the time that first night much like I did the day by just sitting and watching the sky, not able to smoke or find any food.

As the sky morphed from black to blue again, I felt the entire rig begin to slow. I climbed up onto the mound of material where I could just make out a large suspension bridge ahead with the outline of a mid-size city coming into view under an overcast sky. I went to my bag and grabbed a few more pieces of the leftover McDonald's bread and crumbled them in my right hand. I jumped up to the lip of the opening in the container cover and sprinkled a few pieces of bread. I shaved out a flat area in the side of the mound of sandstone, creating a small plateau of the gravelly material and I used the rest of the bread to create a line of crumbs that led under the lid into the shadows. I then crept back into the darkness and crouched down making myself as small and invisible as possible. For good measure as I felt the shadow of the approaching bridge, I made a few 'coo' sounds, and whistled like a bird. Sure enough, my calls got their attention and some of the pigeons from beneath the bridge began to fly down and alight on the rim of the container. A few of the bolder hens flew into the container to gobble up the bread trap. A nice little crowd began to gather when, in a flash of feathers and a rush of escaping birds, I shot out of the shadows and managed to grab three fat hens before the others flew away. Two of the birds I ate immediately, devouring them both in only six bites, leaving only the feet and tail feathers with their spiky cartilage behind which I buried in the mound of sandstone gravel.

388

I waited to see if the sound of the commotion the birds created would attract any human attention but I suspected the crew was too busy concentrating on navigating between the concrete pylons of the bridge to be worried about a kit of pigeons flitting about. Once I felt absolutely sure no one was coming to investigate the bird disturbance, I devoured the rest of my breakfast and retreated to the shadows to study my map. By my calculations, we were passing Cape Giradeau in southeastern Missouri, the biggest town that marked about the halfway point between St. Louis and Memphis. If memory serves me correctly, this area was riddled with the history of the Black Bob Band of the Hathawekela Shawnee and the battles they took part in to counteract the Trail of Tears removals. Here we are, all defeated, dead and reduced to reservations with me being the biggest disappointment. Running around masquerading as some self-proclaimed savior of the goddamned world, now relegated to living in sewers, hiding in a steel container for transportation and eating flying rats for breakfast.

I crept over into the far corner of the container and dug a hole in the sandstone to relieve myself. As I moved back past the opening, I could partially see the tops of the trees on the shoreline. By the pace we seemed to be keeping as we passed the trees, I figured we should reach Memphis in another eight or so hours. The sun would be going down again by then, and I should be able to use the time on land to acquire supplies, change clothes, and eat again before I continue southward.

After a couple of hours of sleep in my hole, I climbed out and just sat on a mound of gravel and passed the time listening to the sounds of the river with my eyes shut. I considered my life up until then and asked myself if this world would even want to change. To finally be able to place blame on and expose the cause of unnecessary misery and unrestrained greed in the world with concrete 100% evidence beyond a shadow of a doubt with all names and receipts all the way down to the nitty gritty? Would that create enough outrage for the public to care enough to want the truth or would they retreat back into their fantasy worlds because knowing the truth requires one to take action? Maybe to even have to change?

I need to somehow put my three hundred plus years of experience to work in extrapolating a way to siphon off a large chunk of their assets and redistribute part of that wealth back to the populace. Hit them where it hurts the most. I need to get their attention. No more playing checkers from here on out. Ever since the late nineties when I read about exchange traded funds and how the web could connect regular computers to the networks of the huge banks and hedge fund portfolios, I knew that if I could somehow siphon off a few trillion, that would surely rattle some cages and let them know that I meant business. Flipping the haves to the have-nots and vice versa overnight.

A horn sounded twice in short friendly bursts from the tugboat, returning my thoughts to my present situation. Probably signaling a fellow barge load passing in the opposite direction. Night was coming on, and I could see the sky turning a pale purple pink as the sun faded into the horizon and the air grew colder as the temperature began to drop again. As soon as it was sufficiently dark, I reached into my bag and took out the small folding knife. The previous night, the pilot waited for a little over an hour after sunset until the sky was completely dark before putting on the navigation spotlights, so I needed to finish my business quickly to avoid being caught. I pulled myself up onto the edge of the container opening, slipped out into the shadows and crouched down behind the lid of another one of the containers. The air against my skin caused my muscles to flex involuntarily against the cold, and my heart rate and breathing increased in kind. I peeked above the lid at the tugboat and saw a large man with a short grey beard and matching ponytail walk out of the helmsman's cabin with a flashlight aiming it down and to his right. The man yelled something that I could not make out over the noise of the boat engine, so I followed his light to see another younger looking crewman with a grey hoodie under and orange vest carrying a bottle in one hand walking towards the stairwell to join his older compatriot on the pilot level.

Unfolding the knife and placing it between my teeth, I moved rapidly toward the front most barge and lowered myself down over the ledge by my fingertips. I turned my body to face the river and held onto the edge of the barge with both hands behind me and my feet against the bow of the boat

390

like a living figurehead. I hung there for about thirty seconds gauging the depth of the water versus the speed of the boat. I folded the knife and put it in my underwear and with one big inhale I dove in headfirst and used my enhanced strength to rocket ahead of the barge and plunge deep into the easily 50 to 75ft deep water. This area should be crawling with catfish, crappie and bass out scavenging for food to use for spawning this early spring evening. As I approached the riverbed, the pressure of the water popped my eardrums and the burn of oxygen depletion began to build. I realized I was not in as good of shape as I was one hundred fifty years ago back when holding my breath for five minutes at a time was child's play.

Amongst the rocks, vegetation, and trash along the river floor, fish, especially catfish, find the perfect homes for sleeping at night during the colder months. I spotted a slow moving medium sized cat and pulled my knife out. I hurled it through the water like a torpedo tagging the fish on its left side. Blood looked like red smoke under water as the catfish unsuccessfully tried to swim away. I zoomed after it and grabbed, snatched it up and made a beeline up to the surface slowing down the last five meters so I did not give myself the bends as I reemerged.

Even in that short period of time it took me to locate and catch the fish my barge ride had traveled about a half a mile downstream. I quickly pulled the knife from the fish folded and stuffed in my underwear. I put the fish in my teeth and I swam using my full strength along with the current of the river to quickly catch up with the barge. I swam up near the starboard side, just right of the dark churning wake of the tugboat. I gathered some oxygen after treading water with one hand free and one hand holding the fish. Using the night and the roar of the tugboat engine to conceal my movements, I swam up along the side of the barge and pulled myself up with my left hand, digging my claws into the slick metal and hanging on the side for a moment in order to watch for any lights being shined in my direction. Unfortunately, the current of the river and the force used to lift me from the water yanked my underwear down to my knees and with the fish in the other hand, I lost my knife and was left indecently exposed. I waited in that position for a minute until I was positive the coast was clear. I tossed my catch onto the slim ledge around the barge and pull my naked ass onto the overhang staying as low as possible. I removed my underwear from my foot and wrapped them around the fish to keep the flesh moist. Moving behind the lid of one of the containers, I glanced back at the tugboat which was still dark and quiet. I crouched down onto the ledge of the container for a minute to allow the air to dry my body before crawling back to my dusty container hiding place. I put my pants on and examined my catch which appeared to be about a three pounder. I counted myself lucky for being able to find something of this size this early in the spring.

With my mission completed, I waited out the rest of the night out on the top of the containers near the tugboat deck tucked behind the front lip of the connector barge and out of sight of the crew and below the sight line of the spotlights. An hour or so before dawn, the spotlights went out again, and I returned to my hole to wait out the day and have my fish head breakfast before removing the guts and splitting my meal in two half filets with my claw. I retrieved a couple of plastic grocery bags from my backpack and wrapped one half of the filets in the plastic and buried it under the cool dirt. Using my claws, I cut the other filet into thin strips and placed it into another plastic bag and buried it in the dirt alongside the first half. I took the leftover guts of the catfish and tossed some over the lip of the container opening. I also scattered a few pieces across the top of the pile of ore with a trail of flesh and guts leading under the covered area of the container. I then chose a shaded spot to sit and wait as the sun rose however, much to my dismay, an overcast sky yielded very few airborne hunters causing the meal I had so graciously presented to be ignored. As the morning progressed and the sun burned off the clouds, the dead flesh began to warm late in the afternoon, and I could now see a group of birds begin to circle and pass above me including a couple of gulls. Toward late afternoon, I spotted a few pelicans, and more gulls began to appear in the sky. I took out the other half of the fish that I cut into filets and flopped a couple pieces onto the pile of ore to simulate movement which attracted a few of the hungry creatures to the top of my hideout. One of the larger more aggressive seagulls pushed out a few greedy smaller gulls already feeding on the entrails and landed directly on the pile of ore and began snatching up the filet strips and a bit of ore with each mouthful. Having had its fill, the seagull flapped its wings and started to take off. In a flash, my hand darted out and grabbed it by the webbed feet and yanked it into the shadows, sending feathers flying and startling the other birds nearby that squawked and flapped away hurriedly. I quickly grabbed another one of the fat gulls before they all scattered and recoiled back into the shadows of the container. I immediately broke both their necks killing them and causing them to go limp in my hands. Fearing the noise and ruckus caused by the quarreling birds most assuredly caught the attention of the ship's crew. I listened and watched the opening of the container for a time before making any large movements as the last of the birds continued to scrap with each other for the last bits of free food. I escaped to a darker corner at the opposite end of the container and sat quietly listening for anyone who may be approaching to investigate the commotion. While waiting, I drained all the blood from the body of the larger bird and after about ten minutes of silent crouching in the shadows, I decided the coast was clear enough to do a more thorough check and see if I had been made. I ventured a look towards the tugboat from the dark corners of the container. No sign that the birds had registered as anything unusual to the crew so I returned to my meal. After draining both birds of all their blood, I removed the head of the larger seagull and as many feathers as I possibly could from both birds. I placed the feathers in a plastic bag and buried them in the sandstone. After completely devouring the larger seagull, I wrapped the rest in a garbage bag from my supplies and placed it under a couple feet of the gravel ore to keep it from spoiling too fast.

That night, a heavy fog rolled in just as the darkness fell, and I resigned myself to just watching the sky and studying my map. To my dismay, the barge passed Memphis without stopping so I readjusted the plan to disembark at Baton Rouge whether the ship stopped there or not. From that point, it should be just a couple of hours to hitch a ride down Interstate 10 to Mobile.

After three very uneventful nights later, we arrived in the waters near the Baton Rouge area. It had been two nights since my last chunk of seagull and since then, I had not been very lucky catching any other nutrients besides a small mouse I nabbed while it was running along the edge of the wheat container. As such, my first point of business when I reached the city would be to get some sustenance. The city lights were dazzling at night as we approached the heart of the downtown, and the ridiculous number of barges

393

and loading docks made it apparent that this was clearly one of the largest shipping hubs south of Memphis. As we approached the Horace Wilkinson Bridge which carried Interstate 10 across the Mississippi River, the spotlights on the tugboat blazed on and illuminated the entire barge and the river ahead of us. I gathered all my belongings into my duffel bag and attached my boots by the laces to the bag and slung it onto my back. I also pulled out of the dirt mound a plastic grocery bag filled with feathers and trash from my earlier meals. I waited barefoot in the dark staring up out of the opening until just as the barge started to move under the bridge. As soon as the spotlights focused ahead of the container that I was hiding in, I squatted down like a frog building energy in my thighs and calves and leapt like a rocket out of the container ripping open the bag of feathers on my way up to make anyone seeing the object moving through the night air think it may be a bird that was stowing away. I landed on the opposite side of the concrete pylon and scurried up and under the steel girders of the bridge into the safety of the shadows.

West of the bridge appeared to be more of an industrial area and was sure to have truck traffic servicing the many shipping companies lining the street. As I clawed my way toward the end of the bridge and the beginning of the highway, the ground below me was a huge train yard labeled BWC Terminal. Even on a cold and dreary night such as this, the irrepressible market forces fostered a transportation system in America that did not miss a beat so there was a constant flow of containers and boxes being moved in every direction at this facility which more than likely operated 24/7 to meet the high demands of our consumption-based society. I planned to continue exploiting that system and hitch a ride with a trucker headed east to Mobile and once there, I should be able to track down Cora at her farm and retrieve my gold and the tools I need to put my plan into motion.

From my perch under the bridge, I could see trucks leaving and entering the various distribution centers below me so there should be plenty of vehicles to choose from heading in multiple directions. I am a quiet, introverted person by nature and my issue with hitchhiking was always finding someone cool and indifferent enough not to pry into my business too deeply while chauffeuring me to my destination. I swung myself down using the steel girders until I was about ten feet above the ground before I jumped barefoot down onto the solid earth. I removed my bag and put my boots, jacket and sunglasses back on and tried to knock as much dust and grime from my clothes as I possibly could. I went into my bag and retrieved from my sealed bag a pack of cigarettes and a can of Brut spray deodorant. In an effort to cover my days of body odor, I sprayed on copious amounts of deodorant in my armpits and onto my other particularly rancid body parts. I followed my stench masking by chain smoking three cigarettes which I had been dying to do since I boarded the barge in St. Louis a week ago. The smells of the river had been driving me absolutely bonkers but I could not risk lighting up for fear of alerting the tugboat crew to my presence.

Halfway through my fourth cigarette I decided to walk toward the main road and suss out my next move. Amongst the trash on the ground, I spotted a piece of cardboard I could make use of. I picked it up, dusted it off and tore it into a rectangle. Then I take a marker out of the front pocket of my bag and scribble the words, *"MOBILE BOUND, WILL PAY $"*. I folded the sign and stuffed it in my back pocket, and continued walking up a street labeled Le Blanc Road.

As I passed the entrance to the Union Pacific railroad yard, I turned my head to avoid a cloud of crushed gravel dust on the road that kept being kicked up by each of the passing trucks and re-covering me with a layer of filth all over again. I decided to take a right on South Westport Drive walking west toward eastbound traffic. I passed numerous companies that transported items ranging from steel, construction stone, piping made of various materials, and even the likes of a truck distribution facility for BP Oil. I found what looked like a suitable spot on the side of the road, pulled out my sign and stuck my thumb out. I made sure to write "MOBILE" in large letters rivaled only by the dollar signs I drew under the words "WILL PAY." I light another cigarette, more to keep the smell of the truck exhaust fumes out of my nose than out of habit, when I noticed that just another 300 yards down the road there was a truck parking lot with a few dozen trucks parked and resting for the next leg of their respective journeys. I can make out a few feminine silhouettes moving between some of the parked rigs. Another example of the irrepressible markets this world is known for. Nothing like a warm body on a cold night.

I continued standing on the side of the road for another hour with no takers, just holding my sign and chain-smoking cigarettes near the entrance of a closed tire shop. I decided it was in my best interest to keep it moving further down the block and not stand in one place for too long lest the cops or someone else mistakes me for a lot lizard.

After a couple miles of walking down the dusty shoulder of the highway with no luck, Providence shone down upon me and the trees just ahead of me opened up to reveal the top of a sign that read one word: Love's. Love's is a chain of gas stations that has been around since the sixties and came equipped to accommodate truck drivers with amenities such as showers, entertainment centers, groceries, tools and supplies. I double time it across the road and shuffle up to the front door, keeping my head down to avoid the cameras that were everywhere.

The first thing I noticed when I entered was an awful smell coming from the hot dogs on display which did not look too appealing turning on the lukewarm rollers at the front of the store. I glanced over into the restaurant lounge area and spotted a police officer standing in line at the bustling Arby's that shared a wall with the gas station. It took me by surprise because I did not see a police cruiser out front but I did not want to take any chances so I decided to leave Love's and cross the highway where I could see a Waffle House and a Burger King sign. I chose Burger King for its more impersonal setting and fortunately there was still half an hour remaining before they closed. I ordered five plain double whoppers and a bottle of water. I sat to eat quickly, only the meat again and I saved half of the buns and discarded the rest. As I left Burger King, the girl who took my order promptly locked the door behind me less out of caution and more to prevent guys like me from walking up and making big orders at closing time.

I crossed the highway again and returned to the Love's truck stop. No police in sight this time so I made my way toward the locker room check in. My body reeked from days without bathing, but there was a 45 minute wait for the showers so I opted to take a whore's bath inside the handicapped stall of the men's restroom. I hustled to the register and requested a fresh carton of Marlboro lights while I paid for a pair of underwear, some terry cloth rags a bar of soap, a gallon of water and a black baseball cap with a white A on it for Alabama Crimson Tide football team, Lynn's favorite. I zipped to the bathroom with my supplies washed and changed into the new underwear and the clothes I bought at the dollar store in St. Louis. I put my old clothes in the garbage can of the bathroom before leaving.

As I exited the Love's, a tall barrel chested black man wearing tortoise shell rimmed glasses entered the store and said "Roll Tide" in my direction. I glanced up to see his round smiling face and I finally register that he was referring to my hat. I raised my right hand to touch the brim in acknowledgement and continued past the man out of the truck stop. I lit a cigarette and walked back toward the main drag to continue in my attempt to find a ride. I was starting to worry if I would be able to catch one before I ran out of darkness. I sauntered back east down South Westport Drive walking with the traffic this time, holding my sign and puffing cigarettes back-to-back. About thirty minutes into my walk, a gleaming white truck with chrome trim pulling a white trailer with the Swift company logo on the side pulled over to the shoulder of the road just ahead of me. The driver stuck his hand out of the window in a beckoning motion for me to hurry up. I flicked my cigarette onto the ground and holding the straps on my pack, I jogged ahead to the passenger door of the truck, opened it, and before me was none other than the smiling face of the man I passed leaving Love's gas station.

"I couldn't let a fellow Bama fan walk in the cold like this," he says in a voice that rings with an accent somewhere between South Carolina and Jamaica as he extends his hand. I shook it and still smiling, he said, "The name's Robert Thompson but I go by Bobby T! I won't ask you for no money for the ride, but I do have one request before we go anywhere."

Still shaking his hand, I glanced down at the .38 special holstered under the handle of the driver's side door.

"Name it," I responded.

"Let me see your eyes behind them glasses", he says. "It was a time when you could give a stranger a ride, black or white, and you didn't have to worry about no murders or rapes or no shit like that. But now, you got all types of crazy muthafuckers running around. Some of 'em they even let drive these damn trucks," Bobby T chuckled. But my Papa would say, *you hafta look a man in his eyes when you is talkin' to him.* Man's eyes is the window to his soul, and I done got to where I need to look at a man in his eyes to tell what type of person he is." He finished and dropped my hand.

"Okay, but I have a problem with my eyes. I just don't want you to be startled when you see them," I warned.

Hell man, I served in 'Nam. Aint nothin' you got can startle me Jack." Bobby T retorts.

I removed my glasses and looked directly at him.

He looked at me expressionless for a moment and then broke into a huge smile. "You got eyes like I ain't seen the likes of since I was a boy in South Carolina. My blind grandaddy tended the farm right up 'til the day he died, but he could get around without help and without a stick by counting the steps everywhere he went. "He could tell which direction he was going at all times by using the warmth coming off of the sun on his face." Bobby laughs.

"My granddaddy could hear a rat piss on cotton, his ears was so sharp. He could tell us kids apart from touchin' our fo'heads and ears and was one of the only negroes to own and be able to ride a unicycle in Moncks Corner."

Bobby T's accent made Monck's Corner sound like he said 'Muskona.

I told him my name and gave him my usual spiel about having sensitive eyes thus the need to wear dark glasses.

"My older sister had to do the same thang when the doctor said she had cataracts so no need to explain nothin' 'bout that. She walked around looking like Arnold Swaznegger in that damn movie every time she left the house. Even to Wednesday night bible study." Bobby T looked at me and laughed to himself again. "As I said, I was born Robert or some folks like to call me Bobby T, but over these roads these big rigs know me by my handle 'Wild Child'. Nice to meet ya."

As I climbed in the truck and closed the door I managed to cough out the fact that it was nice to meet him also.

"I see you like them Marlboro's," Bobby T says, referring to the pack in my front shirt pocket. "I used to smoke 'Reds' myself but my wife and daughter finally got me to quit a couple of years ago. I don't mind if you smoke though so long as you crack the window. Even though I quit, I still like to smell 'em being smoked sometimes ya know?" he tells me.

Bobby T looked to be in his mid to late sixties, dark brown skin with glasses tightly stretched by his round chubby face. He sported a salt and pepper goatee and a trucker's cap with the front logo half scratched off making the letters illegible above the image of a yellow jacket. Robert had an easy, natural demeanor and he liked to talk. I felt that he needed to talk, and he proceeded to tell me his entire life story within the span of our first hour together. He told me how he was born and raised in a small town outside of Charleston, South Carolina, deep in the heart of the Jim Crow South. He beamed as he spoke about his wife and daughter back in Atlanta and how he was proud of his daughter for finishing college at an Ivy League school when he had barely been able to graduate high school. After which he moved to Connecticut started driving trucks and was soon after drafted into the Vietnam war. He told me that the truck he drove was his own free and clear and that his wife managed the accounting for the trucking business. He talked about how he got the name Wild Child from his mischievous younger days as a freight driver— 'tooting powder' and 'fucking any cutie with booty that would stop moving for five seconds, all before he met his wife, he was certain to assure me with a wink.

399

Bobby T must have known that I was looking to move anonymously because he didn't ask me a single question about my own life or much about what business I had in Mobile. Occasionally, he would pause his rant about corrupt politicians and the bigotry that persisted in the trucking industry to pick up the CB radio handset and rattle off some trucker lingo as he passed a semi he recognized. After three and a half hours of colorful banter, I began to see signs for West Mobile which, if I remembered correctly, had always been the moneyed side of town and was still home to some of the old antebellum families that made their fortunes by from owning slaves."

I asked Bobby T if he could drop me at the next cheap motel we came to, and I would be out of his hair for good.

"Man, you don't wanna be walkin' around out here wit dem shades on. The way da' police be knockin' brothers upside they head? Let me take you where you gotta go. I ain't even get to tell ya bout how I ran point for seven months straight over in Vietnam without gettin' even a scratch on me."

I graciously declined his generous offer for I feared any further contact would endanger his life and the lives of his family, especially if I were to allow him to know where Lynn lived. I had already taken a substantial risk in riding with him this far. Although I felt Bobby T to be genuinely kind and generous, I still could not shake the trauma created by decades of constantly living in fear that every person you meet may be a puppet for the Incalculaba, and the paranoia seated deep within my psyche that kept suggesting to me there was a chance that Bobby T could be an agent.

Bobby T interrupted my thoughts stating, "I used to run loads for McGraw-Hill company from the paper mills through Mobile and all over the Southeast years ago when I first moved back south and decided to settle in Georgia wif my wife so I know the area pretty well. If I was a young man again and I was new in town, I would either go to downtown Mobile or stay in Prichard where a brother can lay low and get some thangs done with cash if ya needed to."

Bobby T understood a lot more than he let on. I told him Prichard sounded good, especially if I could get a room for the night with cash.

"If the place is still there, I know just the type of joint you' looking for," he assured me. We exited Interstate 10 onto 65 North toward Prichard, a suburb that rested North of downtown Mobile and happened to be home to much of the Black and Brown population of the city. The shadow of generational poverty coupled with limited access to education loomed large over the people who struggled daily against each other and the machine that kept them literally in the dark. We exited onto the I-65 service road and made a right onto West Rebel Road and then continued onto Whistler Street as the industrial scenery gave way to a more residential fare.

We eventually reached the corner of Whistler and North Shelton Beach Road. Barren trees framed the rundown buildings, and sagging cars reflected the age of the city and the weight of the burdens gripping the people. For every liquor store, there were two churches, and the dreary winter night created a double veil of destitution as we looked down on quiet early morning streets from the perch of the tractor trailer.

Another left onto St. Stephens Road, and we arrived at a horribly dilapidated structure labeled the Azalea Inn that looked like it had been around longer than I have. The parking lot was about half full and a black Honda Civic with tinted windows bumping rap music loudly pulled into the lot and drove around to the side of the building.

"This was the spot we used to take the hookers if we wanted some grits with our eggs," Bobby T said with a wink.

I faked a smile back at him and thanked him, holding out fifty dollars I had already counted out and stuffed in my pocket at the Love's gas station bathroom for flash money to procure a ride.

"I already told ya, I cain't take ya money. Hell, I was already headed this way, and they payin' me damn near two dollars a mile plus all my fuel, Bobby T said to me, smiling like a Cheshire Cat and rubbing his fingers

401

together in the universal money sign. "I was jus' happy to have somebody to talk to instead of listenin' to reruns of Art Bell on the radio or talkin' shit to some of these redneck truck drivers who still don't believe a black man ought to own his own rig."

Clearing my throat and still holding the money out towards Bobby T, I began, "I would appreciate it if..."

"I know," he cut me off. "I ain't gonna say nothing to nobody. I don't talk to the man. Shit I grew up in the sixties. 'My name is Bennett and I ain't in it,' as we used to say. I done picked up all types of folks over the years and some of 'em I regret givin' a ride to just 'cause they spirit didn't sit right with me. But you....you seem like a God fearing, cool cat. Remind me of my cousin Alvin who moved to New York the day we all graduated high school and joined the Panthers instead of going to 'Nam." Robert reached out his hand to shake mine. "So keep ya money and good luck and God bless ya with everythang."

We gave each other the universal soul brother's handshake, and I thanked him again before turning to climb down out of the truck.

As I landed on the ground, I discreetly stuffed the fifty dollars into the door panel and closed the door. With a blast of air from the brakes, Bobby T pulled off as I walked into the dimly lit motel lobby. The clock read '4:57am' and no one was presently behind the counter. The place reeked of Nag Champa incense and mold spores and there were stacks of paperwork strewn behind the counter next to a seriously outdated computer monitor and printer. A 2008 calendar hung on the wall with December's photo being a large ornate statue of Ganesh with the words Pancha Ganapati in large black letters. A small monitor to the left showed a camera view of the parking lot, and I could see the tail of Bobby T's truck pulling slowly out of the parking lot and back onto the highway. The scent of kerosene from a space heater emanated from a room behind the counter, and I could hear the soft snoring of someone napping on the other side of the wall. I knocked loudly on the counter and called out 'Hello' to the empty lobby which interrupted the sound of the snoring. I heard a male voice release a mighty yawn, followed by the creak of a wooden chair, and the shuffle of house-slippers over the linoleum floor. After a short while, a slightly built Indian gentleman, some years past middle aged with salt and pepper hair and a Bindi in the center of his forehead wearing a puffy winter coat, comes out rubbing his hands and blowing on them to warm them.

"Ahem…….Hello…… how can I help you?" the man asked in a still half groggy voice. He let a yawn escape his large mustached mouth as I tell him I would like a room for three nights, and I only have cash to pay with.

"All cash customers must pay in full now for duration of your stay and a 50 dollar fee will be added as deposit for cleaning. Since you are coming at six hours before check out I must charge for today. May I have I.D. please? "the man asked without looking up from his computer.

I handed the guy my passport and enough money for four nights plus an extra $50 fanned out in a way that he could see the amount at a glance. He peered up at me over his bifocals for a brief second, then looked back down at my passport. Then tapped a few times on his computer keyboard before printing out a piece of paper for me to sign. After that, he handed me a key card with the numbers 223 written with a Sharpie on the side.

"Snack machine, ice machine all down hallway to left of lobby building. Your room is around building on right on upper floor." The man points with a finger curving over his shoulder. "If you need towels, please call front desk. Thank you very much, sir, and thank you for choosing Azalea Inn and have a good morning."

Back outside in the parking lot, I could smell cheap weed smoke and see the blue of the new day breaking through the black of the night. I walked around and up the stairs to my room. As soon as I was in, I locked the door behind me and drew the curtains closed.

Chapter 21

Five fifteen in the morning. The scent of cigarettes with a tinge of purple Kush and roach spray seemed to be permanently burnished into the walls and furniture of room 223. I lit up my own cigarette to add to the mix and took in my surroundings. Paint was peeling from the ceiling and the walls, the bed was moldy and dingy just like the rest of the decor. The bathroom reeked of dirty mop water and urine and the roaches were confused on whether or not to scatter because I did not need turn the lights on. There was clear evidence of some rodent living in the closet. It was absolutely spectacular. The Taj Mahal compared to the caves, sewers, and underpasses I was used to.

I stared at the large black box on the dresser and after some minutes, I stood up and grabbed the remote control from the nightstand. The batteries in the remote for the television were dead, of course, and when I approached the television to try and turn it on manually, I noticed that the power cord looked as if something had been nibbling on it. We used to complain about these old-school, cathode-ray tube televisions. Personally, I preferred the soft contrast in the pictures of the old boob tubes in comparison to the digital rubbish the new ‘*smart televisions*’ produce. These new types of television also come fully equipped with surveillance devices that can watch and listen to you as well as you can watch and listen to it.

Sitting and smoking in the darkness, listening to the sounds of the other patrons in the motel was causing my paranoia to swell out of control and would not leave me alone so I opted to walk out of the room and stand out on the balcony to puff a cigarette, listening and scanning for anything like a tail. This sleepy southern town sat silently pregnant with the coming day's potential. There were not as many sirens, gunshots, or traffic sounds to serenade me in the wee hours of the morning like back in good old Chicago. Bird chirps and frog croaks were the ambient soundtrack for this part of the world. A marijuana aroma coming from the room two doors down from mine filled my nostrils with its pungent bouquet, masking all other smells near the front of the hotel. I could make out faint moans with heavy breathing and the rhythmic smack of a loose headboard against the wall coming from one of the rooms below me. Some couple was enjoying their morning, no doubt. At the far corner of the second floor, to my left, I heard laughter and the bass thump of a hip hop beat pulsing steadily in the cool morning. After about a half hour of smoking and silently listening to my surroundings and staring into the darkness, I was finally satisfied with the notion that I had not been followed and that I could relax and return to my room.

Hanging the 'Please Do Not Disturb' sign on the outside of my door as I entered, I closed and locked the door before pushing the old wooden dresser drawer with the television on it in front of the door. That should buy me a few extra seconds to escape in case I was wrong and someone tried to ambush me while I was sleeping. I took a shower and redressed myself with the same clothes I was just wearing before walking back into the main room. I yanked the duvet from the bed and hung it on the curtain rod to fully cover any gaps in the window that the curtain did not cover to block out any traces of the sun.

I laid down on my back on the cool sheets of the queen-sized bed and to my surprise, I was sound asleep in a matter of minutes. I had not been able to relax this well in over fifty years. I slept for nearly eight hours straight, my body must have been sensing the necessity to embrace some deep rest. After getting out of bed and taking a wicked piss, I was about to return to bed for a few more hours of sleep when I noticed a slight glow at the edge of the duvet covering the window. I moved to the window and peeked outside. The sky

405

was grey and overcast enough for me to attempt to venture outside a few hours before nightfall.

I went to my bag and grabbed my collapsible umbrella and made a short trek over to the nearest gas station to get a map of the area. Once I get to Gosport and reunite with Lynn the very first thing I will do is extract the rest of the loot from my stash. Once exchanged, the cash I receive should be more than enough to be able to begin the final phases of the plan to get my revenge against Reichstall and the cabal of oligarchs that were turning this planet into a wasteland.

As I left the motel toward civilization, I lit up my next to last cigarette and started walking east, burying my head in the cup of the umbrella. On the very next block, across South Shelton Beach Road, another message that I was on the right track hit me in the face. A butcher's market specializing in venison and bison called Meatblock Highway 45 Custom Meats sat right on the corner. I was absolutely starving, and the smell of the blood and unprocessed meat was driving me wild. I went in and ordered two pounds of raw brisket and shank and three pounds of top sirloin. After paying for the meat I left the butcher shop and walked down to a small, badly-in-need-of-remodeling, Shell gas station. There were a lot of people in line for lottery tickets and beer but once I reached the register I purchased two copies of USA Today newspaper, disinfectant wipes, garbage bags, fly traps, and a map of Alabama and the Greater Mobile Area before heading back to the hotel.

Once I was back in the room, I spread out one of the newspapers on the floor in front of the bed. I removed my shoes and clothes before opening the package of brisket and devoured most of it while kneeling on the hotel room floor. I had a few bites of the sirloin shank before wrapping up the leftovers and placing them back into the plastic bag. The small motel refrigerator was as disgusting as the rest of the room, and it sounded as if it had compressor issues the way it ran constantly. At least I could store my leftover meat in it without worrying about bugs getting to it even though it may not work well enough to keep the meat from spoiling.

Around 9:00p.m. I decided to go for a walk in the neighborhood down to a bar I noticed across from the gas station. The name above the door of the place read: Freaky's Bar which seemed like another bit of serendipity because I certainly fit into the freak category. The patrons inside seemed to be a mostly forty-plus crowd with a few youngsters sprinkled in. The racial demographic favored the pepper variety with a few specks of salt here and there. The place was more restaurant/lounge than bar, and the bass thump of rap music blasted over the PA system. Ads for their 'March Madness' chicken plates and world-famous onion rings were plastered all around the walls and on placards on every table and there were a few people dancing in front of a large mirror near the restrooms. I took a seat at the bar and ordered a Jack Daniels on the rocks from a voluptuous woman wearing skintight jeans, a white long sleeve shirt, and a black apron.

"Coming right up sugar," says the gorgeous sister tending bar as she flashed her 'southern hospitality' smile and swished her wide hips to the other end of the bar to make my drink and a few others. When she returned, I planned on sliding her an above average tip in hopes that she would be chattier when I started my line of questions about the city.

After taking in my surroundings at the bar, I pretended to be interested in the college basketball on television that had everyone else in the place captivated. The heavy smell of some garlic dish coming from the kitchen began to bother me, making me want to step outside and fill my nostrils with sweet cigarette smoke. I began looking around for a patio area or some other designated smoking pen when I noticed a young couple playing pool together, and I am reminded of the wonder years between myself and Lynn in her youth. How beautiful she used to be in her afro and colorful dresses in the spring. We would hang out in joints like this on Saturday nights. Her Chanel No. 5 perfume was bewitching, and her understanding eyes would meet my ferocity with strength imbued through her ancestral connection to Legba. Her people were enslaved from Benin and her great-grandfather was a papaloi from Louisiana.

The sister who took my order comes back over and places my drink down on a napkin in front of me. Her hands harbor a gold ring or two on every finger including her thumb. I slide her double what the drink costs and tell her to keep the change in a raspy, baritone voice.

"Thanks for the tip, sugar. Where you in here from and how long you plan on stayin'?" she asks me as she refills the pork rinds in the bowl next to me. "They gonna be having the St. Patrick's Day Parade tomorrow, and they gone be doing it B-I-G downtown baby!" she said beaming at me with a huge smile as I took a sip of my Jack Daniels.

Clearing my throat I said, "I am in town on business, I do architecture work."

"Well, go head on, brother". She playfully swatted my hand with hers. "My niece is going to school at Spelman for architecture. With them shades on indoors, I thought you was gonna say you was either a blind musician or a pimp." She chuckled at her own joke.

I began with my usual apology, "Please, do not mistake my glasses as rudeness. My eyes are extremely sensitive to light and…"
"You don't gotta say nothing bout it, baby, I'm just messing with you Sug'," she interjected. "Looking like the chocolate Terminator." She smiled big flashing her pearly whites with their one golden tooth glistening in the light and winked at me to soften the blow of her teasing. "Listen, sugar, I gotta go take care of these orders but…I'll be right back. Rasheeda Hamilton," she extended her hand for me to shake it, which I oblige, "but everybody calls me Peaches cause I'm so sweet." She winked and smiled as she turned with her ample hips and buttocks swaying over to the waiting customers at the other side of the bar.

I took that opportunity to step outside onto the patio to smoke a cigarette and pick up a copy of Auto Trader magazine in the rack at the front of the bar before exiting. It dawned on me that buying a car for cash directly from the owner could be done through the classified ads without needing to prove identity. Having my own vehicle would no doubt be the most direct and safest route to traveling the 75 miles or so to Gosport and reuniting with Lynn. Walking or running the entire way at night would look too suspicious, and there would be no safe place for me to camp during the day if I failed to cover the distance in one evening. I also needed to be able to travel down to Black Hammock Island near the Georgia/Florida line in order to withdraw the lion's share of my stash and exchange that gold for enough cash to finance my revolution

I returned to the bar and asked Peaches if they kept a phone book behind the bar.

"Damn, sugar, you *is* old fashioned. I think that's what I like about you. Somethin' about your accent—You got a old school feeling about you like you been around a while. Like a man that know how to make a woman feel like a woman." She flashes her big gold laden smile again as she stepped to the cash register and athletically squatted down to rummage through some paper and notebooks in a cabinet under the counter. After a short time, she emerged with a small Mobile County Directory and plopped it down in front of me. "Look here, sugar, you ain't got to lie to me. I ain't no police. What kind of architect don't got a cell phone? According to my niece, architects make big money."

I pull a 20 dollar bill from my roll and slide it to her and say, "Thank you for the phone book. If you only knew how old-fashioned I was."

I wink and tip my hat at her, allowing one corner of my mouth to curl up in a grin at her as I take out the pen and pad I took from my room at the Azalea Inn and began to flip through the phonebook to find the telephone numbers for the nearest costume shops and cab companies. I looked up from my task and caught Peaches staring at me. She flashed a smile and skeptically raised one eyebrow as she coyly turned to tend to the other patrons.

I finished my drink and ordered one more, leaving another20 dollar bill on the counter before sneaking out while Peaches was busy speaking with an interracial couple that just arrived at the bar. As I landed outside, I lit up a cigarette and walked back up the street to my hotel room. The rain had stopped, and I spent the rest of the night looking through the Auto Trader magazine for some type of semi-reliable vehicle being sold for cash by the owner. In the bar, I had written down the names, numbers and addresses of the few costume shops I found and the first five cab companies that were listed. I studied the map until I found the streets listed for each costume shop and made note of the ones that were closest to the Azalea Inn. The rest of the night I spent mapping out the best route from the motel to Lynn's place and practicing what I would say to her when I saw her.

I slept from dawn until 10:00a.m. and as soon my feet hit the floor, I began calling about the vehicles I had highlighted in the Auto Trader magazine as potential winners. I found a 1995 Mitsubishi Galant with a little over 193,000 miles on it being sold 'As-is' for 500 dollars in a town east of here called Mauvilla which happened to be in the same county. 500 would be a huge chunk of my remaining money, and I will need extra for gas and incidentals so from here on out I would have to be a little less free with my generosity if I wanted to have enough to make it to Gosport.

The skies were clearer with only a fifteen percent chance of rain so I put on my long sleeve shirt and hat and tried to cover my skin up as best as possible before leaving the hotel. Using the hotel phone, I called a cab and when it arrived I had to grit my teeth and suffer through the pain of my skin burning long enough to tell the cab driver to take me to Bienville Costume Shop near Carlen. When we arrived at the shop it was already busy with customers looking for Saint Patrick's Day accessories. I gave the cab driver an extra 20 bucks to stand by while I shopped. I walked inside, and I purchased some SPF 50 'Dark Brown' makeup, hopped back in the cab and headed back to the hotel room.

Back at the hotel I stood in the mirror and used my fingers to smear on the thick makeup and covered my face and hands and any other exposed skin on my neck and forearm before calling the guy about the Mitsubishi and setting a time to meet him. Since I was at the mercy of the slow cab drivers, I set a rendevous time of 4:00pm which I felt would give me plenty of travel time. For this trip, I dialed a different cab company to avoid anyone becoming familiar with my face and voice.

The cab ride to the Mauvilla took 30 minutes and cost me a whopping $58 which I was none too happy about as my funds were growing ever thinner. The cab pulled up in front of a row of neatly kept, small, one-level duplex homes and I saw my freshly washed future car parked at the sidewalk in front of one of the duplexes which harbored a bunch of other cars in various states of disrepair scattered about the yard. A black rooster strutted around in a patch of brown grass on the side of the carport. The Mitsubishi was grey, and the paint on the hood and roof were discolored due to sun damage. It had new-ish Landspider tires, and tinted windows, with maroon cloth interior. The man selling the car was a short, muscular, Latino gentleman with a thick mustache in his late fifties or early sixties named Ignacio. He wore coveralls and Gravel Gear boots and judging from the music coming from the backyard and the empty beer cans strewn about, he seemed to also be in the midst of enjoying the celebration of Saint Patrick, offering me a Coors Light as I waited for him to retrieve the keys.

I wished only to pay him and going on my merry way, but the man insisted I drive the car first before leaving to ensure that he was honest about it being in good condition. After a short test drive around the block with Ignacio riding shotgun, I gave him the 500 dollars and signed the bill of sale and the title. Ignacio went to his garage and returned with a couple of screws, a screwdriver and a small cardboard sign that read "TAG APPLIED FOR "and placed it on the back of the car.

"Muchas gracias, hermano," I say to Ignacio "Pero si alguien pregunta yo nunca estuve aqui." [If anyone asks I was never here]. And I offered him another fifty dollars, which he refused to take and pushed back towards me.

He shook my hand with a sincere smile and a wink, and bid me a pleasant, "Take care amigo. Esta quinientos es suficiente. Y entiendo tu no tienes preocupar." [What you have given me is more than enough. I understand, no worries]

"Bendiciones mi amigo y adios," I say to Ignacio before jumping in my newly purchased vehicle and taking off. I made it back to Prichard in enough time to make a stop at Meatblock Highway market and pick up two more

411

pounds of the freshest top sirloin they had. I needed something fresh because I didn't trust the refrigerator in the hotel.

I rolled back over to the Azalea Inn and barricaded myself inside once again. I removed all clothing except my pants and washed all the makeup off my hands, face, and neck before I ate my bloody top sirloin shirtless over the tub.

After eating, I sat on the floor of the bathroom brooding over my life. It had been a considerable amount of time since I had touched a woman and tonight, my lower brain was telling me I should stay and proposition Peaches into having some fun before getting on the road and heading north. But out of respect for Lynn, I put the thought out of my head. Having everything I needed for the trip, I decided to cut short my stay in Mobile and head on up to Gosport tonight while everyone was partying and the police had their hands full with the Saint Patrick's Day party crowd. I removed the rest of my clothing and took a long hot shower, washing the blood residue from my meal down the drain. I got dressed and afterwards, I discarded all the bones and any other evidence of my being in the room into the dumpster in the parking lot. Before I left, I wiped the entire room down with disinfectant wipes and hotel towels before making the bed and depositing my key on the dresser and heading out. Outside in the parking lot, I crept over to the black Honda Civic and removed its license plate, using one of my claws as a screwdriver. Discreetly and silently, I attached it to the back of my car before taking my leave of the Azalea Inn. Having an actual tag on my car should bring much less heat as long as I obeyed all the traffic laws and stuck to the main roads, I should not have any trouble from the police. Once I reestablished contact with Lynn I would ask her to register my vehicle and purchase better credentials for me. It had been eleven years since I last had any form of correspondence with Lynn, and she should be in her seventies now. I prayed that she was still alive.

Chapter 22

       Interstate-65 North crosses through Wetumpka, Alabama or Wind Creek, where the Choctaw nation has managed to build and maintain a very large and very successful casino and hotel just north of Freemanville, a small unincorporated town created to settle newly freed blacks and Indians looking to establish their own homesteads and businesses during the reconstruction years. The radio in this part of the South limited my choices to either country music, Latin music, conservative talk, or Christian evangelistic rhetoric. I lit another cigarette as I slowed down to turn north onto Highway 21. The car kicked out a loud backfire and immediately began to sputter like it was losing fuel pressure before picking up speed again. Hopefully it was nothing major, and the car was merely getting adjusted to being driven after being sedentary for a prolonged period. I had no tools to fix anything if it broke down and I needed that baby to last me at least 24 hours without dying. After that, I would drive it into a ditch and burn it as soon as I knew Lynn was safe and her farm was all clear of surveillance.

       I passed the massive Fountain Correctional Facility on my left. Another despicable example of the privately owned and operated prison industrial complex that got their jollies by warehousing and hiring out black, brown, and the disenfranchised white populace to the corporations and state governments for cheap labor. Citizens arrested and charged with offenses that merely reflect the systemic problems in American society. The

413

impoverished, the junkies, and the gangbangers created and propagated by the invisible hand are then funneled into the incarceration side of the capitalist cabal to be so-called "rehabilitated" and released back into society to repeat the same cycle and proliferate ignorance to the next generations. All of it conveniently hidden away in small rural communities throughout the U.S. for marginal local profit and to boost electoral numbers for less populated counties.

And they have the nerve to call me a bloodsucker.

I flicked my cigarette butt out of the window in silent protest as I passed. The two-hour drive from Mobile to Gosport was lined with mostly trees with a few farms dotted throughout the countryside. Everything remained virtually unchanged here for the last hundred years. Only the names on the plots of land were replaced but the balance of power remained in the hands of the conquering minority. The dashboard clock above the radio read 2:46 a.m. as I drove through the dark foggy night. I was tempted to turn off the two sorry excuses for headlights on the Galant and just use my eyes, but it would be my luck to pass a cop who wanted to question why the hell I was driving without a valid license in an unregistered vehicle with no lights at damn near 3:00 in the morning. Highway 21 North became 21 East through Frisco City and then connected with Highway 84 North across the Alabama River and into the heart of old Choctaw country where Lynn and her family have maintained a property for the past forty years.

I put my cigarette out and rolled all my windows down to imbibe the air and let the nostalgia carry me back down the correct roads. Other than the addition of asphalt, most of these old throughways have stayed exactly the same. Just as I passed Pigeon Creek, I saw my landmark, the Mackey Branch Baptist Church. Crafted and built by enslaved men and women and completed just before the Civil War, this church had been an institution of deferred hope in this community from the first days of operation when blacks were made to enter the church through the rear entrance and sit in the balcony and be quiet so as not to upset the white worshippers below them.

Once past the church, I made a right down a partially paved street now labeled Birch Road. As the concrete turned to dirt, I passed multiple mailboxes that were new additions since last I darkened this doorstep. I killed my lights as I approached the last few miles to her home, remembering how nosy 'country' neighbors can be. I pulled into her long gravel driveway but slowed and pulled over to the right into the woods once I was approximately fifty or sixty feet from the entrance. I wanted to wait until morning to confront Lynn in case she or whoever might be living with her might interpret my knocking on the door at 3:00a.m. on a Tuesday after not sending as much as a postcard for more than ten years as rude.

As I sat in the car, I rolled down all the windows and instinctively reached for my pack of cigarettes. But when I was hit with a gust of the crisp morning breeze, I decided to postpone smoking in order to imbibe the smell of the pine trees and the budding muscadine bushes mixed in with new growth dandelions sprouting fresh on this cool March morning.

The scents of the forest began flooding my brain with memories. I thought of Lynn and her love of honeysuckle and gardenias which she would plant in the front yard every spring at our home in East Atlanta. Wild sanguinaria, more commonly known as bloodroot, would grow in large patches in the woods and the fields behind our house, and I would teach her the ways of the Seminoles and how they used the herbs to make medicine.

It was odd that I did not smell any canine presence nearby. Lynn was particularly fond of her pets, and she would always write to me about having at least two or three roaming around and getting into mischief. They were her cheap form of security and somehow they knew without training to bark whenever anyone approached the house. As I stepped out of the car, I noticed something else peculiar about the farm. The grass near the mouth of the driveway and along the shoulder leading to the house was almost two feet high, and there were downed limbs all along the driveway. This seemed odd considering Lynn's obsession with keeping her dwellings as immaculately groomed as humanly possible. She always said that as black people we had to make sure that our property was in good condition because we would be

415

scrutinized twice as hard as the poor whites that lived nearby and kept their properties in varying degrees of disrepair.

Sunrise was a few hours away, and now my anxiousness was building with every minute that passed. I walked further down the drive to listen for any sound emanations from the house. There were too many trees blocking the winding path that led to the house for me to see anything clearly. The weight of the uncertainty began to be too much to bear so I broke down and walked back to the car, reached in, and grabbed my cigarettes from the center console and lit up. I paced back and forth next to the car in the dark while I chain smoked and ruminated on how I should proceed. I entertained the thought of staking out the house from the treetops until morning, but when the sun rose, I would have to climb down and take refuge from the light anyway so I decided to scrap that idea. The only thing I could do was wait.

As the sun started to crack over the tree line, I got back in the car and using the visor mirror, I applied my SPF makeup and went over in my mind what I wanted to say to her beginning with my apologies. I drove the remaining quarter mile up to the main house, and the rest of the place looked as unkempt as the driveway. The property seemed to have been sitting vacant for weeks, maybe months. I parked behind an old tan and white Chevy truck and got out of the car and took a deep breath to check the air for any recent activity. The scent of humans was vague and as I walked closer to the front door, I was careful not to crunch the dried leaves that scattered the yard in case I missed something in my initial scan. I knocked on the door and waited. I knocked even louder for a second and third time and after receiving no response, I tried the doorknob which turned freely, and I entered the living room. Most people in this area did not lock their doors but after living amongst the wolves for so long, I personally always found it odd to be able to walk right into someone's home.

The inside of Lynn's place looked clean and orderly, but the plants were in a withered condition, and again there were no feeding bowls or other signs of the animals that Lynn always kept around. There was a tall stack of mail on the coffee table, the top two envelopes were bills from the county

416

hospital and the bank. In addition, there were two bouquets on the dining room table that were also withered and still had the get well soon cards attached. This I found odd indeed because ever since the incident behind the alley near 16th Street Baptist when Lynn was attacked and I had to share my blood with her, she has not suffered as much as a sniffle and has looked and moved like someone twenty years younger than she was. As my concern grew I began to look around at all the family photos and pictures of Lynn as a young vivacious teacher. Pictures of her and her family on ski vacations or at the beach were on every wall and flat surface in the house. I could not help but smile and envy the warm little place they had managed to carve out in this cold cruel world.

"CLICK CLACK".

        The all too familiar sound of a shotgun cocking was the next thing I heard.
I must have let myself be distracted by my walk down memory lane for me to not have heard or smelled this person's approach.

        "If you move, muthafucka, I'll blow yo ass away," a man's voice said angrily. "They sendin' niggas now to mess with us?" You from the bank?" the man's voice asked sternly?

        I remain silent and staring at the wall ahead of me.

        "I thought we told ya'll that we don't want to sell. I don't know why you bastards are coming around now and how you knew my grandma was sick, but goddammit, if I catch you trespassing here again, I'm gonna bust your fuckin' head to the white meat. Now turn around with your hands in the air where I can see them."

        I turn around with my hands up. The man standing in the doorway looked to be about five foot ten, two hundred pounds, in his early twenties wearing black sneakers, blue jeans, a red and blue Tennessee State Tigers sweatshirt, and a black skull cap.

"How the fuck you see anything in the dark with them Eazy-E shades on?" I knew y'all was dirty, but damn! They done stooped to hiring regular old street niggas to do they dirty work?! Wells Fargo must really be getting desperate." He leveled the gun at my chest. "Now walk on out of here and get in your car and don't fucking come back!"

I just stood there staring at the man, thinking of what I could say that would calm him down enough for me to be able to explain who I was.

"You hear me, nigga?!" He was shaking like a leaf, and his heart was thumping loudly against his rib cage.

I took a step forward as he backed up and flicked on the light switch with his elbow.

"I'm glad the neighbors called me instead of calling the sheriff first because I finally get to catch one of you assholes in the act. Matter fact, are you even with Wells Fargo? Just what fucking bank do you work for? I know the hospital in Grove Hill don't have no black folks working for 'em, so it cain't be them," the man said, and as he raised his head to look me up and down, I could clearly see the family connection between Lynn and this man. His forehead, nose and mouth were all hers.

Now that he could see me fully in the light, the look on his face began changing from pure anger to one of slight puzzlement and query like he was searching his mind on where he had come across my face before.

"I am not an employee of the bank," I began. "I am a former colleague of your grandparents, and I have returned to ask for their assistance in a matter of utmost importance. I was not aware of your grandmother's illness and I do apologize for showing up unannounced and trespassing. I am a friend and I would like to help in any way I can."

The man squinted at me silently," Hold up....wait. I've seen you before."

418

I stop walking towards the door as he holds the gun on me with his head tilted sideways still with a puzzled look.

"Yeah... that's right... in them old pictures with YaYa," the man says, nodding with the gun as his memory tells him that he is on the right track. "But those were the pictures she used to show us of her back in the day during Civil Rights. She had to be in her mid-to-late twenties at the time, and that was damn near fifty years ago. So that would put you at least at 75. I've heard of 'black don't crack' but damn. The glasses are different, but that's you," he motioned toward a picture in the lower left hand corner of the wall. "Or maybe you're his son?"

"Sir, if you would allow me to explain I—"

"How the hell did you find this place?" the man cuts me off. "Up until Papa died, YaYa never spoke much of the details of her Civil Rights activism days. A few months after Papa's funeral, all of a sudden YaYa started keeping that picture of you, or your dad, and her from the sixties on the mantle over the fireplace. YaYa also started opening up more about what life was like for her during those years living under constant fear of being lynched or bombed in the Jim Crow South. She told us a crazy story of how she was almost killed by some white men one night leaving a voter rally, and that the man who saved her was the only man she ever loved other than Papa. As a kid, the couple times I remember her saying anything about her life during the movement days, Papa would get mad and try to change the subject because of the faraway look YaYa would get in her eyes when she spoke of those times." The man seemed to be searching his mind for some lost piece of nostalgia for a second before repositioning the shotgun at my face.

With my hands still in the air, the man circled me with the gun still aimed at my chest and walked over to the table behind the sofa and pulled a stack of photos from a cut-glass bowl. He tucked the shotgun under his right arm as he searched through the stack of photos face up on the table with his left hand and pulled out another picture of Lynn and me at a church dinner in

1966. Her dazzling smile was juxtaposed with my deadpan face. He held the picture up for a comparison.

"Yeah, that's you." he said, looking from me to the photo. "Only thing different is your glasses and hair. Damn, and I thought YaYa aged gracefully. She was always racing with us and keeping up with the school activities of all the grandkids. Hell, I couldn't beat her at basketball until I turned seventeen and even then, I had to really go hard." The man smiled to himself in remembrance.

"When she got sick recently, no one could believe it because she had literally never called out for work a day in her life. Even when her and Papa were in the car accident that he wound up dying from, she ended up healing completely in a few months even though her injuries were thought to be more severe." By this point the shotgun was pointing toward the floor and the man placed the picture of myself and Lynn on a bench nearby. The man seemed to be fighting back tears. I lowered my hands and as he took a seat next to the photograph on the bench I said.

"Your grandmother is an amazing woman. I owe her and your grandfather a debt that can never be repaid and I promise to do what I can to make things right again. I am sorry if I am overstepping my boundaries, but would you happen to know what happened to her prior to her being admitted into the hospital? Was it a complication of the accident you spoke of or had she traveled anywhere odd or been exposed to anything out of the ordinary?" I asked the man.

The man stared at me for a long moment, seeming to struggle with the emotion building inside of him. He took a deep breath and began.

"Well... my sister Tammy seems to think it all started after YaYa had gone to Whatley to give blood. This was way after the accident and Papa dying. The Red Cross had a mobile truck setup to get blood donations for injuries related to a bad tornado that had just torn through North Alabama. A couple days after she got back from Whatley, her phone started ringing nonstop. If it wasn't some rep from the Red Cross calling, it was somebody

420

from the hospital administration calling and calling, over and over, all times of the damn day and night. YaYa started screening any calls she got from numbers that she didn't recognize or that had a unlisted caller ID. The calls got to be so frequent that YaYa stopped answering the house phone altogether. Then they started sending letters about how it was important that she....uhhhh... she needed to *'follow up'* with them or some shit. They wanted her to come back in for uh, what did they call it?"

He snapped his fingers to jog his memory.

"An *'evaluation'* of her blood and that it was crucial that she give more of it because it was very rare and badly needed for their fuckin' research. They even went as far as sending reps from the fuckin' CDC over here to her house to *'recommend'* that she give more of her blood because it was important in helping people with cancer and other diseases like that. My sister who is also a nurse said she was getting *'Henrietta Lacks'* vibes from the whole situation. It was around then that she got freaked out and started calling my mom and my uncles about everything that was going on."

The man who I had confirmed was Lynn's grandson swallowed hard, His eyes became wet with tears as he began his next sentence. He paused and exhaled to regain his composure, wiping his eyes on his sleeve before he began again.

"The neighbors called one day and said that they saw some strange black sedans driving down the road and parking near our property. 'Men in Black' and government type characters walking through the yard and traipsing in the woods behind the house." The man's voice began to crack now as he began his next sentence.

"The next day... one of the neighbors, Ms. Carmen...just happened to be stopping by to wish YaYa a happy holiday and found her collapsed in the yard while hanging the laundry." The man seemed to remember that I was a stranger and attempted to compose himself. He wiped his damp eyes with the sleeve of his sweatshirt before continuing. "YaYa was rushed to the county hospital where..." he paused again. "For some damn reason...the

421

hospital had authorized a full blood transfusion without consulting anyone from the family." Full tears drop from his eyes now and looking down at the ground, he said, "Those muthafuckas wanted her blood bad for some reason man." He composed himself and looked me square in the eye,

"Those punk muthafuckas stole my grandmama's blood!"

He yells in frustration. After a very long, tear stained pause he began again in a more even tone.

"Dammit man!… I didn't mean for all that to come out. I haven't been up here in a while and today for some reason, shit is gettin' me in my feelings." He wiped his eyes again with the sleeve of his sweatshirt.

"I finally get to meet you, and here I am blubbering like a little girl. "My name is Keith." He stands and cradles the shotgun under his left arm as he extends his right hand for me to shake it which I oblige, taking his hand in both of mine as a gesture of sympathy to his emotional state.

"My bad about the gun in your face. I ain't no killer. Far from it," Keith chuckled, embarrassed.

"We all hunt around here since we spent our summers here in the country, but I wasn't gonna shoot ya. I just mad and I wanted to scare off the damn bill collectors and land speculators because I wanted to do something to help YaYa." Keith gestured toward the pile of paperwork and envelopes on the dining room table. "Given that YaYa always had money and always handled all her business on her own, with her being down, it's been hard trying to get all her bills paid. My mother, is YaYa's middle child. We moved back down here from New York to live in Mobile after her and my pops divorced. I started helping YaYa and PaPa on the farm whenever I had time off from school. I've been trying to get back up here to help maintain the place but between work and grad school, I was only able to help relocate the animals to a neighbor's farm who are cool with us and sympathetic to our situation until we can sort out the finances and the day to day upkeep bullshit." Keith sat back down on the bench, putting the shotgun on the floor

422

in front of him he leaned forward and placed his hands over his face to hide his sobs. Broken, powerless and vulnerable.

"I understand this is all very overwhelming for you," I began.

"Thank you for shouldering so much of your family's burdens up until now. I know we just met and you probably still have a lot of questions for me. But if you trust me, I swear I will do everything in my power to bring your grandmother home. Let your mother know that in a week your family will have more than enough money to cover any expenses for the hospital and the farm. Write down the address, phone number and directions to the hospital your grandmother is in and the best number that you can be contacted." I extended my right hand to Keith which he met with a soul brother grip, and I pulled him to his feet. Looking him directly in the eyes with one hand on his shoulder I told him.

"Your grandmother's heart and sacrifices have saved me and countless others over the years, and now it is time to repay her strength with ours."

Keith nodded to me in affirmation, straightened his back, dried his tears and wiped his nose. He walked into the kitchen and after a couple of minutes returned with a sheet of paper with his and his mother's contact information and the address and directions from the farm to the hospital in Grove Hill, Alabama. As we walked outside, I asked to borrow a shovel which Keith retrieved from the tool shed for me and placed it in my trunk.

"Can I meet you back here tomorrow afternoon around 5:30p.m?" I asked Keith.

"I get off work at 5tomorrow and I have one stop to make after that. With traffic, I should be able to make it here by about 6:15 if that's cool?"

"Perfect." I replied.

We shook hands and I walked out of the house and lit a cigarette before getting in my car and driving North on Highway 84 toward the hospital.

•　　　•　　　•

Grove Hill was about six and a half cigarettes northwest of Gosport. A straight shot up U.S. 84 and would be considered the '*big city*' for this part of southern Alabama because most other cities within a 50-mile radius had fewer than two traffic lights; they were so minuscule in population. I was still wearing the SPF makeup so the brightness of the day was way less of a headache, but there was still too much daylight for me to operate at full strength so I opted to lay low and create a plan that would pair better with the nightfall.

I drove up North Jackson Street to the Grove Hill Municipal Park so I could hunker down and sleep in my car without attracting too much attention to myself. I found a nice shady spot and backed my car into an area behind the baseball diamond at the rear of the park. I reclined my seat as far as it would go, locked my doors, and proceeded to close my eyes and rest, albeit lightly. After about three or so hours, my body decided it had had enough, and I reached for my cigarettes, lit one up, and rolled down the window. Nightfall was still several hours away so I opted to just smoke and make notes on future endeavors as I watched the walkers and joggers as they passed me in the park.

At 4:37pm the sun was low enough on the horizon for me to make my way to the hospital to case out a site for an inconspicuous entry and exit point. The hospital consisted of two buildings, an emergency admission ward, and the larger main building behind it where the long-term care patients and, more than likely, Lynn's room was located. The main hospital ward building was a hulking, one-storied affair that matched the small-town architecture motif.

One good thing about small towns is their reluctance to upgrade to newer technology because I miraculously found a pay phone attached to a Marathon gas station a few blocks down from the hospital and called the reception nurse pretending to be a relative of Lynn's to confirm her room number and how I could get there from the main lobby. Once I had directions to Cora's room, I rode back down Jackson Street in order to access the hospital grounds. I circled the campus twice to get the layout of the buildings then using my pen and notepad I drew a crude map of the geography of the area before leaving my car parked at the back of the parking lot and walking a short distance to a Gulf filling station next door to the hospital to buy a fresh pack of Marlboro cigarettes and a local newspaper.

It was dark but the night was still early. Checking my watch, it was barely 7:00 p.m. so I decided to grab a bite to eat. I would have loved something raw but the grocery stores at this time of night were usually full of people shopping after work, and I wanted to draw as little attention to my presence in town as possible. I opted to drive down to the local McDonald's and order a dozen plain hamburgers in the drive thru. I parked in the McDonald's lot and made short work of the meat from the burgers, placing the buns back in the bag. I sat and smoked cigarettes while I studied my homemade hospital map and planned my invasion while the bustle of the busy restaurant continued around me.

I passed the time smoking and reading the newspaper trying to keep my mind off what Keith told me about the CDC snooping around and the hospital stealing Lynn's blood. If the Incalculaba had been alerted that someone with my strain of DNA was living in the area, Myself, Lynn and her entire family could be in grave danger. Before I knew it almost three hours had passed and I had smoked damn near an entire pack of cigarettes. The clock read 9:23 p.m. and the customers swarming McDonald's had thinned out significantly. The whole city seemed to have a collective bedtime where all activity shut down well before midnight.

I ventured back to the hospital parking facility and pulled into a spot in a dark area at the rear of the lot. I removed my hat, shoes, and jacket and zipped into the shadows, running full speed until I was at the tree line behind the main building. The sterile atmosphere of the hospital offered me a greater advantage at distinguishing scents and from what I could tell, there were very few staff on duty tonight. When I called earlier the nurse mentioned to me that visiting hours ended at 9:00p.m. and I figured that there would be staff that did the rounds every couple hours to check the patient's vital signs.

I slipped around to the west side of the building staying in the shadows just out of reach of the streetlamps. A white Clarke County coroner's van was parked near the building, and I quickly crawled under it, holding my body off the ground with my toes and fingertips like a spider. The motor was cold, telling me that this van had not been driven in a while. An unmistakable aroma which I had imprinted on my soul wafted to my nose as someone exited the front doors to the parking lot. I watch a pair of legs wearing green scrubs and grey New Balance shoes pass me and head to their vehicle as I hid under the van. This person must have interacted with Lynn recently because although faint, I was positive I detected the scent of Lynn's skin and hair. Her smell was reaching out to me across the night air, almost as if she was calling to me. I rolled from under the van and ran into the shadows of the building. According to the map I drew, Lynn's room should be the fifth window on the lower tier of the west wing of the building. I slinked down the wall until I'm up directly underneath the correct window. Lynn's scent was more pronounced now, and I turned slowly and reached up to pull myself up onto the windowsill and peeked in through the condensation on the window.

Jackpot.

She was alive...barely. My heart skipped a beat at the sight of her face, now dry with deep wrinkles that made her look much more elderly than she actually was, but still as beautiful as ever. She was sleeping peacefully on her back. Her nose was filled with an oxygen cannula, and the rest of her body was riddled with an assortment of wires and tubes connecting to I.V. drips, catheters, and other assorted equipment.

The clock on the wall read a quarter to ten so I should have at least fifteen minutes to finish my business and get back to my car before the next nurse's inspection. This far south, nobody locked anything so after removing the outer screen with a well-placed claw, I slid the window open and silently poured my body through the 18-inch opening without making a noise. Close up, I could see Lynn's face was gaunt and misshapen, her eyes sunken in, her once black and silver afro was now pure white. I smiled thinking to myself that she would probably prefer to die rather than knowing this was how I saw her for the first time in over a decade.

I could hear voices of the active hospital just on the other side of the door so I proceeded to bite my left thumb with my sharp canine which produced a trickle of blood which I carefully allowed for a few drops to fall into Lynn's mouth before my body closed the wound. I leaned down to kiss her forehead and took one last look at her. As I was standing there looking down at the shell of the woman I once allowed to hold my heart, one of the machines registering her pulse rate began to beep faster and the numbers on her blood pressure monitor slowly began to tick upwards toward more normal levels. Before I could celebrate, I heard the squeak of a tennis shoe near the door as someone approached, and in the next moment, a blonde, full-figured, middle-aged woman wearing blue scrubs and a very pleasant demeanor burst through the door just as I was sliding the window closed.

"Hey hon," she says to the sleeping Lynn, stroking her hair. "You feeling better, girl," the nurse purrs in her syrupy southern accent. "Looks like your vitals are improving, and I'm sure your daughter and the rest of your family will be happy to hear that. I wonder what's done got you all riled up tonight?"

As she made a note of Cora's vital statistics on her clipboard, she paused and looked around the room like she had just noticed something odd.

"Why is it so cold in this darn room? Did you open the window without telling us, miss lady? Did your boyfriend come pay you a secret visit and that's what's got you all lively?" She laughed to herself at the impossibility of what she was suggesting and walked over to the thermostat

427

and tapped it a couple of times to make sure it was working. After checking the I.V. drip and the fullness of the catheter bag the nurse remarked,

"I'll be back in an hour or so now, so sweet dreams hun." The nurse left and closed the door behind her as she continued her rounds for the evening.

Outside the window, I grabbed the torn screen and ran back to the tree line and tossed the screen into the woods behind the hospital. Staying in the darkness, I sprinted back to the car to put my shoes and coat back on and returned to the Shell station where I filled up the Mitsubishi's tank and drove the speed limit back to Gosport. But instead of Cora's farm, I head straight to an uninhabited area near Choctaw Creek and pulled off the road as far into the brush as I could safely go in the sedan without getting stuck in the mud. After making doubly sure I was deep enough in the brush and well hidden from the road, I got out and grabbed the spade shovel from the trunk and walked down into the briars and woods towards a small stream. I followed the flow of the water for another thousand yards until I reached a small, dilapidated man-made wooden bridge that used to connect the two halves of Walker's plantations bifurcated by Choctaw Creek. About three hundred yards from the bridge stood a massive 500-year-old oak tree in a small clearing whose branches and canopy held the stories of the countless lives that have crossed its path. I happened to be this oak tree's oldest living friend. Black people gathered at night under this tree 200 years ago for meetings and worship, and Native Americans employed this mighty tree 200 years before that for their community announcements and marriage ceremonies.

A little over 100 yards south of that tree lay a huge boulder that would require an excavator team to build a road through some of the toughest, most uneven terrain just to get a bulldozer down here that was heavy-duty enough to move this gargantuan stone aside. The boulder sat beautifully defiant, overgrown with vines and covered in moss and leaves, the immovable home to countless generations of insects living beneath it undisturbed for nearly half a century. I chose this area for a hiding place in 1969 when Lynn and I were still together because of its proximity to the property Lynn purchased during our last years together. Removing my jacket and tossing it on the ground I squatted next to the boulder and took a deep breath. I closed my eyes, and the image of Cora's corpse-like body lying stiff in the hospital bed caused my blood to run hot. The thought of one of the handful of people who accepted me unconditionally in this world coming so close to death consumed me. My breathing began to quicken and became more and more shallow. Sufficiently motivated, my eyes sprang open like lightning, and I lunged toward the rock, grabbing it at the roots and digging my claws into it, pressing my body against it with the full strength of my anger. The behemoth stone was slowly disconnected from the earth, yielding to the tremendous force and rolled to the side where it lands with a hollow thump before coming to a stop. After regaining my composure, I walked over and grabbed my shovel and began to dig into the soft dirt under the boulder.

After about 20 minutes of digging, I managed to create a hole about three feet deep and the same measurement as wide. As I plunged the business end of the spade into the earth, there came a wooden and metallic chorus of *'thunk, clang, thunk'* each time I prodded the earth with my shovel. I had reached what I came here to retrieve. I cleared more dirt around the steel box with my hands, enough to be able to drag the heavy box up to the surface by its iron rings. This chest contained approximately 14,500,000 dollars [*adjusted for inflation] in gold and jewelry I liberated from the likes of slavers and imperialists during my time as a pirate with Black Caesar. It was a little less than half of the war chest I kept buried for my revenge against the Reichstalls and the Incalculaba. The majority of my loot was still hidden near Black Hammock Island in north Florida.

I spread my jacket on the ground next to the chest and filled it with a considerable amount of gold and jewels. I quickly resealed the box and placed it back in its hiding place before refilling the hole with the dirt. I rolled the boulder back over the mark, gathered my loot and headed back to my car. An armadillo trotted out from under a bush as I walked back past my friend the oak tree. It had been a few days since I tasted fresh animal flesh, but most armadillos carry leprosy which breaks my skin out into a horrible rash that lasts for a day or two, so I left the family to their business and continued on my way. I got back to the car and grabbed the McDonald's bag from the passenger seat and transferred most of the gold and jewels into it. There was at least 2,000,000 dollar's worth of gems there including two diamond rings and a gold pocket watch that belonged to a particularly vicious slave trader named Bellamy that I confiscated from his decapitated corpse in 1828. The rest of the loot would go into my personal rainy-day fund, and I stashed it neatly in the center console of the car before going around and dropping the shovel back into the trunk. I fired up a cigarette and just sat listening to the quiet of the forest for an hour or so before driving out of the gulch and back onto the road to return to Gosport.

At 2:17 in the morning I was about three miles away from Lynn's farm. I killed my lights well before the street her farm was on to avoid rousing the nosy neighbor's suspicions again. I pulled down the winding driveway with my windows down trying to catch the scent of anything out of the ordinary. No cars in sight besides Lynn's old Chevy. I could not smell any humans nearby. Only faint sounds of woodland creatures skulking amongst the brush thirty feet to my left. A possum or another armadillo, no doubt. I lit up a cigarette and looked up at the millions of lights in the sky as the smoke rose and swirled around my head before disappearing into the ether. Lynn had been a model citizen since the early seventies when the movement became fully hijacked by the Establishment. For the last thirty years, the closest that Cora had come to being involved in anything that remotely resembled activism was the middle school PTA committees and being outspoken at the local city council meetings about the potholes on Main Street in Whatley.

We were extremely fortunate that the Incalculaba and their agents never caught wind of the relationship we had together. Other than the initial contact with Lynn through the hospital administration and the infiltration by the agents Keith mentioned seen snooping around just before her subsequent regression in health, there did not seem to be an Incalculaba presence around the farm. They presumably figured that the situation was 'contained' and the parties involved were such uneducated hicks that they posed no real threat to their agenda so the level of surveillance she was placed under was very light. In all likelihood, the bastards were banking on the fact that she would never leave the hospital. It is also possible that the information about Lynn's blood had not made its way up the food chain yet due to the sheer magnitude of the intelligence networks involved. There was a high probability that some greedy intermediaries wanted to exploit the earnings potential for themselves before reporting it to their handlers.

I finished my cigarette, retrieved the McDonald's bag with the loot from the car, and returned to the house entering through the open back door, locking it behind me. I rummaged through the kitchen drawers and found a flathead screwdriver and used it to open the vent in Cora's room. I placed the bag inside the ductwork and closed the vent. We were always careful about how we contacted each other because she was deeply aware of the merciless, bestial people we were dealing with. I hypothesized that when they analyzed her blood it must have triggered some type of red flag, no pun intended, inside the depraved human trafficking and organ smuggling market created and endorsed by the greedy capitalist medical industry. Those 'men in black' that the neighbors saw could have been a sweeper crew who learned about Cora's rather odd blood results and saw financial gains to be had. Since she had ceased being involved in any revolutionary activity so long ago, they no doubt pegged her as an easy mark. A working class, black widow from the city retiring to a country town, living virtually alone. It would be nothing to exploit her and sweep all the evidence under the rug.

If we are being honest the entire medical establishment from its inception has used misappropriated organs and bodily matter stolen for the so-called *'research'* of so-called *'respected'* universities that served in the financial enrichment of villains from all tiers of society. Once Lynn fell into a coma and was placed in the ICU with limited access to her family, no doubt the hospital assumed there was no longer a witness to prove their crime. Whoever pilfered her blood had yet to realize the true value of the it yet, or else Grove Hill would be under quarantine and the National Guard would have been deployed to enforce martial law if the real devils in the upper echelon of the Incalculaba had gotten wind of the test results. I considered the fact that forty years had passed since she was given my blood and the potency of it had more than likely severely diminished so it may not have triggered the *'contain-control-exploit'* protocols yet. I shuddered to think that if a rival sect within the Incalculaba were to intercept and use the blood to synthesize pharmaceuticals or bioweapons and gain an uneven market share over and against the Reichstall faction, that could trigger an arms race with an even less desirable backlash once they traced the source of the original product. However, at the very least, that scenario would buy us a few months before shit really hit the fan. Either way the Reichstalls and subsequently the Incalculaba would eventually be made aware of the blood's existence and they were bound to want to know where and who it came from.

My paranoia and anxiety began to be more than I could bear so I walked outside to breathe in the cool morning air and tried to calm myself down with another cigarette. To further assist in putting my mind at ease, I opted to scour the entire house and surrounding yard again for any signs of cameras, listening devices, or any other evidence of espionage I may have missed before. After an hour of smoking and searching, I finally convinced myself that the Incalculaba proper were not yet wise to Lynn or her family yet.

The animal pens, chicken coops, and picket fencing on Lynn's little farm had all been painted within the last year. There were buckets neatly stacked and labeled by which feed they contained and even though the garden and flower beds were now overgrown with weeds and withering from neglect, one could see the care and precision that went into aligning the rows just so to allow the plants to achieve maximum potential. From the condition of the property, I inferred that Lynn led a very demure and quiet life that centered around her little homestead with limited interactions with people other than her immediate neighbors and family.

I marched back into the house and ventured back into Lynn's bedroom. Lynn kept a very clean home right up until the day she went into the hospital as her bed was still made and the room was very sparse of clutter and unnecessary furniture. The bedroom looked generic and frozen in place with only a few family pictures smattered about the walls, a chair, an antique vanity, and a modest chest of drawers topped with pictures, vitamins, and various beautification products which gave the room a sense that it was lived in and not a museum exhibit.
The sun should be rising soon, and I elected to just settle in and wait for news from Keith. The windows in Lynn's room were dressed with thick curtains.

Probably an old habit of hers from when we lived together. I sat down on a recliner next to the bed and read an old copy of 'A Gathering of Old Men' that was on the nightstand.

Several hours passed and around 2:00 in the afternoon I caught myself dozing when I was awakened by Cora's landline phone ringing nonstop. I tried to ignore it but after five consecutive minutes of constant ringing, my instinct told me it was someone who knew I was in the house. I checked the caller ID against the number Keith had given me and confirmed that it was him which allowed me to breathe a sigh of relief. I was not expecting to hear from him this early. I picked up the receiver but I didn't say anything just to be on the safe side. The voice on the other end of the line was a total 180 degrees from the melancholy cat I met the day prior.

"I knew it was a long shot to call you here so early, but I couldn't contain myself when I heard the good news. Keith began excitedly. "I was so damn out of it yesterday that it just dawned on me that I never got your name. I understand this is some serious shit and you don't have to say anything but I just need to get this out. I don't know what you did, but I know it was you. As soon as you said you would handle things, YaYa got better.

Since I can't really say nothing to momma and my brother and sister about you, I just wanna say on behalf of my entire family, thank you so very much, brother!"

He sounded as if he was on the verge of tears.

"First of all, the hospital called my mom's and told her that YaYa's vitals had somehow miraculously gotten much stronger overnight, and they were rescinding their recommendation for hospice care. Then, a few minutes later, YaYa *herself* calls against the will of the doctors and nurses who thought it was too dangerous for her to be getting all worked up so soon after her recovery. She then proceeded to call all the doctors and specialists in the room quacks and charlatans and refused to submit to more blood tests before talking to her attorney." Keith paused to laugh before finishing.

433

"She scared the shit out of those doctors saying that she was gonna sue the pants off of 'em because she marched with John Lewis and Martin Luther King, and she wasn't gonna allow injustice to stand on her watch! Man, you should've heard her. I mean, I knew she had a history of that, but man, to hear her go in on all those doctors and nurses in their face was a trip!

When mom passed me the phone so I could speak with YaYa, it took me a while to get word in edgewise but as soon as I mentioned that a man wearing sunglasses came to the house, she immediately calmed down and apologized to the nurses to get them to leave the room. Once she was alone she made me promise to never tell anyone, not even my fiancé or mama about you under any circumstance.

She also told me that I could trust you and that I should follow any instructions you give me to the letter if anything was to ever happen to her again. I've probably already said too much cause you never know who might be listening but just know I owe you big for saving YaYa. See ya in a couple of hours."

And with that Keith hung up the phone.

That night when Keith arrived, I told him my name and I made him swear upon pain of death to never write my name down anywhere electronically or otherwise or to breathe a word about me to anyone other than Lynn especially over the phone.
    I gave him a note to give to Lynn that was written in a Haitian creole shorthand she learned from me in the sixties that I knew only she would be able to read.
The note read as follows:

It was wonderful to see your beautiful face again even though you were asleep. So many memories made in the relatively short amount of time we had together. I am deeply sorry about your husband's passing. He was a good man and I was always happy for you for finding someone who could match your passion for community activism. I would have liked to have contacted you before now but you of all people can understand my proclivities against phone communication and traveling. I am writing to you because once again I need your help. The time to enact the plans we made all those years ago to dismantle this unjust system is upon us. I think it was fate that I met your grandson Keith who seems to carry that same torch for wanting to see fairness and equality in the world that you once did. It would be best if we corresponded through him from now on to put a buffer between yourself and I until this blood transfusion fiasco is completely behind us. I stashed well over a million dollars in gold and jewels inside a bag of McDonald's inside the intake vent of the living room. I will need about $10,000 of it for initial operational cash flow along with a more reliable car with clean tags and registration and new driver's license. You should use the rest of the money to settle any financial issues you have and afterward I suggest that you travel somewhere out of the country for a few years to allow the spotlight placed on you and your family to dissipate. There should be more than enough money for you to sell the farm and relocate if necessary. For good measure I recommend that you obscure your last name by spelling it differently to avoid being hounded by the Incalculaba in the future. Thank you for everything you have done for me over the years.

Love eternally, DuSange

As I prepared to exit I said to Keith, "From here on out you will be my point of contact between myself and your grandmother. I reached in my jacket pocket and gave him the rest of the gold coins and a few jewels. "I want you to use this portion to pay your tuition and any other expenses you or your fiancé may have. I will be contacting you one week from today. And Keith, this is very important. You must swear that you will continue going about life as normally as possible. Nothing about your routine should change. The people we are dealing with have absolutely no scruples and secrecy is our most effective weapon against them."

Before I left Gosport, I visited the local Walmart and bought a generic Samsung phone and a couple of prepaid phone cards, a pair of jeans, a t-shirt, a cheap pair of sneakers, a twin pack of Bic lighters and two pounds of top sirloin. I got fuel and cigarettes at the adjacent gas station before I drove back to Prichard. I booked a few more nights at the Azalea Inn and for the next five days I was holed up in another roach infested room, leaving only to purchase meat, newspapers and cigarettes. On the morning of the sixth day I called Keith on his cell phone.

"Hello" he answered.

"It's me.

   First of all, thank you. The undertaking that we endeavor here could bring about a permanent positive change to the world. However, it will be extremely dangerous. If we are to survive and come out on top, we must always move in the shadows. Any instruction I give you must be followed to the letter or it is game over for us all. Whenever we speak we must keep our calls to less than three minutes. If I need to talk to you, I will call you. The only time you should call me is in an absolute life-or-death emergency. Never under any circumstances send an SMS message to a number I call you from. In three days I will call you with directions to a secure meeting spot. That is where you will bring me a package that your grandmother is putting together for me. Whenever we meet in person we must agree to leave our phones in our vehicles. As briefly as possible, can you tell me what the situation is with your grandmother being discharged from the hospital?"

   "Before anything else I want to thank you. Not just for what you did for YaYa but the money you gave me was enough to pay for my tuition and to cover the expenses for the wedding. YaYa came home Monday night and she has been staying between my mom and my aunt's house all week. After contacting some of Papa's old lawyer friends in Mobile, they tore that hospital a new asshole. Kaiser Permanente's regional director came to personally apologize to YaYa after she threatened to sue the hospital for attempted murder and go to the media with claims of them operating a blood and organ trafficking ring. Ever since she's been out of the hospital she's been going nonstop. It's like she was never sick. Every time I call her, she's in Mobile or Montgomery handling some important business. She and Papa were always good with money and that's how they always taught us to be. Mama said she was anxious to take care of the stuff that got neglected when she was down. I know it's getting close to our time being up but, before you get off the phone...I just want to say thank you again bruh. YaYa is the rock of our family and now that she's back we can all see it. And now I see I gotta get stronger so when she does pass away our family won't fall apart."

'You're a good man Keith, we will talk more when I see you in person. I will call you with the address for the rendezvous point. Until then be safe."

I hung up the phone.

For our next meeting I chose the anonymity of the parking lot of the Monroeville Walmart. Keith handed me a plastic bag with 20,000 dollars in it. Lynn had no issues exchanging most of the gold and jewels for cash and the grand total came out to be way more than I estimated. She was able to buy the car I needed with no problem, but her connections for securing the forged credentials were going to need another two weeks.

On our next call we agreed it would be best if Keith drove the replacement car with the credentials to the Azalea Inn and we swapped cars, titles and all. I got rid of the stolen tag and made a fresh 'Tag Applied For' sign for the Mitsubishi. We shook hands and I reminded Keith to continue going about life normally. It may be months or years before we spoke again and I wanted to reassure him that no matter how long it may take, he must maintain total secrecy for the safety of everyone involved.

The car Lynn purchased for me was a 2004 dark green Nissan Sentra in good condition with only 83,000 miles on it. Now that I had a more reliable car with legitimate paperwork I could move more freely throughout the country. I waited a few hours after Keith had left before I destroyed the pre-paid phone, finished cleaning my motel room, and dumped all my trash in the hotel dumpster before jumping in my car and heading south.
I left Alabama that evening and headed toward the wilderness of the Georgia/Florida Sea Islands where I could check on the largest portion of my loot which was still buried deep in what is now called the Nassau River marshes, a heavy swamp filled with acres and acres of cypress trees, venomous water moccasins, and 16ft. alligators. The absolute perfect hiding spot for anything that you do not want to be found.

On the way down I made a pit stop at a gas station on the Alabama /Florida border to refuel, buy a gallon of water, get a few maps of the area, and restock my cigarette supply. Another few hours of driving and I managed to make it it to the region north of Jacksonville in the east Florida panhandle around 11:30 p.m. As I grew closer to the mark I killed my lights and pulled over to the shoulder on a dark stretch of Cedar Point road into the thick forests just south of Tiger Point. I parked as far into the grass as I could and stripped down to my underwear so my clothes did not get dirty before I exited the car. I covered my car with branches and nearby debris to conceal it from any passersby. The air was cold but there was not much wind. I looked up at the stars to direct me to the grove of 50ft. bald cypress trees which were my markers for where the trail to my stash began. I knew this area very well for I visualized its location often in my idle moments so as to never lose track of its whereabouts over the decades. The solid grass became a muddy soup beneath my feet as I silently moved through the pond scum and leeches counting the steps until my next marker which should be an abnormally bent water tupelo tree at 472 paces. At the odd angled tree, I slogged due east another 1,064 paces toward a large tumor of entangled vines, Spanish moss, and thorny brambles concealed amongst a row of Weeping Willows. In the center of this entanglement of plant life lay another boulder to designate the address of my stash. Not as large as the one I used in Alabama but substantial enough to need at least seven to eight men to move it.

After disentangling the web of vines growing on the boulder, I rolled the giant rock to the side about five feet and began digging in the mud using my bare hands until after about two feet down, I reached the iron trimmed wooden box and pulled it to the surface. I hurriedly carried the heavy chest on my shoulders through the soupy bog back to my car and I took a handful of gold coins out before placing the rotting wooden box in my trunk. I cleared the debris from the car, tossed my muddy underwear and rinsed off with the gallon of water before I hopped back in the car and turned on the heater to dry off a bit before putting my clothes back on. I drove down I-295 to a Walmart in Jacksonville where I purchased an extra set of clothes and shoes, a leather belt, a hunting knife that came with its own sheath, a new prepaid phone, and a combination lock from a Walmart north of town.

I sat parked in Walmart's parking lot waiting for a more suitable time to place my call. At dawn I placed a call to Keith to get a message to Lynn to use her credit card to go online and reserve 10 x 10 unit at a nearby Public Storage facility. Lynn made sure to put me down as an authorized user and had Keith call me to give me the code to enter and exit the security gate. That evening, I used the storage unit to stash the car with the treasure chest locked in the trunk. Before leaving, I disconnected the battery to the car so it would still have some juice when I returned. I exited the storage unit and secured the roll-up door using the combination lock. I hopped the fence at the back of the storage unit and climbed down a retainer wall which sat behind a dilapidated strip mall that featured an old AMC movie theater, a Marshalls clothing store, and Godfather's Pizza. I crushed the prepaid phone in my hand and pitched the debris into a nearby dumpster. I crept into the shadows behind the strip mall where I popped open a sewage drain grate behind the theater and melted down into the catacombs of the city with just the clothes on my back and the 8-inch hunting knife attached to my belt. I left my bag with a change of clothes, a little over eight thousand dollars in cash and a few other essential supplies in the trunk of the car inside the storage facility to be retrieved upon my return.

I traversed the putrid tunnels and canals beneath the city of Jacksonville for three days, using my claws to mark the walls with X's to guide me back to this area once I deemed it safe to return. At the end of the third day, the full moon greeted me as I emerged from the foul sewers at a tributary near Spanish Point and Four Pine Island just south of the St. John's River. The remote, untouched ecosystem of the swamps and marshes of northern Florida made the perfect hiding place for me to dwell as a hermit just outside of human civilization. I built my daytime roost in a thick patch of cypress trees where very little sunlight was able to penetrate and very few humans dared to venture due to the inordinate number of alligators and poisonous snakes in the area. My roost was mainly near the intercoastal waterways by Greenfield Islands near Chicopit Bay, but during my stay, I would travel as far north as the notorious Kingsley Plantation and an area now known as Big Talbot Island State Park. I rested during the day and hunted at night.

My diet consisted mostly of eel, stone crabs, and more marsh rice rats than I care to remember. Only twice during my time in those salt marshes did I come across a white-tailed deer, and I would make a special effort to capture them whenever I picked up their scent. The hot blood of a large mammal was a true treat during my many months in that godforsaken swamp. I ran with large boulders and heavy logs through the thick, muddy bogs to train my muscles and build my speed for future battles. My mind remained focused on one thing: defining what it would take to settle my centuries old grudge against the Incalculaba and come up with a practical and effective plan to cripple and subsequently dismantle the present corrupt, genocidal power structure.

I would reside in those swamps and creek systems for a full year and a half, running through the night wearing only a loincloth made from the tattered flannel shirt I wore when I first entered this jungle. It took me that long to hash out the beginning steps I would need to take to realistically be able to go up against the *behemoth*. Even if everything went exactly according to plan, an inordinate amount of luck would still be required to keep our little scheme from being discovered before we could execute. Prior to leaving the swamp I destroyed my shelter and any evidence of my presence there. I followed the stars in the late November sky back down towards the drainage canal at the mouth of the river. I am greeted by the fragrance of human feces and fatty deposits of cooking grease which are pumped into the precious oceans near the Florida coast 24/7 where I re-enter the murky waters of the sewers sloshing in poorly filtered excrement up to my knees until I reached the main filtration hub where I marked the tunnels that lead back towards the strip mall and the Public Storage. The odor of concentrated waste was destroying my olfactory senses, and I was seriously going to need to find soap and rinse this foul stench from my body before I got back in the car. There were very few signs of human life beneath this city compared to what I was used to, likely due to the climate in Florida allowing for sustainable living above ground for the homeless and displaced, unlike the brutally cold of cities like New York and Chicago that boast huge well established underground communities.

I reached the first 'X' I marked on the tunnel walls and ahead of me, I could see light through the drainage grate that would be my exit. I grab the center teeth of the grate and push the heavy iron up into the air slowly as I climb out from the sewer using footholds in the tunnel wall. It was early morning and only a stray black and white cat was there to witness my return. I replaced the drainage grate back onto the sewer opening and darted into the shadows just below the Marshall's loading dock. There were Z-racks with empty hangers and a couple of stacks of pallets to my left next to a water spigot protruding from the wall. There was a camera pointing directly at the loading dock that I failed to notice before and it would have definitely caught me entering and exiting the sewer so either the camera was inoperable, or the security did not give a shit about some half naked homeless guy hanging out in the sewers underneath their property. I picked up a half brick lying nearby and in one swift motion, I threw my best fastball into the camera which exploded into bits upon impact. I ran towards the building and turned on the spigot and crouched to get my body underneath the flow of water, I rinsed the foul sludge from my skin the best I could within two minutes. I turned the water off and tossed my loincloth into a nearby dumpster before climbing up the retainer wall and scaling the 10ft. iron fence and landing barefoot and naked on the concrete of the closed storage facility. I moved through the shadows expeditiously to avoid the security cameras placed throughout the property. My unit just happened to be directly in front of one of those cameras and even if I did make it inside the unit without being spotted, I still would not be able to leave until after the storage facility officially opened at 9:00 a.m. Destroying this camera may bring more trouble than it's worth so I opt to risk being caught on camera as a naked creeper living in his storage unit rather than being caught by the sunlight without any clothes.

I dashed over to my unit, running on all fours to appear more animal-like and I stood up into a bipedal run the last 20 ft. before I reached the roll-up door. I grabbed lock and quickly entered the code and raised the door just high enough to get my body in and quickly closed it down behind me. I snagged the keys from under the bumper and immediately popped open the trunk of the car and checked to make sure that the treasure chest and cash had not been touched before putting my clothes and shoes on. Once dressed and satisfied that everything was how it should be, I dug out a pack of cigarettes and lit one up. Inhaling deep to replace all the oxygen in my lungs with sweet tobacco and nicotine. I cracked the bottom of the roll-up door

441

just slightly to allow the smoke to escape. I opened the hood of the car and reconnected the battery before walking over to sit in the driver's seat and turning the key to the 'ON' position to check the time which read 5:02 a.m. If this place opened at 9:00 I planned on rolling out of here no later than 9:30.

Using the visor mirror in the car, I covered the skin on my face and hands as best as possible with the remaining makeup I had. My first stop would be to purchase another prepaid phone from Walmart in order to reach out to Keith who by now should have graduated from Tennessee State with his engineering degree and made his fiancé his wife.

I allowed myself a few more cigarettes before the daylight began to creep under the slightly open door. I checked the clock in the car again just after 8:00am and for the next hour and a half until I could, I just sat and waited patiently while brooding on the next steps in my plan.

As soon as 9:30 hit, I booked it out of the storage facility. I prayed that whoever was at the front desk didn't make a stink about me bolting out of there without seeing me come in. After leaving Walmart with my new phone, I located a Pilot Travel Center off I-95 to where I was able to refuel, shower properly and clean myself up enough to look like a decent homeless guy before I made my way back to Mobile. At the gas station I bought some new clothes, a baseball cap, sunglasses and fresh cigarettes. It turned out that this truck stop came equipped with a bank of pay phones which I used to call Keith. Upon hearing my voice, Keith was overwhelmed with joy. He began filling me in on everything that had been happening with his family since the incident and about Lynn and her travels throughout Africa while I had been gone. Despite his rough edges and somewhat rebellious childhood, Keith was able to secure a bachelor's in computer science from Fisk University and a master's in software engineering from Tennessee State University. He was taking a year off to get married and go on a honeymoon before starting the doctorate program at Georgia Tech. Keith had become very proficient in coding and was on the verge of starting a company based around an application he developed that used smart contracts to distribute royalty payments to content creators without the use of third party intermediaries.

With this being the era where a spy satellite can read your tag number clearly from high beyond the stratosphere, we had to be overly careful about how we met and exchanged information. Keith was able to secure burner phones with untraceable sim cards to allow us to communicate outside the network. I would make contact with Keith from a laundromat or diner where I could charge up the phone enough to place the call, and I never spoke for longer than 59 seconds to avoid my voice being recorded by the CARNIVORE systems automatic speech recognition software.

   The treasure chest that I liberated from my Everglades hiding spot held seven million dollars in gold and jewels that Keith managed to launder through various investments in real estate and crypto currency which he used the proceeds to complete his education and relocate Lynn and the immediate family to a safe compound in The Gambia. The remainder of the money was split between establishing Keith's startup software firm and procuring the necessary weapons and equipment essential to the plan.

   It was occasionally necessary to meet in person to discuss crucial details, and Keith and I decided we would meet once every three months on random dates in the backwoods of Choctaw county. Keith was instructed to memorize the routes prior to our meeting to ensure that he always came without phones or other electronic devices and only drove older model cars that were manufactured without microchip technology to one of five designated meeting spots, all within a 10-mile radius of Mackey Branch Church No.1 in Gosport. Our meeting spot was always one of the many old, generic, country dirt roads that riddled southern Alabama. I instructed him to look for a blood red scarf around the branch of a large elm tree that grew near the church to let Keith know whether our meeting had the green light or not. Keith would leave his car parked on the road and walk into the woods for hundreds of yards while I followed from the trees to verify that we were not being followed. We always convened deep in the woods so the sound of our voices could not be picked up by long distance listening devices. Each time I would speak at length about the nature of the beast we were up against and once I educated Keith on the depths of the abyss before us, he became even more eager and determined to help.

"I want my children born into a world of truth and fairness" were the eloquent words Keith used to convey his resolve to me.

The leap in technological advances in surveillance over the next few years led to an atmosphere in the United States where it was virtually impossible to remain covert when using cellular technology, so we decided it was too dangerous to use the burner phones or meet in person anymore and agreed to only contact each other via email. I was back in Chicago where I would do much of my research and emailing at the few internet cafes that still took cash. I did not trust using the computers in the public libraries and eventually I was able to purchase a laptop which I used for research and to store documents. Occasionally I would find free Wi-fi hotspots to email Keith, but I tried to keep that method of communication to a minimum.

Keith had become a wizard at designing software and his skill in the field gave him full access to the computer science department of his doctorate program at Georgia Tech where he disguised his dissertation research as cybersecurity measure to conceive the bug that would exploit the zero-day vulnerabilities needed to undermine the SWIFT world payment allocation system. He christened the bug program M.A.S.C. (Multiple Attack Solvency Commutator), an electronic virus that would handle the siphoning of the Incalculaba's treasure away from their hedge funds and offshore bank accounts at the settlement layer and redistribute the fiat as crypto to individuals and community welfare organizations around the world that had been identified statistically as having the greatest need. The chaos created throughout the financial system would be ruinous to the existing markets, and the world would be forced to reevaluate its core values.

As the years passed and the advancements in technology continued to evolve exponentially, blockchain technology and cryptographic transactions made it possible for Keith and I to communicate using phones that functioned using a private blockchain network. The electronic signals in our voices are 'packaged' by the phone into an encrypted pulse that is translated only by the firmware contained in the other phone. The phone could also be switched to intercept normal cellular data but was limited to only being able to distort speech and text when in cellular mode, not

444

completely encrypt it. We were also able to track each other and use the web over a floating virtual private satellite network.

Chapter 23

"And that is where you come in." I tell Kate, looking over the top of my sunglasses at her.

"I don't follow you," she says with an unsympathetic tone. "I don't understand any of that crypto shit either." She says through a puff of cigarette smoke. "My ex-husband wanted me to pay my alimony to him in that Bitcoin crap, but I told him he was lucky I wasn't paying his sorry ass in pesos!" She downs the rest of her drink for punctuation.

I stand and walk over to her and hold out the phone to her.

" I need you to use your influence in the media to cause enough of a stir for us to put the current Baron Reichstall in a position that the heads of the family will have to make a public appearance to save their business connections with the Central Banks of the G7 countries with the largest economies during the World Economic Forum at Davos. That is where I will be waiting to—"

(Phone Chimes)

We both freeze and turn toward her phone sitting on the ottoman. "I didn't think Amazon delivered packages at the ass crack of dawn," Kate says sarcastically. She stands to pick up the phone and swipes to open the doorbell video application.

Her eyes flash wide as she looks up at me.

"Shit! The cops are back"

My expression doesn't change. I suspected when the helicopter passed over, they were conducting thermal scans of the area.

"Don't worry. I can get them to go away again. I'm a pillar in this community," Kate says confidently. "Give me a minute, I'll send them away. Besides, they need a warrant to gain access to the property, and I highly doubt any of these numbskulls could procure the necessary documents from a judge this time of morning anyway," Kate says, crushing her cigarette in the ashtray before pushing the talk button.

"Yes, officer? Is everything okay? Were you able to find the suspect?" Kate asks sweetly into the phone.

Well, ma'am, our investigation is still ongoing, and with all due respect, our deputies believe the suspect to be holed up on one of the properties in the vicinity. As such, we have a court order to enter and search your premises per our investigation into the incident that happened with one of our deputies last night. Our officers that were here earlier tonight no doubt informed you that we are actively searching for a highly dangerous suspect who fled the scene of a routine traffic stop which resulted in a Dane County officer being critically injured," replies the officer through the phone.

Upon hearing those words, Kate's brow furrows, and she looks me up and down skeptically.

"We have eyewitness reports from local residents that match the description of the vehicle and the driver closely resembling the features of our perpetrator, reported by our officer once he was conscious enough to speak, turning onto this street last night shortly after the incident occurred,"

447

continues the officer. "We have already alerted Mr. and Mrs. Lubovich, your neighbors to the left, who are fully cooperating with another team of officers to ensure the suspect is not taking advantage of the terrain and hiding in an empty barn or stable somewhere on one of the estates in the neighborhood. I assure you, ma'am, the search will not take long, and Sheriff Barrett and Chief Sarben has ordered us to take into consideration your family and the stature and reputation of the other families in this community by requiring that all matters directly or indirectly resulting from our investigation not be reported to any news agencies or media outlets. In situations such as this, time is of the essence, ma'am, and we need to move fast in order to keep the perpetrator from escaping the greater Madison area,"

Kate mutes her microphone before speaking to me. "What now? If they find you here now, your gambit is over before it gets started."

Her handling of this situation showed the strength of her resolve to right the wrongs of her family's past. The ball is in my court now.

"Stall them. Tell them you need five minutes to get dressed and secure your pets. I will contact you exactly 30 thirty days from today, "I tell her.

"But how—"

"We're out of time now!" I cut her off. "Clean up the cigarettes and the evidence of my presence in the living room and go and mess up your bed and turn on the television. Make sure you smoke the whole time you do to make sure the smell is completely throughout the house. Last night, I buried the car under the old hay in the barn and covered my tracks by raking up the crushed grass from driving and walking. After the police complete their investigation, I want you to get in your car not the SUV or the truck and drive to your office in Madison. Once inside the parking garage, they will not be able to track you. We do not want anyone becoming suspicious so, for now, cooperating with the police will be our best bet."

"If I am supposed to act natural, then cooperating with the police will be a dead giveaway that something is wrong," Kate says with a straight face.

"On second thought, just be yourself," and I allow myself to genuinely smile at her before turning and walking towards the back patio door.

"How will you reach me, my number is not listed, and I keep shadow information on the web to discourage stalkers….." were her last words to me as I passed through the sliding glass door and closed it behind me, leaped off the deck and ran into the woods behind the house.

Kate power walks to the bedroom and exchanges her pajamas for a pair of jeans and sweater before putting her hair up in a ponytail. She follows my instructions for tidying up the living room and making her room look slept in and after ten minutes opens the gate. Police vehicles pour onto the property like ants attacking an unattended peanut butter and jelly sandwich at a picnic.

As they clog the cobblestone roundabout with an impossible jumble of vehicles, the officers jump out of their cars and fan out in all directions. The deputy from the call box approaches the house followed by a handful of his subordinates and some forensic types carrying Poliray kits and other crime scene investigation tools. Kate knows something is amiss.

Kate puts on a grand performance demanding to speak to the commanding officer and to see a physical copy of the warrant before anyone was able to set foot inside the main house. Standing at the door she demands that every officer remove their shoes prior to entering. As the sheriff's deputies comb through every room of the house, Kate sits on the sofa smoking a cigarette and stroking the fluffier of the two cats as the officers mill about in their stocking feet through the eleven thousand square foot home, probing under beds and peeking into closets in their futile manhunt.

The officer that initially contacted Kate on the doorbell camera is a tall slender man in his early forties dressed in a shirt and tie with a badge hanging from his neck and a gun on his hip. The officer introduces himself as detective Marchionda and wastes no time in asking Kate, "Ma'am, did you happen to hear or see anything out of the ordinary last night or this morning? Maybe your doorbell camera might have picked up something unusual?"

"Only what I can assume were you people scaring everyone and keeping everyone awake with your helicopters hovering over our rooftops!" Kate says, trying her best to sound utterly perturbed. "I only heard the sounds of my two fur babies and the television. I was in bed all night, and your colleague Sheriff Clark was the only person to ring at the gate around two o'clock I think it was."

Detective Marchionda begins to scribble something onto his notepad. The detective glances at Kate's pocketbook and pointing with his pen, asks her, "May I look through the contents of your purse, ma'am?"

Kate gives the detective the look of death, and says," If it will speed up this charade, I absolutely do not mind," she says with antipathy, and then reaches for the purse and dumps the contents on the coffee table herself exclaiming, "There...are you happy now?" she barks at the detective. As she goes to cross her legs and resume her defiant pose on the couch, she happens to glance down at the freshly vomited cargo of her purse and notices that there are two phones instead of one which causes her to double take and stare at the second phone a bit too long.

"May I?" the slick detective asks as he motions towards the two cell phones now sprawled amongst eyeliner pens, a Gucci wallet, and other miscellaneous innards of Kate's purse.

"You absolutely may not!" Kate shouts. You will need a separate injunction from the court to subpoena my phone. Your priority should be looking for the person who assaulted your colleague, not to investigate me. Get your job straight, buster, before you lose it. One phone call from me, and you'll be bumped all the way back down to assistant crossing guard. The nerve....you really should tread lightly young man!"

The detective stammers nervously. "Listen, I..I..I apologize, Mrs. Reichstall. I certainly did not intend to imply that we suspected you of anything I was just—"

"You were just leaving," Kate snaps at the detective through clenched teeth. "If you'd like to continue working for the Madison police department."

The detective stares at Kate incredulously for a moment then snaps his notepad closed and reluctantly walks into the dining room with another officer who is examining a glass of whiskey left on the table.

"If you're quite done with my role in this charade, I need to go to my office in Bay Creek to meet with my editor early this morning so I can beat traffic into the city. I also have a flight at 10:00a.m. that I do not plan on missing. Cynthia, my house help, will be here any minute, and she can answer any further questions you have about the property." With that, Kate gets up and slides her shoes on, grabs both phones, her wallet, and a few other items and deposits them back into her purse.

The uniformed officers look at Detective Marchionda for instructions on how to proceed, but he is just as powerless as they are in the presence of a woman of such status that she can bend the ear of the chief of police and has the governor's personal cell phone number.

Kate exits into the garage, pushes the switch on the wall to open the tilt-up canopy garage door, and slams the door from the house behind her as she exits. She gets into her car and cranks it up, shifts into reverse, and begins backing out quickly, barely missing the gaggle of police cars clogging access to the driveway.

Inside the house, another officer comes from the bedroom and asks Detective Marchionda, "Ya think it's O.K. to just let her drive off like that?"

To which the detective only taps his note pad with no answer for the man. After a few seconds, Detective Marchionda looks up from the floor and asks rhetorically, "Are you gonna tell a woman from one of the richest families in the world what to do and not to do?"

Not two minutes after Kate peels out from her police-ridden home, Cynthia Perez pulls up to the sprawling estate in a silver Mazda CX5, driving nervously up to the house around the two dozen or so state and county police cars.

"Go out and let her know what's going on, and then escort her in here to speak with me," orders Detective Marchionda to a female subordinate officer.

"Roger that," replies the officer as she exits toward the front door. After few minutes the officer returns with Cynthia Perez: a reserved, 35-year-old naturalized citizen from Panama who owns a cleaning service with her husband and has worked as more of a house sitter than a maid for Kate Reichstall for the past three years.

"Is everything O.K.?" Cynthia Perez asks Detective Marchionda as she is escorted through the door by one of the uniformed officers. "Where's Señora Reichstall? Is she safe? I try to call her and text her when I thought I saw her car past me on Harper Road. I get worry when I see all the police cars when I was driving up but I get no answer. I get really worry you know." Cynthia is wringing her hands and on the verge of tears as she speaks. "They told me they are looking for someone involve with hurting another police. Aye dios mio," Cynthia exclaims, "Way out here?" she asks incredulously to no person I particular "I cannot believe it. Nowhere is safe anymore." She shakes her head holding her face in her hands.

"Yes, ma'am. I know, and unfortunately, we believe the suspect may still be in the area." Detective Marchionda gently places his hand on Cynthia's back to comfort her and pulls a handkerchief from his sport coat pocket and hands it to her. "We have been conducting searches by air and going door to door to try and secure the neighborhood, but checking and securing these massive properties is an arduous task. Especially when many of the residents in this area aren't accustomed to the invasion of privacy our investigations require sometimes," says the detective to the distraught Cynthia.

"Everything is always so quiet here, a big change for me since my family move here from Flint. I cannot believe things like that happening here. Everyone so peaceful here you know," Cynthia exclaims still in disbelief.

"If I may ask, Mrs. Perez, have you been witness to any strange behavior from Mrs. Reichstall or have you seen any evidence of her hiding something or being involved with any suspicious characters? Any noticeable changes in religious or political affiliations?" asks Detective Marchionda.

Cynthia shakes her head, wrings her hands, and looks down at the floor before looking up at the detective. "No... never Mrs. Reichstall is a good woman who—"

(BZZZZ, BZZZZZ)

Detective Marchionda's phone buzzes in his pocket. "I'm sorry, Mrs. Perez. I need to take this", the detective says as he pulls his phone from his right pants pocket.

"Yeah, go", answers the detective.

"Sir, we found tire tracks and some large shoe prints leading down into the lake at the back of the Reichstall property, and they look fresh, sir," says a male voice over the phone. "We also just pinged Deputy Todd's stolen walkie talkie and the signal is faint, but it also seems to be emanating from the lake behind the Reichstall house," the officer says, finishing his report to Detective Marchionda.

"Dammit! I knew she was hiding something" exclaims the detective. Now looking hard at Cynthia, "we're going to need to talk to the judge again to get clearance. We need to get a skimmer out here to check that lake in order to complete a thorough search of the property. If she's on public roads, we can detain her and securing a warrant for a roadside search and seizure in a case involving an officer involved assault should be a piece of cake," the detective says into his phone excitedly as he walks out of the front door. "I want you to radio Huffman and Lars and whoever else we have posted on Troy Dive and Highway 113 and let them know the situation, and then call headquarters and place an all-points bulletin on a 2019 silver BMW 5 series headed toward town. Tag number Romeo, Quebec, X-ray, 3-7-3-0. And have whoever spots her first to radio or call me directly as soon as they have confirmation on the vehicle. Driver is female, white, and highly likely to be uncooperative. Approach with caution. I have a suspicion that she may be trying to smuggle out our fugitive in her trunk."

Cynthia was standing in the threshold of the front door watching the detective leave and at the sound of the word 'fugitive' her eyes grow wide and she covers her head with her hands and begins pacing back and forth shaking her hands.

"Some liberal sycophant Florence Nightingale stunt is what it looks like to me. Classic Stockholm Syndrome, we see it all the time with these far-left types nowadays," states Detective Marchiaonda into the phone, now back in his car and racing down the driveway through the gauntlet of police vehicles and back onto the main road. "I'm on my way now, I think I know where she's headed, and there's only one road that leads to the main highway into town so she couldn't have gotten far. I want at least four squad cars to hang back here and keep an eye out for anything suspicious. They may be trying to pull the old decoy trick and the perp is really still hiding out around here somewhere.

And for God's sake, don't make her get out of the vehicle, and don't tell her anything, just detain her until I get there. Capisce?" finishes Marchionda.

"10-4, sir," comes the reply from the sergeant over the phone. And with that, the detective hangs up the phone and tosses it into the passenger seat as he stands up on the gas pedal leaving tire marks on the pristine driveway. He exits to the main road and makes a sharp left, sending the late model Ford Taurus careening down the highway in hot pursuit of Katherine Reichstall.

A few miles into her journey, Kate is forced to stop at a red light on Highway 240 and Cedar Junction. She looks down at the missed calls from Cynthia and reaches into the center console of the car for a pack of cigarettes. She opens the box, takes one out and lights it in the span of two seconds. She cracks the front windows open slightly for cross-ventilation and exhales a large cloud of smoke. Kate's mind was swirling with mixed emotions. She had to admit to herself that the thrill she's feeling at the moment is something she hasn't felt in many years. A guttural fear that stems from not knowing what was going to happen next. A feeling she now realizes she has always welcomed. Money, fame, and family connections had caused her to become jaded over the years, and as she sped down the empty highway, she is reminded of that tingle in her spine that goes missing when she is not being challenged. This is truly what she craves, and this is exactly why she was always fascinated with unraveling mysteries of the past and present in order to correct and or positively influence the future. Maybe even change the perceptions of evil, depravity, and the association with tyrants and overlords that follows her family name. As the light turns green, Kate speeds off but runs into what looks like morning rush hour traffic ahead of her, and she is forced to pump the brakes as the cars in front of her begin to slow down from some unseen obstruction.

"There's never traffic on this road this early in the fucking morning", Kate thinks to herself. "Something must be going on." Kate veers onto the shoulder of the road to get a better view of what the cause of the traffic is and sure enough, there are two uniformed police officers creating a roadblock bottleneck with their squad cars parked facing each other in the road leaving only enough room for each vehicle to pass down the center of the two-lane highway one at a time.

"Stay calm, "Kate whispers to herself as she reaches for her purse with her right hand to pull her driver's license out of her wallet and then reaches in the middle console and retrieves her press credentials in hopes that it will be enough for them to let her pass. As the pickup truck in front of her is waved forward by the officer on the driver side, Kate pulls forward and rolls down her window with a pleasant but not smiling face and says to the officer politely, "Good morning, officer, My name is Katherine Reichstall." she says holding up her White House press release pass in her attempt to dominate the clearly sheepish officer. "I live not too far from here, and I have level six press clearance. Did something happen up ahead that needs to be brought to the attention of the residents of the area? "Kate asks innocently.

"No, ma'am," begins the officer shakily "...W-we apologize for the inconvenience but we are currently looking for a suspect who we believe may have escaped from the penitentiary at Chippewa Valley Correctional Facility and may be trying to smuggle himself out of the vicinity by hiding in the vehicle of some unsuspecting resident," lies the officer, a younger man of average height but very thin wearing horn rimmed glasses that he pushes back up onto the bridge of his nose as he leans down to look at Kate's identification.

"I'm sorry, Officer....?" Kate inquires.

"Lars," he replies, pointing to his badge on his chest. "Sergeant Jonah Lars," the officer says, now standing with his hands on his hips.

"I'm sorry, Sergeant Lars, but I am on my way to my office in Bay Creek, and I'm on a wicked tight deadline. What exactly gives you the right to be looking through cars without a general search warrant? Not to mention a clear violation of fourth amendment habeas corpus rights. Where is your formally mandated court order issued by a governing authority in the State of Wisconsin that gives you the right to be stopping and harassing every motorist like this?" Kate asks the increasingly paler sergeant. It was then she noticed that the other officer had moved from the passenger side of the car and positioned himself directly in front of her car and was frantically squawking into his Walkie microphone.

"Is everything O.K...?" Kate asks, looking from one officer to the other, still playing the situation as cool as a cucumber.

"Ma'am," Officer Lars exhales. Digging deep within himself to overcome his fears and do what he knows he must. "I do apologize for this, but....I-I- I'm going to have to ask you to pull over to the shoulder of the road so that we can take a quick look in your trunk. It's just a routine—"

"ABSOLUTELY NOT!!!!!!"

 Kate snaps at the officer "You backwater, hayseed cops don't seem to know the law or have the first clue about the rights of the citizens you are supposed to be serving. This is a joke. I need to speak to your supervisor right now."

Just then, another squad car that was posted further up the road to catch runners who tried to flee the roadblock came charging in toward the center of the highway as if to further menace Kate and serve as an additional barrier.

"Please, ma'am, this should only take a moment. Again, we sincerely apologize but unfortunately your vehicle matches the description given by one of the detectives in the investigation and I'm just trying to do my job ma'am," says Sergeant Lars, finding his courage and pleading with Kate to cooperate.

Kate checks her rear view at the long line of cars and trucks forming behind her. She begins to weigh her options. Does she gun the BMW engine and ram the police cruiser and try to give her stowaway a fighting chance at escape, or does she cooperate with the police and let them deal with a pissed off vampire convict and see how far he can get on his own whilst she plays the dumb victim? Kate thinks back over the spectacular tale she has been privy to all evening. The thought then occurs to her that if DuSange is sincere about his ultimate goals for improving the world's condition by exposing and reversing the inhuman governance by the abominable rulers of this planet, then she would like to be remembered by history as one of the heroes that tried to assist him in improving the present state of the world. Considering the fact that ultra wealthy trust fund babies like herself are usually seen as evil and greedy, not doing anything would make her complicit in the ongoing crimes against humanity and planetary vandalism that is inextricably connected to her namesake.

Kate inhales then exhales deeply. She puts the car back in gear and slowly pulls her BMW over to the side of the road. She picks up her cell phone and she sticks her hand out and waves for Sergeant Lars to come closer in an attempt to intimidate him and to buy some more time.

She says, "I'm calling my attorneys now so you better get on the horn with your superiors and let them know that I am not letting you lay a fucking finger on my car without a hard copy of a warrant in my hand." She lights another cigarette and exhales the smoke in the now panicked face of the young Sergeant Lars before continuing. "If this takes a second longer than five minutes. I am going to have you all brought up on harassment and procedural jurisdiction imprudence," Kate says scoldingly and loud enough to be certain that everyone outside and inside the car could hear her intentions clearly.

The Dane County and Madison police all were conscious of the fact that every property within this zip code was owned by either a rich corporate tycoon, a high-level politician, or some kind of villainous combination of the two. The residents here have been known to band together to prohibit ownership by entertainers or athletes that attempt to purchase homes in the area unless they are able to prove to a board of regents that they are somehow a noteworthy figure in society that fits their stringent criteria. This area was so exclusive that applicants needed to have some big-league connections outside of their profession, or possess a net worth of no less than five hundred million dollars just to get an appointment to look at a property. Every civil servant in the tri-state area knew Kate and knew she carried the Reichstall name which sat at the pinnacle of wealth and connections amongst the billionaire class. Kate knew this and was always reluctant to use her clout, but under the circumstances, she was left with no choice but to flex her prestige if she was to buy some time and figure out how to smuggle her stowaway out of town.

"Ma'am," says Sergeant Lars as he approaches the driver's side window of Kate's car once more. "We truly and sincerely apologize for any inconvenience this may be causing, but we promise to have you out of here and back on your way in no time," the Sergeant coyly reassures Kate.

Kate exhales smoke through the opening and into the sergeant's face again and says, "Four minutes," as she sits with her arms crossed facing forward, the civilians in the line of cars ogle her as they pass slowly through the roadblock. In her rear view, she can see an unmarked Ford Taurus barreling down the shoulder of the road towards the roadblock intersection with flashing blue and red lights in the dash and front grille of the car.

The car blows past the squad car barrier and screeches to a halt 10 feet behind Kate's car. "Who the fuck is this?" she thinks to herself.

A tall man leaps out of the car almost before it comes to a complete stop. In his hand is a document and now Kate can clearly see that this is Detective Marchionda coming in hot.

"What is it now, Detective? Kate asks angrily, still trying to bluff her way through. "I told your subordinates that you have exactly two minutes before I drive away," she says to the detective staring directly at him with her arms folded across her chest as she takes a drag of the cigarette.

"With all due respect, ma'am, I am politely going to have to ask you to exit the vehicle so that myself and my fellow officers may conduct a routine search of your car as an extension of your home in pursuance of an unlawful suspect per our warrant and under Section 817.43 of the Wisconsin criminal investigation procedures," Detective Marchionda says as he holds up the phony but very convincing warrant, also bluffing on the hunch that the only possible place that he had not checked was Kate's trunk where he was absolutely sure his suspect was hiding.

"Turn the car off and please exit the vehicle, Ms. Reichstall," commands Detective Marchionda

.

"I assure you that all of this is for your own safety. I don't know if you may be the victim of some type of extortion scheme or be under the influence of prescription medications that may be clouding your judgment, but as a resident of this state, you are lawfully bound to obey this warrant. I do not plan to repeat myself," the detective barks, taking a few steps back from Kate's door to allow her space to exit the vehicle.

Kate fumes at the temerity of Detective Marchionda's tone but she realizes painfully that she is out of options.

Before Detective Marchionda could react, Kate guns the engine on the BMW 535i and the tires squeal loudly, releasing smoke and gravel into the air and flying into the face of the detective. As the wheels catch the concrete, the back end of the car bottoms out and the front end of the chassis raises up as the German engineered machine peels off sideswiping the front of another squad car that was parked at an angle in the center of the road to block the oncoming lanes, flattening the back tire of the police car in the impact. Kate runs over a slew of cones and smashes into an orange and white construction barrel before righting the car and speeding past two other police officers who were scrambling to get back to their vehicles to give chase.

"Shit!"

yells Marchionda who is vindicated that his hunch was right. He hated the idea of the ultra-rich being able to do whatever they wanted and live above the law simply because they paid the politicians to look the other way. He turns to run back to his car and thinks of all the stories of villainy and past underhanded deeds connected to the origins of the Reichstall family's wealth and their 'devil may care' attitude towards the rest of the world which serves to piss him off even more as he jumps on the gas pedal, screeching the tires and fishtailing the Taurus in hot pursuit of Kate. He grabs his radio and roars into it.

"This is Marchionda. I got a Echo-2 priority. I want a 10-53 spike strip deployed at the intersection of Highway 240 and Legrand Avenue, and I want

460

it right fucking now!" After a brief pause, "10–4 detective" comes the reply, "Echo-2 clearance confirmed. Dispatching officers in the vicinity into position now. Over." squawks the radio in reply.

Kate is barreling down the road, weaving in and out of the light but annoying early morning country traffic. As she crests the hills, she sees two patrol cars up ahead on either side of the intersection. Two officers were outside of their cars standing in the middle of the road, one in the center of each lane of the highway with one hand up waving frantically and the other hand down on their hip astride their service weapons.

Over the radio, Marchionda is heard yelling, "And for God's sake, under no circumstance does anyone fire on that vehicle!! 10-38 only! I repeat 10-38 only!"

Seeing that the road beyond the officers was clear, Kate decides to call their bluff on shooting her and accelerates toward the officers, running toward her now down the middle of the road. Approximately five meters from impact, the officers dive out of the way of the car and Kate stands up on the gas pedal again. Just before the intersection, a loud 'BANG' goes off and a black metal device comes flying out into the road near a squad car behind which two unseen police deputies are crouched down firing a remote spring-loaded spike strip onto the road just in front of Kate's tires as she zooms by. The high-tech car disabling device inserts carbon fiber tubing into the tires which are supposed to deflate normal steel belted tires within five to fifteen seconds of making contact. Kate's BMW is equipped with very high-grade Kevlar infused steel fiber run-flat tires that are supposed to withstand such an attack to allow her to continue driving for a few miles following the initial puncture.

Unfortunately, the shock of the noise made by the initial deployment of the spike strip caused Kate to swerve sharply and overcorrect to her right in an attempt to avoid them. She never quite regained control of the vehicle and the back of her car begins to fish tail violently, slowing her forward progress greatly.

Detective Marchionda accelerates to unsafe speeds, driving like a maniac, feeling personally slighted by Kate's defiant and belittling manner of speaking to him in front of his colleagues. Marchionda, hopelessly consumed by anger, erroneously misjudges his speed and in an attempt to perform a pit maneuver to nudge Kate's car off the road as police are trained to do in pursuit situations, the detective unintentionally flies in a bit too hot. Just as Kate regains control and is righting herself, he slams into the left rear fender of the BMW hard, sending it sliding off the shoulder of the road and slamming into an embankment of solid dirt just beyond the drainage ditch.

Dust and smoke kicked up by the accident covered the scene as the other squad cars arrived, screeching to a halt and their drivers and passengers jumped out with guns drawn and moving towards Kate's now disabled, motionless car. Marchionda wildly hops out of his vehicle and runs toward the wrecked BMW, moving in with his service Glock .19 in his right hand and speaking into the radio in his left hand he pleads breathlessly,

"Dispatch, this is special Detective Marchionda." "Request emergency services to Highway 240 mile marker 31..... we have a V.I.P that needs EMT... advise neck injury stabilization. ASAP. Over."

"Dane County EMT and fire department have been alerted and are on their way to your twenty, Detective. ETA less than ten. Over," comes the voice of dispatch over the radio.

He clips the radio back onto his waistband and cautiously approaches the driver side of the car. He can't tell the extent of Kate's injuries through the dust and smoke.

"Mrs. Reichstall, ma'am.

Can you hear me?

I'm truly sorry things had to end like this but fleeing the scene of an active criminal investigation is unlawful and could result in serious legal repercussions even for someone of your stature," Detective Marchionda yells as he approaches.

No response from Kate whose curly disheveled hair cushions her head against the headrest and her eyes remain closed as if she is merely resting. The hot deflating airbag whispers out steam as the smoke and dust begin dissipating. Marchionda motions to the other approaching officers to cover the trunk as he reaches in and unlocks the driver door to Kate's car and opens it. He briefly glances at Kate for any visible signs of head or neck trauma. He holsters his gun and touches her neck to check her pulse and breathing which he deems to be normal. Gesturing to the officers behind him with two fingers to keep their eyes peeled, Marchionda gives a little nod to the other cautiously approaching officers creeping up slowly with their guns trained on the back of the car. The state troopers along with Dane County Sheriff's Department have both directions of Highway 240 cordoned off causing traffic for miles in each direction. Detective Marchionda slowly reaches down past the unconscious Kate and under the dashboard to the left of the steering column and pushes the trunk latch release button which unlocks the trunk.

"He's going to fucking kill you all," whispers Kate. Her raspy voice causes Detective Marchionda's blood to run cold as he stares down at Kate who still has her head back against the headrest of the seat with her eyes closed.

Marchionda gathers all his courage as he approaches the now slightly ajar trunk. From the report he was given by the medical examiners who admitted officer Todd, whoever they were dealing with was incredibly strong. They concluded it was possible some junkie hopped up on PCP could have done that damage. The report also included a direct account of the incident from Officer Todd but most of what they could get from him were stories about a demon attacking him just before he blacked out. Whoever or whatever attacked officer Todd, if it's hiding in this trunk, then it was as good as dead Marchionda thought to himself.

"This is the Dane County Police! You are surrounded! You have until the count of three to come out of the trunk with your hands where we can see them!" yells Detective Marchionda towards the back of the car.

One.... two.... three!"

Detective Marchionda lunges at the trunk, throwing it open with his left hand whilst training his pistol on the trunk with his right. As the other officers leap back, startled by the blur of black and brown fur that darts out deftly through the legs of the dumbfounded officers and into the woods. Kate's fuzzy cat Gilgamesh disappears into the woods in a flash. Gone, never to be seen again.

The detective's mouth drops as he stares down into the trunk of the car and is horrified to find nothing but an old handmade quilt, some files, some of Kate's research books, and a turd that more than likely belonged to Gilgamesh.

Detective Marchionda rushes back to Kate's window, now absolutely livid at this embarrassment and dreading the fact that he will have to explain why he brought out half the police force of the state Wisconsin to track down a fucking house cat.

"Who is going to kill us all?" The detective who is now growing unhinged yells at Kate. "You said someone was trying to kill us all, who, who the fuck were you talking about?" the detective shouts, speaking through his raw anger and frustration, all pretense and procedural niceties gone. No longer able to contain his open contempt for Kate and what she stands for, Detective Marchionda slams his walkie-talkie to the ground in frustration.

Kate's eyes open and she just stares at the seething Marchionda for a moment before uttering,

"My ex-husband..... My ex-husband is going to kill you all for losing his cat." With that Kate just smiles and closes her eyes again and says, "you'll be hearing from my attorney soon." She smiles and lights up a cigarette, blowing the smoke into the face of the now hysterical detective.

Chapter 24

Many hours after the excitement of the day had worn down, I emerged into the darkness from the trunk of a navy-blue Ford Taurus belonging to one Mr. Francis Marchionda. The car was parked in the heart of downtown Madison, Wisconsin in a parking garage structure adjacent to a posh apartment building labeled The Mifflander. I slowly poured myself out of the car and onto the ground and move into the shadows. It is 3:00a.m., and the cold streets were dead silent. The first storm drain cover I came across I quickly and quietly removed the heavy lid and dropped down into the tunnels beneath the city where I used the drainage passageways to connect to the wastewater tunnels that lead out of the metro area to the district treatment plant. The modern wastewater treatment facilities use state of the art imaging technology that direct the flows and the filtration processes automatically and in turn, these operations require fewer human employees than was necessary in the past making it much easier to navigate through the city without worrying about being spotted by the police.

I popped up from the catacombs beneath Madison around 6:00 am. Underneath the cloud filled night I ran in an easterly direction toward Milwaukee through acres of forests at speeds approaching 40 miles an hour. I stopped briefly in an uninhabited area near the city of Lake Mills to remove my pants and boots to allow more flexibility in my stride and so I wouldn't destroy them with friction created by my speed. I rolled my pants up tight and stuff the cloth cylinder into the inner sleeve of my jacket and tied the shoelaces of my boots together and slung them over my shoulder before continuing my race against the sunlight. Including the times I was forced to deviate from the direct path because of a large body of water I could not leap over or a few instances where I was forced to hide until it was clear of human activity before continuing, I was able to make the almost 70 mile run to Milwaukee in two and a half hours.

I reentered the sewers on the outskirts of town near the city of Waukesha. The wooded areas give way to suburbs and gradually more populated areas. Metropolitan Milwaukee supports a combined sewer system that collects wastewater and stormwater runoff in the same pipes to be treated at nearby facilities. This, in turn, required the civil engineers to bore out some very wide spaces beneath the ground to accommodate the pipes required for the increased amounts of material flow. These massive pipes made for a relatively comfortable journey for anyone choosing to travel by drainage pipe.

After getting lost in the labyrinth of tunnels beneath Milwaukee for two days, I finally regained my bearings and was able to travel as far south of the city as the sewers would take me. I ascended from the sewer tunnels in a wooded area known as Gorney Park located in the city of Caledonia, Wisconsin. The sky was cold and clear, and I was able to use the stars to guide me further south until I ran into Interstate 94. This area was heavily populated, and dodging human activity and any camera surveillance was proving to be very difficult. I needed a more direct route back to Chicago and back to my original base of operations deep below Millennium Park.

I pulled my pants out of my sleeve and put them and my boots back on. I stopped to grab a few tennis ball size rocks from the ground at the base of the concrete barrier from the side of the interstate and from the shadows, I hurled the stones at the 50ft. mast LED streetlights illuminating this section of the highway. I was successful in smashing six of them and one surveillance camera. I promptly climbed the concrete pylon holding the huge green signs generic to every interstate across the United States. This sign pointed southward to my destination. The unexpected strength of wind currents above the interstate caused by the stream of cars and trucks almost knocked me down into the flow of traffic. From this angle every eighteen-wheeler was like a huge missile, some carrying loads of upwards of forty tons barreling down the road at no less than 75 miles an hour. They were moving much too fast for me to risk jumping and miscalculating the landing velocity so I opted to get closer and shrink the gap between the sign and my target. I lowered myself down through the truss behind the sign and hung from my feet just out of sight of the bottom edge of the sign. I flexed hard to prepare my upper body muscles for the impact and my claws began to elongate instinctively. I ready myself and just before the next truck passed below me, I leapt from the metal sign towards my target. Woefully I was a nano second too late and missed grabbing the front edge of the trailer. The speed of the truck and the force of the wind ripped me along the top of the truck. I scrambled to flip my body over onto my stomach. At the very last moment, just before I slid off the top of the truck and onto the highway to be plowed through by another vehicle, the claws on my left hand managed to dig into the metal of the trailer enough to stop me from slamming onto the highway. Using the claws on both hands, I dragged myself back onto the top of the trailer and lay as flat as I possibly could. The freezing cold night wind blasted me relentlessly for the entire 60-mile journey. A thin layer of frost covered my entire body as the truck pulled off the highway in Niles, Illinois, and stopped at a Costco Wholesale center where I stiffly dismounted the truck and reentered the sewers through a drainage pipe near the loading dock. It took another couple of days traversing tunnels and drainage canals, but I finally made it back to Chicago and my refuge deep beneath Millenium Park.

I was hiding in Detective Marchionda's trunk the entire time Kate was read her rights and taken by ambulance to the Windsor Hills medical center to be treated for the minor injuries she received in the crash. Detective Marchionda, still on his power trip, had the nerve to require Kate to be taken into custody to be booked in downtown Madison after she was released from the hospital. The Reichstall family attorneys were waiting at the police precinct for Kate when she arrived and by the time they were done, the entire incident became an extreme embarrassment for Dane County Sheriff's Department, the Madison Police and damn near the entire state of Wisconsin. Chief Barnes and Mayor Conway were required to publicly apologize and in the fastest settlement ever reached by an American city government in a civil lawsuit, the state and city were forced to jointly pay 3.7 million dollars in damages and legal fees to Kate for physical and psychological duress. The illegal and improper search of her property was called off and all evidence collected there became inadmissible due to procedural missteps on the part of local law enforcement. From what I read online years later, Detective Marchionda was forced to resign weeks after the fiasco pointed to him as the main culprit in the police overreach case. He now works as a security guard at a mall jewelry store in Kenosha, Wisconsin. Fortunately, everything worked out in our favor that night, but the plan was affected by being pushed back much farther than I had intended.

Nearly two years have passed since that fateful day. Since that time, I extracted every drop of treasure I had collected over the last two hundred years, which I grossly underestimated the value of. I did not account for the insane inflation the world had undergone. When all was said and done, what I thought was about 13 million dollars of gold and jewels in fact amounted to be well over 37 million dollars. A little more than a third of the money went into the creation of a software development firm that Keith dubbed Kemetech. The primary focus of the firm was the development of data transfer privacy protocols and blockchain related security applications. Another large portion of the loot went towards securing a very diligent team of attorneys that helped form a myriad of shell companies loosely connected through his legitimate software development business that allowed him to buy a multi acre property in a suburb of Venice, Italy, and to anonymously purchase a small cottage condominium in St. Moritz, Switzerland, a ski resort municipality that sits in the heart of the Swiss Alps property that he made a killing on by renting it through Verbo and UltraVilla. This condo would later serve as a crucial rendezvous point once the mission was complete.

It took us another 4 million dollars and an additional 18 months to secure weapons and supplies that would be crucial to the mission. We planned, plotted, and calculated every foreseeable angle possible to ensure that the operation was infallible. Critical to the mission would be a cache of human blood packs and other specialty items that would certainly be frowned upon if they were presented through normal customs protocols. To get me and my equipment to Switzerland we found a company called

Rowland Brothers that specialized in international repatriation for the living and the deceased. Keith used one of his hacker connections to infiltrate their systems and change the pickup location of his *'dead'* uncle from a funeral home in upstate New York to a storage facility in Queens where a special casket containing yours truly and a small arsenal of weapons and supplies would be waiting. The casket was to be delivered to Keith's property in Zuccarello, a small province in the northeastern section of the boot of Italy. About five miles north of the Aeroporto Internazionale de Venezia. Due to severe lack of ground space for in-earth burials, Italians inter their dead in huge mausoleums that warehouse bodies and ashes for future visits by relatives and loved ones. To guarantee that everything went smoothly, Keith hired a management company in Mestre, Italy, to receive the casket at the property and have it delivered to one of these ossuaries.

One day after the casket arrived in Italy, Keith flew himself in from his offices in New York to be the sole attendant of the funeral where he poured out a small sandwich bag full of red clay that he had saved from his time living in Alabama to place on top of my casket before being carried off to a nearby mausoleum. A few hours after my entombment, I turned on my NSA type 1 encryption satellite phone which sent a code to the sealing mechanism to disengage the inner locks of the casket.

The foot of my specially made casket was built with a hinge on the bottom panel that was supposed to release once I unlocked it. For some reason it was malfunctioning so I was forced to kick my way out. With the limited space and all my equipment and weapons, it was proving to be impossible to bend my knees enough to kick the false door open and push the concrete slab seal away from the bottom of the casket. Not to mention the fact that my body had grown very stiff from lying still in this cramped box for the last four days. With some effort, I managed to shimmy downward in the casket and pushing down hard, I kicked the hinged foot of the casket out. The force of my kick sent the iron slab that the mausoleum had set in place flying and the sound of the metal falling to the hollow marble floor echoed loudly throughout the enormous corpse lined auditorium. I quickly wriggled my way out of the tight rectangular tomb with my duffel bag full of weapons and personal items in tow and locked the casket up before replacing the seal.

The sound of the seal hitting the floor made way more noise than I bargained for but luckily there was usually no security on patrol and most mausoleums had no need for CCTV systems on the property because, culturally, no one in Italy would ever dream of defaming a cemetery. I ducked out of the main sanctuary past a statue of a winged angel weeping with her head down on a large ornate pedestal that read: *Perdonami*. I moved into the night air soundlessly as a cat passing through the shadows of headstones of soldiers, dignitaries, and various well to do people who could afford the high cost of being placed in the ground. I ran until I was able to reach the darkness made by the moon and the streetlight beyond the large mausoleum courtyard wall.

Pulling my duffel bag up and cinching it to my back, I jumped up and grabbed the stone of the wall, digging in with my claws as I climbed up and over the 20ft. enclosure. Once over the top, I dropped down into a thick michelia figo hedge growing at the bottom of the mausoleum wall. I used the relative cover of the thick bushes to relieve my full bladder now that I was outside of the sacrosanct crypt. Pissing on the graves of strangers was not the vibe I wanted to start this mission with. I remained behind the hedge barricade to check the time and to read any messages from Keith.

I had an email that read: "Walk east down the hedge wall to the end of the building and cross the road that runs adjacent to the mausoleum. There is a row of buildings labeled Donato and Sons at the corner. Wait there."

I brushed off my clothes, straightened my hat and adjust the duffel bag on my back to look more like a typical 'backpacker on an adventure through Europe' as much as possible before I walked out of the shrubbery. I strolled the lane as coolly as possible next to the perfectly manicured lawn alongside the front entrance of the mausoleum. The property was accented with an ornate display of very lifelike Peperino stone sculptures depicting forest creatures and winged children scattered throughout the exterior garden. As I came out from the darkness there were no cars or pedestrians to be seen along the road in this sleepy country village. I checked my watch again and looked down either side of the street casually as if expecting someone. About fifty meters to my right, I spotted the hand-painted Donato e Figli sign above multiple doors of an all brick, one-story office front. The headlights of a car approached me as I trotted across the street. A red Volkswagen Jetta carrying a young couple, animated in conversation, flew past me without casting a glance in my direction. I arrived at the corner of via Ugo Fuscolo and via Praello where the Donato and Sons strip mall building ended. I took my bag off my shoulder and reached in the front pocket and pulled out my half empty box of cigarettes and a lighter. I turned away from the street and used my hand to block the wind preventing me from enjoying my nicotine. Once lit, I inhaled deeply and exhaled through my nose, purging the smell of that stale coffin.

About halfway through my cigarette, another set of headlights crested the hill from the direction that the Volkswagen came and as the lights got closer, they began to slow and a black Volvo S60 pulled up next to me and rolled down the driver window. Keith was grinning at me like the Cheshire Cat from the driver's seat.

"Did I miss the joke?" I asked him.

"You ever heard of Henry "Box" Brown?" he asked with a chuckle.

"Who do you think he got the idea from?" I say to him sarcastically as I flicked my cigarette away and walked to the passenger side and got in.

There was an insidious emotion that accompanied having absolute power and control over the entire planet for hundreds of years. It is this singular emotion that has most often been the catalyst for the downfall and destruction of all empires. A very small handful of the great nation states have been able to postpone its ruinous influence but, with no exception, they have all eventually fallen susceptible to it. That emotion is simply known as arrogance. And with arrogance comes its close friend complacency. Our plan to disrupt the controlling elite through their financial instruments and to strike a psychological blow to their uninterrupted hegemony by physically

471

attacking their economic and political representatives was made terribly easy by the fact that most of the large players of the global markets all conduct financial transactions in Switzerland. More than a quarter of the world's wealth resides in Swiss Bank accounts.

A large portion of the scientific and intellectual property of the ruling elite is also concentrated in Switzerland in the form of the Large Hadron Collider. CERN, the mega corporation that manages the Large Hadron Collider and its experiments, is the direct brainchild of the global elites who want to control time, matter, and energy. So much so that they are willing to spit in the face of the universe and conduct outrageous experiments that could ultimately result in tearing open the fabric of the space time continuum itself. All done in an attempt to reign over the cosmos and physical reality just as readily as they rule nations. The disgusting cost of CERN to build and maintain is enough to provide food and clothing for every single poor person on the planet five times over. The Swiss also are privileged to host the World Economic Forum in Davos every year placing all the wealth, privilege, and authority on the planet in one place, and at one time, flaunting their perceived invulnerability that stems from having fantastic wealth and influence. Much of their comfort is buttressed by the surety that their regimes are guarded by one of the most comprehensive security forces on the globe in the form of the Federal Intelligence Service.

The Federal Intelligence Service or FIS is a Swiss security firm that 99% of civilians have never heard of. Their sole purpose is early perception of espionage, cyberattacks, terrorist, and extremist assaults or any other perceived threats to political leaders. They work with and create policy for the likes of the Mossad, the C.I.A., the D.G.S.E., MI6, Scotland Yard, and the Mabahith to name just a few of the more well-known government agencies. The FIS also stays abreast of the latest and greatest in world affairs by maintaining close ties to underground elements like the Yakuza , La Cosa Nostra , the Belgian Milieu, Boko Haram, Solntesvskaya Bratva, and numberless other so called 'criminal' organizations in order to 'keep a spoon in every pot. During major events like the World Economic Forum conference at Davos, the FIS takes the lead in securing the city and surrounding areas. In addition to the already platinum level security that the FIS provides, many of the high-level individual attendees have been known to retain their own big name private security firms such as Triple Canopy or GS4 Global which are usually composed of former special forces and commandos who provide the most highly trained and technically sound security forces in the world. Employing the latest in state-of-the-art technology available, these private 'mercenary' groups go to great lengths to ensure that their assets are safe and secure. The ability to operate within this level of security allows the purveyors of tyranny to rest easy on their laurels knowing that they are protected by the best bodyguards and cutting-edge science that money can buy. What their haughtiness did not factor into account was that there was a 300-year-old freak of nature like me with a grudge and a long memory that would hold them accountable for the sum of their misdeeds and transgressions upon myself and the rest of humanity. The shadow that plagues Mother Earth is about to experience a glimmer of righteousness.

The first part of our plan was the easiest— creating a time release software bug that would infiltrate the entirety of the U. S. international foreign exchange and derivative markets which clocks an average of 11.3 trillion dollars moved across computer screens every day. Most of that currency is bounced between the major hedge fund and legacy trust managers that manipulate markets to make their own pockets fatter while the rest of the world starves. Keith came up with the brilliant idea of using a small Swiss cryptocurrency exchange called Bitnuk to upload and hide our Stuxnet-like bug as a stowaway that propagated using a trading bot that would create orders every six hours for the remaining 10 ten months leading up to the World Economic Forum in Davos. Once activated, the bug would seek out the accounts of whales in the blockchain system and siphon fractions of pennies from their accounts. Whatever fiat the money is being held in would be transferred to an address holding bitcoin wrapped with Ethereum using smart contracts that would track the wallets connected to those tiny transactions. At a time specified by us, the bug would distribute those funds into various decentralized exchanges and wait for our redistribution order. The beauty of the program was that it was all coordinated over the dark web using private open-source software in cyberspace, a floating VPN, .dot crypto accounts, emails, and blockchain tech so at no point was there any hardware that they could trace back to us.

473

The second and arguably most dangerous part of the plan involved physically getting into the main hall of the Davos meeting during the opening ceremony of the World Economic Forum, where all the major dignitaries from around the world will be gathered to further their selfish agenda.

In the 40 year history of the World Economic Forum and their Davos agenda meetings, there has never been anyone even remotely able to infiltrate their impeccable security. All personnel are thoroughly and repeatedly screened for the remotest of connections to any criminal or terrorist organizations. None of the staff who have been employed for less than three years are allowed to work the opening ceremony because of the security risk. All private citizens and businesses in and around Davos must register with the FIS who processes all the data while working in coordination with multiple law enforcement and security agencies using state of the art identification and communication devices. Each organization all agree to fall under Swiss rules of engagement in an endeavor to better coordinate their security efforts. There are bomb and weapon sniffing Grosser Schweizer Sennenhunds and anti-personnel animals in the form of vicious German shepherds, trained grey wolves, and trained harpy eagles.

The two-legged threats are equally as ferocious. Many of the mercenaries hail from Europe and the United States' special forces units, some of whom are equipped with prototype biomechanical exoskeleton suits that give them enhanced strength, speed, and stamina. These soldiers were also equipped with Belgian FN SCAR's with twenty round magazines of armor piercing tracer rounds, along with AI enhanced battle visors that provide real time updates and communication with their tactical mobile headquarters and can toggle between zoom, night vision, and infrared vision.

The entire campus of the Kongresszenstrum Davos complex where the opening ceremony is to take place is in the center of downtown Davos. The city and the area around where the meeting is held will be absolutely riddled with cameras that can see in all conditions and various spectrums. There are pressure plates and laser beams throughout the convention grounds and the surrounding forest that can differentiate between the weights of humans and animals. The intruder detection systems they have installed provide a detailed map of the entire area every two minutes using a wide array LIDAR scanner in and around the district surrounding the main venue. There are also drones that patrol the sky that are backed up by multiple spy satellites owned jointly by the Swiss and French governments, all focused down on the zone where the meeting is to take place. There are even rumors that there are small autonomous robots disguised as insects, birds, and squirrels that also serve to patrol the area secretly. Our research confirms the presence of anti-aircraft and anti-tank missile silos dotted throughout the property resting in underground servos that can be activated remotely when either airspace is breached, or the weight and movement of a tank-like vehicle is detected within the defense parameters. Unfortunately, even with all their firepower and precautionary measures, that still will not be the most difficult part of our plan to pull off.

  The third and most difficult part of the plan was not because it was the most technical or physical risk involved but because for this part of the plan to work, it involved a huge gamble that we could manipulate the global political atmosphere in a way that forced our targets to come out of hiding and appear at the next forum. With only a year until the execution of our ploy, there was precious little time to move all the chess pieces into the right position for our checkmate. It was time to activate our ace in the hole.

Chapter 25

Over three years had passed since that fateful night I had my face-to-face meeting with Kate Reichstall that ended in a botched manhunt by the Wisconsin police. The police in Madison were unable to find a shred of evidence that connected me or Kate to the assault on Officer Todd but there is still an open file for the case. The Dane County Sheriff's department was forced to drop any further investigations against Kate and her estate. She also received an official letter of apology from Governor Evers. There was always a lot of criticism surrounding Kate and her family and after the settlement they were once again placed in the spotlight for seemingly playing the victim card and receiving money from the state even though they were already wealthy beyond imagination. With all the new renewed media attention there was no way I could risk contacting her. After a few months Kate was eventually able to return to her relatively normal life but a small place in the back recesses of her mind buzzed with memoires of me and the gripping story I recounted to her.

To get a boost in ratings the mainstream media would periodically report on her family's history of deceit and their connection to political influence and misdeeds. One of these reports delved into an incident that even Kate had never heard of before. The story chronicled a subsidiary company owned by her great grandfather who over one hundred years earlier had embezzled money from an insurance conglomerate that he oversaw the accounting for. Kate took it upon herself to investigate further into the claims of the report which led to her discovering many more connections that her family had with organized crime syndicates and the persuasion of governmental policies within the parliamentary decisions of over a dozen countries.

Kate considered herself as a woman who, despite being born into wealth, had always been able to roll with the punches life threw at her. She was far from being a creampuff by any sense of the word. She never allowed anyone to define who she was and what her goals should be. As a journalist she was regularly required to be pushy and overbearing in order to handle business effectively and be taken seriously by her colleagues. But ever since our encounter something inside of her had shifted. With a bit of digging through her family's private archives she was able to corroborate every word I had told her. Kate's research led her to discover that many of the world's current infirmities such as war, rampant inflation and deadly weather anomalies were directly or indirectly linked to actions done through subsidiaries of the Reichstall family conglomerate. This knowledge sickened her to the point of depression. The more she uncovered about the dark history of the Reichstall's the more it served to change her personality, and a good chunk of her audacious attitude had been diminished.

In the years that followed our encounter, Kate made it a point to spend more time with the genuine friends she had made. She also began spending less time buried in research and being a recluse and began taking more time for herself, something she had not been able to do for a long time.

One beautiful summer Sunday morning, Kate was having mimosas in the city with her old college roommate Natasha, one of the few close friends Kate had managed not to alienate and who also served as the lead attorney on Kate's personal legal team.

"I still can't believe you, of all people, agreed to pay that asshole for a fucking cat!" Natasha exclaimed, "I mean what sane person puts a clause in their divorce filings about specifications on 'feline care'. I knew he was a psychopath when you married him, but I think at the time you weren't speaking to me because of the bridal shower fiasco," Natasha says between sips of mimosa while Kate sat staring into the ether. "You know when I drink Tequila I lose my shit," Natasha chuckled. She glanced over at Kate who was a total space cadet.

"Hellooooo? Katheriiiinnneee?" Natasha said in a sing-song way, snapping her fingers as if to focus Kate back on the conversation.

"Sweetie, this is not the Kate I know who doesn't miss a chance to talk about her piece-of-shit ex-husband. What is wrong with you, my dear?" Natasha asked.

Kate looked up from pushing around the same piece of risotto on her plate and sighed. "I'm sorry. I just have been overwhelmed since—.

She was interrupted by an annoying ringtone.

They both stop and look at each other. Again the annoying ringtone sounds.

"Is that your phone?" Kate asked.

"My phone is on silent because I'm not rude," Natasha quipped.

"Excuse me, but my phone is also on silent and even when it's not, I wouldn't have that stupid ringtone. It would drive me absolutely insane," Kate retorts.

Again the ringtone sounded.

"That is definitely coming from your pocketbook, Kate."

Kate picked up her purse just as the annoying ringtone sounded again.

She reached in the side pocket of the Telfar bag and pulled out her iPhone which was still on silent and showed three emails and a text message from Cynthia, her housekeeper. The sound of the phone continued to come from her purse. Kate stared at the purse for a second before it dawned on her.

She had been faithfully carrying the phone DuSange had given her everywhere she went for the last three years. It had become such a habit for her to take the phone with her wherever she went that she had totally forgotten about it. She could not quite place why she so ardently held on to the phone because it seemed to be dead. Even when she tried to charge the phone, it would never turn on. Maybe it was a longing to believe in something? Maybe it was a need to feel a connection to something positive after all the negativity she had encountered?

As if in a daze, Kate put the designer bag on top of her unfinished food and slowly reached down into the bottom of the bag. Natasha's eyes go wide in disbelief at the sight of her usually very astute friend acting so oddly. After rummaging around in her purse for a second or two, Kate pulled out the strange phone that now rang loudly outside the bag and read one word: UNKNOWN.

"H-h-hello?"

Kate asked breathlessly, her pulse racing and her palms sweating. She took a deep breath and closed her eyes to regain her composure. Now holding the phone with both hands, covering the receiver and her mouth as if to keep anyone from reading her lips.

"Is that you?" Kate whispers into the phone. "Are you here? I thought something might have happened to you that day with the police an—"

"I will call you back in exactly one hour. Please be alone," a familiar voice said to her and then hangs up the phone.

"Wait I..., I -I-need—" Kate begged into the phone but it was too late. She looked up at Natasha who had put down her wine and cigarette, completely nonplussed at her usually shrewd and logical friend.

"Is everything okay sweetie?" Natasha asked with a look of concern.

"I'm sorry Tash," Kate said as she stood and picked up her purse out of the half-finished plate of risotto which dropped from the bottom of the bag in clumps as she slung it over her shoulder.

"An emergency came up, and I have to go to my office for a meeting and—"

"Listen, Kate," Natasha began cutting Kate off mid-sentence. "You forget that I know you better than most people, and I know that if something has the mighty Katherine Reichstall flustered enough to leave a spa day with her bestie, then it must be the absolute pinnacle of emergencies," Natasha quipped sarcastically.

"I'll call you," Kate yelled to Natasha as she power-walked out of the Bistro, heels clicking loudly with each stride.

Natasha watched her until she was completely out of the door and then motioned to the waiter to bring her another Vietti Moscato d'Asti.

Exactly sixty minutes later Kate was sitting in her car near the intersection of East Gorham Street and North Butler Street, across from James Madison Park in downtown Madison, Wisconsin. The phone rang exactly one hour to the second.

"Hello," Kate said expectantly into the phone.

480

"Before I begin, I need you to go somewhere away from any cars and if you have your iPhone, please make sure you are at least thirty feet away from it and any other Bluetooth capable devices including your car. They are always listening so we must be very careful," I emphasized to her.

Kate proceeded to dig the key fob out of her purse and exited the car holding only it and the phone that I gave her. One 'beep' was heard as the lock sound the car makes as Kate pushed the corresponding button on the key fob. She walked hurriedly towards the intersection before the park holding the phone to her ear instead of using the speaker function.

"Okay, I'm here….I'm outside…. it should be safe to speak now," Kate said.

"I must be brief. I apologize for not contacting you within thirty days, but as the saying goes, 'the best laid plans…' Thank you for trusting me. We have reached the point in our stratagem that involves you, and we only have about 10 months before our deadline." I told her.

Kate trotted across the street and entered the park as she asked breathlessly,

"Where are you? How did you get away from the police that day? You could have at least warned me and not been so fucking cryptic about everything." She began with a touch of agitation in her voice.

"Two…almost three fucking years of radio silence, and I've been lugging around this brick of a phone like a mad woman because I didn't know what might have happened to you, and for the longest time, for some reason, I blamed myself. I figured you were dead or in prison, but for the life of me, I could not figure out why I gave a damn… But now I think I know why," she paused a moment before continuing.

"I've always wanted to change the world, but I could never bring myself to understand the 'why' of it other than the challenge it presented to fling myself against the ruling class and everything my last name stood for. Always forcing myself to march forward even though deep in my heart I knew

481

it was pointless and futile. But since you spoke with me that night, I have done a lot of reflecting and thinking. That is to say that I have finally come to realize that there are many things I don't and may never understand, but knowing that there are people in this world fighting much harder and for much longer than I could have ever dreamed of, that gives me hope that there may be a microscopic fraction of a chance that we can actually change the future of this world," she finishes solemnly, wiping the building tears from her eyes.

After a long awkward pause, I responded.

"I sincerely apologize but as you well know, secrecy is our greatest weapon against a foe who monitors the very airwaves. Knowing my comings and goings would put you in a danger greater than anything you could fathom. Even though you are bloodline, they would not hesitate to eliminate you, with prejudice, if you posed a serious threat to their wealth and predominance. If at all possible, I would like to keep your involvement to a minimum so nothing can be traced back to you," I added.

"My intention is to make the Incalculaba understand that they can no longer suppress the will of the masses. Recent research has discovered that they are able to create colossal negative energy fields using the immense voltage generated by CERN. That power is then harnessed during their Davos World Economic Forum meeting which is nothing more than a large seance or group chant to invoke demons and evil apparitions from alternate dimensions through modern adaptations of blood ritual magic. Spells found in esoteric manuscripts such as the Lesser Keys of Solomon and the Heptameron are used to amplify their powers of control over the masses, to keep them asleep, and invoke demons that create disharmony across the globe. The world continues to suffer unduly because of this, and I have been a witness to this madness for over three hundred years. Unfortunately, I only see it getting worse if nothing is done about it".

"You do realize these are impossible odds," Kate said. "How in the hell do you expect to get the drop on them first of all?" Kate asked seriously.

"These people control everything and although you may be immortal, you're still only one man."

I smiled wide so she can hear my amusement over the phone.

"For once in your life, you are wrong about something, for you see, Katherine... I am much more than a man."

"Touché," Kate retorted.

"Again, I must be brief for now. I will answer all your questions in full once this operation is complete," I told her. "First of all, we must assume that we are always under surveillance so please try and remain extraordinarily discreet whenever you are conducting your research. I will need you to provide me with all information you can about the attendees of the World Conference Forum for the last five years. I would also like for you to use your journalistic influence to instigate fears that the Reichstall multinational conglomerate may be losing its foothold on all their alpha positions of market share capitalization evidenced by their loss in financial dominance. Maybe you could attribute it to their reluctance to move from traditional banking into decentralized financial systems that are purely web based in the emerging Asian and African markets. Thirdly and most importantly, I need you to propagate rumors of their occult practices. My research as found that your family has employed an Ancient One such as myself as a bodyguard for the main heads of the family for the last one hundred fifty years.

This being is alleged to hail from the eastern Romanian, Latvian bloodline and has access to the Ars Groetia, an ancient encyclopedia filled with various spells that allow the user to travel as mist and grant them the ability to shape-shift into different creatures of the night. He or she can also influence the actions of humans by connecting to their unconscious mind through dreams. An extremely dangerous individual who would pose a serious threat to our plan were we to encounter them during our assault. I will need you to confirm the existence of such a person for me on our next call which I promise will be an actual thirty days from today." Kate looked at the phone skeptically. "The phone is programmed to only receive calls and to remain in sleep mode to preserve battery. There are no words profound enough to express my gratitude," I tell her. "Unfortunately, no one will ever be able to know that you saved the planet from following a path to certain destruction. Until next time, be safe and stay dangerous." I hung up the phone.

"I wanted to ask you— "

Kate blurted out quickly, but it was too late. She looked at the phone which was now a black mirror again. Kate looked around the park at the various people walking dogs, jogging and riding bicycles along the paved areas of the park. No one seemed to even notice her, but now she could get my warning 'assume we are always under surveillance' out of her mind. She walked back to her car and deposited the phone in the lower storage of the middle console. She cranks up the car and checks her rear and side mirrors before she pulled onto the street and drove straight to her office and logged into her computer to begin researching and compiling the necessary information.

Chapter 26

The opening day of the World Economic Forum's Davos Agenda meeting was less than two months away. From that day forward, the power structure that has kept the planet earth in a low vibrational field for hundreds of years will be shaken to its core. The Incalculaba and globalist elites will be put on notice that the people will no longer tolerate a below average standard of living. The planet itself was about to experience a revolution.

It had been three months since I had what would be my last conversation with Kate before the operation began. The phone was programmed to self-destruct on receipt of a specific text message to ensure that no one could tie her in with the mayhem that was certain to ensue. Even with all of our careful planning and my near immortal body the odds of me surviving this ordeal and escaping from that den of monsters will be slim to none.

Our plan to shame the upper echelon of the organization had worked perfectly. Kate began by writing scathing op-ed reports in Bloomberg, Forbes, the New York Times, the Wall Street Journal, and several other well-known publications, convincingly painting the current head of the Reichstall family and various other top global elites as out of touch and pompous with no clue on how global markets should be run.

By the same token, Kate also took to the web to energize the dislike for the global aristocracy by bringing to light various international corruption scandals via Twitter(X), Reddit, Parler, Tik Tok, Discord, and other outlets, manipulating the millennial voices on all sides of the political spectrum. By using social media to circumvent the mass communication control of the elites, Kate was able to plant a seed that spread like wildfire. Her scathing reports circulated through various influencers and then to celebrities and politicians who used Kate's familial ties to the Reichstall family as proof that the disclosures were genuine and thusly provided the impetus for further investigations by independent reporters trying to make a name for themselves. All types of pundits and armchair news anchors on the internet began creating videos speaking about everything from the elite's purposeful mismanagement of the economy that was contributing to massive inflation, to their entanglements in the pandemic debacle.

Kate even went as far as exposing the establishment ties to sex trafficking profits being funneled through various offshore accounts that could directly be linked back to corporate profits and stock buybacks. Even with their use of shadow banning and using large tech companies to suppress negative and dissenting voices at their disposal, the elites were unable to completely quell all the unwanted press. This led the high society families on every continent and financial region notably the Bogdanoffs, the Windsors, the Rockerfellers, the Sauds, the Wallenbergs, the Ambanis, and the Dangotes to name a few, to institute their own counter public relations campaigns in order to distance themselves from their perceived negative histories.

The political climate got so hot that even the media channels that were owned and funded by the super-rich were forced to run stories against their benefactors to remain relevant in the eyes of the public. Kate leveraged the power of social and independent media against the wealthy elite and was able to reach all the way down into the pits of Hades and drag out the carcass of the current Baron Alesteir von Reichstall himself who was forced out of seclusion to make statements publicly on behalf of the family and put to bed rumors that they owned more than half the wealth of the world and were the architects of all wars, and poverty on earth amongst other antagonistic rumors being spread.

The Baron held his press conference just after sundown at one of his many French chateaus in an undisclosed location. The entire charade was filmed by a handpicked documentary film crew and broadcast to all the major mainstream and social media outlets. The video briefly showed a tall white haired man wearing sunglasses standing behind the baron. This man we believed to be the presumed Ancient Blooded One that was recruited by the Reichstall family as a personal aide and bodyguard. There was very little information to be found about this individual. Not one picture existed of this person in any of the facial recognition protocols Keith ran on the footage.

Kate was miraculously able to get access to all the attendee information for the World Economic Forum over the last twenty years and there was still no trace of this person's existence. Even with Kate's seemingly unlimited access to classified information, we were only able to find the names *Ubiytsa*, *Zabijak*, or *Ucigas* associated with this man, words that all translate to mean murderer or killer in Eastern European languages.

All my research and data compilations over the decades combined with and all the data Keith and Kate were able to scrape was still only able to yield very scant information about the inner circle of the Incalculaba and the current leaders of the Reichstall family. I do know that their employ of such a being as their loyal bodyguard at their beck and call must come at an astronomical price. When the time comes, I will need to separate this person from Baron Reichstall which may prove to be very problematic. I am counting on his weaknesses to be the same as mine and in case they happen to be well versed in occult magic, I will be sure to bring talismans and a Kabbalah amulet to ward off any negative spiritual energy. If he has even a fraction of my strength and speed, then it will be imperative that I find a way to delay or subdue him during my initial assault or else I will lose the precious seconds I need to surprise and suppress the hordes of military, mercenaries, and Secret Service agents that will be swarming the area.

Six weeks before the Davos Agenda meeting, our plan was set into motion. Keith had been working nonstop and collaborating anonymously with other genius hackers and programmers via Fiver, 4chan, Github, Discord, and a sundry of other internet brain trust sites to tweak the distribution arm of our redistribution plan to best help masses. In addition to nipping at Forex trades, the currency siphoning bug software was also developed to seek out and identify the accounts of private banks, sovereign wealth funds, family offices, hedge funds and other organizations that serve ultra-high-net-worth individuals who have made large transactions within the span of the last year. The programmable bug would in turn create a link that would siphon money from their accounts on a time delay trigger coincided with the date of our attack on the Davos Agenda Meeting.

That money would then also be redistributed to people who have been chosen demographically to be the most in need financially. This part of the software functions by seeking out the statistically poorest countries and communities based on an extremely sophisticated algorithm that even considered the number of miles a candidate walks per day for work as one of the many determining factors of their poverty level. We really wanted to get this right and Keith and his team worked day and night to ensure that every aspect of life was included in the metric to determine the degree of need. And once a certain parametric quantity is met, the program will redistribute the money equally via online checking accounts, funds credited to EBT cards, debit cards, Cash App, Google Pay, M-PESA, Alipay, PayPal, and the hundreds of other electronic payment vectors throughout the world. The markets will be in absolute chaos and as a cherry on top, there was no paper trail because the entire thing had been created as an open-source program in cyberspace disguised as the premise for a video game.

A little over a month before the World Economic Forum's Davos Agenda meeting, it was time for me to head to Switzerland to do some recon for my ground assault. We needed a foolproof guise to get me close enough to Davos without alerting any part of their vast security network. Keith decided the best way was to disguise ourselves as tourists to gain access to the grounds surrounding the meeting. I was adamant that Keith did not involve himself further than he already had and that I would travel through Europe using the Bernina Express from Toriano to one of the surrounding municipalities like Poschiavo or St. Moritz and then continue by foot at night over the Easter Alps to reach Davos in a little over a week.

"There are too many uncontrollable variables if you ride the train," Keith argued. "What if someone asks you to remove your hat and sunglasses for identification purposes at the ticket booth? Cameras will be everywhere, brother," he adds for emphasis. "And you know since the pandemic, there are infrared and facial recognition algorithms running constantly. Not to mention the lingering concerns with European countries and how they view foreign nationals these days. What if they ask to take you to test or show vaccination proof? And how in the bloody hell do you expect to get there with that in your bag?"

He points to the wall of the basement apartment which holds my specially made sword. I cashed in a large percentage of my treasure to have this one-of-a-kind weapon created. It was forged by combining graphene flakes with enormous heat and pressure to create a virtually unbreakable metal blade that was five percent the density of steel but had ten times the strength. Sharpened beyond a razor's edge with the ability to separate matter on a micron level.

"You're gonna need a better way, brother, and I have the perfect solution that will get you in the country undetected and keep our connection a secret." Keith said as he smiled and raised his hand to give me dap. I gripped his hand in return and we gave each other the standard 'bro' shake and hug before Keith left to go to his office.

Three days later Keith flew his wife and daughter from Atlanta to San Liberale, Venice, to spend a few weeks traveling the European countryside. Ever since he began developing the money siphoning bug more than a year ago he had not seen his family in person for fear of getting them involved in our plan before we could execute it. For the trip, Keith rented a Fiat Ducato motorhome with all the bells and whistles complete with an enclosed cargo trailer to haul all the luggage and supplies. Keith had become very familiar with the northern Italian roads and had been carefully planning this vacation for months as a surprise 'thank you' to his family for dealing with his crazy work schedule that kept him out of the country for the majority of the last year and a half.

The trip itinerary entailed traveling through various tourist localities in southern Switzerland such as the breathtaking vistas at Ponte Tibetans Carasc and the exorbitant resorts located in Ancona, and Locarno. After spending a few days there, they will continue into the heart of the Bellinzona for a week-long stay in the picturesque villas in the municipality of Arbedo-Castione.

I built a false wall inside the rented trailer by conjoining two 4x8 pieces of plywood painted white to match the interior to safely store myself and my equipment for the mission. The space would be just larger than the width of my shoulders. Enough for me to lie or sit sideways, with my duffel bag and sword. Keith's wife Mauricia and their daughter Sundari made good use of the rest of the space in the trailer, filling it to the brim with Harmon and Louis Vuitton luggage packed with enough clothes to set up a designer boutique. As if that was not enough, they also brought two large Italian leather handcrafted Paoli trunks filled with shoes, jewelry, hats, and other fashion accessories for the ladies to lavish on themselves over the course of a fortnight. For zipping around the town, Keith brought two adult size and one child size Carrera folding electric mountain bikes, ironically shipped from Great Britain. For refreshments there were cases of Perrier water and a large cooler full of American snacks for what was only supposed to be a two-week excursion.

Once we reach the Italian Alps, I plan to cross the perilous mountains by traveling at night and when it is overcast enough for me to travel during the day. From that point on, there will be no more contact with Keith or anyone for that matter to ensure that there is no one they can link to me and use as a pawn to force me to yield. In our original plan, we thought of stealing the identity of one of the janitors at the conference center and infiltrating the old-fashioned way, but the employees that work the conference are screened exhaustively, similar to the treatment received by the civilian workforce at Area 51. No one who has been working there for under a year is even allowed anywhere near the main conference hall. All food and beverages undergo multiple scans by exceptionally sensitive cameras programmed with artificial intelligence that can break down substances to their elemental content.

Our reports also showed that a handful of the more powerful countries have allocated spy satellites to take pictures and video of the area around the venue for at least thirty days prior to the conference. All footage is then analyzed by specialized programs on par with what the N.S.A. use that can scan the footage and report any anomalies instantly. These satellites not only track all moving creatures larger than a fruit fly that approach within ten miles of the city limits of Davos, but they also simultaneously cross reference current satellite feed data and any significant meteorological atmospheric data between respective countries satellites that would indicate any changes in weather that could pose a threat to the conference. DARPA has even begun implementing artificial telepathy to communicate instructions to the commandos in the field by vibrating the bones in their individual skull frequencies rather than using other forms of message transmission that require a surgical procedure such as a Neuralink chip or individual soldiers wearing bulky electroencephalography caps under their helmets. The Swiss Guard that are deployed in and around the conference have been known to utilize a combination of all these technologies to correspond seamlessly across great distances, allowing soldiers in the field to act in a coordinated manner without fear of their messages being intercepted and decoded by enemy agents.

The element of surprise will be my best weapon. Switzerland was carved out purposely to take advantage of the natural defenses created by the colossal Alpine Mountain range. The probability of a human successfully crossing these daunting peaks without camping supplies, rope or climbing equipment, and traveling in the pitch-dark night without a vehicle to reach the heart of Davos undetected was so astronomically inconceivable that the Swiss government had never been faced with a real threat from invading forces since it officially became a country almost two hundred years ago. According to our intel, for the last few decades, the Swiss government has used fewer human sentries as opposed to electronic ones when it comes to monitoring their borders. I analyzed maps of the terrain until I had them committed to memory and giving myself a month in advance to make my approach will provide ample time for me to hide and lie in waiting before they realize that their perimeter has been compromised.

"Give em Hell," Keith says to me as we give each other the 'soul brother' handshake for what may be the last time before I am loaded and sealed into the false wall of the trailer the night before the family is supposed to leave on their trip. As I sit in the dark stillness of my accommodations, I twist my body into a position where I can lean my upper torso up on one elbow in the cramped trailer compartment and go over my inventory.

In order to be able to move at maximum speed over the inconstant, craggy terrain at night, my kevlar boots are designed with small pointed titanium cleats that will grip the rocky ,snowy, and icy terra beneath me and are flexible and durable enough to allow me to sprint at speeds of over fifty miles an hour. I paid a small fortune to a Japanese company that specialized in forging vintage weaponry to craft a pair of Tekagi Shoku or hand claw attachments from a chunk of molybdenum. These will help me climb and burrow into the cold dirt and rock of the Swiss terrain and cling to the sheer walls of the Alpine Mountains, saving my own claws for rending the flesh of the Incalculaba and their cohorts.

My Kevlar bag also holds two Glock 19 pistols: one with live ammo utilizing armor piercing tips and the other modified to shoot tranquilizer shell darts. Both come complete with five 17 round magazines for additional ammo each. I packed one Sig Sauer P220 with two special magazines of eight, .45-caliber sterling silver bullets. My guess is that during my direct attack on Reichstall his vampire bodyguard will blunder in their arrogance and allow the bullets to hit them thinking they are standard rounds. If there are multiple bodyguards, the difficulty of neutralizing them with a gun increases exponentially. I will have to fire at very close range if I am to have a snowball's chance in hell of shooting another vampire in a vital spot without the element of surprise.

My tactical suit was purchased from a private company that contracts regularly with the Pentagon to design high tech military equipment. Not only does it utilize nano-silver particles added to the outer layer, making it extremely resistant to dirt and moisture, the suit itself is made of a special polyethylene glycol with nanoparticles of silica layer and an added layer of magnetorheological fluid inside of a Kevlar skin. This material is so advanced that it immediately hardens upon impact and can be hardened even further in response to certain electromagnetic field manipulators attached to sensors inside the suit itself that activate during combat. With the added resistance of my nigh immortal physiology, I should be able to withstand calibers up to .50mm and multiple stinger or equivalent missile and artillery blasts with no ill effects. The tactical suit is also covered with infrared blocking material and is programmable to match the colors and textures of the surroundings that the soles of my feet are in contact with, making the suit virtually invisible in multiple environments. The only drawback being that the suit is battery powered and the active camouflage only has about eight hours of electricity before the system needs a recharge.

I was also able to procure five C4 shape charges and seven compact M84 stun grenades equipped with radio receivers that I can transmit a detonation signal remotely with my indestructible smart watch. Two pints of blood, humanely donated from a vegan athlete friend of Keith's would serve as my secret weapon to replenish my strength and restore any grave injuries more rapidly. The bags of blood were kept in a small, battery powered titanium lunchbox cooler that carries a charge for up to three months. I plan to hunt for chamois and red deer native to the European countryside at dusk and during the night to quench my hunger and keep up my stamina over the course of the weeks before the raid. Several Ka-Bar self-sharpening knives made of tool steel adorn my tactical suit in various areas for ease of access during close quarters combat and for skinning and fileting any animal flesh.

At the bottom of my duffel bag rests a Viper A3 ballistic helmet with adjustable mandible attachment and bullet proof visor. My weakest point in any battle has always been my lungs. This is the main reason why I have focused much of my physical training on breath control and functioning within low oxygen environments. But as an added measure, I also purchased an Avon M59 CBRN gas mask, the best money can buy. I had it modified to cover only my nose and mouth which gives me the added advantage of being able to be worn under my ballistic helmet apparatus. The last and most important item with me is my unbreakable graphene katana. This sword has been honed beyond a razor's edge and coated with a sterling silver alloy. It is sheathed in a Kevlar scabbard that magnetizes to my back. The blade of this weapon can cut through tempered steel as if it were paper.

The next morning, after being loaded with all the amenities and clothing to accommodate the entire royal family, the RV finally pulls out from Zucarrelo at 10:45 A.M. UCT(Universal Coordinated Time). We decided it would be best to leave on a Sunday because in Italy trucks are not allowed on the autostrada. Moving at a snail's pace at first, Keith gradually learned to navigate the weight of the trailer through the narrow Italian streets. After our slow start, we finally make it to the main highway, E-route 55 which runs into E-route 70.

After about three and a half hours of driving, I feel the RV pull off the highway and come to a stop. I look at my map out of boredom and surmise that by the elapsed driving time, we should be about an hour outside of Milan in an area near the city of Bergamo in Northern Italy. By the smell and sounds of it, Keith and his family have stopped to refuel. I can hear him in a seemingly tense discussion with his wife about why they need to find a taste of home before going up into the mountains by locating the nearest Italian McDonald's. Keith's daughter Sundari, who was only eleven years old at the time, chimed in begging Keith to stop there because she saw on Tik Tok that the Italian McDonald's served cheese fries and you could order wine if you were sixteen.

Back on the road after our pitstop, I can feel the subtle air pressure changes as we enter what must be the Autostrada dei Laghi or the "Motorway of the Lakes", which takes us up into the higher elevations and closer to the Swiss-Italian border. We stop again after another hour and a half of driving which by the map places us near the city of Chiasso. According to what I can hear of the traffic around me and intermittent movement of the RV, there seems to be a bit of a traffic jam created by a toll collection. Once through the toll, I can feel the engine of the RV roar to life again to meet the ever-increasing incline of the road. I can smell the crisp water as we cross the Melide Causeway into Switzerland proper as we push north past what is known as the Lugano PreAlps in the canton of Ticino. Not long now before we reach the resort in Bellinzona. The hours spent on the ride west down Euro Route A70 in the walled compartment pass by as smooth as butter. Just as we calculated to the minute, 643 kilometers or a little over 400 miles translated to about about seven and a half hours of driving exactly, including stops.

The placements of the major cities around the world are no mere coincidences or arbitrary happenstances of development. The largest cities rest on very powerful electromagnetic emanations from the earth that 99.9% of humans have lost the ability to feel consciously but nonetheless are drawn to these areas involuntarily by an invisible force. From London to Cairo, human beings cannot resist the siren song of these unseen muses. Geneva, Switzerland, has one of the largest amounts of energy by many orders of magnitude emanating from its bowels. Second only to Giza where the Great Pyramids and the Sphinx were built to contain and harness that extraordinary power rising quietly from the geographical center of the earth. Even now, as we drive closer to the Swiss border, I can sense the ethereal traces of energy spilling out into the peaks and valleys of the alpine wilderness.

A little over a month from now, at the stroke of midnight, the organization known only to the most sagacious as the Incalculaba will perform a forbidden ritual to harness this energy and redirect it for their nefarious purposes. At that moment, all the world's political and industrial leaders who make up the 'invisible hand' that controls the globe will be assembled to directly absorb that vile energy to promote and perpetuate malevolent acts against humankind. Fomenting anger and maintaining a low vibrational frequency in the minds of the populace is the goal of these devils. They amplify the reach of the control ritual by harnessing the energy produced by the Large Hadron Particle Collider at CERN which is fired up immediately before the ceremony for the purpose of opening portals into extra dimensional realms. We found that they have perfected the widespread use of the same artificial telepathy techniques utilized by the military to target specific frequencies upon which the human skull vibrates on to send messages to the unsuspecting populace and literally put negative thoughts into their minds. This is all done in a desperate attempt to counteract a spiritual awakening that would naturally occur if it were not for these adversarial forces pushing everyone to embrace the ugliest aspects of humanities character. 2012 was the first year the ritual was broadcast worldwide and ever since that year, there have been many temporal anomalies and time dilations that place an unsustainable strain on the timeline of planet earth.

The RV carrying myself and Keith's family arrives at a beautiful three-bedroom AirBNB home tucked within the rustic hills of Mount Carasso in the canton of Ticino, adjacent to the Tibetan Pointe. I cannot see what the property looks like yet, but I can hear and smell the signs of a large concentration of vegetation or a garden. I can also hear the low rumble of a pool pump or some other type of water cycling system. I hear the doors of the car shut and hear jubilations from Sundari for finally arriving.

Mauricia is visibly impressed by the estate from her remarking cheerfully, "Oh, honey, this place is absolutely fabulous!" A moment later the thick smell of Drakkar Noir cologne hits my nose followed shortly by a male voice in a thick Italian accent.

"Welcome to Monte de Carasso! The mountain overlooking the mouth of the Bellinzona. My nome is Matteo. It is my pleasure to have you here. Signor Robinson, I am very upset, sir. Ju' keep secrets from Matteo. How you not tell me you have two beautiful daughters?" I hear the man say.

"I like him," Mauricia remarks, and I hear feet shuffling and a jumble of jovial banter as they exchange hugs and handshakes accompanied by traditional kisses on either side of the face.

"Matteo is my chief of staff, and he just happens to be from a town just south of here called Giaubiasco so he agreed to help us get settled in, and for the rest of the week. He has vowed to treat us all to the 'non-*turista*' version of southern Switzerland," I hear Keith say.

"Come, come, come," Matteo begins again. "Surely you are weary from you driving mio amico. We will have plenty of time to visit the wonders of my country. Tomorrow, we begin by having *prima colazione* at the market followed by croissants and bread cake con *marrons glaces.* I will take you breath away with magnificent lakefronts and mountain views of the village, much like the one you are experiencing now, okay?" Their voices become a jumble of sound again and footsteps trail off as they leave the area around the RV and head into the house, and I am left again with the music of nature bustling all around me.

The balmy temperatures and lack of ventilation in this cramped position is causing me to sweat profusely, and I shift my bag and sword down under my legs so my back is completely touching the cool floor of the trailer. After a few minutes, I can make out the voices and footsteps of two people approaching the trailer. I hear what must be Keith opening the lock and unfastening the latch to open the trailer door. As the door slides open, I hear Matteo exclaim,

"Che Diavolo! Jou planning to move to Italy, signore?!" he asks Keith sarcastically.

"Oh, you know… women, "Keith responds as I hear him and Matteo grunting and cursing as they struggle to carry the many pieces of luggage, boxes of groceries, and supplies into the house which, from the sounds of it, takes several tedious trips.

I hear the trailer door being shut just before I hear Keith's voice cry out, "Don't worry about closing and locking the trailer door, Matteo. I'm sure no one's going to bother us way out here."

"If you say so, signore Keith," replies Matteo.

The door reopens and footsteps trail away toward the house before it is quiet once more. I lie still and meditate for the next couple of hours until I hear and smell the sounds of day giving way to cool night. After waiting a few hours more, I sit up and begin to gather myself and prepare for my exit. The music and laughter coming from the house has been going on for a good while now. Through the walls of the trailer, I can hear Matteo singing traditional Italian songs and playing an acoustic guitar.

I begin the process of unscrewing the inner bolts with one hand while holding on to the handle I installed on the plywood wall to secure it in place as I prepare to make my exit. I push the wall open and a gust of fresh night air rushes into my lungs invigorating my spirit as I look toward the sparkling lights of the Bellinzona Valley below the looming heights of the Alps. I shove the fake wall to one side while I gather my bag and sword. After reinstalling the fake wall, I creep my way out into the darkness and stretch my muscles after being cramped in such a small space for so long.

The rental house and the surrounding garden and pool are just as magnificent as Keith and his family made it sound from inside the trailer. A split-level garden surrounded by olive and fruit trees. Stone floors and walls with a traditional red tile roof lined with solar panels. The entire property slopes down the side of the lower part of Mount Carasso and overlooks the bulk of the city. At the rear of the house there are multiple stone stairways that lead down to the pool level of the property. As I am taking in the beauty of the scenery, I hear the family wish Matteo a goodnight which is my cue to rush back up the hill and into the shadows. I move to the driver door of the maroon Alfa Romeo, open it, push the boot release hatch, and place myself, my duffel bag and my sword inside. After a few minutes of waiting patiently in the dark, I hear the car crank up and the now slightly inebriated Matteo clumsily makes his way back down the mountain to his home in Giubiasco which lies on the opposite side of the Bellinzona near the Dragonato River.

The opposite side of the valley is exactly the area I need to be in to begin my trek across the Alps over the next week or so before planting myself under the convention center in Davos and awaiting my prey. Keith made sure to mention where Matteo was from in earshot of the trailer to let me know that riding with him would be my ticket into the heart of the Alps where there has not been anyone bold enough to bring an army through since the time of Hannibal.

Matteo's estate consisted of a nice home in the northeastern section of town. On arrival, he hurriedly made his way into the house under some great urgency. The need to release all the wine he had been drinking, I presumed, by the way he was driving. After I could no longer hear Matteo, I pull the trunk release latch and peer out of a slit in the trunk to make sure that there was no one seeing me exit the vehicle. I merge with the shadows and move swiftly between the homes, following the stars east until I run into the tree line at the Dragonato river.

There are only five hours left before dawn so I have to push myself to run at full speed for at least the first two hours in order to make it to the foot of the MarMontana which starts the eastern ridge of the Swiss-Italian or Lepontine Alps as they are called. From there begins about a 100-mile journey up and over steep and dizzying mountain ranges including but not limited to the Piz Corbet and the snowy peaks of the Piz Platta in the Oberhalbstein Alps. The Piz Calderas are the highest summits I will have to cross within the Albula section of the Alpine region and that should spit me out near the Alplihorn in the canton of Graubunden just southeast of Davos.

During the second night of my trek, the moon was full and bright in the sky. The Alps are filled with stars creating a dazzling tapestry of lights above me. There were many times along my trek that I was obliged to duck out of sight from campers and other Alpine enthusiasts who had also decided to brave these steep cliffs in order to chronicle the magnificent, pristine scenery. Because of my sense of smell, I was usually able to spot civilians long before I reached them, and I am keen to keep within my domain of shadows whenever humans are present. At the first sight of dawn on that second morning, I had the providence of being able to find a cave high upon the northeast face of the Tre Cime Di lava redo Dolomites just before the sun fully rose. Unfortunately, it was a shallow cave. I was out of time to secure a more secluded resting spot. I received very little rest that second day on account of my paranoia from having to pass the sunlight hours in a cave so small that a curious hiker could easily poke their head into and find me hiding. Woe be it to any human who may have the unfortunate fate as to stumble upon my sanctum during the day for I cannot afford to have anyone divulge my presence until I have seen my mission through to completion.

Moving only at night, it took me a little over seven days to reach Sertig Valley just east of the main city of Davos. There is a very small farm town at the mouth of Davos Clavadel near an even smaller river called the Sertibach which will serve as the perfect access into the bowels of the city where I should be able to loiter in the sewers and underground tunnels until the night of the attack. The dawn is just breaking on my eighth day of traveling. In six days, Davos will enter a strict lockdown to secure the city for the arrival of the world's richest and most powerful men and women. Elite guests' airplanes will be escorted by Swiss Air Force F/A-18C's(F-5E's) armed to the teeth with the latest in state-of-the-art programmable missile systems and laser targeting instruments.

Tonight, I will dine upon my last meal before I resign myself into hibernation under the Kongresstrum Convention Center Davos until the night of the ceremony. As I enter the thicket of trees, I can smell the marking urine of red deer in the area. I remove my sword, pack, and boots before unzipping my tactical suit which has a 7-digit passcode that must be entered on the wristwatch interface before the suit will respond to voice commands that can deactivate it in order for me to remove it for the hunt. After hiding my gear in a marked tree near the Sertigbach Creek, I chose two 5-inch throwing knives from my collection and proceed into the thicket. I stalk my prey through the treetops as they approach the creek for a drink of cool mountain water. I let fly with one of my knives which hit a large doe in the side of the neck startling her and her companions. As they scatter, I drop down from my perch to pursue on foot. The adrenaline in the doe's body pushes her to run full speed, desperately crashing through the bush. Her damaged arteries pulse hot blood that sprinkles across the plant life and the floor of the forest. I quickly run her down and grab her by the neck slamming her to the ground while I drain the rest of the warm blood from her thrashing body. Her legs kick and spasm as the hot life empties from her. Her heavy panting becomes slow shallow breaths which deteriorate into sporadic attempts at respiration until she is finally still. Fear and turmoil experienced at the brink of death tends to give the raw meat of animals a repugnant flavor which is why humans must add salt and other seasonings to the flesh of animals to make them palatable. Fortunately, I am not human.

As the night falls on my ninth night of my journey, I find myself at the edge of the large forest where I killed the doe. The overwhelming smell of horses crashes my nose, and I see a sign on the fence of a stable that reads Reitschule Davos Judith von Guten GmbH. It is a sprawling multi building facility that trains adults and youth to ride horses. The Landwasser River flows south from Lake Davos directly in front of this horse-riding school making a 'T' with the Sertigbach Creek. I cross the Landwasser River via a walking bridge which ran adjacent to the main road leading into the city by climbing under it and clawing my way along the girders and I-beams, staying as far away from the light as possible. Streetlamps and cameras outnumber the blades of grass in this city so I have to be extremely careful as I get closer to the venue.

It is only 10pm, so I decide to wait a few more hours under the bridge to give the moon some time to travel across the sky and give any night owls ample time to return to their dwellings and settle down for the evening. I move into the darkest corner at the far end of the bridge and go over my map of the territory and the most direct path to the convention center again even though I have already committed the route to memory. Just after midnight, the city is dead silent, and I creep from under the bridge and begin to make my way past a small cluster of industrial buildings into a large open patch of grass adjacent to the Reformierte Kirche Davos Fraunenkirch: a large Evangelical church sitting in the middle of a field at the foot of the mountain. There is a huge avalanche splitting wedge attached to the back of the church and a cemetery directly alongside it. I glide between the shadows, sprinting west in the direction of the forest that lies just on the other side of the Davos Altien parish.

I make the length of three football fields across the perfectly manicured lawn from the church to the tree line in under 20 seconds. Once safe inside the grove of pine trees, I stop and take inventory of everything in case I may have dropped something on the run. This will be the most difficult part of my approach because we had a major problem with obtaining intel on the most recent layout of the city of Davos. The Swiss government more than likely purposely obfuscated any information about the city's topography to prevent an attack like the one we are planning due to their proclivity to host the global elite and the mega wealthy. Entering an urban area is always tricky because it greatly increases the risk of my being spotted by someone or picked up on camera or motion sensors that track animal movement. It is 2:00 a.m. on a Monday morning, and there is a bright moon and clear sky above me tonight. Not ideal conditions for sneaking into one for the most heavily secured areas on the globe. Until I reach the main hub of the city, I won't be able to shake this feeling of paranoia about my chances of going undetected. One slip up and it's game over.

After about half a mile carefully creeping into the dense forest I come across one of the many roads that cut through these mountain provinces. No vehicles in sight so I sprint across the highway and into a small thicket of topiaries surrounding what looks to be an apartment complex of some sort. As I continue forward, I check my watch again. Only three hours until the sun begins to make its way across the horizon. I slink my way across the 200 or so meters of residential area quickly but cautiously, and I do not stop running until I am at least 50 meters into another cluster of evergreens before I stop to find my bearings. There are signs of recent human activity as I pass a deer stand five meters up into one of the pine trees and frayed rope around a piece of buried barbed wire that suggests this area was once pastoral lands. I claw my way up to the top of a thick tall pine tree to better surveil the city. According to the map, the heart of Davos is just a little over two miles northeast of my present position. I need to move faster to get as near to the city as I possibly can if I am to establish a proper nest before the deadline. In a few days, the annual security protocols will kick in, and this place will become the most secure metropolis on the face of the planet in anticipation of hosting the yearly World Economic Forum Conference.

I come across another one of the winding roads that cut through the forest of this resplendent country. I elect to take to the trees to avoid any sensors or wildlife cameras as I cross the larger mountain thoroughfares such as the Obere Albertistrasse and the Gruenistrasse. I dash under the cloudy night sky over rocky creek beds and through the occasional grassy meadows that dot the countryside. The hoots of distant owls out hunting hares and pikas in the early morning darkness catch my attention as I move silently through the thicket. I can smell the urine of domesticated animals, alerting me to the fact that there are human dwellings scattered amongst the trees on this mountainside. I freeze at the crest of a large chestnut tree and grab the trunk tightly when I notice a camouflaged deer stand 60 meters to my left attached to a large pine tree. It appears to be about five meters from the ground and empty. I am well above it on my perch hidden by the thick green branches but if there are humans with guns nearby, that could potentially be an issue. I don't sense anyone to be inside of the deer stand, but I am reminded of my encroachment on a densely inhabited city and that to dawdle or lose focus could mean failure for the plan.

This serene and elegant landscape owes its wealth and subsequent peace to the banking system that it has been famous for touting for years. A Swiss bank account is and has always been the gold standard in privacy and discretion allowing wealth from all over the world to be stored safely from the prying eyes of regulatory authorities and tax revenue collectors. This country specializes in managing the dirty money of enslaving capitalists, the pedophilic bloodline elites, and allowing some of the most despotic regimes who enrich themselves on the resources of their citizenry to sleep easily knowing that their ill-gotten gains are safe.

On top of housing the world's largest particle accelerator at CERN, Switzerland is also home to the offices of the World Trade Organization, the World Health Organization, the International Labour Organization, and the main building for the headquarters of the Bank of International Settlements to name just a few of the institutions orchestrating the corruption. Dragon lines or ley lines dictate the flow of spirit through the planet and are what the electromagnetic energy grid configurations are called. As I have mentioned before, they can have a great influence over human behavior. I can feel these subtle yet highly influential energies in remarkable abundance throughout the Alps and particularly through Switzerland, which renders it the perfect hub for all manner of inter-dimensional entities to travel to and from earth realm. Entities such as the fabled Saurians or Lizard People and the Grey Aliens who are theorized to feed on the fear and misery of humans and are presumed to be the true puppet masters behind the Incalculaba and their insatiable appetite for mankind's suffering.

The city of Davos, Switzerland, has allocated its wealth exceedingly well toward creating a very comfortable resort town atmosphere nestled between the Plessur and Albula mountain ranges. Top three in my list of cleanest urban environments that I have had the pleasure of exploring next to Ashgabat, Turkmenistan and Kobe, Japan. Every lawn here is manicured and maintained by the civil service in such meticulous detail that the city is lauded for its impeccable maintenance of its roadways and city streets.

As the dawn draws nearer a heavy layer of clouds roll in, covering the moon, and just before daybreak it began raining. I try to keep myself and my equipment as dry as possible as I attempt to rest through the day hours by sitting straddled on a branch with my back against the trunk of a large evergreen. The gods bless me with an overcast night sky blocking any clear visuals for surveillance satellites and bestowing the perfect amount of darkness preferable to infiltrate the city later that evening. Further northeast of my position lies the heart of the city and once I cross the Albertibach River, the landscape becomes riddled with roads leading to various ski resorts and neighboring villages, so I am forced to enter the city well south of my main target to avoid being seen.

At 9:45p.m. UCT, I descend from my perch and make my way east. At the edge of the forest, I can see a road and a small resort hotel about 350 yards in front of me. I tear through the darkness and make it close enough to the resort to read the sign marking the Zwillingsh of Davos, the exact spot Keith had in mind for entry into the city's sewer system. This multi-structure resort connected readily to the tunnels running toward one of the city's prodigious high tech wastewater treatment plants. The correct navigation of these modern-day labyrinths which will be quintessential to my infiltration mission. Steam rises from my chosen manhole cover into the cool air, and using the index finger on my right hand, I twist the center of the metal valve cover bearing the seal of Saint George slaying the dragon and lift the heavy iron lid off. The rusted metal makes a louder than expected 'clank' against the concrete as the seal is broken, causing me to hasten my descent and replace the cover above me before anyone appears to investigate the noise. The rushing sound of the water through the spillway is deafening making it impossible to hear anything and the odor of raw sewage being churned and filtered is preventing me from using my nose, so essentially even though I have my keen eyesight, my sensory field is greatly reduced.

The water levels are elevated due to the recent rains, and the sewage has bubbled up onto the walking platforms at places as much as three inches. My tactical suit conveniently resists moisture by fusing high density neoprene material with nanotechnology and actively seals the areas around my wrists and ankles to preserve the heat in my body even in subarctic temperatures. The suit also rebuffs any residue that I come in contact with that would otherwise hold odors and stains. This nebulous world beneath the streets is a paradox that lies beneath the city and provides a buffer for the surface world who, brush their teeth, bathe, and remove waste from their bodies without giving a second thought to the hard work and technology that goes into maintaining a hygienic living environment for vast groups of people.

I periodically stop to check my map which is a few years old and seems to not account for any of the upgrades made to the waste management system in the last twenty years. Given the tight security on the city schematics, it was the best we could do with the time and money we had available. Confident that I am still on the right track, I continue past huge valve systems and elaborate concrete sloops and PVC piping that travel for miles beneath the city. Many of the tunnels and passageways here start to look very similar, and I am forced to retrace my steps several times as I run into dead ends and unforeseen blockages caused by the recent deluge of rain. As I slosh through the muck and mire in a northeasterly direction, my thoughts drift over my life and the countless amount of unnecessary death and corruption I have witnessed up until this point. I allow myself to bask in a bit of pride at the contemplation that my 300-year lust for revenge and retribution have finally manifested into a concrete plan, and I will be able to finally feel as if I am using my curse to strike back against those who have robbed myself and the rest of the world of peace.

As I advance deeper into the city center, I begin to encounter a mixture of the old aqueduct plumbing scabbed together with the latest in filters and waste management engineering. New polymer material used for the massive storm water drains and for the sanitary sewer pipelines become a more routine occurrence as I get closer to the city center. I walk for hours and begin to notice that for a city of this size there are little to no signs of human activity in these sewers. I suppose it is to be expected for a town that caters to the wealthy clients seeking the multitude of ski resorts that promulgate in the area. At times, there is barely enough space in the tunnels for me to crawl through which forces me to drag my duffel bag and sword behind me. Alas I was hoping to snag a few trout in the Albertibach River before descending into the city, but the rains and the considerable amount of human activity in the area caused my fishing dreams to be canceled, as I chose to err on the side of be prudence to avoid being spotted by someone. I think of this and let out a small sigh as I peel back the skin of one of two Swiss rats which will serve as my last meal before I go into a month-long hibernation under the Kongresszentrum Davos, the facility where the opening ceremonies for the World Economic Forum Conference is being held. I check my map again and notice that the huge fiber optic cable pipeline next to me correlates perfectly with the path suggested as our Plan A trajectory for entering the building. Along with a very robust and efficient waste removal system, there is also a huge amount of elaborate communications infrastructure running silently underneath the ground of this entire country.

Our intel was able to get vital information about a massive structure beneath the convention center that houses a secret underground entrance that connects with the Kongress Hotel and the Engadin Airport in Samedan, Switzerland which is astonishingly over forty kilometers away. Attendees of the forum can travel to and from the event completely privately utilizing a hyper loop train, accessible only to the mega rich or politically influential. It's hard to imagine the wealth and influence required to create a secret railway system through the cooperation of multiple European governments that goes under and through the bedrock of four Alpine mountain ranges right into the heart of the city Davos. The entire apparatus is built and maintained by Elon Musk's Boring Company. As I reach the lowest plumbing level in the Congress Center structure, below me lies a series of massive pumps that service the upper and lower levels and manage the liquid and solid waste connected to the physical plant operations of the Kongresszentrum Davos Center itself. To ensure that the convention center and the hotel remain running smoothly these facilities are managed separately from the city's main waste removal apparatus. The recent precipitaion have caused a buildup in storm water drainage around the underground structures beneath the building so the pumps are currently active in removing the excess rainwater. The narrow causeway echoes with the loud whirring sounds of the giant machines above me as I walk bent over along a metal scaffolding bridge towards the main tanks and pressure release valves of the system.

The Incalculaba were able to commandeer one of the many underground springs created from the melting snow and ice that trickles down from the bordering Alps that lead into the city to install a separate water supply for the patrons of the Kongress Center and the residents of Kongress Center Hotel. There is an elaborate security grid around the reservoir and intake pipes for this private spring, and this will serve as my ingress into the main building. There are sensors on every access panel and a state-of-the-art laser grid that detects contaminants and tampering along sensor plates that periodically scan for life forms identified as pests. Fortunately for us, we had a brilliant scientist at Keith's software firm named Taraja Ramsees who earlier in his career had helped design the hardware that many of these industrial filter mechanisms and their scanner technologies used. Dr. Ramsees specialized in electrical engineering and led Keith's research team which developed the countermeasures needed to circumvent the security systems such as the one surrounding the reservoir and private spring water supply beneath Davos. Dr. Ramsees was also able to devise a small localized electromagnetic pulse generator, or EMP, small enough to be the size of a graphing calculator yet powerful enough to send multiple pulses that would knock out all electrical equipment in a 50-meter range. With an elaborate detection framework such as the one under The Kongress Center, the EMP blasts will give me slightly less than two minutes before the backup systems kick in and reboot the security measures.

On my way to the main access conduits, I take the precaution of hunting and capturing another rat which I keep alive to save as my wingman. I tie the creature's paws and muzzle with bits of paracord from my bag and drop it in a utility pouch on my waistband. As I approach the main water recycling facility, I dig in my bag to retrieve the electromagnetic pulse device. I take a deep breath and exhale before I turn the dial on the EMP to maximum range before flipping the switch. The laser beams surrounding the reservoir apparatus flicker and disappear, and there is a large whirring sound that slows and stops like a turbine coming to a halt as the main systems go offline. My suit becomes heavy and burdensome as the nanobots within the material power down.

I leap twenty feet up to the filtration pipe and claw my way across the bottom until I am just below the test valve release. I crawl around to the top of the pipe, spin the wheel of the valve, take a deep breath, and then open it allowing water to rush out forcefully, almost knocking me off the pipe and down onto the concrete floor below. At the release of the pressure, the water begins to subside enough for me to slide into the pipe and reseal the door above me by twisting the nut of the valve bolt with my bare hands. I have already wasted 25 seconds and I have not even begun to travel the length of the pipe. I shimmy down the narrow, waterlogged tube dragging myself onward with my elbows and knees as fast as possible with my bag and sword being pulled behind me by its strap. Now with seconds left, I can see the grate and last filter before the reservoir tank used by the Congress Center. Four bolts to unscrew and re-screw in 20 seconds.

The speed of my movement causes my muscles to begin burning from lack of oxygen but I should be able to hold my breath for at least a minute longer even after all the decades of cigarette smoke. The physical activity of shimmying up this pipe coupled with the psychological pressure of the time crunch before the alarms and sensors reset trapping me in here are causing me to feel smothered and somewhat unsteady. I shake it off and regain my composure as I twist the final bolt off and swim through into the inner reservoir supply tank. I yank my bag through and swim for dear life. I have only enough time to replace two of the bolts on the grate before I must move on. My muscles activate like long dead engines roaring awake out of necessity created by the stress hormones. My heart pumps like a steam engine and the chemicals being churned out by my adrenal glands are something akin to rocket fuel for my body. My limbs kick and claw through the water brilliantly moving me up through the tube impossibly fast. My lungs are fried as the rest of my body devours all the oxygen for it to be able to move at this speed.

By my calculation, I have 35 seconds before the EMP blast wears off and systems will reset and I will be trapped in this tank. I slam into the final filtration grate with my right elbow with no results. I manage to pull my left hand up and use both hands to quickly turn the four bolts holding the outer screen of the filter. As I push against the filtration gradient which should now be free, to my horror, it does not budge.

Only 20 seconds left, and I am not even inside the reservoir tank. Without thinking, I push off against the grate as hard as I could, considering the space, sending me back down the tube only a few feet before the force of the water behind me pushed me forward again, But as I shoot back toward the stubborn filtration grate, I make a fist and give the grate a quick right jab with the strength of the desperation of 300 years of pain behind it and knock the grate out of the way as I blast through into the main reservoir tank with my bag rocketing out of the supply tube at my heels. I grab my bag in one hand and the filtration grate in the other and quick as a flash, I jam the screws into the four holes stripping the teeth on the metal pins but with enough force that they hold the grate firmly in place again. I push off from the bottom of the tank, rocketing upward to the top valve of the fifty thousand gallon tank and stretch my nose and mouth into the small pocket of air where the curve of the wheel valve door juts up from the tank and I take a small life-giving breath before I twist the bolt spinning the outer wheel and push the door open to climb out of the reservoir into the darkness of the underground physical plant with only two seconds to spare.

As the power is restored, the nano-fibers in the fabric are already drying my tactical suit by actively channeling the heat from my body and distributing it evenly throughout the threads. It really came in handy so I do not leave a moisture trail and to prevent mold and fungus from developing on the suit and my skin. I hop down from the top of the reservoir tank just as the lights and machinery of the physical plant begin to regain power. This facility houses the furnace and maintains the industrial machinery to measure water pressure and distribution to the various segments of the building. I can hear the hum of the servers rebooting the system and the buzz of the sodium vapor lights begin to glow as they warm up to full power. With all the detailed intel we were able to enlist for this mission, we were unable to procure any information beyond the reservoir tank, so it is up to me to figure out a hiding place that is safe from the sensors and cameras for another 29 days before the convention.

There are precious few seconds before the security measures fully reboot so I pivot my body slowly taking care to move my feet in such a way that I can search for a refuge without triggering the motion sensors. I quickly scan the colossal hangar for a place to conceal myself as more sounds of machinery booting up and turbines coming online to supply air and pump water for this massive subterranean complex are heard all around me. They will certainly be sending technicians to check the system and make sure that no security breaches occurred during the power outage.

Searching high and low, I spot a platform leading to a staircase under a large metal sliding door. Probably one of the main entryways for the upper floors. The platform lies approximately 200 feet from my position and will most likely be where the employees will access this floor at any moment. I reach for the pouch on my belt and loosen the drawstring and undo the velcro seal to pull out the waterlogged rat. I untie its mouth and feet while it is biting and scratching to free itself from my grasp. I toss the rat in the opposite direction and run full speed towards the platform. On my first footfall, the motion sensors ignite and the blare of the alarm is deafening in the enclosed room. I close the distance to the platform in a second and leap onto the stairs and climb under the platform and underneath onto the steel girders and pull myself up between the 12-inch I-beams on either side of the support apparatus for the walkway leading from the door into the reservoir tank hangar. I tuck myself up against the wall and the support joists making myself as small as possible in the shadow created by the platform. This nook will actually be perfect if it pans out because it is at an angle that is well out of sight of the cameras and above the motion detectors and pressure sensors of the floor. At any rate it will certainly be one hell of a test of fortitude to remain here virtually still for a month.

The alarm continues to blare loudly, and the emergency lights flash red all around the room. Between horn blasts, I can hear approaching footsteps as multiple people approach with an urgent cadence to their movements. The door bursts open, and I see the beams of flashlights waving around the still dim room in search of intruders. As they descend the stairs, I can tell by the insignias on their uniforms that these are the heavily armed members of the notorious Swiss Guard.

The soldier leading the group is the only person whose rifle is on his back and not in his hands, carrying only what looks to be a Sig P365 9mm handgun in his right hand with a flashlight attachment and looking down and following a display on his left forearm that seems to be guiding them towards something on the opposite side of the large room.

The last soldier in the group spins in my direction and flashes the light at the end of his rifle just in front of my hiding spot before lowering the barrel and searching the corners and crevices below me. Whatever the lead soldier was following on his display must have changed course because he makes an abrupt right turn and quickens his pace to match the speed of the trespasser. He holds up his fist and the rest of the soldiers freeze. He then makes two quick gestures with his left hand and the soldiers change formation and split to either side of the lead two soldiers to surround the prowler and neutralize it. Flushed out, I watch in amusement as the terrified rat runs straight toward the lead soldier who after seeing it holsters his weapon and then raises his boot and brings it down, forcefully crushing the skull of the poor creature. He then spits on the floor in disgust and speaks in German to someone over his wrist communicator radio.

"Wartungsrbeiten sofort mit der reiningungsmannschaft hierher schicken. Dies ist das critter Jahr dass schadlinge einen fehlalarm ausgelost haben." [Send maintenance down here immediately with the cleaning crew. This is the third time this year that pests have caused a false alarm.]

"Holen sie dieses verdammte schadlings problem in den griff oder sie werden das gleiche schicksal wie die Ratten treffen." [Get this pest problem under control or you lot will meet the same fate as the rat.]

After this exchange, the soldiers begin to make their way towards the main door, simultaneously inspecting the room one last time before ascending the stairs and exiting the now fully lit room as the sodium vapor lights reach full power. I hold my breath as their jackboots rattle the metal of the platform above me. Although their arm bands displayed a Swiss Guard coat of arms their gear was Soviet issue. Built specifically to address soldier fatigue during combat missions, the Russian Ratnick-2 armor is designed with passive carbon-fiber exoskeletons that are incorporated into the suit to absorb heavy physical burdens for soldiers in the field while providing full protection from enemy fire from calibers as high as 7.62 x 39mm and 7.62 x 54mm rounds.

Three minutes pass since the last soldier exited, and I hear the door open again, More sounds of buttons being pressed onto a keypad. I see the lasers along the floor power down allowing two men and a woman dressed in dark green coveralls to descend the stairs without triggering the alarm mechanism. The two men carry cleaning supplies including garbage bags, a rolling bucket, and a mop respectively and the woman carries an iPad device. After making a brief note near the mess in the center of the floor, she begins to walk around the room to inspect the servers and the digital pressure gauge indicators near the reservoir tank. For five minutes or so, the woman wrote down measurements and made a visual inspection of all the hoses and valves along the wall while the two men cleaned up the remains of the rat and the bloody footprints left by the soldier. I watch the woman speak into her wristwatch and moments later, a team of four people dressed in hazmat suits and wearing Hudson sprayers on their backs assemble before the woman who seems to be giving instructions as she points to various areas around the room.

The woman and the two maintenance men exit and the four members of the hazmat team begin to spray some type of horrible smelling chemical in the nooks and crannies of the room. I thought for sure I would be discovered because I would have a coughing fit at any second. My lungs have barely healed from holding my breath in the tank and this gas may linger indefinitely so trying to hold my breath was not going to be an option. Seeing the mist from the steaming liquid fill the room for some reason made me think that if I survive the mission the first thing I plan on doing is smoking a cigarette under the light of the moon. I slowly pull my gas mask from my bag and place it over my nose and hold it to my face without strapping it around my head. After having thoroughly saturated the room with the anti pest chemicals, the hazmat team begins to leave the room and on the exit of the last person, I hear the keypad being pressed which reactivates the motion and pressure sensors within the room. My eyes watered and my muscles burned but I managed to wait nearly half an hour for the stench to subside enough for me to safely remove my mask and place it back in the bag. I position the right side of my body against the I-beam and span four of the girders lying at a 45-degree angle with my pack against my chest. Cradled by the I-beam, I am virtually invisible to anyone just glancing casually in my direction and not making a thorough inspection of the undercarriage of the platform.

My original blueprints suggested it and from my current observations, I deduce that since the entire system is automated as long as I do not trigger the alarm, I should be safe.

During my time in the bush, I found that like many other earth creatures, I have the ability to control blood flow throughout my body. This explained my ability to survive on very little food and oxygen. I can also depress my metabolic rate at will to ration energy usage in my body and slow my heart rate and organ function to an absolute minimum, similar to insects and animals who hibernate when cold and aestivate when it is warm. This is probably the reason my kind has garnered the reputation of being the undead, appearing as such to the profane.

After securing my duffel bag to my chest. I tie a length of paracord around my feet and the girder directly below them and secure them tightly against the beam. Sitting forward with my bag still against my chest, I wrap another longer piece of rope around the girder that goes across the center of my back and lie down before tying it around my torso tightly to prevent my body from falling off the platform while I am resting. I set my watch alarm for 28 days, 7 hours, and 52 minutes from now. The watch is designed with a special setting that gives me the option of not only vibrating but also sending multiple jolts of electricity into my wrist to bring me out of deep suspended animation sleep.

I close my eyes and attempt to clear my mind, but my thoughts are occupied with the bittersweet fragments of over 300 years of life.

My mother...

Colette...

Jessie...

Lynn...

Revenge...

Mistakes...

The amount of death I have caused, whether directly or indirectly...

My heartbeat slows gradually until it is a mere five pulses per minute, and I fall into a catatonic state.

Chapter 27

Attack

I have the exact same dream over and over again…

    I am sitting on the grass under the warm sun in a grassy meadow, talking with my mother who is seated on a chair next to me wearing a white dress with her hair wrapped in a scarf sitting high on her head like a crown. We talk for hours on end about my father and her childhood and the times of peace and the celebrations amongst the different tribes. These festivals would last for days taking place betwixt the beautiful lakes and mountains that surrounded her village. The latter part of my dream would find me being able to walk in the full sunlight slowly down red clay roads talking and holding hands with Colette. I catch myself staring into her beautiful dark brown eyes, with my back erect and wearing shoes like a true gentleman. The sun is shining on her beautiful brown skin intermittently through the leaves of the trees and she is smiling at me. My heart is just bursting with happiness.

    In the next moment, I look down and notice a large wasp on my wrist and it is actively stinging me over and over again, the pain of the stings becoming ever sharper. As I reach out to shoo the wasp away, Colette and the beautiful country lane slowly disappear, taking my heart along with it. I open my eyes to the dark grey steel of the metallic catwalk. I can no longer hear the songs of birds and the low hum of the bees, only the rumblings of water pumps and the hum of a large power generator. I slowly begin to remember that I am still under the trellis strapped to the girders beneath the platform inside the underground physical plant of the Kongress Center in Davos. The muscle atrophy experienced during this suspended animation sleep sends sharp pains throughout my body as the arteries and capillaries swell with the life-giving fluid, and my extremities begin to tingle in response to the increased blood flow.

After five minutes or so, I am able to flex my arms and hands enough to begin to untie the rope holding me tightly across my chest. Pain and stiffness from lying in such an awkward position slowly begins to subside, and I reach into my pack while still lying down and pull out the small battery powered cooler with the packets of blood. I bite into the edge of one of the packets and drain it of all its contents. The effect is immediate and dramatic, healing my muscles and restoring my vitality completely. I sit up moving extremely slowly in order to untie my feet from the girders and not set off the motion detectors. I take a deep breath and exhale and look down at my watch which reads 23:56 UCT.

At midnight before the first day of the World Economic Forum, there is a ceremony held involving only the leaders of all the major economic powers. Presidents, prime ministers, kings, queens, leaders of the corporatocracy, you name it, all gather in a Bohemian Grove style ritual wearing Druidic robes and chanting demonic incantations and verses from demonic texts. This demonic liturgy is performed to manifest lowering of the vibration of the earth realm and allowing creatures from other dimensions who feed on human misery to proliferate throughout the planet. The conjurors of these entities are shielded from their influence while they collude to become richer and more powerful through despicable acts of violence and exploitation. The Large Hadron Collider in Geneva is fired up five days before the event in order to achieve maximum power 24 hours in advance of this ritual and should be running at full capacity by now in time for their spells to harness their dimension warping power and to have a maximum effect on the planet and surrounding galaxy. This is one of the few rare occasions that the true leaders of the Incalculaba must expose themselves to the public because they are connected by blood to the progenitors of the ritual and must be the focal point of distribution of the

516

wickedness that certain inter-dimensional beings have in store for planet earth.

The main conduit person by bloodline and high priest for this year's event has been identified as the current Baron Alesteir Reichstall who is well into his nineties but still wields control over all branches of the family. An empire totaling more than 500 trillion dollars in wealth. The Baron is so secretive concerning his public appearances and his day-to-day whereabouts are so unknown that until Kate's investigations pressured him to resurface, there had not been a clear picture taken of him since the late 1990's when he was just around 70 years old. The data of his last singular appearance where the initial picture of the vampire bodyguard was taken was only revealed when a British tabloid journalist cyber-bullied a former high-level employee at the hotel in Davos who, was attempting to pursue a political career in a small county in Port Moresby, New Zealand. The tabloid people got him by hacking into his personal computer and finding child pornography and blackmailing him into spilling the beans on extremely classified information about certain V.I.P.s at the conference or else they would disclose to his wife and family the type of lifestyle he was really into.

My wrist display now reads 23:58. Once the ceremony starts, the entire Kongress Center Complex goes into lockdown mode for a full 33 minutes. No one is allowed in or out, and no cameras or electronic devices are allowed inside the banquet hall whatsoever. Members with pacemakers or hearing aids that cannot be removed are excluded from attending the convocation because of the risk that the devices could be used to record or leak the proceedings to the outside world.

I reach into my bag and remove my tranquilizer gun and my .45 caliber Sig Sauer P220 Legion with the silencer tip and the armor piercing shells. At the stroke of midnight, I drop down from the girders landing with my full weight on the floors pressure sensors. The lights in the room go red, and the alarm begins to sound just like when the rat was scurrying across the floor a little less than a month ago. I holster the tranquilizer gun in the small of my back and holster the .45 on my chest as I sling the sword into its sheath on my back and then pull my pack onto my shoulders fully and securely before pulling the .45 again and racing up the stairs to wait for my guests. No sooner do I reach the door, it begins to slide open, and I leap into the air and one-handed grab a steel girder above me and pull my legs up just before five commandos in full armor storm in with their guns raised and pointing in every direction.

The leader griped in German. ["If this is another rat, I swear I'm gonna stick my rifle up that bitch's ass and pull the trigger. I'm not going down over fucking Mickey Mouse because she can't figure out how to seal this place up. This is the absolute worst possible time for this shit to be happening."] he turns and shouts at his subordinates, ["Locate this fucking thing, and smash it to bits. Shut the alarm down now or else we are Hackepeter."]

The second-in-command behind the leader quickly types something into a display on his arm and shuts off the siren but the lights remain red. The door slides shut behind the last soldier who is looking down at a handheld sonar device like the one they had before that led them straight to the location of the rat. Thinking that there must be a malfunction in the device, the man taps the machine and rereads the room measurements and radar in disbelief.
Impatiently, the lead soldier turns around and shouts at the man holding the portable imaging device.

"Nun, wo ist es? (Well, where is it?)"

The soldier stammers back (in German), ["I think there is something wrong with this machine. The pressure sensors are reading something much larger than a rat here… and…"] He squints at the machine as the alert indicates that the *something* larger than a rat was practically on top of him. He looks up just as I drop out of the darkness onto the floor.

I spin kick him in the head, shattering his display visor and probably most of the bones in his face, sending his body flying back into the leader. Then one…two…three…headshots to the remaining soldiers who are dead on their feet before they knew what hit them. I run to the spot where the lead

518

soldier landed and put a bullet in his brain and pluck out one of his eyes. Behind me, the door slides open again and the two members of the maintenance crew are standing at the door with a mop, a bucket of cleaning supplies and a water hose filling their respective hands. I reach behind me and pull the tranquilizer gun and fire a shot directly into their solar plexus before they can react. They drop their cleaning supplies and turn to run but their legs turn to jelly and within three seconds, the smaller of the two men collapses. Two seconds later the other man collapses to his knees and woozily drops on his side like a sack of potatoes onto the floor. The woman that accompanied the maintenance team the last time is nowhere to be seen, but I proceed with caution through the door quickly having already used the retinal scan ID from the lead soldier to deactivate the flashing red lights.

The hallways are too narrow to use my sword effectively, so I holster my tranquilizer gun and race down the hall holding the silenced .45. The cameras lining the walls are no doubt witnessing my approach, and I anticipate a swarm of soldiers to burst through one of the doors along this corridor at any second. If I can make it to the main courtyard and confront them there, I will have plenty of room to swing my sword freely. I plan to cut all the mercs and soldiers down quickly and speed through to the main ceremony hall to disrupt the ritual and confront the Baron and the other members of Incalculaba personally before they can escape.

At this very moment, world financial markets should be experiencing a massive nightmare. Accounting firms are scrambling to figure out how balance sheets of trillion dollar asset hedge funds have been drained by no less than fifty percent of their assets, and regular ordinary people are receiving notices on their phones and laptops that their bank accounts have huge balances or they have received a large chunk of Bitcoin, Ethereum, Cardano, USDT, British Pound, Naira, Rand, Shekel , Peso, and an innumerable variety of other fiat currencies to spend as they please. The richest of the rich that are in attendance at the ceremony tonight will not find out until after their annual prayer to Beelzebub is complete. We determined that this would be the perfect window to strike with the computer virus because of the ironclad restriction by the security forces to never interrupt the conjuring ceremony under any circumstance or risk facing the wrath of their short-tempered masters.

The door to the stairs is secured with a magnetic lock at the top of the frame that is normally controlled from a centralized switchboard or unlocked locally with a digital key. I blast the magnet mechanism above the door with two bullets shattering the apparatus enough to yank the door open and run through. I sprint up three flights of stairs to the lobby courtyard level just outside the main event and banquet halls and freeze in my tracks. I smell them just before I hear them reach the door downstairs. An entire commando squad of at least five men with automatic rifles are coming up the stairs behind me through the busted door. A pincer maneuver is surely incoming because I wager that on the other side of that courtyard door is a small army with no less than fifty mercenaries waiting for me to step out and get blown away by their high caliber machine guns.

I holster my weapon and take off my bag and before it hits the floor, I am down the stairs stabbing the lead soldier before his unfortunate brain could register the pain of being stabbed through the vital organs. In the same motion, I push my sword through the armor and into the heart and lung of the second soldier. My speed overwhelms them before either could fire a single shot. I lift them up on the hilt of my sword and using the downward momentum, I kick them into the third and fourth soldier causing them to clip the third soldier and sending him flying into the wall. The fourth soldier quickly dodges right and levels his weapon at my face. The sound of metal 'tings' the air as I slice his gun in half along with most of his left forearm. As my right hand swings the sword, my left hand goes to my chest and pulls the .45, dumping three shots into the fifth soldier knocking him back into the door just as another soldier sticks his gun through the opening and fires off a quick burst of three shots that bury themselves in the concrete wall behind me before the door slams on the muzzle of his gun. I stab my sword into his heart through the gap created in the door, then turn and holster the .45, leap over the bodies clogging the floor, resheath my sword and hurtle back up the three flights of stairs to the lobby floor. I grab my bag and remove a shape charge, set it for two minutes and sixty seconds and attach it to the center of the door. I pull out a small vial of weaponized nitric acid from the tool pouch on the top side of my bag, and I take a deep breath to avoid inhaling the fumes created by the melting steel and then proceed to pour the acid onto the hinges of the door. I rip the door closer mechanism from the plate above it and once the hinges are soft enough, I grab the door knob with both hands and pull the heavy steel door towards me to unseat it from the door jamb, holding it against my body like a shield.

I take three steps forward into the banquet hall when all hell breaks loose and a barrage of bullets rain down on my position and riddle the steel door stopping me in my tracks. Three gas canisters fly overhead, striking the wall and bouncing back into the room quickly filling the large space with some form of nerve agent. Holding my breath with three seconds left on the timer, and I spin, holding the door in one hand and launching it like a frisbee into the fray of soldiers reloading their weapons after their initial flurry of bullets. I dash to the left taking a few bullets in the side and back before diving for cover behind a large pillar.

"KATHOOOOOOMMM!!!!!"

The door explodes, rocking the room with a cacophonous shockwave and sending smoke and shrapnel from the door in a hundred different directions, scattering the brigade of soldiers guarding the main event halls. In the seconds after the explosion, I put on my gas mask and helmet, toss my bag behind a concrete bench and draw my sword, emerging from the smoke like an arrow shot from a bow, slicing through armor, flesh and bone of each of my enemies, one after the other, moving between opponents too fast for any one soldier to get a clear shot off. I rip open the helmet of one soldier and bash another with the hilt of my sword crushing his gas mask and exposing them both to the tear gas smoke filling the hall.

I move like a madman, faster than anything their training has taught them to react to. One soldier manages to get off a few rounds, two of which ping my helmet. A close call indeed if it was not bulletproof. I kick him in his chest, sending him flying into the wall and knocking him unconscious. I can hear a man who must be their commander screaming at the top of his lungs in German to regroup as the entire banquet hall has fallen into pure chaos.

The phantom smell of blood reaches me as I slice through the commandos' ballistic TALOS battle armor like paper. I jet towards the side of the room making a circle back towards my bag running like a bat out of hell, using the smoke from the gunfire, explosions, and tear gas canisters to my advantage. Killing, maiming and incapacitating dozens of adversaries in my wake. I grab my bag and run full speed toward the thick glass doors leading to the inner courtyard and the main auditorium beyond which I should be able to confront the management level devils and complete my mission.

I slice through the ballistic glass and no sooner than I breach the exit door to the dark courtyard, I hear a loud whirring sound like swarms of bees or locusts filling the night air. I look up just as a spotlight springs on from above and a loud electronic voice repeats in English, French, and German for me to

"Surrender"

I see three heavily armed copter style military drones closing fast on my position. At the other end of the expanse, a group of soldiers carrying anti-personnel shields enters from either side of the cloister followed by two nine foot armored ATLAS humanoid robots with M61 Vulcan 20mm autocannons attached to their frames. Like a marching band getting into formation, they all align themselves across from my position. I reload the .45 with a fresh clip and go on a strafing run, concentrating on the drones first. It takes me six shots to disable the rotors of two of the attack drones, placing them out of commission before the sound of the autocannons on the robots begin to spin.

Steel plates drop down in front of the glass doors I just came through sealing me within the concrete walls of the courtyard. I turn to run so swiftly my feet take a second to get traction when the wall explodes with gunfire. I have never moved so fast in my life. The bullets from the autocannons are right on my heels dimpling the steel and chipping the concrete in their wake as I tear across the courtyard. My speed and the durability of my tactical suit was the only factor keeping me from being ripped in half by the salvo of bullets. As I move, the robots are forced to pivot rapidly as their targeting systems dictate. I make a quick motion to dodge fire from the remaining drone as they continue to fire recklessly at such a high rate of speed that the robot on the left strikes the arm of the adjacent robot, sending bullets ricocheting into the shielded commandos. The sudden hail of misfired bullets knocks them back and causes them to stumble over each other to avoid the friendly fire, toppling the line and breaking their tight formation.

The robot's AI kicks in and it adjusts by ceasing fire out of caution for the commandos while its companion robot repositions itself by moving laterally to avoid future crossfire incidents. This gave me the precious seconds I needed to close the gap between myself and the closest shield-wielding commando. Using my momentum, I unleash a vicious spin kick on the carbon fiber ballistic shield, knocking the shield to the side, exposing his body. I chop his hands away from the shield, grab it and turn to face the group of soldiers now firing at me sporadically from behind their own shields. I strafe to the left as they regroup and take up a formation behind the two robots again for another onslaught of gatling gun fire. I sprint straight towards the two robots holding my newly acquired shield in front of me. Just as the lethal autocannons begin to target me again, I lunge forward and make a downward slash at the lead robot. To my surprise, the droid responds quick enough to bring its free arm up in time to absorb the impact of the blow but my sword slices right through the carbon steel of the arm and the rest of the metal alloy body of the droid like a hot knife through butter, putting it totally out of commission. The second robot opens fire at point blank range with a barrage from the M61 Vulcans just as I raise my shield, and I am blown backwards by the impact, sending me flying forty feet and skidding across the ground into a concrete wall. My right shoulder absorbs most of the impact, and I let go of the shield as I roll wildly on the ground.

I quickly get to my feet and dive behind a concrete bench which is riddled with bullets immediately. I pull my duffel bag from my back, reach into the side zippered pouch of my bag and pull out my electromagnetic pulse device which still carries two more charges. I turn the dial and flip open the cover on the switch. Staying low, I pivot toward the robot who is approaching with the remainder of the shielded soldiers not far behind. All of these soldiers seem to be wearing tech enhancements that interact with the sensors on the robot who is using some sort of sophisticated tracking method other than a mere infrared sensor because it is uncannily accurate at following and targeting me relentlessly, even in my suit's stealth mode.

I get to my feet, swiftly ducking behind the decor of the courtyard which is being ripped apart by enemy fire. I blast through a section of the thick shrubbery and dive roll towards the hulking machine tucking the EMP as I roll, flicking the switch in mid motion. Everything goes dark. My tactical suit becomes heavy, and I watch the lights go out on the mechanical monster and the huge machine drops face first to the floor. A few of the soldiers in the vicinity of the blast wearing exoskeleton suits fall to their knees now that their armor is incapacitated. They are forced to remove their enhancements and retreat behind cover. I was luckily able to catch a couple of the battle drones in the blast radius of the EMP, all of which came crashing down hard onto the concrete.

Everything was in a state of confusion as the soldiers and mercenaries' communications and targeting systems were now temporarily offline. Many of these soldiers had come to rely on their tech enhancements to guide them on the battlefield and now were forced to use only their own God-given senses in the darkness against me. In the tumult, I take up my sword and run full speed into the fray of soldiers delivering fatal blows and slicing through their body armor effortlessly. I slice up the downed drones and disable the robot just as reinforcements pour into the plaza from an unseen trapdoor at the far side of the room near where I entered. These soldiers carry high powered rifles and immediately drop into a firing formation in an attempt to take me out from long range. Again, I was way too fast for them. On the run, I use my .45 to blast out the emergency flood lights above the courtyard to lower their visibility. I take a few direct hits as I close in on my opponents, but the pain doesn't register and using my bloody sword, I begin dispatching the slow moving heavily armored combatants who looked to be a large faction of mercenaries for they bore no military insignia on their now bloodstained uniforms. These are the hired guns that come at the highest prices for their willingness to go wherever and do whatever it takes, no matter how heinous the request. Many are rewarded with the latest in high-tech devices that put them head and shoulders above most military regiments of even developed countries. This edge fosters an even greater desire for them to act as judge, jury, and executioner in the field because there is essentially no unified force who can stand against them. They, in turn, get to decide whose political regime is important according to their ability to pay.

Even with all their battle experience and superior military gear, nothing could have prepared them for a creature like myself.

I cleared a path paved with scores of bodies of the exterminated mercs. One after the other, they met their gruesome end. My speed and sword technique overwhelmed their forces with ease which begins to worry me because something about the battle felt too easy. We calculated that there would be a much larger contingency of soldiers and mechs this close to the ceremonial chambers. I tried to hold on to the notion that since no one could have reasonably conceived that one person could have made it this far into the inner sanctum that there was no contingency plan in place to alert the majority of their forces and have them scramble together outside the main hall in enough time to try and slow my advance.

My tactical suit starts to reactivate and the lights in the courtyard begin to glow as they reenergize. I make a beeline for the only set of doors on the windowless building at the far side of the courtyard. According to my map, they lead to the inner lobby structure where the ceremony should still be in progress. I begin to take fire from another large and growing group of soldiers from the opposite side of the courtyard that causes me to divert my path. I run and rip a shield from the arm of one of the dead soldiers to protect my flank from the steady gunfire while my suit is still booting up and vulnerable to armor piercing rifle fire. As I run back towards the lobby doors, I suddenly feel a gust of wind at my back. I instinctively dive like a major league baseball player stealing home plate to retrieve another one of the fallen shields. I grab both sides of the two shields as best I can while still holding my sword and roll to my right a nanosecond before the flash of a small rocket being fired from a drone lights up the night sky and hits my double shield barricade at near point blank range. The recoil of the blast sends the drone flying out of control only to smash fatally into one of the large topiaries in the courtyard. The explosion slams me into the concrete, , and knocks the wind utterly from my chest, causing my ears to bleed and filling my brain with a loud ringing noise.

I lie there unable to move my body wondering if I may have lost a limb or been blown in half because for about three seconds, I could not lift my head to look at the status of my body. The hot smoking twisted carbon fiber alloy of the shields sat melted and smoldering about six feet to my left, ripped from my now sore hands in the blast. It has been over a century since I was forced to push myself like this, and the technology of the enemy has gotten exponentially more lethal. The double shields and my now re-powered tactical suit seem to have taken the brunt of the impact and after another moment or two, I shake off the grogginess and look to my numb right hand. Panic grips me when I realize I am no longer holding my sword. I have still not fully recovered from the shock of the blast, but I will my body to move again.

All at once, I hop unsteadily to my feet amongst the thick smoke and swirling debris. I can hear the soldiers approaching my position, but visibility is low. All of my equipment, especially my sword, was outfitted with specialized air tags that allow me to track my belongings.

"Find sword."

I say into my watch and a high pitch whistle that only animals and the most sensitive listening devices can hear is emitted from the cross guard of my katana. I wipe the dust from my visor to get a better look at the display which says it is 37 feet behind me. I pull the .45 from its holster and begin blasting my way out of the smoke, striking two of the closest soldiers that were approaching my position from my right. One of the soldiers took a bullet in the neck, dropping him like a bag of rocks. The other soldier was able to charge headlong into the gun blasts of my armor piercing bullets, no doubt due to his next generation Sotnik battle armor that was rumored to be in development as standard issue for special ops in the Russian military and highly sought after by discriminating mercenaries with unlimited resources.

As he leveled his weapon at me, I explode towards him, grabbing the muzzle of his rifle just as he fires, bending the metal of the gun upward as I snatch his rifle away and punch him hard in the face, crushing his gas mask and sending blood and broken teeth spurting from the man's twisted visage. I push him aside and straightaway race towards my sword currently lying in a patch of red mulch when machine gun fire from behind sends bullets whizzing past me and dimpling the concrete next to me. I holster the .45 and scoop my sword up mid-run. Pivoting towards the wall, I turn to head towards the door leading to the ceremonial chamber when one of the mercenaries fires a grenade launcher from less than 50 feet in front of me. The hair bristles down my spine as I watch the grenade flying towards me in slow motion. With my reflexes being multiple times faster than a cobras, I was able to jump and twist my body through the air to avoid being hit directly by the shell, but the explosion and subsequent shockwave of the blast when it hit the floor threw me off balance, and I took a severe blow to the head which I involuntarily used to break my fall onto the concrete. If not for my helmet I would have sustained a serious injury.

The blast was fortunate in a sense because I land on my stomach less than twenty feet from the front of the doors leading to the inner lobby and main meeting halls. I jump up, sword in hand, and book it towards the exit. The mercenaries and soldier reinforcements, taking note of my close combat success, deliver overwhelming suppression fire to keep me away from my goal as they advance on my position. Even with the protection my tactical suit provided, there are too many of them to turn my back on while I attempt to hack my way through the locked metal doors. I grab a stun grenade from a side pocket on my belt and toss it into the oncoming mercenaries.

Sweat was pouring down the inside of my tactical suit which was taking considerable punishment from some of the more accurate hits landed by the sophisticated targeting modules equipped by the mercenaries. These cutting-edge weapons can track movement using air vibrations along with heat signatures. I grab the barrel of an enemy gun and kick the merc holding it in the chest, sending him flying and flip the gun in my hand in order to use it as my own. However, as I suspected, all of their weapons came equipped with "smart gun" trigger technology that only fire if the user is wearing a

527

corresponding bluetooth device, usually a watch or ring of some sort, that tells the gun it can fire safely. In all the confusion and mayhem, I feel a familiar sharp pain of electrical shock in my left wrist which I recognize as the alarm on my watch telling me that there is only fifteen minutes left before the ritual will be over. I glance up and notice that the clouds above the courtyard seem to be swirling in an unnatural way. Using another stun grenade as cover, I double back towards the group firing on me to thin their ranks as I slice, kick, and punch my way towards the doors to the corridor leading to the main hall.

Even through my mask I can tell the entire place stinks of war and blood. The charred smell of fire and the stench of men evacuating their bladders and bowels as they take their last breath on the bare concrete floor engulf the courtyard. I continue killing and maiming all who stand in my way, slicing my opponent's bodies in two before they even realize they have been cut. I recognize some of the government sanctioned soldiers scattered amongst the other mercenaries by their Swiss Guard insignia on their arm bands. These soldiers seem to carry the more sophisticated weaponry and give the impression of being in charge as they relay orders to the rank-and-file shooters. I run toward one of these officers and as he coolly levels his gun and pulls the trigger. I quickly narrow the space between us, dodging most of his bullets, coming under his line of sight and delivering a crushing uppercut to his chin knocking him high into the air. I slice through the AR-15 of his colleague standing behind him, grab him by the neck, and hoist him up with my left arm using his T.A.L.O.S. armored body as a shield as I ran towards the bank of doors on the north end of the courtyard. I ran brazenly straight through the hail of bullets, the soulless soldiers mercilessly firing into the body of their now deceased fellow comrade. Draping him over my shoulder to absorb the bullets, I hold his bloody left hand on the palm scanner as the remaining mercenaries advanced forward.

The display flashes red as all access has likely been shut down throughout this part of the building. The soldiers keep firing relentlessly at me and the seemingly bulletproof glass doors but seem reluctant to approach me any further in my current position at the door access panel. It was as if they wanted me to open the door. As if they were herding me toward this

528

entrance. My instinct screamed "trap," but I paid it no heed. Drawing back my sword, I stabbed straight through the dark bullet-proof glass and yanked back my sword, quickly leaving a two-inch crack in the glass. I flip the hilt in my hand and using the bottom of my sword, I slam into the crack in the glass with all my might, causing the small crack to become a larger crack with each hit. After five quick blows, the two top pieces of thick glass split in two, and I dive into the corridor leaving my human shield behind. To my surprise, this corridor is completely empty. As soon as I scramble to my feet, I hear a rumbling behind me and turn to see a huge steel plated fire door dropping down on either side of the narrow corridor and imprisoning me inside.

Meanwhile, within an unseen control room far beneath my current position, one of the analyst soldiers reports to his commanding officer:

(IN GERMAN) ["Colonel Konigsmark, the intruder has been clocked by our drone sentries as running through the courtyard at speeds upwards of eighty miles an hour without a discernible exo-suit and has managed to take out our Russian and Swiss front guards including several autonomous battle drones and two MegaAtlas sentry bots carrying M61 Vulcans. Our troops have never witnessed anything move like that in live combat. We were forced to slow down the video feed just to figure out if what they were encountering was in fact humanoid. Must be some sort of new cyborg tech built into that suit because there is no way a human being can move like that after taking so many direct hits. Approximately 74% of our first responder ground forces have been neutralized sir and casualties are high. The hostile has been reported to have discharged an electromagnetic pulse device that is said to have damaged one of the main nodes powering the electromagnetic perimeter field. We had to allocate additional troops in order to beef up our perimeter defense personnel in anticipation of accomplices attacking the building while our defenses were down. Locally, there is a system-wide wattage drain caused by the Large Hadron Collider, so we usually don't activate our reserve generators prior to the end of the ceremony in case there is a brownout in the capital. Normally, this is the only time when we are forced to increase our ground forces throughout the perimeter but because of the threat caused by this one bastard being able to defeat our first responders and penetrate our impregnable sensor systems, we are at a serious disadvantage right now.] Pausing his rant, the analyst soldier spins in his chair to face his computer again and begins frantically entering the code to deploy more drones and two additional robotic sentries to the courtyard area.

(In German) ["No bio suit that exists today can perform like that,"] replied the commanding officer Colonel Konigsmark, chewing on the unlit remains of a cigar and staring at the footage of the intruder with uncharacteristic worry in his eyes.

["I've only seen movements like that once about fifteen years ago at the G7 summit. A stupid protester jumped a barricade and made a quick lunging movement towards one of the Reichstall heirs while he was being escorted through the crowd into the UN building. This protester guy had a box cutter and was slippery enough to get within arm's length of Reichstall. At that instant this woman seemed to just appear from thin air. She was holding the protester, who was twice her size, up off of the ground by his neck with one arm before slamming his flailing body into the ground, knocking him unconscious and fracturing his skull in the process. We all ran in to cuff the guy and take him into custody and I only got a quick glimpse of the woman who foiled the attack. She wore dark sunglasses and had pale skin but makeup seemed to be caked upon her face. She seemed to be in her mid-twenties but her hair was pure white. It was all over in a matter of seconds, and she walked away and got into the back seat of the Baron's vehicle without saying one word to anyone."] Colonel Konigsmark finishes his story staring intently at the looping footage of DuSange rampaging through the Kongress Center

["don't even bother deploying the Osprey to capture that thing. Detach that security corridor and launch the anti-aircraft missiles to disintegrate that creature immediately,"] Colonel Konigsmark says, calmly lighting his cigar and watching the CCTV monitors as DuSange kneels down and reaches into his bag.

Colonel Konigsmark places his huge rough hand on the shoulder of the analyst soldier and looks down at him with a grim look on his scruffy, scarred face and says flatly, ["Prepare to evacuate A1 and all other clients using the Hyperloop cars, and divert all above ground forces to the lower levels. Somehow this...'thing' has figured out that this building was a diversion,"] he continues gravely.

The eyes on the computer specialist soldiers go as wide as dinner plates. Another high-ranking analyst standing near the colonel speaks up.

(German) ["Sir, with all due respect, that knowledge is such restricted classification that 98% of our own personnel have no clue that the structure they've been tasked with protecting is a decoy. How can you be so sure this man knows even though he walked right into our trap?"]

Colonel Konigsmark does not answer him. He only continues staring at the screen.

Another technician makes an announcement. ["The V-22 Osprey will make visual contact with the security corridor in less than two minutes. Sir, do you think we should still call for evacuation also?" the analyst naively asks the colonel. "Once the Osprey makes contact and attaches the magnet to the structure, it takes less than thirty seconds to detach and lift the adamantine box away, causing no further threat to our clients and delivering the intruder to our disposal facility in Geneva. A trap made for the world's most resilient rats,"] the technician says smugly as he watches his on-screen display tracking the progress of the disposal vehicle arriving at their location.

Silence only from Colonel Konigsmark who continues to watch the screen intently.

"Is he setting a shape charge in that small space?" the analyst monitoring the screen asks rhetorically. "It's suicide if he sets off anything powerful enough to blow through the walls of that container in such a small enclosure," he says loudly, looking questioningly up into the colonel's emotionless face as a child would who searches his parents' visage for answers about the many mysteries of life."

Back inside the now-sealed security corridor is filling up with all manner of deadly gases that would surely have put me in a very vulnerable position were it not for the mask inside my helmet. As soon as the doors closed behind me, I realized it. There was no way they would allow me reach the corridor in which, just beyond, sat the most powerful people on the planet. The reckless way that those soldiers were shooting at me made me suspect that the ritual was really taking place elsewhere within the facility. I use my sword to carve a row in the six inch thick steel floor of my cage. Then I reach inside my bag and pull out my shape charges and the remainder of the nitric acid. I pour a little of the acid inside the divot, place a large wad of C4 explosive over that and top it off with an RF receiver trigger device. I set the timer for ten seconds with my wristwatch transmitter and retreat towards the corner of the room and crouch into a ball facing the walls with my hands on my helmet where my ears would be.

"KAHHHHTHOOOOMMM!!!!"

The explosion rocks me to the core, the force being multiplied inside the titanium alloy compartment before pushing its way through the bottom of the container, making a small, twisted metal exit wound in the floor about two feet in diameter. The inside of my skull rang like the Freedom Bell, and my body felt like I had plummeted from seventy stories high into a belly flop onto solid concrete. My tactical suit and helmet absorbed most of the ground zero blast, and after a long thirty seconds, I was able to slide up on my wobbly legs like a newborn calf and stumble over to look down through the hole at what lies before me. As I peek in, I am smacked in the face with the dust and debris from the explosion being kicked up by the wind turbines from some vehicle now hovering above my location. Below me from what I can make out, there seems to be a large underground military complex. I drop down through the hole onto the top of a structure with industrial air movers on the roof. According to every blueprint and schematic we found on the city of Davos, a facility of this magnitude is not supposed to exist. From the looks of the building, this probably serves to house the personnel residency facility for private staff and long standing employees that service the Elites while on the premises that Keith and I knew existed but could not figure out the mystery of where it was hidden.

I run to one of the large air handlers and rip off the grate, toss my bag in, then jump feet first holding my sword up as I slide down into the vent. I scurry backwards down the duct and soon after I feel my bag has stopped its descent against a large soffit. I kick open the vent cover and drop down with my bag and sword into a women's bathroom. I quickly take inventory of my remaining gear and bolt towards the exit. In the hall outside the bathroom, this top floor appears to be domicile rooms, much like a hotel or apartment building with brown wooden doors uniformly numbered up and down both sides of the hall. There are no signs of any other people present, but there is a red flashing alarm light signaling an emergency, so I run full speed towards the fire exit to try and follow wherever they were headed. I shove my way into the stairwell and jet down nine flights of stairs. I remove my helmet and gas mask to take a deep breath of air when I reach the second to last floor.

The recent smell of humans, heavily covered with cologne and hairspray, leads further downstairs and towards a set of double doors into the adjoining structure. I ran full speed following the aroma into a wide corridor that connected to an underground shuttle depot waiting area which I suppose is the personnel entrance for the servants and assistants that accompany the elite. My intrusion must have prompted them to be evacuated in order to wait safely for their masters and patrons outside the 'actual' ceremonial altar space. I believed myself well versed in the lengths that the Incalculaba would go to maintain their power but even I am taken aback at their ability to be able to construct a full-scale city below ground without one shred of information being leaked about it.

As I look around frantically for clues on which direction to go, I begin to realize that even with all my senses, it would be impossible to find the meeting hall in time because of the sheer magnitude of this underground facility. No one in our intel network calculated that the entire affair on the surface was a decoy and that the real ceremony was taking place dozens of feet below the earth directly under the real Kongrsszentrum Davos meeting hall.

With my helmet and mask removed, my senses are all at maximum again and above me I can hear the heavy footfalls of boots in the stairwell. The mercenaries have finally caught up to me and are coming to hunt me down. Another prolonged sharp jolt of electricity in my wrist from my timer alarm let me know that the festivities would be ending soon and that if I did not step on the gas, I would fail the mission and have to wait another millennium in order to have an opportunity to strike at the head of the dragon.

I put my gas mask and helmet back on and high tail it down a long passageway now following the multiple rows of pipes and conduit along the walls and ceiling that most likely supply water, power, and internet to the corridor and subsequent facilities deeper inside the headquarters. I brace myself for the shock of any electrical discharge and drawing my sword, I leap into the air and with a quick downward slash, I sever the aluminum piping and the wires that they protect in one swift chop, sending sparks and a bright flash of light as the exposed current dies in the air with no place to go. My attack served in killing the power to the lights in the corridor and plunging everything into darkness. Only the glow from the battery powered keypad guarding the door around thirty meters ahead of me could be seen. As I hurriedly reached the entrance next to the keypad, the high-quality steel material that the door was made of led me to believe that I was on the right track. Another wave of soldiers should be arriving soon, and I am already out of time due to our miscalculations on the true location of the ceremony. I stab through the keypad next to the door with one of my knives and shoot the magnet apparatus just above the door a few times to deactivate it and enter the room. Servers and computers line the walls of this chamber which seems to be a data hub connected to a research facility. This room still had electricity so it must run on a separate circuit from the lights and air handlers.

I survey the sterile concrete room and spot a large air register twenty feet above a door across the room. Underground headquarters such as this one are the gold standard in protection against enemy attacks, but one of the drawbacks associated with operating an underground facility of this size is the need to constantly recycle the air to prevent stagnation and sickness. I sheath my sword into the magnetic scabbard on my back and jump ten feet up the wall and dig my claws into the painted cinder block making my way up to the air vent, rip off the grate and toss it to the ground. My body will not fit with my duffel bag on my back so, holding on to the opening of the vent with my left hand, I pull myself up and swing my legs up and into the opening. Half hanging out of the open ductwork, I grab the sword from the scabbard on my back with my right hand and with my left hand, I remove the bag slung over my head and slide feet first down into the aperture using my knees and elbows to hastily scuttle backwards and down into the abyss of the air vent. The space is cramped, and I am forced to crawl down the long air duct with the space just barely being more than shoulder width. As I move along for what seems like a mile, I can hear the high pitch whine of a mag lev train starting and stopping. This vent most likely runs parallel to an underground tram for moving the elite clientele secretly between venues using hyper-loop rails. The duct I was in leads into into a slightly larger pipe, and I crawled backwards another 75 meters before I begin to hear voices and feel light emanating from the grate opening behind me.

It was impossible to make out their conversation through my helmet but there seemed to be a sense of urgency in their tones. My plan to cut the power seems to have had no effect on this area of the site which doubtlessly serves as the nerve center of operations for the entire underground sanctum. There were no sensors attached to the grate and no detectable cameras installed inside the shaft. In their arrogance, the builders of this facility never dreamed that anyone could make it past all the advanced technology and the finest army of sanctioned mercenaries and soldiers that only a coalition of the richest people in the world could afford.

I blindly blast through a metal grate with my knee hoping that I would get lucky and my entry point would be somewhere near the assembly hall. To my surprise, I drop directly down into a large sterile white room with rows and rows of computer desks and large LED screens displaying multiple images of what looked to be various military installations in different countries around the world.

As soon as I land, I toss my bag into a cubicle on my left, draw my .45 and reload with a fresh magazine of the armor piercing shells. I duck down

535

when I hear a door burst open at the other side of the room followed by the familiar sounds of heavy booted men entering. I glance down at my watch which is flashing red indicating that I am out of time and should be getting the hell out of here as soon as possible.

I pop up from behind the computer desk and blast away at the approaching soldiers. The few technicians and unarmed employees who got trapped by my surprise visit were already scrambling to escape when I burst through the ceiling vent begin screaming and diving under the nearest workstations as the soldiers return fire without regard for the safety of the non-combatants. I spring from behind the desk as it is being riddled with bullets, blasting away in midair and striking two soldiers in the thigh and hand respectively, dropping them and creating a gap in the defense formation just wide enough for me to glimpse through the glass doors behind them. There was another cluster of six soldiers running in the opposite direction behind a petite woman dressed in a dark colored business suit and heels with white hair pushing someone in a wheelchair hastily towards a bank of three elevators at the far end of the adjacent room.
"Shit," I scream internally. If the evacuation of the ceremony attendees has progressed this far then I am too late to intercept the Baron and the high ranking Incalculaba members in the midst of the blood ritual. My mission is now officially a failure.

Dammit! I say to myself. All those years of planning down the toilet. After today, they will no doubt increase the security to a level that an army of vampires could not penetrate and the Incalculaba will continue to sleep well knowing its unfettered propagation of misery and corruption will continue without consequence. My blood begins to boil at the thought of what the consequences of my failure will mean to so many people.

Pinned down by enemy machine gun fire, I lie behind a cubicle wall and look at my watch to note the time. I quickly pull another mag from an inner pocket in my tactical suit and reload the .45. I place my sword down momentarily, grab a rolling desk chair recently vacated by a technician, and lob it like a baseball towards the soldiers. Taking up my sword again and moving the speed of greased lightning, I scurry behind the desks in a lateral direction, forcing the enemy to pivot while firing faster than their targeting mechanisms can adjust. The soldiers' bullets shred the computer stations and cubicles, sending debris and shrapnel from computer monitors, glass doors, and office furniture flying everywhere. My movements are sharp and deliberate. Anger and desperation fuel my attack, and I change direction on a dime. While dodging their fire, I rush headlong into the garrison of mercenaries. At this speed, the force of each swing of my blade made the sound of water being divided into two as I sliced through battle armor, cloth, skin, muscle, and bone of my opponents. I am laser focused on reaching this person in the wheelchair whom I presume to be one of the high-ranking members from the Incalculaba. If the woman guarding him is what I think she is, I absolutely cannot let this opportunity elude me. I plan to catch and pass ultimate judgment on this person as an example to the rest of the Incalculaba whom I hold responsible for the unnecessary hardship experienced by 99% of the populace of the planet.

I unload the clip from the .45 into two soldiers keeping their distance and firing at me as I chopped up their comrades. Blood and entrails covered the white floors and furniture. In the room just beyond the now shattered glass doors, the woman and the person in the wheelchair were entering the middle elevator with three of their mechanized mercenaries. As the doors of the elevator were closing, the remainder of the garrison following them turned to face me and began unloading their Fn P90 and MP5s with hundred round magazines. I spring forward and run full speed taking a serpentine path and using pillars along the corridor as cover to avoid the hail of bullets. I manage to get within twenty meters or so from in front of the elevators when one of the mercenaries launches an incendiary device that I successfully dodge, leaping up over it at the last second. The force of the explosion threw myself and a couple of computer workstations into the air, filling the room with dust and smoke and leaving me vulnerable to attack. I land ungracefully hard on my back, but I am up in a flash and using the swirling smoke as cover. I charge at the remaining soldiers like a bull. Ten meters away from the nearest soldier, I toss my sword up and grab it in the center with my thumb and fist and throw my sword javelin style straight as an arrow into the right shoulder of the chap who was third farthest away from me as he was just finishing the process of reloading his grenade launcher. Dropping his arm, he clumsily fires a grenade into a thick concrete wall to his left creating a shockwave and another cloud of dust and debris that showers down upon the mercenaries. Ordinarily, an explosion like that at point blank range would have knocked the toughest of soldiers on their asses, but these X-17 Sabertooth Series Powered Exoskeleton wearing commandos were merely stunned momentarily. I use that brief instance to close on the nearest commando. To my surprise, he has already recovered from the recoil explosion and is raising his weapon at me.

KRRAAOOW!
KRRAAOOW!

He manages to get off two shots from his rifle, one of which strikes me in the chest. The impact of the bullet was not enough to penetrate the suit but at that range, the liquid armor suit could only do so much and I feel as if one of my ribs has been shattered. I lunge forward and grab the mercenary's weapon by the hand guard on the barrel and pull him towards me. I can feel the strength in his exoskeleton cyber enhancements but alone, he is no match for me. I head-butt him in the face to stun him, crushing his face shield and breaking his nose, causing him to drop his rifle. I grab his left forearm at the wrist with my left hand and grasp his left hand with my right and twist his arm and hand in opposite directions back and forth breaking his bones and flesh and ripping his left hand from his arm causing him to howl and scream in pain. I release him as he stumbles backwards in agony, grab up his rifle in a rolling move and using my newly acquired hand that carried the required DNA signature to fire the gun, I quickly turned and leveled the rifle at the commando to my right, striking him in the throat and putting him out of commission. I then turn on my heels and unload the rest of the magazine on the other commando positioned about five meters away while strafing right towards the victim of my sword attack who was unsuccessfully trying to pull the embedded blade from his shoulder. As he moves towards his compatriot in order to use his cover fire to buy more time to remove the sword, I level my weapon at his head but my next pull of the trigger was answered with the click of an empty magazine. I drop the severed hand and run like the clappers of hell toward the last two soldiers.

538

My overwhelming speed again proves to be too much for the pair and as I reach the wounded commando, I strike him in the front of his helmet with the butt of the gun, crushing his gas mask covered face. In one second I drop the gun, pivot behind him, wrap my left arm around his neck placing him in a headlock from behind and hoist his lifeless body up as a shield between me and his accomplice. I rip my sword from his shoulder with my right hand and charge at the last commando who attempts to back away to put enough distance between himself and I to safely fire. I move extraordinarily quickly considering I was carrying a three hundred plus pound armored soldier and bringing my sword upward, I slice through most of his right leg and his left arm up to the elbow. With the next blow he was nearly decapitated and I drop his friend on top of his corpse, sheath my sword on my back, pick up his weapon and the severed left forearm and ran over to the lift access doors. I place the gun and arm down in front of the divide in the elevator door, and I use my strength to overcome the interlocking mechanism and pry them open just enough to push the arm and weapon through with my foot and slide my body sideways through the doors and into the elevator shaft. I quickly scooped up the bloody forearm and the weapon and aim upwards. Puppeteering the severed left forearm with my own left hand, I remove the safety on the grenade launcher, and pull the trigger.

KABOOOOOOOMMMM!!!!!

The explosion inside the closed elevator shaft amplifies the shockwave tenfold flattening me to the ground as the pieces of the elevator came crashing down around me. My helmet protected my eardrums from being destroyed by the blast, but I was momentarily stunned by the concussive force of the blowback from the explosion.

Despite my ringing head and inability to see from the smoke, I push myself up from the floor and leap halfway up the elevator shaft and begin scaling the walls. My head begins clearing and the buzzing in my ears begins to diminish as I move closer to the newly created opening in the bottom of the lift. As I reached the top of the elevator shaft and peeked over the landing, I could see that the explosion had taken out the three armored sentries that must have been near the elevator when it exploded. One of the sentries' corpses was bounced against an adjacent concrete wall, another lay motionless on his stomach twenty feet in front of me, his body peppered with glass and metal shrapnel. Another lay a few feet from the entrance covering his bloody face with both hands and writhing on the ground in pain.

Ahead of me, running along a platform that led to one of the Hyper-loop pods, was the white-haired woman and the old man in the wheelchair. With their force spread so thin from my initial attack and the elevator access to this level now destroyed, there was no quick way to get reinforcements up here. Now unguarded, this unlucky pair will be the first of many to absorb the wrath of the great unwashed. I charge down the empty platform after them when suddenly the woman stops dead in her tracks.

I hear the old man in the wheelchair then say to the woman hoarsely, "This is certainly an outrageous turn of events. Are you sure that one of your people has not betrayed us?"

The white-haired woman who wore an all-black business suit, black stockings, and black heels turns to look at me over her shoulder dismissively while still keeping both hands on the handlebars of the wheelchair. In a tenth of a second, the woman was planting her fist in my sternum. My eyes could barely follow her movements. Her initial attack had so much force behind it, she was able to break at least three ribs through the polyethylene glycol liquid armor tactical suit and send me sliding across the floor on my ass. I somehow managed to hang on to my sword in the assault, and I look up from lying flat on my back to see this woman descending from twenty feet above my head to deliver a crushing blow with her high heel stiletto pumps. These shoes must be made of some type of incredibly durable carbon steel fiber material to be able to stand up to the pressure and force exerted by this creature who is clearly one of the apex predator vampires in this world. This geezer must be a Reichstall or someone with incredible wealth on par with theirs because he must be paying her very handsomely to negate the iconoclastic nature of powerful vampires like her.

As she plummeted towards me, I push up from the ground swinging my sword in attempt to chop her leg off as soon as she was in range, but she read my movements and was able to spin her body in mid-air and change trajectories so suddenly that I whiff the air in my first swing. She lands a few feet away and I roll backwards in order to put some space between us. This woman possesses the physical capability to take out an entire army, I cannot give her a nanosecond of a chance or she will most certainly kill me. My helmet, although extremely durable and useful in combat, has the huge drawback of not allowing me to use my keen senses to the fullest making it very difficult to fight someone of this caliber on equal ground. I can barely follow her movements with just my eyes and fighting instincts. Time slows to a crawl, my fangs were at full bore. As she darts at me with her right hand extended in front of her, claws pointed like knives, I uncharacteristically lost my cool by blindly swinging into what I knew she would dodge and be able to counterattack by exploiting my being off balance. Incredibly, this woman catches my sword between her hands, clapping them together on the blade, and twists it out of my hands in one swift spinning motion kicks me in my stomach, puncturing a hole in my tactical suit and my abdomen before sending me flying into the wall. She mercilessly comes at me with my own sword held high above her head ready to chop me in half as I lay sprawled on my back. Still stunned from the force of the kick and barely able to move, I will myself into action and quickly reach into my tactical suit and produce the gun I had secreted away for just such a desperate situation.

I blast away with the .45 caliber loaded with pure Argentium silver tipped shells, and she uses my own sword to block most of the bullets that she does not bother to dodge. Fortunately, I was able to make contact with a few rounds. The metal toxins secreted by these specially made artillery have an immediate effect on vampires being that they greatly inhibit and ultimately retard the regeneration process of our species. I roll out of the way as the white-haired woman falls and drops the sword as her body tumbles across the floor landing face down. Her body convulses with pain for a moment before going completely still. Black blood starts to pool under the body of the now motionless vampire woman.

I stand up holding the wound in my stomach and gingerly stoop to retrieve my sword and sheath it on my back. I turn to find the old man slowly wheeling himself toward the doors of the Hyper-loop car on the opposite end of the platform. As soon as my eyes are on him, he seems to notice even though he is not facing me and turns his chair around slowly. He looks ancient. His bald, age-spot speckled head, cruel nose, dry withered and wrinkled skin hanging from his jowls and neck as if he is melting. His eyes sit deep in his wrinkled forehead and the dull grey cloudiness could be seen as he raises one thick white eyebrow at the sight of his billion-dollar centurion now sprawled lifeless atop the floor. I begin moving towards him and as I get closer, our eyes meet. In the next instant, his dull muddy blue iris' turn a familiar steel grey, like a wolf and he glares at me with palpable contempt.

"Lower your gaze, you dog," the old man rasps with a sneer and begins to turn his motorized wheelchair around and leave as if dismissing me after looking at me and surmising that I was not worth his time.

I close the gap between us in a millisecond. My clawed hand clutches the back of his elderly throat, and I lift him up roughly from the wheelchair and turn him around to face me with his arms and legs sprawling in the air. That was when I felt it. The icy cold skin with a surreal texture, more akin to scales than human flesh. In my anger, I neglected to remain cautious, and I was repaid for my blunder immediately. In the next moment, I felt a tremendously sharp pain in my forearm and when I looked down, I could see the pain was coming from the old man's almost skeletal hand which was clamped on my arm applying a tremendous amount of pressure. I could not withdraw from his grasp no matter how hard I tried, and that is when it dawned on me that I may have been set up with this feeble carcass posing as one of the billionaire Elite. Could it be a reptilian shapeshifter serving as a Trojan horse for the Incalculaba and I stupidly fell right into their trap?

My left hand sprang up to grab his to pry myself away from his grasp, but I continued struggling to free myself from this superhuman skeleton of a man. All at once, I felt the leathery icy cold skin begin to turn fire hot. That was when it dawned on me, and I knew immediately why he did not flee when I was busy scuffling with his guardian. And why he seemed so calm in the face of what was surely impending death at my hands. At first, I pondered as if his great strength stemmed from his ingesting or being infused with the blood of another ancient one. Maybe the white-haired woman was his donor, hence their close relationship. Something unfathomably more sinister was at play here and I was unprepared for what happened next. The aura emanating from this withered man's being commenced to vibrate and my ears began to ring with a high-pitched frequency as if someone was blowing a dog whistle directly on either side of my head. I clench my teeth in order to bring all my strength to bear. Flexing hard against him and staring directly into his shape shifting eyes. This unearthly strength started troubling me. In my fatigued state, it was all I could do to pry two of his fingers away from this antiquated man's grip. His pale feeble arms and shoulders seem to be growing larger and filling out his tailored Armani business suit.

He spoke again but this time his voice was stronger and more guttural. It reminded me of the demonic voice of Asmodeus that Nathan Reichstall used two hundred years ago when I was forced to witness one of the few people I have ever loved, murdered like an animal before my very eyes.

"You dare put your filthy hands upon a being such as I? I... A being whose lifetime would make your centuries look as but scarcely a day. I am known as The Count of Saint Germain by you mortals, amongst many other monikers and I have tamed your kind when I was but a whelp in Lemuria. Parnassus was my fellow pupil as I sat in the sacred Halls of Amenti at the feet of Thoth called Hermès Trismegistus! You have no clue as to what level of despair and anguish that is to come to pass because of your intrusion upon our hallowed ceremony, you foul black monkey."

His mouth movements became disembodied from his voice and crashed into my ears violently, booming as if from a speaker in every corner of the room. The skin on the back of my neck where the silver brand was embedded deep in my flesh began to throb with an excruciating burning sensation. All the while his grip is tightening down on my arm like a vice. His eyes flaring and changing color between a cloudy bluish-purple to a piercing steel grey. Seeming to calm down after a momentary outburst of anger his voice came normally and not from all corners of the room again.

"That girl you killed there was one of many that I have at my disposal. Over the decades, we have finally perfected the procedure to imbue normal humans with powers such as yours. And soon we will no longer need to beg and barter from your kind while you look down on humans like they do cattle."

The old man looks smugly down his nose at me as he shape shifts into a younger form. I recognize him now as being the reclusive Belgian multi-billionaire Baron Kristoff von Reichstall.

"Our hundreds of millions of dollars spent on gene research and D.N.A science was missing one impossibly rare ingredient that we had unfortunately lost long ago when you decided to go missing. Thousands of man-hours went into our exhaustive efforts to capture you again, the last major attempt being around the late eighties if I remember correctly. You disappeared just before the gene-splicing techniques were perfected, and we proliferated a secret mandate amongst every law enforcement agency on the planet to scour the earth for you. Lamentably, we were unsuccessful in locating you again."

He smiles at me now, his teeth growing whiter and grey stubble on his face grows darker and fuller. I am dumbfounded as I grapple against this man, his strength advantage over me slowly begins to increase. Such Herculean strength from this flabby armed old man was holding me stock-still in place without registering any strain within his voice as he spoke. I attempt to reposition my hands to regain lost leverage and to my astonishment the body of the man calling himself St. Germain began to grow before my eyes. His physique and facial features rapidly reversed in aging, hair begins growing from a once bald spotted noggin and turn as black as midnight. Those steel grey eyes began to turn blood red. The resonance of Reichstall's voice began to fluctuate again and grow deeper and more metallic sounding after each syllable.

"To our most pleasant surprise, we finally found a D.N.A. match several years ago thanks to a chance encounter with, now that I think of it,

544

what must have been your blood incubating inside some black bitch from Alabama."

At the mention of Lynn and the blood they stole from her that almost killed her, my mind goes into an empty rage. A feral state of being seasoned with hate and revenge that has been cultivated for almost three hundred years. I rear back my head and violently and repeatedly smash my bulletproof helmeted skull into the half-old/half-young face of this sinister bastard, destroying the helmet and splitting it in two halves, but in the process crushing Baron Reichstall's nasal cavity and maxilla mid-transformation. The force of the blows impels him to release his vice grip on my arms as he winces back in pain holding his bloody face which is already beginning to heal itself.

With my helmet and mask destroyed, my nostrils fill with all the smells of gunpowder and fried electronics. Blood trickles from my nose which I believe to be broken from the savage smashing against Baron Reichstall's skull. I turn to run just as the door from the Hyper-loop pod access bursts open and an ungodly amount of heavily armed Kommando Spezialkrafte (German special forces) soldiers pour into the room and a hail of bullets unloads behind me. As I speed away to dive back down the elevator shaft, I glimpse the bloody spot where the vampire woman was lying a minute earlier but her body was no longer there. I run and dive headlong into the elevator shaft to avoid the barrage of enemy fire. In my haste, my foot catches on a pile of debris from the initial explosion, and I tumble awkwardly down the 25-meter shaft head first.

"Fuck!"

I yell, as I land in an awkward position that does not absorb the impact of the fall properly and severely sprain my left ankle. My tactical suit senses the major injury and cinches around my ankle and lower leg accordingly to create a stint and contain any internal bleeding that may occur. I pry open the doors again and and slip through the crack into the control room just as, above me, mercenaries begin unloading their AK-104 rifles at me while others were preparing to repel down the shaft in hot pursuit.

I stand up on my good leg and begin hobbling as fast as possible to retrieve my bag from the cubicle in the far corner of the room. If the enemy were to use gas or airborne neurotoxins or sonic equilibrium destabilizers right now, I would be totally vulnerable so I focus on retrieving my bag and escaping before I am captured and enslaved once again. I reach the cubicle and remove the debris I covered it with and open it to find everything stained with red liquid. The container carrying my extra pint of blood had been dented and crushed in such a way that it ruptured the bag inside. I suck out the remaining quarter pint of blood and then grab the last of the C4 shape charges from their plastic pouches which kept them clean and dry. I stuff two ignition receivers inside the wads of C4, toss them into my bag and close it. I place the transmitter in the pocket of my tactical suit. I throw the duffel bag towards the open elevator shaft and remove my sword and place it firmly between my teeth. Leaping up onto the wall on my good ankle, I dig my claws in and start scaling the wall towards the air vent. Just as I am ripping up one corner of the vent cover, the first soldiers to repel down the elevator shaft reach the bottom floor and commence to search the room for me. I cannot avoid making noise from the sound of the metal being ripped from the wall, and the commandos quickly open fire on my position. I jam my hand down into my pocket and pull out the transmitter and palm it in my left hand. Grabbing my sword from my mouth, I pull myself up and into the open vent and as soon as I am inside, I flick the switch for the transmitter button cover and press the button and start crawling as fast as my knees and elbows would take me.

Three seconds later,

'KRRRRAAAATTTHHHOOOOOOOMMMMMMMM!!!!!!!!!!'

The sound was ear splitting due to the resonance inside the vent. The soldiers and most of the hardware in that room were obliterated by the explosion which had the added effect of causing a partial power outage in the east wing of the complex. The soldiers and mercenaries were now too busy with fire management and damage control to pursue me, and I scurried through the maze of air ducts for what seemed like a mile, using my nose to guide me toward the fresh air intake. The tunnel I happened to be in connected to a large duct that provided fresh air from the mountain ranges and pumped it in constantly as exhaust fans located high in the perms of the underground facility escorted the filthy air out. As I get closer to the pumps, the force of the air becomes greater and the sound of the fans progressively louder.

As I reach the fan mechanism, I realize my lack of leverage from being in such an awkward position was going to make it difficult to hack and punch my way through the intake turbine. I can barely bend my arm to stab at the fan blades and without being able to swing, I cannot create enough force to puncture through the metal harness in any substantial manner. The soldiers and mercenaries are no doubt already regrouping and closing in on my location at this very moment so I need to act fast.

Critically out of time and options, I commence to jabbing my sword into the corners of the gearbox cover, just enough to puncture the outer metal grate through the filter. I continue puncturing holes in a V-shaped pattern like opening a tin can with a knife until I was sure the hole would be large enough to accommodate my shoulders and using my left hand, I punch the triangular metal pattern out with a series of short powerful strikes that left blood all over the grate and trickling from my knuckles as I pushed and shimmied my way through the broken fan and out of the machine cabinet.

The stars shine above me as I emerge into the crisp night air. I cannot smell or sense any soldiers in the immediate area, and I spin 360 degrees before looking up above at the stars to get my bearings. According to the constellations, I crawled all the way to the southern end of the campus to the top of one of the secondary annex buildings that presumably serves as one of the physical plants that maintain the above ground mechanisms needed to supply the massive subterranean complex with clean air. I sheath my sword and run to the edge of the building; my ankle had healed enough for me to put my full weight on it. I was hoping to fully revitalize my body with the extra pack of blood, but that plan went awry. My leg is still too weak to build up enough momentum to leap to another rooftop and trying to exit through the building is much too dangerous. The instant they use gas or any airborne chemicals, I would be unguarded. Without my helmet, I also leave myself vulnerable to headshots from snipers. My instincts were correct to get to higher ground but immediately the pit of my stomach drops out as I hear a loud buzz converging on my location. Several high-speed drones are closing in fast on my position from the east campus and I can hear the footsteps of a slew of soldiers charging up the stairs inside the building. The west side of the building led away from the approaching drone attack so I decide to exploit the opening and try to make a swift retreat to the sewers.

I draw my sword and hop over the ledge wall over the side of the building into a 80 foot dead drop, gripping my sword over my head plunger style with two hands. I jam it into the wall a little better than ten feet from the ground. My sword gets stuck in the concrete, and the inertia of the fall forces me to jerk away from the sword and hit the ground hard, punching the air from my chest as I smack my back on the stone ground. As soon as I pop up, I am hit with a beam from a flashlight and then multiple flashlight beams. I jump to grab my sword and the area I was just standing in is riddled with bullets. I grab my sword and using my good foot, I plant it against the wall and pull hard but the sword is stuck deep and it only releases slightly. As I reach down with my other hand to give it more leverage, I am hit with multiple shotgun slugs that force me to let go of my sword and fall back to the ground. In an instant, I am surrounded by four more Kommando Spezialkrafte armored troops wearing a new model of full exoskeleton attachments covering their limbs. The strength of their cybernetic accouterments was tremendous. These uniquely crafted limb attachments were a type of special hunter model that gave the soldiers a more insect-like than humanoid appearance. They all begin pummeling me and grabbing at my limbs as I fight their attacks tooth and nail in a last-ditch effort to escape certain doom. My body is at its limit from all the physical strain. My speed and brute strength are my only weapons as I brawl bare knuckle style against these mechanical monstrosities. My animosity is my only fuel to keep rapidly firing bloody punches and kicks. Blind anger gives me the impetus to continue to go heads up and stand my ground with no weapon against the four of these cyborgs despite their clear advantage.

One of the armored soldiers catches me square on the nose with the butt of his gun as I spin around from knocking the shit out of one of his colleagues. I grab the bastard and lift him over my head and 'powerbomb' him onto the concrete. As I jump up from the ground and turn to face off against another motorized mercenary, I am hit with extremely high voltage stun prods fired from the wrist cannon of one of the cyborgs, dropping me to my knees and causing my body to convulse uncontrollably for a few seconds. As I rip the leads from my chest and get back to my feet, I am hit with another whack, this time from a cybernetically amplified uppercut to the back of the skull. The blow from the metal fist knocks me off balance, and I grab the mercenary in front of me to avoid going down, sinking my claws into his metallic forearms and stumbling forward before he catches his balance, we lock up in a test of strength. I use his aggression against him and as he attempts to push me back towards his crowd of colleagues, I pull him toward me and Judo flip him onto his back while still holding fast to his forearms. I plant my foot in his chest with a vicious stomp and begin to pull as if to rip his arms out of their sockets.

Suddenly, I am hit in the chest damn near point blank from a shotgun slug that loosens my grip and knocks me back on my ass. In a flash, the three still vertical mechanical monsters are all over me. These cyborgs are in an entirely different class than any technology I thought was on the market and available to even the most elite of security forces. They are exponentially more advanced than the armored soldiers and exoskeleton extensions I fought in the courtyard earlier. Their speed and durability have been greatly amplified, and I am running on fumes trying to fend them off and create enough of an opening in order to make a break for the safety of the sewers.

Above us, the spotlights of the hovering drones illuminate our battle waiting for the outcome and ready to launch an all-out missile attack in the event I defeat this first wave of mechanical mercenaries. One of the cyborgs delivers a vicious blow to my chest with two metal hands while the other two move into positions on either side of me, each grabbing one of my arms together while the third cyborg mercenary delivers another crushing two-fisted blow to my face, this time breaking my nose and bouncing my brain off the back of my skull, severely stunning me as I struggled to free myself from

549

the unyielding grasp of the other two cyborg assailants. As the cyborg cocks his fist up again to reload for another crushing blow to my face, I realize that I cannot afford to keep taking blows like this to vital areas of my body if I am to survive this fiasco. I frantically twist my shoulders and yank my body violently left and bring my right knee up high enough to absorb the blow from the mercenary. I twist my body in the opposite direction with just as much force bringing my left foot up and into the face of the bastard trying to put my lights out, flattening the side of his helmet and causing him to stumble backwards and fall on his back unconscious from the force of the blow. Even with my enhanced stamina due to my rapid healing factor, the overwhelming fatigue from the battle begins to set in, and the muscles in my arms begin to burn from the frenetic wrenching of them back and forth to free myself from these machine men.

In my peripheral, I catch a glimpse of another small battalion of mercenaries approaching with flashlights and a pair of them at the forefront carried between them a heavy metallic object shaped like the letter 'M.'

'ZZZZZZTTT-ZZZZZZZZTTT'

The lumbar region of my back explodes in pain, I was hit with some type of high voltage cattle prod weapon which sent a devastating shock to my nervous system that almost causes me to lose consciousness. The momentary pause induced by the shock of the stun gun creates sufficient stoppage in my movement for the mercenaries to get close enough to clamp my arms in the openings of the 'M' shaped device which turns out to be a magnetic shackle made of some type of heavy duty osmium alloy making them impossible to break. My claws were out of commission, but I continued to try and free myself, thrashing wildly at anyone within range of the heavy metal club now attached to my arms up to the elbow. I was successful in breaking away from the cyborgs momentarily while using my new handcuffs to smash the skulls of several of the arresting mercenaries before they could fall back to a safe distance. I shifted right and rolled onto my feet to put some space between myself and the cyborg mercenaries who immediately opened fire on me again as I tried to escape behind the buildings. I remain at a severe disadvantage due to my head being exposed and it was only a matter of time before more reinforcements would arrive and they would finally overpower me.

The anxiety I was feeling causes me to go berserk and somewhere deep within my psyche, instinct took over and I am barely conscious of my movements as I leap and roll to dodge gunfire still wearing the heavy arm shackles. I use my handcuffs to block some of the gun blasts and as a bludgeon against one of the larger of the commandos Again I am hit with another high voltage stun cartridge that lodges in my right shoulder blade this time. The searing pain from the flood of voltage stops my forward progress long enough for the mercenaries and soldiers to surround me again, and they began taking their turns pummeling me and trying to kick my knees out and throw me off balance enough to drop me to the ground and subdue me further. For some reason the image of the shapeshifting Kristoff von Reichstall pops into my head. He was one of the founding thirteen members of the current Incalculaba. I am positive now that I recognize him as one of the leader of the Easter European arm of the Reichstall clan that reportedly had perished in a plane crash twenty years ago. Blood begins to pour down my face, my tactical suit and onto the concrete below me.

Despite my pitiful circumstances, I continue to thrash and swing around my heavy manacles like a weapon with the abandonment of a madman. My fighting style went from calculated and methodical to erratic and wild. I made a vow on my mother's soul that I will fight these bastards until every spark of life left in my body is gone. Tonight, I will accept nothing less than death. I vow never to be the tool of these devils ever again. I will give them a battle that they will never forget. I have come to terms with death, and I have resigned myself to going down fighting on my feet. This is the only way I will accept my demise. Head on, so that I may finally be acquainted with peace. I know beyond a shadow of a doubt that if I am captured here, I will be tortured for information about my accomplices and imprisoned for all eternity as the plaything of those sick depraved monsters masquerading in human flesh.

Tears begin to mix with the blood flowing down my face as I think of all the sacrifice, all the money and all the years of careful planning and hard work that went into this mission and I still failed. I was too weak. Too weak to prevent the continuation of the conjuring of the low spiritual beings that will feast upon the misery of humankind for another year, unabated. Innocent men, women, and children worldwide are unknowingly once again placed under the Spell of Leviathan and forced to live inside the negative energy trap of the Incalculaba.

I was being kicked and punched, stabbed and shot by mercenaries and soldiers from every side now. They rushed me from all directions and were taking turns inflicting damage on every part of my body while nimbly avoiding my wild swings of the heavy arm cuffs. Firing at me at point blank range as I roll and somersault away from the gunfire, blocking as many blows as I could with the osmium shackles, still refusing to fall to my knees. Thoughts flood into my mind of my mother, Colette, Jessie, Lynn and all the people I tried to be strong for throughout the centuries but have been too weak to protect from these devils.

BLAAKOW!

A cacophonous, point-blank shotgun blast and the searing pain in the back of my left leg forces me to drop onto one knee. Time begins to distort again, and I can barely see through my swollen bloody eyes. Seconds seem like hours as the blows continue to rain down on me and the night sky is shrouded by the enraged faces of these misguided men sent here to subdue me by any means necessary. I instinctively curl up into a ball and close my eyes to fully embrace the sorrow and the vexation in my heart. For a moment, I feel something that I believe to be the icy clutch of death embracing me from the massive loss of blood and severe beating that I had been taking for the last few minutes. But somewhere in the abyss of my soul, a barely audible rumble begins to build at the exasperation I felt due to my failure. That rumble turns into an odd sensation that can only be described as if one were conscious of being birthed into this world. The brink of death has caused something inside me to be unlocked. An extraordinary feeling, born of anger and frustration, wells up inside of me and begins to burn my very limbs with indignation. Rage and resentment are absorbed within my body at the cellular level. I can still feel the soldiers and mercenaries firing on me at point blank range and striking my body repeatedly with metal clubs and melee weapons, but the sensation of pain came less and less, and the blows begin to feel more like a pressure that became lighter and less effective with each passing moment. Internally, my body gave the impression that it was undergoing preparations to explode, and I could feel my muscles and tendons tightening and growing all throughout my being.

The blood stopped flowing from my more severe injuries, and the cuts and wounds on my body began to heal at a phenomenal rate. The shackles on my hands became impossibly tight as if they were constricting in response to my newfound vigor. My shoulder blades felt like exactly one thousand knives were being inserted in the center of my back and pushed out through my chest. My upper and lower mandible began to expand, and I could feel my fangs growing larger and forcibly shedding both rows of teeth like a shark to make way for what could only be described as daggers in my mouth. In the next moment I felt the strength building within my body so rapidly that it felt as if my skin would burst open as it was unable to contain the metamorphosis taking place, a feeling like nothing I have experienced in my more than three hundred years of life. I flex hard and rip off the shackles covering my forearms like they were wet noodles, knocking the soldiers and mercenaries who were dog piling on top of me away like bowling pins and scattering them in all directions. I grew at least a foot taller and about 75 pounds heavier. My muscles begin tightening and coiling upon themselves becoming increasingly denser to the consistency of organic iron. My upper torso feels constricted by the too small tactical suit, I reach up and I rip open the front zipper and peel the top of my suit off to the waist. The excruciating pain from the metamorphosis racking my body is concentrated mainly in my shoulder blades and chest very acutely and in the very next moment the skin on my back erupted open and two newly minted thick leathery wings burst through the flesh above my shoulder blades. Razor sharp talons burst forth on my toes, ripping through the seams in my Kevlar coated steel toe boots like tissue. I took one step and leapt fifty feet straight into the air as my huge wings flexed hard against the dark night. My now incredibly formidable back muscles instinctively gave a mighty flap and lifted me soaring even higher into the night sky, higher and faster than the drones could maneuver. The power and lift from my wings rocketed me out of the range of the mercenaries' weapons in seconds, flying westwardly through a cloud bank and over the mountain forests at subsonic speeds. A new being forged in the furnace of hell. A new weapon in the fight against global oppression.

THE END...

About the Author

Konrad Quincy Lewis is a native of Nashville, Tennessee born in 1977 to Jerry and Lucille Lewis who are both college graduates that met in their hometown of Birmingham, Alabama during the civil rights movement. Konrad left Nashville to pursue a Computer Science degree from Morehouse College and currently works as an On-set Dresser in the burgeoning Georgia film industry. Some of the more recent projects he has worked on include Suicide Squad 2, The Color Purple, Black Panther: Wakanda Forever and Captain America: Brave New World. As a youth Konrad fell in love with the written word and is an avid reader of books of all genres. His love for science fiction stems from his fascination with Greek Mythology and his love for the superhero stories in comic books, movies and television shows of the 80's and 90's. He is the esteemed husband of one Mrs. Natasha Lewis and the proud father of two daughters, Simone and Olivia.

www.ingramcontent.com/pod-product-compliance
Lightning Source LLC
Chambersburg PA
CBHW080715020726
47501CB00010B/2440